OXFORD ENGL

General Editor: JAN

ANNA ST. IVES

THOMAS HOLCROFT

ANNA ST. IVES

Edited with an Introduction by

PETER FAULKNER

OXFORD UNIVERSITY PRESS

LONDON   OXFORD   NEW YORK

1973

Oxford University Press

LONDON OXFORD NEW YORK

GLASGOW TORONTO MELBOURNE WELLINGTON

CAPE TOWN IBADAN NAIROBI DAR ES SALAAM LUSAKA ADDIS ABABA

DELHI BOMBAY CALCUTTA MADRAS KARACHI LAHORE DACCA

KUALA LUMPUR SINGAPORE HONG KONG TOKYO

ISBN 0 19 281141 X

Introduction, Notes, Bibliography, and Chronology
© *Oxford University Press 1970*

First published in the OXFORD ENGLISH NOVELS *series*
(General Editor: James Kinsley)
by Oxford University Press, London, 1970
First issued as an Oxford University Press paperback 1973

Printed in Great Britain
at the University Press, Oxford
by Vivian Ridler
Printer to the University

CONTENTS

INTRODUCTION

THOMAS HOLCROFT belongs to that tenacious and independently minded species, the self-taught man of letters. Born in 1745 in London, the son of a shoemaker, he spent his childhood in poverty (his parents at one time being reduced to peddling), became a stable-boy at Newmarket, later a strolling player, and eventually a well-known and respected figure in the literary London of the later eighteenth century. This career is vigorously recounted in the *Memoirs* completed by Hazlitt from material supplied to him by Mrs. Holcroft after her husband's death in 1809. Reviewing the *Memoirs* on their eventual publication in 1816, *The Gentleman's Magazine* praised Holcroft's example as

a gentleman who, from the lowest degree of human condition, rose, by perseverance and industry, to a celebrity which even those born in higher spheres, with the advantage of a classical education, supported by the gifts of fortune, can very seldom attain.

The determination which lay behind Holcroft's career may be appreciated from Coleridge's rueful remarks recorded by Hazlitt in 'My First Acquaintance with Poets':

We talked a little about Holcroft. He had been asked if he was not much struck *with* him, and he said, he thought himself in more danger of being struck *by* him.

A lively and convincing evocation of Holcroft (whose conversation seems, in its copiousness and variety, to have resembled Coleridge's own) is given by Thomas Ogle in a letter to Ralph Griffiths in 1792:

Of a truth that Mr. Holcroft is an oddity. He has indeed gone before the world, as he says; and the world, whip and spur, will never catch him! His conversation at Turnham Green was sufficiently curious to make one desirous of learning a few of the arcana of his system, and he himself furnished a clue by which I hoped to get at some of the contents of that compressed head of his, which promised to contain 'more than your philosophy ever dreamt of'. I did get at it indeed, but not without labour: for no sooner had he set his face toward London, than, with a body as stiff as a poker, but inclined toward the ground so as to form with it an angle of about 45 degrees, off he set at the rate of $5\frac{1}{2}$ miles an hour. Well might he pity those who travelled in carriages: they crept at snail's pace.

On the walk, Holcroft talked mainly about the superiority of mind:

it is nonsense to say that we must all die; in the present erroneous system I suppose that I shall die, but why? because I am a fool!—Hurra! said I:—but if a man chops your head off?—It will be impossible to chop your head off: chopping off heads is error, and error cannot exist.—But if a tree falls on you and crushes you? Men will know how to avoid falling trees:—but trees will not fall: falling of trees arises from error.

Holcroft's vigour, amusingly reflected here, is attested to by all who knew him.

The bulk of Holcroft's writing was done for the theatre, and included many adaptations from the French and German as well as original plays. The most successful of these were *The School for Arrogance* (1791) and *The Road to Ruin* (1792). The latter, according to Hazlitt, 'carried his fame as a dramatic writer into every corner of the kingdom, where there was a play-house'. Mrs. Inchbald, in the introductory 'Remarks' to her edition of the play in *The British Theatre* Vol. XXIV in 1808, described it as 'among the most successful of modern plays' and praised it as being 'perfectly natural'. Both these plays, unlike those which had preceded them, had a strong flavour of political radicalism in their criticisms of some aspects of the *status quo* in England in the years immediately after the French Revolution.

For these were years of heightened political consciousness in England, during which a real struggle of ideas was taking place. A focal point in the struggle was the publication of Burke's *Reflections on the Revolution in France* in November 1791, which provoked numerous replies. These have been interestingly discussed by Professor J. T. Boulton in *The Language of Politics in the Age of Wilkes and Burke* (1963). But in addition to the pamphlets, radicalism found expression in the novel. Thus J. M. S. Tompkins in her account of *The Popular Novel in England 1770–1800* (1932) calls *Anna St. Ives* 'the first full-blown revolutionary novel'. Bage's *Man as He Is*, also of 1792, makes similar criticisms of English society and contains an overt reply to Burke; other novels in the same spirit in the next few years were to be Godwin's *Caleb*

Williams in 1794, Bage's *Hermsprong* and Mrs. Inchbald's *Nature and Art* in 1796, and Holcroft's *Hugh Trevor* in 1794 and 1797. Contemporary readers were well aware of the political context of these novels, whose guiding principles were as much polemical as aesthetic.

Hazlitt's account, in the first chapter of Book IV of the *Memoirs*, of English Radical feeling inspired by the French Revolution is of classical authority, and deserves to be placed with Wordsworth's evocation of the mood in Book XI of *The Prelude*. Holcroft's principles are clearly suggested:

He was a friend to political and moral improvement, but he wished it to be gradual, calm and rational, because he believed no other could be effectual.

The resemblance between his ideas and those of Godwin (whom he met in 1785 or 1786) is obvious, and Godwin paid tribute to the stimulating effect of Holcroft's personality upon him:

My mind, though fraught with sensibility, and occasionally ardent and enthusiastic, is perhaps in its general habits too tranquil and unimpassioned for successful composition, and stands greatly in need for stimulus and excitement. I am deeply indebted on this point to Holcroft.

V. R. Stallbaumer has emphasized the similarity of the thought in *Political Justice* and *Anna St. Ives*, though for him Godwin's work has a 'lucidity and cogency' not to be found in 'the rambling and discursive style of Holcroft's novel'. It is perhaps unnecessary to contrast the two works: according to Crabb Robinson, the novel helped to prepare the ground for the treatise.

In *Anna St. Ives* the ideals of the new radical outlook are embodied in the eponymous heroine and the like-minded hero, Frank Henley. In their conversations they share a vision of the future in which arrogance and selfishness shall have given way to co-operation and benevolence. This vision is most eloquently expounded by Frank and recorded by Anna in Letter LXXXII:

Frank was present; and his imagination, warm with the sublimity of his subject, drew a bold and splendid picture of the felicity of that state of society when personal property shall no longer exist, when the whole torrent of mind shall unite in enquiry after the beautiful and the true, when it shall no longer be diverted by those insignificant pursuits to which the absurd follies that originate in our false hearts give birth, when individual selfishness shall be unknown, and when all shall labour for the good of all!

For Frank and Anna, 'the claims of truth and reason' are alone admissible; family relations are irrelevant. 'What, indeed, has relationship to do with truth?' asks Frank in Letter LXVII, and the implicit negative answer parallels the universal ethic of *Political Justice*. In Letter LXXIX Anna tells Clifton, 'Reason and not relationship alone can give authority'.

Holcroft was experienced enough a writer to realize that the exposition of the new ideals would in itself be inadequate to make an interesting novel. There needed also to be an exciting plot, and this he based on the simple tug-of-war principle, with the heroine between two contrasting suitors. Holcroft's experience of the theatre is evident in his handling of the story. For instance, the openings and endings of each of the seven volumes are managed with theatrical *élan*—effects which are lost in the compression of the second edition into five volumes. Similarly, the most Utopian passages occur in the middle of the sixth volume, when Frank and Anna are looking forward to a future together of social usefulness and personal felicity: they are followed immediately by the implementation—which the reader has been expecting—of the villain's evil plans.

In the villain himself, Coke Clifton, Holcroft created a vivid piece of theatrical characterization. Henley, the virtuous son of the steward of Anna's father, has his anti-type in Clifton, the witty and urbane rake, excellently described by R. M. Baine in his recent monograph on Holcroft's novels as 'the son of Lovelace by a strolling player'. Clifton enters at the start of the second volume with a brilliantly vivacious and cynical account of his experiences as a man of pleasure in Italy, and outlines his voluptuary's philosophy. His energy is felt in the language of his letters, which is quite different from that of the rationalists Anna and Frank. Frank uses the second person singular in his letters to his friend Oliver Trenchard, thus giving a sense of provincial simplicity. Anna, at a moment of strain, asks, 'Poor Frank. Where art thou?' which emphasizes the depth of her concern. Clifton employs a plethora of references to the classics, and both by direct reference and quotation shows his familiarity with Shakespeare, especially the tragedies. He wishes to take Anna to see Garrick in *Richard III*; Anna is to him 'this cloud-capt lady' and also an 'ill-starr'd wench'; he refuses to imitate the dilatory Hamlet, and he is driven by

passion to quote Othello's jealousy of Desdemona. His attempts
to screw himself up to the point of assaulting Anna are couched in
an extravagant post-Shakespearian rhetoric of undoubted force—
splendid fustian—bringing the tone close to that of the contemporary Gothic novels which Holcroft despised. And Clifton's
reluctance at the end to provide the 'exemplary reformation'
which is asked of him by Anna and Frank leads him to a quasi-
Renaissance exclamation of pride: 'I am Clifton'.

Equally lively and more amusing are Clifton's sarcastic and
inventive comments on his rival Frank. A wide variety of references
and a splendid vigour of rhythm make some of these denunciations
particularly effective. Letter XXVIII is outstanding in this way, with
its allusions to celebrated stoic philosophers in whom Clifton sees
the nearest analogies to Frank's self-control: 'The legitimate son
of Cato's eldest bastard, he! A petrified Possidonius, in high preservation.' Similar in tone and vitality is Letter XXV to his sister
Louisa, who has given him some good moral advice. In reply, he
suggests that she should dedicate herself to good works: 'Get a
charm to cure the ague, and render yourself renowned. Spin, sew,
and knit. Collect your lamentable rabble around you, dole out your
charities, listen to a full chorus of blessings, and take your seat
among the saints.' Surprisingly, Clifton is able to achieve a
measure of pathos in Letter CXIX. Now his inner conflict between
love for Anna and the desire to dominate her has reduced him to a
sense of futility: 'Should I be obliged to come like Jove to Semele,
in flames, and should we both be reduced to ashes in the conflict,
I will enjoy her!—Let one urn hold our dust; and when the fire
has purified it of its angry and opposing particles, perhaps it may
mingle in peace.' The creation of Clifton is what gives verve to
the novel.

The minor characters provide further interest. Sir Arthur St.
Ives is an amusing satirical sketch of a self-impoverishing land-
owner with an insatiable urge to 'improve' his grounds, to the
great profit of his steward; Letters IX and LXII amusingly reveal
the absurdity of his ambitions. At the same time he is basically an
affectionate father with a 'difficult' and puzzling daughter. The
crafty steward Abimelech Henley—'honest Aby'—is charac-
terized by the use of a grotesque language compounded of dialect,
cant, and mis-spelling. (The sources of his vocabulary have been

well discussed by R. M. Baine.) The full flavour is appreciated if the letters are read as rapidly as their orthography allows, remembering that most of the obscure terms are either synonyms for Aby's favourite object, money—among these are kole, shiner, rhino, omnum gathrum, dust, marygolds, gillyflowers, yellow boys, super nakullums, yellow hammer, and chink—or terms of abuse directed at his son Frank for his lack of self-interest—such as Sir jimmy jingle brains, Nicodemus, Gaby goose, Timothy Tipkin, and Peter Grievous. Aby's letters are not so frequent as to become irritating, and he serves as a contrast to his virtuous son. His belief is in wealth as the index of value: 'When a man has got the wherewithals, why a begins to be somebody, and mayhap a's as good as another'. This attitude helps to draw attention to the true egalitarianism embodied in Frank and Anna, Frank being unusual even in radical novels as a man of mean family as well as the highest integrity. Finally, the Irish bravo MacFane uses a different form of cant indicative of his nation as well as of his dishonesty and aggressiveness.

It may also be suggested that there is more complexity in the rendering of Anna and Frank than is at first obvious: 'rational' is not all that they are. Although they both use the term 'reason' to point to the highest value, they are (as Clifton realizes) deeply in love with one another. Anna sets off for France at the beginning of the novel with 'the divine Sterne' for her reading: the *Sentimental Journey* would hardly appeal to a strict rationalist. Moreover, the style of Frank's early letters is broken and chaotic, a reflection of the strength of his inner feelings; he wants to read the romantic poetry of Petrarch. Later, he is found reading, and being moved by, a translation of Rousseau's *La Nouvelle Héloïse*, which both appear to know well. He excels also in the reading aloud of Shakespeare. When Frank is wounded, Anna exhibits 'angelic sensibility', and in Letter LXVIII she refers to the revolt of 'the impassioned heart' against 'the cold apathy of reason', when affected by a sense of her father's affection for her. Although Holcroft does not develop these suggestions in overt discussion, they do—together with the development in Anna herself—interestingly modify the view that the ideals of Holcroft's radicalism are coldly rationalistic. The contrast is not so much between reason and passion as between altruism and egotism.

NOTE ON THE TEXT

THE first edition was published in seven volumes by Shepperson and Reynolds of Oxford Street in 1792. There are Errata notices at the end of Volumes II and VII; the corrections have been incorporated into the present text. This is printed from the copy of the first edition in the University Library, King's College, Aberdeen: I am grateful to the Librarian for the loan of these handsome volumes. The British Museum copy was used for a page missing from the Aberdeen copy.

The only later edition is that of 1800, in five volumes, published by G. G. and J. Robinson, of Paternoster Row. This is a very careless reprint of the first edition which appeared while Holcroft was on the Continent, and has no independent authority. I am grateful to the Keeper of Printed Books at the Bodleian Library for the opportunity to consult this rare edition.

The core of the new morality is contained in Frank's argument to Clifton against duelling: 'No man can be degraded by another.' This conviction enables Anna to defy the would-be rapist Clifton in a different spirit from that of Richardson's Clarissa. At the end of the novel, Clifton comes to see the contrast when he says of himself, by now ironically, 'I am a man of honour, a despiser of peasants, an asserter of rank.' In *Caleb Williams* two years later Godwin was to create Falkland, the embodiment of the same mistaken aristocratic ideal: 'I was the fool of fame.' But whereas Godwin made of the clash of ideals a tragedy, with Williams's abandonment of his own self-sufficiency for a concern for external reputation, Holcroft created a vigorous melodrama culminating—in a theatrical rather than a probable manner—in the victory of the new over the old, of principle over selfishness. Most readers will agree with Mary Wollstonecraft, who reviewed the novel on its first appearance, that Anna's behaviour is 'so remote from everything that we observe in real life, that we must pronounce it highly improbable, if not wholly unnatural'. But they may also be able to discern, in the variety of characterization and the management of the plot, the reasons why Hazlitt considered it 'interesting, lively and vigorous'. It is also evidence of a pacific social idealism which has done much to enrich the English political tradition.

SELECT BIBLIOGRAPHY

There is no collected edition of Holcroft's works.

BIBLIOGRAPHY

Elbridge Colby, *A Bibliography of Thomas Holcroft* (New York Public Library, 1922). This is not complete.

BIOGRAPHY AND CRITICISM

The primary sources are the *Memoirs of the Late Thomas Holcroft*, completed by Hazlitt from Holcroft's autobiographical writings, in 3 volumes (1816), and Kegan Paul's *William Godwin, his Friends and Contemporaries*, 2 volumes (1876). The *Memoirs* were reprinted in 1852 in Longman's Travellers' Library, and in 1926 in the World's Classics series; they also form the third volume of P. P. Howe's edition of Hazlitt's *Complete Works* (1932). There is no modern biography, but there is a greatly expanded edition of the *Memoirs*, in 2 volumes, by Elbridge Colby, entitled *The Life of Thomas Holcroft* (1925). T. V. Benn has written on 'Holcroft in France', *Revue de la littérature comparée*, vi (1926), 331-7.

Early criticism includes Mary Wollstonecroft's brief review in the *Monthly Review*, viii (June 1792); the *Anti-Jacobin Review* dealt characteristically with Holcroft, i (July 1798). Hazlitt's discussion of the novels in the *Memoirs*, mainly in the first two chapters of Book IV, is the most thorough early criticism. Saintsbury is vigorous if sardonic in *The English Novel* (1913), chapter iv; in *The Peace of the Augustans* (1916), chapter iii; and in Volume IX of the *Cambridge History of English Literature* (1932), chapter xiii. Modern scholarship is represented by Allene Gregory, *The French Revolution and the English Novel* (New York, 1915), chapter ii; J. M. S. Tomkins, *The Popular Novel in England 1770-1800* (1932 and 1962), esp. chapter viii; V. R. Stallbaumer, 'Thomas Holcroft

B

as a Novelist' in *English Literary History*, iii (1948), 194-218, and
'Holcroft's Influence on *Political Justice*' in *Modern Languages
Quarterly*, xiv (1953), 21-30; S. S. Morgan, 'The Damning of
Holcroft's *Knave or Not?* and O'Keefe's *She's Eloped*' in *Hunting-
don Library Quarterly*, xxii (1958), 51-62; W. L. Renwick, rather
cavalierly, in *English Literature 1789-1815* (1963), chapter iv;
R. M. Baine sensibly in *Thomas Holcroft and the Revolutionary
Novel* (University of Georgia Monographs No. 13, 1965); and
H. R. Steeves breezily in *Before Jane Austen* (1966), chapter xviii.

A CHRONOLOGY OF
THOMAS HOLCROFT

ANNA ST. IVES

A NOVEL

VOLUME I

LETTER I

Anna Wenbourne St. Ives to Louisa Clifton

Wenbourne-Hill

HERE are we, my dear girl, in the very height of preparation. We begin our journey southward at five tomorrow morning. We shall make a short stay in London, and then proceed to Paris. Expectation is on tiptoe: my busy fancy has pictured to itself Calais, Montreuil, Abbeville, in short every place which the book of post roads enumerates, and some of which the divine Sterne has rendered so famous.[1] I expect to find nothing but mirth, vivacity, fancy, and multitudes of people. I have read so much of the populousness of France, the gaiety of its inhabitants, the magnificence of its buildings, its fine climate, fertility, numerous cities, superb roads, rich plains, and teeming vineyards, that I already imagine myself journeying through an enchanted land.

I have another pleasure in prospect. Pray have you heard that your brother is soon to be at Paris, on his return from Italy?—My father surprised me by informing me we should probably meet him in that capital. I suspect Sir Arthur of an implication which his words perhaps will not authorize; but he asked me, rather significantly, if I had ever heard you talk of your brother; and in less than five minutes wished to know whether I had any objections to marriage.

My father is exceedingly busy with his head man, his plotter, his planner; giving directions concerning still further improvements

that are to be made, in his grounds and park, during our absence.
You know his mania. Improvement is his disease. I have before
hinted to you that I do not like this factotum of his, this Abimelech
Henley. The amiable qualities of his son more than compensate
for the meanness of the father; whom I have long suspected to be
and am indeed convinced that he is artful, selfish, and honest
enough to seek his own profit, were it at the expence of his em-
ployer's ruin. He is continually insinuating new plans to my father,
whom he Sir Arthurs, and Honours, and Nobles, at every word,
and then persuades him the hints and thoughts are all his own.
The illiterate fellow has a language peculiar to himself; energetic
but half unintelligible; compounded of a few fine phrases, and an
inundation of proverbial wisdom and uncouth cant terms. Of the
scanty number of polite words, which he has endeavoured to
catch, he is very bountiful to Sir Arthur. 'That's noble! That's
great your noble honour! Well, by my truly, that's an *elegunt ideer!*
But I always said your honour had more *nobler* and *elegunter ideers*
than any other noble gentleman, knight, lord, or dooke, in every
thing of what your honour calls the grand gusto.' Pshaw! It is
ridiculous in me to imitate his language; the cunning nonsense of
which evaporates upon paper, but is highly characteristic when
delivered with all its attendant bows and cringes; which, like the
accompaniments to a concerto, enforce the character of the composition, and give it full effect.

I am in the very midst of bandboxes, portmanteaus, packing-
cases, and travelling trunks. I scarcely ever knew a mind so sluggish
as not to feel a certain degree of rapture, at the thoughts of travelling. It should seem as if the imagination frequently journeyed so
fast as to enjoy a species of ecstasy, when there are any hopes of
dragging the cumbrous body after its flights.

I cannot banish the hints of Sir Arthur from my busy fancy.—
I must not I ought not to practise disguise with any one, much less
with my Louisa; and I cannot but own that his questions suggested
a plan of future happiness to my mind, which if realized would be
delightful. The brother of my dear Louisa, the chosen friend of
my heart, is to be at Paris. I shall meet him there. He cannot but
resemble his sister. He cannot but be all generosity, love, expansion, mind, soul! I am determined to have a very sincere friendship
for him; nay I am in danger of falling in love with him at first sight!

Louisa knows what I mean by falling in love. Ah, my dear friend, if he be but half equal to you, he is indeed a matchless youth! Our souls are too intimately related to need any nearer kindred; and yet, since marry I must, as you emphatically tell me it will some time be my duty to do, I could almost wish Sir Arthur's questions to have the meaning I suspect, and that it might be to the brother of my friend.

Do not call me romantic: if romance it be, it originates in the supreme satisfaction I have taken in contemplating the powers and beauties of my Louisa's mind. Our acquaintance has been but short, yet our friendship appears as if it had been eternal. Our hearts understand each other, and speak a language which, alas, we both have found to be unintelligible to the generality of the world.

Once more adieu. You shall hear from me again at London. Direct to me as usual in Grosvenor Street.

Ever and ever your

A. W. ST. IVES

P.S. I am sorry to see poor Frank Henley look so dejected. He has many good, nay I am well persuaded many great, qualities. Perhaps he is disappointed at not being allowed to go with us; for which I know he petitioned his father, but was refused; otherwise I could easily have prevailed on Sir Arthur to have consented.

I am determined to take King Pepin* with me. It is surely the most intelligent of all animals; the unfeathered bipeds, as the French wits call us two-legged mortals, excepted. But no wonder: it was my Louisa's gift; and, kissing her lips, imbibed a part of her spirit. Were I to leave it behind me, cats, and other good for nothing creatures, would teach it again to be shy, and suspicious; and the present charming exertion of its little faculties would decay. The development of mind, even in a bird, has something in it highly delightful.

Why, my Louisa, my friend, my sister, ah, why are not you with me? Why do you not participate my pleasures, catch with me the rising ideas, and enjoy the raptures of novelty? But I will forbear. I have before in vain exhausted all my rhetoric. You must not, will not quit a languishing parent; and I am obliged to approve your determination, though I cannot but regret the consequence.

* A goldfinch which the young lady had so named.

LETTER II

Louisa Clifton to Anna Wenbourne St. Ives

Rose Bank

HEALTH, joy, and novelty attend the steps of my ever dear and charming Anna! May the whirling of your chariot wheels bring a succession of thoughts as exhilarating as they are rapid! May gladness hail you through the day, and peace hush you to sleep at night! May the hills and valleys smile upon you, as you roll over and beside them; and may you meet festivity and fulness of content at every step!

I too have my regrets. My heart is one-half with you; nay my beloved, my generous mamma has endeavoured to persuade me to quit her, arguing that the inconvenience to her would be more than compensated by the benefit accruing to myself. The dear lady, I sincerely believe, loves you if possible better than she does me, and pleaded strenuously. But did she not know it was impossible she should prevail? She did. If my cares can prolong a life so precious but half an hour, is it not an age? Do not her virtues and her wisdom communicate themselves to all around her? Are not her resignation, her fortitude, and her cheerfulness in pain, lessons which I might traverse kingdoms and not find an opportunity like this of learning? And, affection out of the question, having such high duties to perform, must I fly from such an occasion, afflicting though it be? No! Anna St. Ives herself must not tempt me to that. She is indeed too noble seriously to form such a wish. Answer, is she not?

Oh that I may be deceived, but I fear you expect too much from my brother. Oh that he might be worthy of my Anna! Not for my own sake; for, as she truly says, we [That is our souls, for I know of no other we. We] cannot be more akin; but for his own. He is the son of my beloved mother, and most devoutly do I wish he might be found deserving of her and you. He would then be more deserving than any man, at least any young man, I have ever known. Though brother and sister, he and I may be said to have but little acquaintance. He has always been either at school, or at college, or in town, or on his travels, or in some place where I did not happen to be, except for short intervals. I have told you that his person is not displeasing, that his temper appears to be prompt and daring, but gay, and that his manners I doubt are of that free kind which our young gentlemen affect.

To say the truth however, I have heard much in favour of Coke Clifton; but then it has generally been either from persons whose good word was in my opinion no praise, or from others who evidently meant to be civil to me, or to the family, by speaking well of my brother. I believe him to have much pride, some ambition, a high sense of fashionable honour; that he spurns at threats, disdains reproof, and that he does not want generosity, or those accomplishments which would make him pass with the world for a man whose alliance would be desirable. But the husband of my Anna [you perceive I have caught your tone, and use the word husband as familiarly as if there were any serious intention of such an event, and as if it were any thing more than the sportive effusion of fancy, or rather the momentary expansion of friendship] the husband of my Anna ought to be more, infinitely more, than what the world understands by such phrases; if it can be said to understand anything. Forgive the jingle, but, to pair with her, he ought to be her peer. And yet if she wait till time shall send her such a one, and that one every way proper for her alliance, in her father's opinion as well as in her own, I am afraid her chance of marriage will be infinitely small.

Were I but assured that Coke Clifton would be as kind and as worthy a husband, to Anna St. Ives, as any other whom it were probable accident should ever throw in her way, I should then indeed seriously wish such a thought might be something more than the transient flight of fancy. But enough. You are on the wing to the city where you and he will probably meet. Examine him well; forget his sister; be true to yourself and your own judgment, and I have no fear that you should be deceived. If he prove better even than a sister's hopes, he will find in me more than a sister's love.

I like Sir Arthur's favourite, Abimelech Henley, still less than you do. My fears indeed are rather strong. When once a taste for improvement [I mean building and gardening improvement] becomes a passion, gaming itself is scarcely more ruinous. I have no doubt that Sir Arthur's fortune has suffered, and is suffering severely; and that while that miserly wretch, Abimelech, is

destroying the fabric, he is purloining and carrying off the best of
the materials. I doubt whether there be an acre of land in the occupation of Sir Arthur, which has not cost ten times its intrinsic
value to make it better. It is astonishing how Sir Arthur can be
[pardon the expression, my dear] such a dupe! I have before
blamed, and must again blame you, for not exerting yourself
sufficiently to shew him his folly. It concerns the family, it concerns yourself, nearly. Who can tell how far off the moment is
when it may be too late? My mamma has just heard of a new mortgage, in procuring of which the worthy Abimelech acted, or pretended to act, as agent: for I assure you I suspect he was really the
principal. During my last visit, if I do not mistake, I several times
saw the pride of wealth betraying itself; and only subdued by the
superior thirst of gain.

Poor Frank Henley! Is it not miraculous that such a father
should have such a son? I am tempted to give utterance to a
strange thought! Why should I not? What is the opinion of the
world; what are its prejudices, in the presence of truth? Yet not to
respect them is to entail upon ourselves I know not what load of
acrimony, contempt, and misery! I must speak—I never yet met
a youth whom I thought so deserving of Anna St. Ives as Frank
Henley! The obstacles you will say are insurmountable. Alas!
I fear they are. And therefore 'tis fortunate that the same thought
has not more strongly occurred to you. Perhaps my caution would
have been greater, but that I know your affections are free; and
yet I confess I wonder that they are so. If it be the effect of your
reason, the praise you merit is infinite: and I hope and believe it is;
for, notwithstanding all the tales I have heard and read, my mind
is convinced of nothing more firmly than that the passion of love
is as capable of being repressed, and conquered, as any other
passion whatever: and you know we have both agreed that the
passions are all of them subject to reason, when reason is sufficiently determined to exert its power.

I have written a long letter; but, writing to you, I never know
when to end.

Heaven bless my Anna St. Ives!

                                                    LOUISA CLIFTON

LETTER III

Frank Henley to Oliver Trenchard

Wenbourne-Hill

OLIVER, I am wretched! The feeble Frank Henley is a poor miserable being! The sun shines, the birds warble, the flowers spring, the buds are bursting into bloom, all nature rejoices; yet to me this mirth, this universal joy, seems mockery—Why is this? Why do I suffer my mind thus to be pervaded by melancholy? Why am I thus steeped in gloom?

She is going—Thursday morning is the time fixed—And what is that to me?—Madman that I am!—Who am I? Does she, can she, ought she to think of me?—And why not? Am I not a man; and is she more than mortal?—She is! She is!—Shew me the mortal who presumes to be her equal!

But what do I wish? What would I have? Is it my intention or my desire to make her wretched? What! Sink her whom I adore in the estimation of the world; and render her the scoff of the foolish, the vain, and the malignant?—I!—I make her wretched! —I!—

Oliver, she treats me with indifference—cold, calm, killing in-difference! Yet kind, heavenly kind even in her coldness! Her cheerful eye never turns from me, nor ever seeks me. To her I am a statue——Would I were! Why does she not hate me? Openly and absolutely hate me!—And could I wish her to love? Do I love? Do I? Dare I? Have I the temerity so much as to suspect I love? —Who am I? The insignificant son of ——!

And who is she? The daughter of a Baronet—Pshaw! What is a Baronet?—Away with such insolent, such ridiculous dis-tinctions. She is herself! Let Folly and Inferiority keep their distance!

But I?—Low bred and vulgar let Pride and Error call me, but not villain! I the seducer of men's daughters! Noble men and still nobler daughters! I! Why, would I be so very vile a thing? Would I, if I could?

Yet who shall benumb the understanding, chain up the fancy, and freeze sensation? Can I command myself deaf when she sings, dead when she speaks, or rush into idiotism to avoid her enchantments?

Despise me, Oliver, if thou wilt, but the deep sense I have of my own folly does but increase the distemper of my brain. She herself pities me, yet does not suspect my disease. 'Tis evident she does not; for her soul is above artifice. She kindly asked—was I not well? I owned I was not quite so cheerful as I could wish to be; and [wouldst thou think it?] was presumptuous enough to hint that I thought the enlivening air of France might do me good. Thou seest how frantic I am! She answered with the utmost ease, and without the most distant suspicion of my selfish, my audacious motive, that she would speak to Sir Arthur. But I was obliged to request her to forbear, till I had first tried to gain my father's consent, of which indeed I had but feeble hopes.

Every way miserable, why am I obliged to think and speak of my father with so little respect? Indeed he is——Well, well!—He is my father——I am convinced he is become wealthy; nay indeed he gives me to understand as much, when he wishes to gain any purpose, by endeavouring to excite avarice in me, which he hopes is, and perhaps supposes must be, mine and every man's ruling passion. Yet, no; he cannot: his complaints of me for the want of it are too heartfelt, too bitter.

He has kept me in ignorance, as much as was in his power. Reading, writing, and arithmetic is his grand system of education; after which man has nothing more to learn, except to get and to hoard money. Had it not been for the few books I bought and the many I borrowed, together with the essential instruction which thy excellent father's learning and philanthropy enabled and induced him to give me, I should probably have been as illiterate as he could have wished. A son after his own heart! One of his most frequent and most passionate reproaches is 'the time I *waste* in reading.'

I scarcely need tell thee he was almost in a rage, at my request to accompany Sir Arthur to France; stating, as I did, that it ought to be and must be at his expence. Otherwise he cares but little where I go, being rather regarded by him as a spy on his actions than as his son. Thou canst not conceive the contempt with which he treats me, for my want of cunning. He despises my sense of philanthropy, honour, and that severe probity to which no laws extend. He spurns at the possibility of preferring the good of society to the good of self——But, once again, he is my father.

Prithee lend me thy Petrarch,[1] and send it in return by Thomas. I had nothing to say, though I have written so much, except to ask for this book, and to burden thee with my complaints. Remember me kindly to thy most worthy father, and all the family. Thine,

F. HENLEY

LETTER IV

Anna Wenbourne St. Ives to Louisa Clifton

London, Grosvenor Street

OH, Louisa! I have such a narrative! Such accidents! Such—! But you shall hear.

We are arrived; and, thank God and good fortune, are all alive; which, every thing considered, is no small consolation. The chaise was at the door punctually at five on Thursday morning. Abimelech Henley had been very busy with Sir Arthur over night; and was in close conference with him again previous to our departure.

Frank too was there, as disconsolate and as attentive as ever; active and watchful that every thing was as it should be. How the difference between soul and soul discovers itself in such scenes! I very much fear his father treats him unkindly, and that he grieves more than he ought; nay more than a person of his youth, strong form, and still stronger mind, could be supposed to grieve. I understand he very much laments the loss of a college education, which the miser his father could very well have bestowed upon him, had not his heart been as contracted as the mouth of his purse.

Mr. Trenchard, luckily for Frank, early discovered his genius, and gratuitously aided him in his studies. Frank reveres him as a more than father, and loves his son Oliver like a brother. He is but too sensible that a true father feeds the mind, and that he who only provides for the body is no better than a step-father. I have some fear that there is another cause for his dissatisfaction, and that he has cherished some silly thoughts of an impossible nature. If so, an effort must be made which I hope will restore him to reason. And yet what right have I to conclude that he reasons erroneously?

Have I sufficiently examined? This is a question which has several times lately forced itself upon my mind. I am not insensible of his high worth: it opens upon me daily. What I am going to relate will picture that worth better than any praise of mine. I will therefore continue my narrative.

Every thing being adjusted, off we went; I, Laura, and Sir Arthur, in the chaise, and one footman only with us, who was to ride before as our courier, and prepare horses.

I told you of my intention to take King Pepin with me; but the morning of our departure was all hurry, and it seldom happens that something is not forgotten, amid the tumult into which the passions seem to plunge as it were with delight, gratified with the confusion which themselves create. I must own I was vexed and offended with myself, when I found that the something over-looked on this occasion was the gift of my Louisa. Ingratitude with all its reproaches rose up to sting me; and I immediately resolved to punish myself, by informing my Louisa how unworthy I am of the gifts of such a friend. It was at the first stage where we changed horses that I made this discovery. One moment I was inclined to petition Sir Arthur to stay, while a messenger should be sent; but the next I determined that my fault should incur its due pains and penalties.

Every thing was ready; but just as we had seated ourselves in the chaise, and were again proceeding on our journey, one of the servants of the inn called to Sir Arthur to stop, for young Mr. Henley was coming up full speed on the bay mare. Frank and the bay mare are both famous through the whole country. My father immediately prognosticated some bad accident, and I began to be alarmed. Our fears however were soon dissipated, his only errand being to bring my charming favourite.

I confess I was not a little moved by this mark of attention, which indeed is but one among many, as well as by the peculiarity of the youth's manner in delivering the bird. He was fearful, visibly fearful, that his desire to oblige should be thought officious. He attempted to apologize, but knew not what to say. I thanked him very sincerely, and in the kindest manner I could; and, seeing him booted, the thought instantly struck me to request Sir Arthur's permission for him to accompany us to London, which I imagined might give him pleasure.

The request happened to coincide with some new project of alteration which Sir Arthur had conceived, and which, he said, after having further digested, he could better communicate to Frank than describe on paper. The mare is said to be one of the best travellers in the kingdom; and, as she was very capable of performing the journey, and the carriage being rather heavily loaded, he accordingly kept pace with us.

During the day we passed many delightful scenes, and enjoyed the charming prospects which the rich cultivation of England, and the road we travelled, afford. Frank Henley was scarcely ever out of sight, though he was rather watchfully assiduous than communicative.

Sir Arthur, for his part, did not forget to point out to us what a charming park such and such grounds might be turned into; how picturesque a temple, or a church steeple, would look in this place; what a fine effect a sheet of water would have in that bottom; and how nobly a clump of trees would embellish the hill by which it was overlooked.

I believe I am a sad wicked girl, Louisa! I was once strangely tempted to tell him I was much afraid his father had mistaken the trade to which his genius was best adapted, when he made him a baronet instead of a gardener. However I had the grace to bite my tongue and be silent. He might have had the retort courteous upon me, and have replied that gardening was much the most honourable trade of the two. But he would never have thought of that answer.

Thus the day, as I tell you, passed pleasantly and whimsically enough. But the night! Oh!—The night!——You shall hear.

It was the dusk of evening when we were at Maidenhead. We had then three stages to go, and Sir Arthur began to be alarmed by the rumours of depredations which had lately been committed on the road. I really do not know what to say to it; but there appears to be something deeper in the doctrine of sympathies than such silly girls as I can either account for or comprehend. I endeavoured with all my might to oppose the sensation, and yet I found my father's fears were catching. Frank Henley indeed begged of me, with great energy, not to be alarmed; for that he would die sooner than I should be insulted. Upon my honour, Louisa, he is a gallant youth!—You shall hear—But he is a brave, a gallant youth.

I cannot say but I wished I were a man; though I am convinced it was a foolish wish, and that it is a great mistake to suppose courage has any connexion with sex; if we except, as we ought, the influence of education and habit. My dear mother had not the bodily strength of Sir Arthur; but, with respect to cool courage and active presence of mind, I must say, Louisa, there was no comparison.

We set off, however, Frank having first provided himself with a hanger and a pair of pistols; and he now kept close to the chaise-door, without once quitting his station. I believe Sir Arthur was heartily glad at being thus provided with a guard, as it were un-expectedly, and without any foresight of his own. For, not to mention gold watches and trinkets, he had more money with him than he would have chosen to have lost, fright out of the question.

We proceeded thus without molestation as far as Brentford; but not without receiving fresh hints that it was very possible we might be visited; and then, though it began to be drawing toward midnight, Sir Arthur thought the danger chiefly over. As it hap-pened he was mistaken. He was indeed, my dear! I assure you I could tremble now with the thoughts of it, but that my woman-hood forbids. I remember how valiant I have been in laughing at the pretty fears of pretty ladies, with their salts, hartshorn,[1] fits, and burnt feathers.[2] Beside, I would not have my Louisa think too meanly of me. Yet I assure you it was a terrible night.

We had just passed the broad part of Turnham Green, as Frank has since told me, and were near the end of a lane which strikes into the Uxbridge road, when the postillion was stopped by one high-wayman, while almost at the same instant another dashed his pistol through the side-glass into the chaise, full in Sir Arthur's face.

Frank was on my side—Notwithstanding the length of the journey, he seemed to infuse his own ardour into the spirited animal on which he rode, and was round instantaneously—It was really dreadful!—The highwayman saw, or rather heard him coming, for it was prodigiously dark, and fired. Poor Frank was shot!—In the shoulder—But he says he did not feel it at first—He returned the fire; and the highwayman exclaimed, with a shocking oath, 'I am a dead man!' He rode away however full speed; and his associate, who stood to guard the post-boy, rode after him. Frank imagines that, owing to the darkness of the night, and his being so close under the chaise, they had not perceived him when they came to the attack.

But here let me tell you, for I am sure I ought, our protector, our hero is not dangerously wounded. He indeed makes very light of it; but I am persuaded he would do that if he had lost an arm. The moment the highwaymen were gone, he rode round to me to intreat me not to be alarmed, for that all was safe.

Imagine whether I did not thank him, and bless him; at least in ejaculation. Imagine what I felt, after what I *had* heard, at hearing him talk to me, and at being convinced that he was actually alive. I had not the least suspicion of his being wounded, he spoke so cheerfully; yet I naturally enquired if he were hurt. His answer was—'No no—Not *hurt*'—But he spoke with an emphasis that immediately raised my apprehensions. I repeated my question— 'Are you sure you are not hurt; not wounded?' He could not say no to that, and therefore answered—'He believed he felt a slight contusion in the shoulder; but that he was convinced it was trifling.'

I was now seized with a fit of terror much greater, in effect, than my former panic. I fervently intreated Sir Arthur to let the servant take the bay mare, and ride for help! I begged, urgently, violently, for God's sake, that he would take my place in the chaise! I would mount the mare myself! I would do any thing! All the replies I could get were still more vehement intercessions from Frank Henley, that I would not be alarmed, assurances that there was not the least danger, the most obstinate determination not to quit his post, and, notwithstanding the pain which he could not but feel, a persisting to reload the discharged pistol, and then to proceed.

I know not myself how my fears were so far pacified as to yield to this, except that his energy seemed to overpower mine. Indeed I suffered dreadfully the rest of the way. I knew the youth's generous spirit, and my imagination was haunted with the idea, that the blood was flowing every foot of the road, and that he would rather drop from the horse than be subdued. It is impossible, indeed it is, to tell you what I felt.

At last we arrived in Grosvenor Street; and sure enough the poor fellow was faint with the loss of blood. 'My God!'—said I to Sir Arthur, when the light was brought, and I saw him—

C

'Send for a surgeon! Good Heavens! Run! Somebody run for help!'—He still insisted he was but slightly hurt, and began to resume all his earnestness to quiet me. Sir Arthur did it more effectually by sending as I desired, and by telling me that, if I continued to agitate by contending with him so much, I might very possibly throw him into a fever, and make a wound, which most probably was not in itself dangerous, mortal.

I said not another word, except seriously and solemnly requesting him to calm his mind, for his own sake, if not for mine; for that, after being wounded in defence of me and my father, to die by my fault were dreadful indeed. He retired with more apparent satisfaction in his countenance than I think I ever saw before.

I was resolved however not to go to bed, till I had received some account from the surgeon. He came, the wound was examined, and word was immediately sent me, by the express command of Frank, who had been told I was sitting up for that purpose, that there was, as he had assured me, no danger. The surgeon indeed thought proper to qualify it with no *great* danger. It is an old remark that surgeons are not prone to speak too lightly of the miracles they perform. This short syllable, great, did not fail however to disturb me very considerably. I waited till the ball was extracted, and [Would you believe it?] brought us; for I insisted upon seeing it. Sir Arthur called me a mad girl, adding there was no ruling me. I persisted in questioning and cross-examining the surgeon, till I was convinced that, as he said, there was no *great* danger; and I then retired to rest: that is, I retired to the same swimming motion which the chaise had communicated to my nerves, or my brain, or I know not what, and to dreaming of swords, pistols, murdered men, and all the horrid ramblings of the fancy under such impressions.

To convince me how trifling the hurt was, the gallant Frank insisted the next day on coming down to dinner; though he was allowed to eat nothing but chicken broth, and a light pudding. I never saw him so lively. His only present danger of death, he said, was by famine; and complained jocularly of the hardship of fasting after a long journey. I could almost have persuaded him to eat, for indeed he is a brave, a noble youth.

I know I never need apologize to my Louisa for the length of my letters. How can we enjoy equal pleasure to that of thus conversing in despite of distance, and though separated by seas and mountains? Indeed it is a kind of privation to end; but end I must—therefore—Adieu.

A. W. ST. IVES

LETTER V

Frank Henley to Oliver Trenchard

London, Grosvenor Street

YOU did not expect, dear Oliver, to receive a letter from me dated at this distance. By the luckiest accident in the world, I have been allowed to accompany her thus far, have ridden all day with my eye fixed upon her, and at night have had the ecstatic pleasure to defend, to fight for her! Perhaps have saved her life! Have been wounded for her!—Would I had been killed!—Was there ever so foolish, so wrong, so romantic a wish? And yet it has rushed involuntarily upon me fifty times. To die for her seems to be a bliss which mortal man cannot merit! Truth, severe truth, perhaps, will not justify these effusions. I will, I do, endeavour to resist them. —Indeed I am ashamed of myself, for I find I am very feeble. Yet let not thy fears be too violent for thy friend: he will not lightly desert his duty.

Let me tell thee, before I proceed, that my wound is slight.— We were stopped by a couple of highwaymen. Thou never wert a witness of such angelic sensibility as the divine creature discovered, when she found I had received some hurt. She alarmed me beyond description, by the excess of her feelings. Oh! She has a soul alive to all the throbs of humanity! It shoots and shivers in every vein!—Then too when we arrived, when candles were brought [I had bled somewhat freely, and I suppose looked rather pale] thou hast no conception of, it is impossible to conceive the energy with which she insisted on sending for the best and most immediate help.

We had another battle of sensibility; for I assure thee I was almost as much [Did I not know her I should say more.] alarmed for her as she could be for me.

Yet do not imagine I am fool enough to flatter myself with any false hopes. No: it was humanity; it was too deep a sense of a slight benefit received; it was totally distinct from love.——Oh no! Love, added to such strong, such acute sensations, surely, Oliver, it would have shrieked, would have fainted, would have died!—— Her fears and feelings were powerful I grant, but they were all social, and would have been equally awakened for any creature whom she had known, and had equal cause to esteem. And she esteems all who have but the smallest claims to such respect; even me!—Did I tell thee it was she who petitioned Sir Arthur to lay his commands on me to attend them to London, knowing I wished it; and that this was in return for the trifling favour I had done her, in galloping after her with her favourite bird? Oh! She is all benignity! All grace! All angel!

Never did I feel such raptures as since I have received this fortunate, this happy wound!——Yet why?——Is not her heart exactly what it was? It is. I should be an idiot not to perceive it is. Strange contradiction! Hopeless yet happy!—But it is a felicity of short duration.

Would it were possible for me to accompany her to France! My restless foreboding imagination has persuaded me she will be in danger the moment she is from under my protection. Vain fool! Who, what am I?—Because a couple of dastardly highwaymen have galloped away at the first report of a pistol, my inflated fancy has been busy in persuading me that I am her hero!

Yet I wish I might go with her! Tell me, Oliver, wouldst not thou wish so too? Would not all the world wish the same? Didst thou ever in thy life behold her without feelings unusual, throbs, doubts, desires, and fears; wild, incoherent, yet deriving ecstasy from that divinity which irradiates her form and beams on every object around her?—Do!—Think me a poor, raving, lovesick blockhead! And yet it is true! All I have said of her, and infinitely more, is true! Thou nor the world cannot disprove it! Would I might go with her!

I have seen the fellow with whom I had the rencounter. His wound is much more severe than mine. Sir Arthur sent information to the office in Bow Street. Wouldst thou think a highwayman could be so foolish a coxcomb as to rob in a bright scarlet coat, and to ride a light grey horse? The bloodhunters [I am sorry that our absurd, our iniquitous laws oblige me to call them so] the bloodhunters soon discovered the wounded man. Forty pounds afforded a sufficient impulse.[1] They were almost ready to quarrel with me, because I did not choose to swear as heartily as they thought proper to prompt. Thou knowest how I abhor the taking away the life of man, instead of seeking his reformation.

After persisting that it was impossible for me to identify the person of the highwayman, as indeed it really was, and luckily prevailing on Sir Arthur to do the same [though he, like most folks who have any thing to lose, was convinced it would be an excellent thing if all rogues could be instantly hanged, like dogs, out of the way] I paid the poor wretch a visit, privately, and gave him such a lecture as, I should hope, he would not easily forget. It was not all censure: soothing, reasoning, and menace were mingled. My greatest effort was to convince him of the folly of such crimes; he had received some proof of the danger. He was in great pain, and did not think his life quite secure. He promised reformation with all the apparent fervour of sincerity, prayed for me, blessed me very heartily, and praised me for my bravery. He says the Bow Street runners will leave nothing unattempted to secure the reward, and take away his life. I have therefore engaged to hire a lodging, and bring a hackney coach for him myself, at seven in the morning, the hour least likely for him to be watched or traced. I believe I was more earnest to prevent harm happening to him than he himself was; for, having met a man upon the stairs, whose physiognomy, dress and appearance led me to suspect him, I questioned my penitent, who owned it was his accomplice; a determined fellow, according to his account; an Irish gambler, whose daring character led him, after a run of ill luck, to this desperate resource. It was with some difficulty I could persuade him the fellow might betray him, and join the Bow Street people. The gambler, as he says, expects a supply, and has promised him money. But he has consented to leave his lodging; and I think I have convinced him of the folly, danger, and guilt of such connections.

I found he was poor, and, except a few shillings, left him the trifle of money which I had; endeavouring by every means to restore a lost wretch to virtue and society. The fellow was not flint. The tears gushed into his eyes, and I own I came away with hopes that my efforts had not been wholly ineffectual.

I have written by the first post, that you mayst know what is become of me. Farewell.

F. HENLEY

LETTER VI

Louisa Clifton to Anna Wenbourne St. Ives

Rose Bank

I HAVE only time for a single line, but I cannot forbear to tell you how great the emotions have been which I felt, my dear Anna, at reading your last. Ten thousand thanks for your history; for so it may well be called. You have quite filled my mind with the pictures, incidents, and adventures of your journey. ——Then your deliverer!—Such courage!—Such fortitude!— Such——!

I must not finish my sentence. I must not tell you all I think concerning him. There were two or three passages in your letter which raised doubts in my mind; but of these I was soon cured by recollecting a sentence at the beginning—'An effort must be made which will restore him to reason. Yet the question must be examined.'—Certainly—You could not be Anna St. Ives, and act or feel otherwise.

But I absolutely adore this youth, this Frank Henley!

The boy is waiting; he will be too late for the post. Be that my excuse for the briefness of this; but do not fail, my dear dear Anna, to write fully every thing that passes. Your last has both warmed my feelings, nay in some measure my fears, and excited my curiosity.

Yours eternally,

L. CLIFTON

P.S. I will write more at length tomorrow.

LETTER VII

Abimelech Henley to Sir Arthur St. Ives, Baronet

Wenbourne-Hill

MOST onnurable Sir, my ever onnurd Master,

The instructions* you wus pleased to give me have bin kept in mind. Your onnur's commands is my duties; your precepts is my laws. For why? Your noble onnur knows how to command, and I knows how to obey.

The willow dell is fillin up; all hands is at work. I keeps 'em to it. The sloap of the grande kinal will be finisht and turft over in 3 wekes; and I have chosen the younk plants for the vardunt hall: nice wons they be too, your onnur!

But I have a bin ponderaitin[1] on all these thinks, and sooth an trooth to say, your onnur, I doubt as how the bitt[2] [I mean the kole,[3] your onnur] witch your noble onnur has a bin pleesd to stipilate and lay by for these here improvements [And glorious improvements they will be, let me tell your onnur. I think I knows a sumthink of the matter; thos to be sure I must a say as how I am no more nur a chit, a kintlin,[4] to your onnur, in matters of taste and the grande goosto, and all a that there; but I'll give your onnur my two ears if there be any think at all komparissuble or parallel to it in all England.] But as I wus a sayin to your noble onnur—I am afeard we shall want cash; and I am a sure that would be a ten m̅[5] of pitties. Especially if your onnur thinks any think more of the vister, with another church steepil in prospekshun. And to be sure it was a noble thoft; I must say it would be a sin and a shame to let sitch an elegunt ideer a slip through your fingurs. And then, pardn me your onnur, but for what, and for why, and for wherefore?

* The editor has sometimes found it very difficult to translate the letters of this correspondent, out of bad spelling into English. Had they been left as they were written, they would have been half unintelligible.

The editor however has used his own judgment, in suffering various words to retain their primitive dress; the better to preserve what would otherwise have been too much unlike its author, had the orthography been rendered perfect.

It would have been assassination to have omitted any of the dialectic or cant terms, in which this honest Abimelech takes so much delight: for which reason they have been carefully retained.

Besides all witch, your onnur wus a menshinnin a willdurness, and a hermmutidge, and a grotto; all witch as your onnur said would conceal the dead flat anenst the 3 old okes. And would your onnur think of stoppin short, after havin a done all that your onnur has a done, to bring Wenbourne Hill into vogue an reppitaishun, and make it the talk of the hole kuntree? Nay, for the matter of that, it is a that already; that I must say. But then, as your onnur says, in answer, nothink is done till every think is done.

And so I have paradventerd umbelly to speak my foolish thofts, on this here business. For why? I knows a what your onnur will say. Your onnur will tell me, when your onnur comes back, Ay, honest Aby, I wish the shiners[1] that I a spent and a bamboozild[2] in that there France had a bin strewed over these here grounds. For, over and above of what I a bin a menshinnin to your onnur, there is the tempel beside a the new plantation, of a witch your onnur has so long a bin talkin of a buildin of. And then there is the extenshun and ogmenshun of the new ruins. So that all together, I must say that if simple honest Aby might paradventer to put in my oar to so generous and so noble a gentleman, and moreover won of his majesty's baronets, why I would keep the money now I had a got it; since, as your onnur finds, money is not so easy to be a come at. Pray your onnur, I beesiege your onnur dont forget *that*; money is not so easy to be a come at.

And so I most umbelly rimmane, with the blessin of almighty mercifool praise, your onnur's most umbel and most obedient, very faithfool and very thankfool, kind sarvent to command,

ABIMELECH HENLEY

P.S. I pray your onnur to think of the vister, and the willdurness, and the hermmutidge; I pray your onnur doo ee; not forrgettin the tempel. Think of the money your most dear gracious noble onnur; and think to what vantidge I could a lay it out for your onnur; that is, take me ritely your most exceptionable onnur, a savin and a sayin under your wise onnur's purtection, and currection, and every think of that there umbel and very submissive obedient kind. Bring me the man that a better knows how to lay out his pound or his penni than myself; that is, always a savin and exceptin your noble onnur, as in rite and duty boundin. And then as to forin parts! Why, lawjus mighty! Your noble onnur has 'em

at your fingur's ends. The temple will stand; blow or snow, a there
it will be; I'll a answer for that; a shillin's worth for every shillin:
but ast for the money a squitterd[1] a here and a there in forin parts,
what will your most noble onnur ever see for that? I most umbelly
condysend to beg and beesiege your good and kind onnur's noble
pardn for all this audacious interpolation, of and by witch any but
your most disrespectfool onnur would say wus no better but so
much mag:[2] but I hopes and trusts your onnur, as you always have
bin henceforth in times passt, is in the mind a well to take what a
well is meant.

And so I wonce and again most perrumptallee beg leave, in all
lowliness by the grace and blessin of God in his infinit goodness
and mercy to superscribe meself

ABIMELECH HENLEY

LETTER VIII

Anna Wenbourne St. Ives to Louisa Clifton

London, Grosvenor Street

FRANK HENLEY'S accident has necessarily delayed our journey
for a fortnight; nay, it was within an ace of being delayed for
ever, and [Would you think it possible?] by the artful remonstrances of this Abimelech Henley. I have been obliged to exert
all my influence, and all my rhetoric, upon Sir Arthur, or it
would have been entirely given up. Rapacious and narrow in
his own plans, this wretch, this *honest Aby*, as my father calls
him, would not willingly suffer a guinea to be spent, except
in improvements: that is, not a guinea which should not pass
through his hands. A letter from him to Sir Arthur has been the
cause of this contest.

I hope however, my dear, that Sir Arthur's affairs are not
in so bad a train as your fears [expressed in your letter of the
third] cause you to imagine. Should they be so, what will become
of my brother? A mere man of fashion! Active in the whole
etiquette of visiting, dressing, driving, riding, fencing, dancing,
gaming, writing cards of compliment, and all the frivolous follies

of what, by this class of people, is called *the world*; but indolent in, or more properly incapable of all useful duties.

I stand rather high in his opinion, and he has done me the honour to consult me lately on a family affair. The Edgemoor estate, of eight hundred per annum, is entailed on him, as the heir of St. Ives, by my grandfather's will; with right of possession at the age of twenty-four. Sir Arthur I suppose does not find it convenient to abridge his income so materially, and has been endeavouring to persuade him that it is his duty and interest not to insist upon possession; at least for the present. My brother is not pleased with the proposal, and has complaisantly written to ask my opinion, with an evident determination to follow his own, he having now almost completed his twenty-fourth year. My answer was an attempt [I fear a vain one] to call to his mind the true use of money; and, unless he should have found the art of employing it worthily, I advised him to shew his filial affection and oblige Sir Arthur.

I can prophesy however that he will have no forbearance. Not to mention debts, he has too many imaginary and impatient wants to submit to delay. Neither have I any great desire that he should; being convinced that the want of money is the only impediment that can put a stop to Sir Arthur's improvements.

But this honest Aby!—The same post that brought me your letter of the eleventh,* brought one for Sir Arthur; and while I was meditating on the contents of yours, and not a little chagrined at the confirmation of your intelligence concerning the mortgage— [Chagrined that my father should be the instrument, the tool of such a fellow: chagrined that his family should be in danger, and himself made a jest]—while I was considering what were the best means, if there were any, of inducing Sir Arthur to abandon projects so foolish, and so fatal, Laura came running with the news that our journey to France was all over, that orders to that effect had been given, and that a chaise was to be at the door in an hour, to take Sir Arthur back to Wenbourne-Hill.

This incident, in my then temper of mind, produced its full effect. I knew Sir Arthur's way: I knew he would not willingly see me himself; and, immediately suspecting that his letter was from

* This and other letters are occasionally omitted, as not containing any new information.

honest Aby, I determined if possible he should not escape me. He
was in his own room; and how to draw him out? An hour would
soon be gone! I therefore employed an artifice, which, on after
recollection, I am convinced was wrong; very wrong! I went into
the drawing-room, and bade the footman go to him and announce
Miss Wenbourne. I have a maiden aunt of that name, whom I was
christened after, who lives in London, and whom I believe you
never saw. The trick succeeded, and Sir Arthur came into the
drawing-room. He looked disconcerted at seeing me, and the
following dialogue began.

Heydey, Anna! Where is your aunt?

Sir, I am afraid I have done an unjustifiable thing. [My conscience then first smote me, with a conviction that what I had
persuaded myself was a defensible artifice was neither more nor
less than a direct falsehood; which of all crimes, you know, I think
one of the most mean, hateful, and pernicious. The just confusion
I felt had nearly ruined my cause.]

Why!—What!—What do you mean?—Where is your aunt?

She is not here, sir. It was I who wished to speak to you.

You! And send in your aunt's name?

My name is Wenbourne, sir.

Your name is St. Ives, miss.

I feel, sir, how exceedingly culpable I am; and perhaps do not
deserve that you should pardon me. [My father began to suspect
the reason of my wishing to speak with him, and did not know
whether good nature or ill would serve his cause the best. I perceived him cast an eye toward the door.]

This is extraordinary!——Very extraordinary, upon my soul!

[I saw it was time to recover my spirits.] I have heard something
which I scarcely can believe to be true, sir.

What have you heard? What have you heard?

That you are going back to Wenbourne-Hill.

Well, what then?

And that you do not intend we should visit France.

Who told you so?

The servants have orders to that effect.

The servants are a parcel of busy blockheads!

What can have occasioned you, sir, to change your opinion so
suddenly?

My affairs. [He looked again toward the door, but he felt it was too late; and that he must now either defend or abandon his cause.] The journey will be too expensive.

If, sir, the journey would in the least embarrass your affairs, and if I did not daily see you entering into expences so infinitely greater than this, I would not answer a word to such an argument. I think it my duty to be as careful of your property as you yourself could be; and for that reason have often wished I could prevail on you, in some measure, to alter your plans.

I have no doubt, miss, of your prodigious wisdom; you remind me of it daily. Your plans to be sure would, as you say, be infinitely better than mine. When you are married, or I am dead, you may do as you please; but, in the mean time, suffer me to act for myself. I do not choose to be under tutelage.

I am sorry, my dear papa, to see that I offend you; but indeed I mean the very reverse. Indeed I do! It is my zeal for your interest, my love of you, [I ventured to take his hand] that oblige me to speak—

And plainly to tell me you do not approve of my proceedings!

Plainly to tell you the truth, because I believe it to be my duty.

Upon my word! A very dutiful daughter! I thought the duty of children was to obey the wills of their parents.

Obedience—[Pardon my sincerity, sir.]—Obedience must have limits. Children should love and honour their parents for their virtues, and should cheerfully and zealously do whatever they require of them, which is not in itself wrong.

Of which *children* are to judge?

Yes, sir: of which children are to judge.

A fine system of obedience truly!

They cannot act without judging, more or less, be they obedient or disobedient: and the better they judge the better will they perform their duty. There may be and there have been mistaken parents, who have commanded their children to be guilty even of crimes.

And what is that to me? Upon my word, you are a very polite young lady! A very extraordinarily polite miss!

God forbid, my dear papa, that you should imagine I think you one of those parents.

I really don't know nor don't care, madam, what you think me. —My plans, indeed!—Disapproved by you!

If I saw any person under a dangerous mistake, misled, wronged, preyed upon by the self-interested, should I not be indolent or cowardly, nay should I not be criminal, if I did not endeavour to convince such a person of his error? And what should I be if this person were my father?

Upon my honour, miss, you take intolerable liberties! The license of your tongue is terrible!

It were better, sir, that I should subject myself to your displeasure, and make you think unkindly of me, than that others, who pretend to be your servants and your humble but friendly advisers, should injure—should—I know not what! We have often heard of stewards, who have acted the mortgagee to their own masters. [This hint was a thunder stroke. Sir Arthur was wholly disconcerted. His mind apparently made several attempts to recover itself; but they were all ineffectual.]

Well, well—I, I—I know what the meaning of all this is. You—You are vexed at being disappointed of your journey—But make yourself easy, child; you shall go: you shan't be disappointed.

'Tis true, sir, I wish to visit Paris; but not if it will be in the least inconvenient to you, in money affairs. Though I own I should indeed be vexed to see the small sum you had appropriated for this journey wrested from you, to throw up a hill, or build a fantastic temple in some place where its very situation would render it ridiculous.

Upon my word!—Was ever the like of this heard?—Don't I tell you, you shall go?

Indeed, sir, going is but a small part of the subject: there is another point, which, if I could but gain, would give me infinitely more pleasure.

Pshaw! Girl! I can't stay to argue points with you now! I tell you, you shall go. I give you my word you shall go; and so let's have no more of it.—Do you hear, Anna? I am too old to be schooled. I don't like it! Mind me! I don't like it!

I am very sorry, sir, that I cannot find words to speak the truth which would be less offensive.

I tell you again there is no truth to be spoken! Have not I promised you shall go? There's an end of the business. You shall go.

And away went Sir Arthur; apparently happy to get rid both of me and himself: that is, of the disagreeable ideas which, as he thought, I had so impertinently raised. You blamed me in your last for not exerting myself sufficiently, to shew him his folly. You see the sufficiently is still wanting. Perhaps I have not discovered the true mode of addressing myself to Sir Arthur's passions. For, though my remonstrances have often made him uneasy, I cannot perceive that they have ever produced conviction. And yet I should suppose that a certain degree of momentary conviction must be the result of such conversations. But the fortitude to cast off old habits, and assume new, is beyond the strength of common mortals.

Frank Henley is a favourite with you, and very deservedly. But, in answer to the surprise in your former, my dear, that he has never engaged my affections, as well as to the cautionary kind hints in your two last, for so I understand them, let me say that, had I imagined love to be that unconquerable fatality of which I have been speaking, I do not know what might have happened: but, having been early convinced that a union between him and me must be attended with I know not what scenes of wretchedness, in short, knowing the thing in a certain sense to be impossible, it has always been so considered by me, and therefore I have no reason to think myself in any danger. Doubts occasionally rise in my mind, but in general soon disappear. Should they return I will not conceal them.

I remember it was a remark of yours that 'Admiration is the mother of love.' So it is, of love such as I bear to my Louisa; and of such perhaps as angels might be supposed to bear to angels. I admire Frank Henley, greatly, ardently admire him; yet I certainly do not love: that is, I certainly do not permit myself to feel any of those anxieties, alarms, hopes, fears, perturbations, and endearments, which we are told are inseparable from that passion. I extinguish, I suffocate them in their birth.

I am called for: Adieu, my ever dear Louisa.

A. W. ST. IVES

LETTER IX

Sir Arthur St. Ives to Abimelech Henley

London, Grosvenor Street

I HAVE received your letter, good Abimelech, and own your reasoning has its force. Much is yet to be done to Wenbourne-Hill. Year after year I have said—'This shall be the last: we will now bring affairs to a finish.' But improvement is my delight; walking, talking, sitting, standing, or lying, waking or sleeping, I can think of nothing else. We live you know, honest Aby, only to amend: so that, instead of concluding, I find more things to do at present than ever.

I have the wilderness very much at heart: but the soil is excellent, and I scarcely know, Aby, how we shall make the land sufficiently barren. Yet it would have a fine effect! Yes, that it certainly would, and we will try our utmost. The hermitage too at the far end! The moss-grown cell, Aby! With a few scattered eglantines and wild roots! We will plant ivy round the three old oaks, and bring a colony of owls to breed! Then at the bottom of all a grotto: Oh! it will be delicious!

Shells will be expensive, for we are not within forty miles of the sea. But no matter: it must and it shall be done, for I have set my heart on it. Nay, from what you said to me, honest Aby, knowing you to be a careful thrifty fellow, full of foresight, I was so warm in the cause that I had determined to take your advice, and renounce or defer the journey to France; but the blabbing servants got a hint of the matter, and it came to my daughter's ears. So, for peace and quietness sake, I think I must e'en indulge her, and take her a short trip to the continent. But we will go no further than the neighbourhood of Paris. Beside I wish, for my own part, to see how the country is laid out. I am desirous to know whether all France has any thing to equal Wenbourne-Hill.

And yet, Aby, I find it is impossible to please every body. You know what continual improvements I have been making, for these last twenty years; for you have superintended them all. I have planted one year, and grubbed up the next; built, and pulled down; dug, and filled up again; removed hills, and sent them back to their old stations; and all from a determination to do whatever could be done. And now, I believe, there are no grounds in all England so wooded and shut in as those of Wenbourne-Hill; notwithstanding its situation on a very commanding eminence. We are surrounded by coppices, groves, espaliers,[1] and plantations. We have excluded every vulgar view of distant hills, intervening meadows, and extensive fields; with their insignificant green herbage, yellow lands, and the wearisome eternal waving of standing corn.

And yet, Aby, after having done all this, comes me Sir Alexander Evergreen, and very freely tells me that we have spoiled Wenbourne-Hill, buried ourselves in gloom and darkness, and shut out the finest prospects in all England! Formerly the hall could be seen by travellers from the road, and we ourselves had the village church in view, all of which we have now planted out of sight! Very true: but, instead of the parish steeple, have we not steeples of our own in every direction? And, instead of the road, with the Gloucestershire hills and lessening clouds in perspective, have we not the cedar quincunx?[2] Yet see the curse of obstinacy and want of taste! Would you think it, Aby? Of this Sir Alexander complains!

It is in vain to tell him that we are now all within ourselves; that every body is surprised to see how snug we are; and that nobody can suspect so many temples, and groves, and terraces, and ascents, and descents, and clumps, and shrubberies, and vistas, and glades, and dells, and canals, and statues, and rocks, and ruins are in existence, till they are in the very midst of them. And then! Oh how have I enjoyed their admiration! Nothing is so great a pleasure to me as to bring a gentleman of taste, who knows how to be struck with what he sees, and set him down in the middle of one of my great gravel walks! For all the world allows, Abimelech, that our gravel walks at Wenbourne-Hill are some of the broadest, the straightest, and the finest in the kingdom.

Yet observe how men differ, Abimelech. Sir Alexander wants me to turf them over! He says that, where you may have the smooth verdure, gravel walks are ridiculous; and are only tolerable in common pathways, where continual treading would wear away the greensward. But I know what has given him such a love for the soft grass. Sir Alexander is gouty, and loves to tread on velvet.

Beside he is a cynic. He blames all we have done, and says he would render one of the deserts of Arabia the garden of Eden,

with the money we have wasted in improving Wenbourne-Hill;
which he affirms, before we touched it, was one of the most beautiful spots in the three kingdoms.

I confess, Aby, that, if as I said I did not know him to be a cynic,
I should be heartily vexed. But it either is, or at any rate it shall be,
one of the most beautiful spots in the three kingdoms, ay or in the
whole world! Of that I am resolved; so go on with your work,
Abimelech. Do not be idle. The love of fame is a noble passion;
and the name of Arthur St. Ives shall be remembered at Wenbourne-Hill, long after his remains are laid in their kindred clay,
as the poet says.[1]

I desired your son Frank to accompany us to London. He is a
spirited young fellow, and behaved well on the road, where he had
an affair with a highwayman, and got a slight wound; but he is in
no danger. He is a fine fellow, a brave fellow, and an honour to you,
honest Aby.

Some grounds which I saw on my journey, with water purling,
meandering, and occasionally dashing down a steep declivity, or
winding along a more gentle descent, as it happened to be, suggested an idea to me. It came into my mind that, as we lie high, if
we had but a lake sufficiently large on the top of the hill, we could
send the water down in rivulets on every side. But then the difficulty
struck me how to get it up again. Perhaps it may be overcome. It
would have a charming effect, and we will think of it hereafter.

When you have received my address at Paris, do not fail to let
me know, once a week, how every thing proceeds. Be particular in
your accounts, and do not be afraid of wearying me. My heart is
in my grounds and my improvements; and the more places and
things you name the more pleasure you will give me. Write to me
too concerning my herd of deer, my Spanish sheep, my buffaloes,
my Chinese pheasants,[2] and all my foreign live stock.

I will make my journey as short as possible; it shall not be long
before I will re-visit my Wenbourne-Hill. To own the truth, honest
Aby, after reading your letter, I had ordered the chaise to the door
to come down again; but Anna St. Ives would not hear of it, so I
was obliged to yield. But, as I tell you, my heart is with you;
Wenbourne-Hill is never out of my mind.

I could wish you to be cautious in your communications,
Abimelech, concerning our money matters. My daughter gave me

D

a hint about the last mortgage, which I did not half like. Children think they have a right to pry into a father's expences; and to curb and brow-beat him, if the money be not all spent in gratifying their whims. Be more close, Abimelech, if you would oblige me.

ARTHUR ST. IVES

LETTER X

Louisa Clifton to Anna Wenbourne St. Ives

Rose-Bank

I AM excessively angry with myself, my dear Anna. I have not treated you with the open confidence which you deserve, because I have had improper fears of you. I have doubted lest an excess of friendship and generosity should lead you into mistake, and induce you to think well of my brother rather for my sake than for his own. But the more I reflect the more I am convinced that duplicity never can be virtue.

Your last letter has brought me to a sense of this. The noble sincerity with which you immediately accused yourself, for having practised an artifice [which I, like you, do not think was innocent, because artifice cannot be innocent] has taught me how I ought to act; and Sir Arthur's caprice is an additional incitement.

I have for some time known that it has been very much desired by my mamma to see you and Coke Clifton united. She mentioned her wish to Sir Arthur, and he seemed pleased with the idea. She did me the honour to consult me; and I opposed precipitate proceedings, and strenuously argued that all such events ought to take their natural course.

This was the origin of your present journey to Paris; and I consequently was enjoined secrecy, of the propriety of which I doubted at the moment. I am now convinced that secrets are always either foolish or pernicious things, and that there ought to be none.

The fickleness of Sir Arthur however, relative to this journey, both surprises and pains me. It shews his weakness as well as the power of his favourite, Abimelech, to be greater than even I imagined; and my former thoughts were not very favourable.

After having concerted this plan with my mamma, and after preparing and proceeding a part of the way, I can scarcely imagine what excuse he would have made to her.

His mentioning my brother to you likewise surprised me. In conversing with my mamma, I had told her that, if such an event were to take place, it were desirable that you and my brother should become acquainted, before any hint or proposal ought to be made to you. I at present believe this to have been wrong and weak advice; but it prevailed, and the arrangement was that my mamma should write to Coke Clifton, to direct his route through Paris; that he should be there at a fixed time, to transact some pretended business for her; that Sir Arthur and you should make a journey thither on a party of pleasure, which we all knew would be agreeable to you; and that you and my brother should meet as if by accident. But it appears that Sir Arthur, when he has any favourite project in view, can scarcely forbear being communicative, not from principle but from incontinence.

With respect to my brother, having told you all that has passed, I have only to add, it is my earnest advice that you should be careful to put no deception on yourself, but to see him as he is. His being the brother of your friend cannot give him dignity of mind, if he have it not already. Were I a thousand times his sister, I could not wish him another wife so deserving as my Anna. But sister shall be no motive with me to make me desirous of seeing persons united whose sentiments and souls may be dissimilar. Had I not so much confidence in your discernment, and truth to yourself, I should not be without uneasiness. My opinion is that the parties should themselves reciprocally discover those qualities which ought mutually to fit them for the friendship of marriage. Is not that the very phrase, Anna; *the friendship of marriage?* Surely, if it be not friendship, according to the best and highest sense in which that word is used, marriage cannot but be something faulty and vicious.

I know how readily you will forgive the wrong I have done you by this concealment; because you will perceive I acted from well meant but mistaken sentiments. I have told my mamma my present thoughts, and have shewed her all the former part of this letter, which she approves. Her affection for me makes her delight in every effort of my mind to rise superior to the prejudices that bring misery into the world; and I often fear lest this affection should deprive her of that force, and acumen, which in other instances would be ready to detect error, whenever it should make its appearance.

I need not tell my Anna how tenderly she joins with me, in wishing her a safe and pleasant journey. All other matters she entirely commits to my Anna's penetration, and discretion.

Adieu.

L. CLIFTON

P.S. My brother is not rich, but has great expectations. This as I imagine occasioned Sir Arthur to receive the proposal with pleasure; and my mamma tells me they had some talk of settlements. He was exceedingly warm and active, in contriving this journey, for a few days; after which I thought I observed his ardour abate. And the probability is that Abimelech, from the first, had opposed the excursion; but that further conversations with my mamma, and the pleasure which the projected journey had given you, kept Sir Arthur to his purpose. I own I began to suspect that, should such a match take place, the recollection of parting with money, which he would willingly have expended on improvements, had influenced his conduct; and it is some relief to hope that he was rather acted upon than acting, if he really did feel any wish to retract. How far he may be, or may have been, acted upon in other instances, as well as this, is still a further question.

I cannot shake off a doubt which hangs on my mind; though I have been debating all morning whether I ought to mention it or be silent. I suspect that you yourself have not solved it entirely to your own satisfaction. Frank Henley!—It is I think indubitable that he loves you.—He would make you happier than perhaps any other man could upon earth. Be not swayed by your affection for me: beware of any such weakness. That you could love him if you would permit yourself, nay that you are obliged to exert your whole force not to love him, I am convinced. You are conscious of it yourself.— Is your decision just?—Indeed it is a serious question. What is the magnitude of the evil which would result from such a union; and what the good? Enquire—I give no opinion. There is a mist before my eyes, and I dare not give any, till I can see more distinctly. Think, be just, and resolve. Your own judgment ought to determine you.

LETTER XI

Frank Henley to Oliver Trenchard

London, Grosvenor-Street

OLIVER, what are we? What is man? What is virtue? What is honour?—My pride has received a wound much more acute than that which the ball of the highwayman inflicted on my body—I have had money palmed upon me—Money!—A man cannot behave as he ought, and as it would be contemptible not to behave, but he must be paid! His vices are paid! His virtues are paid!—All is mercenary! I to be sure must be one of the number!—A twenty pound bank note, I tell thee, forced upon me by Sir Arthur!—No, no—Not by him—He never could have made me accept what I supposed [falsely, however; as fact and reflection have since led me to suspect] it was mean and degrading to accept. She only could prevail. She whose commands are irresistible, and who condescended to entreat!—Her eye glistening with a tear, which she with difficulty detained in its beauteous orbit, she entreated!—There was no opposing such intercession! Her eloquence was heavenly! God be praised that it was so! For, as it has happened, I am persuaded it has preserved a poor distressed creature from phrensy—Have patience, and I will tell thee.

I had removed my penitent, and had been taking a short airing in the park; and, as I was returning, I saw a crowd collected in a court. Led by curiosity to enquire what was the matter, I was told that two men had just been pursuing a third over the roofs of the neighbouring houses; and that, having been obliged to descend through a trap-door, they had followed him, where it was supposed he had at last been taken. I asked what his crime was, but nobody knew. Some believed him to be a thief, some thought it was a press-gang, and others conjectured they were bailiffs.

It was not long, however, before a decent, well-looking, and indeed handsome young woman, with a fine child in her arms, came running up the court, made her way through the crowd with terror in her countenance, and with the most piercing cries demanded—'Where is he?—Where is my dear Harry?—Who has seen him? Where is he?'

Some of the people pointed out the house. She knocked violently, continued her cries and lamentations, and at last gained admittance.

Her grief was so moving, so sympathetic, that it excited my compassion, and made me determine to follow her. Accordingly I elbowed my way, though I felt that I rather disturbed the surgeon's dressing; but that was a trifle. I followed her up stairs without ceremony. With respect to her, affection, 'masterless passion, had swayed her to its mood;'[1]—she was not to be repulsed.

The prisoner and his pursuers had descended to the second floor, in which the poor fugitive had endeavoured to seek refuge, but not soon enough to find protection from the bailiffs, as they proved and as he knew them to be. Never didst thou see terror so strong, nor affection so pathetic, as this excellent young woman, his wife, discovered. Excellent I am certain she is. She wrung her hands, she fell on her knees, she held up her babe; and, finding these were ineffectual, she screamed agonizing prayers to save her Harry. The idea she had conceived of the loss of liberty, and the miseries of a prison, must have been dreadful. But tears and prayers and cries were vain; she was pleading to the deaf, or at least to the obdurate.

As soon as the violence of her grief gave a momentary respite, I enquired what the sum was for which he was in thraldom, and found it to be sixteen pounds, beside costs. It was not a debt originally contracted by himself; it was for a note, in which he had joined to serve his wife's brother. It seemed they are a young couple, who by their industry have collected a trifling sum, with which they have taken a small shop. I did not ask of what kind. She serves her customers, and he follows his trade, as a journeyman carpenter. It did not a little please me to hear the young creature accuse her brother of being false to his friend; while the husband defended him, and affirmed it could be nothing but necessity. I could perceive however that she grieved to think her brother was not so good as she could have wished him to be.

The horrors of a jail were so impressed, so rooted in her fancy, that she was willing to sell any thing, every thing; she would give them all she had, so that her Harry might not be dragged to a damp, foul dungeon; to darkness, bread and water, and starving. Thou canst not imagine the volubility with which her passions flowed, and her terrors found utterance, from the hope that it was not possible for Christian hearts to know all this, and not be moved to pity.

I am well persuaded however that, had I not been there, those good Christians the bailiffs would have paid no other attention to her panic than to see how it might be turned to profit. The miscreants talked of five guineas, for the pretended risk they should run, in giving him a fortnight to sell his effects to the best advantage. They too could recommend a broker, a very honest fellow—By what strange gradations, Oliver, can the heart of man become thus corrupt? The harpies looked hatefully.

Luckily I happened to have the twenty pound note, which pride had bidden me reject with so much scorn, in my pocket. Thou, I am certain, wilt not ask what I did with it. I immediately tendered those same Christians I told thee of their money. The rascals were disappointed, and would have been surly; but a single look silenced their insolence. One of them was dispatched, according to form, to see that there were no detainers; and, being paid, they then set their prisoner free.

Now, if thou thinkest, Oliver, thou canst truly figure to thyself the overflowing gratitude of the kind young creature, the wife, thou art egregiously mistaken. She fell on her knees to me, she blessed me, prayed for me, and said I was an angel from heaven, sent to save her dear Harry from destruction; she kissed him, hugged, God blessed, and half smothered her heavenly infant, as she truly called it, with kisses; nay she kissed me—in spirit, Oliver —I could see she did: ay and in spirit I returned her chaste caresses.

She entreated me with so much humble love and gratitude to come and see her poor house, which I had saved, and to tell her my name, that she might pray for me the longest day she had to live, that I could not forbear gratifying her so far as to go with her. As for my name, I told her it was man. The quick hussey understood me, for she replied—No, it was angel.

I found her house, like her person, neat, and in order. What is still better, her Harry seems a kind good young man, and alive to as well as deserving of her affection.

Wouldst thou think it, Oliver?—The pleasure I had communicated had reverberated back upon myself; yet the sight of a couple thus happy gave birth to a thought of such exquisite pain

that——! Something shot across my brain—I know not what—
But it seemed to indicate I should never be so mated!

Still, this money, Oliver——Prithee be at the trouble to examine
the question, and send me thy thoughts; for I have not been able
to satisfy myself. What is the thing called property? What are
meum and *tuum*? Under what circumstances may a man take money
from another? I would not be proud; neither would I render myself
despicable.

Thou seest how I delight to impart my joys and griefs to thee.
Thou tellest me thou partakest them; and, judging by myself, I
cannot but believe thee. Tell me when thou art weary of me; I have
long and often been weary of myself.

Yet she is very kind to me, and so kind that I have lately been
betrayed into hopes too flattering, too ecstatic to be true. Oh!
Should she ever think of me! Were it only possible she ever should
be mine!—The pleasure is too exquisite! It is insupportable!—Let
me gaze and wonder at humble distance, in silence and in awe!—
Do not call me abject—Yet, if I am so, do; tell me all that ought to
be told. It is not before her rank that I bend and sink. Being for
being I am her equal: but who is her equal in virtue?—Heavens!
What a smile did she bestow on me, when I took the money I
mentioned to thee! It has sunken deep, deep in my heart! Never
can it be forgotten! Never! Never!

Peace be with thee.

F. HENLEY

LETTER XII

Anna Wenbourne St. Ives to Louisa Clifton

London, Grosvenor-Street

MUST I be silent? Must I not tell my Louisa how infinitely her
candor and justice delight me? With the voice of a warning angel
she bids me enquire, examine my heart, and resolve. I think I
have resolved; and from reasons which I believe are not to be
overcome. Yet I will confess my opinion, strong as it is, receives
violent attacks; as, Louisa, you will be convinced, when you have
read the whole of this letter.

My friend cautions me against being partial, even in favour of her brother. Such a friend is indeed worthy to advise, and I will remember her precepts. This brother may be a degenerate scion from a noble stock: yet I can hardly think the thing possible. That he may have fallen into many of the mistakes, common to the world in which he has lived, is indeed most likely. But the very qualities which you describe in him speak an active and perhaps a dignified nature.

We have duties to fulfil. Few opportunities present themselves to a woman, educated and restrained as women unfortunately are, of performing any thing eminently good. One of our most frequent and obvious tasks seems to be that of restoring a great mind, misled by error, to its proper rank. If the mind of Clifton should be such, shall I cowardly decline what I believe it to be incumbent on me to perform? Let him be only such as I expect, and let me be fortunate enough to gain his affections, and you shall see, Louisa, whether trifles shall make me desist.

What high proofs of courage, perseverance, and of suffering, do men continually give! And shall we wholly renounce the dignity of emulation, and willingly sign the unjust decree of prejudice, that mind likewise has its sex, and that women are destitute of energy and fortitude?

But Frank Henley!—Let me not hide a thought from my Louisa. He is indeed worthy of being loved, every day more worthy. I have a new story to tell, which will be more effectual praise than any words of mine. Like you I am persuaded he has some affection for me. I am not insensible to his worth and virtues: I ought not to be. Were I to indulge the reveries into which I could easily fall, I might be as much misled by passion as others, who are so ready to complain and pity themselves for being in love. But a wakeful sense of the consequences is my safeguard. It cannot be. I should render my father, my relations, and friends, miserable. I should set a bad example to my sex. I, who aim at shewing them mind is superior to sex.

Such are the thoughts that protect me from the danger. His mental excellence perhaps I love as truly as heart could wish. But, as the lover who is to be the husband, no! I will not suffer my thoughts to glance in that direction. I might, but I will not. Nothing but a conviction that my principles are wrong shall ever make me; and that conviction I hold to be impossible.

Do not imagine I am guilty of the mistake of supposing myself
his superior. Far the reverse. The tale which I am now about to
relate will inform you better of the true state of my feelings.

You must know, my dear, that on our arrival in town, Sir Arthur,
with my help, prevailed on Frank Henley to accept a twenty pound
bill, that he might have the means of gratifying his inclinations, and
enjoying the pleasures which at his age it is natural he should wish
to enjoy. These means I had but too good reason to be convinced
had been denied him by his father, which I suspected to be, and
am now satisfied was, the true reason that Frank refused to attend
us on our journey.

The youth has quite pride enough, my dear: he is desirous to
confer, but not to accept obligations; is ready enough to give, but
not to receive. As if he had not only a right to monopolize virtue,
but to be exempt from the wants which are common to all, and to
supply which men form themselves into societies. He seems to
shrink with exquisite pain from the acceptance of money. However I was determined to conquer, and conquer I did. Nor can I
say, considering them as I do, that I was sorry to offend the false
feelings even of Frank Henley, for whom I have an infinite esteem.

After receiving this present, he accompanied me two or three
times to those public places to which crowns and half guineas gain
admittance; and, as you may imagine, was far from appearing
insensible of the powers of poetry and music. Suddenly however
he refused to be any more of such parties, for which I own I could
divine no reason. I knew he had been educated in habits of œcon-
omy, and therefore could not suppose, generous though I knew
him to be, that he had squandered away his pocket-money in so
short a time. I endeavoured both to rally and to reason, but in
vain; he was positive even to obstinacy; and I rightly conjectured
there must be some cause for it which I had not discovered.

You have heard me speak, I believe, my dear, of Mrs. Clarke,
as of a careful good woman, and a great favourite with my dear
mamma, when living. She was then our housekeeper in the country, but has lately been left in the town house; because the furniture
is too valuable to be entrusted to a less attentive person. This Mrs.
Clarke had a sister whose name was Webb, and who left a son
and a daughter, who are both married. The son, as you will soon
hear, has been a wild and graceless fellow; but the daughter is

one of the most agreeable and engaging young creatures I think I ever saw.

Yesterday my good Mrs. Clarke and her niece were shut up together in close conversation for a considerable time; and I perceived that their cheeks were swelled, their eyes red, and that they had been crying violently. I almost revere Mrs. Clarke as my mother, because of the excellence of her heart and the soundness of her understanding. I therefore could not forbear earnestly enquiring whether it were possible for me to remove her cause of grief; for grieved, I told her, I could plainly perceive she was. She burst into tears again on my questioning her, and endeavoured to express feelings that were too big for utterance. Turning to her niece she said—'I must inform my dear young lady.' 'For God's sake don't! For the Lord's sake don't!' cried the terrified creature. 'I must,' replied the aunt. 'It is proper.' 'He will have no mercy shewn him! He will be hanged!' exclaimed the other, in an agony. 'You do not know this lady,' said the aunt. 'Indeed she does not,' added I, 'if she supposes I would have any creature upon earth hanged.' 'Retire, Peggy,' said the aunt, 'while I relate the vile, the dreadful tale.' 'No, no! For mercy's sake no!' replied the niece. 'I must stay, and beg, and pray, and down on my knees for my brother! He is a wild and a wicked young man, but he is my brother.' 'Pray let her stay,' said I to the aunt. 'And fear nothing, my kind-hearted Peggy. Be assured I will not hurt a hair of your brother's head. I will do him good if I can, but no injury.' 'The God of Heaven bless and reward your angelic ladyship!' cried the half frantic grateful Peggy.

Mrs. Clarke attempted to begin her story. She was almost suffocated. I never heard so heart-rending a groan as she gave, when she came to the fatal sentence! Would you believe it, Louisa? This nephew of the worthy Mrs. Clarke, this brother of the good Peggy, is the very highwayman who shot Frank Henley!

His benevolent aunt has been with him, for he is still under the surgeon's hands; and he has confessed to her [I am angry with myself, Louisa, to find I wonder at it] he has confessed that the brave, the humane, the noble-minded Frank has visited him several times, and has set the folly of his wicked pursuits in so true and so strong a light, that the man protests, with the utmost vehemence, if he can but escape punishment for the faults he has

committed, he will sooner perish than again be guilty of his former
crimes.

The first time Frank visited him he gave the poor wretch a
guinea; and went himself in search of another lodging for him, as
well to remove him from the knowledge of his wicked companions
as to protect him from the forty pound hunters. The man wants to
escape over to the continent; and appears to be so sincere, in his
resolves of reformation, that Frank has undertaken to furnish him
with the means.

You cannot imagine, Louisa, the heart-felt praises which the
worthy Mrs. Clarke bestowed on the youth. And Peggy said that
she hoped she should some time or another live to see him, that
she might fall down and kiss his footsteps! But, added she, with
great ardor, I find indeed there are very good men in the world!

Still there appeared something enigmatical to me, between
Frank and the money account. I could not conceive how he should
want the means immediately to furnish such a sum as would have
been sufficient for the poor fugitive. And this again reminded me
how assiduously Frank had lately avoided every occasion of
expence.

While we were in the midst of our discourse, who should enter
the room but Frank! Never was I present at such a scene!———
'Good God Almighty!' exclaimed Peggy, the moment she saw
him. 'This is he! This is the very blessed, dear gentleman, that
saved my poor Harry from those terrible jailors.'

'Is it possible?' cried Mrs. Clarke.

'It is, it is he! He himself!' said the full-hearted Peggy, falling
down on her knees, and catching the flap of his coat, which she
kissed with inconceivable enthusiasm.

Poor Frank did not know which way to look. Good deeds are
so uncommon, and so much the cause of surprise, that virtue
blushes at being detected almost as deeply as vice. I knew Frank
had a noble heart; and I own, Louisa, I was not much amazed
when Peggy, with abundance of kind expressions and a flow of
simple eloquence, related the manner in which Frank had saved
her husband from the bailiffs, by paying a debt which with costs
amounted to upward of eighteen pounds.

I did not however forbear severely to reprove myself, for having
dared so much as to imagine that a youth with such high virtues

could not, in a city like London, find opportunities of expending so small a sum as twenty pounds in acts of benevolence. I ought at least to have supposed the thing probable; yet it never once entered my mind.

The thanks, blessings, and prayers of Peggy were endless. Finding him not only to be what she knew, the man who relieved her from the most poignant distress, but likewise the vanquisher and the saviour of her brother, she said and protested she was sure there was not such another angel upon earth! She was sure there was not! Frank was ashamed of and almost offended at her incessant praise. It was so natural and so proper for him to act as he did, that he is surprised to find it can be matter of wonder.

I must insist however upon seeing him reimbursed; and I persuade myself there is one thought which will make him submit to it quietly. I have but to remind him that the good of others requires that men, who so well know the use of it, should never be without money.

Adieu. I have not time to write more at present.—Yet I must, for I ought to add, that, though I thought myself so fully convinced when I began this letter, concerning Frank and the only right mode of acting, doubts have several times intruded themselves upon me, while I have been writing. I will think when the fancy is not so busy as at present; and when I have thought do not fear my resolution.

Ever most affectionately yours,

A. W. ST. IVES

LETTER XIII

Frank Henley to Oliver Trenchard

London, Grosvenor-Street

IT is an intolerably strange thing, Oliver, that a man cannot perform the mere necessary duties of humanity, without being supposed almost a prodigy. Where is the common sense, I will not say delicacy, which should teach people that such suppositions are an insult, not only to the person but to all mankind? I am young, I grant, and know but little of the barbarity which it is pretended is universal. I cannot think the accusation true. Or, if it be, I am convinced it must be the result of some strange perversion of what may be called the natural propensities of man. I own I have seen children wrangle for and endeavour to purloin, or seize by force, each others apples and cherries; and this may be a beginning to future rapacity. But I know the obvious course of nature would be to correct, instead of to confirm, such mistakes. I know too that there are individual instances of cruelty, and insensibility. But these surely are the exceptions, and not the rule.

I visited a man whose vices, that is whose errors and passions were so violent as to be dangerous to society, and still more dangerous to himself. Was it not my duty? I thought myself certain of convincing him of his folly, and of bringing back a lost individual to the paths of utility and good sense. What should I have been, had I neglected such an opportunity? I have really no patience to think that a thing, which it would have been a crime to have left undone, should possibly be supposed a work of supererogation!

I saw an industrious rising family on the brink of ruin, and in the agonies of despair, which were the consequences of an act of virtue; and I was not selfish enough to prefer my own whims, which I might choose to call pleasures, to the preservation of this worthy, this really excellent little family. And for this I am to be adored! For no word is strong enough to express the fooleries that have been acted to me. They were well meant? True. They were the ebullitions of virtue? I do not deny it. But either they are an unjust satire upon the world in general, or it is a vile world. I half suspect, indeed, it is not quite what it ought to be.

In addition to all this, I have been obliged to receive a sum equal to that which I thought it my duty to bestow. This is the second time; and perhaps thou wilt tell me I am not difficult to persuade. Read the following dialogue, which passed between me and the most angelic of Heaven's creatures, and judge for thyself. She is really a prodigy! I never knew another mind of such uncommon powers! So clear, so collected, so certain of choosing the side of truth, and so secure of victory!

I am an ass! I am talking Arabic to thee. I ought to have begun with informing thee of a circumstance which is in itself odd enough. The highwayman and Peggy. [Pshaw! The woman whose husband was arrested.] They are not only brother and sister, but the nephew and niece of Mrs. Clarke. Think of that, Oliver! The nephew of so worthy a woman so audaciously wicked! Well might the distressed Peggy express anger which I could perceive was heartfelt, though she herself at that time knew not of this act. But to my dialogue. Listen to the voice of my charmer, and say whether she charm not wisely!

You have made a generous and a noble use, Frank, of the small sum which you were so very unwilling to accept. [She treats me with the most winning familiarity! What does she mean? Is it purposely to shew me how much she is at her ease with me; and how impossible it is that any thing but civility should exist between us? Or is it truly as kind as it seems? Can it be? Who can say? Is it out of nature? Wholly? Surely, surely not. These bursting gleams of hope beget suspense more intolerable than all the blackness of despair itself.]

I acted naturally, madam; and I confess it gives me some pain to find it the subject of so much wonder.

It is no subject of wonder to me. Your inferiors in understanding I know would not act like you; but the weak do not give law to the strong. I own that I have been dull enough, unjust enough, not to suspect your true motive for refusing, as you have done lately, to accompany us to public places. But this is a heavy penalty on you which an act of virtue ought not to incur.

If it be a penalty, madam, I am sure it is one which you have too much generosity to wish to deprive me of the pleasure of paying.

I understand your hint: but I am not so generous as you think me; for I am determined, and you know what a positive girl I am, to share both the penalty and the enjoyment with you.

I beg your pardon, madam, but that cannot be.

Oh! But, in spite of your serious and very emphatical air, it must be.

Excuse me, madam. I am certain you have too high a sense of justice to impose laws to which you yourself would not submit.

Very true. Prove me that and I am answered. Nay, so confident am I of the goodness of my cause, that I will not require you to take up this [Laying down another bank note, of equal value with the former.] unless I can on the contrary prove it to be nothing but false pride, or mistake, which can induce you to refuse. You

perceive, Frank, I am not afraid of offending you by speaking the
plain truth. Pray tell me, when you saw the worthy couple whom
you relieved in distress, had you persisted in your refusal of the
paltry bit of paper which I before prevailed on you to receive,
what would you have said to yourself, what would have been your
remorse, when you found yourself unable to succour the unfortunate, merely because you had been too proud to receive that which
you wanted, and which therefore you had no right to refuse. [You
see, Oliver, she snatched my own sword from my side, with which
to dispatch me. If thou art too dull to understand me, consult my
last letter.] You were ready to protect, though at the risk of your
life, those very persons at whose favours, as they are falsely called,
your spirit is so equally ready to revolt. Perhaps in defending us
you did no more than you ought; but we cannot be ignorant how
few are capable of doing so much. And, since you are thus prompt
to perform all which the most austere morality can require, so
long as it shall be apparent to the world that your motives are not
selfish, proceed a step further; disregard the world, and every
being in it; that is, disregard their mistakes; and, satisfied that
your motives are pure, defy the false interpretations to which any
right action may subject you. Neither, while you are actually discharging the highest offices of humanity, deny to others the right
to fulfil some of the most trivial.

I could not act otherwise than I did, on both the occasions to
which you allude, madam. I believe it is our duty always to be
guided by circumstances; but not to be guilty of an impropriety,
because it is possible such circumstances may again occur.

You are right. We only differ concerning the meaning of the
word. Impropriety, or propriety, we shall come to presently. You
have promised your wounded penitent money, to facilitate his
escape, and you have none.

I have some trifling useless property, madam.

But you have a journey to make back to Wenbourne-Hill,
according to your present intentions.

Do you imagine, madam, I cannot fast for a day?

Oh yes! I doubt it not; for a week, Frank, to effect any great,
any laudable purpose. But I must be plain with you. It is un-
generous of you to wish to engross all virtue and sensibility.
Beside, you have duties to perform to yourself, which are as

pressing as any you owe to society, because they are to fit you for
the social duties. [Hearken to the angel, Oliver!] It is as much my
duty, at present, to afford you the means which you want, as it
was yours to visit the wounded highwayman, or aid the distressed
Peggy. You ought to suffer me to perform my duties, both for my
sake and your own. You ought not to neglect, while you are in
London, to seize on every opportunity which can tend to enlarge
your faculties. You have no common part to act; and, that you may
act it well, you should study the beings with whom you are to associate. You must not suffer any false feelings to unfit you for the high
offices for the execution of which men like you are formed. [Didst
thou ever hear such honeyed flattery, Oliver?] Something more—
You must accompany us to France.

Madam!——Impossible.

Hear me, Frank. The journey will be of infinite service to you.
A mind like yours cannot visit a kingdom where the manners of
the people are so distinct as those of the French must be from the
English, without receiving great benefit. Your father is rich.

That he denies, madam.

To you; and you and I know why. If your delicacy should object
to a gift, I am sure it cannot with propriety to a loan. Going with
us, your expences will in fact be only casual. I can supply you with
such money as you want, which you may hereafter repay me, when
I may perhaps be glad that I have such a debtor.

My father's property, madam, is of his own acquiring; I have
no legal claim upon it; and it would be dishonest in me to spend
that, upon speculation, which perhaps never may be mine.

Yes; to spend it in unworthy purposes would be dishonest. But
I again recur to your duties. However, since you are so tenacious
on the subject, I will become a usurer to pacify your feelings, and
you shall pay for risk. Fifty pounds, unless you meet with more
Peggies, I dare say will bear you free. [It is twenty pounds more,
thou knowest, than I asked of my father.] You shall give me eighty
whenever you have a thousand pounds of your own.

Madam!——

Well, well! You shall give me a hundred——[Very seriously]
It almost vexes me, Frank, to be refused so very slight a favour;
for I can read refusal and opposition in your eye. But, if you persist,
you will give me great pain; for you will convince me that, where

E

your own passions are concerned, you are not superior to the paltry
prejudices by which the rest of the world are governed.

I own, madam, my mind has had many struggles on the subject;
and I am afraid, as you say, it has been too willing to indulge its
prejudices, and its pride. But if you seriously think, from your
heart, it is my duty to act in this case as you direct—

I do, seriously, solemnly, and from my heart, think it is your
duty.

Then, madam, I submit.

Why that's my kind Frank! As noble in this instance as in every
other——I could love you for it if you would let me—[In a moment
my heart was alarmed! I could feel myself change colour! I am
certain she saw my agitation; her manner told me so, for she
instantly added, with a kind of affectionate significance which I
know not how to interpret—] I would say as much to the whole
world, but that it is a foolish world, and wants the wit to conceive
things truly as they are meant.

She was gone in an instant, smiling, sailing,[1] and her countenance brightening with heavenly radiance, as she departed.

What can this be? Her words are continually resounding in my
ears!——*She could love me, if I would let her!*——Heavens!——
Love me?——Let her?—Let her!—Oh!—*It is a foolish world*——
She fears its censures——Love me!—Is it possible?——Tell me,
Oliver, is it possible?——*It wants the wit to conceive things truly as
they are meant*——Was this forbidding me to hope; or was it
blaming the world's prejudices?——I know not——Ah! To what
purpose warn the moth, unless she could put out the light?—Oh,
blasphemy!——Love me if I would let her?——I cannot forget it,
Oliver!——I cannot!——Oh! I could weep like a child, at my own
conscious debility.

Why should I despair?——With a modern miss, a fine lady, I
might; but not with her. She has a mind superior to the world,
and its mistakes. And am I not convinced there ought to be no
impediment to our union? Why should I doubt of convincing her?
She dare do all that truth and justice can demand—And she could
love me if I would let her—Is not my despondency absurd?—
Even did I know her present thoughts, and know them to be
inimical to my passion, what ought I to do? Not to desert my own
cause, if it be a just one: and, if it be the contrary, there is no

question: I will make none. Let me but be convinced of my error, and it shall be renounced. Yes, Oliver, I dare boldly aver—it shall! But shall I forego a right so precious, if it be mine?—No! Kingdoms shall not tempt me!—Why is this timidity? Why does my heart palpitate? Why with inward whispers do I murmur thoughts which I dare not speak aloud? Why do they rise quivering to my lips, and there panting expire, painfully struggling for birth, but in vain? Oh! How poorly do I paint what so oppressively I feel!

I would have thee read my whole heart. I shudder to suppose it possible I should be a seducer. Falsely to be thought so would trouble me but little. But tamely to yield up felicity so inestimable, in compliance with the errors of mankind to renounce a union which might and ought to be productive of so much good, is not this a crime?——Speak without fear. Shew me what is right. Convince me, then blame me if I quail.

And now, Oliver, it is probable thou wilt not see me for these three months. Delicate as these money favours are become in the transactions of men, contemptible as they often are in themselves, and unwilling as I have been to subject myself to them, I am glad that she has conquered. I would not have hesitated a moment; for obligation, if obligation it were, to her would be heaven: but she has her own wants, her own mode of doing good. These I was very desirous not to abridge. But, since I must either comply or remain behind, I am glad to have been so honourably vanquished.

My father, I know, is willing enough I should go to France, or where I please, so that I do not ask him for money. Indeed he told me as much. He thinks it matters not what becomes of a fellow so useless, and so idle, as he supposes me to be. However I have written to inform him of my intention, and once more to remind him, though certainly in vain, of the manner in which he ought to act.

Ever thine,

F. HENLEY

P.S. Thou art an unwilling, sluggish correspondent. I have just received thine of the 21st. I find I am in no danger of reproof, from thee, for the acceptance of these pecuniary obligations: but I half suspect, from the tenor of thy letter, that thou wouldst bid me take all that any body is willing to give. Be just to thyself and thy friend,

Oliver; shrink not from wholesome severity. Let not thy suavity of temper, or thy partial kindness to me, sway thee to the right or the left; lest hereafter I should make the fearful demand of my lost principles, or at least relaxed and enfeebled, from thee. Beware of the kindness of thy heart.

Do not omit my most respectful and kind acknowledgments to thy father and family.

LETTER XIV

Anna Wenbourne St. Ives to Louisa Clifton

London, Grosvenor-Street

I HAVE had a strong contest, my dear, with our favourite youth, to overcome what I believe I have convinced him is prejudice; and I hope he is cured of false delicacy, for the future. He is to go with us to France, and is no longer under the necessity of abstaining from innocent and instructive amusements, because he is possessed of sensibility and a high respect for virtue.

But he had no sooner accepted this supply than away he was gone to his convert. This I suspected. For which reason I had previously dispatched Mrs. Clarke to visit her nephew. The good woman could not be prevailed on to receive any money for his relief; urging that she was very capable of supplying him herself. That being so, I did not choose violently to contest the matter with her; as I do not wish to encourage the most distant approaches to a spirit of avarice. I only told her it would be unjust should she ever want money, for useful and virtuous purposes, if she did not apply to me: and she with much good sense answered she thought as I did, and would certainly act accordingly. She is a very worthy woman.

She was with her nephew when Frank came in; and the scene, as described by her, was affecting. The poor culprit had been repeating all his obligations to the generous Frank, praising his bravery, and dwelling, with a degree of conviction which gave Mrs. Clarke great pleasure, on the effects of goodness; since it could render a man so undaunted, so forgiving, so humane, and so much as he said like a saint. You know, my dear, that saint, in the language of such people, does not mean an impostor, who pretends to carry burning coals in his hands, drive rusty nails into his legs, adore a morsel of rotten wood, or decayed bone, and pretend to work miracles, or preach exclusive doctrines of faith and salvation. A saint with them is a person more perfect, in the discharge of the highest moral duties, than they believe any other earthly being to be. Let us accept their definition, and enroll the name of Frank Henley in our calendar.

Frank was disappointed, and in some measure displeased, that any person should offer his reformed friend, as from the best of motives he called him, money but himself; and the reason he gave was not without its force. This is a memorable epocha in the life of a mistaken man, said he; and no means, which can move his mind to a better performance of his duties than he has hitherto attempted, should be left untried. It is but natural that he should think more of me than of most other persons: ['I can think of no one else!' Exclaimed the poor fellow, with enthusiasm.] and, the more cause he shall have to remember me with affection, the more weight will the reasons have with him which I have urged.

The culprit acknowledged that, from ill advice, vicious example, and violent passions, he had become very wicked. But, said he, I must be wicked indeed if I could ever forget what this gentleman has said, and done, to save my family from shame and ruin, and me from destruction and death.

There is the greater reason to hope, because Mrs. Clarke says that he has been what is called well educated, his station in life considered: and indeed of this I imagine she herself had taken care.

Peggy came in, and by her excess of gratitude, and which is better of admiration for her hero, she drove the over delicate Frank away. This is one of his defects, for which we must endeavour to find a remedy. Men are not exposed to the fulsome praise which we unmarried females are calmly obliged to hear, or be continually at war; or Frank would be more patient. Indeed he ought to be; because, in this instance, the praises he receives are the effusions of persons who had never before seen virtue exert herself with so much ardour.

Though the nephew be not an old or hardened offender, he has committed some depredations of the consequences of which, were they proved upon him, he himself is ignorant. His accomplice has discovered his retreat; another more private lodging has therefore been taken for him, to which he is to remove with all possible caution. And when he is sufficiently recovered, which Mrs. Clarke tells me will be soon, he is then to depart for the continent and work at his trade, which is that of a cabinet-maker. English workmen are in high esteem abroad, and he will easily find employment. He is more than reconciled to labour, he is eager to begin; and, as it appears, does not want activity of mind; of which the dangerous expedients to which he resorted are some proof.

So much for the history of a highwayman; which I think is at least as deserving of remembrance as that of many other depredators.

I have been making some efforts to decide the question, not of love, but, of duty. Love must not be permitted, till duty shall be known. I have not satisfied myself so well as I could wish, yet my former reasons seem invincible. Ought my father and my family to be offended? Ought I to set an example that might be pernicious? Is it most probable that by opposing I should correct or increase the world's mistakes? The path before me is direct and plain; ought I to deviate?

In vain I fear should I plead his extraordinary merit. Would the plea remove the load of affliction with which I should overwhelm those who love me best? At present they think well, nay highly of me. I sometimes have the power to influence them to good. What power shall I have when they imagine I have disgraced both myself and them?

Who ever saw those treated with esteem who are themselves supposed to be the slaves of passion? And could the world possibly be persuaded that a marriage between me and the son of my father's steward could ever originate, on my part, in honourable motives?

Ought I to forget the influence of example? Where is the young lady, being desirous to marry an adventurer, or one whose mind might be as mean as his origin, who would not suppose her favourite more than the equal of Frank? For is not the power of discrimination lost, when the passions are indulged? And ought my name to be cited? Ought they to be encouraged by any act of mine?

Yet the opposing arguments are far from feeble. His feelings are too strong to be concealed. Perhaps the only weakness I can think him capable of is that of loving me. For if love be contradictory to reason, it is a weakness; but should he answer that love and reason are in this instance united, we must come to proofs. That he loves is too visible to admit of doubt. I have seen the word trembling as it were on his tongue. I am almost certain that a silly thing which I said, with a very different intention, would have produced an avowal of his passion, had I not added something to prevent it, and hurried away.

Well then! Am I certain I am guilty of no injustice to him? And why ought I not to be as just to him as to any other being on earth? Who would be more just to me? Who would be more tender, more faithful, more affectionate?

I know not whether I ought to shrink from the vanity which seems annexed to the idea, for I know not whether it be vanity, but I cannot sometimes help asking myself whether the good that might result from the union of two strong minds, mutually determined to exert their powers for the welfare of society, be not a reason superior even to all those I have enumerated.

If this be so, and if our minds really possess the strength which I am so ready to suppose, I then know not what answer to give. I reject the affectation of under estimating myself, purposely that I may be called a modest humble young lady. Humility I am persuaded, though not so common, is as much a vice as pride. But, while avoiding one extreme, I must take care not to be guilty of another. The question is embarrassing; but I must not by delay suffer embarrassment to increase.

With respect to your brother, I can at present conclude nothing, and can conjecture but little. The idea which has oftenest occurred, and which I have before mentioned, is the infinite pleasure of seeing an active mind in the full possession of its powers; and of being instrumental in restoring that which mistake may have injured, or in part destroyed. It seems a duty pointed out to me; attended perhaps with difficulty, and it may be with danger; but these increase its force. And if so, here is another argument to add to the heaviest scale.

Yes. It must be thus. The more I examine, and while I am writing perhaps I examine the best, the more I am confirmed in my former decision.

Pity for Frank ought not to be listened to. It is always a false motive, unless supported by justice. Frank will never condescend to endeavour to incite compassion; it is not in his character. He will rather assert his claims, for so he ought. I do not mean that a complaint will never escape him. The best of us are not always so perfectly master of our thoughts as never to be inconsistent. But his system will not be to win that by intercession which he could not obtain by fair and honourable barter. The moment I have entirely satisfied and convinced myself, I have no doubt of inducing him to behave as nobly on this as he has done on every other trying occasion.

And now, my dear Louisa, for the present farewel. I do not suppose I shall write again, except a line to inform you of our safe arrival after having crossed the channel, till we come to Paris. I expect to be amused by the journey. Though I cannot but own I think that, as far as amusement was concerned, the good ladies under the reign of the Tudors, who travelled twenty miles a day, on a strong horse and a pillion, that is when summer made the roads passable, had much better opportunities for observation than we, who, shut up in our carriages, with blinds to keep out the dust, gallop further in two days and two nights than they could do in a month. This hasty travelling, when haste is necessary, is a great convenience. But nothing, except the inordinate ardour of the mind to enjoy, could induce people on a journey of pleasure to hurry, as they do, through villages, towns, and counties, pass unnoticed the most magnificent buildings, and the most delightful prospects that forests, rivers, and mountains can afford, and wilfully exclude themselves from all the riches of nature. To look about us, while thus surrounded, seems to be a very natural wish. And if so, a portable closet, or rather a flying watch-box, is but a blundering contrivance.

You know your Anna: her busy brain will be meddling. And perhaps she trusts too much to the pardoning affection of friendship.

Once again, adieu.

Yours ever and ever,

A. W. ST. IVES

LETTER XV

Frank Henley to Abimelech Henley

SIR,

London, Grosvenor-Street

That I may not appear to neglect any filial duty, all of which it has been my most earnest wish to fulfil, I write to inform you that, at the request of the family, I am preparing to accompany Sir Arthur to France. From our last conversation I understood you had no objection to the journey, except that of furnishing me with money; for it was your pleasure to remind me that a man so idle, as you suppose I am, may be or go any where, without the world suffering the least loss. I own, did I imagine the same of myself, it would make me wretched indeed.

You thought proper, sir, to refuse me the small sum which I requested of you for this purpose. I do not wish to wrest what you are unwilling to give. You understand your own reasonings best; but to me they appear to be either erroneous or incomprehensible. I wished to explain to you what my plan of life was, but you refused to hear me. I had no sooner said that I thought it my duty to study how I could best serve society, than you angrily told me I ought first to think how I could best serve myself. From a recollection of the past, I am convinced this is a point on which we shall never have the same opinion. For this I am sincerely sorry, but as I hope not to blame.

Suffer me however once more to repeat, sir, that though my young lady has kindly offered to furnish me with money, I still think it wrong that you should permit me to accept her offer; having as I am well convinced the means to supply me liberally yourself. I assure you, sir, I would forbear to go, or to lay myself under the necessity of asking you for money, were I not fully persuaded of its propriety. In order to perform my duty in the world, I ought to understand its inhabitants, its manners, and principally its laws, with the effects which the different legislation of different countries has produced. I believe this to be the highest and most useful kind of knowledge.

Could I fortunately induce you to think as I do, you certainly would not refuse my request. Thirty pounds to you would be but a trifle. But from my late failure I have so little hope, that I rather write to execute a duty, than with any expectation of success.

I submit this to your consideration, and have the greatest desire to prove myself your dutiful and affectionate son,

F. HENLEY

LETTER XVI

Abimelech Henley to Frank Henley

Wenbourne-Hill

HERE's a hippistle! Here's tantarums! Here's palaver! Want to pick my pocket? Rob me? And so an please ee he's my dutyfool and fekshinait son! Duty fool, indeed? I say fool—Fool enough! And yet empty enough God he knoweth! You peery?[1] You a lurcher?[2] You know how to make your 3 farthins shine, and turn your groats into guineas?—Why you're a noodl! A green horn! A queezee quaumee[3] pick thank[4] pump kin![5] A fine younk lady is willin to come down with the kole,[6] and the hulver headed hulk[7] wants to raise the wind on his own father! You face the philistins![8] Why they will bite the nose off a your face!

Thirty pounds too! The mercy be good unto me! Me thirty pounds! Where must I get thirty pounds! Does the joult head[9] think I coin? Would he have me go on the highway? Who ever giv'd me thirty pounds? Marry come up! Thirty pounds? Why I came to Wenbourne-Hill with thrums[10] immee pouch. Not a brass farthin more. And now show me the he or the hurr—Shiner for shiner[11]—Hool a cry hold first?—Thos as to the matter of that, younker, why that's a nether here nor there; that's a nothink to you dolt. I never axt you for nothink. Who begottee and sentee into the world but I? Who found ee in bub and grub[12] but I? Didn'tee run about as ragged as any colt o' the common, and a didn't I find duddz[13] for ee? And what diddee ever do for me? Diddee ever addle[14] half an ounce in your life without being well ribb rostit?[15] Tongue pad[16] me indeed! Ferrit[17] and flickur[18] at me! Rite your hippistles and gospels! I a butturd my parsnips finely!

Am I a to be hufft and snufft o' this here manner, by a sir jimmee jingle brains[1] of my own feedin and breedin? Am I to be ramshaklt out of the super nakullums[2] in spite o' my teeth? Yea and go softly! I crack the nut and you eat the kernel!

I tellee once again you've an addle pate o' your own! Go to France to learn to dance, to be sure! Better stay at home and learn to transmogrify[3] a few kink's picters into your pocket. No marry come fairly! Squire Nincompoop! He would not a sifflicate[4] Sir Arthur, and advise him to stay at home, and so keep the rhino[5] for the roast meat! He would not a take his cue, a dunder pate! A doesn't a know so much as his a, b, c! A hasn't so much as a single glimm of the omnum gathrum[6] in his noddl! And pretends to hektur and doktur me! Shave a cow's tail and a goat's chin, an you want hair.[7]

And then again what did I say to ee about missee? What did I say? Didn't I as good as tellee witch way she cast a sheepz i? That indeed would a be summut! An you will jig your heels amunk the jerry cum poopz,[8] you might a then dance to some tune. I a warruntee I a got all a my i teeth imme head. What doesn't I know witch way the wind sets when I sees the chimblee smoke? To be sure I duz; as well with a wench as a weather-cock! Didn't I tellee y'ad a more then one foot i'the stirrup? She didn't a like to leave her jack in a bandbox[9] behind her; and so missee forsooth forgot her tom-tit, and master my jerry whissle an please you[10] galloped after with it. And then with a whoop he must amble to Lunnun; and then with a halloo he must caper to France! She'll deposit the rhino;[11] yet Nicodemus[12] has a no notion of a what she'd be at! If you've a no wit o' your own, learn a little of folks that have some to spare. You'll never a be worth a bawbee[13] o' your own savin. I tellee that. And ast for what's mine why it's my own. So take me ritely, now is your time to look about ee. Then indeed! If so, why so be it; yea ay and amen, a God's name, say I. The fool a held his mouth open, and a down a droppt the plumb.

Not after all that it would a be any sitch a mighty mirakkillus catch nether, as I shall manage matters mayhap. But that's a nether here nor there. And so you know my mind. Take it or leave it or let it alone. It's all a won to I. Thos and I gives all this here good advice for nothink at all, what do I get by it? Give me but the wide world and one and 20, with 5 farthins ten fingurs and a tongue,

and a turn me adrift to morrow; I'de a work my way: I'de a fear
nether wind nor weather. For why? I'de a give any man a peck of
sweet words for a pint of honey. What! Shall I let the lock rustee
for a want of a little oilin? Haven't I a told ee often and often, that
a glib tongue, smooth and softly, always with the grain, is worth a
kink's kinkddum?

So mind a what ee be at. Play your cards out kuninlee; and then,
why if so be as thinks should turn up trumps, why we shall see.
That is, take me ritely; and I has a no notion that ee should take it
into your nobb noddl[1] that I means to suppose that I shall come
down with the dust.[2] No forsooth! For what and for why and for
wherefore? We shall see—Why ay to be sure!—But what shall we
see? Why we shall see how generous and how kappaishus[3] my
younker will be, to his poor old father: we shall see that.

Not but if the ready be wantin, plump do you see me, down on
the nail head, and if Sir Arthur should a say as it must be so, why
so. Mayhap we—But I tell ee again and again that's a nether here
nor there. Besides leave me to hummdudgin[4] Sir Arthur. Mind
you your hitts with missee, I'll a foistee fubb[5] he.

And so now show your affection for all this my lovin kindness
and mercy; and crown my latter days with peace and joy, witch
nothink can xseed but the joys of heaven in his glory everlastin,
witch is a preparin for me and for all kristshun soles, glory and
onnur and power and praise and thanks givin, world without end,
for ever and ever, God be good unto us, and grant us his salvation;
amen, and it be his holy will.

                                                    ABIMELECH HENLEY

LETTER XVII

The Honourable Mrs. Clifton to her son, Coke Clifton

                                                         Rose-Bank

I DIRECT this letter to you, my dear son, at Paris; where it
will either find you, or lie at the banker's till your arrival. A
packet accompanies it, which contains the accounts of your late
uncle with Monsieur de Chateauneuf; by which it appears there

is a considerable balance in his favour, which as you know by will devolves to me.

I hope, when you have settled this business, you will be disposed to return to England; and that I shall once again have the happiness to see you before I die. Do not imagine I speak of death to attract any false pity. But my state of health obliges me to consider this serious event as at no great distance; though I do not think myself in immediate danger.

Sir Arthur St. Ives and his lovely daughter will soon be in Paris. They requested letters from me; and, among others, I thought I could not recommend them to any one with more propriety than to my son. There is an intimacy between our families at present; which was first occasioned by an affection which your sister Louisa and Anna St. Ives conceived for each other, and which has continually increased, very much indeed to my satisfaction. For, before I saw this young lady, I never met with one whom I thought deserving of the friendship of your sister, Louisa; whose strength of mind, if I do not mistake, is very extraordinary for her years. Yet even I, her mother, and liable enough to be partial, have sometimes thought she must cede the palm to her friend, the charming Anna.

My reason for writing thus is that you may be guilty of no mistakes of character, which indeed I think is very unlikely, and that you will shew Sir Arthur all possible respect, as well as his daughter, in justice to yourself, and as the friends of the family. Your sister writes under the same cover; and I cannot doubt, whenever you read her letters, but that you must receive very great satisfaction, to find you have such a sister.

I scarcely need tell you, Clifton, that though you have resided but little with me, I feel all the fond affection of a parent; that I am earnestly desirous to hear of your happiness, and to promote it; and that no pleasure which the world could afford to me, personally, would equal that of seeing you become a good and great man. You have studied; you have travelled; you have read both men and books; every advantage which the most anxious desire to form your mind could procure has been yours. I own that a mother's fondness forms great expectations of you; which, when you read this, be your faculties strong or weak, you will very probably say you are capable of more than fulfilling. The feeble,

hearing their worth or talents questioned, are too apt to swell and
assume; and I have heard it said that the strong are too intimately
acquainted with themselves to harbour doubt. I believe it ought
to be so. I believe it to be better that we should act boldly, and
bring full conviction upon ourselves when mistaken, than that a
timid spirit should render us too cautious to do either good or
harm. I would not preach; neither indeed at present could I. A
thousand ideas seemed crowding upon my mind; but they have
expelled each other as quickly as they came, and I scarcely know
what to add. My head-achs disqualify me for long or consistent
thinking; and nothing I believe but habit keeps me from being
half an idiot.

One thing however I cannot forget; which is, that I am your
mother, Clifton; and that I have the most ardent and unremitting
desire to see you a virtuous and a happy man. In which hope my
blessing and love are most sincerely yours.

M. CLIFTON

LETTER XVIII

Louisa Clifton to Her Brother, Coke Clifton

Rose-Bank

IT is long, my dear brother, since I received a letter from you;
and still longer since I had the pleasure to see you. How many
rivers, seas, valleys, and mountains have you traversed, since that
time! What various nations, what numerous opposite and characteristic countenances have you beheld! From all and each of
them I hope you have learned something. I hope the succession
of objects has not been so quick as to leave vacuity in the mind.

My propensity to moralize used formerly [And our formerlies
you know, brother, are not of any long duration.] to tease and half
put you out of temper. Indulge me once more in hoping it will not
do so at present; for I believe I am more prone to this habit than
ever. What can I say to my brother? Shall I tattle to him the
scandal of the village, were I mistress of it? Shall I describe to him
the fashion of a new cap; or the charms of a dress that has lately

travelled from Persia to Paris, from Paris to London, and from London to Rose-Bank? Or shall I recount the hopes and fears of a sister; who has sometimes the temerity to think; who would be so unfashionable as to love her brother, not for the cut of his coat, not for the French or Italian phrases with which he might interlard his discourse, not for any recital of the delight which foreign ladies took in him and which he took in foreign ladies, not for a loud tongue and a prodigious lack of wit, not for any of the antics or impertinences which I have too frequently remarked in young men of fashion, but for something directly the reverse of all these: for well-digested principles, an ardent desire of truth, incessant struggles to shake off prejudices; for emanations of soul, bursts of thought, and flashes of genius. For such a brother, oh how eager would be my arms, how open my heart!

Do not think, my dear Clifton, I am unjust enough to mean any thing personal; to satirize what I can scarcely be said to have seen, or to condemn unheard. No. Your faculties were always lively. You have seen much, must have learned much, and why may I not suppose you are become all that a sister's heart can desire? Pardon me if I expect too much. Do we not all admire and seek after excellence? When we are told such a person is a man of genius, do we not wish to enquire into the fact? And, if true, are we not desirous of making him our intimate? And do not the ties of blood doubly enforce such wishes, in a brother's behalf? From what you were, I have no doubt but that you are become an accomplished man. But I hope you are also become something much better. I hope that, by the exertion of your talents, acquirements, and genius, I shall see you the friend of man, and the true citizen of the world.

If you are all that I hope, I think you will not be offended with these sisterly effusions. If you are not, or but in part, you may imagine me vain and impertinent. But still I should suppose you will forgive me, because you are so seldom troubled with such grave epistles; and one now and then, if not intolerably long, may be endured from an elder sister.

Yet why do I say elder? Neither age nor station have any just claim; for there can be none, except the claims of truth and reason; against which there is no appeal. I am eighteen months older than my brother, and up rises the claim of eldership! Such are the habits, the prejudices we have to counteract.

My dear mamma has mentioned Sir Arthur St. Ives, in her letter, and his lovely daughter, Anna; more lovely in mind even than in form, and of the latter a single glance will enable you to judge. I need not request you to be attentive and civil to her, for it is impossible you should be otherwise. Your own gratification will induce you to shew her the public places, and render her every service in your power; which will be more than overpaid by associating with her; for it is indeed a delight to be in her company. For grace and beauty of person, she has no equal; and still less can she be equalled, by any person of her age, for the endowments of wit and understanding. I am half angry with myself for pretending to recommend her; when, as you will see, she can so much more effectually recommend herself.

I have nothing to add except to say that, when my dear brother has a moment's leisure, I shall be glad to hear from him; and that I remain his very affectionate sister,

L. CLIFTON

P.S. On recollection, I am convinced it is a false fear which has prevented me from mentioning another person, very eminently deserving of esteem and respect; a fear of doing harm where I meant to do good. We ought to do our duty, and risk the consequences. The absurd pride of ancestry occasions many of our young gentlemen to treat those whom they deem their inferiors by birth with haughtiness, and often with something worse; forgetting that by this means they immediately cut themselves off as it were from society: for, by contemning those who are a supposed step below them, they encourage and incur contempt from the next immediately above them. This is in some measure the practice: and, were it true that birth is any merit, it would be a practice to which we ought to pay a still more strict attention. The young gentleman however whom I mean to recommend, for his great and peculiar worth, is Mr. Frank Henley, the son of a person who is gardener and steward to Sir Arthur; or rather what the people among whom you are at present would call his *homme d'affaires*. But I must leave my friends to speak for themselves; which they will do more efficaciously than can be done by any words of mine.

END OF VOLUME I

VOLUME II

Coke Clifton to Guy Fairfax, at Venice

Paris, Hotel de l'Université, près le Pont Royal

I WRITE, Fairfax, according to promise, to inform you that I have been a fortnight in France, and four days in this city. The tract of country over which I have passed, within these three months, is considerable. From Naples to Rome; from Rome to Florence; from Florence to Venice, where we spent our carnival; from Venice to Modena, Parma, and Genoa; from thence to Turin; from Turin to Geneva; then, turning to the left, to Lyons; and from Lyons to Paris. Objects have passed before me in such a rapid succession, that the time I have spent abroad, though not more than a year and a half, appears something like a life. The sight of the proud Alps, which boldly look eternity in the face, imparts a sensation of length of time wholly inadequate to the few hours that are employed in passing them. The labour up is a kind of age; and the swift descent is like falling from the clouds, once more to become an inhabitant of earth.

Here at Paris I half fancy myself at home. And yet, to timid people who have never beheld the ocean, and who are informed that seas divide France and England, Paris appears to be at an unattainable distance. Every thing is relative in this world; great or small near or distant only by comparison. The traveller who should have passed the deserts, and suffered all the perils all the emotions of a journey from Bengal by land, would think himself much nearer home, at Naples, than I do, coming from Naples, at Paris: and those who have sailed round the world seem satisfied that their labour is within a hair's breadth of being at an end, when they arrive, on their return, at the Cape of Good Hope.

F

You, Fairfax, have frequently asked me to give you accounts of this and that place, of the things I have seen, and of the observations I have made. But I have more frequently put the same kind of questions to myself, and never yet could return a satisfactory answer. I have seen people whose manners are so different from those of my own country, that I have seemed to act with them from a kind of conviction of their being of another species. Yet a moment's consideration undeceives me: I find them to be mere men. Men of different habits, indeed, but actuated by the same passions, the same desire of self-gratification. Yes, Fairfax, the sun moon and stars make their appearance, in Italy, as regularly as in England; nay much more so, for there is not a tenth part of the intervening clouds.

When molested by their dirt, their vermin, their beggars, their priests, and their prejudices, how often have I looked at them with contempt! The uncleanliness that results from heat and indolence, the obsequious slavishness of the common people, contrasted with their loquacious impertinence, the sensuality of their hosts of monks, nay the gluttony even of their begging friars, their ignorant adoration of the rags and rotten wood which they themselves dress up, the protection afforded to the most atrocious criminals if they can but escape to a mass of stone which they call sacred, the little horror in which they hold murder, the promptness with which they assassinate for affronts which they want the spirit to resent, their gross buffooneries religious and theatrical, the ridiculous tales told to the vulgar by their preachers, and the improbable farces which are the delight of the gentle and the simple, all these, and many other things of a similar nature, seem to degrade them below rational creatures.

Yet reverse the picture, and they appear rather to be demi-gods than men! Listen to their music! Behold their paintings! Examine their palaces, their basins of porphyry, urns and vases of Numidian marble, catacombs, and subterranean cities; their sculptured heroes, triumphal arches, and amphitheatres in which a nation might assemble; their Corinthian columns hewn from the rocks of Egypt, and obelisks of granite transported by some strange but forgotten means from Alexandria; the simplicity the grandeur and beauty of their temples and churches; the vast fruitfulness of their lands, their rich vineyards, teeming fields, and early harvests; the

mingled sublime and beautiful over the face of nature in this
country, which is sheltered from invaders by mountains and seas,
so as by a small degree of art to render it impregnable; their
desolating earthquakes, which yet seem but to renovate fertility;
their volcanos, sending forth volumes of flame and rivers of fire,
and overwhelming cities which though they have buried they have
not utterly destroyed; these and a thousand other particulars, which
I can neither enumerate nor remember, apparently speak them a
race the most favoured of heaven, and announce Italy to be a
country for whose embellishment and renown earth and heaven,
men and gods have for ages contended.

The recollection of these things appears to be more vivid, and
to give me greater pleasure than I believe the sight of them afforded.
Perhaps it is my temper. Impatient of delay, I had scarcely glanced
at one object before I was eager to hunt for another. The tedious-
ness of the Ciceroni[1] was to me intolerable. What cannot instantly
be comprehended I can scarcely persuade myself to think worthy
of the trouble of enquiry. I love to enjoy; and, if enjoyment do not
come to me, I must fly to seek it, and hasten from object to object
till it be overtaken.

Intellectual pleasures delight me, when they are quick, certain,
and easily obtained. I leave those which I am told arise from patient
study, length of time, and severe application, to the fools who think
time given to be so wasted. Roses grow for me to gather: rivers
roll for me to lave in. Let the slave dig the mine, but for me let
the diamond sparkle. Let the lamb, the dove, and the life-loving
eel writhe and die; it shall not disturb me, while I enjoy the
viands. The five senses are my deities; to them I pay worship
and adoration, and never yet have I been slack in the performance
of my duty.

What! Shall we exist but for a few years, and of those shal.
there be but a few hours as it were of youth, joy, and pleasure,
and shall we let them slip? Shall we cast away a good that never
can return; and seek for pain, which is itself in so much haste
to seek for us? Away with such folly! The opposite system be
mine.

The voluptuous Italian, as wise in this as in other arts, knows
better. He lives for the moment, and takes care not to let the
moment slip. His very beggars, basking in the sun, will not remove,

so long as hunger will suffer them to enjoy the happiness of being idle. Who so perfectly understand the luxury of indolence as the Lazaroni[1] of Naples?

The Italian, indeed, seems to exert all the craft for which he is so famous, to accomplish this sole purpose of enjoyment. He marries a wife, and the handsomest he can procure; that, when the ardour of desire is satiated, she may fleece some gallant, who shall pay for his pleasures elsewhere. And, as variety is the object of all, gallant succeeds to gallant, while he himself flies from mistress to mistress, and thus an equal barter is maintained.

This office of Cicisbeo[2] is however an intolerably expensive one; especially to our countrymen. The Signora is so inventive in her faculties, there are so many trinkets which she dies to possess, and her wants, real and artificial, are so numerous, that the purse is never quiet in the pocket. And every Englishman is supposed to be furnished with the purse of Fortunatus.[3]

The worst because the most dangerous part of the business is, the ugly and the old think themselves entitled to be as amorous as the young and beautiful; and a tall fellow, with a little fresh blood in his veins, is sure to have no peace for them. Prithee, Fairfax, tell me how the Contessa behaved, when she found I had escaped from her amorous pursuit. She began to make me uneasy; and I almost thought it was as necessary for me to have a taster as any tyrant in Christendom. Poison and the stiletto disturbed my dreams; for there were not only she, but two or three more, who seemed determined to take no denial. I congratulated myself, as I was rolling down mount Cenis,[4] to think that I was at length actually safe, and that the damned black-looking, hook-nosed, scowling fellow from Bergamo, whom I had so often remarked dogging me, was no longer at my heels.

But I have now bidden adieu to the *Cassini*, the *Carnivali*, and the *Donne*;[5] and soon shall see what provision this land of France affords. For the short time that I have been here, I have no occasion to complain of my reception. I do not know why, Fairfax, but we Englishmen seem to be in tolerably good repute every where, with the ladies. Well, well, pretty dears, they shall find me very much at their service. I should be sorry to bring disgrace upon my nation, Fairfax. Would not you?

I expect to find you a punctual correspondent. Fail not to let me know, when, weary of being a *Cavaliere servente*,[1] you shall leave the proud banks of the Adriatic, and the wanton Venice, for some other abode; that our letters may never miss their aim. I will relate every thing that happens to me, when it can either afford you amusement to read, or me satisfaction to write. You have too much honour and honesty not to do the same. Or, if not, I will try what a threat can do: therefore remember that, unless you fulfil the terms of our agreement, and give me an account of all your rogueries, adventures, successes, and hair-breadth escapes, I will choose some other more punctual and more entertaining correspondent.

Observe further, and let that be a spur to your industry, I have a tale in petto;[2] a whimsical adventure which happened to me yesterday evening; but which I shall forbear to regale you with, for three substantial reasons: first because it is my good pleasure; secondly because I like it; and lastly such is my sovereign will. Nay, if that be all, I can give you three more: first because I am almost at the end of my paper; next because I may want a good subject when I write again; and finally because the post is a sturdy unceremonious fellow, and does not think proper to wait my leisure.

So farewell; and believe me to be very sincerely yours,

COKE CLIFTON

P.S. I have this moment received information that Sir Arthur St. Ives and his daughter arrived yesterday in the afternoon at Paris. I have heard that the daughter is the most beautiful woman in England, and that her wit is even superior to her beauty. I am very glad of the accident, for I have a great desire to see her. My mother's last was partly a letter of business, but chiefly of recommendation, particularly of the young lady: and in it was enclosed one from my sister, Louisa, which gives a very high character of her friend, Anna St. Ives. They have become acquainted since I have been abroad. The letter is loaded with advice to me, at which as you may well think I laugh. These girls, tied to their mother's apron-strings, pretend to advise a man who has seen the world! But vanity and conceit are strange propensities, that totally blind the eyes of their possessors. I have lived but little at home, but I always thought the young lady a forward imperious miss; yet I never before knew her so much on the stilts. I expect she will soon put on boots and buckskin,[1] and horsewhip her fellows herself; for she improves apace.

Once more farewell.

LETTER XX

Anna Wenbourne St. Ives to Louisa Clifton

Paris, Hotel d'Espagne, Rue Guenegaude,
Fauxbourg St. Germain

AFTER abundance of jolting in carriages, sea sickness, and such-like trifling accidents, incidental to us travellers, here we are at last, dear Louisa. My very first demand has been for pen ink and paper, to inform my kind friend of our safe arrival: though I am so giddy, after this post haste four day's hurry, that I scarcely can write a straight line. Neither do I know whether I have any thing to say; though I seemed to myself to have acquired an additional stock of ideas, at the very moment that I first beheld Calais and the coast of France.

What is there, my dear, in the human mind, that induces us to think every thing which is unusual is little less than absurd? Is it prejudice, is it vanity, or is it a short and imperfect view; a want of discrimination? I could have laughed, but that I had some latent sense of my own folly, at the sight of a dozen French men and women, and two or three loitering monks, whom curiosity had drawn together upon the pier-head, to see us come into port. And what was my incitement to laughter?—It was the different cut of a coat. It was a silk bag, in which the hair was tied, an old sword, and a dangling pair of ruffles; which none of them suited with the poverty of the dress, and meagre appearance, of a person who seemed to strut and value himself upon such marks of distinction.

Sterne was in my pocket,[2] and his gentle spirit was present to my mind. Perhaps the person who thus excited a transient emotion of risibility was a nobleman. For the extremes of riches and of poverty are, as I have been informed, very frequent among the nobility of France. He might happen to think himself a man highly unfortunate and aggrieved. The supposition occasioned my smile to evaporate in a sigh.

But the houses!—They were differently built!—Could that be right? They were not so clean! That was certainly wrong. In what strange land is the standard of propriety erected?—Then the blue and brown jackets of the women; their undaunted manner of staring; their want of hats, and stays; the slovenly look of slippers not drawn up at the heel; the clumsy wooden shoes of some, and the bare feet of others; nay their readiness to laugh at the uncouth appearance of the people who were condemning them for being ridiculous; what could all this be? But how came I so unaccountably to forget that children and beggars sometimes go barefoot in England; and that few people, perhaps, are more addicted to stare and laugh at strangers than ourselves? Oh! But the French are so polite a nation that even the common people are all well bred; and would enter a drawing-room with more ease and grace than an English gentleman!—Have you never heard this nonsense, Louisa?

The character of nations, or rather of mind, is apparent in trifles. Granted. Let us turn our eyes back to the shores we have so lately left: let us examine the trifles we hang about ourselves. How many of them, which characterize and as it were stamp the nation with absurdity, escape unobserved! We see them every day; we have adopted and made them our own, and we should be strangely offended, should any person take the liberty, having discovered the folly of them, to laugh at us.

I wrote thus far last night; but learning, on enquiry, that Tuesdays and Fridays are foreign post days, I left off; being rather indisposed after my journey. 'Tis only a swimming in the head, which will soon leave me; though I find it has returned upon me occasionally all the morning. But to my pleasing task; again let me prattle to my friend.

The innkeepers of Calais come themselves, or send their waiters, to watch for and invite passengers to their houses; and will not be dismissed without difficulty. The most daring endeavour to secure customers, by seizing on some of their trunks, or baggage. But we had determined to go to Dessein's, and the active Frank soon made way for us.

I was amused with the handbill, stuck up against the walls of this inn, or hotel, as it is called; announcing it to be the largest, the completest, the most magnificent, with a thousand et cæteras, in the universe; and recounting not only its numerous accommodations, but the multifarious trades which it contained within its own walls; to all which was added a playhouse. A playhouse it is true there was, but no players; and as for trades, there were at least as many as we wanted. Sir Arthur took over his own carriage; otherwise this first of inns in the universe would not have furnished him with one, but on condition of its being purchased.

Sir Arthur observed it was strange that the French innkeepers should not yet have discovered it to be their interest to keep carriages for travellers, as in England. To which Frank Henley shrewdly answered, that the book of post roads, in his hand, informed him government was in reality every where the innkeeper; and reserved to itself the profits of posting. And the deepest thinkers, added Frank, inform us that every thing in which governments interfere is spoiled. I remarked to him that this principle would lead us a great way. Yes, said he, but not too far: and, playing upon my words, added, it would lead us back to the right way, from which we appear at present to have strayed, into the very labyrinth of folly and blunders.

Frank is earnestly studious of the effects of governments, and laws; and reads the authors who have written best on such subjects with great attention, and pleasure. He and Sir Arthur by no means agree, in politics; and Sir Arthur has two or three times been half affronted, that a man so young and so inferior to himself, as he supposes Frank to be, should venture to be of a different opinion, and dispute with him; who was once in his life too a member of parliament. I am obliged now and then slily to remind him of the highwayman and Turnham Green.

And now, Louisa, traveller like, could I regale you with a melancholy narrative, relating how the fields in this country have no hedges; how the cows are as meagre as their keepers; how wretched the huts and their owners appear; how French postillions jump in and out of jack-boots, with their shoes on, because they are too heavy to drag after them; how they harness their horses with ropes; how dexterously they crack the merciless whips with which they belabour the poor hacks they drive; how we were obliged to pay for five of these hacks, having only four in our carriage, and two of them frequently blind, lame, or useless; with many other items, that might be grievous to hear, could I but persuade myself thoroughly to pity or be angry at the whole French nation, for not exactly resembling the English. But do they themselves complain? Mercy on us! Complain?—Nothing is so grateful to their hearts, as the praise of that dear country, which English travellers are so prone to despise!

Frank as usual has been all attention, all ardour, all anxiety, to render our journey as pleasant as possible. His efforts have been chiefly directed to me; my ease, my satisfaction, my enjoyment, have been his continual care. Not that he has neglected or overlooked Sir Arthur. He overlooks no living creature, to whom he can give aid. He loses no opportunity of gaining the esteem and affection of high and low, rich and poor. His delicacy never slumbers. His thirst of doing good is never assuaged. I am young it is true, but I never before met a youth so deserving. Think of him myself I must not; though I would give kingdoms, if I had them, to see him completely happy.

And now, dear Louisa, I am soon to meet your brother. Why do I seem to recollect this with a kind of agitation? Is there rebellion in my heart? Would it swerve from the severe dictates of duty? No. I will set too strict a watch over its emotions. What! Does not Louisa honour me with the title of friend, and shall I prove unworthy of her friendship? Forbid it emulation, truth, and virtue!

How happy should I be were your brother and Frank Henley to conceive an immediate partiality for each other! How much too would it promote the project I wish to execute! I have been taxing my invention to form some little plot for this purpose, but I find it barren. I can do nothing but determine to speak of Frank as he deserves; which surely will gain him the love of the whole world. And for his part, I know how ready he will be to give merit its due.

I have more than once purposely mentioned your brother's name to Sir Arthur, when Frank was present; in some manner to prepare and guard him against surprise. But I could not but remark my hints had an effect upon him that betrayed how much his heart was alarmed. He thinks too favourably, and I fear too frequently of me. What can be done? The wisest of us are the slaves of circumstances, and of the prejudices of others. How many excellent

qualities are met in him! And for these to be rejected—! Alas!—
We must patiently submit to the awful laws of necessity.

Neither is Sir Arthur without his fears and suspicions. His
discourse betrays his alarms. He cannot conceive that a love of the
merits of Frank can be distinct from all love of his person. The
crime of disobedience in children, the ruin of families by foolish
and unequal marriages, and the wretchedness which is the result
of such guilty conduct, have been hinted at more than once lately;
and though not with many words, yet with a degree of anxiety that
gave me pain, for it taught me, being suspected, half to suspect
myself.

But I must conclude: my travelling vertigo I find is not immediately to be shaken off. I imagine that a few hours calm sleep will
be my best physician. Adieu. I shall wait, with some impatience,
for a letter from my dear Louisa.

A. W. ST. IVES

LETTER XXI

Frank Henley to Oliver Trenchard

Paris, Hôtel d'Espagne, Rue Guenegaude,
Fauxbourg St. Germain

MY emotions, Oliver, are too strong to permit me to narrate
common occurrences. I can only tell thee our journey is ended,
that we arrived yesterday, and that we are now at Paris. My feelings are more tumultuous than they ought to be, and seek relief
in the mild and listening patience of friendship.

First however I must relate a singular adventure, which
happened yesterday evening.

After I had seen our baggage properly disposed of, curiosity led
me, though night was approaching, to walk out and take a view of the
famous façade of the Louvre. From thence I strayed, through the
gardens of the Thuilleries, to the Place de Louis XV; being delighted
with the beauties around me, but which I have not now time to
describe. A little farther are the Champs Elysées, where trees planted
in quincunx afford a tolerably agreeable retreat to the Parisians.

It was now twilight. The idlers had retired; for I suppose, from what followed, that it is not very safe to walk after dark, in these environs. Ignorant of this, and not apprehensive of any danger, I had strayed to a considerable distance among the trees, against one of which I stood leaning, and contemplating the banks of the Seine, the Palais Bourbon, and other surrounding objects. All was silent, except the distant hum of the city, and the rattling of carriages, which could but just be heard.

Amid this calm, I was suddenly alarmed by voices in anger, and approaching. They spoke in French, and presently became more distinct and loud.

Draw, sir, said one.

Mort de ma vie, come along, answered the other.

Draw, sir, I say; replied the first. I neither know who you are nor what your intentions may be. I will go no further. Draw!

Sacristi, answered his antagonist, we shall be interrupted: the guard will be upon us in a moment.

The first however was resolute, and in an imperious voice again bade him draw. Their swords were instantly out, and they began to assault each other. Thou mayst imagine, Oliver, I would not cowardly stand and be a spectator of murder. They were not twenty paces from me. I flew; when, to my great surprise, one of them called, in English, Keep off, sir! Who are you? Keep off! And, his enemy having dropt his guard, he presented his point to me.

It was no time to hesitate. I rushed resolutely between them; holding up my open hands above my head, to shew the Englishman, who seemed apprehensive of a conspiracy, he had nothing to fear from me. His anger almost overcame him: he held up his sword, as if to strike with it, and with great haughtiness and passion again bade me begone. Have patience, sir, answered I. Men shall not assassinate each other, if I can prevent it.

Let us retire, said the Frenchman: I knew we should be interrupted.

You shall not fight. I will follow you, added I, I will call for help.

You are a damned impertinent fellow, said the Englishman.

Be it so; but you shall not fight, was my answer.

The combatants, finding me so determined, put up their swords, and mutually exchanged their address; after which they separated.

So that it is probable, Oliver, my interference has done no good. But that I must leave to chance. I could not act otherwise.

This incident, so immediately after my arrival, in a place so strange to me, and coming so suddenly, made too great an impression upon me not to tell it thee. Though I have another topic much nearer my heart; the true state of which has been shewn me, by an event of which I will now inform thee.

We are lodged here in the first floor, consisting of many chambers, each of which is a thoroughfare to the most distant. It is not ten minutes since I was seated, and preparing to write to thee, when Anna came to pass through the room where I was, and retire to her own apartment. She was fatigued, I imagine, by the journey; though I frequently fear the ardour of her mind will injure her constitution. She walked with some difficulty, was evidently giddy, and staggered. I was alarmed, and was rising, when she called to me faintly,—'Help me, Frank!'

I sprung and caught her as she was falling. I received her in my arms! And my agitation was so violent, that it was with difficulty I could preserve strength enough to support her, and seat her in the chair I had quitted.

The house to me was a kind of wilderness. I knew not where to run, yet run I did for water. I called Laura, with a latent wish that nobody might help her but myself; and, as it happened, nobody heard. I returned; she recovered, thanked me, with her usual heavenly kindness, and I conducted her to her apartment, she leaning on my arm.

Oh! Oliver, is it wrong to feel what I feel, at the remembrance? If it be, reprove me sternly; teach me my duty, and I will thank thee. Surely there is something supernatural hovers over her! At least she resembles no other mortal! Then her kindness to me, her looks, her smiles, her actions, are all intentional benignancy. She is now but three chambers distant from me; enjoying as I hope refreshing slumbers. Angels guard her, and inspire her dreams. No matter for the nonsense of my words, Oliver; thou knowest my meaning. She desired me to bid Laura not disturb her; and here I sit, watchful of my precious charge. Grateful, heart-soothing office!

And now, Oliver, what am I to think? My fears would tie my tongue; but, either I am deluded or hope brightens upon me, and I want the self-denying resolution of silence. Yes, Oliver, I must repeat, there is such sweetness in her countenance, when she speaks to me, such a smile, so inviting, so affirmative, that I am incessantly flattering myself it cannot but have a meaning. I have several times lately heard her sigh; and once so emphatically that I think it impossible I should be deceived. I and Sir Arthur were conversing. I was endeavouring to shew the pernicious tendency of the pre-judices of mankind, and inadvertently touched upon the absurdity of supposing there could be any superiority, of man over man, except that which genius and virtue gave. Sir Arthur did not approve the doctrine, and was pettish. I perhaps was warmed, by a latent sense of my own situation, and exclaimed—'Oh! How many noble hearts are groaning, at this instant, under the oppres-sion of these prejudices! Hearts that groan, not because they suffer, but because they are denied the power effectually to aid their very oppressors, who exert the despotism of numbers, to enforce claims which they themselves feel to be unjust, but which they think it dishonourable to relinquish!'——It was then the sigh burst forth of which I told thee. I turned and found her eyes fixed upon me. She blushed and looked down, and then again bent them toward me. I was heated and daring. We exchanged looks, and said—! Volumes could not repeat how much!—But surely neither of us said any thing to the other's disadvantage.

Oh! The bliss to perceive myself understood and not reproved! To meet such emanations of mind—! Ecstasy is a poor word! Once more she seemed to repeat—*She would love me if I would let her.*

Tell me, then—Have I not reason on my side? And, if I have, will she not listen? May she not be won? Shall I doubt of victory, fighting under the banners of truth? Alas!—Well well—

My own sensations, Oliver, are so acute, and I am so fearful lest they should lead me astray, that I could not forbear this detail— Let us change the theme.

Well, here we are, in France; and, wonderful to tell, France is not England!

I imagine it is impossible to travel through a foreign country, without falling into certain reveries; and that each man will fashion his dreams in part from accident, and in part according to the manner in which he has been accustomed to ruminate. Thy most excellent father, Oliver, early turned my mind to the consideration of forms of government, and their effects upon the manners and morals of men. The subject, in his estimation, is the most noble that comes under our cognizance; and the more I think myself capable of examining, and the more I actually do examine, the more I am a convert to his opinion. How often has it been said of France, by various English philosophers, and by many of its own sages, What a happy country would this be, were it well governed! But, with equal truth, the same may be said of every country under heaven; England itself, Oliver, in spite of our partialities, not excepted.

How false, how futile, how absurd is the remark that a despotic government, under a perfect monarch, would be the state of highest felicity! First an impossible thing is asked; and next impossible consequences deduced. One tyrant generates a nation of tyrants. His own mistakes communicate themselves east, west, north, and south; and what appeared to be but a spark becomes a conflagration.

How inconsistent are the demands and complaints of ignorance! It wishes to tyrannize, yet exclaims against tyranny! It grasps at wealth, and pants after power; yet clamours aloud, against the powerful and the wealthy! It hourly starts out into all the insolence of pride; yet hates and endeavours to spurn at the proud!

Among the many who have a vague kind of suspicion that things might be better, are mingled a few, who seem very desirous they should remain as they are. These are the rich; who, having by extortion and rapine plundered the defenceless, and heaped up choice of viands and the fat of the land, some sufficient to feed ten, some twenty, some a hundred, some a thousand, and others whole armies, and being themselves each only able to eat for one, say to the hungry, who have no food—'Come! Dance for my sport, and I will give you bread. Lick the dust off my shoes, and you shall be indulged with a morsel of meat. Flatter me, and you shall wear my livery. Labour for me, and I will return you a tenth of your gain. Shed your blood in my behalf, and, while you are young and robust, I will allow you just as much as will keep life and soul together; when you are old, and worn out, you may rob, hang, rot, or starve.'

Would not any one imagine, Oliver, that this were poetry? Alas! It is mere, literal, matter of fact.

Yet let us not complain. Men begin to reason, and to think aloud; and these things cannot always endure.

I intended to have made some observations on the people, the aspect of the country, and other trifles; I scarcely now know what: but I have wandered into a subject so vast, so interesting, so sublime, that all petty individual remarks sink before it. Nor will I for the present blur the majesty of the picture, by ill-placed, mean, and discordant objects. Therefore, farewell.

F. HENLEY

P.S. Examine all I have said, and what I am going to add, relative to myself, with severity. Mine is a state of mind in which the jealous rigour of friendship appears to be essentially necessary. I have been seized with I know not what apprehensions, by some hints which she has two or three times lately repeated, concerning the brother of her dear and worthy friend, Louisa; who, it seems, is to give us the meeting at Paris. Is it not ominous? At least the manner in which she introduced the subject, and spoke of him, as well as the replies of Sir Arthur, were all of evil augury. Yet, why torment myself with imaginary terrors? Should the brother resemble the friend—! Well! What if he should? Would it grieve me to find another man of virtue and genius, because it is possible my personal interest might be affected by the discovery? No. My mind has still strength sufficient to reject, nay to contemn, so unworthy a thought. But he may be something very different! Love her he must: all who behold her love! The few words she has occasionally dropped, have led me to suspect 'more was meant than met the ear.' Whenever this chord is touched, my heart instantly becomes tremulous; and with sensibility so painful as fully to lay open its weakness; against which I must carefully and resolutely guard. It is these incongruous these jarring tokens that engender doubt, and suspense, almost insupportable.

LETTER XXII

Anna Wenbourne St. Ives to Louisa Clifton

Paris, Hotel d'Espagne, Rue Guenegaude,
Fauxbourg St. Germain

THE oddest and most unlucky accident imaginable, Louisa, has
happened. Your brother and Frank have unfortunately half
quarrelled, without knowing each other. I mentioned a giddiness
with which I was seized; the consequence, as I suppose, of travelling. I was obliged to retire to my chamber; nay should have fallen
as I went, but for Frank. I desired he would tell Laura not to disturb me; and he it seems planted himself sentinel, with a determination that neither Laura nor any other person should approach. I
am too often in his thoughts: he is wrong to bestow so much of his
time and attention on me. Sir Arthur was gone to look about him;
having first sent a note, unknown to me, to inform your brother of
our arrival; and requesting to see him, as soon as convenient.

Away hurried your brother, at this mal apropos interval, with
Sir Arthur's note in his pocket, to our hotel. He enquired for my
father?

He was gone out.

For me?

Laura answered she would call me.

She was running with great haste, for this purpose, but was inter-
cepted by Frank; who, agreeably to my desire, would not suffer her
to proceed. She returned; and your brother, referring again to Sir
Arthur's note, was much surprised, and rather vexed.

He asked by whose order she was sent back.

She answered by the order of Mr. Frank.

Who was Mr. Frank?

A young gentleman; [Laura has repeated all that passed] the
son of Mr. Aby Henley.

And who was Mr. Aby Henley?

The steward and gardener of Sir Arthur; his head man.

Steward and gardener? The son of a gardener a gentleman?

Yes, sir. To be sure, sir, among thorough bred quality, though
perhaps he may be better than the best of them, he is thought

no better than a kind of a sort of a gentleman; being not so high born.

Well, said your brother, shew me to this son of Mr. Aby; this peremptory gentleman; or, as you call him, kind of a sort of a gentleman!

Laura obeyed; and she says they were quite surprised at the sight of each other; but that I suppose to be one of the flourishes of her fancy. Your brother, however, as I understand, desired, with some haughtiness, that Frank would suffer the maid to pass, and inform me he was come, agreeably to Sir Arthur's request, to pay his respects to me. Frank resolutely refused; alleging I was not well. Not well! Said your brother. Is not this Sir Arthur's handwriting? Yes, replied Frank; but I assure you she is not well: and I am afraid that even our speaking may awaken her, if she should chance to be asleep. I must therefore request, sir, you would retire.

The oddness of the circumstances, and the positiveness of Frank, displeased your brother. Sir Arthur happened to return; and he went to him, scarcely taking time for first compliments, but asking whether it were true that I was not well. Sir Arthur was surprised: he knew nothing of it! I had not thought a giddiness in the head worth a complaint. Laura was again sent to tell me; and was again denied admittance. Sir Arthur then, with your brother, came to question Frank; who continued firm in his refusal; and when Sir Arthur and your brother had heard that I was so dizzy as to be in danger of falling, had not he supported me, they were satisfied. But such a meeting, between Frank and your brother, was quite vexatious: when the very reverse too was wished! However he is to visit us this morning; and I will then endeavour to do justice to the worth of Frank, and remove false impressions, which I have some reason to fear have been made.

I will pause here; but, if I find an opportunity, will write another short letter, under the same cover, by this post: that is, should I happen to have any thing more to say—This accident was exceedingly unlucky, and I seem as if I felt myself to blame; especially as I am quite in spirits this morning, and relieved from my giddy sensations. I am sorry; very sorry: but it cannot be helped.

A. W. ST. IVES

G

LETTER XXIII

Coke Clifton to Guy Fairfax

Paris, Hotel de l'Université, près le Pont Royal

I T was well I did not tell my tale in my last, Fairfax; it would have been spoiled. I knew it only by halves. It has ended in the most singular combination of circumstances one could well imagine.

You remember I told you of the arrival of Sir Arthur St. Ives, and his daughter; I believe it was in the postscript; and that I was immediately going to—Pshaw! I am beginning my story now at the wrong end. It is throughout exceedingly whimsical. Listen, and let amazement prop your open mouth.

You must have observed the ease with which Frenchmen, though perfect strangers to each other, fall into familiar conversation; and become as intimate in a quarter of an hour, as if they had been acquainted their whole lives. This is a custom which I very much approve. But, like all other good things, it is liable to abuse.

The other day I happened to be taking a walk on the Boulevards, it being a church festival, purposely to see the good Parisians in all their gaiety and glory; and a more cheerful, at least a more noisy people, do not, I believe, exist. As I was standing to admire a wax-work exhibition of all the famous highwaymen, and cut-throats, whose histories are most renowned in France, and listening to the fellow at the door, bawling—*Aux Voleurs! Aux grands Voleurs!*—Not a little amused with the murderous looks, darkness, dungeons, chains and petty horror which they had mimicked, a man uncommonly well-dressed, with an elegant person and pleasing manners, came up and immediately fell into discourse with me. I encouraged him, because he pleased me. We walked together, and had not conversed five minutes before, without seeming to seek an opportunity, he had informed me that he was the Marquis de Passy, and that he had left his carriage and attendants, because he like me took much pleasure in observing the hilarity of the holiday citizens. He had accosted me, he said, because he had a peculiar esteem for the English; of which nation he knew me to be, by my step and behaviour.

We talked some time, and though he made no deep remarks, he

was very communicative of anecdotes, which had come within his own knowledge, that painted the manners of the nation. Among other things, he told me it was not uncommon for valets to dress themselves in their masters clothes, when they supposed them to be at a distance, or otherwise engaged, assume their titles, and pass themselves upon the *Bourgeoisie* and foreigners for counts, dukes, or princes. It was but this day fortnight, said he, that the Marechal de R—— surprised one of his servants in a similar disguise, and with some jocularity publicly ordered the fellow to walk at his heels, then went to his carriage, and commanded him, full dressed as he was, to get up behind.

He had scarcely ended this account before another person came up, and with an air of some authority asked him where his master was, what he did there, and other questions.

To all this my quidam acquaintance, with a degree of surprise that seemed to be tempered with the most pleasing and unaffected urbanity, replied, without being in the least disconcerted, sir, you mistake me: but I am sure you are too much of a gentleman to mean any wilful affront.

Affront! Why whom do you pretend yourself to be, sir?

Sir, I am the Marquis de Passy.

You the Marquis de Passy?—

Yes, sir; I!—

Insolent scoundrel!—

No gentleman, sir, can suffer such language; and I insist upon satisfaction.——And accordingly my champion drew his sword. His antagonist, looking on him with ineffable contempt, answered he would take some proper opportunity to cane him as he deserved.

I own I was amazed. I reasoned a short time with myself, and concluded the person was mistaken; for that it was impossible for any man to counterfeit so much ease, or behave with so much propriety, who was not a gentleman. I therefore thought proper to interfere, and told the intruder that, having given an insult, he ought not to be afraid of giving satisfaction—

And pray, sir, said he, who are you?

A gentleman, sir, answered I—

Yes. As good a one as your companion, I suppose—

You know, Fairfax, it is not customary with me to suffer insolence to triumph unchastised, and I ordered him immediately to draw.

What, sir, in this place, said he? Follow me, if you have any valour to spare.

His spirit pleased me, and I followed. I know not what became of the fellow, whose cause I had espoused; for I saw him no more.

My antagonist led me across the rue St. Honoré, to a place which I suppose you know, called the Elysian Fields. It began to be late, and I am told there is danger in passing the precincts of the guard. I apprehended a conspiracy, and at last refused to proceed any farther. Finding me obstinate he drew, but said we should be interrupted.

He was no false prophet; for we had not made half a dozen passes before a youth, whom from his boots and appearance I supposed to be English, came running and vociferating—Forbear! I was not quite certain that his appearance might not be artifice; I therefore accosted him in English, in which language he very readily replied. He was quite a sturdy, dauntless gentleman; for, though our swords were drawn, and both of us sufficiently angry, he resolutely placed himself between us, declaring we should not fight; and that, if we went farther, he would follow.

Nothing was to be done; and I now began to suspect the person, with whom I had this ridiculous quarrel, to be really a gentleman. I gave him my address, and he readily returned his; after which we parted, he singing a French song, and I cursing the insolence of the English youth, who seemed to disregard my anger, and to be happy that he had prevented the spilling of blood.

Remember that all this happened on the preceding evening, after I had written the greatest part of my last long letter. The next morning I finished it, and received a note from Sir Arthur St. Ives, as I mentioned.

As soon as I could get dressed, I hastened away; and, arriving at the hotel, enquired for the knight?

He was gone out.

For his daughter?—

She had retired to her apartment.

I sent in my name. The maid went, and returned with an answer that Mr. Frank did not think it proper for her mistress to be disturbed. Now, Fairfax, guess who Mr. Frank was if you can! By heaven, it was the very individual youth who, the night before, had been so absolute in putting an end to our duel!

I was planet-struck! Nor was his surprise less, when he saw me, and heard my errand and my name.

I found my gentleman as positive in the morning as in the evening. He was the dragon; touch the fruit who dared! Jason himself could not have entrance there![I] And he was no less cool than determined. I was almost tempted to toss him out of the window.

However I am glad I contained myself; for, on the entrance of Sir Arthur, we came to an explanation; and I find the young lady was really indisposed. But, considering his mongrel birth and breeding, for he is the son of a gardener, I really never saw a fellow give himself such high airs.

Sir Arthur received me with great civility. I have not yet seen the daughter, but I expect to find her a beauty. She is the toast of the county where her father resides. I am to be with her in half an hour; and, as I suppose I shall be fully engaged with this and other affairs for some days, I shall seal up my letter: you must therefore wait for an account of her, till inclination and the full tide of events shall induce me again to indite of great matters.

I shall direct this, agreeably to your last, to your banker's, in Parma. Do not fail to tell me when you shall be at Turin.

Yours very sincerely,

C. CLIFTON

P.S. My opponent of the Elysian Fields has just paid me a visit. He is a man of family; seems to be of a slightly pleasant humour; and acknowledged that what he had heard convinced him he had mistaken my character; for which he was very ready either to cut my throat or ask my pardon. His ease and good temper spoke much in his favour; and I laughed, and answered, in mercy to my throat, I would accept his apology. In consideration of which we are to cultivate an acquaintance, and be sworn friends.

LETTER XXIV

Anna Wenbourne St. Ives to Louisa Clifton

Paris, Hotel d'Espagne, Rue Guenegaude,
Fauxbourg St. Germain

I RETURN eagerly to my Louisa. Mr. Clifton, my dear, has this
instant left us. I give you joy! Yes, he is the brother of my friend!
I do not say he is her equal, though I am not quite sure that he is
her inferior. He is all animation, all life. His person is graceful,
his manners pleasing, and his mind vigorous. I can say but little
from so short an acquaintance; except that I am convinced his
virtues, or his errors, if he have any, [And who is without?] are
not of the feeble kind. They are not characterised by dull medio-
crity; which, of all qualities, is the most hopeless, and incapable.
He gave his earnest desire to see me, when he was refused by
Frank, the air of a handsome compliment; politely accusing himself of improper impatience, when he was in expectation of what
he was pleased to call an uncommon pleasure. Though it was our
first interview, he felt no restraint; but said many very civil things
naturally, and with an exceedingly good grace.

I purposely turned the conversation on Frank, related some
anecdotes of him, and bestowed praise which was confirmed by
Sir Arthur. Your brother, whose imagination is warm and active,
called him a trusty Cerberus;[1] and said he had a mouth to answer
each of the three; meaning Laura, himself, and Sir Arthur. Various
remarks which escaped him shew that he has a fondness for pleasant satire, and similes of humour.

He praised Frank, after hearing our account of him; but his
praise was qualified with the word obstinacy. There was an
appearance of feeling that the gentleman ought not to have been
so sternly repulsed, by the son of a steward.—And was this his
kindred equality to my friend?—Forgive me, Louisa—It was unjust in me to say I was not quite sure he is your inferior—However
I can very seriously assure you, he is not one of your every day
folks.

Frank came in, and your brother addressed him with good
humour, but in a tone denoting it was the gentleman to the sort of

a gentleman. I own it pleased me to observe the ease with which Frank, by his answers, obliged Mr. Clifton to change his key. But I soon had occasion to observe that the warmth of your brother's expressions, his eagerness to be immediately intimate with us, and the advances which he with so little sense of embarrassment made to me, had an effect upon Frank which, I greatly fear, was painful. I must look to this; it is a serious moment, and I must seriously examine, and quickly resolve. In the mean time, your brother has kindly insisted upon devoting himself wholly to our amusements; to attend on us, and shew us the public buildings, gardens, paintings, and theatres; as well as to introduce us to all his friends.

And what must we do in return for this well-meant kindness? Must we not endeavour to weed out those few errors, for few I hope they are, which impoverish a mind in itself apparently fertile and of high rank?—Yes, it instantly suggested itself to me as an indispensable act of duty—The attempt must be made—With what obstinate warfare do men encounter peril when money, base money is their proposed reward! And shall we do less for mind, eternal omnipotent mind?

He is returned. Adieu. You shall soon hear again from your

A. W. ST. IVES

LETTER XXV

Coke Clifton to His Sister, Louisa Clifton

Paris, Hotel de l'Université, près le Pont Royal

I WRITE agreeably to your desire, sister, to thank you for all obligations, not forgetting your advice. Not but I am excessively obliged to you; I am upon my soul, and seriously, for having done me the favour to bring me acquainted with your charming friend. I have seen many women and in many countries, but I never beheld one so sweet, so beautiful, so captivating! I had heard of her before I left England, her fame had reached Italy, and your letters had raised my expectations. But what were these? The accomplishments and graces of her person, the variety, the pleasure inspiring heaven of her countenance, the cupids that wanton in her dimples, and the delights that swim and glisten in her eyes, are each and all exquisite beyond imagination!

Whatever you may think of me, Louisa, I do persuade myself I know something of women. I have studied them at home and abroad, and have often probed them to the soul. But I never before met with any one in the least comparable to the divine Anna! She is so unreserved, so open, that her soul seems to dwell upon her lips. Yet her thoughts are so rapid, and her mind so capacious, that I am persuaded it will cost me much longer time to know her well than any other woman with whom I ever met.

Having thanked you very heartily and sincerely for this favour, I shall just say a word or two in answer to yours.

And so you really think you have some morality on hand, a little stale or so but still sound, which you can bestow with advantage upon me? You imagine you can tell me something I never heard before? Now have you sincerely so much vanity, Louisa? Be frank. You acknowledged I have crossed rivers, seas, and mountains; but you are afraid I have shut my eyes all the time! *A loud tongue and a prodigious lack of wit! Antics and impertinences of young men of fashion!* Really, my dear, you are choice in your phrases! You could not love your brother *for any recital of the delight which foreign ladies took in him, and which he took in foreign ladies!* But you could be in ecstatics for a brother of your own invention.

Do not suppose I am angry! No, no, my dear girl; I am got far above all that! Though I cannot but laugh at this extraordinary brother, which you are fashioning for yourself. If, when I come into your sublime presence, I should by good luck happen to strike your fancy, why so! My fortune will then be made! If not, sister, we must do as well as we can. All in good time, and a God's name. Is not that tolerable Worcestershire morality?

I am obliged to lay down my pen with laughing at the idea of Miss Louisa's brother, supposing him to be exactly of her modelling. I think I see him appear before her; she seated in state, on a chair raised on four tressels and two old doors, like a strolling actress mimicking a queen in a barn! He dressed in black; his hair smugly curled; his face and his shoes shining; his white handkerchief in his right hand; a prayer book, or the morals of Epictetus[1] in his left; *not interlarding his discourse with French or Italian phrases,* but ready with a good rumbling mouthful of old Greek, which he had composed, I mean compiled, for the purpose! Then, having advanced one leg, wiped his mouth, put his left hand in his breeches pocket, clenched his right, and raised his arm, he begins his learned dissertation on *well digested principles, ardent desire of truth, incessant struggles to shake off prejudices*, and forth are chanted, in nasal twang and tragic recitative, his *emanations of soul, bursts of thought*, and *flashes of genius!*

But *you would not be satirical*. Gentle, modest maiden! And surely it becomes the tutored brother to imitate this kind forbearance. *My faculties were always lively?* And *I must pardon you if you expect too much?*——Upon my soul, this is highly comic! Expect too much! And there is danger then that I should not equal your expectations?—Prithee, my good girl, jingle the keys of your harpsichord, and be quiet. Pore over your fine folio receipt book, and appease your thirst after knowledge. Satisfy your longing desire to do good, by making jellies, conserves, and caraway cakes. Pot pippins, brew rasberry wine, and candy orange chips.[1] Study burns, bruises, and balsams.[2] Distil surfeit, colic, and wormwood water.[3] Concoct hiera picra,[4] rhubarb beer, and oil of charity;[5] and sympathize over sprains, whitloes, and broken shins. Get a charm to cure the argue, and render yourself renowned. Spin, sew and knit. Collect your lamentable rabble around you, dole out your charities, listen to a full chorus of blessings, and take your seat among the saints.

You see, child, I can give advice as well as yourself; aye and I will bestow it most plentifully, if you happen to feel any desire after more. I hate to be ungrateful; you shall have no opportunity to utter your musty maxim upon me—'That the sin of ingratitude is worse than the sin of witchcraft.' You shall have weight for weight, measure for measure, chicken; aye, my market woman, and a lumping pennyworth. Brotherly for sisterly *effusions!*

As for the right of eldership, I recollect that a dozen years ago I envied you the prerogative; but now you are welcome to it with all my heart. If, among your miraculous acquirements, you have any secret to make time stand still, by which you can teach me to remain at sweet five-and-twenty, and if you will disclose it to me, I will not only pardon all your *impertinences*, as you so *pertinently* call them, but do any other thing in reason to satisfy you; except turn philosopher and feed upon carrots! Nay I will allow you to grow as old as you please, you shall have full enjoyment of the rights of eldership.

In the mean time, sister, I once more thank you for bringing me acquainted with your friend. You seem to have 'put powder in her drink;'[1] and I freely tell you I wish she loved me half as well as she professes to love her immaculate Louisa. But these I suppose are the *flashes of genius*, which you have taught her. However she is an angel, and in her every thing is graceful.

As for your other prodigy, I scarcely know what to make of him; except that he seems to have quite conceit enough of himself. Every other sentence is a contradiction of what the last speaker advanced. This is the first time he ever ventured to cross his father's threshold, and yet he talks as familiarly of kingdoms, governments, nations, manners, and other high sounding phrases, as if he had been secretary of state to king Minos,[2] had ridden upon the white elephant,[3] and studied under the Dalai Lama![4] He is the Great Mogul[5] of politicians! And as for letters, science, and talents, he holds them all by patent right! He is such a monopolizer that no man else can get a morsel! If he were not a plebeian, I could most sincerely wish you were married to him; for then, whenever my soul should hunger and thirst after morality, I should know where to come and get a full meal. Though perhaps his not being a gentleman would be no objection to you, at least your letter leads me to suspect as much.

Do not however mistake me. I mean this jocularly. For I will not degrade my sister so much, as to suppose she has ever cast a thought on the son either of the gardener or the steward, of any man. Though, tied to her mother's apron-string and shut up on the confines of Worcestershire, she may think proper to lecture and give rules of conduct to a brother who has seen the world, and studied both men and books of every kind, that is but a harmless and pardonable piece of vanity. It ought to be laughed at, and for that reason I have laughed.

For the rest, I will be willing to think as well of my sister, as this sister can be to think of her catechised, and very patient, humble, younger brother,

                                                        C. CLIFTON

P.S. I have written in answer to my mother by the same post. From the general tenor of her letter, I cannot but imagine that, just before she sat down to write, she had been listening to one of your civil lectures, against wild brothers, fine gentlemen, and vile rakes. Is not that the cant? One thing let me whisper to you, sister: I am not obliged to any person who suspects or renders me suspected. I claim the privilege of being seen before I am condemned, and heard before I am executed. If I should not prove to be quite the phœnix which might vie with so miraculous so unique a sister, I must then be contented to take shame to myself. But till then I should suppose the thoughts of a sister might as well be inclined to paint me white as black. After all, I cannot conclude without repeating that I believe the whole world cannot equal the lovely, the divine Anna St. Ives: and, whatever else you may say or think of me, do not lead her to imagine I am unjust to her supreme beauty, and charms. An insinuation of that kind I would never forgive—Never!

LETTER XXVI

Sir Arthur St. Ives to Abimelech Henley

Paris, Hotel d'Espagne, Rue Guenegaude,
Fauxbourg St. Germain

YOU cannot imagine, honest Aby, the surprise I am in. Is this their famous France? Is this the finest country in the whole world? Why, Aby, from Boulogne to Paris, at least from Montreuil, I am certain I did not see a single hedge! All one dead flat; with an eternal row of trees, without beginning, middle, or end. I sincerely believe, Aby, I shall never love a straight row of trees again. And the wearisome right lined road, that you never lose sight of; not for a moment, Aby! No lucky turning. No intervening hill.

Oh that I were but the Grand Monarch! What improvements would I make! What a scope for invention, Aby! A kingdom! A revenue of four hundred millions of livres, and a standing army of three hundred thousand men! All which, if the king were a wise man, it is very evident, Abimelech, he might employ in improvements; and heaven knows there is a want of them. What are their petty corvées, by which these straight roads have been patched up, and their everlasting elms planted? I would assemble all my vassals—[Your son Frank, Aby, has given me much information concerning the present governments of Europe, and the origin of manors, fiefs, and lordships. I can assure you he is a very deep young man; though I could wish he were not quite so peremptory and positive; and has informed me of some things which I never heard of before, though I am twice his age. But he seems to have them so fast at his finger's ends that I suppose they must be true. I had often heard of entails, and mortmain, and lands held in fee or fief, I don't know which, and all that you know, Abimelech. One's deeds and one's lawyers tell one something, blindly, of these matters; but I never knew how it had all happened. He told me that—Egad I forget what he told me. But I know he made it all out very clear. Still I must say he is cursed positive.]— However, Aby, as I was saying, I would assemble all my vassals, all my great lords and fief holders, and they should assemble their vassals, and all hands should be set to work: some to plan, others to plant; some to grub, some to dig, some to hoe, and some to sow. The whole country should soon be a garden! Tell me, Aby, is not the project a grand one*? What a dispatch of work! What a change of nature! I am ravished with the thought!

As for any ideas of improvement to be picked up here, Abimelech, they must not be expected. I shall never forget the sameness of the scene! So unlike the riches of Wenbourne-Hill! Sir Alexander would have a country open enough here, at least. He would not complain of being shut in. The wind may blow from what point it pleases, and you have it on all sides. Except the road-side elms I mentioned, and now and then a coppice, which places they tell me are planted for the preservation of the game, I should have supposed there had not been a tree in the country; had I not been told that there were many large forests, to the right, and the left, out of sight. For my part I don't know where they have hidden them, and so must take their word for the fact. 'Tis true indeed that we travelled a part of the way in the dark.

I was mentioning the game, Aby. The game laws here are

* The plan is in reality much grander than the good knight suspected; if embraced at the will of a nation, instead of at the will of an individual.

excellently put in execution. Hares are as plenty as rabbits in a warren, partridges as tame as our dove-house pigeons, and pheasants that seem as if they would come and feed out of your hand. For no scoundrel poacher dare molest them. If he did, I am not certain whether the lord of the manor could not hang him up instantly without judge or jury.

Though Frank tells me they have no juries here: which by the bye is odd enough; and as he says I suppose it is a great shame. For, as he put the case to me, how should I like to have my estate seized on, by some insolent prince or duke? For you know, I being a baronet in my own right, Aby, no one less in rank would dare infringe upon me. Well! How should I like to have this duke, or this prince, seize upon my estate; and, instead of having my right tried by a special jury of my peers, to have the cause decided by him who can get the prettiest woman to plead for him, and who will pay her and his judges the best? For such Frank assures me is the mode here! Now really all this is very bad; very bad indeed, and as he says wants reforming.

But as for the game laws, as I was saying, Aby, they are excellently enforced; and your poor rascals here are kept in very proper subjection. They are held to the grindstone, as I may say. And so they ought to be, Aby. For, I have often heard you say, what is a man but what he is worth? Which in certain respects is very true. A gentleman of family and fortune, why he is a gentleman; and no insolent beggar ought to dare to look him in the face, without his permission. But you, Aby, had always a very great sense of propriety, in these respects. And you have found your advantage in it; as indeed you ought. It is a pity, considering what a learned young man you have made your son, that you did not teach him a little of your good sense in this particular. He is too full of contradiction: too confident by half.

Let me have a long and full and whole account of what you are doing, Aby. Tell me precisely how forward your work is, and the exact spot where you are when each letter comes away. I know I need not caution you to keep those idle fellows, the day labourers, to it. I never knew any man who worked them better. And yet, Aby, it is surprising the sums that they have cost me; but you are a very careful honest fellow; and they have done wonders, under my planning and your inspection.

I do not wish that the moment I receive a letter it should be known to every lacquey; especially here; where it seems to be one entire city of babblers. The people appear to have nothing to do but to talk. In the house, in the street, in the fields, breakfast, dinner, and supper, walking, sitting, or standing, they are never silent. Nay egad I doubt whether they do not talk in their sleep! So do you direct to me at the Café Conti—However I had better write the direction for you at full length, for fear of a mistake. And be sure you take care of your spelling, Aby, or I don't know what may happen. For I am told that many of these French people are devilish illiterate, and I am sure they are devilish cunning. Snap! They answer before they hear you! And, what is odd enough, their answers are sometimes as pat as if they knew your meaning. Indeed I have often thought it strange that your low poor people should be so acute, and have so much common sense. But do you direct your letters thus—

A Monsieur Monsieur le Chevalier de St. Ives, Baronet Anglois, au Café Conti, vis-à-vis le Pont Neuf, Quai Conti, à Paris.

And so, Abimelech, I remain

A. ST. IVES

LETTER XXVII

Frank Henley to Oliver Trenchard

Paris, Hotel d'Espagne, rue Guenegaude,
Fauxbourg St. Germain

THE black forebodings of my mind, Oliver, are fulfilled! I have been struck! The phantom I dreaded has appeared, has flashed upon me, and all the evils of which I prophesied, and more than all, are collecting to overwhelm me; are rushing to my ruin!

This brother of Louisa! Nothing surely was ever so unaccountable! The very same whom I prevented from fighting, in the *Champs Elysées!* Ay, he! This identical Clifton, for Clifton it was, has again appeared; has been here, is here, is never hence. His aspect was petrifying! He came upon me this second time in the strangest, the most insolent manner imaginable; just as I had sent away my last letter to thee; when I was sitting the guardian of a treasure, which my fond false reveries were at that moment flattering me might one day be mine! Starting at the sight of me! Nothing kind, nothing conciliating in his address; it was all imperious demand. Who was I? By what right did I deny admission to the young lady's woman, to inform her he was come to pay her his respects? He!—Having a letter from Sir Arthur, inviting him thither!——Were such orders to be countermanded by me? Again and again, who was I?——Oliver, he is a haughty youth; violent, headstrong, and arrogant! Believe me he will be found so.

What do I mean? Why do I dread him? How! The slave of fear? Why is my heart so inclined to think ill of him? Do I seek to depreciate? She has mentioned him several times; has expected, with a kind of eagerness, he would resemble her Louisa; has hoped he and I should be friends. 'Did not I hope the same?' Oliver, she has tortured me! All benevolence as she is, she has put me on the rack!

I must not yield thus to passion: it is criminal. I have too much indulged the flattering dreams of desire. Yet what to do?—How to act?—Must I tamely quit the field the moment an adversary appears; turn recreant to myself, and coward-like give up my claims, without daring to say such and such they are? No. Justice is due as much to myself as to any other. If he be truly deserving of preference, why let him be preferred. I will rejoice.——Yes, Oliver, *will*.——He who is the slave of passion, is unworthy a place in the noble mind of Anna.

But this man is not my superior: I feel, Oliver, he is not; and it becomes me to assert my rights. Nay, his pride acts as a provocative——Oliver, I perceive how wrong this is; but I will not blot out the line. Let it remain as a memento. He that would correct his failings must be willing to detect them.

The anxiety of my mind is excessive; and the pain which a conviction of the weakness and error that this anxiety occasions renders it still more insupportable. I must take myself to task; ay and severely. I must enquire into the wrong and the right, and reason must be absolute. Tell me thy thoughts, plainly and honestly; be sure thou dost; for I sometimes suspect thee of too much kindness, of partiality to thy friend. Chastise the derelictions of my heart, whenever thou perceivest them; or I myself shall hereafter become thy accuser. I am dissatisfied, Oliver: what surer token can there be that I am wrong? I weary thee—Prithee forgive, but do not forget to aid me.

F. HENLEY

P.S. He—[I mean Louisa's brother; for I think only of one he and one she, at present.] He has not yet taken any notice of our strange first meeting; and thou mayst imagine, Oliver, if he think fit to be silent, I shall not speak. Not that it can be supposed he holds duelling to be disgraceful. I have enquired if any rencounter[1] had taken place; for I was very apprehensive that the champions would have their tilting-match another time. However, as I can hear of no such accident, and as Mr. Clifton is here continually, I hope I have been instrumental in preventing such absurd guilt. The follies of men are scarcely comprehensible! And what am I? Dare I think myself wise? Oliver, my passions are in arms; the contest is violent; I call on thee to examine and to aid the cause of truth.

LETTER XXVIII

Coke Clifton to Guy Fairfax

Paris, Hotel de l'Université

I HAVE found it, Fairfax! The pearl of pearls! The inestimable jewel! The unique! The world contains but one!—And what?— A woman! The woman of whom I told you!—Anna St. Ives!— You have seen the Venus de Medicis?—Pshaw!—Stone! Inanimate marble! But she!——The very sight of her is the height of luxury! The pure blood is seen to circulate! Transparent is the complexion which it illuminates!——And for symmetry, for motion, for grace, sculptor, painter, nor poet ever yet imagined such! Desire languishes to behold her! The passions all are in arms, and the mere enjoyment of her presence is superior to all that her sex beside can give!

Do not suppose me in my altitudes:[2] all I can say, all you can imagine, are far short of the reality.

Then how unlike is her candour to the petty arts, the shallow cunning of her sex! Her heart is as open as her countenance; her thoughts flow, fearless, to her lips. Original ideas, expressed in words so select, phrases so happy, as to astonish and delight; a brilliancy and a strength of fancy that disdain limitation, and wit rapid and fatal as lightning to all opposition; these and a thousand other undescribable excellencies are hers.

I love her—Love?——I adore her! Ay——Be not surprised—— Even to madness and marriage!——No matter for what I have beforetime said, or what I have thought, my mind is changed. I have discovered perfection which I did not imagine could exist. I renounce my former opinions; which applied to the sex in general were orthodox, but to her were blasphemy.

I would not be too sudden; I have not yet made any direct proposal. But could I exist and forbear giving intimations? No. And how were they received? Why with all that unaffected frankness which did not pretend to misunderstand but to meet them, to cherish hope, and to give a prospect of bliss which mortal man can never merit.

She is all benevolence! Nay she is too much so. There is that youngster here; that upstart; he who bolted upon us and mouthed his Pindarics[1] in the Elysian Fields; the surly groom of the chamber This fellow has insinuated himself into her favour, and the benignity of her soul induces her to treat him with as much respect as if he were a gentleman.

The youth has some parts, some ideas: at least he has plenty of words. But his arrogance is insufferable. He does not scruple to interfere in the discourse, either with me, Sir Arthur, or the angelic Anna! Nay sets up for a reformer; and pretends to an insolent superiority of understanding and wisdom. Yet he was never so long from home before in his life; has seen nothing, but has read a few books, and has been permitted to converse with this all intelligent deity.

I cannot deny but that the pedagogue sometimes surprises me, with the novelty of his opinions; but they are extravagant. I have condescended, oftener than became me, to shew how full of hyperbole and paradox they were. Still he as constantly maintained them, with a kind of congruity that astonished me, and even rendered many of them plausible.

H

But, exclusive of his obstinacy, the rude, pot companion loquacity of the fellow is highly offensive. He has no sense of inferiority. He stands as erect, and speaks with as little embarrassment and as loudly as the best of us: nay boldly asserts that neither riches, rank, nor birth have any claim. I have offered to buy him a beard, if he would but turn heathen philosopher. I have several times indeed bestowed no small portion of ridicule upon him; but in vain. His retorts are always ready; and his intrepidity, in this kind of impertinence, is unexampled.

From some anecdotes which are told of him, I find he does not want personal courage; but he has no claim to chastisement from a gentleman. Petty insults he disregards; and has several times put me almost beyond the power of forbearance, by his cool and cutting replies. His oratory is always ready; cut, dry, and fit for use; and damned insolent oratory it frequently is.

The absurdity of his tenets can only be equalled by the effrontery with which they are maintained. Among the most ridiculous of what he calls first principles is that of the equality of mankind. He is one of your levellers! Marry! His superior! Who is he? On what proud eminence can he be found? On some Welsh mountain, or the pike of Teneriffe?[1] Certainly not in any of the nether regions! What! Was not he the ass that brayed to Balaam?[2] And is he not now Mufti[3] to the mules? He will if he please! And if he please he will let it alone! Dispute his prerogative who dare! He derives from Adam; what time the world was all hail fellow well met! The savage, the wild man o' the woods is his true liberty boy; and the orang outang his first cousin.[4] A Lord is a merry andrew, a Duke a jack pudding, and a King a tom fool:[5] his name is man!

Then, as to property, 'tis a tragic farce; 'tis his sovereign pleasure to eat nectarines, grow them who will. Another Alexander, he; the world is all his own! Ay, and he will govern it as he best knows how! He will legislate, dictate, dogmatize; for who so infallible? What! Cannot Goliah[6] crack a walnut?

As for arguments, it is but ask and have: a peck[7] at a bidding, and a good double handful over. I own I thought I knew something; but no, I must to my horn book. Then, for a simile, it is sacrilege; and must be kicked out of the high court of logic! Sarcasm too is an ignoramus, and cannot solve a problem: Wit a pert puppy, who can only flash and bounce. The heavy walls of wisdom are not to be battered down by such popguns and pellets. He will waste you wind enough to set up twenty millers, in proving an apple is not an egg-shell; and that *homo* is Greek for a goose. Dun Scotus[1] was a school boy to him. I confess, he has more than once dumb-founded me by his subtleties.—Pshaw!——It is a mortal murder of words and time to bestow them on him.

My sister is in correspondence with my new divinity. I thought proper to bestow a few gentle lashes on her, for a letter which she wrote to me, and which I mentioned in my first from Paris, insinuating her own superiority, and giving me to understand how fortunate it would be for the world should I but prove as con-summate a paragon as herself. She richly deserved it, and yet I now wish I had forborne; for, if she have her sex's love of vengeance in her, she may injure me in the tenderest part. Never was woman so devoted to woman as Anna St. Ives is to Louisa. I should suspect any other of her sex of extravagant affectation; but her it is impos-sible to suspect: her manner is so peculiarly her own: and it comes with such unsought for energy, that there is no resisting con-viction.

I have two or three times been inclined to write and ask Louisa's pardon. But, no; that pride forbids. She dare not openly profess herself my enemy. She may insinuate, and countermine; but I have a tolerably strong dependance on my own power over Anna. She is not blind. She is the first to feel and to acknowledge superior merit; and I think I have no reason to fear repulse from any woman, whose hand I can bring myself to ask.

One of Anna's greatest perfections, with me, is the ready esteem which she entertained for me, and her not being insensible to those qualities which I flatter myself I possess. Never yet did woman treat me with affected disdain, who did not at last repent of her coquetry.

'Tis true that Anna has sometimes piqued me, by appearing to value me more for my sister's sake even than for my own. I have been ready to say dissimulation was inseparable from woman. And yet her manner is as unlike hypocrisy as possible, I never yet could brook scorn, or neglect. I know no sensation more delicious than that of inflicting punishment for insult or for injury; 'tis in our nature.

That youngster of whom I have prated so much, his name is

Frank Henley, denies this, and says that what the world calls nature is habit. He added, with some degree of sarcasm as I thought, that it was as natural, or in his sense as habitual, for some men to pardon, and to seek the good even of those by whom they were wronged, as it was for others to resent and endeavour to revenge. But, as I have said, he continually makes pretensions to an offensive superiority. You may think I do not fail to humble the youth, whenever opportunity offers. But no! Humble him, indeed! Shew him boiling ice! Stew a whale in an oyster-shell! Make mount Caucasus into a bag pudding! But do not imagine he may be moved! The legitimate son of Cato's eldest bastard, he! A petrified Possidonius,[1] in high preservation!

There is another thing which astonishes me more than all I have mentioned. Curse me, Fairfax, if I do not believe that [God confound the fellow!] he has the impudence to be in love with Anna St. Ives! Nay that he braves me, defies me, and, in the insufferable frothy fermentation of his vanity, persuades himself that he looks down upon me!

I must finish, for I cannot think of his intolerable insolence with common patience; and I know not what right I have to tease you, concerning my paltry disputes with a plebeian pedant, and my still more paltry jealousies. But let him beware! If he really have the arrogance to place himself in my way, I will presently trample him into his original nonentity. I only forbear because he has had the cunning to make himself so great a favourite.

This must be horribly stupid stuff to you, Fairfax: therefore pay me in my own coin; be as dull as you sometimes know how, and bid me complain if I dare.

C. CLIFTON

LETTER XXIX

Louisa Clifton to Coke Clifton

Rose-Bank

I WRITE, dear brother, in answer to your last, that I may not by any neglect of mine contribute to the mistake in which you are at present. Your letter shews that you suppose your sister to be vain, presumptuous, and rude; and, such being your feelings, I am far from blaming you for having expressed them.

Still, brother, I must be sincere, and I would by no means have it understood that I think you have chosen the best manner of expressing them; for it is not the manner which, if I have such faults, would be most likely to produce reformation. But your intention has been to humble me; and, desiring to be sarcastic, you have not failed in producing your intended effect. I am sincerely glad of it: had you shewn that desire without the power, I should have been as sincerely sorry. But where there is mind there is the material from which every thing is to be hoped.

I suppose I shall again incur chastisement, for rising thus as you call it to the sublime. But I will write my thoughts without fear, and I hope will patiently listen should they deserve reproach. If I have sinned, it is in most fervently wishing to find my brother one of the brightest and the best of men; and I have received more pleasure from the powers he has displayed, in reproving me, than I could have done by any dull expression of kindness; in which, though there might have been words, there would neither have been feeling, sentiment, nor soul.

The concluding sentence of your letter warns me not to defame you with my friend. I must speak without disguise, brother. You feel that, had you received such a letter, revenge would have been the first emotion of your mind. I hope its duration would have been short. I will most readily and warmly repeat all the good of my brother that I know: but I will neither conceal what ought to be said, nor say what I do not know. I take it for granted that he would not have me guilty of duplicity.

Adieu, dear brother; and believe me to be most affectionately your

L. CLIFTON

LETTER XXX

Frank Henley to Oliver Trenchard

Paris, Hotel d'Espagne, Rue Guenegaude,
Fauxbourg St. Germain

HOW severe, Oliver, are the lessons of truth! But to learn them
from her lips, and to be excited to the practice of them by her
example, are blessings which to enjoy and not to profit by would
shew a degenerate heart.

I have just risen from a conversation which has made a deep
impression on my mind. It was during breakfast. I know not
whether reflecting on it will appease, or increase, the sensations
which the behaviour of this brother of Louisa hourly exacerbates.
But I will calm that irritability which would dwell on him, and
nothing else, that I may repeat what has just happened.

The interesting part of what passed began by Mr. Clifton's
affirming, with Pope, that men had and would have, to the end of
time, each a ruling passion. This I denied, if by ruling passion were
meant the indulgence of any irregular appetite, or the fostering of
any erroneous system. I was asked, with a sneer, for my recipe to
subdue the passions; if it were not too long to be remembered.
I replied it was equally brief and efficacious. It was the force of
reason; or, if the word should please better, of truth.

And in what year of the world was the discovery of truth to be
made?

In that very year when, instead of being persecuted for speaking
their thoughts, the free discussion of every opinion, true or false,
should not only be permitted, but receive encouragement and
applause.

As usual, the appeal was made to Anna: and, as usual, her decision was in my favour. Nothing, said she, is more fatal, to the progress of virtue, than the supposition that error is invincible. Had I
persuaded myself I never could have learned French, Italian, or
music, why learn them I never could. For how can that be finished
which is never begun? But, though all the world were to laugh
at me, I should laugh at all the world, were it to tell me
it is more difficult to prevent the beginning, growth, and excess

of any passion, than it is to learn to play excellently on the piano
forte.

Is that really your opinion, madam? said Clifton.

It is.

Do you include all the passions?

All.

What! The passion of love?

Yes. Love is as certainly to be conquered as any of them; and
there is no mistake which has done more mischief than that of
supposing it irresistible. Young people, and we poor girls in particular, having once been thoroughly persuaded of the truth of such
an axiom, think it in vain to struggle, where there are no hopes of
victory. We are conquered not because we are weak, but because
we are cowards. We seem to be convinced that we have fallen in
love by enchantment, and are under the absolute dominion of a
necromancer. It is truly the dwarf leading the giant captive. Is it
not—[Oliver! She fixed her eyes upon me, as she spoke!]—Is it
not, Frank?

I was confounded. I paused for a moment. A deep and heavy
sigh involuntarily burst from me. I endeavoured to be firm, but I
stammered out—Madam—it is.

I am convinced he is jealous of me. Nay he fears me; though he
scorns me too much to think so meanly of himself. Yet he fears me.
And what is worse, Oliver, I fear him! I blush for my own debility.
But let me not endeavour to conceal my weakness. No: it must be
encountered, and cured. His quick and audacious eye was searching me, while I struggled to think, and rid myself of confusion;
and he discovered more than gave him pleasure.—She continued.

I know of no prejudice more pernicious to the moral conduct of
youth than that of this unconquerable passion of love. Any and all
of our passions are unconquerable, whenever we shall be weak
enough to think them so. Does not the gamester plead the un-
conquerableness of his passion? The drunkard, the man of anger,
the revengeful, the envious, the covetous, the jealous, have they
not all the same plea? With the selfish and the feeble passion succeeds to passion as different habits give birth to each, and the last
passion proves more unconquerable than its predecessor. How
frequently do we see people in the very fever of this unconquerable
passion of love, which disappears for the rest of their lives, after a

few weeks possession of the object whom they had so passionately loved! How often do they as passionately hate; while the violence of their hatred and of their love is perhaps equally guilty!

Sir Arthur I observed was happy to join in this new doctrine; which however is true, Oliver. I am not certain that he too had not his apprehensions, concerning me: at least his approbation of the principle was ardent.

This was not all. After a short silence, she added, and again fixed her eyes on me—Next to the task of subduing our own passions, I know none more noble than that of aiding to subdue the passions of others. To restore a languishing body is held to be a precious art: but to give health to the mind, to restore declining genius to its true rank, is an art infinitely more inestimable.

She rose, and I withdrew; her words vibrating in my ear, where they vibrate still. Perceivest thou not their import?——Oliver, she has formed a project fatal to my hopes! Nay, I could almost fear, fatal to herself! Yet what, who can harm her? Does the savage, the monster exist, that could look upon her and do her injury? No! She is safe! She is immaculate! Beaming in beauty, supreme in virtue, the resplendent ægis of truth shields her from attaint!

Yes, Oliver, her answers were to him; but the intent, the soul of them was directed to me. It was a warning spirit, that cried, beware of indulging an unjustifiable passion! Awake, at the call of virtue, and obey! Behold here a sickly mind, and aid me in its recovery!— To me her language was pointed, clear, and incapable of other interpretation.

But is there not peril in her plan? Recover a mind so perverted? Strong, I own, nay uncommon in its powers; for such the mind of Clifton is: but its strength is its disease.

And is it so certain that for me to love her is error, is weakness, is vice? No. Or, if it be, I have not yet discovered why. Oliver, she shall hear me! Let her shew me my mistake, if mistaken I be, and I will desist: but justice demands it, and she shall hear me.

We are going to remove, at his repeated instances, to the hotel where he resides. He leads Sir Arthur as he pleases; but it grieved me to see her yield so readily. Now that I have discovered her intentions, I no longer wonder. Omnipotent as the power of truth and virtue is, I yet cannot approve the design. The enterprises of virtue itself may have their romance—I know not—This to me at least is fatal—Could I—? I must conclude!—Lose her?— For ever!—For ever!—I must conclude—

F. HENLEY

LETTER XXXI

Anna Wenbourne St. Ives to Louisa Clifton

Paris, Hotel de l'Université

THE assiduity of Clifton, my dear Louisa, is so great that we already seem to be acquaintance of seven years standing. This is evidently his intention. His temper is eager, impatient of delay, quick in resolving, and, if I do not mistake, sometimes precipitate. But his intellectual powers are of a very high order. His wit is keen, his invention strong, his language flowing and elegant, and his ideas and figures remarkable, sometimes for their humour, and at others for their splendour. His prejudices are many of them deep; nor are they few; but he speaks them frankly, defends them boldly, and courts rather than shuns discussion. What then may not be hoped from a mind like his? Ought such a mind to be neglected? No!—No!—Eternally no!—I have already given a strong hint of this to Frank.

I am persuaded that, since you saw him, he is greatly improved in person. The regularity of his features, his florid complexion, tall stature, and the facility and grace of all his motions, are with him no common advantages.

He has attached himself exceedingly to us, and has induced Sir Arthur to take apartments in the *Hotel de l'Université*, where he resides himself, and where the accommodations are much better, the situation more agreeable, and the rooms more spacious.

A little incident happened, when we removed, which was characteristic of the manners of the people, and drew forth a pleasing trait of the acuteness of Clifton, and of his turn of thinking.

One of the men who helped us with our luggage, after being paid according to agreement, asked, as is very customary with these people, for *quelque chose pour boire*; which Sir Arthur, not being very expert in the French idiom, understood literally. He accordingly ordered a bottle of the light common wine, and being thirsty poured some into a tumbler and drank himself first, then poured out some more, and offered the porter.

The man took the glass as Sir Arthur held it out to him; and, with some surprise and evident sense of insult in his countenance, said to Sir Arthur—*à moi, monsieur?* To which Sir Arthur, perfectly at a loss to comprehend his meaning, made no answer; and the man; without tasting the liquor, set the glass down on a bench in the yard.

Clifton, well acquainted with the manners of the people, and knowing the man imagined Sir Arthur meant to insult him, by giving him the same glass out of which he had drunken, with great alacrity took it up the moment the man had set it down, and said—*Non, mon ami, c'est à moi*—and drank off the wine. He then called for another tumbler, and filling it gave it to the man.

The French are a people of active and lively feelings; and the poor fellow, after receiving the glass from Clifton, took up the other empty tumbler, poured the wine back into it, said in his own language forgive me, sir; I see I am in the wrong; and immediately drank out of the tumbler which he had before refused.

Each country you perceive, Louisa, has its own ideas of delicacy. The French think it very strange to see two people drink out of the same vessel. Not however that I suppose every porter in Paris would refuse wine, if offered, for the same reason. Neither would they all with the same sensibility be so ready to retract.

The good humour as well as the good sense of Clifton's reproof pleased me highly; and we must all acknowledge him our superior, in the art of easily conforming to the customs of foreigners, and in readily pardoning even their absurdities. For foreigners, Louisa, have their absurdities, as well as ourselves.

But I have not yet done. I have another anecdote to relate of Clifton, from which I augur still more.

I had observed our Thomas in conversation with a man, who from his dress and talking to Thomas I knew must be an Englishman; and the care which it becomes me to take, that such well-meaning but simple people should not be deceived, led me to inquire who he was. Thomas began to stammer; not with guilt, but with a desire of telling a story which he knew not how to tell so well as he wished. At last we understood from him it was a young English lad, who had neither money, meat, nor work, and who was in danger of starving, because he could find no means of returning to his own country. Poor Thomas finding himself among a kind of heathens, as he calls the French, pitied his case very sincerely, and had supplied him with food for some days, promising that he would soon take an opportunity of speaking to me, whom he is pleased to call the best young lady in the world; and I assure you, Louisa, I am proud of his good word.

Your brother heard this account, and immediately said——[For indeed I wished to know what his feelings were, and therefore did not offer to interrupt him.] 'Desire him to come up. Let me question him. If he be really what he says, he ought to be relieved: but he is very likely some idle fellow, who being English makes a trade of watching for English families, and living upon this tale.' So far said I to myself, Clifton, all is right. I therefore let him proceed. The lad came up, for he was not twenty, and your brother began his interrogations.

You are an English lad, you say?

Yes, sir.

Where do you come from?

Wolverhampton.

What is your trade?

A buckle plater.

And did you serve out your apprenticeship?

No.

How so?

My master and I quarrelled, he struck me, I beat him, and was obliged to run away.

Where did you run to?

I went to London. I have an aunt there, a poor woman, who chairs for gentlefolks, and I went to her.

How came you here?

She got me a place, with a young gentleman who was going on his travels. I had been among horses before I was bound 'prentice, and he hired me as his groom.

But how came you to leave him?

He is a very passionate gentleman. He has got a French footman, who stands and shrugs, and lets him give him thumps, and kicks;

and one morning, because one boot was brighter than t'other, he
was going to horsewhip me. So I told him to keep his hands off, or
I would knock him down.

Why you are quite a fighting fellow.

No, sir; I never fought with any body in my life, if they did not
first meddle with me.

So you quarrelled with your master, beat him, ran away from
your apprenticeship, got a place, came into a foreign country, and
then, because your master did not happen to please you, threatened
to knock him down!

The poor fellow was quite confounded, and I was half out of
breath from an apprehension that Clifton had taken the wrong side
of the question. But I was soon relieved——This tale is too artless
to be false, said he, turning to me.——You cannot conceive, Louisa,
the infinite pleasure which these few words gave me——I still
continued silent, and watching, not the lad, but your brother.

So you never meddle with any body who does not meddle
with you?

No, sir, I would scorn it.

But you will not be horsewhipped?

No, sir, I won't; starve or not starve.

I need not ask you if you are honest, sober, and industrious; for
I know you will say you are.

Why should I not, sir?

You have nobody to give you a character, have you?

My master is still in Paris; but to be sure he will give me
a bad one.

Can you tell me his address—where he lives?

I can't tell it in French, but here it is.

Can you write and read?

Yes, sir.

And how long have you been out of place?

Above seven weeks.

Why did not you return to England, when you received your
wages?

I had no money. I owed a fellow servant a guinea and a half,
which I had borrowed to buy shirts and stockings.

And those you have made away with?

Not all. I was obliged to take some of them to Mount Pity.

Mont Piété, you mean*.

Belike yes, sir.

Well, here's something for you, for the present; and come to me to-morrow morning.

The lad went away, with more in his countenance than he knew how to put into speech; and I asked Clifton what he meant by desiring him to come again. I intend, madam, said he, to make some inquiries of his master; and if they please me to hire him; for I want a servant, and if I am not deceived he will make a good one.

Think, Louisa, whether I were not pleased with this proof of discernment. By this accident, I learned more of Clifton's character in ten minutes than perhaps I might have done in ten months. He saw, for I wished him to see, that he had acted exactly as I could have desired.

He appears indeed to be a favourite with servants, which certainly is no bad omen. He is Laura's delight. He is a free gentleman, a generous gentleman, [I suppose he gives her money] a merry gentleman, and has the handsomest person, the finest eye, and the best manner of dressing his hair she ever beheld!——She quite overflows in his praise.

In a few days we are to go to the country seat of the Marquis of Villebrun, where we intend to stay about a fortnight. Your brother has introduced us to all his friends, among whom is the marquis; and, as we are intimate with our ambassador, we have more invitations than we can accept, and acquaintance than we can cultivate. Frank is to go with us.

And now, Louisa, with anxiety I own, my mind is far from satisfied. I have not thought sufficiently to convince myself, yet act as though I had. It is little less than open war between your brother and Frank. The supposition of a duty, too serious to be trifled with, has induced me to favour rather than repulse the too eager advances of Clifton; though this supposed duty has been but half examined.

The desire to retrieve mind cannot but be right; yet the mode may be wrong.

At this moment my heart bitterly reproaches me, for not proceeding on more certain principles. The merit of Frank is great,

* The general receptacle for pledges. Among other monopolies and trades, government in France used to be the common pawnbroker.

almost beyond the power of expression. I need not tell my Louisa which way affection, were it encouraged, would incline: but I will not be its slave. Nor can I reproach myself for erring on that side; but for acting, in resistance to inclination, with too little reserve. No arguments I believe can shew me that I have a right to sport with the feelings of my father, and my friends; though those feelings are founded in prejudice. But my inquiries shall be more minute; and my resolves will then be more permanent and self-complacent.

Adieu, my best and dearest friend. Write often: reprove me for all that I do amiss——Would my mind were more accordant with itself! But I will take it roundly to task.

A. W. ST. IVES

LETTER XXXII

Coke Clifton to Guy Fairfax

Paris, Hotel de l'Université

THIS brief memorandum of my actual existence, dear Fairfax, will be delivered to you by the Chevalier de Villeroi; a worthy gentleman, to whom I have given letters to my friends, and who will meet you at Turin.

I have not a moment to waste; therefore can only say that I am laying close siege; that my lines of circumvallation do not proceed quite so rapidly as my desires; but that I have just blown up the main bastion; or, in other words, have prevailed on Sir Arthur to send this hornet, this Frank Henley, back to England. The fellow's aspiring insolence is not to be endured. His merit is said to be uncommon. 'Tis certain he strains after the sublime; and in fact is too deep a thinker, nay I suspect too deep a plotter, not to be dangerous. Adieu.

C. CLIFTON

I am in a rage! Curse the fellow! He has countermined me; blown up my works! I might easily have foreseen it, had I not been a stupid booby. I could beat my thick scull against the wall! I have neither time nor patience to tell you what I mean; except that here he is, and here he will remain, in my despite.

LETTER XXXIII

Frank Henley to Oliver Trenchard

Paris, Hotel de l'Université

I T is as I told thee, Oliver. He fears me. He treats me, as he thinks, with the neglect and contempt due to an unqualified intruder: but he mistakes his own motives, and acts with insidious jealousy; nay descends to artifice. His alarmed spirit never rests; he is ever on the watch, lest at entering a room, descending a staircase, stepping into her carriage, or on any other occasion, I should touch her hand. He has endeavoured to exclude me from all their parties; and, though often successfully, has several times been foiled.

But his greatest disappointment was this very morning. Sir Arthur sent for me, last night, to inform me I must return to Wenbourne-Hill, with some necessary orders, which he did not choose to trust to the usual mode of conveyance. I immediately suspected, and I think I did not do him injustice, that my rival was the contriver of this sudden necessity of my return.

I received Sir Arthur's orders, but was determined immediately to acquaint Anna.

Clifton was present. She was surprised; and, I doubt not, had the same suspicions as myself; for, after telling me I must not think of going, she obliged Clifton himself to be the intercessor, with Sir Arthur, that I should stay. His reluctance, feigned assent, and chagrin were visible.

Her words and manner to me were kind; nay I could almost think they were somewhat more. She seemed to feel the injustice aimed at me; and to feel it with as much resentment as a spirit so benignant could know.

What!——Can he not be satisfied with half excluding me from her society; with endeavouring to sink me as low in her estimation as in his own; and with exercising all that arrogance which he supposes becoming the character of a gentleman?

Oliver, I am determined in my plan: my appeal shall be to her justice. If it prove to be ill-founded, why then I must acquiesce. I am angry at my own delay, at my own want of courage; but I shall find a time, and that quickly. At least, if condemned I must be, I will be heard; but equity I think is on my side—Yes—I will be heard.

F. HENLEY

LETTER XXXIV

Frank Henley to Oliver Trenchard

Paris, Hotel de l' Université

AID me if thou canst, Oliver, to think, or rather to unravel my own entangled thoughts. Do not suffer me to continue in a state of delusion, if thou perceivest it to be such. Be explicit; tell me if thou dost but so much as forebode: for at moments I myself despond; though at others I am wasted to the heaven of heavens, to certainty, and bliss unutterable. If I deceive myself?—Well!—And if I do, what is to follow?—Rashness?—Cowardice?—What! Basely abandon duty, virtue, and energy?—No!

Looks, words, appearances, daily events are all so contradictory, that the warfare of hope and fear increases, and becomes violent, almost to distraction! Clifton is openly countenanced by Sir Arthur, treated kindly by her, and is incessant in every kind of assiduity. His qualities are neither mean, insignificant, nor common. No: they are brilliant, and rare. With a person as near perfection as his mind will permit it to be, a knowledge of languages, a taste for the fine arts, much bravery, high notions of honour, a more than common share of wit, keen and ungovernable feelings, an impatience of contradiction, and an obstinacy in error, he is a compound of jarring elements, that augur tempests and peril. Vain, haughty, and self-willed, his family, his fortune, his accomplishments and himself are the pictures that fascinate his eye. It is attracted, for a moment, by the superior powers of another; but all his passions and propensities forebode that he is not to be held, even by that link of adamant.

And is she to be dazzled then by this glare? Can her attention be caught by person, attracted by wit? And does she not shrink from that haughty pride which so continually turns to contemplate itself; from those passions which are so eager to be gratified; and from those mistakes which it will be so almost impossible to eradicate? Even were I to lose her, must I see her thus devoted?— The thought is—I cannot tell what! Too painful for any word short of extravagance.

Impressed by feelings like these, the other day I sat down and threw a few ideas into verse. The mind, surcharged with passion, is eager by every means to disburthen itself. It is always prompt to hope that the expression of it's feelings, if any way adequate, cannot but produce the effect it wishes; and I wrote the following song, or love-elegy, or what thou wilt.

> Rash hope avaunt! Be still my flutt'ring heart;
> Nor breathe a sorrow, nor a sigh impart;
> Appease each bursting throb, each pang reprove;
> To suffer dare—But do not dare to love!
>
> Down, down, these swelling thoughts! Nor dream that worth
> Can pass the haughty bounds of wealth and birth.
> Yes, kindred feelings, truth, and virtue prove:
> Yes, dare deserve—But do not dare to love!
>
> To noble tasks and dang'rous heights aspire;
> Bid all the great and good thy wishes fire,
> The mighty dead thy rival efforts move,
> And dare to die—But do not dare to love!

Thou knowest her supreme excellence in music; the taste, feeling, and expression with which she plays; and the enchanting sweetness and energy with which she sings. Having written my verses, I took them, when she was busied elsewhere, to the pianoforte; and made some unsuccessful attempts to please myself with an air to them. Sir Arthur came in, and I left my stanzas on the desk of the instrument; very inadvertently I assure thee, though I was afterward far from sorry that they had been forgotten.

I have frequently indulged myself in sitting in an antichamber, to listen to her playing and singing. I have thought that she is most impassioned when alone, and perhaps all musicians are so. The next day, happening to listen in the manner I have mentioned, I

I

heard her singing an air which was new to me, and remarked that she once or twice stopped, to consider and make alterations.

I listened again and found she had been setting my verses!

By my soul, Oliver, I have no conception of rapture superior to what I experienced at that moment! She had collected all her feelings, all her invention, had composed a most beautiful air, and sung it with an effect that must have been heard to be supposed possible. The force with which she uttered every thought to the climax of daring, and the compassion which she infused into the conclusion—'But do not dare to love'—produced the most affecting contrast I ever heard.

This indeed was heaven, Oliver! But a heaven that ominously vanished, at the entrance of Clifton. I followed him, and saw her shut the book, and wipe the tear from her eye. Her flow of spirits is unfailing, but the tone of her mind was raised too high suddenly to sink into trifling. She looked at me two or three times. I know not for my part what aspect I wore; but I could observe that the haughty Clifton felt the gaiety of his heart in some sort disturbed, and was not pleased to catch me listening, with such mute attention, to the ravishing music she had made.

Once again prithee tell me, Oliver, what am I to think? It was impossible she should have sung as she did, had not the ideas affected her more than I could have hoped, nay as much as they did myself. She knew the writing. Why did she sigh? Why feel indignant? Why express every sentiment that had passed through my mind with increasing force?——What could she think?—— Did she not approve?—She sung as if she admired!——The world shall not persuade me that her looks were not the true expressions of her heart; and she looked—! Recollect her, and the temper of mind she was in, and imagine how!—Remember—*She could love me if I would let her!*

I was displeased with the verses when I had written them: they were very inadequate to what I wished. I discovered in some of the lines a barren repetition of the preceding thought, and meant to have corrected them. But I would not now alter a word for worlds! She has deigned to set and sing them; and what was before but of little worth is now inestimable.

Yet am I far from satisfied with myself. My present state of mind is disgraceful; for it cannot but be disgraceful to be kept in doubt by my own cowardice. And if I am deceiving myself—Can it be possible, Oliver?—But if I am, my present error is indeed alarming. The difficulty of retreating momentarily increases, and every step in advance will be miles in return.

Clifton will suffer no impediment from the cowardice of which I complain; for I much mistake if he has been accustomed to refusal; or if he can scarcely think, when he deigns to sue, denial possible.

I find myself every day determining to put an end to this suspense, and every day delaying. The impulse however is too great to be long resisted; and my excuse to myself continually is that I have not yet found the proper moment.

If, Oliver, this history of my heart be troublesome to thee, it is thy duty to tell me so. But indeed thou tellest me the contrary; and I know not why at this instant I should do thee the injustice to doubt thy sincerity. Forgive me. It is a friendly fear, and not intended to do thee wrong. But I wish thee to judge of me and my actions; and even to let thy father judge, if thou shouldest at any time hesitate, and fear I am committing error. Do this, and continue thy usual kindness in communicating thy thoughts.

F. HENLEY

P.S. The day after tomorrow, we are to set off for the Chateau de Villebrun; on a party of pleasure, as it is called. Thus men run from place to place, without knowing of what they are in search. They feel vacuity; a want of something to make them happy; but what that something is they have not yet discovered.

LETTER XXXV

Anna Wenbourne St. Ives to Louisa Clifton

Paris, Hotel de l'Université

I FEAR, my dear Louisa, I am at present hurried forward a little too fast to act with all the caution which I could wish. My mind is not coherent, not at peace with itself. Ideas rush in multitudes, and more than half obscure my understanding.

I find that, since we left Wenbourne-Hill, Frank has grown upon
my thoughts very strangely. Indeed till then I was but partially
acquainted with his true character, the energy of which is very uncommon. But, though his virtues are become more conspicuous,
the impediments that forbid any thought of union are not lessened.

My chief difficulty is, I do not yet know how to give full effect to
my arguments, so as to produce such conviction as he shall be
unable to resist. Let me do but this, and I have no doubt of his
perfect acquiescence, and resignation. But, should I fail, the warfare of the passions will be prolonged; and, for a time, a youth
whose worth is above my praise rendered unhappy. A sense of
injustice, committed by the person of whom, perhaps, he thought
too highly to suppose it possible that either error or passion should
render her so culpable, may prey upon his peace, and destroy the
felicity of one to whom reason and recollection tell me I cannot
wish too much good.

I am convinced I have been guilty of another mistake. I have
on various occasions been desirous of expressing approbation,
mingled with esteem and friendship. He has extorted it from me.
He has obliged me to feel thus. And why, have I constantly asked
myself, should I repress or conceal sensations that are the dues of
merit? No: they ought not to have been repressed, or concealed,
but they ought to have been rendered intelligible, incapable of
misconstruction, and not liable to a meaning which they were
never intended to convey. For, if ever they were more than I suppose, I have indeed been guilty.

Yes, my Louisa, let me discharge my conscience. Let no
accusation of deceit rest with me. I can endure any thing but self-
reproach. I avow, therefore, Frank Henley is, in my estimation,
the most deserving man I have ever known. A man that I could
love infinitely. A man whose virtues I do and must ever love. A
man in whose company my heart assures me I could have enjoyed
years of happiness. If the casuists in such cases should tell me this
is what they mean by love, why then I am in love.

But if the being able, without a murmur, nay cheerfully, to marry
another, or see him properly married, if the possession of the power
and the resolution to do what is right, and if an unshaken will to
exert this power prove the contrary, why then I am not in love.

When I may, without trespassing on any duty, and with the full approbation of my own heart, yield up its entire affections, the man to whom they shall be devoted shall then find how much I can love.

My passions must be, ought to be, and therefore shall be, under my control; and, being conscious of the purity of my own intentions, I have never thought that the emanations of mind ought to be shackled by the dread of their being misinterpreted. It is not only cowardly, but in my opinion pernicious.

Yet, with respect to Frank, I fear this principle has led me into an error. Among other escapes of this kind, there is one which has lately befallen me, and for which I doubt I am reprehensible.

Frank has written a song, in which his feelings and situation are very strongly expressed. He left it on my music desk, by accident; for his character is too open, too determined, to submit to artifice. The words pleased me, I may say affected me, so very much that I was tempted to endeavour to adapt an air to them; which, when it was written, I several times repeated, and accompanied myself on the piano-forte. Your brother came in just as I had ended; and, from a hint which he purposely gave, I suspect that Frank had been listening in the antichamber.

The behaviour of Frank afterward confirmed the supposition. He followed your brother, and sat down while we conversed. His whole soul seemed absorbed; but not, as I have sometimes seen it, in melancholy. Satisfaction, pleasure, I know not whether rapture would be too strong a word for the expressions which were discoverable in his countenance.

My own mind had the moment before been impassioned; and the same sensations thrilling as it were through my veins might mislead me, and induce me to suppose things that had no existence. Still I do not think I was mistaken. And if not, what have I done? Have I not thoughtlessly betrayed him into a belief that I mean to favour a passion which I should think it criminal to encourage?

I know not why I delay so long to explain my sentiments. It is the weak fear of not doing justice to my cause; of not convincing, and of making him unhappy, for whom I would sacrifice my life, every thing but principle, to make him the very reverse.

However this must and shall soon be ended. I do not pretend to fix a day, but it shall not be a very distant one. I will arrange my thoughts, collect my whole force, and make an essay which I am

convinced cannot fail, unless by my fault. The task is perhaps the
most severe I have ever yet undertaken. I will remember this, and
I hope my exertions will be adequate.

Adieu, my dear Louisa: and, when you come to this place,
imagine me for a moment in your arms.

A. W. ST. IVES

LETTER XXXVI

Coke Clifton to Guy Fairfax

Chateau de Villebrun

NEVER was fellow so pestered with malverse accidents as I am;
and all of my own contriving! I am the prince of Numskulls! The
journey to the Chateau was a project of my own; and whom should
I meet here but the Count de Beaunoir! The very same with whom
I was prevented from fighting, by this insolent son of a steward!
They knew each other instantly; and the whole story was told in
the presence of Anna. My foolish pride would never before let me
mention to her that a fellow, like him, could oblige me to put up
the sword I had drawn in anger. Nor can I now tell why I did not
run him through, the instant he dared to interfere!

I cut a cursed ridiculous figure! But the youth is running up a
long score, which I foresee he will shortly be obliged to discharge.
Damn him! I cannot think of him with common patience! I know
not why I ever mention his name!

I have raised another nest of wasps about my ears. The French
fops, here, all buzz and swarm around her; each making love to
her, with all the shrugs, grimaces, and ready made raptures of
which he is master; and to which I am obliged patiently to listen,
or shew myself an ass. These fellows submit to every kind of
monopoly, except of woman; and to pretend an exclusive right to
her is, in their opinion, only worthy of a barbarian. But the most
forward and tormenting of them all is my quondam friend, the
Count; who is half a lunatic, but of so diverting a kind that, ere a
man has time to be angry, he either cuts a caper, utters an absurdity,
or acts some mad antic or other, that sets gravity at defiance.

Not that any man, who had the smallest pretensions to common sense, could be jealous, either of him or any one of these apes. And yet jealous I am! My dotage, Fairfax, is come very suddenly upon me; and neither you, nor any one of the spirited fellows, whose company I used to delight in, can despise me half so much as I despise myself——A plebeian!——A——! I could drink gall, eat my elbows, renounce all my gods, and turn Turk!——Ay, laugh if you will; what care I?—

I have taken a turn into the park, in search of a little cool air and common sense.

All the world is met here, on purpose to be merry; and merry they are determined to be. The occasion is a marriage, in the true French style, between my very good friend, the Marquis de Villebrun, an old fellow upwards of sixty, and a young creature of fifteen; a child, a chit, just taken out of a convent; in which, but for this or some such preposterous match, she might have remained, till time should have bestowed wrinkles and ugliness as bountifully upon her as it has done upon her Narcissus, the bridegroom. The women flock busily round her, in their very good-natured way, purposely to form her. The men too are very willing to lend their aid; and, under such tuition, she cannot but improve apace. Why are not you here, Fairfax? I have had twenty temptations to take her under my pupillage; but that I dare not risk the loss of this divinity.

The purpose of our meeting however is, as I said, to be joyous. It is teeming time therefore with every brain, that has either wit, folly, or fancy enough to contribute to the general festivity. And various are their inventions, and stratagems, to excite surprise, attract visitors, and keep up the holiday farce of the scene. Musicians, painters, artists, jugglers, sages, all whose fame, no matter of what motley kind, has reached the public ear, and whom praise or pay can bring together, are assembled. Poets are invited to read their productions; and as reading well is no mean art, and writing well still much more difficult, you may think what kind of an exhibition your every day poetasters make. Yet, like a modern play, they are certain of unbounded applause.

Last night we had a *Féte Champêtre*; which, it must be granted, was a most accurate picture of nature, and the manners of rustics!

The simplicity of the shepherd life could not but be excellently represented, by the ribbands, jewels, gauze, tiffany, and fringe, with which we were bedaubed; and the ragouts, fricassees, spices, sauces, wines, and *liqueurs*, with which we were regaled! Not to mention being served upon plate, by an army of footmen! But then, it was in the open air; and that was prodigiously pastoral!

When we were sufficiently tired of eating and drinking, we all got up to dance; and the mild splendour of the moon was utterly eclipsed, by the glittering dazzle of some hundreds of lamps; red, green, yellow, and blue; the rainbow burlesqued; all mingled, in fantastic wreaths and forms, and suspended among the foliage; that the trees might be as fine as ourselves! The invention, disposition, and effect, however, were highly applauded. And, since the evil was small and the mirth great, what could a man do, but shake his ears, kick his heels, cut capers, laugh, sing, shout, squall, and be as mad as the best?

To-morrow night we are to have fireworks; which will be no less rural. I was in a splenetic humour, and indulged myself in an exclamation against such an abominable waste of gunpowder; for which I got reproved by my angelic monitress, who told me that, of all its uses and abuses, this was the most innocent.

I suppose our stay here will not be less than a fortnight. But I have left orders for all letters to be sent after me; so that your heroic epistles will come safe and soon to hand.

Which is all at this present writing from your very humble servant

to command,

C. CLIFTON

LETTER XXXVII

Anna Wenbourne St. Ives to Louisa Clifton

Chateau de Villebrun

IN compliance with the very warm entreaties of our kind French friends, we have been hurried away from the metropolis sooner than was intended. We are at present in the country, at the Chateau de Villebrun; where, if we are not merry, it is not for the want of laughing. Our feet and our tongues are never still. We dance, talk, sing, ride, sail, or rather paddle about in a small but romantic lake; in short we are never out of exercise.

Clifton is as active as the best, and is very expert in all feats of agility. With the French he seems to dance for the honour of his nation; and, with me, from a desire to prove that the man who makes pretensions to me, which he now does openly enough, is capable of every excellence.

You know, Louisa, how much I despise the affectation of reserve; but he is so enterprising a youth that I am sometimes obliged, though very unwillingly, to exert a little mild authority.

The French, old or young, ugly or handsome, all are lovers; and are as liberal of their amorous sighs, and addresses, as if each were an Adonis. Clifton is well acquainted with foreign manners, or I can perceive their gallantry to me would make him half mad. As it is, he has been little less than rude, to one or two of the most forward of my pretended admirers.

I speak in the plural, as if we were rather in town than at a country seat; and so we appear to be. The French nobility do not seem to have any taste for solitude. Their love of variety induces them to change the scene; but the same tumult of guests and visitors, coming and going, is every where their delight. Whatever can attract company they seek with avidity. I am dear to them, because I am an English beauty, as they tell me, and all the world is desirous of paying its court to me.

Clifton has equal or perhaps greater merits of the same kind. And I assure you, Louisa, the women here can pay their court more artfully and almost as openly as the men.

Frank is idolized by them, because he reads Shakespeare.[1] You would wonder to hear the praises they bestow upon him, and which indeed he richly deserves, though not one in ten of them understands a word he says. *C'est beau! C'est magnifique! C'est superbe! C'est sublime!* Such is their continual round of good-natured superlatives, which they apply on all occasions, with a sincere desire to make others as happy as they endeavour to persuade themselves to be. Frank treats their gallantry with a kind of silent contempt, otherwise he would be a much greater favourite.

Perhaps you will be surprised to find me still guilty of procrastination, and to hear me describing French manners, instead

of the mode in which I addressed a youth whom I have accused
myself of having, in a certain sense, misled, and kept in suspense.
I can only answer that my intentions have been frustrated; chiefly
indeed by this country excursion, though in part by other accidents. My mind has not indulged itself in indolence; it could not;
it is too deeply interested. But, the more I have thought, the more
have I been confirmed in my former opinion. This is the hour of
trial: this is the time to prove I have some real claims to that
superiority which I have been so ready to flatter myself I possess.
Were there nothing to regret, nay were there not something to
suffer, where would be the merit of victory?—But, on the other
hand, how much is there to gain!—A mind of the first order to be
retrieved!—A Clifton!—A brother of Louisa!

This appears to be a serious crisis. Again I must repeat how
much I am afraid of being hurried forward too fast. An error at
this moment might be fatal. Clifton is so much alarmed by the
particular respect which the Count de Beaunoir [A pleasant kind
of madman, who is a visitant here.] pays me, that he has this
instant been with me, confessed a passion for me, in all the strong
and perhaps extravagant language which custom has seemed to
authorise, and has entreated, with a degree of warmth and earnestness that could scarcely be resisted, my permission to mention the
matter immediately to Sir Arthur.

It became me to speak without disguise. I told him I was far
from insensible of his merits; that a union with the brother of my
Louisa, if propriety, duty, and affection should happen to combine, would be the first wish of my heart; that I should consider
any affectation and coyness as criminal; but that I was not entirely
free from doubt; and, before I could agree to the proposal being
made to Sir Arthur, I thought it necessary we should mutually
compare our thoughts, and scrutinize as it were each other to the
very soul; that we might not act rashly, in the most serious of all
the private events of life.—You know my heart, Louisa; at least as
well as I myself know it; and I am fearful of being precipitate.

He seemed rather disappointed, and was impatient to begin the
conversation I wished for immediately.

I told him I was unprepared; my thoughts were not sufficiently
collected; and that the hurry in which we at present exist would

scarcely allow me time to perform so necessary a duty. But, that I might avoid the least suspicion of coquetry, if it were his desire, I would shut myself up for a day from company, and examine whether there were any real impediments; that I would ask myself what my hopes and expectations were; and that I requested, or indeed expected that he should do the same. I added however that, if he pleased, it would be much more agreeable to me to defer this serious task, at least till we should return to Paris.

He repeated my words, if it would be much more agreeable to me, impatient and uneasy though he owned he was, he must submit.

I answered I required no submission, except to reason; to which I hoped both he and I should always be subject.

Love, he replied, was so disdainful of restraint that it would not acknowledge the control of reason itself. However, by representing to him how particular our mutual absence from the company would seem, unless we could condescend to tell some falsehood, which I would not I said suppose possible to either of us, I prevailed on him to subscribe to this short delay.

His passions and feelings are strong. One minute he seemed affected by the approbation which, as far as I could with truth, I did not scruple to bestow on his many superior gifts; and the next to conceive some chagrin that I should for a moment hesitate. The noblest natures, Louisa, are the most subject to pride, can the least endure neglect, and are aptest to construe whatever is not directly affirmative in their favour into injustice.

With respect to the Count de Beaunoir, he has been more passionate, in expressing how much he admires me, than my reserve to him can have authorised; except so far as he follows the manners of his country, and the impulse of his peculiar character. I suppose he means little; though he has said much. Not that I am certain. He may be more in earnest than I desire; but I hope he is not; because, if I am to be your sister as well as your friend, I should be sorry that any thing should excite a shadow of doubt in the mind of Clifton.

The Count is one of the Provençal nobility; a whimsical creature, with an imagination amazingly rapid, but extravagant. Your brother calls him Count Shatter-brain; and I tell him that he forgets he has some claim to the title himself. The Count has read

the old Provençal poets, and romance writers, till he has made
himself a kind of Don Quixote; except that he has none of the Don's
delightful systematic gravity. The Count on the contrary amuses
by his want of system, and his quick, changeable incongruity. He
is in raptures one moment with what he laughs at the next. Were
it not for the mad follies of jealousy, against which we cannot be
too guarded, the manner in which he addresses, or in his own
language adores me, would be pleasant. If I wished to pass my life
in laughing, I would certainly marry the Count.

I am called to dinner. Adieu.

Ever and ever yours,

A. W. ST. IVES

LETTER XXXVIII

Anna Wenbourne St. Ives to Louisa Clifton

Chateau de Villebrun

MY alarms, Louisa, increase; and with them my anxious wishes
for an eclaircissement[1] with Frank. Clifton has too strongly
imbibed high but false notions of honour and revenge. His quick,
apt, and versatile talents are indubitable. He wants nothing but
the power to curb and regulate his passions, to render him all that
his generous and excellent sister could desire. But at present his
sensibility is too great. He scarcely can brook the slightest tokens
of disapprobation. He is rather too firmly persuaded that he
deserves applause, and admiration; and that reproof he scarcely
can deserve: or, if he did, to submit to it he imagines would be
dishonourable.

Frank and he behave more than usually cool to each other: I
know not why, unless it has been occasioned by an incident which
happened yesterday. Clifton has bought an English hunter, from
one of his countrymen at Paris, which he was exhibiting to his
French friends, whose horsemanship is very different from ours,
and who were surprised to see him ride so fearlessly over gates and
other impediments. They continued their airing in the park of
Villebrun, and turned round to a kind of haha, which was both

deep and wide, and about half full of water, by the side of which they saw a party of ladies standing, and me among the rest. Frank was with us.

One of the gentlemen asked whether the horse could leap over the haha: to which Clifton made no answer, but immediately clapped spurs to his hunter, and over he flew. The whole company, gentlemen and ladies, broke out into exclamations of surprise; and Clifton turned his horse's head round, and regained his former place.

While they were wondering, Frank Henley happened to make it a matter of doubt whether a man or a horse could leap the farthest; and Clifton, continually in the habit of contending with Frank, said it was ridiculous to start such an argument, unless he would first shew that he himself could make the same leap. Frank, piqued in his turn, retired a few yards; and, without pulling off his coat or deigning to leap, he made a short run and a hop and sprung over.

You may imagine that the kind and good folks, who love to be astonished, and still more to tell the greatness of their astonishment, were manifold in their interjections. Frank, in order to rejoin the company, was obliged a second time to cross the haha; which he did with the same safety and truly amazing agility as he had done before.

Clifton, indulging his wrong habits, though I have no doubt admiring Frank as much as the rest, told him in a kind of sarcastic banter that, though he could not prove the equality of mankind, he had at least proved himself equal to a horse. To which Frank replied he was mistaken; for that he had shewn himself equal to the horse and his rider.

This answer I fear dwells upon the mind of Clifton; and I scarcely myself can tell whether it were or were not worthy of Frank. How can Clifton be wilfully blind to such courage, rectitude of heart, understanding and genius?

The stern unrelenting fortitude of Frank, in the cause of justice, and some symptoms of violence in the impetuous Clifton, have inspired me with apprehensions; and have induced me to behave with more reserve and coldness to Frank than I ever before assumed.

Yet, Louisa, my heart is wrung to see the effect it produces. He has a mind of such discriminating power, such magnanimity, that an injury to it is a deep, a double sin; and every look, every action testify that he thinks himself injured, by the distance with which I behave. Oh that he himself might be impelled to begin the subject with which my mind is labouring!

This is wrong; I am ashamed of my own cowardice. Yet would there not be something terrifying in a formal appointment, to tell him what it seems must be told?—Yes, Louisa, must——And is there not danger he should think me severe; nay unjust?—Would it were over!——I hope he will not think so of me!—It must be done!—Must!—Must!——

Indeed, Louisa, I could be a very woman——But I will not!—No, no!—It is passed——I have put my handkerchief to my eyes and it is gone——I have repressed an obstinate heaving of the heart——

Let her blame me, if I deserve it, but my Louisa must see me as I am—Yet I will conquer——Be sure I will—But I must not sing his song any more!

A. W. ST. IVES

LETTER XXXIX

Frank Henley to Oliver Trenchard ,

Chateau de Villebrun

OH, my friend, my heart is torn! I am on the rack! My thoughts are all tumult! My passions rebel! I seem to have yielded up the best prerogative of man, reason; and to have admitted revolt, anarchy, and desolation!

Her manner is changed! Wholly! She is become cold, reserved; has marked me out for neglect; smiles on me no more; not a sigh escapes her. And why? What have I done? I am unconscious. Have I been too presuming? Perhaps so. But why did her looks never till now speak her meaning as intelligibly as they do at present? I could not then have mistaken them. Why, till now, has she seemed to regard me with that sweet amenity which was so flattering to hope?

Perhaps, in the distraction of my thoughts, I am unjust to her. And shall I, pretending as I do to love so pure, shall I become her accuser? What if she meant no more than that commerce of grateful kindness, which knits together human society, and renders it delightful?

Yet this sudden change! So evidently intentional! The smiles too which she bestows on the brother of Louisa, and the haughty airs of triumph which he assumes, what can these be? Confident in himself, ardent in his desires, unchecked by those fears which are the offspring of true delicacy, his passions violent, and his pride almost insufferable, he thinks he loves. But he is ignorant of the alarms, the tremors, the 'fitful fevers'[1] of love.

I cannot endure my present torture. I must seek a desperate end to it, by explanation. Why do I delay? Coward that I am! What worse can happen than despair? And is not despair itself preferable to that worst of fiends, suspense? What do I mean by despair? Would I, being rejected, desert my duty, sink into self, and poorly linger in wretchedness; or basely put an end to existence? Violently end that which ought to be devoted to the good of others?—— How did so infernal a thought enter my mind?——Can I be so very lost a thing?——No!——Despair is something confused, something horrid: I know not what. It may intrude upon me, at black and dismal intervals; but it shall not overwhelm me. I will shake it off. I will meet my destiny.

The clouds are gathering; the storm approaches; I hear the distant thunder rolling; this way it drives; it points at me; it must suddenly burst! Be it so. Grant me but the spirit of a man, and I yet shall brave its fury. If I am a poor braggart, a half believer in virtue, or virtuous only in words, the feeble victim then must justly perish.

I cannot endure my torments! Cannot, because there is a way to end them. It shall be done.

I blush to read, blush to recollect the rhapsodies of my own perturbed mind! Madman! 'Tis continually thus. Day after day I proceed, reasoning, reproving, doubting, wishing, believing and despairing, alternately.

Once again, where is this strange impossibility?——In what does it consist?——Are we not both human beings?—What law of Nature has placed her beyond my hopes?—What is rank? Does

it imply superiority of mind? Or is there any other superiority?——
Am I not a man?——And who is more? Have the titled earned their
dignities by any proofs of exalted virtue? Were not these dignities
things of accident, in which the owners had no share, and of which
they are generally unworthy? And shall hope be thus cowed and
killed, without my daring to exert the first and most unalienable
of the rights of man, freedom of thought? Shall I not examine what
these high distinctions truly are, of which the bearers are so vain?

This Clifton——! Thou knowest not how he treats me. And can
she approve, can she second his injustice?—Surely not!—Yet does
she not dedicate her smiles to him, her conversation, her time?
Does she not shun me, discountenance me, and reprove me, by her
silence and her averted eyes?

Once again it must and shall have an end!——I have repeated
this too often; but my next shall shew thee I am at length determined.

F. HENLEY

LETTER XL

Anna Wenbourne St. Ives to Louisa Clifton

Chateau de Villebrun

AN affair has just happened in this country which is the universal
topic of conversation. The daughter of a noble and wealthy family
has fallen in love with a man of uncommon learning, science, and
genius, but a musician. In consequence of his great skill and
reputation, he was employed to teach her music; and she it appears
was too sensible, at least for the decorum of our present manners,
of his worth.

The ability to discover his merit implies merit in herself, and
the musician and lady were equally enamoured of each other. A
plan for elopement consequently was laid, and put in execution;
but not effectually, for, before the lovers had passed the confines of
the kingdom, they were pursued and overtaken.

The musician knew his own personal danger, and by a stratagem
fortunately escaped from his bonds, and attained a place of safety.

The lady was brought back; and, from the severity of the French laws and the supposed atrocity of the crime, it is generally affirmed that the musician, notwithstanding his talents and fame, had he been secured, would have been executed.

I have mentioned this adventure, my dear Louisa, not so much for its own sake as for what relates to myself. It was natural that I should feel compassion for mistakes, if mistakes they be, which have so great an affinity to virtue; and that I should plead for the lovers, and against the barbarity of laws so unjust and inhuman. For it is certain that, had not the musician been put to death, his least punishment would have been perpetual imprisonment.

In a former letter I mentioned the increasing alarms of Sir Arthur; and this was a fit opportunity for him to shew how very serious and great those alarms are. He opposed me, while I argued in behalf of the lovers, with what might in him be called violence; affirmed it was a crime for which no merit or genius could compensate; highly applauded those wholesome laws that prevented such crimes, and preserved the honour of noble families from attaint; lamented the want of similar laws in England; and spoke of the conduct of the young lady with a degree of bitterness which from him was unusual. In fine, the spirit of his whole discourse was evidently to warn me, and explicitly to declare what his opinions on this subject are.

Had I before wanted conviction, he fully convinced me, on this occasion, of the impossibility of any union between me and Frank Henley; at least without sacrificing the felicity of my father and my family, and from being generally and sincerely beloved by them, rendering myself the object of eternal reproach, and almost of hatred.

Previous to this conversation, I was uneasy at the state of my own mind, and particularly at what I suppose to be the state of Mr. Henley's; and this uneasiness is at present very much increased.

Once again, Louisa, it must immediately have an end. I can support it no longer. I must be firm. My half-staggering resolution is now fixed. I cannot, must not doubt. My father and family must not be sacrificed to speculative probabilities. Frank is the most deserving of mankind; and that it should be a duty to reject the most deserving of mankind, as the friend of my life, my better self,

K

my husband, is strange; but I am nevertheless convinced that a duty it is. Yes; the conflicts of doubt are over. I must and will persevere.

Poor Frank! To be guilty of injustice to a nature so noble, to wring a heart so generous, and to neglect desert so unequalled, is indeed a killing thought! But the stern the unrelenting dictates of necessity must be obeyed. The neglect the injustice and the cruelty are the world's, not mine: my heart disavows them, revolts at them, detests them!

Heaven bless my Louisa, and give her superior prudence to guard and preserve her from these too strong susceptibilities! May the angel of fortitude never forsake her, as she seems half inclined to do her poor

A. W. ST. IVES

END OF VOLUME II

VOLUME III

LETTER XLI

Anna Wenbourne St. Ives to Louisa Clifton

Chateau de Villebrun

AT last, my dear Louisa, the charm is broken: the spell of silence is dissolved. Incapable any longer of restraint, passion has burst its bounds, and strong though the contest was, victory has declared for reason.

My change of behaviour has produced this effect. Not that I applaud myself: on the contrary, I am far from pleased with my own want of fortitude. I have even assumed an austerity which I did not feel.

I do not mean to say that all appearances, relative to myself, were false. No. I was uneasy; desirous to speak, desirous that he should speak, and could accomplish neither. I accused myself of having given hopes that were seductive, and wished to retract. In short, I have not been altogether so consistent as I ought to be; as my letters to you, my friend, will witness.

Various little incidents preceded and indeed helped to produce this swell and overflow of the heart, and the eclaircissement that followed. In the morning at breakfast, Frank took the cakes I usually eat to hand to me; and Clifton, whose watchful spirit is ever alert, caught up a plate of bread and butter, to offer me at the same instant. His looks shewed he expected the preference. I was sorry for it, and paused for a moment. At last the principle of not encouraging Frank prevailed, and I took some bread and butter from Clifton. It was a repetition of slights, which Frank had lately met with, and he felt it; yet he bowed with a tolerable grace, and put down his plate.

He soon after quitted the room, but returned unperceived by me.

The young marchioness had breakfasted, and retired to her toilet;
where some of the gentlemen were attending her. She had left a
snuff-box of considerable value with me, which I had forgotten to
return; and, with that kind of sportive cheerfulness which I rather
encourage than repress, I called—'Here! Where are all my esquires?
I want a messenger.'

Clifton heard me, and Frank was unexpectedly at my elbow.
Had I known it, I should not have spoken so thoughtlessly. Frank
came forward and bowed. Clifton called—'Here am I, ready, fair
lady, to execute your behests.'

I was a second time embarrassed. After a short hesitation, I
said—'No—I have changed my mind.'

Frank retired; but Clifton advanced, with his usual gaiety,
answering,—'Nay, nay! I have not earned half a crown yet this
morning, and I must not be cheated of my fare.' I would still have
refused, but I perceived Clifton began to look serious, and I said
to him—'Well, well, good man, here then, take this snuff-box to
the marchioness, she may want it: but do not blunder, and break
it; for if you do I shall dismiss you my service. Recollect the picture
in the lid, set with diamonds!'

It was fated to be a day of mortification to Frank. His complaisance had induced him to comply with the request of the
marchioness, that he would read one of the mad scenes in Lear,
though he knew she had not the least acquaintance with the
English language. But she wanted amusement, and was pleased
to mark the progress of the passions; which I never saw so distinctly and highly expressed as in his countenance, when he reads
Shakespeare.

I happened to come into her apartment, for the French are
delightfully easy of access, and the reading was instantly interrupted. I was the very person she wanted to see. How should we
spend the evening? The country was horribly dull! There had
been no new visitors these two days! Should we have a dance?
I gave my assent, and away she ran to tell every body.

I followed; Frank came after me, and with some reluctance,
foreboding a repulse, asked whether he should have the pleasure
to dance with me. His manner and the foregone circumstances
made me guess his question before he spoke. My answer was—
'I have just made a promise to myself that I will dance with

Mr. Clifton.' It was true: the thought had passed through my mind.

Mr. Clifton, madam!

Yes——

You—you—

I have not seen Mr. Clifton? Right—But I said I had made the promise to *myself*.

Poor Frank could contain no longer! I see, madam, said he, I am despised; and I deserve contempt; I crouch to it, I invite it, and have obtained a full portion of it—Yet why?—What have I done?—Why is this sudden change?—The false glitter that deceives mankind then is irresistible!——But surely, madam, justice is as much my due as if my name were Clifton. Spurn me, trample on me, when I sully myself by vice and infamy! But till then I should once have hoped to have escaped being humbled in the dust, by one whom I regarded as the most benignant, as well as the most deserving and equitable of earthly creatures!

This is indeed a heavy charge: and I am afraid much of it is too true. Here is company coming. I am sorry I cannot answer it immediately.

I can suffer any thing rather than exist under my present tortures. Will you favour me so far, madam, as to grant me half an hour's hearing?

Willingly. It is what I wish. Come to my apartment after dinner.

Clifton came up, and I have no doubt read in our countenances that something more than common had passed. Indeed I perceived it, or thought so; but his imagination took another turn, in consequence of my informing him, that I had been just telling Frank I had promised myself to be his (Clifton's) partner. He thanked me, his countenance shewed it as well as his words, for my kindness. He was coming, he said, to petition, the instant he had heard of the dance. But still he looked at Frank, as if he thought it strange that I should condescend to account to him for my thoughts and promises.

Dinner time came, and we sat down to table. But the mind is sometimes too busy to attend to the appetites. I and Frank ate but little. He rose first from table, that he might not seem to follow me. His delicacy never slumbers. I took the first opportunity to retire. Frank was presently with me, and our dialogue began. The struggle of the feelings ordained that I should be the first speaker.

I have been thinking very seriously, Frank, of what you said to me this morning.

Would to heaven you could forget it, madam!

Why so?

I was unjust! A madman! A vain fool! An idiot!—Pardon this rude vehemence, but I cannot forgive myself for having been so ready to accuse one whom—! I cannot speak my feelings!—I have deserted myself!—I am no longer the creature of reason, but the child of passion!—My mind is all tumult, all incongruity!

You wrong yourself. The error has been mutual, or rather I have been much the most to blame. I am very sensible of, and indeed very sorry for my mistake—Indeed I am—I perceived you indulging hopes that cannot be realized, and—

Cannot, madam?

Never!—I can see you think yourself despised; but you do yourself great wrong.

My mind is so disturbed, by the abrupt and absurd folly with which I accused you, unheard, this morning, that it is less now in a state to do my cause justice than at any other time—Still I will be a man—Your word, madam, was—Cannot!—

It was.

Permit me to ask, is it person—?

No—certainly not. Person would with me be always a distant consideration. [You, Louisa, know how very far from exceptionable the person of Frank is, if that were any part of the question.]

You are no flatterer, madam, and you have thought proper occasionally to express your approbation of my morals and mind.

Yet my expressions have never equalled my feelings!—Never!

Then, madam, where is the impossibility? In what does it consist? The world may think meanly of me, for the want of what I myself hold in contempt: but surely you cannot join in the world's injustice?

I cannot think meanly of you.

I have no titles. I am what pride calls nobody: the son of a man who came pennyless into the service of your family; in which to my infinite grief he has grown rich. I would rather starve than acquire opulence by the efforts of cunning, flattery, and avarice; and if I blush for any thing, relative to family, it is for that. I am either above or below the wish of being what is insolently called well born.

You confound, or rather you do not separate, two things which are very distinct; that which I think of you, and that which the world would think of me, were I to encourage hopes which you would have me indulge.

Your actions, madam, shew how much and how properly you disregard the world's opinion.

But I do not disregard the effects which that opinion may have, upon the happiness of my father, my family, myself, and my husband, if ever I should marry.

If truth and justice require it, madam, even all these ought to be disregarded.

Indubitably.

Did I know a man, upon the face of the earth, who had a still deeper sense of your high qualities and virtues than I have, who understood them more intimately, would study them, emulate them more, and profit better by them, I have confidence enough in myself to say I would resign you without repining. But, when I think on the union between mind and mind—the aggregate—! I want language, madam—!

I understand you.

When I reflect on the wondrous happiness we might enjoy, while mutually exerting ourselves in the general cause of virtue, I confess the thought of renouncing so much bliss, or rather such a duty to myself and the world, is excruciating torture.

Your idea of living for the cause of virtue delights me; it is in full concord with my own. But whether that great cause would best be promoted by our union, or not, is a question which we are incapable of determining: though I think probabilities are for the negative. Facts and observation have given me reason to believe that the too easy gratification of our desires is pernicious to mind; and that it acquires vigour and elasticity from opposition.

And would you then upon principle, madam, marry a man whom you must despise?

No, not despise. If indeed I were all I could wish to be, I am persuaded I should despise no one. I should endeavour to instruct the ignorant, and reform the erroneous. However, I will tell you what sort of a man I should wish to marry. First he must be a person of whom no prejudice, no mistake of any kind, should induce the world, that is, the persons nearest and most connected with me in the world, to think meanly—Shall I be cited by the thoughtless, the simple, and the perverse, in justification of their own improper conduct?—You cannot wish it, Frank!—Nor is this the most alarming fear—My friends!—My relations!—My father!——To incur a father's reproach for having dishonoured his family were fearful: but to meet, to merit, to live under his curse! —God of heaven forbid!

Must we then never dare to counteract mistake? Must mind, though enlightened by truth, submit to be the eternal slave of error?—What is there that is thus dreadful, madam, in the curse of prejudice? Have not the greatest and the wisest of mankind been cursed by ignorance?

It is not the curse itself that is terrible, but the torture of the person's mind by whom it is uttered!——Nor is it the torture of a minute, or a day, but of years!——His child, his beloved child, on whom his hopes and heart were fixed, to whom he looked for all the bliss of filial obedience, all the energies of virtue, and all the effusions of affection, to see himself deserted by her, unfeelingly deserted, plunged in sorrows unutterable, eternally dishonoured, the index and the bye-word of scandal, scoffed at for the fault of her whom his fond and fatherly reveries had painted faultless, whispered out of society because of the shame of her in whom he gloried, and I this child!

Were the conflict what your imagination has figured it, madam, your terrors would be just—But I have thought deeply on it, and know that your very virtues misguide you. It would not be torture, nor would it be eternal—On the contrary, madam, I, poor as I am in the esteem of an arrogant world, I proudly affirm it would be the less and not the greater evil.

You mistake!—Indeed, Frank, you mistake!—The fear of poverty, the sneers of the world, ignominy itself, were the pain inflicted but confined to me, I would despise. But to stretch my father upon the rack, and with him every creature that loves me, even you yourself!—It must not be!—It must not be!

I too fatally perceive, madam, your mind is subjected by these phantoms of fear.

No, no—not phantoms; real existences; the palpable beings of reason!—Beside what influence have I in the world, except over my friends and family? And shall I renounce this little influence, this only power of doing good, in order to gratify my own passions, by making myself the outcast of that family and of that world to whom it is my ambition to live an example?——My family and the world are prejudiced and unjust: I know it. But where is the remedy? Can we work miracles? Will their prejudices vanish at our bidding?—I have already mortally offended the most powerful of my relations, Lord Fitz-Allen, by refusing a foolish peer of his recommendation. He is my maternal uncle; proud, prejudiced, and unforgiving. Previous to this refusal I was the only person in our family whom he condescended to notice. He prophesied, in the spleen of passion, I should soon bring shame on my family; and I as boldly retorted I would never dishonour the name of St. Ives—I spoke in their own idiom, and meant to be so understood ——Recollect all this!—Be firm, be just to yourself and me!—— Indeed indeed, Frank, it is not my heart that refuses you; it is my understanding; it is principle; it is a determination not to do that which my reason cannot justify——Join with me, Frank—— Resolve——Give me your hand——Let us disdain to set mankind an example which would indeed be a virtuous and a good one, were all the conditions understood; but which, under the appearances it would assume, would be criminal in the extreme.

My hand and heart, madam, are everlastingly yours: and it is because this heart yearns to set the world an example, higher infinitely than that which you propose, that thus I plead!—This opportunity is my first and last—I read my doom—Bear with me therefore while I declare my sensations and my thoughts.—The passion I feel is as unlike what is usually meant by love as day to night, grace to deformity, or truth to falsehood. It is not your fine form, madam, supremely beautiful though you are, which I love. At least I love it only as an excellent part of a divine whole. It is your other, your better, your more heavenly self, to which I have dared to aspire. I claim relationship to your mind; and again declare I think my claims have a right, which none of the false distinctions of men can supersede. Think then, madam, again I conjure you, think ere you decide.——If the union of two people whose pure love, founded on an unerring conviction of mutual worth, might promise the reality of that heaven of which the world

delights to dream; whose souls, both burning with the same ardour
to attain and to diffuse excellence, would mingle and act with
incessant energy, who, having risen superior to the mistakes of
mankind, would disseminate the same spirit of truth, the same
internal peace, the same happiness, the same virtues which they
themselves possess among thousands; who would admire, animate,
emulate each other; whose wishes, efforts, and principles would all
combine to one great end, the general good; who, being desirous
only to dispense blessings, could not fail to enjoy; if a union like
this be not strictly conformable to the laws of eternal truth, or if
there be any arguments, any perils, any terrors which ought to
annul such a union, I confess that the arguments, the perils, the
terrors, and eternal truth itself are equally unknown to me.

We paused for a moment. The beauty, force, and grandeur of
the picture he had drawn staggered me. Yet it was but a repetition
of what had frequently presented itself to my mind, in colours
almost as vivid as those with which he painted. I had but one
answer, and replied—

The world!—My family!—My father!——I cannot encounter
the malediction of a father!——What! Behold him in an agony of
cursing his child?—Imagination shudders and shrinks from the
guilty picture with horror!——I cannot!—I cannot!—It must not
be!—To foresee this misery so clearly as I do, and yet to seek it,
would surely be detestable guilt!

Again we paused—He perceived my terrors were too violent to
cede to any efforts of supposed reason. His countenance changed;
the energy of argument disappeared, and was succeeded by all
the tenderness of passion. The decisive moment, the moment of
trial was come. His features softened into that form which never
yet failed to melt the heart, and he thus continued.

To the scorn of vice, the scoffs of ignorance, the usurpations of the
presuming, and the contumelies of the proud, I have patiently submitted: but to find my great and as I thought infallible support
wrested from me; to perceive that divine essence which I imagined
too much a part of myself to do me wrong, overlooking me; reject-
ing me; dead to those sensations which I thought mutually pervaded and filled our hearts; to hear her, whom of all beings on earth
I thought myself most akin to, disclaim me; positively, persisting,
un——

Unjustly?——Was that the word, Frank?—Surely not unjustly!
—Oh, surely not!

And could those heavenly those heart-winning condescensions
on which I founded my hopes be all illusory?—Could they?—Did
I dream that your soul held willing intercourse with mine, beaming divine intelligence upon me? Was it all a vision when I thought
I heard you pronounce the ecstatic sentence—*You could love me
if I would let you?*

No; it was real. I revoke nothing that I have said or done. Do
not, Frank, for the love of truth and justice do not think me insensible of your excellence, dead to your virtues, or blind to mind
and merit which I never yet saw equalled!—Think not it is pride,
or base insensibility of your worth! Where is the day in which
that worth has not increased upon me?—Unjust to you?—Oh!—
No, no, no!—My heart bleeds at the thought!—No!—It is my
love of you, my love of your virtues, your principles, and these alone
are lovely, which has rendered me thus inflexible. If any thing
could make you dearer to me than you are, it must be weakness;
it must be something which neither you nor I ought to approve.
All the good, or rather all the opportunities of doing good which
mortal or immortal being can enjoy do I wish you! Oh that I had
prayers potent enough to draw down blessings on you!—Love
you?—Yes!—The very idea bursts into passion. [The tears,
Louisa, were streaming down my cheeks.] Why should you doubt
of all the affection which virtue can bestow? Do you not deserve
it?—Oh yes!—Love you in the manner you could wish I must not,
dare not, ought not: but, as I ought, I love you infinitely! Ay, dear,
dear Frank, as I ought, infinitely!

Louisa!—Blame me if thou wilt—But I kissed him!—The
chastity of my thoughts defied misconstruction, and the purity of
the will sanctified the extravagance of the act. A daring enthusiasm
seized me. I beheld his passions struggling to attain the very pin-
nacle of excellence. I wished to confirm the noble emulation, to
convince him how different the pure love of mind might be from
the meaner love of passion, and I kissed him! I find my affections,
my sensibilities, peculiarly liable to these strong sallies. Perhaps
all minds of a certain texture are subject to such rapid and almost
resistless emotions; and whether they ought to be encouraged or
counteracted I have not yet discovered. But the circumstance,

unexpected and strange as it was, suffered no wrong interpretation
in the dignified soul of Frank. With all the ardour of affection, but
chastened by every token of delicacy, he clasped me in his arms,
returned my kiss, then sunk down on one knee, and exclaimed—
Now let me die!——

After a moment's pause, I answered—No, Frank! Live! Live
to be a blessing to the world, and an honour to the human race!

I took a turn to the window, and after having calmed the too
much of feeling which I had suffered to grow upon me, I continued
the conversation.

I hope, Frank, we now understand each other; and that, as this
is the first, so it will be the last contention of the passions in which
we shall indulge ourselves.

Madam, though *I still think, nay feel a certainty of conviction, that
you act from mistaken principles*, yet you support what you are
persuaded is truth with such high such self-denying virtue, that
not to applaud, not to imitate you would be contemptible. You
have and ought to have a will of your own. You practise what you
believe to be the severest precepts of duty, with more than human
fortitude. You resolve, in this particular, not to offend the prejudices of your family, and the world. I submit. To indulge sensibility but a little were to be heart-broken! But no personal grief
can authorise me in deserting the post I am placed in; nor palliate
the crime of neglecting its duties. *To the end of time I shall persist
in thinking you mine by right*; but I will never trouble you more with
an assertion of that right——Never!—Unless some new and
unexpected claim should spring up, of which I see no probability.

He bowed and was retiring.

Stay, Frank, I have something more to say to you—I have a
requisition to make which after what has passed would to common
minds appear unfeeling and almost capricious cruelty; but I have
no fear that yours should be liable to this mistake. Recollect but
who and what you are, remember what are the best purposes of
existence, and the noblest efforts of mind, and then refuse me if
you can—I have formed a project, and call upon you for aid—
Cannot you guess?

Mr. Clifton, madam—?

Yes.

I fear it is a dangerous one; and, whether my fears originate in selfishness or in penetration, they must be spoken. Yes, madam, I must warn you that the passions of Mr. Clifton are, in my opinion, much more alarming than the resentment of your father.

But they are alarming only to myself. And ought danger to deter me?

Not if the good you design be practicable.

And what is impracticable, where the will is resolved?

Perhaps nothing—But the effort must be great, must be uncommon.

Has he not a mind worthy of such an effort? Would not his powers highly honour truth and virtue?

They would.

Will not you give me your assistance?

I would, madam, most willingly, would he but permit me. But I am his antipathy; a something noxious; an evil augury.

You have been particular in your attentions to me.

And must those attentions cease, madam?

They must be moderated; they must be cool, dispassionate, and then they will not alarm.—I cannot possibly be deceived in supposing it a duty, an indispensable duty to restore the mind of Clifton to its true station. If I fail, the fault must be my own. I am but young, yet many men have addressed me with the commonplace language of admiration, love, and I know not what; or rather they knew not what; and, except yourself, Frank, I have not met with one from whom half so much might be hoped as from Clifton. He is the brother of my bosom friend. Surely, Frank, it is a worthy task—Join with me!——There is but one thing I fear. Clifton is haughty and intemperate. Are you a duellist, Frank?

No, madam.

Then you would not fight a duel?

Never, madam, no provocation, not the brand of cowardice itself, shall ever induce me to be guilty of such a crime.

Frank!—Oh excellent, noble youth!

Here, Louisa, our conversation abruptly ended. The company had risen from table, and we heard them in the corridor. I requested him to retire, and he instantly obeyed.

Oh! Louisa, with what sensations did he leave my mind glowing!—His conviction equals certainty, *that I act from mistaken principles!—To the end of time he shall persist in thinking me his by right!*—Can the power of language afford words more strong, more positive, more pointed?—How unjust have I been to my cause!—For surely I cannot be in an error!—'Tis afflicting, 'tis painful, nay it is almost terrifying to remember!—*Persist to the end of time?*—Why did I not think more deeply?—I had a dark kind of dread that I should fail!—It cannot be the fault of my cause!—Wrong him!—Guilty of injustice to him!—Surely, surely, I hope not!——What! Become an example to the feeble and the foolish, for having indulged my passions and neglected my duties? —I?—His mind had formed a favourite plan, and could I expect it should be instantly relinquished?—I cannot conceive torment equal to the idea of doing him wrong!—Him?——Again and again I hope not! I hope not! I hope not!

Then the kiss, Louisa? Did I or did I not do right, in shewing him how truly I admire and love his virtues? Was I or was I not guilty of any crime, when, in the very acme of the passions, I so totally disregarded the customs of the world? Or rather, for that is the true question, could it produce any other effect than that which I intended? I am persuaded it could not. Nor, blame me who will, do I repent. And yet, my friend, if you should think it wrong, I confess I should then feel a pang which I should be glad not to deserve. But be sincere. Though I need not warn you. No false pity can or ought to induce you to desert the cause of truth.

Adieu—My mind is not so much at its ease as I hoped, from this conversation; but at all times, and in all tempers, believe me to be, ever and ever,

Your own dear

A. W. ST. IVES

LETTER XLII

Frank Henley to Oliver Trenchard

Chateau de Villebrun

ALL is over!—My hopes are at an end!—I am awakened from a dream, in which pain and pleasure were mingled to such excess as to render its continuance impossible.

Nor is this all. This trial, severe as it was, did not suffice. To the destruction of hope has been added the assault of insolence, accompanied with a portion of obloquy which heart scarcely can sustain —Oh, this Clifton!—But—Patience!

Yet let me do her justice. Mistaken though I am sure she is, the motives of her conduct are so pure that even mistake itself is lovely in her; and assumes all the energy, all the dignity of virtue. Oh what a soul is hers! Her own passions, the passions of others, when she acts and speaks, are all in subjection to principle. Yes, Oliver, of one thing at least she has convinced me: she has taught me, or rather made me feel, how poor a thing it is to be the slave of desire.

Not that I do not still adore her!—Ay, more than ever adore! But from henceforth my adoration shall be worthy of herself, and not degrading to me. From her I have learned what true love is; and the lesson is engraven on my heart. She can consider personal gratification with apathy, yet burn with a martyr's zeal for the promotion of universal good.

And shall I not rise equal to the bright example which she has set me? Shall I admire yet not imitate?

Did she despise me? Did she reject me for my own sake?—No! —All the affection which mind can feel for mind she has avowed for me! And shall I grieve because another may be more happy?— And why more?—In what?—Is not the union of souls the first the most permanent of all alliances? That union is mine! No power can shake it. She openly acknowledges it; and has done, daily, hourly, in every word, in every action. Whither then would my wishes wander?

Oliver, I am a man, and subject to the shakes and agues of his fragile nature!—Yet it is a poor, a wretched plea; a foolish, and a false plea. Man is weak because he is willing to be weak. He crouches to the whip, and like a coward pities while he lashes himself. His wilful phrensy he calls irresistible, and weeps for the torments which he himself inflicts.

But once again this Clifton!—Read and tell me how I ought to act—I have received a blow from him, Oliver!—Yes, have tamely submitted to receive a blow!—

What intolerable prejudices are these! Why does my heart rebel so sternly, at what virtue so positively approves?

I had just left her; had that instant been rejected by her for his

sake; had been summoned to aid her, in weeding out error from
his mind. She shewed me it was a noble task, and communicated
to me her own divine ardour. Yes, Oliver; I came from her, with a
warmed and animated heart; participating all her zeal. The most
rigid, the most painful of all abstinence was demanded from me;
but should I shrink from a duty because I pity or because I love
myself? No. Such pusillanimity were death to virtue. I left her,
while my thoughts glowed with the ardour of emulating her heroism; and burned to do him all the good which she had projected.

He was at the end of the corridor, and saw me quit her apartment. His hot spirit caught the alarm instantaneously, and blazed
in his countenance. He accosted me—

So, sir! You are very familiar with that lady! What right have
you to intrude into her apartments?

When she herself desires me, sir, I have a right.

She desire you! 'Tis false!

Sir?

'Tis false, sir!

False?

Yes, sir. And falsehood deserves to be chastised!

Chastised? [It is in vain, Oliver, to endeavour to conceal the
truth from myself; my folly incurred its own punishment—I
repeat] Chastised? [I was lunatic enough to walk up to him, with a
ridiculous and despicable air of defiance. He re-echoed my words,
and instantly in contempt struck me on the cheek with the back
of his hand.]

Yes, sir; chastised!

His rashness restored me to some sense of the farcical heroism
which I had been aping. I hurried from him, without another word.

Oliver, I can conceive nothing more painful than this wresting,
this tearing of passion from its purpose.

I walked a few minutes to calm my thoughts, and wrote him the
following note.

'SIR,

'I feel at present the humility of my situation: but not from your
blow; for that has brought me to myself, not humbled me. No man
can be degraded by another; it must be his own act: and you have
degraded yourself, not me. My error is in having, for a moment,

yielded to the impulse of passion. If you think I fear you, continue to think so; till I can shew my forbearance is from a better motive. Cowardice might make me kill you; but true courage will teach me calmly to hear the world call me coward, rather than commit an act so wicked, so abhorred, as that of taking or throwing away life. I wished to seek your friendship; and even now I will not shun you. Make the world imagine me a coward; imagine me one yourself, if you can. I will live under the supposed obloquy; and leave the tenor of my life to shew whether living be the act of fear, or of reason. I pardon you, sir, and leave you to pardon yourself.

F. HENLEY'

My forbearance and this letter mitigated my sense of pain. Yet I am very ill satisfied with myself. Am I so easily to be moved? 'Tis true the scene I had just quitted was fermenting, as it were, in my veins, and shaking my whole system.

What is worse, I am child enough to be tormented, in my own despite, by the recollection of having received a blow! And why? In many countries, and even in my own, among the class in which I was born, the stigma is none, or trifling—Stigma? Absurd!—Cowardice!—Murder!——If vanity were ever becoming, I have perhaps more reason to be vain, considering the danger to which I had exposed myself, of this than of any act of my life.

Well, well, Oliver—I hope these agitations are over; and that from this time thou wilt begin to think better of me.

I communicate my whole thoughts to thee. If the experiments made upon my mind can be of any use to thine, my letters will then answer the best of the purposes for which they are written.

F. HENLEY

L

LETTER XLIII

Coke Clifton to Guy Fairfax

Chateau de Villebrun

YOUR last, Fairfax, pleased me. You say truly, and I like your remark, 'Such fellows ought not to claim a moment's attention from me. I should brush them away, like flies from my forehead, when they presume to tease or settle themselves upon me.' I have taken your advice, and fly-slapped the wasp that was more willing than able to sting.

I have lately grown dissatisfied with myself; I know not how, or why. I suspect this youth, in part, has made me so, with his visionary morality. I hate such sermonizing. Who has a right to control me? Whose slave am I? I was born to rule, not to be ruled. My appetites are keen, my desires vast, and I would enjoy. Why else am I here? Delay to me is insufferable; suspense distracts me; and the possibility that another should be preferred to myself drives me mad! I too heartily despise the tame creatures, that crawl upon the earth, to suffer opposition from them. Who would be braved by bats and beetles, buzzing in his ears?

I never before saw a woman whom any temptation could have induced me to marry; and now I have found one I am troubled with doubts, infested with fears, and subjected to the intolerable penance of procrastination. Impeded in my course; and by what? Why, I am told to scrutinize myself, and to discover whether I am quite as perfect as it is necessary I should be! 'Tis unjust! 'Tis unkind! I did not doubt of her perfections; and both love and pride, equally jealous of their honour, demand that mine should have been taken for granted.

The time has been when this would have been revenged. But I seem to be half subdued. My fierce spirit, before so untameable, declines contending with her. Not but I frequently feel it struggling with suffocation, kindling, and again ready to burst into a more furious blaze.

Yet let me do her justice. Mild, gentle, and affectionate, she conquers my impetuosity with prayers, and soothing, and with kindness irresistible. Still she conquers.

Then she suffers these animals to torment me. I am angry to think that, in so short a space, I should have so entirely lost all power over myself!

But where is the mortal that can look and not love? Were I myself not an actor in the play, how should I enjoy the perplexity of these French *amoureux!* There are I know not how many of them; each more busy than the other. 'Tis laughable to see with what industry they labour to make love according to her liking; for they find that their own trifling manner is inefficient, and can never succeed with her. One of them, that said crazy Provençal Count, is very earnest indeed, in his endeavours; but she keeps him in due awe. And it is well perhaps for him that she does, or I would. Still however he is damned troublesome and impertinent; and I could wish she were more peremptory. Yet it is unjust to blame her, for the animal is so full of antics, that it is impossible to be angry.

After all, I am far from satisfied respecting myself and this youth, whom I condescended to chastise. It was beneath me. It gave him a sort of right to demand satisfaction: but he affects forbearance, because, as he pretends, he despises duelling. And I hear he has actually given proofs of the most undaunted courage. He wrote a short note of only three or four sentences on the subject, after I had struck him, which produced a very uncommon effect upon me, and made me half repent, and accuse myself of haughtiness, rashness, and insult.

But these things torture me. I am out of patience with them. What right has any pedant, because he thinks proper to vex and entangle his own brain with doubts, to force his gloomy dogmas upon me? Let those who love sack-cloth wear it. Must I be made miserable, because an over-curious booby bewilders himself in inquiry, and galls his conscience, till, like the wrung withers of a battered post-horse, it shrinks and shivers at the touch of a fly's foot? What, shall I not enjoy the free air, the glorious sun, the flowers, the fruits, the viands, the whole stores of nature? Who shall impede, who shall dare disturb the banquet? Were it even a dream, the meddling fool that waked me should dearly repent his rashness.—Let speculative blockheads brew metaphysical nectar, make a hash of axioms, problems, corollaries and demonstrations, and feed on ideas and fatten. Be theirs the feast of reason and the

flow of soul.[1] But let me banquet with old Homer's jolly gods and
heroes, revel with the Mahometan houris,[2] or gain admission into
the savoury sanctorum of the gormandizing priesthood, snuff the
fumes from their altars, and gorge on the fat of lambs. Let cynic
Catos truss up each his slovenly toga, rail at Heliogabalus,[3] and
fast; but let me receive his card, with—'Sir, your company is
requested to dine and sup.'

I cannot forget this gardener's son. I am sometimes angry that
I should for a single instant trouble myself with a fellow so much
beneath me; and at others equally angry, for not shewing him the
respect which he claims. There are moments in which I have even
feared him as a rival; for when she speaks to him, which she is very
ready to do, the usual mildness and benevolence of her voice and
features are evidently increased. She must, she shall be more
circumspect. Indeed I have made her so within these few days.

Prithee forgive all this. My mind is not at ease; but I know not
why I should infect you with its malady. Write, relate something
pleasant; tell me what has happened to you last, and relieve the
dissatisfaction I feel by your unaffected flow of gaiety. Adieu.

                                                    C. CLIFTON

LETTER XLIV

Anna Wenbourne St. Ives to Louisa Clifton

Chateau de Villebrun

I CANNOT sufficiently applaud the resolute propriety of Frank,
since our last conversation. Indeed, Louisa, his fortitude is admirable! He does not indulge self-compassion, by brooding over his
own loss. Nor does he, like other mistaken people whose affections
have met disappointment, suppose himself into sufferings, which
swell into existence in proportion as they are imagined to be real.
His evident determination is not to permit any selfish motive to
detach him from the great purposes of life; but cheerfully to submit to what is inevitable, without thinking it an evil.

In the mean time, I have been indulging a hope, which at
moments has appeared almost a certainty, that Clifton, by our

mutual efforts, shall acquire all this true ardour, which is so lovely in Frank. How sorry am I to observe that the haughtiness of Clifton and the coldness of Frank seem to be increasing! To what can this be attributed? Their behaviour is so peculiar that I almost dread something has happened, with which I am unacquainted.

But perhaps it is the present temper of my mind: the effect of sensations too irritable, doubts too tremulous, and fears too easily excited. I cannot forget the conversation: it haunts me; and, did not Frank set me the example of fortitude, I have sometimes doubted of my own perseverance.

Oh, how mean is this in me! Is not the task I have proposed to myself a worthy and a high one? Am I not convinced it is an inevitable duty? And shall he, even under a contrary conviction, outstrip me in the career?—Generous and excellent youth, I will imitate thy most eminent virtues!

The Count de Beaunoir still continues to be particular, in what he calls his adoration of me; but his tone and style are too romantic to authorize me in any serious remonstrance. Clifton is not pleased, and the Count and he have fallen into a habit of rallying each other, and vaunting of what lovers dare do, to prove their affection. Their irony took so serious a turn, yesterday, that Clifton proposed they should load their pistols, and both holding by the corner of a handkerchief, fire at each other. Considering the temper in which they were, and the constitutional extravagance of the Count, the proposal was terrifying: but I had the presence of mind to give it an air of ridicule, by saying—You do not understand the true point of gallantry, gentlemen. You should go to Japan, where one noble-blooded person draws his sabre, and dispatches himself, to prove he is acquainted with the high punctilio and very essence of honour; while another, enraged that he should be in waiting and have a dish to carry up to the emperor's table, requests he would condescend to live till he can come down again, that he may shew he knows what honour is as well as his disingenuous enemy, who had taken such an unfair advantage.

The Count laughed, and Clifton I should hope was not displeased that it was impossible the conversation should again assume the same desperate and absurd tone.

I took an opportunity to ask him privately how he could indulge such intemperate passions; but I was obliged to soften my admonition by all possible mildness. I know not whether I did right, but I even took his hand, pressed it between mine, and requested of him, with an ardour which I think must sink deeply in his mind, to do justice to himself, to exert those powers of thought which he certainly possessed, and to restrain passions which, if not restrained, must deter me, or any woman worthy of him, from a union that would be so dangerous.

The impression would have been stronger, but that unfortunately his quick sensations took a different turn. Feeling me clasp his hand, he dropped on his knee, and with an ecstasy which he seemed unable to resist kissed both mine, talked something of bliss unutterable, and, recollecting the conclusion of my sentence, added that the very thought of losing me was madness. We were interrupted, and I began to fear lest my true motive should have been misunderstood.

Oh! Louisa, what a world is this! Into what false habits has it fallen! Can hypocrisy be virtue? Can a desire to call forth all the best affections of the heart be misconstrued into something too degrading for expression?

I know not, but I begin to fear that no permanent good can be effected at present, without peril. If so, shall I listen only to my fears; shrink into self; and shun that which duty bids me encounter? No. Though the prejudices of mankind were to overwhelm me with sorrows, for seeking to do good, I will still go on: I will persevere, will accomplish or die.

Yet I know not why I am in this mood! But so I am, and Louisa will forgive me. I talk of sufferings? What have I suffered? What can those who, mature in reason, are superior to prejudice suffer?

But who are they? My prejudices hourly rise up in arms against me. Every day am I obliged to combat what the day before I thought I had destroyed. Could we, at the same moment that we correct our own mistakes, correct those of the whole world, the work were done at once. But we have to struggle and to struggle; and, having to-day shaken off the burs that hung about us, to-morrow we give a glance and perceive them sticking as closely and as thick as ever!

I wish to question Frank, concerning these alarms; but he seems purposely to avoid giving me an opportunity. Perhaps however I am mistaken; and I hope I am. The restless fancy is frequently too full of doubts and fears. Oh, how beautiful is open, artless, undisguised truth! Yet how continually are dissimulation and concealment recommended as virtues! Whatever mistakes, public or private, they may think they have discovered, and however beneficial it might be to correct them, men must not publish their thoughts; for that would be to libel, to defame, to speak or to write scandal!

When will the world learn that the unlimited utterance of all thoughts would be virtuous? How many half-discovered half-acknowledged truths would then be promulgated; and how immediately would mistake, of every kind, meet its proper antidote! How affectionately and unitedly would men soon be brought to join, not in punishing, nor even in reproving, but in reforming falsehood! Aided and encouraged by your dear and worthy mother, we have often discoursed on these things, Louisa: and the common accidents of life, as well as those peculiar to myself, render such conversations sweet to recollection.

I must conclude: for though we write best when thoughts flow the most freely, yet at present I find myself more inclined to think than to write.

Affectionately and ever

A. W. ST. IVES

LETTER XLV

Anna Wenbourne St. Ives to Louisa Clifton

Chateau de Villebrun

I KNOW not, Louisa, how to begin! I have an accident to relate which has alarmed me so much that I am half afraid it should equally alarm my friend. Yet the danger is over, and her sensations cannot equal ours. She can but imagine what they were. But it is so incredible, so mad, so dreadful! Clifton is strangely rash!

He had been for some days dissatisfied, restless, and disturbed. I knew not why, cxccpt that I had desired time for mutual consideration, before I would permit him to speak to Sir Arthur. He

has half terrified me from ever permitting him to speak—But then
he has more than repaired all the wrong he had done. There is
something truly magnanimous in his temper, but it has taken a
very erroneous bent. The chief subject of my last was the distance
which I observed between him and Frank Henley. Little did I
know the reason. But I will not anticipate: only, remember, be
not too much alarmed.

Frank was but one of the actors, though the true and indeed
sole hero of the scene I am going to relate. Indeed he is a wonderful,
I had almost said a divine youth! It took birth from the Count de
Beaunoir.

In my last, I mentioned the strange defiance of the pistols and
the handkerchief: and would you think, Louisa, a conversation so
frantic could be renewed? It is true it shewed itself under a new
though scarcely a less horrible aspect.

We were yesterday walking in the park, in which there is a
remarkable lake, small but romantic. I before spoke I believe of
our rowing on it in boats. We were walking beside it on a steep
rock, which continues for a considerable length of way to form
one of its banks. The Count and Clifton were before: I, Frank
Henley, and a party of ladies and gentlemen were following at a
little distance, but not near enough to hear the conversation that
was passing between your brother and the Count.

It seems the latter had first begun once again to talk of times of
knight errantry, and of the feats which the *preux chevaliers* had performed for their ladies. The headlong Clifton, utterly despising the
pretended admiration of what he was persuaded the Count durst in
no manner imitate, after some sarcastic expressions of his contempt,
madly but seriously asked the Count if he durst jump off the rock
into the lake, to prove his own courage. Shew your soul, said he, if
you have any! Jump you first, said the Count——! ******!

Imagine, Louisa, if you can, the shock I received when, not
knowing what had passed, but in an apparent fit of frenzy, I saw
him desperately rush to the side of the rock, and dash himself
headlong down into the water! It was at an angle, and we had a
full view of him falling!

Every soul I believe shrieked, except myself and perhaps Frank
Henley. Never had I so much need of the fortitude to which I have
endeavoured to habituate my mind.

The gentlemen all ran to the side of the rock. — They saw Clifton, after rising to the surface, sink! He had jumped from a place where the shelving of the rock, under water, by projecting had stunned him as he fell.

Frank perceived the danger: he threw off his hat and coat, and ran to another part, where the height was still more dreadful! Indeed, Louisa, it excites horror to look at the place! But he seems to be superior to fear. He plunged down what might well be called an abyss; and, after rising for a few seconds to breathe, dived again in search of poor Clifton.

He was twice obliged to rise and take breath. The third time he found him, rose with him, turned him upon his own back, and swam with him a very considerable distance before he could find a place shallow enough to land.

To all appearance Clifton was lifeless! But the excellent, most excellent when you shall hear all, the heroic Frank immediately applied himself to the remainder of his office. He stayed not a moment to rest, but lifted him a seeming corpse from the earth, threw him once more on his back, and ran faster than any of us to the chateau, carried him up stairs, undressed him himself, put him between the blankets, and gave every necessary order with as much presence of mind as if there had been neither accident nor danger. Wet as he was he lost not a thought upon himself.

Never shall I forget the indefatigable assiduity with which he laboured to restore your brother to life; the anxiety which he struggled to conceal; the variety of means he employed; the ingenuity of his conjectures and the humanity of every motion!

Two hours were I and he and all of us held in this dreadful suspense. At last he was successful; and the relief I felt, the load that seemed removed from my heart, it is impossible to describe!

When your brother was perfectly come to himself, Frank suffered him to be bled. For it had been proposed before; but Frank, with a determination that could not be withstood, refused to admit of it; though he had been intreated, and at last openly and loudly blamed, by the surgeon and those who believed in him, for his pertinacity. But Frank was not to be shaken, even by the very serious fear of future accusation. He followed, as he tells me, the opinion of John Hunter;[1] and well might he think it of more worth than that of the person who pretended to advise. But it requires no common degree of resolution to persist, in this manner, in the right; and wholly to despise calumny and its consequences.

If you think, Louisa, that after this I can add nothing in praise of Frank you are greatly mistaken; for what is to come raises his character almost to an enviable dignity.

Could you imagine that this very Frank Henley, this undaunted, determined, high-souled Frank, who had flung himself down the horrid precipice after your brother, who had swum with him, run with him, risked being supposed in some sort his murderer, and at last restored him to life, had the very day before received from the hand of this same brother—a blow!——If, Louisa, there be one being upon earth capable of attaining virtues more than human, it is surely Frank Henley!

Much praise however, as well as blame, is justly due to Clifton. I never saw a heart more painfully wrung, by the sense of an injury committed and of a good so unexampled received, as his has been. It was he who told of his own behaviour. His total want of power to make retribution is the theme by which he is pained and oppressed.

Frank, uniform in generosity, disclaims any superiority, and affirms Clifton would have done the same, had he been in the same danger. I think I would, answered Clifton, in a tone that shewed he felt what he spoke: but I know myself too well to suppose I should have so unremittingly persevered, like you, in the performance of an office of humanity which seemed hopeless.

The distinction was just, disinterested, and worthy the discernment of a mind like that of your brother.

Clifton says that, though he cannot think like Frank [We hope to make him, Louisa.] yet he cannot but admire the magnanimity with which he acts up to his principles, and proves his sincerity.

Oh, my friend! You can conceive all the terrors of the scene! So fine a youth, so accomplished, so brave, the brother of my Louisa, brought to Paris to meet an untimely death! I the cause of his coming thither! I the innocent instigator of this last rash act! The eyes of all upon me! The horror of suspense!——It was indeed a trial!

Yet who knows what accidents may occur in life? Who can sufficiently cherish fortitude; and by anticipating defy misfortune? Violently as my feelings were assaulted, there yet may

be, there are, shocks more violent, scenes more dreadful in the
world. Nor is it impossible but that such may be my lot. And if
they were, I hope I still should bear up against them all.

It is true I may not always have a Frank Henley to cherish and
inspire hope. His constant theme was—'He is not dead!' And I
once heard him murmuring to himself, with a kind of prophetic
energy—'He shall not die!'—It was this *shall not* by which he was
saved: for, with any other creature upon earth, I am persuaded he
had been gone for ever. Oh this noble perseverance! It is indeed a
godlike virtue!

The Count is less in spirits, less extravagant, since this accident.
It seems to hang upon his mind, as if he had been out-braved. His
anxiety, as might well be expected from such a temper, was excessive, while Clifton was in danger: but he seems to repent now, that
he did not follow the mad example. *Parbleu! Madame, je suis
Provençal; on dit que j'ai la tête un peu chaude; mais Messieurs les
Anglois vont diablement vite aux épreuves! Mes compatriotes même
ne sont pas si fous!—Je ne suis pas content de moi—J'aurais du faire
le saut—J'aurais sauvé la vie à mon rival!—Voilà une belle occasion
manquée, et beaucoup de gloire à jamais perdue pour moi!**

My mind at present is not entirely tranquil. The recollection of
a temper so rash as Clifton's preys upon me. Yet, where there are
qualities so high, and powers so uncommon, shall I despair? Shall
I shrink from an act of duty? It is a task I have prescribed to myself. Shall I witness the fortitude of Frank, and be myself so easily
discomfited? No, Louisa. Clifton shall be ours——*Shall be!*—
Shall be the brother of Louisa, the friend of Frank, and the better
part of Anna. Yes, I too will be determined! I like Frank will say—
'He is not dead! He shall not die!'

A. W. ST. IVES

---

* 'Sdeath! Madam, I am a native of Provence, and they tell me I am a little crazy:
but these Englishmen are in a confounded hurry to come to the proof!—My own
countrymen are less lunatic!——I am not satisfied with myself. I ought to have
leaped after him: I should have saved the life of my rival! It was losing a glorious
opportunity; and I have robbed myself of thus much fame for ever!

LETTER XLVI

The Honourable Mrs. Clifton to Frank Henley

Rose-Bank

SIR,

If the praises, prayers, and thanks, of a woman whom disease has robbed of more than half her faculties, could be of any value, if the overflowing heart of a mother could but speak its throbs, if admiration of gifts so astonishing and virtues so divine could be worthy your acceptance, or could reward you for all the good you have done us, I would endeavour to discharge the unexampled and unmerited obligation.

But no, sir; you are superior to these. I write not for your sake, but for my own; that I may endeavour to relieve myself of sensations that oppress me. I feel it incumbent on me to write; yet what can I say? I have no words. I despair of any opportunity of retribution: I am aged, infirm, and feeble. I am going down to the grave; but still I have life enough to revive and feel a new existence, at the recital of your virtues!

Forgive this short effusion, from the exuberant heart of a mother, who wishes but is wholly unable to say how much she admires you.

M. CLIFTON

LETTER XLVII

Louisa Clifton to Frank Henley

Rose-Bank

SIR,

I, like my dear mamma, am impelled to endeavour to return thanks for benefits, at the recollection of which the heart sinks, and all thanks become inadequate and vain. Yet suffer a sister's thanks for a brother spared, pardoned, and restored to life! Restored at the hazard of your own, and after a mortal affront received! Restored by the energies of fortitude, sagacity, and affection!

Indeed, sir, I cannot tell you what I feel. It is utterly impossible. Imagine me your friend, your sister. Command my life, it is yours. Yours not so much because the youth you have saved happened to be my brother, as for the true esteem I have for qualities so exalted. This is not the first time you have excited my admiration, and permit me to add my love. Your heart is too noble to misunderstand me. I love virtue, in man or woman; and if that be sin may I be ever sinful!

I would wish you the joys of heaven, but my wishes are vain; you have them already: nor can a mind like yours be robbed of them, by all the powers of man or accident.

L. CLIFTON

LETTER XLVIII

Louisa Clifton to Anna Wenbourne St. Ives

Rose-Bank

YOUR three last letters, my dear Anna, have affected me in a very uncommon manner. The pure passion, the noble resignation, and the fortitude of Frank Henley are unparalleled. Not to admire, not to esteem, not to love such virtues is impossible. His unshaken patience, his generosity, his forgiveness, his courage, his perseverance, are inimitable proofs of his superiority. Who can forbear wishing him success? Ought he not to command it; to say it is mine; truth and justice dare not deny it to me?

Indeed, Anna, my mind is strangely in doubt. To be guilty of injustice to such worth is surely no common guilt. And yet my brother—Headlong lunatic! Whose intemperance is every moment hurrying him into extremes.—I grant, my friend, his mind is worthy of being retrieved; and it is a generous, a noble enterprize. Nay I own I sometimes persuade myself it cannot fail, when Anna St. Ives and Frank Henley, from motives so pure and with so much determination, engage in the cause. But at others, I see peril at every step! I find my heart reproaching me for not adjuring my friend to desist; for not exciting her to bestow her hand on the man who of all others can most justly claim it, as his right.

That I desire to see my brother all that emulation and wisdom could make him, the friend and husband of my Anna, the rival of her virtues, and the bosom intimate of him whom she is willing to forego for this brother's sake; that I desire this, ardently, vehemently, is most true. If the end be attainable, it is a noble enterprize. But the difficulties! What are they? Have they been well examined?—I, with my Anna, say mind can do all things with mind: truth is irresistible, and must finally conquer. But it has many modes of conquering, and some of them are tragical, and dreadful.

To see my Anna married to strife, wasting her fine powers to reform habits which, though they may be checked, may perhaps be too deep ever to be eradicated, to see all her exquisite sensibilities hourly preyed upon by inefficient attempts to do good, for which instead of praise and love she might meet neglect, reproach, or perhaps stern insult—Oh! It is a painful thought! She would not pine; she would not weakly sink into dejection, and desert her duties, in pity to her own misfortunes.—No—But still it is an unhappy, nay, it is an abhorred state.

I am bewildered. One train of reasoning overturns another, and I know not what to advise. There are times in which these consequences appear most probable; and there are others in which I say no, it is impossible! Brutality itself could not be so senseless, so destructive of its own felicity! Anna St. Ives would win a savage heart! And my brother evidently has quick and delicate sensations; capable of great good. But then are they not capable of great harm? Yes: but are they, would they be capable of harm with her? Would not she command them, regulate them, harmonize them? Again, and again, I know not.

One thing however let me add. Let me conjure the friend of my bosom not to suffer herself to be swayed, by the remembrance of that friendship. Nay, if she do not feel a certainty of success, let me intreat, let me admonish her to desist, before it be too late; and before further encouragement shall seem to authorize the presuming Clifton, for presuming I am convinced he will be, to found claims upon her kindness.

Oh that he were indeed worthy of her! Would that he could but rise to something like that enviable dignity! And can he not? —Indeed I would not plead against him; but neither would I be instrumental in rendering my friend, who is surely born a blessing to the earth, miserable.

I am angry with myself for my own indecision: but in vain; I have no remedy. I sometimes conclude this indecision ought to act as a warning, and for that reason I have painted my feelings as they are. If yours should resemble them, I firmly and loudly say— Anna, desist! If not, I then have no advice to give. For this I blame myself, but ineffectually.

Be assured however that, under all circumstances of future life, be they adverse or prosperous, my best wishes will be with you, and my heart and soul ever yours.

L. CLIFTON

P.S. My mamma and I have mutually written to Frank Henley: you may easily imagine in what tone and style. But I could wish my brother to see our letters. We have both thought it best to forbear writing to him; his temper being wayward, and tetchy. We would much rather he should be obliged to feel, indirectly, what our opinions and sensations are, than learn them from any formal address, which he is so liable to misconstrue. It is most probable that Frank will not mention these letters. But, if you shew him this, and being of my opinion will join in the request, I have no doubt he will then comply. There is one sentence in my letter which makes me likewise wish that Clifton should know I have requested Frank would permit him to see what I have written; otherwise that sentence might very probably by him be misinterpreted. When you read the letter, you will instantly know which I mean; the word love makes it conspicuous; and you will then perceive my reason. To raise the mind, which is habituated to the suspicious practices of the world, above those practices, and to make it feel that the pure heart defies the pusillanimous imputation of want of delicacy, is a difficult task. But let us, my Anna, continue to act and speak all that our thoughts approve, void of the fear of accusation.

LETTER XLIX

Anna Wenbourne St. Ives to Louisa Clifton

Paris, Hotel de l'Université

WE are returned to Paris. The Marquis and his bride have taken leave of their country pleasures, and are gone to Fontainebleau, to be presented at court.

The strange incident of Clifton excited much conversation, in which my name and his were frequently joined. The Count de Beaunoir became less particular in his behaviour to me, in consequence of the reserve which I thought it right to assume. I find however that he told Sir Arthur, after running over a great number of enthusiastic epithets, in his wild way, all in my praise, that he perceived at present I preferred another; and that he had too high a sense of honour to put any restraint on a lady's inclinations. But if my mind should change, and his person, fortune, sword, and life could give me pleasure, they should eternally be at my command. He likewise means in a few days to follow the court to Fontainebleau, as he said; and he again repeated he had lost a fine opportunity of convincing me how he adored me; and that he was *diablement fâché*.

Clifton has entirely altered his behaviour to Frank; he now treats him with unaffected freedom and respect. But his impatience relative to me has not abated. Tomorrow we are to have some conversation, after which I imagine he wishes to make proposals to Sir Arthur.

Would you think, Louisa, that I sometimes suffer myself to be surprised into fears; and that I then find myself ready to retract, or at least questioning whether I ought to proceed.

There is something fatally erroneous in the impatient propensities of the human mind. How seldom does it stay so fully to examine a question as to leave no remaining doubt, and to act on a preconcerted and consistent plan! Yet it never acts with safety, or with satisfaction, except when it has or imagines it has made this examination. If our motives be few, slow, and feeble, we then are heavy, dull, and stupid: if they be quick, numerous, and strong, we are too apt implicitly to obey first impulses, and to hurry headlong into folly and extravagance. Yet these last only can give energy; and, having them, wisdom will consist in being able to curb them, so as to give full time for consideration.

The conscious want of this in myself is what I blame. How often am I surprised by unexpected circumstances, which I ought to have foreseen, and against which I ought to have provided! If I have any doubts of myself, if I am not certain of producing those effects on the mind of Clifton which I know I ought to be able to produce, it becomes me to recede. Or rather it becomes me to apply myself, with the resolution of which I am so ready to vaunt, to attain that which is attainable, to discover the true means, the clue to his mind, and to persevere.

I have sometimes suspected myself of being influenced by his fine form, and the charms of his wit and gaiety. At others I have even doubted whether I were not more actuated by an affection for my Louisa, than by a sense of incumbent duty. But, consider the subject how I will, that there is a duty, and that I am called upon to fulfil it, is an unerring decision.

There must be no concealment. I must explain my whole chain of reasonings to him: for nothing appears more indubitable to me than that duplicity never can conduce to good. The only fear is that I should be deficient in my detail, and present my plan so as to give it a false appearance. Truth partially told becomes falsehood: and it was a kind of blind consciousness of this which first induced men to countenance dissimulation. They felt their inability to do justice to truth, and therefore concluded hypocrisy was a virtue, and, strange to tell, truth itself sometimes a vice. It was a lamentable mistake. It is partial truth, or in other words falsehood, which is the vice.

Clifton has from the beginning been a great favourite with Sir Arthur. He contradicts none of my father's prejudices; he admires grounds and parks beautifully laid out; has a taste for architecture; points out the defects and excellencies of the buildings of France with much discrimination; has a great respect, like Sir Arthur, for family, and prides himself in being the son of an honourable mother; recounts, in a pleasant and lively manner, the anecdotes he has heard; and relates his own adventures, so as to render them amusing. There is therefore no fear of opposition from Sir Arthur.

He has another advantage with the family. My uncle, Lord

M

Fitz-Allen, is at present in Paris, on his return from Switzerland, and Clifton has been introduced to him by his kinsman, Lord Evelyn, who is making a short excursion to the south of France. The near relationship of your brother to this noble lord has given him great consequence with my uncle, who has once more condescended to restore me to favour. Could I or did it become me entirely to conceal those feelings which his arrogance inspires, I should stand much higher in his esteem. As it is, he acts more from the love of his rank and family, that is of himself, than of me; and has accordingly signified his mandatory approbation to Sir Arthur. As nothing however in the way of family advantage is to be expected from him, he having several children and a prodigious quantity of dignity to maintain, his behest is not altogether so omnipotent as it might otherwise be.

My brother, agreeably to his grandfather's will, has taken possession of the Edgemoor estate, which is eight hundred a year. This I imagine will oblige Sir Arthur, in despite of his predilection, to retrench some of his improving expences. He mentioned the circumstance to me, and I thought that a good opportunity once more to attack his ruling passion. Our conversation soon became animated. I boldly descanted on the use and abuse of riches, on the claims of honest distress, and on the turpitude of seeking self-gratifications, and neglecting to promote the great ends for which men ought to live, the spreading of truth, the rewarding of genius, and the propagation of mind.

But it was to little purpose. Sir Arthur did not understand me; and I was more angry at myself than at him, as well I might be, for wanting the power to render myself intelligible. He as usual was amazed to hear he had not a right to do what he pleased with his own, and to be told it was not his own. Nor was he sparing in pettish reproof to the self-sufficient young lady, who thought proper to dispute the propriety and wisdom of his projects.

The question that continually occurs to me is, when shall those beings who justly claim superiority of understanding, and thence a right to direct the world, find some simple and easy mode of convincing the mistaken, and by conviction of eradicating error?

Adieu. Blessings be with you. I shall most probably write by the next post, for I wish you to be as perfectly acquainted as possible with every thing that passes, that I may profit by the advice of a friend so dear, so true, and so discerning.

A. W. ST. IVES

P.S. Your last letter is this moment come to hand, and has strongly revived trains of ideas that of late have repeatedly passed through my own mind. It confirms me in the resolution of being very sincere with your brother. But, unless my sincerity should so far offend him, as to induce him voluntarily to recede, it likewise shews me it is my duty to persist. At least such is the result of all the arguments I hold with myself, whenever the subject presents itself to me, either through the medium of my own imagination, or pictured by others. I will write soon. I approve the reasoning in your postscript, will shew it to Frank, and will ask him to let me and Clifton see the letters, who shall likewise know it is by your desire.

LETTER L

Sir Arthur St. Ives to Abimelech Henley

Paris, Hotel de l'Université

I HAVE received yours of the 30th ult.* honest Aby, and it gave me great pleasure to hear you had so much dispatch. Wenbourne-Hill is the garden of Eden. The more I see the more I am convinced. What is there here to be compared to my temples, and my groves, and my glades? Here a mount and a shrubbery! There a dell concealed by brambles! On your right a statue! On your left an obelisk, and a sun-dial! The obelisk is fixed, yet the dial shews that time is ever flying. Did you ever think of that before, Aby?

Apropos of this dial: Sir Alexander I remember said it was useless half the day; because it was shaded from the sun to the west and the north, by the old grove. His advice was that the grove should be grubbed up; but it certainly would be much easier to remove the sun dial, obelisk, and all.

I am so delighted with the recollection of these things, Abimelech, that I had half forgotten the reason of my writing to you.

* Omitted.

The subject is disagreeable enough; and I should not be sorry if
I were never to remember it more.

I very much fear we must stop our improvements. My son has
claimed and entered upon the Edgemoor estate. I thought myself
sure that he would remain satisfied as he was till my death. What
could be more reasonable? I argued with him to the very utmost,
but to no purpose. He is in great haste to set up for himself; and
I don't know whether he would not eject me out of Wenbourne-
Hill, if he had the power. In vain did I tell him that his pay in the
guards, added to the three hundred a-year which I had before
allowed him, was more than any young man knew how properly
to spend. He has only himself to think of; and he very positively
declares he never means to have a family, for he will never marry.
I believe he is quite serious in his declaration: and if so, what does
he want with an estate of eight hundred a-year? He ought to consider that; and to remember that a provision must be made for his
sister. But no; he considers only himself.

Indeed I hear but an indifferent account of him: he is a fashionable gentleman, and would rather squander his money at the
gaming-table, than suffer it to remain in the family. He has been
a wild youth. I have sometimes wondered where he got all the
money which I am told he has spent. Not from me I am sure. And
though I have often heard of his deep play, I do not remember to
have ever heard of his winning. But he follows his own course.
My arguments that I had the family dignity to support, his sister
to marry, and mortgages to pay off, were all in vain.

He was equally deaf when I pleaded the improvements that I
was making; all for his sake. For you know, Aby, he is to have
them when I am gone: and go I must, some time or another.

He had even the confidence to tell me that, if Wenbourne-Hill
were his, he would quickly undo every thing that I have been
doing.

Is not this a sad thing, Aby? For what have I been labouring?
Have not we both spent our lives in contriving? How many charming thoughts have we had! What pleasure have we taken in planting
and pulling up, digging and scattering, watering and draining,
turfing and gravelling!

Talking of water, Aby, I cannot forbear mentioning a most
delightfully romantic lake, which I have met with in the park of

the Marquis de Villebrun. It is the only thing, in the laying out of grounds, that I have seen to please me in all France. One part of it a fine level: such a sweep! At the other extremity nothing but rocks and precipices. Your son Frank threw himself headlong down one of them, into the water, to save a gentleman's life. Were you but to see it, you would be astonished. They have called it the Englishman's leap. I would not do such a thing for a million of money. I should be dead enough if I did.

But Frank is a bold young man, and I assure you, Aby, highly esteemed by my daughter; ay and by myself too, and by every body: very highly indeed. He was the whole talk for I know not how many days.

But about this money, Aby. I shall soon want a good round sum, if I am not mistaken. I may venture, Aby, to give you a hint that I expect very soon, indeed I don't know how soon, a proposal should be made to me for my daughter: and if it be, I am so pleased with the party, who let me tell you is a fine spirited young fellow, that I assure you I shall not think of refusing my consent; especially as he is so much in the good graces of my daughter. In this case, I cannot do less than pay twenty thousand pounds down.

I am afraid, honest Aby, we must renounce the wilderness! But when you know the party, I think you will allow I could not act otherwise.

Indeed, I find, however we may please ourselves, we can never satisfy our children. Here too has Anna been lecturing me, about money thrown away, as she is pleased to conceive; and has said a great deal indeed, against what I thought could not have been found fault with. But so it is! Friends, relations, children, all are wiser than ourselves! All are ready enough to discover or to suppose blemishes! Would you think it possible for any body to be acquainted with Wenbourne-Hill and do any thing but admire? My hope, nay my determination was to have made it the paradise of England, and to have drawn strangers far and near to come and be delighted with its beauties. But these rubs and crosses put one out of heart with the most excellent thoughts and contrivances.

Let me know what you think can be done in these money matters, if things should be as I expect. You are perfectly acquainted with the state of my affairs. I see no way but that of mortgaging more deeply.

It is exceedingly vexatious to think of stopping our proceedings, Aby. But what can be done? However, as I do not intend to stay much longer here, we can talk more to the purpose on these matters when we meet in England.

Perhaps it would be better to begin by discharging the workmen gradually; which you will find proper opportunities to do, Aby. And if you were, by way of talk in the neighbourhood, to say that you thought nothing more could be done to Wenbourne-Hill, and that you had reason to believe that was my opinion likewise, such a report might tie the tongues of cavillers: for I would not have it thought we stop for want of money.

You may write to me here, in answer to this; for we shall not leave Paris before your letter will come to hand. And so, good Abimelech, farewell.

A. ST. IVES

P.S. I will not tell you the name of the party from whom I expect the proposal, honest Aby; because if he should be shy of speaking, as youngsters sometimes are, it might come to nothing; but I may hint to you, that you are well acquainted with his family; and I dare say you will not be sorry for the match, it being so agreeable to my daughter's inclination; though I grant it may not be so good a one as my sister Wenbourne, and others of the family, have been expecting; because of Anna's beauty and accomplishments, which I own might well merit a man of higher birth and fortune. But the little hussy has been so nice, and squeamish, that I began to fear she would take up her silly spend-thrift brother's whim, and determine to live single: therefore I shall not balk her, now she seems in the humour.

LETTER LI

Abimelech Henley to Frank Henley

Wenbourne-Hill

WHY ·ay! To be sure! This will do! I shall be fain to think a summut of ee, now you can flamgudgin[1] 'em a thisn. I did'nt a think it was innee. Why you will become a son of my own begettin.

I write to tellee the good news, and that ee mightn't a kick down the milk.[1] You have a sifflicated[2] Sir Arthur. I could a told ee afore that you had a sifflicated Missee. But I was afeard as that you wur a too adasht.[3] But I tellee it will do! Father's own lad! An ear-tickler! Ay, ay! That's the trade! Sugar the sauce, and it goes down glibly.

Listen to me. I a learnt the secret on't. What was I, I pray you? Pennyless Aby! Wet and weary! And what am I now? A tell me that. Why I'm a worth—But that's a nether here nor there, I tellee. And what may you be an you please? What should I a bin, an I ad had your settins out? Why Ide a bin what Ide a pleased. A dooke, mayhap; or a lord mayor of Lunnun?—No—A sekittary prime minister?—No—A member of parliament?—No—Ide a bin treasurer!—Treasurer of the three kinkdums. Ide a handled the kole!—I've a feathered my nest as it is; and what would I a done then thinkee?

Stick close to Sir Arthur. Mind your hits, and you have him a safe enough. Didn't I always tellee you must catch 'n by the ear? A cunnin curr always catches a pig by the ear. He expects a pro-posal for Missee; he does not a know how soon. And who does he expect to propose? Guess, Nicodemus,[4] if you can. Do you mind me? He shan't refuse his consent. Mark you me that! They are his own words. Twenty thousand pounds down! His own words again. What do you say to me now? It's all your own! I mean it's all *our* own—Do you mind me? For who have you to thank for it? I tellee it is but ask and have—And how do I know that?—— What's that to you, Dolt?—No, no—You are a no dolt now—You are a good lad.

I tellee I'm in the secret! So do you flamdazzle[5] Missee. I a heard of your jumpins and swimmins: and so that you do but swim to the main chance, why ay! That's a summut! I a bin to Clifton-Hall. For why? I begind to smell a rat! And there I talked with t'other Missee. I a palavered her over. I a ferretted[6] and a feagued[7] and a worked and a wormed it all out of she. Your name is up! You may go to bed! Do you mind me? You may go to bed to twenty thousand pounds! It is as good as all your own.

I am a to find the kole: that is, I first havin and holdin the wherewithalls, and the whys, and the wherefores. And so do you see me, I expect to have the handlin ont—But that's a nether here

nor there. Sir Arthur as good as said it to me—So don't a stand
like a Gabriel Gallymaufry[1] all a mort,[2] shilly shally, I would if I
durst—A dip in the skimmin dish and a lick of the fingur—That's
a not the way with a maiden—What! A don't I know?—Make up
to Missee, and say to her, Missee! Here am I! My name is Frank
Henley! My father's name is Abimelech Henley! A's a cunnin
warm old codger—A tell her that—And says you, here Missee says
you am I, at your onnurable Ladyship's reverend sarvice. My
father has a got the rhino[3]—A don't forget to tell her that—Smug
and snug and all go snacks[4]—Do you mind me? And so, says you,
I have a paradventerd umbelly to speak my foolish thofts, says
you. That is take me ritely, your Ladyship, says you; under your
Ladyship's purtection and currection, and every think of that
there umbel and very submissive obedient kind, says you. And so
says you, do ee see me Missee, I onnurs and glorifies your Ladyship; and am ready to have and to hold, says you; go fairly go
fouly, be happy be lucky, any day o'the week, says you; I and my
father, honest Aby, says you. He can raise the wind, says you! He
can find the wherewithalls to pay for lawyer's parchment, says
you—But mind, that's a nether here nor there—So a here Missee
stands I, says you; I and my honest old father—A's got the marygolds,[5] says you! The gilly flowers,[6] the yellow boys,[7] says you!
Golore!—But that's a nether here nor there.

So do you tell her all a that I bid ee, and a mind your pees and
cues. Who knows but Wenbourne-Hill itself may be one day all
our own? I say who knows? There be old fools and young fools—
I tellee that—Old planners, and improvers, and bite bubbles;[8]
and young squitter squanders,[9] gamblers, and chouse chits[10]—
Mark you me that—And there be wax and parchment too—Ay
and post obits*; and besides all doosoors[11] and perkissits. A what
is money good for but to make money? A tell me that.

And so in the name and the lovin kindness of the mercifool
sufferins of almighty goodness, and peace and glory and heavenly
joys, no more at present.

ABIMELECH HENLEY

* The original reads—postt-off bites. The context suggested post obits, which
reading is confirmed by succeeding letters. The syllable *bits* might very naturally,
in the mind of honest Aby, be changed into *bites*. Dates have for certain reasons
been omitted; but, from this and other passages, we may perceive that the date of this
correspondence is antecedent to the bill for protecting minors against usury.[12]

LETTER LII

Abimelech Henley to Sir Arthur St. Ives

Wenbourne-Hill

MOST onnurable Sir, my ever onnurd Master,

For certainly your noble onnur knows best. And thof I have paradventerd, now and tan, umbelly to speak my foolish thofts, and haply may again a paradventer, when your most exceptionable onnur shall glorify me with a hearing, in sitch and sitch like cramp[1] cases and queerums[2] as this here; yet take me ritely, your noble onnur, it is always and evermore with every think of that there umbel and very submissive obedient kind.

My younk Lady Missee is as elegunt a my Lady younk Missee as any in the three kink's kinkdums. A who can gain say it? She is the flour of the flock, I must a say that. The whole country says it. For why, as aforesaid, a who can gain say it? A tell me that! Always a savin and exceptin your noble onnur, as in rite and duty boundin. What, your most gracious onnur, a hannot I had the glory and the magnifisunce to dangle her in my arms, before she was a three months old? A hannot I a known her from the hour of her birth? Nay, as a I may say, afore her blessed peepers a twinkled the glory of everlastin of infinit mercifool commiseration and sunshine? A didn't I bob her here, and bob her there; a up and a down, aback and afore and about, with a sweet gracious a krow and a kiss for honest poor Aby, as your onnur and your onnurable Madam, my Lady, ever gracious to me a poor sinner used then to call me?

Not but those times are a passt. But, a savin and exceptin your noble onnur, that's a nether here nor there. I may hold up my head as well as another. A why not? When so be as a man has no money, why then, a savin and exceptin your onnur's reverence, a's but a poor dog. But when so be as a man as a got the rhino, why then a may begin to hold up his head. A why not? Always a savin and exceptin your noble onnur, as aforesaid.

Your noble onnur knows that I'm a be apt to let my tongue mag[3] a little, when my wits be a set a gaddin; and whereupon the case is as witch your noble onnur was pleased to sifflicate[4] me upon, in your last rite onnurable and mercifool letter. For why? A man's

son as I may say is himself; and twenty thousand pounds, thof it
be not a penny too much, is somethink. For witch the blessin and
glory of goodness and praise be with the donors. Nevertheless that
there will likewise be the wherewithalls, mayhap, notwithstandin,
when my head comes to be laid low. Thof if so be I cannot but say
that a man would rather a not think of that there, if a could help it.
A savin and exceptin that the blessin and glory and power and
praise of the saints, and the martyrs, and the profits, and the
cherubims and serafims, and the amen allelujahs, might a be summut to a dyin soul; when a has had, god be mercifool unto us, time
for repentance, and the washin away of the sins of this wickedness
world, by good deeds, and charity, and mercy, and lovin kindness
unto all men; when the poor miserable sinner, with groans, and
tears, and eternal terrifyins of the flamin prince Lucifer Belzebub
of darkness everlastin is at last obliged to take leave of the soul
from the body. Ah, a well a day! Man is a reprobation race! A's
a given over to sin, and to shame, and to backslidins, and to the
slough of despond, and to the valley of the shaddow of death, and
if a has not, miserable sinner, a time to repent, of a witch be evermore granted unto us all, world without end. Amen! Amen!

Ah, dear a me, what have I a bin talkin to your most gracious
onnur? I was a meant to tell your noble onnur that the twenty
thousand pounds mayhap might a be forth cummin; on proper
occasions, and certificates, and securities, and doosoors,[1] and
perkissits; all of the witch, as my ever onnurd master aforetime
knows, there is no a doin a business without. For why?—Money
is money, and land is land; and there be troubles, and takins, and
seekins, and enquirins, and profit and loss, and ifs and mayhaps,
and all a that there; of the witch there is no a doing without. But
nevertheless I dares to say, likewise and notwithstandin as aforesaid, that the money may be a forth cummin.

Nay and if so be the witch that I might a paradventer to advise,
but that to be sure I should not a like to have it a thoft that I should
perk and put in my oar, all agog to my betters, and moreover one
of his majesty's baronets, otherwise I should say nevertheless as
aforesaid that the younk lady is the flour of the flock; and if so
be as I had the onnurable grace and blessin to be her father, I
would a give her and a make over to her, now and evermore hereafter, all a that the law would a let me. And a let 'em tell me, your

noble onnur, who desarves it better. What! Is n't she, as I may say,
the very firmament of the power and glory of praise? What is ivory
and alablaster a parallel to her? Let 'em a tell me that! If I wus the
onnurable father of sitch ever mercifool affability, would a not I
be fain to give her gems and rubies, and carbuncles, if I had 'em?
Who should gain say me? A savin and exceptin your ever exceptionable and noble onnur. I would n't a be meant to be thoft to
put in a word for meself, by no manner of account; no, no; far
be it from me; but in other partikillers, if so be that it wus me
meself, I should n't a grutch her kinkdums. And ast to thwartin
and knatterin[1] and crossin the kindly sweet virginal soul, ever
blessed as she is, in love, for what truly? Your noble onnur has
too much bowels of fatherly miseration. No, no!—Your noble
onnur has a clencht it; take her now she is in the humour. Whereby
maidens be wayward and fain and froward and full of skittish
tricks, when they be happen to be crossed in love. Take her in the
humour your wise and alwise noble onnur.

Whereof your onnur was a menshinnin a stagnation to be put
in the spoke of the wheel of improvements. Whereof if I might a
paradventer to put in my oar, I should say why that should be as
it might a be happen. When if as I should ever live to see the
glorious day of this marriage match rejoice the heart of Wenbourne-
Hill, why then I should know how to speak my poor thofts. For
why? All would then be clear and above board; and we should all
a know who and who was together. That would be summut! We
might then a be happen to raise the wind; and the wherewithalls
might a be forth cummin.

And so, as matters and thinks is likely to turn out, to be sure I
must say that your onnur has a hit the nail on the head. Whereof
as your onnur has a ushered your commands, I shall begin to
take care of the kole, and send them there rapscallions a packin.

And as to the flickers and fleers[2] of the neighbours, your onnurable onnur, a leave me to humdudgin[3] they. I'll a send their wits a
wool-gatherin. For why? Your onnurable onnur has always a
had my lovin kindness of blessins of praise, as in duty boundin.
For certainly I should be fain to praise the bridge that a carries
me safe over. And now that your onnur is a thinkin of a more of
lovin kindness and mercies, to me and mine, why a what should
I say now? Why I should say and should glorify, to all the world,

that your onnur is my ever onnured and rite most mercifool
bountifool faithfool and disrespectfool kind master; and that I be
your ever rite and most trusty true honest Aby; and every think of
that there umbel and very submissive obedient kind, as in duty
boundin.

But I a bin a thinkin, your ever gracious onnur, that a behap the
kintlin[1] may stand alooft, and a hang** ****, and a be adasht. And
a what is to be done then? Why then, whereupon if that your ever
gracious onnur would but be so all mercifool in goodness as to say
the word, why we should be upon sure ground, and all our quips[2]
and quandaries and afterclaps[3] would a be chouse clickt.[4] I most
umbelly pray and besiege your onnur to be so mercifool as to
think o' that there! Do ee, your ever gracious onnur! I pray your
onnur, doo ee! Then we should a be all sound and safe over, and
it would all a be holiday at Wenbourne-Hill! A that would be a
glorified day! The lawjus mighty, ay! It would!

Witch is all in praise and onnur of the glory and peace to come,
thanksgivin and gladness; umbelly beggin leave to super scribe
me self,

ABIMELECH HENLEY

I needn't a say nothink of a concernin of a dockin of the entail,
to your onnur. For why? As your onnur knows, nothink can be
done, in the way of the kole and the wherewithalls, without a that
there. But ast for that, a that argufies nothink. For why? His
younk onnur, I knows, will be a willin enough; that is, settin the
case of a proviso of a doosoor consideration[5] in ready rhino for
himself. A told me himself, his younk onnur, that a will have that.
A says a will sell his chance, and a does n't a care how soon; but a
wonnot give it away. Witch if so be as it be not to be helpt, why a
what be to be done, your onnur?

LETTER LIII

Anna Wenbourne St. Ives to Louisa Clifton

Paris, Hotel de l'Université

YOUR brother has this moment left me. Our conversation has been animated; and, as usual, I sit down to commit what has passed to paper, while it is fresh on my memory.

He began with the warmest expressions of the force of his passion. I have no reason to doubt of their sincerity; and, if affection can be productive of the end which I hope, its strength ought to give me pleasure. He would scarcely suffer me to suppose it possible there could be any cause of difference between us: let me but name my conditions and they should be fulfilled. He would undertake all that I did, all that I could require; and it was with difficulty that I could persuade him of the possibility of promising too fast. This introduced what was most material in our dialogue.

My heart assures me, madam, said he, that I never gave you the least cause to suspect the sincerity and ardour of my passion: and I should hope that the fears, which I have sometimes thought you too readily entertained, are now dissipated.

My fears are chiefly for, or rather of, myself. I doubt whether any person has so high an opinion of the powers and energy of your mind as I have: but I think those powers ill directed, and in danger of being lost.

I own, madam, I have been sometimes grieved, nay piqued, to perceive that you do not always think quite so well of me as I could wish.

You wrong me. You yourself do not think so highly of yourself as I do.

Yet you suppose me to be in danger?

Of being misled. Some of my opinions and principles, or some of yours, are erroneous, for they differ; I cannot at this moment but perceive how liable I am to be misunderstood. I cannot be insensible of the awkwardness of the situation in which I now place myself. My age, my sex, the customs of the world, a thousand circumstances contribute to cast an air of ridicule upon what ought to be very serious. But I must persist. Do you endeavour to forget these circumstances; and consider only the words, not the girl by whom they are spoken.

It is not you, madam, but I who ought to dread appearing ridiculous. But for your sake—Let me but obtain your favour, and make me as ridiculous as you please.

I told you so!—Should the lordly lettered man submit to have his principles questioned, by an untutored woman? Be sincere: your mind revolts at it?

I feel the justness of your satire. Men are tyrants.

Prejudice is a tyrant: there is no other tyranny.

Madam!

That is one of my strange opinions.

It may be true; I am willing to think it is. Such things are indifferent to me. Let me but have your consent, to speak to Sir Arthur, and I have accomplished all I wish. I do not desire to trouble myself with examining opinions, true or false. I am determined to be of your opinion, be it what it will.

That is, you avow that the gratification of your desires is the chief pursuit of your life. We have now found the essential point on which we differ.

Is not happiness, madam, the universal pursuit? Must it not, ought it not to be?

Yes. But the grand distinction is between general and individual happiness. The happiness that centres in the good of the whole may for the present find momentary interruption, but never can be long subverted: while that individual happiness, of which almost the whole world is in pursuit, is continually blundering, mistaking its object, losing its road, and ending in disappointment.

Then, madam, we must all turn monks, preach self-denial, fast, pray, scourge away our sins, live groaning, and die grieving.

[I smiled. It is his usual way, when he thinks I am got a little in the clouds, to draw some humorous or satirical picture, to bring me down to what he esteems common-sense. But, as I am convinced that truth only need to be repeated, and insisted on, whenever there is an opportunity, in order finally to be received, the best way is always to join in the laugh, which is inoffensive, unless pettishness give it a sting.]

You find yourself obliged at present to consider me as a whimsical girl, with a certain flow of spirits, and much vanity, desiring to distinguish herself by singularity?

No, madam, Whatever you may think of me, my heart will not endure a thought to your disadvantage.

Nay, nay, forbear your kind reproaches. Every time you differ with me in sentiment, you cannot but think something to my disadvantage. It is so with all of us. The very end of this present explanation is sincerity. We each think well of the other: but do we think sufficiently well? Is there a certainty that our thoughts are in no danger of changing? Of all the actions of private life, there is not one so solemn as that of vowing perpetual love: yet the heedless levity with which it is daily performed, proves that there is scarcely one on which less serious reflection is bestowed. Can we be too careful not to deceive ourselves? Ought we not minutely to examine our hopes and expectations? Ought not you and I, in particular, to be circumspect? Our imaginations are vivid, our feelings strong, our views and desires not bounded by common rules. In such minds, passions, if not subdued, become ungovernable, and fatal.

I am very conscious, madam—

Nay, do not fancy I seek to accuse: my purpose is very different. My mind is no less ardent than yours, though education and habit may have given it a different turn. It glows with equal zeal to attain its end. Where there is much warmth, much enthusiasm, I suspect there is much danger. We had better never meet more, than meet to be miserable.

For heaven's sake, madam, do not torture me with so impossible a supposition!

You expect one kind of happiness, I another. Can they coalesce? You imagine you have a right to attend to your appetites, and pursue your pleasures. I hope to see my husband forgetting himself, or rather placing self-gratification in the pursuit of universal good, deaf to the calls of passion, willing to encounter adversity, reproof, nay death, the champion of truth, and the determined the unrelenting enemy of error.

I think, madam, I dare do all that can be required of me.

I know your courage is high. I know too that courage is one of the first and most essential qualities of mind. Yet perhaps I might and ought to doubt, nay to ask, whether you dare do many things.

What is it, madam, that I dare not do?

Dare you receive a blow, or suffer yourself falsely to be called liar, or coward, without seeking revenge, or what honour calls satisfaction? Dare you think the servant that cleans your shoes is your equal, unless not so wise or good a man; and your superior, if wiser and better? Dare you suppose mind has no sex, and that woman is not by nature the inferior of man?—

Madam—

Nay, nay, no compliments; I will not be interrupted—Dare you think that riches, rank, and power, are usurpations; and that wisdom and virtue only can claim distinction? Dare you make it the business of your whole life to overturn these prejudices, and to promote among mankind that spirit of universal benevolence which shall render them all equals, all brothers, all stripped of their artificial and false wants, all participating the labour requisite to produce the necessaries of life, and all combining in one universal effort of mind, for the progress of knowledge, the destruction of error, and the spreading of eternal truth?   .

There is such energy, madam, in all you say, that, while I listen to you, I dare do any thing, dare promise any thing.

Nay, but the daring of which I speak, must be the energy of your own mind, not of mine.

Do not distress yourself and me with doubts, madam. I have heard you yourself say that truth ultimately must prevail. I may differ with you in some points; but I am willing to hear, willing to discuss; and, if truth be on your side, there can be no danger.

The only danger is in the feeble or false colouring which the defenders of truth may give it, and not in truth itself.

I am too well convinced of your power to feel your doubts. You oblige me to see with your eyes, hear with your ears, believe what you believe, and reject what you think incredible. I am and must be whatever you please to make me. You have but to prescribe your own conditions.

Prescribe I must not. If I can persuade, if I can win upon your mind—

If—! You won my whole soul the very first moment I saw you! Not a word or action of mine but what has proclaimed the burning impatience of my passion!

True: the burning impatience—Your eagerness to assent will

not suffer you to examine. Your opinions and principles are those which the world most highly approves, and applauds: mine are what it daily calls extravagant, impracticable, and absurd. It would be weak in me to expect you should implicitly receive remote truths, so contradictory to this general practice, till you have first deeply considered them. I ask no such miracle. But if I can but turn your mind to such considerations, if I can but convince you how inestimable they are, even to yourself as well as to the world at large, I shall then have effected my purpose.

Of that, madam, be sure—You shall see!—Upon my honour, you shall!—I will order a fur-cap, a long gown, a white wand, and a pair of sandals this very day! No Grecian ever looked more grave than I will! Nay, if you desire it, razor shall never touch my chin more.

Well, well; equip yourself speedily, and I will provide you with a wooden dish, a lanthorn, and a tub.[1]

But then, having made your conditions, you now grant me your consent?

That is obliging me once more to put on my serious face—The danger in which I so lately saw you hangs heavily on my mind; that and the warm passions by which it was occasioned.

And my excess of ardour, to demonstrate my love, you regard as a proof of my having none.

How passion overshoots itself! Your conclusion is as precipitate as was your proof.

I cannot be cool, madam, on this subject. I wonder to see you so! Did affection throb and burn in your bosom, as it does in mine, I am persuaded it would be otherwise.

We are neither of us so entirely satisfied with each other as we ought to be, to induce either me to consent or you to apply to Sir Arthur.

For heaven's sake, madam—

Hear me patiently, for a moment. Previous to this conversation, I was convinced of the folly and danger of excessive haste. Should you imagine I have any self-complacency or caprice to gratify, by delay, you will do me great injustice: I solemnly protest I have none. My own interest, had I no better motive, would make me avoid such conduct. The inconsistencies and vain antics of the girl, which are justly enough stigmatized by the epithets flirting

N

and coquetry, are repaid tenfold upon the wife. I would deal openly,
honestly, and generously; but not rashly. I have every predilection in your favour which you could wish; such doubts excepted
as I have declared. But I must not give either you or the world
cause to accuse me of levity. My consent to speak to Sir Arthur
would be generally understood as a pledge to proceed; not it is
true by me, if I saw just cause to retract: but, though I earnestly
desire to reform, I almost as earnestly wish not unnecessarily to
offend the prejudices of mankind.

Nay let me beg, let me conjure you—[He took both my hands
with great ardour.]

And let me beg too, let me conjure you, not to think meanly or
unkindly of me, when I tell you that I must insist on a short delay.

I will kneel! I will do any thing—!

Do nothing which your heart does not approve; it never can be
the way to forward any worthy suit. For my part, I must tell you,
which you may reckon among my faults, that when I have once
considered a subject, I am a very positive and determined girl.
This may be thought obstinacy; but such I am, and such therefore
you ought to see me.

And when, madam, may I now presume to hope?

Do not speak as if you were displeased. Indeed it is far from my
intention to offend.

You are too well acquainted, madam, with your own power of
pleasing, to fear giving offence.

Far the contrary, for I fear it at this moment.

You are kind and killing both in a breath.—Be doubly kind, and
suffer me immediately to speak to Sir Arthur.

I told you I am fixed, and I assure you it is true.

When then may I hope?

I could have wished to have seen my friend, your sister, first:
but perhaps Sir Arthur may make some stay in London, and I
should be sorry to delay a moment longer than seems absolutely
necessary. Let us both consider what has passed this morning, and
provided no new accident should intervene—

Another leap from a rock?

Provided our approbation and esteem for each other should
continue, and increase, I will ask for no further delay, after we
come to London.

Well, well. It is the poor lover's duty to thank his mistress for the greatness of her condescension, even when he thinks she uses him unkindly.

I was going to reply, but my enterprising gentleman—[Indeed, Louisa, your brother is a bold youth]—snatched an unexpected embrace, with more eagerness than fear, and then fell on one knee, making such a piteous face for forgiveness, so whimsical, and indeed I may say witty, that it was impossible to be serious. However, I hurried away, and thus the conference ended.

And now, after reviewing what has passed, tell me, Louisa, ought I to recede? Are not my hopes well founded? Must not the reiteration of truth make its due impression, upon a mind like Clifton's? Can it fail? Is he not the man who, for all the reasons formerly given, truly merits preference?

I must not forget to tell you that Frank readily complied with your request, and Clifton has seen the letters. He seems oppressed, as it were, with a sense of obligation to Frank; which the latter endeavours to convince him is wrong. Reciprocal duties, he says, always must exist among mankind; but as for obligations, further than those, there are none. A grateful man is either a weak or a proud man, and ingratitude cannot exist; unless by ingratitude injustice be meant. Frank's opinions appear to Clifton to be equally novel with mine; and must be well understood, to escape being treated with mockery.

It is infinitely pleasing to me to perceive the fortitude with which Frank resists inclination. He is almost as cheerful, and quite as communicative, and desirous of making all around him happy, as ever. His constancy, however, is not to be shaken, in one particular. I could wish it were! It pains me to recollect that he will *persist, to the end of time, in thinking me his, by right!*

I cannot proceed!

A. W. ST. IVES

LETTER LIV

Coke Clifton to Guy Fairfax

Paris, Hotel de l'Université

LAUGH at me if you will, Fairfax. Hoot! Hiss me off the stage!
I am no longer worthy of the confraternity of honest, bold, free
and successful fellows. I am dwindling into a whining, submissive,
crouching, very humble, yes if you please, no thank you Madam,
dangler! I have been to school! Have had my task set me! Must
learn my lesson by rote, or there is a rod in pickle for me! Yes! I!
That identical Clifton; that bold, gay, spirited fellow, who has so
often vaunted of and been admired for his daring! You may meet
me with my satchel at my back; not with a shining, but a whindling,[1] lackadaisy,[2] green-sickness[3] face; blubbering a month's
sorrow, after having been flogged by my master, beaten by my
chum, and dropped my plum cake in the kennel.

'Tis very true, and I cut a damned ridiculous figure! But I'll
remember it. The time will come, or say my name is not Clifton.

Yet what am I to do? I am in for it, flounder how I will. Yes, yes!
She has hooked me! She dangles me at the end of her line, up
the stream and down the stream, fair water and foul, at her good
pleasure! So be it. But I will not forget.

Then she has such a way of affronting,[4] that curse me if she does
not look as if she were doing me a favour: nay and, while she is
present, I myself actually think she is; and, if vexation did not come
to my relief, I believe I should so continue to think. She is the most
extraordinary of all heaven's creatures: and, in despite of my railing, I cannot help declaring a most heavenly creature she is!
Every body declares the same. I wish you could but see her; for a
single moment, Fairfax; and, having gazed, could you but listen!
——Her very soul is music. Form, features, voice, all are harmony.
Then were you to hear her sing, and play——

But why the devil does she treat me thus? It is something to
which I am unaccustomed, and it does not sit easily upon me. If I
tamely submit to it may I——! I lie, in my teeth! Submit I must,
bounce how I will. I have no remedy—

She gives me the preference, 'tis true. But what sort of a

preference? Why a cold, scrutinizing, very considerative, all wisdom and no passion preference. I do not think there is, upon the
face of the whole earth, so nauseous a thing as an over dose of
wisdom; mixed up, according to the modern practice, with a
quantum sufficit[1] of virtue, and a large double handful of the good
of the whole. Yet this is the very dose she prescribes for me! Ay,
and I must be obliged to swallow it too, let me make what wry
faces I please, or my very prudent lady is not so deeply in love but
she can recede! And shall I not note down this in my tablets?—

I was sufficiently piqued at the first delay. Why delay, when I
offer? Would you have thought, Fairfax, I should have been so
very ready with a tender of this my pleasant person, and my dear
freedom? And could you moreover have thought it would have
been so haughtily rejected?—No—Curse it! Let me do her justice,
too. It is not haughtily. She puts as many smiles, and as much
sweetness, and plausibility, into her refusal as heart could desire.
But refusal it is, nevertheless.

I must be further just to her: I must own that I have acted like
a lunatic—I am mad at the recollection!——

I told you of the young fellow—Frank Henley—Whom I talked
of chastising. Curse on my petulance! He has doubly chastised me
since! He has had his full revenge! And in such a generous, noble
manner—I am ashamed of myself—He has saved my life, and damn
me if I do not feel as if I could never forgive him. There was an
end of me and my passions. What business had he to interfere?—
He did it too in such an extraordinary style! He appears to have
risked more, laboured more, performed more for me than man
almost ever did for his dearest and sworn friend.

Mine was an act of such ridiculous phrensy that I am half
ashamed to tell what it was. I jumped headlong down a declivity,
because I knew I was a good swimmer, into a lake; but, like a
blockhead, never perceived that I should get stunned by the
shelving of the rock, and consequently drowned. And for what,
truly? Why to prove to a vapouring, crack-brained French Count,
that he was a coward; because perhaps he had not learned to swim!
When I look back I have absolutely no patience with myself!—

And then this generous Frank Henley!—After a still more
seemingly desperate leap than mine, and bringing me out of the
water, dead as a door nail, two hours did he incessantly labour to

restore me to life! I, who a few hours before had struck him! And here do I live to relate all this!

I think I could have forgiven him any thing sooner than this triumph over me. Yet he claims and forces my admiration. I must own he is a dauntless fellow—Yes, he has a heart——! Damn him! I could kiss him one minute and kill him the next!

He has been the hero of the women ever since. But they are safe enough, for him. He has principles! He is a man of virtue, forsooth! He is not the naughty cat that steals the cream! Let him be virtuous. Let him lave in his own imaginary waters of purity; but do not let him offend others, every moment, by jumping out and calling—'Here! Look at me! How white and spotless I am!'

As I tell you, the women are bewitched to him; are all in love with him! My sister, Louisa, does not scruple to tell him so, in her letter! But she is one of these high-flyers. Nor can I for the soul of me persuade myself that, family pride excepted, she—ay, she herself, my she, would not prefer him to me. But these gentry are all so intolerably prudent that, talk to them of passions, and they answer they must not have any. Oh, no! They are above such mundane weakness!

As for him, he sits in as much stern state as the Old Red Lion of Brentford.[1] Yes, he is my Lord Chief Justice Nevergrin! He cannot qualify, he! He is prime tinker to Madam Virtue, and carries no softening epithets in his budget.[2] Folly is folly, and vice vice in his Good Friday vocabulary——Titles too are gilt gingerbread, dutch dolls, punch's puppet show. A duke or a scavenger with him are exactly the same—Saving and excepting the aforesaid exceptions, of wisdom, virtue, and the good of the whole!

Did you never observe, Fairfax, how these fellows of obscure birth labour to pull down rank, and reduce all to their own level?

Not but it is cursed provoking to be obliged to own that a title is no sufficient passport for so much as common sense. I sincerely think there is not so foolish a fellow in the three kingdoms, as the noble blockhead to whom I have the honour to be related, Lord Evelyn: and, while I have tickled my fancy with the recollection of my own high descent, curse me if I have not blushed to acknowledge him, who is the head and representative of the race, as my kinsman! I own however he has been of some service to me in the present affair; for by his medium I have been introduced to the uncle of my deity, Lord Fitz-Allen, who has considerable influence in the family, and the very essence of whose character is pride. He is proud of himself, proud of his family, proud of his titles, proud of his gout, proud of his cat, proud of whatever can be called *his*; by which appellation in his opinion his very coach-horses are dignified. I happen to please him, not by any qualities of mind or person, of which he is tolerably insensible, but because there is a possibility that I may one day be a peer of the realm, if my booby relations will but be so indulgent as to die fast enough.

Once more to these catechumenical inspectors of morality, these self-appointed overseers of the conscience.

I do not deny that there is some nay much truth in the doctrines they preach to me. But I hate preaching! I have not time to be wisdom crammed. What concern is it of mine? What have I to do with the world, be it wrong or right, wise or foolish? Let it laugh or cry, kiss or curse, as it pleases! Like the Irishman in the sinking ship, ''Tis nothing to me, I am but a passenger.'

But, notwithstanding these airs, I have my lesson set me. Ay and I must con it too; must say it off by rote; no parrot better!

There is no resisting one's destiny; and to be her slave is preferable to reigning over worlds! You have, for you can have, no conception of her and her omnipotence! She is so unlike every other woman on earth! I wonder while I hear her, am attentive, nay am convinced! What is most strange, though the divinest creature that ever the hand of Heaven fashioned, the moment she begins to speak you forget that she is beautiful!

But she should not hesitate, when I offer. No—She should beware of that! At least to any other woman the world contains, it would have been dangerous; and I am not sure that even she is safe.

However, I must learn to parse my lesson, for the present, and be quiet. Yes, yes; she shall find me very complaisant. I must be so, for live without her I cannot. She must she shall be mine. It is a prize which I am born to bear away from all competitors. This is what flatters and consoles me.

You, Fairfax, think yourself more in luck. You continue to range at large. You scorn to wear the chain to-day which you cannot shake off laughingly to-morrow—Well I envy you not——

When you see her, if you do not envy me may I be impaled and left to roast in the sun, a banquet for the crows.

Good night.

C. CLIFTON

LETTER LV

Frank Henley to Oliver Trenchard

Paris, Hotel de l'Université

SOME events have happened, since I wrote to thee, on which I meant to have been silent, till we had met; but I want thy advice on a new incident, and must therefore briefly relate what has passed. I have had an opportunity of appeasing that hungry vanity, which is continually craving after unwholesome food. I have proved to Clifton that it was not fear which made me submit to obloquy, which in his opinion could only be washed away in blood. I have been instrumental in saving his life.

There is a half lunatic count, who was a visitor at the Chateau, and who is enamoured of her whom all are obliged to love and admire. I know not whether it be their climate, their food, their wine, or these several causes combining and strengthened by habit, or whether it be habit and education only which give the natives of the south of France so much apparently constitutional ardour; but such the fact appears to be. This count is one of the most extravagant of all the hot-brained race I have mentioned. He indulges and feeds his flighty fancy by reading books of chivalry, and admiring the most romantic of the imaginary feats of knight-errantry.

The too haughty Clifton, angry that he should dare to address her to whom he openly paid his court, fell into habitual contests with him, daring him to shew who could be most desperate, and at last gave a tolerably strong proof that, though he has an infinitely more consistent mind, he can be at moments more mad than the count himself. He leaped down a rock into a lake, where it is probable he must have perished, but for me.

One would have imagined that what followed would have cooled even a Marseillian fever of such phrensy. But no: the count has been brooding over the recollection, till he had persuaded himself he was a dishonoured man, and must find some means to do away the disgrace. I thought him gone to Fontainebleau; but instead of that he has just been here. He came and inquired of the servants for the monsieur who had taken the famous leap; cursing all English names, as too barbarous to be understood by a delicate Provençal ear, and wholly incapable of being remembered. The servants, thinking he meant me, for I was obliged to leap too, introduced him to my apartment.

Luckily Clifton was out for the day. She and Sir Arthur were with him. I am hourly put to the trial, Oliver, of seeing him preferred——But——Pshaw——

After a torrent of crazy compliments from the count, who professes to admire me, I learned at last it was Clifton and not me he wanted; and I also learned in part what was the purport of his errand. His mind was too full not to overflow. Knowing how hot, unruly, and on such subjects irrational, the spirits were that were in danger of encountering, I was immediately alarmed. The most effectual expedient I could conceive to prevent mischief was to shew its actual absurdity. I saw no better way than that of making it appear, as it really was, its tragical consequences excepted, ludicrous. But the difficulty was to give it the colouring which should produce that effect on a mind so distorted.

Mort de ma vie! said the count, I shall never pardon myself for having lost so fine an opportunity! I am not so heavy as he. I should not have been hurt by the fall. I should have saved the life of my rival, and been admired by the whole world! My triumph would have been complete! Every gazette in Europe would have trumpeted the exploit; and the family of Beaunoir would have been rendered famous, by me, to all eternity! No! I never shall forgive myself!

I think, sir, you ought rather to be angry with me than with Mr. Clifton.

Parbleu! I have been thinking of that. Why did you prevent me? The thought could not long have escaped me, if you had not been in such devilish haste!

True. The only danger was that, while you were waiting for the thought, the gentleman might have been drowned.

Diable m'emporte! I had forgotten that. Well then, I must have satisfaction of Monsieur Calif—Morbleu!—What is the gentleman's name?

[I wish I could confide enough in my French to write the dialogue in the language in which it passed; but I must not attempt it. The ideas however are tolerably strong in my memory, and they must suffice.]

Clifton.

Oui da—Califton—Monsieur Califton must give me satisfaction for the *sanglante* affront I have received.

But I cannot conceive, sir, how any man's thinking proper to kill himself can be an affront to another.

Comment, Monsieur? Peste! But it is, if he kill himself to prove me a coward!

Then, sir, I am afraid there is not a madman in Bedlam who does not daily affront the whole world.

How so, sir?

By doing something which no man in his senses dare imitate.

Nom d'un Dieu! Monsieur, I am a man of honour! The family of Beaunoir is renowned for its noble feats, it shall not be disgraced by me. I have been defied, and I will have satisfaction.

But you were not defied to sword, or pistol. You were defied to leap.

Well, sir?

And before, as a man of honour, you can have any right to give a second challenge, you must answer the first.

Is that your opinion, sir?

Nay, I appeal to yourself.

Allons!—If so, I must leap! Will you do me the favour to accompany me? I will order post-horses instantly. You shall be my witness that I perform the first condition.

Can you swim?

Ventrebleu! What a question! I am not heavy enough to sink. Besides, sir, I was born at Marseilles.—Yes, we will go together; you shall see me make the leap; after which I may then return and publish my defiance to the whole universe.

No, sir! If you leap you will never publish your defiance! How so?

You will be killed! The whole universe could not save you!

Comment, diable! Look at me! Look at Monsieur Calif! I am as light as—! *Peste!*

Yes; but you are not so strong as he: you cannot leap so far. His effort was prodigious! I have examined the place: and, had he fallen half a foot short of where he did, he must have been dashed to pieces.

Fer et feu!—In that case, I must die!—Yes, I must die! There is no remedy! I must not dishonour my family! No man on earth must brave the Count de Beaunoir! I must die!

And be laughed at?

Laugh, sir! *Mort de ma vie!* Who will dare to laugh?

When you are dead, of what should they be afraid?

Morbleu! That's true.

He would be a rash fool who should dare to laugh at you while you are living.

Foi d'un honnête homme, monsieur, you are a man of honour: a gentleman. You are brave yourself, and know how to honour brave men, and I esteem you.

Sir, if you really esteem me—

Ventrebleu! Sir, I esteem you more than any man on earth! Command my purse, my sword! I would serve you at the hazard of my life!

Then let me prevail on you, sir, to consider well what I say. I solemnly assure you, I would not advise you to any thing which I would not do myself.

Pardieu! Monsieur, I am sure you would not. You have too much honour.

I have too much regard to truth.

C'est la même chose*.

Men honour themselves most by opposing, nay by acting in the very teeth of the prejudices of mankind; and he is the bravest man who opposes them the oftenest. The world makes laws, and afterward laughs at or despises those by whom they are obeyed. He proves the nobleness of his nature best who acts with most wisdom. Recollect the madness with which Mr. Clifton acted, how much he was blamed by every body, and imagine to yourself the temper of your own countrymen; then ask whether you would not be laughed at, instead of applauded and admired, were you so madly

* That is the same thing.

to throw away a life which you ought to dedicate to your country.
The Parisians would write epigrams, and songs, and sing them in
every street, on the nobleman who, instead of living to fight the
battles of his country, should toss himself like a lunatic down a
rock, and dash out his brains.

Que Dieu me damne, *monsieur*, but you are in the right! Yes!
I am a soldier! My country claims my sword! I hear we are soon
to have a war with England; and then——! *Gardez-vous bien,
Messieurs les Anglois**!——Where is Monsieur Calif—?

Mr. Clifton will not be at home to-day.

Well, sir, be so kind as to present my compliments to him, and
tell him I would certainly have run him through the body, if you
had not done me the honour to say all that you have said to me.
I have appointed to set off for Fontainebleau tomorrow morning;
but I intend to visit England: we may have the good fortune hereafter to meet, and then we will come to an explanation.

After a thousand whimsical, half crazy but well meaning, and I
believe very sincere compliments, and offers of service, he left me;
and I hope the danger is over.

But as I told thee, Oliver, the chief purpose of my writing is to
ask thy advice. Principle, as thou well knowest, is too severe to
admit of falsehood; direct, or indirect. To mention this dialogue
to Clifton might be dangerous. It ought not to be, I grant, but still
it might. One would imagine that, instead of feeling anger, he must
laugh, were he told of what has passed: but there is no certainty.
And is not silence indirect falsehood? The count has been here;
his errand was to Clifton. Ought he not to be told of it, and suffered
to judge for himself? And is not concealment an indirect falsehood? To me it appears the contrary. He is full as likely to take the
wrong as the right side of the question. I see a possibility of harm,
but no injury that can be done by silence. Nor do I myself perceive
how it can be classed among untruths. Still the doubt has occurred
to my mind, and I have not hitherto answered it to my own
satisfaction.

I forgot to tell thee with what ardour the count declared himself
an admirer of her who is most admirable; and the romantic but
very serious effervescence with which he called himself her champion; one who had devoted himself to maintain her superiority

* Englishmen, beware!

over her whole sex, which he would die affirming; and to revenge
her wrongs, if ever mortal should be daring or guilty enough to do
her injustice. But as I tell thee he is an eccentric and undefinable
character.

I have lately received a letter from my father, from which I find
he has been led, by I know not what mistake, to conclude that Sir
Arthur thinks of me for his son-in-law. His letter, as usual, is a
strange one; and such as I believe no man on earth but himself
could write.

Direct thy next to me in Grosvenor Street; for we shall be on
our return, before I shall receive an answer.

Farewell.

F. HENLEY

LETTER LVI

Anna Wenbourne St. Ives to Louisa Clifton

London, Grosvenor Street

WHAT strange perversity of accidents is it, Louisa, that has made
me most deeply indebted to that man, above all others on the face
of the earth, who thinks I have treated him unjustly? We are
under fresh obligations, nay in all probability we again owe our
lives to Frank Henley.

We left Paris on Sunday last; and, after waiting a day and a
night for a fair wind at Calais, we embarked on board the packet-
boat; the wind still continuing unfavourable, though it had changed
a little for the better. The channel was very rough, and the water
ran high, when we went on board. Sir Arthur would willingly
have retreated; but Clifton was too impatient, and prevailed on
him to venture.

Before we had reached the middle of the channel, Laura, Sir
Arthur, and soon afterward I, were very sea-sick. It is a most disagreeable sensation when violent, and would certainly be more
effectual in rendering a coward fearless of death than the dying
sentiments of Seneca, or Socrates himself.

The wind increased, and the captain laboured several hours, but in vain, to make the port of Dover. He at last told us we were too late for the tide, and that the current set against us, and must drive us down to Deal. We proceeded accordingly, and it was dark before we came within sight of the town of Deal; where the captain, in the sea phrase, was obliged to come to an anchor.

The Deal boatmen, who are always on the watch, and are the most noted as we are told on the whole coast for their extortion, soon came up to the ship, inviting us to be put on shore, but refusing to take us for less than ten guineas. Frank and Sir Arthur were desirous that we should not be imposed upon; but Clifton pleaded my sea sickness, and would not listen to any proposal of delay. He is very peremptory, when his passions are excited; and especially when he conceives, as he then did, that reason is on his side. There were three boats; but they had agreed among themselves, and two of them kept aloof. This we are told is their common practice, that they may not spoil their market by competitorship.

We were not above a mile from shore: Clifton however agreed to their extravagant demand, and we went into the boat.

We had not been there many minutes before we perceived that the five boatmen, who managed it, were all in liquor, especially he who seemed to be their head man; and that we were much more at the mercy of winds and waves, in our present than in our former situation. Clifton and Frank endeavoured to make them attentive, by reproving them; and probably did some good; though the answers they received, in the rugged vulgar idiom of the sea, were not very conciliatory. We were much tossed by the roughness of the water, but made however toward the shore, though evidently in an awkward and dangerous way.

Most part of the beach, at Deal, is excessively steep; and, when the weather is stormy, the waves break against it very abruptly, and dangerously to boats which are managed by men that are either ignorant or have drunken away their senses. When the boat approached the beach, the man at the helm, being stupid and it being dark, did not do his duty, and the side of the boat was dashed against the beach. The shock almost overset the boat, and it was half filled by the wave which broke over it. The water is always a fickle and perilous element; but in an agitated sea, when the winds howl and the waves roar, foam, dash, retreat, and return with additional threats and raging, it is then truly terrific! I shall never forget that night! I think on it even now with horror! One of those poor drunken creatures, Louisa, was in an instant washed overboard and lost; almost without a cry; not heard, not aided, scarcely remarked; no attempt made to save him, for all attempt was absolutely impossible: we were within a few yards of land, yet were ourselves almost certain of perishing. The remaining men were little better than helpless; for it was the most active of them who was thus miserably drowned!—Indeed, Louisa, it was dreadful!

The reflux of the water was in half a minute likely to be equally violent. Frank, whose presence of mind never forsakes him, saw what the nature of our danger was; and, shaking off poor Laura, who clung round him, begging of him for God's sake to save her precious life, he flew to the helm, turned the head of the boat in its proper direction, and called with that imperious kind of voice which on such occasions enforces obedience, for somebody to come to the helm. Clifton was there in an instant. Keep it, said Frank, in this position.

Every motion was necessarily rapid. Frank was immediately out of the boat, and almost up to the shoulders in the sea. He caught hold of the side of the boat, retreated a step or two, set his feet against the steep beach, and steadied it, to resist the returning wave. It had no sooner retreated than he called to me, took me in his arms, and in a moment I found myself in safety on shore!

He returned and brought my father next!

Poor Laura shrieked, with fear and impatience! She was the third whom he landed.

He then ordered the boatmen to take care of themselves; and, drunk and refractory though they were, they did not neglect to obey the mandate. After which Clifton, leaving the helm, jumped into the water, the servants having gone before, and we all found ourselves safe, after some of us had concluded we were lost beyond redemption.

Our peril appears to have been wholly owing to the inebriety of the boatmen; for, had they been able to do their duty, there would have been none, or certainly very little: and it was averted by the active and penetrating mind of Frank, which seems as if it were most accurate and determined, in its conclusions and expedients, in proportion to the greatness of the danger, when common minds would be wholly confused and impotent.

Clifton, though he did not so immediately perceive what was best to be done, saw the propriety of it when doing, and immediately assented, and aided, by keeping the boat in the position Frank directed, almost as essentially as his co-adjutor. I am more and more convinced it is accident only that has kept him from possessing one of the most enlarged of human understandings. But I must likewise allow that this said accident has rendered him petulant, impatient of contradiction, too precipitate to be always aware of mistake, and too positive to be easily governed. But these are habitual errors, which time and care will cure.

I must add too that his affection for me displays itself in a thousand various forms. He is apparently never satisfied, except when it is exercised to give or procure me pleasure. I know not whether the passion, which infuses itself into all his words and actions that relate to me, ought to inspire all that sympathetic sensibility which he intends; but I own it sometimes alarms me. His ardour is astonishing. He seems to wish, and even to design, to make it irresistible. Yet it is mingled with such excess of tenderness that I have half lost the power of repressing it.

But I must not, no, I will not, stand in awe of his impetuosity. Ardour is a noble quality, and my study shall be how to turn it to his advantage. The more I look round me the more I perceive that fear enfeebles, withers, and consumes the powers of mind. Those who would nobly do must nobly dare. Rash people, perhaps, are those who feel the truth of this principle so strongly that they forget it is necessary not only to dare, but to discover the best method of daring.

Clifton now avoids argument, and appears systematically determined to be of my opinion; or rather to say as I say. The only opposition he affords is now and then a witty, sarcastic, or humorous reply. But he is generally successful in his continual attempts to give the conversation a new turn, when his favourite opinions are opposed: for I do not think it wise to obtrude too many painful contradictions upon him at a time. Truth must be progressive. Like a flash of lightning, it stuns or kills by excess.

Clifton will not long suffer me to rest, now we are returned; and
consequently my dear Louisa may soon expect another letter from
her most affectionate

A. W. ST. IVES

LETTER LVII

Frank Henley to Oliver Trenchard

London, Grosvenor Street

WE have now been in London four days, Oliver; and, known
places reviving old ideas, it almost seems as if we had never moved
from the spot where we are at present. I fall into the same trains
of thinking; except that I am more restless, more inclined to
melancholy, to inaction, to a kind of inanity, which no trifling
efforts can shake off.

I have received thy letter, and find thy reasoning in some respects similar to my own. I was ashamed of remaining in doubt, on
a question which only required a little extraordinary activity of
mind to resolve. It appears to me that nothing can be classed among
falsehoods, except those things the tendency of which is to gener-
ate falsehood, or mistake. Consequently, not to tell what has passed
to Clifton is acting according to the dictates of truth: for, to tell
would be to run an imminent danger of false conclusions. Not, it is
true, if the whole could be told: that is, if all possible reasonings,
and consequences, could be fairly recollected, and stated. But
memory is first to be feared; and still more that prejudice which
will not have the patience to lend mute attention. I therefore think,
with thee, that silence in this case is truth.

We have been in some danger, owing to the drunkenness of the
Deal boatmen; but saved ourselves by a little exertion. One of
the poor inebriated wretches however was lost. We saw him only the
instant of his being washed overboard; and he was hurried away
into the sea by the recoiling waves, in the roaring of which his last
cry was overpowered, without our being able so much as to attempt
to give him aid! By which thou mayest judge that we ourselves
were in considerable jeopardy.

O

When we reflect how near danger is to us, daily and hourly through life, we are apt to wonder that we so continually escape. But, when we again consider how easily even great dangers, that is such as take us by surprise, may be warded off, the wonder ceases.

My mind, Oliver, is not at ease: it is too much haunted by fear. At least I hope it is; for my fears are for one whom it is almost torture to suppose in peril. Thou never knewest so enterprising, so encroaching a youth as this Clifton! Nay I am deceived if encroachment be not reduced to system with him; and, strong as her powers are, impossible as I know it to be to shake her principles, yet, who can say what may happen, in a moment of forgetfulness, or mistake, to a heart so pure, so void of guile?

Such terrors are ridiculous, perhaps thou wilt say; and perhaps they are; at least I most devoutly hope they are. But his temperament is sanguine, his wishes restless, ungovernable, and I almost fear ominous, and his passion for her is already far beyond the controul of reason, to which indeed he thinks it ought not to be nor can be subject.

As for me, all is ended. Jealous I must not, no, I will not be! And surely I am above the meanness of envy. Yet I own, Oliver, I sometimes blame her. I think her too precipitate, too fearless, nay too ready to imagine her power, her wondrous power, greater than it is. She makes no secret of her thoughts, and she tells me that she and I, she doubts not, shall transform him to all that we ourselves could desire. Be not surprised at her kindness to me; for she has a heart that is all benevolence, all friendship, all affection. If I can aid her, thou needest not doubt my will. But Heaven grant she may not be mistaken!—Heaven grant it!

And yet, I cannot say. I even sometimes hope and acquiesce; for his talents are indeed extraordinary. But his pride, and the pitiless revenge which he shews a constant propensity to take, when offended, are dangerous symptoms.

For her, she seems to act from motives wholly different from those of her age and sex. It is not passion, not love, such as it is usually felt and expressed; it is a sense of duty, friendship for Louisa, admiration of great talents, an ardent desire to give those talents their full value, and the dignified pride she takes in restoring such a mind to its proper rank. By these she is actuated, as all her words and actions demonstrate.

Well, well, Oliver! She soars a flight that is more than mortal! But she leaves a luminous track, that guides and invites, and I will attempt to follow. Thou shalt see me rise above the poor slavish wishes that would chain me to earth!—

Oliver, my mind, like a bow continually bent, is too much upon the stretch. Such is the effect of my situation, of which my thoughts, my language, and my actions partake. But I will calm this agitation. Fear not: thou shalt find me worthy to be thy friend, and the pupil of thy most excellent father.

No! I will not, Oliver, be a child; though the contest be indeed severe. By day I am with her; for hours I listen, while she sings, or plays, or speaks. I am a witness of her actions! Her form is never absent from me! The sound of her voice is unceasing harmony to my ears! At night, retiring to darkness and thought, I pass her chamber door! In the morning again I behold the place where all that is heavenly rests! I endeavour after apathy. I labour to be senseless, stupid, an idiot! I strain to be dead to supreme excellence! But it is the stone of Sisyphus;[1] and I am condemned to eter——!

Indeed, Oliver, this weakness is momentary! Indeed it is—— Fear not: thou shalt find me a man; be assured thou shalt. Though the furies, or, worse than all that invention can feign, the passions throng to assault me, I will neither fly nor yield. For to do either would be to desert myself, my principles, my duties.

Yet this encroaching spirit that I told thee of!—But then, what is the strength of him, compared to hers? What is there to fear? What do I fear? Why create horrible shadows, purposely to encounter them?—No: it cannot be!

Farewell.

F. HENLEY

LETTER LVIII

Anna Wenbourne St. Ives to Louisa Clifton

London, Grosvenor Street

YOUR brother has gained his point. The deed is done. My consent
is given. For, in reality, to have withheld it would have had more
the appearance of a coquette than of the friend of my Louisa.
After sufficiently strong hints in the course of the two first days,
on the third after our arrival, Clifton came. His intention was evidently to take no denial. It was with difficulty that I could bring
him to listen, for a few minutes, while I repeated principles before
declared, and required an avowal of how far he thought them an
impediment to future happiness. To every thing I could ask he
was ready to accede. 'He had nothing to contend, nothing to contradict; and, if he did not think exactly like me in every particular, he
was determined not to think at all, till he could. Beside, my own
conclusions, in favour of truth, were my safeguard. I had not any
doubt that reason, if attended to, must finally prevail; and I could
not deny that he was at all times ready to pay the strictest attention.'

Indeed he seemed at first resolved, as it were, not to enter into
any conversation, but to claim my promise. But I was still more
determined to exert myself; that the due influence which reason
ought always to have, over passion, might not be lost, and sink
into habitual and timid concession. When he perceived there was
no resisting, he then listened with a tolerably good grace; but still,
as I said, with an apparently preconcerted plan not to contend;
urging, and indeed truly, that fair arguments could desire nothing
more than patient hearing; and this he pledged, in his energetic
and half wild manner, honour, body, and soul to give. I could not
desire more sincere asseverations than he made; and that they
were sincere I cannot doubt. Nor do I regret that they were strong.
Where there is energy there is the material of which mind is
fashioned: and the fault must be mine, if the work be incom-
plete. Our conversation however was long; and when at last
obliged to enter into the subject, the acuteness and depth of his
remarks were strong proof of his powers, had any proof been
wanting—Yes, Louisa, the attempt must be made. It is a high and

indispensable duty; and I must neither be deterred by the dread of danger, nor swayed by the too seducing emotions of the heart— They must be silenced!—They must!

I have an assistant worthy of the cause. Frank does not shrink from the task: though it is but too evident that he has not changed his opinion! I know not why, but so it is, those two particular sentences continually reverberate in my ear—*I feel a certainty of conviction, that you act from mistaken principles*——*To the end of time I shall persist in thinking you mine by right!*——Oh, Louisa!

Sir Arthur of course made no difficulty in giving his consent; I imagine Mrs. Clifton will this post receive a letter from her son, and perhaps another from my father, requiring her acquiescence.

Sir Arthur has shewn me one of the most strange, eccentric, and perhaps comic letters, from *honest Aby*, that I think I ever read. I am glad it is not quite so intelligible to Sir Arthur as it is to me; for I see no good that could result, were he to understand its true sense. The old——! I can find no epithet for him that pleases me ——Well then—*Honest Aby* is excessively anxious that I should marry a son of whom he is so unworthy. But his motives are so mean, so whimsical, and so oddly compounded and described, peering as it were through the mask of cunning, with which he awkwardly endeavours to conceal them, that nothing but reading his letter can give you an idea of its characteristic humour. This post I suppose will likewise shew him his mistake. How he will receive the news I know not; though I suspect he will raise obstacles, concerning the money which Sir Arthur wants, in order to pay my portion. But this will soon be seen.

I likewise learn, from his letter, that my brother is to join in docking the entail of the hereditary estate; and that he is willing, provided he may share the spoil. How would my heart bleed, were I not cured of that prejudice which makes happiness consist in the personal possession of wealth! But the system of tyranny would be more firm and durable even than it is, did not this mutation of property daily exist; and were not the old and honourable families, as they call themselves, brought to ruin by their foolish and truly dishonourable descendants.

Every thing confirms me in the suspicion that honest Aby has been playing a deep game; and that both Sir Arthur and my brother have ceded to all the extortions of craft and usury, to have their whims and extravagancies supplied.

My brother persuades himself that he is determined never to marry; and I suppose has formed this determination purposely that he may spend all he can obtain, without being teased by any qualms of conscience. For the destructive system of individual property involves a thousand absurdities; and the proud but inane successor of a Sydney or a Verulam,[1] instead of knowing how difficult the subject of identity[2] itself is, instead of perceiving that man is nothing but a continuity, or succession, of single thoughts, and is therefore in reality no more than the thought of the moment, believes there is a stable and indubitable affinity between him and his great ancestor.

I must now be more than ever determined to accomplish the task I have undertaken; and to give to the arms of my best, my dearest Louisa, a brother worthy of a heart so pure, and a sister such as she herself could wish to be that brother's other half——Very true, Louisa! It is the old story: I am Sir Arthur's vapouring hussey! But I comfort myself with reflecting that, after the battle is won, the rashness of the attack is never remembered; or, if it be, it is always applauded; and that all generals, great or small, confide in their own plans, till defeat has proved them to be abortive. Something must be ventured, ere any thing can be won.

Not knowing what might be the notions of Sir Arthur, or even of Mrs. Clifton, concerning the silence they might think it necessary to keep, I forbore to mention their plan, of which my friend, with her consistent frankness, informed me, till our last conference: but I then thought it an indispensable duty to relate the truth; otherwise it might have come, at some unlucky moment, in the disguise of falsehood, and have done mischief. Secrets are indeed absolutely contrary to my system. 'Tis pride or false shame that puts blinds to the windows either of the house or of the mind. Let the whole world look in, and see what is doing; that if any thing be wrong, it may have an opportunity to reprove; and whatever is right there is some hope it may imitate. Clifton was pleased to find himself treated with undisguised sincerity. Yes, Louisa, fear not: you will find him your brother, in virtue as well as in blood.

Ever and ever most affectionately,

A. W. ST. IVES

LETTER LIX

Sir Arthur St. Ives to The Honourable Mrs. Clifton

London, Grosvenor Street

DEAR MADAM,

Our plan has succeeded to our wish: Mr. Clifton is as I may say quite smitten with my daughter. And indeed I do not wonder at it; for, though she is my child, I must say, she is the sweetest, most charming, lovely girl I ever beheld! She has always been my darling! I have a true fatherly fondness for her; and, though I own it will not be very convenient to me, I mean immediately to raise twenty thousand pounds, to pay down as her portion. If at my death I should have the power to do more, she shall not be forgotten: but I promise nothing.

As I remember, dear madam, this was the sum which you said was necessary, to redeem certain mortgages, pay off encumbrances, and enable Mr. Clifton to appear in England, in a manner becoming the heir of the Clifton family. And this sum I think it very fit the daughter of Sir Arthur St. Ives should receive. I shall accordingly write to my agent, and put every thing immediately in train; after which, you shall hear from me without delay.

If any alteration should have happened in your own views, or affairs, which may impede or forward our plan, you will be kind enough to inform me.

I am, madam, with the truest respect, your very obedient humble servant,

A. ST. IVES

LETTER LX

Coke Clifton to The Honourable Mrs. Clifton

London, Dover Street

I WRITE to you, dear and honoured madam, with a grateful and happy heart, to thank you for a project so maternally and wisely conceived in my favour, and of which I have just been informed, by the frank-hearted and lovely Anna St. Ives. Of all the blessings for which, madam, I hold myself indebted to you, this last, of discovering and endeavouring to secure for your thankful son a gem so precious, a lady so above all praise, I esteem to be the greatest.

You, dear madam, are acquainted with the propriety with which she thinks and acts, on every occasion; and I have no doubt will join with me, in applauding the entire undisguisedness of relating all that had passed, which appeared to her delicate mind at this moment to be absolutely necessary.

After obtaining her consent for that purpose, I have spoken to Sir Arthur; who, at my request, has promised immediately to write to you. And, it being a project, dear madam, a kind one, of your own forming, I have no fear that it should be discountenanced by you. My only doubt is of delay. Let me entreat you, my dear mother, to remove all impediments with every possible speed; and not to lose a moment in writing to me, as soon as you and Sir Arthur have arranged the business, that I may solicit her, from whom I am certain to receive all possible bliss, to name a time, when suspense shall joyfully end.

Do not, dear madam, let impatience seem a fault in me. Remember the lady; who she is, and all she is; and think, if her perfections could make the impression which they seem to have done upon your heart, what must they have made upon mine! I, who, with all the fire of youth and constitutional eagerness, in consequence of your own wise plan, am become a wishing and expecting lover!

My sister, I am sure, is too generous, the happiness of her friend and brother being pledged, not to join me in the request I now make: and I certainly will not forget a kindness which, I acknowledge, I know not how I shall ever repay.

I am, dear madam, your ever affectionate and dutiful son,

C. CLIFTON

END OF VOLUME III

VOLUME IV

Coke Clifton to Guy Fairfax

London, Dover Street

I AM caught, Fairfax! Spring guns and man traps have been set for me, and I am legged! Meshed! Shot through the heart! I have been their puppet! They have led me, with a string through my nose, a fine dance! From the farthest part of all Italy here to London, in order to tie me up! Noose me with a wife! And, what is more strange, I am thanking and praising and blessing them for it, in spite of my teeth! I swallow the dose as eagerly as if it had been prepared and sweetened by my own hand; and it appears I have had nothing to do in the matter! I am a mere automaton; and as such they have treated me!

Is it not cursed odd that I cannot be angry? And yet, when I recollect all this, I really suspect I am not pleased. Damn it! To be made their convenient utensil! To be packed up, their very obedient jack in a bandbox,[1] and with a proper label on my back, posted with other lumber from city to city, over hills and seas, to be taken out and looked at, and if not liked returned as damaged ware! Ought I to sneak and submit to this? Tell me, will not the court of honour hoot me out of its precincts? Will not the very footmen point after me, with a—'There goes the gentleman that miss had upon liking?' Why it is not yet full two months, since I was the very prince of high blooded noble sportsmen, in the romantic manors, domains, coverts and coveys of Venus! By what strange necromancy am I thus metamorphosed, thus tamed?

I feel myself a husband by anticipation! I am become as pretty a modest, well-behaved, sober, sentimental gentleman, as any you shall see on a summer's day! I get phrases by rote, and repeat them too! I say 'God bless you, madam,' when the cat sneezes: and mumble amen to grace after meat!

I told you that I had my catechism to learn; and, what is worse, it is not the questions and commands of good old mother church, with all the chance-medley promises and vows of godfathers and godmothers made in my name, [For which, by the bye, I think both godfathers and godmothers are fools, and knaves.] but I have the Lord knows how much more to learn than ever I supposed the most outrageous morality could have exacted. And I am obliged to answer yes, and no, and I thank you kindly, while my finger's ends are smoking, tingling, and aching under the stroke of the ferula! Yes! I, Coke Clifton, with my sweetmeats in one hand and my horn-book in the other, am whipped till I pule, coaxed till I am quiet, and sent supperless to bed, if I presume to murmur!

Why what the devil is the English of all this, say you, Clifton? What does it mean? My head is so full of it, and I have it so all by rote myself, that it had totally escaped me that every word I have uttered must be heathen Greek to you. Nay I had forgotten to tell you we have changed the scene, which now is London.

And as for accidents, by sea and land, why we have had some of them too. Frank Henley has again shewn his dexterity. I could eat my fingers, to think that he should hit upon a certain and safe mode of acting, in a moment of danger, sooner than I! But so it is. He seems born to cross me! We should all have been tossed into the sea, and some of us certainly drowned at the very water's edge, if we had not been alert. He took the command upon himself, as imperiously as if it were his by right indisputable; and I saw no expedient but to obey, or perhaps behold her perish. For curse upon me if I know whether any other motive, on earth, could have induced me to act as his subordinate. But, as it was, I did as he bid me; and sat grinding my teeth at the helm, while I saw him reap all the honour of taking her in his arms; and after her the rest, and landing them in safety! If, Fairfax, you can conceive any anguish on earth more excruciating than this, why tell it; and you shall be appointed head-tormentor to the infernal regions, for your ingenuity!

What was I going to say?—My brain is as murky as the clouds under which I am writing——Oh!—I recollect—She had no hand in spreading the trammel,[1] into which, buzzard like, I have been

lured. It was the scheme of my very good and careful mother; for
which I have been very sincerely writing her a letter with more
thanks than words; and of the wise Sir Arthur; who, wise though
he be, is not one of the magi. She knew nothing of it for some time,
nor would have known but for my communicative sister; and, as
she scorns deception, for by my soul she scorns every thing that is
base, or derogatory, it was she who informed me of the trap in
which I have been taken; of which otherwise perhaps I might have
remained in eternal ignorance.

But still and once again, say you, what trap? What do you
mean?—

Three words will explain the whole.

I have been brought from Naples to Paris, not as I supposed to
settle a few paltry debts of a deceased uncle, but to see, fall in love
with, and be rib-hooked[1] to this angel. This my good mother as I
understand thinks the kindest act of her life.—Nay, I think so too;
and yet I am not satisfied. And merely I suppose because I feel I
have been tricked. I will not be the gull of man or woman. What is
it to me that they mean me well? I will judge for myself. It is
insolent in any one to pretend to know what befits me better than
I myself know.

In short, I would quarrel, and bounce, and curse a little, if I
knew how—But they offer an apology so ample, so irresistible, that
there is no demanding to exchange a shot; they present Anna St.
Ives as their excuse, and a fico[2] for resentment.

And now there is nothing on earth for which I so earnestly wish
as to be yoked! What think you, Fairfax; shall I bear my slavish
trappings proudly? Shall I champ upon the bit, and prance, and
curvet, and shew off to advantage? I doubt I shall stand in need of
a little rough riding. And yet I know not; let her but pat me on the
neck, and whisper two or three kind epithets in my ear, and she will
guide me as she pleases: at least she does. No! Hopes there are
none of my ever again returning to my native wilds, and delightful
haunts! Never was seen so fond a booby as I am, and am likely to
remain!

Nor do I believe I should grumble, had she not such a super-
abundance of discretion. She smiles upon me it is true; is all
gentleness, all benevolence; but then she does just the same to
every body else. For my part, I see no difference; except that I

sometimes think she has a kinder smile for Frank Henley than she ever yet had for me! But he is just as discreet as herself; so that it seems impossible to be jealous. Yet jealous I am! Ay and jealous I should be of my cat, if she were as ready to purr and rear her back to be stroked by every coarse unwashed hand as by mine.

Is it not a cursed shame that, when you feel a continual propensity to quarrel with a man, he should be such a prince Prim as never to give you an opportunity? And why have I this propensity?—I know not!—Confound the fellow, why does he make himself so great a favourite? Why does he not contrive to be hated a little? And then perhaps I might be induced to love him. I dislike to have friendship or affection forced upon me, as a duty. I abhor duties, as I do shackles and dungeons. Let me do what I like. I leave others to examine whether or no my conduct be rational: 'tis too much trouble for me.

This marriage is never out of my head! I wish for it, sigh for it, pray for it, and dread it! It may well be said there is no resisting our destiny! If I could but find out the key to her master passion— Well! What then?—What do I want? What do I hope? To hope any thing short of the noose is mere madness. Beside, could I think of living without her?—No!—I would be eternally in her company, for she is eternal novelty: she is all the world in one. She is herself a million of individuals; and not the stale, dull repetition of the same; which is so horrible to imagination.

One thought has struck me.—She has the utmost confidence in what she calls the force of truth. It cannot fail! That is her constant language. I am to be her first convert. I have humoured this whim lately; except when my irritable fancy breaks loose, and runs riot. If she have any folly, it is this said confidence: and whether it be one, or be not, is more than I have yet been able to determine. But she has furnished me with an argument, which I might carry to I know not what extent. 'You,' I urge to her, 'you need not act with the timid and suspicious caution of your sex. You are sure of your principle; and to proceed with distrust and fear would prove doubt instead of certainty.' She boldly replies,—Yes, she is sure; and therefore she speaks and behaves with all that undisguise and sincerity which are so uncommon in the world, and which some would deem so blameable.

She says true: she rises totally superior to the petty arts and tricks of her sex. I seem to participate the trust which she reposes in herself; and the confidence which she appears to place in me, when she so openly declares all she thinks and all she means, is highly pleasing. But, if my views were different from what they are, I doubt whether madam Confidence might not be brought to lull madam Caution so fast asleep, at some lucky moment or another, as to suffer me to purloin her key, and afterward to rob her of all her treasure. Nor should I fail, under certain circumstances, to try the experiment.

Neither is that intriguing spirit which has so long been in restless habits of continual pursuit entirely idle. My first care as usual was to secure the prime-minister of my charmer, whose name is Laura. The hussey is handsome, cunning, and not without ambition. An occasional guinea and a few warm kisses, when it was certain that all was safe, for caution is necessary, have bound her to me. The poor fool is fond of me, and often finds some ingenious chambermaid's excuse to pay me a visit. It does not appear that I shall need her agency; otherwise here she is, properly prepared to be wholly at my devotion. Anna St. Ives affords the fancy full employment; with any other woman an amour without plot and stratagem, attack and defence, would be too insipid to be endured.

Not but I sometimes find my conscience reproach me, for suffering such active talents as mine to lie concealed and unknown; being as they are capable of acquiring renown so high. When in Italy, having even there, in that land of artifice, rendered myself the superior of all competitors, I used to glory in the havoc I should make on my return to England. But this the will of fate opposes, at least for the present: and of what duration my honeymoon is to be is more than any prescience of mine can discover.

Write, Fairfax, and tell me freely your opinion of all this; only remember that, if you make your calculations and conclusions from any comparison with woman whom you have ever yet seen, they will be all error. Tell me however what you think, and all you think.

I forgot to say that twenty thousand pounds is the sum to be paid me down, for condescending to accept this jewel. I am informed it is wanted, to pay off I know not what encumbrances and arrears—Pshaw!—I care not—I have never yet troubled myself about wants, nor do I wish to begin. My father lived fast, and died soon. Well! And is not that better than croaking and crawling over this dirty globe, haunted by razors, halters, and barebones;[1] sobbing in your sleep, groaning when awake, vegetating in sorrow, and dying in the sulks? Let me kick my heels in mirth and sunshine. Or, if clouds intervene, let pleasure and fancy create suns of their own. Those who like them, may find gloom and November enough any day in the year. Tell me, Fairfax, may they not? Write, and tell me.

C. CLIFTON

LETTER LXII

Sir Arthur St. Ives to Abimelech Henley

HONEST ABY,

London, Grosvenor Street

WE are once more arrived in England; for which I am not sorry. Though I cannot say that I repent my journey into France. My former suspicions are confirmed: I had visited the country before, but at that time my taste was not formed; I did not then understand laying out, and improving, as I do at present. I had heard that the French had begun to imitate our best gardens tolerably well; but I have seen some of those that are in most fame, and what are they to Wenbourne-Hill?——No, no, Aby.—I am now convinced that, as they say of their Paris, there is but one Wenbourne-Hill.

I do not know when the family will return to the country. The young people wish to enjoy the diversions and pleasures of the town; and I rather suppose we shall stay here all the winter. Perhaps we may take a jaunt or two, between this and the meeting of parliament. Not that any such plan is yet settled. And as for me, I shall be down with you occasionally, as affairs shall require. I shall take great delight, in once again treading over all my grounds, and walks, and dells; and in visiting places that are never out of my mind.

I cannot forget the hermitage, and the grotto, and the wilderness, of which, the moment you mentioned them, I had formed so charming and so excellent a plan. The picture clings to me, as it were; and it grieves me to give it up. But so it must be.

However, as I say, I shall come down more than once: and, for my part, I wonder how these young unthinking people can prefer the dirty streets of London, to all the delights and riches of nature, and of art; which may be said to be waiting for and inviting them, at Wenbourne-Hill.

I am very glad to find, honest Abimelech, that money is so certainly to be had. But you were always intimate with the warm old fellows, that provide themselves plentifully with what you so aptly call the wherewithalls. You have followed their example, and learned to increase your own store. I am glad of it, and am pleased to find you do not forget your first and best friends. I must own, Abimelech, that you have always appeared to me to understand your situation very properly, and to pay respect where it was due. I have seen your proud, upstart stewards carry their heads as high as their masters! Ay, and instead of studying their tempers and humouring them, as it was their duty, have been surly, and always ready with their ifs, and ands, and objections, and advice! As if it were any concern of theirs, what a gentleman shall please to do with his money! But you, Aby, have known how to comport yourself better; of which I believe you have no cause to repent.

As to the entail, as you say, it must be docked. I know no remedy. And since my son is so positive, and determined to stickle for a good bargain, why we must do the best we can.

I was once sorry at his resolving never to marry; but I think that is partly over now; I care little about the matter. My daughter's son will be as much my grandchild as his son would have been; and, as for names, they may easily be changed. I am certain, were any body to ask me which is the wisest, my son or my daughter, I should not stop a moment to consider about that.

Ay, ay! She is my own child! Every body used to tell me, when she was a baby, how like me she was!

She has some of her mother's features too; who, as you well know, Aby, was a very good sort of an excellent kind of a lady, and very much respected: ay, very much. Indeed the greatest fault of Lady St. Ives was that she would not always be of my opinion. But we are none of us perfect. If it were not for that one thing,

I really should think my daughter a young lady of more good sense, and good taste, and indeed every thing of that kind, than any young person I was ever acquainted with: but she too is a declared enemy to planning, and improving. It is very strange; and I can only say there is no accounting for these things!

My son however knows as little of the matter as she does; nay I believe less. And, as to other kinds of knowledge, he is a child to her! It delights me to hear her talk, and debate points, and chop logic, with your Frank, who is one of her own sort; and with Mr. Clifton, the young gentleman whom I intend for my son in law. I gave you an account in my last, Aby, that the thing was in expectation; and it is now as good as concluded. I have written to Mrs. Clifton; the lawyer is ordered to make a rough sketch of marriage articles, and every thing will be got ready, while my attorney is preparing the necessary deeds down in the country, according to your instructions, and you are raising the money.

Be sure however, honest Aby, to make as good a bargain for me as you can. I know money is not to be had without paying for it; and I trust to you not to suffer me to pay too dearly. Better security you know, Aby, cannot be offered; and I begin to feel, my improvements excepted, which indeed I hold to be inestimable, that I am not so rich as I was fifteen years ago. But, as my son means never to marry, and as the families of Clifton and St. Ives are to be united in one, I have no doubt, some time or another before I die, of seeing every thing retrieved; though I grant there are heavy mortgages, and other impediments to overcome.

Pray has my son told you what sum he expects? If not, endeavour to learn, and let me know. Though on second thoughts you need not, for I hear he is to be in town next week. He must recollect the estate of eight hundred a-year, of which he has lately taken such violent possession. But he is a dissipated young man, and recollects nothing but his pleasures.

I always said, Aby, you were a man of sense; and you are very right in thinking I cannot do too much for my daughter. I hope to contrive to leave Wenbourne Hill her own. It is a rich spot! And, though she be an economist, and no friend to what she thinks a waste of money in improvements, yet I am sure, at my request, she will not be guilty of what I may well call sacrilege, and pull down my temples, and dedicated groves, and relics of art, and ruins; nor, as my son would, destroy with a Gothic hand, as the poet says,[1] and tear away beauties, which it would rend my heart-strings not to suppose durable, as I may say, for ages! I would have my name, and my taste, and my improvements be long remembered at Wenbourne Hill! I delight in thinking it will hereafter be said— 'Ay! Good old Sir Arthur did this! Yonder terrace was of his forming! These alcoves were built by him! He raised the central obelisk! He planted the grand quincunx!' And ah, Aby! if we could but add, 'He was the contriver of yonder charming wilderness!' I then should die in peace.

Let me beg, good Abimelech, that you would write your thoughts in as plain and straight forward a manner as you can; for, I assure you, I have been very much puzzled with some parts of your last letter; which I cannot yet say that I understand. In some places it is very plain that you hint at Mr. Clifton, and wish me not to dally with him; and, as I know you have my interest at heart, and speak in a style at which no gentleman can be offended, why I rather thank than blame you, for your desire to give good advice. Though I must say, Aby, that I do not think I have any need of it. I am mistaken if I could not advise others. I wish all the world would be governed by my plans, and principles. That's a favourite word with my daughter, Aby, and a very apt one.

I once took some delight in such things; I mean in what is called polite learning, Aby. Indeed I was remarkably fond of Ovid's Metamorphoses. But then, as I did not like to puzzle myself with the Latin, I read Garth's, or Rowe's, or Pope's, or I don't know whose translation.[2] And I do believe it was that, and a visit to Lord Cobham's,[3] which first made me study taste and improvement. Nothing is wanting but riches, Aby, to proceed to much greater lengths than any we have yet thought of. What richness of imagination is there in Ovid! What statues might we form, from the wonderful tales which he relates! Niobe at the head of the canal, changing into stone! To be sure we should want a rock there. Then on one side Narcissus, gazing at himself in the clear pool, with poor Echo withering away in the grove behind! King Cygnus, in the very act of being metamorphosed into a swan, on the other! It would be so apropos, you know; a swan, and a canal, and king Cygnus! And then at the further end Daphne, with her arms and legs sprouting into branches, and her hair all laurel leaves!

P

You cannot imagine, Aby, all the fancies which came into my head the other day, when I happened to lay my hand on Tooke's Pantheon,[1] which brought all these old stories fresh to memory.

But, as I was saying, good Aby, write your thoughts as plainly as you can; for I sometimes did not know whom you were talking of, and there were one or two places which made me think you wish something should be done for your son, Frank. And indeed he is a very deserving, and a very fine young fellow; and I have been thinking it would not be amiss, since he has really made himself a gentleman, if we were to purchase him an ensign's commission. What say you to it, honest Aby? He would make a fine officer! A brave bold figure of a man! And who knows but, in time, he might come to be a general; ay and command armies! For he fears nothing! He has lately saved us a dipping, nay and for aught I know a drowning too, and we really should do something for him; for he is a great favourite, and a very good young man. However, I thought it best to mention the matter first to you, and will expect your answer.

A. ST. IVES

LETTER LXIII

Anna Wenbourne St. Ives to Louisa Clifton

London, Grosvenor Street

I MUST write, dear Louisa. My heart feels as if it were estranged by silence, and thinks it has a thousand things to repeat; though, when it comes to enquire what, they seem as if they had all vanished. Not but I have a little incident to relate, which interests us both; the Dramatis Personæ being, as usual, Clifton, Frank Henley, and the friend of my Louisa.

We yesterday paid a visit to my aunt Wenbourne, at her summer villa of Richmond. But I ought to premise, that I am sorry to see Clifton again looking on Frank Henley with uneasiness, and a kind of suspicion that might almost be called jealousy.

Having consulted Sir Arthur, I mentioned it, as a pleasant excursion, to Clifton; and added, as soon as Frank Henley should

come, I would desire him to hold himself in readiness. Sir Arthur
was present; and Clifton, in a pouting kind of manner, whispered
me—'Can we never go any where, without that young fellow
dogging us at the heels?'

I smiled it off, rapped him on the knuckles with my thimble, told
him he was naughty, and said we must not suffer merit to think
itself neglected. Clifton began to sing Britons strike home;[1] which
he soon changed to Rule Britannia:[2] sure tokens that he was not
pleased; for these are the tunes with which he always sings away
his volatile choler. But one of the columns, on which I raise my
system, is a determination to persist in the right. Frank Henley was
therefore invited, and accompanied us.

Clifton endeavoured to pout; but, as I did not in the least change
my good humour, knowing how necessary it was rather to increase
than diminish it, he could not long hold out, and soon became as
cheerful and as good company as usual; and his flow of spirits, and
whimsical combinations, are very exhilarating.

After dinner, my good old aunt presently got to wordy wars
with Frank; in which, as you may suppose, she had little chance
of victory. But she called in Clifton, to be her auxiliary; and he
fell into the same pettish, half-haughty, half-contemning kind of
manner, in which he had so improperly indulged, previous to the
accident of the lake, in France. I looked at him; he understood me,
and endeavoured, but rather awkwardly, to change his tone.

The conversation continued, and he was again becoming warm;
and, while Frank was laying down the law to my aunt, at which I
could perceive his tongue tingled, I took an opportunity to warn
him to beware, for that I had more than one crow to pluck with
him[3] already.

However, as the best and securest mode was, from the temper of
the parties, to put an end to the conversation, I rose, and proposed
a walk, and my proposal was accepted.

I was particularly cautious to say as little to Frank as I could,
purposely that Clifton might have no retort upon me; though a
part of my plan is to accustom him to see me just to the merits of
Frank, without indulging any unworthy suspicions. But this I did
not think a fit occasion for such experiments.

We returned to town, and I purposed, when Clifton should
come to pay me his morning visit next day, to read him a gentle

lecture. Of this he was aware; and, feeling, as I suppose, that he should make a bad serious defence, knew a comic one would better serve his turn: for his fancy and humour appear to be inexhaustible.

The first thing he did, when he entered the room, was to fall down on his knees, like a child to his school-mistress, holding his hands pressed flatly together, with a piteous face and a 'Pray, pray!' I laughed, and told him he was a very bad child. His 'Pray, pray!' was repeated, with another strangely pleasant contortion of countenance. But I still answered—'No, indeed—I should not forgive him, till I had made him truly sensible of his fault.' On which he rose from his knees, pulled out a paper fool's cap, which he had been carving and fashioning for himself, fixed it on his head, and placed himself, with a new kind of penitential countenance, in a corner; continuing such quaint mimickry, of a child in sorrow, that there was no resisting fair and downright laughter.

I still made two or three attempts to begin to argue; but they were ineffectual; they were all answered with some new antics, and I was obliged at last to say—'Well, well! I find you are sensible how much you deserve punishment; and therefore I dare say you will take care not to offend in future.'

After this, he gave the whole discourse a comic and a witty cast, embellishing it with all the flights of his rich and strong imagination, on purpose to avoid the possibility of remonstrance. This is a certain sign that it must be very painful to him; unless indeed we allow for the pleasure which he cannot but take, in exhibiting the activity of his mind. Yet painful I am sure it is. Contradiction is a thing to which he has not been accustomed. He has no doubt led the opinions of his companions; partly by conforming to and strengthening their favourite prejudices, though chiefly by his superior talents: and to be too often encountered, by any one whose intellects are more clear and consistent than his own, is a kind of degradation to which he scarcely knows how to submit.

With respect to Frank Henley, whenever he is pleading the cause of truth, he is inflexible. I have sometimes indeed known him silent, when he was hopeless of doing good: but at others I have heard him blame himself for this, and assert that we never ought to despair; for that truth, no matter how violently opposed at the moment, would revive in the mind, and do her office, when the argument and the anger should be wholly forgotten.

I believe the observation to be just. But he is no common thinker! No! I am almost persuaded he is the first of human beings! Equal, nay I have sometimes even thought superior, to Louisa herself!

As you perceive, dear friend of my heart, that I know you too well to fear offending you, I am sure you will do me the justice at the same time to confess that I do not seek to flatter.

Thus, dear Louisa, you perceive, we do not perhaps make quite so swift a progress as we could wish: but we must be satisfied. The march of knowledge is slow, impeded as it is by the almost impenetrable forests and morasses of error. Ages have passed away, in labours to bring some of the most simple of moral truths to light, which still remain overclouded and obscure. How far is the world, at present, from being convinced that it is not only possible, but perfectly practicable, and highly natural, for men to associate with most fraternal union, happiness, peace, and virtue, were but all distinction of rank and riches wholly abolished; were all the false wants of luxury, which are the necessary offspring of individual property, cut off; were all equally obliged to labour for the wants of nature, and for nothing more; and were they all afterward to unite, and to employ the remainder of their time, which would then be ample, in the promotion of art and science, and in the search of wisdom and truth!

The few arts that would then remain would be grand; not frivolous, not the efforts of cunning, not the prostitution of genius in distress, to flatter the vanity of insolent wealth and power, or the depraved taste of an ill-judging multitude; but energies of mind, uniting all the charms of fancy with all the severe beauties of consistent truth.

Is it not lamentable to be obliged to doubt whether there be a hundred people in all England, who, were they to read such a letter as this, would not immediately laugh, at the absurd reveries of the writer?—But let them look round, and deny, if they can, that the present wretched system, of each providing for himself instead of the whole for the whole, does not inspire suspicion, fear, disputes, quarrels, mutual contempt, and hatred. Instead of nations, or rather of the whole world, uniting to produce one great effect, the perfection and good of all, each family is itself a state; bound to the rest by interest and cunning, but separated by the

very same passions, and a thousand others; living together under
a kind of truce, but continually ready to break out into open war;
continually jealous of each other; continually on the defensive,
because continually dreading an attack; ever ready to usurp on the
rights of others, and perpetually entangled in the most wretched
contentions, concerning what all would neglect, if not despise, did
not the errors of this selfish system give value to what is in itself
worthless.

Well, well!——Another century, and then——!

In the meantime, let us live in hope; and, like our worthy hero,
Frank, not be silent when truth requires us to speak. We have
but to arm ourselves with patience, fortitude, and universal
benevolence.

Pardon this prattle!—The heart will sometimes expand; and it
is then weak enough to plead that the effusions of friendship claim
attention, and respect. This is among the prejudices of our education, and I know not who has hitherto overcome them all. I can
only say, dear Louisa, it is not her who is most affectionately your

                                                              A. W. ST. IVES

P.S. Clifton is quite successful with my relations: he has won
the heart of my aunt. Every moment that he was absent was
lavished in his praise. 'He was a handsome man, prodigiously handsome, exceedingly well bred, a man of great understanding, and
what was more a man of family. His pretensions were well founded;
it was a very proper connection, and was very much approved by
her.' Nor did the good old lady omit various sarcastic hints glancing at Frank, and which were not softened by the opposition he
made to her opinions. But he is too great a lover of truth to betray
it for the sake of self; and she too much an admirer of her own prejudices not to be offended at contradiction. Once more, Louisa,
we are the creatures that education has made us; and consequently
I hope we shall hereafter be wiser and better.

LETTER LXIV

Louisa Clifton to Anna Wenbourne St. Ives

Rose-Bank

AN odd circumstance, my dear Anna, has happened here, of which I think it necessary to inform you immediately.

Honest Aby has again been with us. He came and enquired for my mamma. Disappointment, chagrin, and ill-humour were broadly legible on his countenance. He talked in his odd dialect; which I cannot remember accurately enough to repeat; said he had just received a letter from Sir Arthur, from which he understood something that to him appeared to be matter of great surprise; which was that Sir Arthur intended to bestow your hand on my brother; and, in a half submissive half authoritative way, wanted to know whether it were true; and whether my mamma knew any thing of the business.

She acknowledged that such were the intentions of the two families: and he answered that, for his part, he thought they might as well think no more of the matter; muttering the words *wherewithal*, and *coal*.

Mrs. Clifton desired him to be explicit; but he continued in half sentences, repeating that the ready was not so easy to be had, and rhino was a scarce commodity. Neither could he tell what might happen. There were foreclosures, and docking of entails, and many things to be settled; and cash must come from where it could be got; but not from him, he believed.

My mamma, mild as she is, was obliged to check his growling inclination to be insolent; and then he had his whole bead-roll of fine words, with which he has so often tickled the ear of Sir Arthur, at his tongue's end; and ran them off with his usual gracious, and very humble obedient volubility.

Had I not received your last,* his discourse would have been more enigmatical to me: but, as it was, I understood him tolerably well. The bitterness of gall is at his heart. The greatness of his visible disappointment shows how high his hopes had been

---

* Letter LVIII: whence we may conclude that the letter immediately preceding this was not come to hand.

raised; and I suspect he is determined they shall not be very easily pulled down. For, after having acted all his abject humility, he could not forbear again to murmur over his threats, as he was leaving the room; and there was an air of self-sufficient confidence so apparent in his face that, I am persuaded, the obstacles he has the power to raise are much greater than you, my dear friend, have ever supposed.

I cannot describe to you, my best Anna, how deeply my mind is agitated, at times, concerning this marriage. I censure myself very severely, for seeming to indulge improper fears, one minute; and perhaps, the next, am more angry with myself for not disinterestedly pleading the cause of Frank Henley. If there could be a miracle in nature, I should think his being the son of *honest Aby* one. What can I say? My doubts are too mighty for me! I know not how, or what, to advise. The reasons you have urged are indeed weighty: yet they have never made an impression so deep upon my mind, as not to take flight, and leave their opponent arguments in some sort the victors.

Nor can I be more angry with myself, on any occasion, than I am at this moment. I distress and trouble you with my fears, when I ought to keep them to myself; unless I could determine whether they were or were not well founded. They are even increased by the recollection that, in all probability, Clifton could now much less bear disappointment than the strong-minded and generous Frank.

Then, my Anna! Should ill happen to her, from an undertaking the motive of which is so worthy, so dignified, what should I say? Should misfortune come, how could I excuse myself, for having neglected to dissuade, and to urge such reasons as have appeared to me the strongest? What could I say, but repeat the diffidence of my mind, the want of full and satisfactory conviction, and the fear of mistake?

The only buckler, with which I oppose these insurrections of reason, is the omnipotence of truth, and Anna St. Ives! And, when I recollect this, my terrors are hushed, and I think her sure of conquest.

The very affirmative tokens which Aby displayed of his own consequence, convince me however that there will be delay. How Clifton will submit to it is to be seen. His letter to my mamma is all impatience, and expectation. But I have talked with her, and she appears to be determined that nothing can be done, till Sir Arthur is ready to pay the sum he proposed.

My Anna will not be very ready to attribute this to avarice; for no one can think more highly of her than Mrs. Clifton does. But my father, at his death, left the family in absolute distress, from which she has retrieved it, by her economy and good sense: retrieved it, that is, in part; for there are still many heavy debts to pay, and mortgages to be cleared. Her plans have been severe; and of long continuance; deeply thought on, and perseveringly executed. To convince her that any part of them ought to be relinquished scarcely appears possible. Nor am I sure that, obliged as we are to conform to the present system of things, they are not all just. Beside which she is not in a state of health to support the fatigue of argument, or the pain of contradiction.

She likewise considers Sir Arthur as a weak old gentleman; who, if this opportunity were abandoned, would perhaps never have the spirit or the power, hereafter, to do his daughter justice: and she thinks that, for your sake, she ought not in the least to relax. Should you, my dear Anna, reason differently, I am still certain that you will reason charitably.

With respect to my brother, it may perhaps be fortunate, should the suspense afford you time for further trials; and we may have cause to rejoice at the accident, which had checked the precipitate impatience of passion.

Though I expect a letter from you by tomorrow's post, I think this of too much consequence to suffer any delay: I shall therefore seal it, and send it off immediately.

Heaven bless and eternally preserve my dear Anna!

L. CLIFTON

LETTER LXV

Abimelech Henley to Sir Arthur St. Ives

Wenbourne-Hill

MOST onnurable Sir, my ever onnurd Master,

Your onnur has a thrown me quite into a quandry! I couldn't
have thoft it! For why? My thofts were all in the mercifool praise
and glorification of your onnur; and I had a done nothink but say
how good and gracious your onnur had a bin, to me and mine. But
I do find, a savin and exceptin your ever onnurable onnur, 'tis all
a gull queerum![1] Whereof the face of affairs is quite transmogrified![2] And so, ast for raisin the wind of twenty thousand pounds,
I find the think is neither komparissuble[3] nur a parallel to common
sense. For why? It is not to be had. A man's money is his own,
your onnur; and when a has got it, there's as good law for he as for
a dooke. Always a savin and exceptin your most exceptionable
onnur, as in duty boundin. For as I wus a sayin, your onnur, when
a man has a got the super nakullums,[4] who shall take it from him?
Because why, it is his own.

If so be as the whats and the whys and the wherefores had a bin
a forth cummin, why then the shiners might a seen the light of
day, mayhap. But a man's son, why a's his son; a's his own; a's
his goods and chattels, and law and rite; bein of the race of his
own begettin, feedin, and breedin. Whereby I cannot but say, love
me love my dog. Always a savin and exceptin your onnurable
onnur, as aforesaid.

And ast for the rhino, why some do save, and some do spend,
and some do hold, and some do let go, and some do have, and
some do want. Whereupon if so be as he as a has the most a may
be as good as another. Why not? Always a savin and exceptin your
ever onnurable onnur, as aforesaid. But when so be as a man has
the wherewithalls, why a let him begin to hold up his head, I say.
Why not? For why? It is the omnum gathurum[5] that makes the
man. And if I do a doff my hat to my betters, there a be and a bin
the whats and the whys and the wherefores for it. But I can a doff
my hat, or I can a keep it on my head; and mayhap a can begin to
look my betters in the face, as well as another. Why not? Always

a savin and exceptin your ever exceptionable onnur, as in duty boundin.

And ast for famalies and names, I axes nothink about they. A tell me who has the most kole! I axes that! Mayhap Henley may be as good a name as Clifton. And ast for famalies, why it is notorious that Adam and Eve wus the begettin of us all; always a savin and exceptin your onnurable onnur. Whereof a there's an end of that.

Whereby your onnurable onnur wus a menshinnin the mort-gages; and of a seein of every think a treeved[1] and settled, afore your onnur do die. But as thinks do be likely to turn out, why every man for himself, and God for us all. There be foreclosures mayhap, that a be to be thoft of. For why? There a be wheels within wheels.

If so be indeed as if thinks had a turned up trumps, why then ay, it would a bin summut; all smooth and go softly, and there might a behappened to be sunshine and fair weather at Wenbourne-Hill. For why? Every think would then a bin clear and above board. Thinks would a then a bin safe and sure to all sides; and your onnurable onnur would mayhap a seen that your onnur would a lost nothink by the bargain. For why? Missee my younk lady might a paradventered to have had all, in the upshot; and an ever gracious and glorious and mercifool my younk lady missee she would a then a bin. Whereby as matters be likely to turn out, why thinks must a take their course. Thof a mayhap folks may go further and fare worse. Whereof if so be as lives have a bin saved, by land and by water, and a man's son is thoft to be somebody, why mayhap a may not a take it so kindly to be chouse flickurd.[2]

For my part, I thoft as thof all thinks had a bin as good as settled; and that in all partikillers missee my younk lady, of ever mercifool affability, would a bin left to please herself. Why not? When precious lives have a bin saved, and when there a bin shootins, and leapins, and swimmins, and sousins, I say as aforesaid, why that's a summut; and a man's own son mayhap won't a like to be flamdudgind.[3]

And so as to mortgages to be paid off, your onnurable onnur, why mayhap that's a sooner said nur done. For I say as aforesaid, that it seems as if whereby, if it had not a bin for some folks, some folks would a now a bin in their salt water graves: always a savin and exceptin your ever exceptionable onnur, as in duty boundin.

Whereby take me ritely, your onnurable onnur, I means nothink
amiss. If thinks be a skew whift, why it be no fault of mine. It is
always a savin and exceptin of your onnurable onnur: being as I
be ready to glorify to the whole world of all your futur lovin kindness of blessins of praise, a done and a testified to me and mine.

Whereof as to frippery jerry my gingle red coats and cockades,[1]
why they be nothink of my seekin. For why? They be the betokens
of the warnins of the signs of the bloody cross of antichrist, and
the whore of Babilon, and of the dispensation of the kole, and the
squitter squanderin[2] of the wherewithalls, and the supernakul-
lums. Whereby an honest man's son may become to be bamboozild,
and addle brained,[3] and foistee fubbd,[4] belike, as finely as his
neighbours. So that if so be as I have a bin a ponderaitin[5] that there
a be nothink to be got by it. Always a savin and exceptin of the
blessins of praise, and mercifool glory, of your ever exceptionable
onnurable onnur's lovin kindness, and goodness; and every think
of that there umbel and very submissive obedient kind, as in duty
boundin.

Witch is all at present, beginnin and endin to the everlastin
power of almighty joys eternal; umbelly beggin leave to superscribe meself

ABIMELECH HENLEY

LETTER LXVI

Abimelech Henley to Frank Henley

Wenbourne-Hill

WHY what be all a this here? What is it that a be about, dolt?
Here's a rumpus! Here's a fine to do! You be a pretty squire
Nicodemus Nincompoop![6] You a son of my own begettin, feedin,
and breedin! You seeze the fulhams![7] Why they would a draw
your i teeth for ee! Marry come fairly! You the jennyalogy of my
own body and loins? No, by lady! And so squire my lord Timothy
Doodle has a bin flib gibberd,[8] and queerumd,[9] after all? Thof if
so be as notwithstandin a that Missee, my younk lady, had as good
as a bin playin at catch me come kiss me,[10] and all in the dark

with'n; and thof I had a sifflicated[1] the Sir Dandle Dunderpate, a
here a do stand, a suckin his thumbs! Thof so be as how I told him
to make up to Missee, and the twenty thousand pounds! What, a
did n't I put words into your mouth, as good as a ready butterd,
as I may say? What, a did n't I give ee all your pees and cues?
Because as why, I did a know a wus a quaumee[2] kintlin.[3] And so a
has played with the mouse and has a lost it at last! A fine kettle of
fish a's made on't! Whereof forsooth, so as that now as that all
o'the fat's in the fire, why I must a be set to catch the colt if I can.
Why ay, to be sure! Whereby if so be as the Gaby goose[4] may now
go barefoot! And a whose fault is that? No! A would n't a be akin
to a good estate; not he!

But harkee me chit! Mind what I be about to say to ee, Simon the
simple, and mayhap thinks may become to be komparissuble[5] and
parallel to the yellow hammers[6] and the chink,[7] for all of all this
here rig royster.[8] For why? I can put a spoke in the wheel of the
marriage act and deed. Madam Clifton wonnot a budge a finger,
to the signin and sealin of her gratification of applause, whereby
as if so be as that the kole a be not a forth cummin, down on the nail
head. And where now might Timothy Tipkin[9] sifflicate[10] that it
may behappen to be for to come from? Pummel thy pumkin, and
a tell me that, Peter Grievous.[11] Where, but out of my pouche,
Gaby? That is, I first havin and holdin the wherewithalls, and the
whys, and the wherefores. Do you take me now? So that forsooth,
some folks may behappen to cry peccavi.[12]

Whereby mind what I do tell ee. For why? I've as good as a told
Sir Arthur the wind is a not to be raised for any of a sitch of a
flammbite[13] of a tale of a tub.[14] Whereby I a told'n a bit of my mind.
And if so be as if a will wince, a mayhap it may come to pass that
I can kick. A shall find I was not a bred and a born and a begotten
yesterday. An a champ upon it, let'n. An a will run rusty,[15] mayhap a may belike to get his head in a hedge. So mind what I do say
to ee; and tell 'em that they may a behappen to find that your father
is somebody, and that you are his son. A tell 'em that.

So do you strike up to Missee boldly. Mind what ee be at; and
let 'em like it or leave it. For if so be as when a man has a got the
Marygolds, why then let'n begin to speak for himself. Why not?

Whereby I have now once again given the costard monger[16] his
pees and his cues. So that if so be as if a do find that sweet sauce be

good for goose, why let'n a give his tongue an oilin. But if so be as a do find a be Sir Arthur Crabvarjus o'the high ropes,[1] why then says you, look ee me says you, honest Aby is my father; and when a man has a got the wherewithalls, why a begins to be somebody, and mayhap a's as good as another. A tell 'em that.

And so no more at present; a savin and exceptin of the all bountifool glory of the everlastin praise of joys eternal, livin and hopin for time to repent us of all our manifold sins, and of a dyin in peace and charity with all men. Whereby we shall be sure to partake of the resurrection of the just sheep, and of the virgin oil in our lamps, and of the martyrs and of the profits and of the saints everlastin rest.

ABIMELECH HENLEY

LETTER LXVII

Frank Henley to Oliver Trenchard

London, Grosvenor Street

OLIVER, it is not half an hour since I ended writing one of the most undutiful and bitter Philippics, that ever was addressed by a son to his father. I say undutiful, because this wise world has decreed that to abhor, reprove, and avoid vice in a father, instead of being the performance of a duty, is offensive to all moral feeling.

I have just received a letter from him, chiding and blaming me, with his usual acrimony, for a supposed want of cunning; and for not aiding him in what I perceive now to be the design he has most at heart; which is my marriage with the divine Anna. He has almost disgusted me with myself, for having, though ineffectually, endeavoured to aid him so well. Nay I have been tempted to shew his letter to Sir Arthur. But, on recollection, I have thrown the Philippic I mentioned into the fire; and have determined on silence: for I perceive harm that may result from a contrary conduct, but no good. To swerve, to the right or the left, from the direct path of principle and truth, because of the selfish, narrow, and unwise views of others, is to be weak and culpable.

What, indeed, has relationship to do with truth? No human ties can bind us to error: and, while we rigorously act according to the rules of truth, as far as we know them, the comments, mistakes, disapprobation, and even resentment, of relation, friend, or father, ought to be disregarded.

I must own, however, I have still the folly to feel additional grief that errors of so mean, so selfish, so dishonest a nature should have taken such firm possession of the mind of my father: and I am afraid I could support them better in the person of another.

Having determined not to write to him, I have written to thee, to give vent and relief to these feelings. Of course thou wilt tell me if thou seest any reason, which I have not discovered, why I ought to communicate the contents of his letter to Sir Arthur; whom he vaunts of having in his power, and whom he is determined not to supply with money, for the projected marriage with Clifton. My conviction is that to shew this letter would but increase their mutual anger, and render compliance on my father's part, whose temper I know, still less probable than it is; if less it can be.

Adieu.

F. HENLEY

LETTER LXVIII

Anna Wenbourne St. Ives to Louisa Clifton

London, Grosvenor Street

I WRITE, at present, to my dear Louisa, that by writing I may divert the perturbation of my mind. But I must begin calmly; for I have so much to say, that I scarcely know what to say first. Our mutual conjectures, concerning honest Aby, are in part verified. I conclude thus, not from having seen any more of his letters, but from knowing more have been received; which, instead of having been shewn me, have, if I do not mistake, thrown Sir Arthur into some of the most serious reflections he ever experienced. I never knew him so grave, thoughtful, and pensive, as he has been for some days——

My brother too!—But more of him by and by.

Observing the efforts of reflection, and desirous of aiding, alleviating, or increasing them, as should be most prudent, I took an opportunity, after breakfast, when Sir Arthur and I were alone, of speaking to him; and we had the following dialogue.

I think, sir, you seem more thoughtful lately than usual. I am afraid there is something disturbs you. Can I—?

No, no—Nothing—Not much. Worldly matters, which you do not understand.

I am far from wishing, sir, to intrude into your private concerns; except they were such as might relate to me, and—

Mere money matters, child; of which you have no knowledge— [We paused; Sir Arthur seeming as if his mind laboured with a subject which he knew not how to begin]—Where is Mr. Henley?

Retired to his apartment, sir. This is his time of day for study.

He is a very learned young man.

Not so learned I believe, sir, as wise.

Are not they the same thing?

I think not, sir.

Well then, a very wise young man—You think him so; do you not, Anna?

I do, sir.

You have a very high opinion of him?

I have, sir.

Perhaps a higher than of any other young gentleman, with whom you are acquainted.

I am indeed afraid, sir, I have never seen his equal.

Humph!—You—You are not sparing of your praise.

You asked me a question, sir, and would not have me guilty of equivocation, or falsehood.

No, child: I am pleased with your sincerity; and I hope and expect you will be equally sincere in every thing you say.

Of that, sir, you may be assured.

What are your reasons for thinking so exceedingly well of Mr. Henley?

My reasons, sir!

Yes; your reasons.

I own I am a little surprised at this question from you, sir; who have been a witness to so many of his virtues, and their effects.

[I then briefly recapitulated the progress of Frank from a child in virtue, insisting on the numerous proofs of which we so lately had been witnesses. I recounted the histories of the highwayman, and of Peggy and her husband; the adventure of the lake; and the protection we found from his skill, strength, and courage at Deal; not forgetting the attendant incidents of each, nor neglecting to give such brief but strong touches as feeling dictated.]

I must own, he is a very extraordinary young man!

Yet we can know but a part of the good effected by a mind so active, and so virtuous. Though I perhaps know more than you, sir.

Ay!—What? Let me hear.

You think me partial already, sir.

No, no. Let me hear.

The very night we arrived at Paris, he prevented Mr. Clifton and the Count de Beaunoir from fighting a duel.

Indeed!

Yet never mentioned it; nor perhaps ever would, had not we afterward met with the Count at the Chateau de Villebrun.

That was very odd!

Nay more, sir, but a day or two before that he saved the life of Mr. Clifton, he had submitted to the insult of a blow from him, rather than fight a duel.

A blow——?

He does not want courage, sir, you are convinced.

No, no—It is what he calls one of his principles not to fight duels—He is a very extraordinary young man!——And not I think much like his father.

As opposite, sir, as day and night, grace and deformity, virtue and vice.

You think but indifferently of Abimelech.

I think very ill of him, sir. I think him selfish, cunning, covetous, and dishonest.

Dishonest?

In the eye of equity, though not perhaps of the law.

Why did not you tell me your opinion sooner?

I did, sir.

I do not remember it.

No, sir: it made no impression, because you did not think it true.

May be so—And you do not find any of these bad qualities in the son?

Q

Bad!—If all the highest gifts of intellect; if memory, perspicuity, perception, and genius; added to all the virtues, wisdom,
benevolence, philanthropy, and self-denial; if to be the active
friend of man and the declared enemy of error, and of that alone;
if these can entitle him to esteem, admiration, reverence and praise,
why then esteem, admiration, reverence and praise are justly his
due.

You are warm in your encomiums.

Indeed, sir, I think I am cold.

How so?

Because my encomiums are so very much beneath his deserts.

Anna——[Sir Arthur assumed a very serious tone, and look.]

Proceed, sir—Do not be afraid of questioning me. You shall
find, my dear father, a child that will answer truly, affectionately,
and I hope dutifully.

[I kissed his hand, pressed it, and wet it with an unwilling tear.
The impassioned heart, Louisa, will sometimes rebel against the
cold apathy of reason; but such revolt is but of short duration.]

Are you aware, Anna, of the state of your own affections?

I think so, sir.

You think?

Well then, I am certain.

You say Mr. Henley has no equal?

In my opinion, none, sir.

Look you there!

But do you think, sir, I will not emulate the virtues I admire: or
that, because I have a just sense of his worth, I will trespass against
my duties to the world, my sex, my family and my father?

Anna!—Child!—[The tears stood in Sir Arthur's eyes. He
stretched out both hands, and I flew to his arms.—After a short
interval of silence, Sir Arthur proceeded.] Tell me, Anna: What
are your thoughts of Mr. Clifton?

I think him, sir, a very extraordinarily gifted gentleman.

But not a Mr. Henley?

Not at present, sir. Time I hope will make him one.

No, child, never.

Why so, sir?

I cannot tell why, but I am sure it never will. They are two very
different men.

Mr. Clifton, sir, has uncommon powers of mind.

May be so; I suppose so; I only say they are very different men. Their tempers are different, their opinions, their manners, every thing.

I do not imagine, sir, they will ever exactly resemble each other; but I think myself sure they will continually approach.

Indeed!

Yes, sir.

May be so; but I own I doubt it. Mr. Clifton is a gentleman, both by birth and education.

That I own, sir, may be a great disadvantage; but—

Disadvantage, child!

Our conversation was here interrupted, Louisa, by a letter brought me from my brother. Read it, and judge of what I felt.

'Dear Sister,

'I am a ruined man, unless I could command a sum of money which it is impossible for me to raise. I last night lost three thousand pounds, upon honour, which I am totally unable to pay. And, what is worse, I did not lose it to a gentleman, but to a sharper; who, the very last throw he made, let a third die fall upon the table. But this is of no avail; he is an unprincipled, daring fellow; denies any foul play with imprecations and threats, and insists on being paid. I know you cannot help me to such a sum; and I suppose my father will not. For my part, I can neither pay it nor think of living, under the disgrace and infamy which must follow.

EDWARD ST. IVES'

Sir Arthur saw my agitation; and, had I been desirous, it would have been difficult to have concealed the letter, or its contents. I shewed it him, and his perplexity and pain I believe exceeded mine. It was impossible, he said, for him immediately to pay the money: it would greatly distress him at any time. It likewise shewed the deplorable state of my brother's affairs. The Edgemoor estate, every thing gone!

Sir Arthur knew not how to act. I was in a tremor, and could not persuade myself there was any way so safe as that of consulting Frank Henley. This I proposed; Sir Arthur instantly acquiesced, and he was sent for down. After reading the letter, the only expedient, he said, which he could think of, was to visit my brother; either accompanied by or under the sanction of Sir Arthur. My father absolutely refused to go himself; but he gave Frank full powers to act for him, and as he should think most prudent. Before he went, he endeavoured to calm our fears; saying he thought it impossible, if such a rascal as this gambler were properly dealt with, but that he must be glad to renounce his claim.

Frank is now absent on this desperate business; sent, by my officiousness, to encounter a practised ruffian!

What could I do? A brother threatening his own life! Yet what is the life of such a brother, to that of Frank Henley?

I hope he is not in danger! I think I was obliged to do as I have done; though indeed I am very ill satisfied with myself.

The chief purpose of my writing this long dialogue, which I had with Sir Arthur, was to ward off fears: for surely it is but a folly to anticipate misfortune. I should else not have written till tomorrow. And must I alarm my friend, by sending this before I know the result of so dangerous an affair? I think I ought not.

Clifton has just been with me. It could not long escape his quick penetration that my thoughts were deeply occupied. He was earnest with me to accompany him, in the evening, to see Garrick in Richard III,[1] but could not prevail. He taxed me with absence of mind, and was kindly earnest to know why I was so serious. I told him at last it was a family concern; and this did but increase his eagerness to know of what nature. I was obliged to own he was too impetuous to be trusted at such a critical minute. Frank Henley I hoped would effect every thing that could be done.

He repeated, with great chagrin, 'Frank Henley!——He was sorry not to be thought as worthy of a trust of danger, and as zealous for the honour of the family, as even the favourite Frank Henley.'

I replied my mind was not enough at ease, to give a proper answer to such a remark; which however was far from a just one.

He felt the rebuke, and apologized; with praises of Frank Henley's prudence, and accusations of his own intemperate haste. 'But wise people knew how to be cool. Prudence and wisdom were cold blooded qualities. Good or harm, of any moment, if done by him, must be done in a kind of passion. It was his temper, his

nature, which he tried in vain to correct. Neither was he quite
certain that such a temper was not the best: at least it was the most
open and honest.——'

I told him he was mistaken in most of these fancies: but he
seemed not to hear me, and went on——

'He could not but own, he was piqued, and almost grieved, to
find he must despair of meriting the preference; and that he was
destined to find a rival, where rivalship ought perhaps least to be
expected.'

My temper of mind did not permit me to argue with him; I
could much rather have indulged the woman, and burst into tears;
but I subdued my feelings, and could think of no better mode of
reproving him than to retire. I accordingly withdrew, without
answering, and left him making ineffectual struggles with his pride,
his consciousness of error, and his desire of being heard, and
reconciled to himself, and me.

He told me, yesterday, he was surprised at not receiving an
answer from Mrs. Clifton, and at the silence of Sir Arthur. I made
no reply, because I had not considered how I could address myself
to him with the best effect. But I mean, when he mentions it again,
to inform him of the probability of delay. I, like you, my friend,
think delay rather a fortunate incident than otherwise.

But why, Louisa, should you suppose it necessary to justify the
conduct of Mrs. Clifton to me? I am well acquainted with her
virtues, and the purity of her intentions. Whether I should act
with exactly the same caution, under the same circumstances, is
more than I can say: but neither can I say that my prudence, and
foresight, would equal hers.——I think I hear Frank Henley. I am
all impatience and alarm. Adieu.

                                              A. W. ST. IVES

LETTER LXIX

Anna Wenbourne St. Ives to Louisa Clifton

London, Grosvenor-Street

FRANK has this moment left me. He is still in pursuit of this business, which is by no means brought to a conclusion. He has been with my brother, and has met the gambler; with whom two very characteristic dialogues have passed, which Frank has repeated with considerable humour. My brother was only present at and bore his part in the second. The man is a perfect master of his vile trade; a practised duellist; as expert, Frank says, in killing of men as in cogging of dice.[1] A Hibernian bravo; determined to pursue the most desperate means to effect his purpose.

Energy in vice or virtue, Frank remarks, is the characteristic of the Irish. It is a noble quality, of which no nation perhaps has more, if any so much; but it is frequently abused by them, and made productive of the most hateful effects.

Frank was with my brother in his dressing-room, when the man came and was shewn into an anti-chamber by the servant. Edward was sufficiently unwilling to see him, and readily agreed to the proposal Frank made, of first conversing with him, as my brother's friend.

Frank accordingly went to him, and says he was struck at the sight of the man, being much deceived if he be not an old acquaintance. I was and still am surprised at what Frank told me; but he begged I would suspend my curiosity, till he himself should be better satisfied; and proceeded with his dialogue.

Your name I believe, sir, is Mr. Mac Fane.

At your sarvice, sir.

I am the friend of Captain St. Ives.

Then to be sure, sir, you are a gintleman, and a man of honour. I am a gintleman and a man of honour mysilf.

Do you say that from your conscience, sir?

From my conscience? Ay, sir! Why not? When all my debts due are duly and truly paid, why I shall have ten thousand pounds in my pocket.

There are people, sir, heretical enough to suppose that even ten thousand pounds are no absolute proof of honour.

No, indeed!—Why then, for those very scrupulous people, I have an excellent pair of proof pistols, which I believe are absolute enough. Because I would take the odds that they would hit a bird's eye flying.

Those arguments I own are difficult to withstand.

Stand!—Faith, and if any man shall think proper to stand, I will fetch him down.—[Remember, Louisa, I am imitating this man's language, as delivered by Frank; though I believe my memory is tolerably correct.] But I should be proud to speak a word with your friend; becase that will be more to the point.

He requested me to inform you, sir, he should be glad if you would delay your visit an hour or two; and I think it will be the safest; for you I perceive, sir, are rather warm; and his temper, as you may imagine, cannot be so cool, just at present, as usual.

His temper!—Faith, sir, and the devil a care care I about his temper! And as for warm and cool, I can be either, or neither, or both. I have won the money, and the Captain must pay it; or else d'ye see, sir——!

You'll hit the bird's eye flying?

Ay; flying, or lying, or any way!—However, I will take a turn and come back by and by. I have two or three calls to make on some peers of my acquaintance. I am a man of nice honour, sir.

And you imagine, nice though it is, that your honour is suspected.

By my soul, sir, I imagine no such thing. Because as why, I think it would not be very safe. I tell you very seriously, sir, that I have a sure sacrit to cure any impartinent suspicions of my honour; as I beg you would inform your friend, Captain St. Ives; who, being a man of honour himsilf, knows what belongs to the business. These, sir, are tender points, with every gintleman. And so, sir, I wish you a good morning for the present.

Frank says he was desirous of conversing with the man, that he might discover his character, previous to his concerting any plan of action.

After he was gone, he endeavoured to lead my brother into a discussion on the state of his affairs. But Edward avoided all detail; satisfying himself with affirming he was a ruined man, and unable to pay the sum. He had no objection to meet the fellow in the field; though certainly the chances were a hundred to one in his disfavour. He might as well die that way as any other. With respect to victory, of that there were but little hopes, with so expert a ruffian, who had practised pistol shooting till he was sure of his mark, which my brother had wholly neglected.

Frank then enquired at what house the money had been lost; and found it had been at one of the common receptacles for gamblers of the second order. No person was present but the groom porter, whom Frank immediately determined to see, and went thither for that purpose. But, on enquiry at the house, he found the man had absconded.

He returned, and had some difficulty to convince my brother that his honour would not suffer by delay; for it was plain that Mr. Mac Fane was resolved on immediately pushing the matter to an extreme. However, on communicating his own conjectures concerning this man of nice honour, Edward consented to permit Frank to act in his behalf. Frank observes that our men of fashion seem agreed to overlook a portion of insolence from these gamblers, under the affectation of despising them, which the tamest of the fine gentlemen among them would scarcely brook from each other.

In about two hours, Mr. Mac Fane returned; and, being introduced to my brother and Frank, another conversation very similar to the former ensued. The man began.

Your servant, gintlemen. I told you last night, Captain, that I would give you a call this morning: and as it is an affair in which your honour is concerned, why I was determined to be very punctual. Becase why, you know, I am extremely nice and punctual mysilf, upon points of honour.

I am sorry to be obliged to tell you, sir, that Captain St. Ives neither knows nor owns any such thing; and that I have good reason to believe the very reverse.

Sir!—You—! [Frank says the man put on the true look of a desperado, resolved on mischief if opposed: but that, after pausing a moment, he began, with a kind of humorous anger, to rub the side of his face, as if it were benumbed] Faith, on recollection, I believe I got a bit of a cold last night, which makes me rather dull of hearing.

Sir, I repeat—

Repate!—Boo!—There is no occasion to repate, at all at all.
I remember very well that my friend, Captain St. Ives, owes me
three thousand guineas; and, it being a dibt of honour, why, to be
sure he will pay it, without any repating about the matter.

Sir, said my brother, give me leave to tell you—

That you will pay me. You need not tell me that.

Sir—!

There never yet was man that refused to pay me, but oh! The
almighty thunder! I gave him a resate in full for the dibt. I made
him repint after his death the day that ever he was born.

There's the door, sir, said Frank.

Faith and I know there's the door, sir; but where's the money,
Captain?—That is, I don't mane the ready cash: that is not to be
expected, from a gentleman—A bond in these cases you know,
Captain, is customary.

Sir, there's the door.

I find that your friend, here, is disposed to be a little upon the
Captain Copperthorne[1] this morning; and so I shall leave you for
the present to consider the matter. I have no doubt but I shall
hear from you, Captain, in the course of the four and twenty hours.
It is now full three weeks since I heard the whiz of a bullet; and
I would advise you, as a friend, not to waste any of your powder
and ball upon the prisent occasion. It would only be a buz and
blow by business, Captain: for, by the holy limb of Luke, I never
yet saw lead that durst look me in the face.

We should be glad to be alone, sir.

Faith, sir, you may be as bluff as you please; but, when the
Captain is a little cool, I shall expict to receive a bit of a message
from him; or may I never look on the bald pate of the blessed Peter
but he shall receive a bit of a message from me. And so once more,
gintlemen, good morning.

Frank did not lose a moment after he was gone, but hastened
home; first to inform us of his proceedings, thus far; and next to
make the researches on which he is now absent. Here, therefore,
my dear Louisa, I must pause; and once again subscribe myself,
most affectionately,

                                          A. W. ST. IVES

P.S. I have reason to believe that Clifton is more seriously
offended than I ever knew him before. When I refused going to the

play with him, he persisted in saying I might change my mind
before night, and that he would come again in that hope. His
manner of parting with me, after being told Frank was entrusted
with a business which we had not dared confide to him, was, as I
have described, unusual, and accompanied with more coldness
and reserve than either of us had ever before assumed. It is now
eight o'clock, and I have not seen him since. If he have resolution
enough to keep away the whole evening, which I suspect he will
have, the proof of the truth of my conjectures will be indubitable.

I know not, when he comes to hear the business, whether he
will be convinced that he was less proper to transact it than Frank;
otherwise I should not be sorry, could he but certainly feel himself wrong: for it is by a repetition of such lessons that the good we
intend must be effected.

Be it as it will, let us neither recede nor slacken our endeavours.
I suspect that every worthy task must be a task of difficulty, and
often of danger.

LETTER LXX

Anna Wenbourne St. Ives to Louisa Clifton

London, Grosvenor Street

FRANK is returned; and, as usual, crowned with success.

I had been puzzling myself to no purpose, concerning Mr. Mac
Fane being one of our old acquaintance. It appears he was the
accomplice of the highwayman, Webb, the brother of Peggy, who
was shot by Frank at Turnham Green. He forebore to tell me, in
part because he had not time to connect and relate the grounds of
his suspicion; though his chief reason was lest a whisper, heard by
Laura or any other, should have betrayed and overturned his whole
scheme.

He went immediately to question Mrs. Clarke, concerning her
nephew. She knew not what was become of him; for, after having
determined to go abroad, he changed his mind; and, being reproved and discountenanced by her, he had forborne his visits.
She had even refused to hear his name mentioned. But she believed

her niece, Peggy, had some knowledge of him; though she was not certain.

Frank thought proper to confide in Mrs. Clarke, and they immediately went in quest of the niece. From her they learned that he had been promoted to the office of groom-porter at a gambling house: and in fact he proved to be the very man who had been present at the transaction between Edward and Mr. Mac Fane.

Peggy was next questioned concerning his present hiding-place. She was confused; she stammered, and trembled. Was not her brother in danger? Could she be sure no harm would come to him?——At last however the mild and humane reasoning of Frank, and the authority of Mrs. Clarke subdued, her terrors— He was in the house.

It seems the moment he knew it was Captain St. Ives, my brother, whom Mr. Mac Fane had been plundering, he refused to appear, or have any further concern in the affair: and being violently threatened by the gambler, who wanted to force him to come forward as his witness, he concealed himself for fear; not knowing to what excess so desperate a man might be carried by his passions. He and Peggy had just been debating on the propriety of appearing to bear testimony in my brother's behalf; but were too much alarmed to decide.

Frank lost no time. He took the man with him in the carriage, and hastened to my brother's apartments; where he left him, and immediately drove away to Bow-street, to procure the assistance of the police. Previous to this, Mr. Mac Fane, having received some intimation that there was danger, had written to my brother. The following is a copy of his letter; and no bad specimen of the man.

'SIR,

I find you think that there is a bit of a blunder in this business, and that you doubt the doctors.[1] I understand too that Webb, the groom porter, is under obligations to your honourable family; for which raison the lying spalpeen[2] pretends that he smoaked a bale of Fulhams[3]—To be sure it is all a mistake —I am a man of honour; and you, Captain, are a man of honour also; for which I give up the coal to your ginerosity; in raison whereof hush is the word. And so in that case, I remain your most obadient humble sarvant. But if not, why the bull dogs must bark.

PHELIM MAC FANE'

Is it not a pity, Louisa, that so much courage and ability should be perverted to such vile ends? The man, by means of the wealth he had so rapidly collected in this manner, had secured more than one spy among the Bow-street runners. This we learned from Peggy's brother; and it is confirmed by the event; for he has forsaken all his former haunts, and it is conjectured is either gone off for the continent, or, which is more probable, is lying concealed till he can discover how far he is in danger. He was constantly provided with disguises, has been to sea, and is intimately acquainted with the manners of the vulgar; so that, were any strict search made, he would not easily be caught. But he need not fear; his supposed enemy takes no delight in blood; and this he will probably soon learn, and soon again be upon the town.

You wonder, no doubt, how Frank should recognise a man who, attempting to rob us on a dark night, had stationed himself at the head of the çarriage. Had he seen no more of him, he would have been in little danger of detection. But, on one of the visits which Frank made to Webb, the brother of Peggy, he had met him on the stairs. Mr. Mac Fane as he descended was opposite the window on the landing place, and his face was full in the light; while Frank could scarcely be seen by him, being then several steps below him. His countenance is a remarkable one; it has a deep scar above the left eye; and Frank, suspecting him to be the accomplice of the man he was going to visit, had fixed it in his memory.

Frank has since been talking very seriously with this brother of Peggy; and appears to have convinced him that his present profession is as much that of a thief as his former. However, in this short space of time, without understanding the vile arts of a gambler, he has collected between two and three hundred pounds. Such is the folly with which money is squandered at these places. While Mr. Mac Fane is absent, he thinks himself in no danger; and should he return, he has been promised the protection of our family, which he thinks a sufficient guarantee; being rather afraid of him as a desperado than as an accuser. Webb has therefore agreed to take a shop, and exercise his trade as a master. He is a man of quick intellects; and, notwithstanding all that he has done, has many good propensities. As a proof of these, his poor sister, the kind Peggy, has infinite affection for him; and is sure now that he will do well.

Sir Arthur and Edward have both been very sincere and hearty in their thanks to Frank: to which he answers, and answers truly, it was a stroke rather of good fortune than of foresight. But he has gained himself a character; and they are partly of opinion, that every thing must prosper which he undertakes. Aunt Wenbourne too overflows in his praise. Edward is her favourite; and Frank stands now almost as high on her list as he was but a little while ago the reverse; for Edward is continually talking of him to her, and every word he says is orthodox. But opinions like these are too light, too full of prejudice, too mutable to be of much value.

Clifton kept away all the evening; however, after hearing the whole story, he was obliged to acknowledge that, let his other qualities be what they would, he could not have been so successful as Frank in this affair; because he could have known nothing of Mr. Mac Fane. But he did not forget that this was an accident, unforeseen at the time when Frank was trusted.

My constant rule, of equanimity of temper, has restored him to his wonted good-humour. But I perceive he regrets the possibility of any man equalling him in the esteem of those whose friendship he cultivates. Alas! Why does he not rather seek to surpass them, than to envy their virtues?

He says he will propose an eulogium on Frank, and give a prize himself to the French Academy; for he finds he will never get sufficiently praised in England. He never knew so eternal a theme for panegyric. In fine, it is evident, in despite of his efforts to conceal it, that his jealousy increases: and I suspect he feels this last decision against him more sensibly than any preceding circumstance.

Adieu. Most truly and dearly, your own

A. W. ST. IVES

LETTER LXXI

Coke Clifton to Guy Fairfax

London, Dover Street

WAR! Fairfax, war!—It is declared!—Open war!—My wrathful
spirits are in a blaze, and I am determined. Hear and blame me if
you can. But do I not know you? Does not the temper of your
letters tell me you will applaud my just anger, and fixed revenge?

Yes, Fairfax, longer to palliate, or wilfully be blind to the partial
edicts and haughty ordonnances of this proud beauty, were idiotism! She has presumed too far; I am not quite so tame a creature as
she supposes. She shall find I am not the clay, but the potter. I will
mould, not be moulded. Poltron as I was, to think of sinking into
the docile, domesticated, timid animal called husband! But the
lion's paws are not yet pared; beware then, my princess!

The lady would carry it with a high hand, Fairfax. But let her!
If I not note her freaks, if I forget her imperious caprice, if my
embittered mind slumber in its intents, say not I am the proud-
spirited Clifton you once knew; that prompt, bold, and inflexible
fellow, whom arrogance could rouse, and injury inflame, but a
suffering, patient ass; a meek pitiful thing, such as they would
make me!

Wonder not that I now am angry, but that I have so long been
torpid. A little phrensy has restored the palsied soul to life, and
again has put its powers in motion. I'll play no more at questions
and commands—Or, if I do, it shall only be to make sure of my
game.

I have been reproved, silenced, tongue-tied, brow-beaten;
have made myself an ape, been placed behind the door, and have
shewed tricks for her diversion. But I am not muzzled yet: they
shall find me one of the *feræ naturæ*.[1]

A most excellent project, forsooth! When I am sufficiently
familiarized to contradiction, rebuke, fillips[2] on the forehead, and
raps on the knuckles, she will then hear me my prayers, pack me
off peaceably to bed for tonight, and graciously bestow a pat and
a promise upon me for tomorrow! There is danger in the whim,
lady; beauteous though you are, and invincible as you may think

yourself. Model me!———No!—I am of a metal which not even your files can touch. You cannot knead, dough-bake, and temper me to your leaven.

Fairfax, she had fascinated me! I own it! There is such incantation, in the small circle of her eye, as mortal man scarcely can resist! I adored her; nay still adore! But she knows me not. I have a soul of fire. She has driven me beyond the limits of patience.

Her wisdom degenerates into rhodomontade. She will prescribe the hour and minute when she shall begin to love. She does not pretend to love me yet; and, if she did, her looks, her manner would betray the falsehood of her heart.

Yet let me not wrong her, vexed though I am. Double dealing is not her error: she is sufficiently sincere.

Why would I hide it from myself? Her partialities all lead another way: ay and her passions too, if passions she have. But this most incomprehensible, this tormenting, incoherent romance of determining not to have any, I believe from my soul, in part produces the effect she intends, and almost enables her to keep her determination!

Still and eternally, this fellow! This Frank! Oh that I were an Italian, and that my conscience would permit me to deal him the stilletto!—Let him beware!———He is employed, preferred, praised! It is eulogium everlasting! Had Fame as many trumpets as she has tongues and lies, they would all be insufficient. And not only she but the whole family, father, brother, aunts, the devil knows who, each grateful soul is oozing out the froth of its obligations!

Had they less cause, perhaps I should be less irritated: but he has rescued the poor being of a brother, Edward St. Ives, who had neither courage nor capacity to rescue himself, from the gripe of a gambler. This Edward, who is one of the king's captains, God bless him, and who has spent his fortune in learning the trade, not of a man of war, but of a man of fashion, having lost what ready money he had, staked his honour against a cogger of dice,[1] and was presently tricked out of three thousand guineas; which he was too poor in pocket to pay, and, if I guess right, too poor in spirit afterward to face the ruffian whom he had made his companion.

So Mr. Henley, and it please, you, was chosen, by father and daughter. Though she owns she proposed it first; for she does not

scruple to own all which she does not scruple to act. The holy
mission was his, to dole out salutary documents of reproof, and
apothegms of Epictetus;[1] and to try whether he could not release
the bird-limed owl. I was overlooked! I am unfit for the office!
I am but little wiser than the booby brother! Whereas Solomon
himself, and the seven sages to boot, are but so many men of
Gotham,[2] when he is present. The quintessence of all the knowledge, wit, wisdom, and genius that ever saw the sun, from the
infantine days of A B C and king Cadmus,[3] to these miraculous
times of intuition and metaphysical legerdemain, is bottled up in
his brain; from which it foams and whizzes in our ears, every time
discretion can be induced to draw the cork of silence.—Once
again, let him beware!

I then am selected for no other purpose but for her morality to
make experiments upon.——She is called wife, and wife she may
be; nay wife she is, or at least all other women, she being present,
are intolerably foolish. But, by heaven, this is no proof of her
wisdom! I am the scape-goat!——I!——Be it so!——Should she
be caught in her own springe, who can say I am to blame?

She has seen my anger, for I could not hide it; but she has seen
it only in part. A hypocrite she wants, and a hypocrite she shall
have. I will act the farce which she is composing; let her look to the
catastrophe.

I begin to think that marriage and I shall never meet; for, if I
withstand her, woman cannot tempt me. And her I shall withstand. At least I never will have her till I have humbled her; and
then perhaps I shall not be in the humour. And yet my heart tells
me that I shall. For in spite of all its anger, in spite of her injustice
and glaring indifference, the remembrance of which puts me in a
fever, it would be misery to know her, recollect her, and live
without her.

But, patience! Her pride shall first be lowered. I must command, not be commanded: and, when my clemency is implored,
I will then take time to consider.

My brain is in a ferment, and its various engines are already in
commotion. She herself, her hated favourite, her father, her
brother, her aunt, her uncle, her maid, every creature that surrounds her must each and all contribute to my purposes and plots.
Parts fit for the actors must be assigned. The how and what I

know not yet precisely, for I have scarcely sketched the canvas;
but I have conceived some bold and masterly strokes, and I foresee the execution must be daring and impassioned. I am in haste
to begin, and my hot oscillatory spirits can with difficulty be tamed
to the still pause of prudence and premeditation: they are eager for
the fight, and think caution a tardy general, if not a coward.

I know not how it is, but when I am angry, very angry, I feel as
if I were in my element. My blood delights to boil, and my passions to bubble. I hate still water. An agitated sea! An evening
when the fiery sun forebodes a stormy morning, and the black-
based clouds rise, like mountains with hoary tops, to tell me
tempests are brewing! These give emotion and delight supreme!
Oh for a mistress such as I could imagine, and such as Anna St.
Ives moulded by me could make! One that could vary her person,
her pleasures, and her passions, purposely to give mine variety!
Whose daily and nightly study all should centre in me, and my
gratifications! Whose eyes should flash lightning to rouse the
chilled sensations, and shed appeasing dews to quench the fire of
rage. These are the objects in which I could delight; these the
devotions I require. Change for me. A true English day; in which
winter and summer, hail, rain, and sunshine meet and mingle.

I had almost forgotten one chief cause of my resentment;
though the most fortunate one I could have wished for to promote my purpose. This Sir Arthur dallies with me. I find, from
various items which the candour of her mind has suffered to
escape, that the motive is poverty. I am glad of it. I will urge and
hurry her into a promise to be mine. The generosity of her temper will aid me. I will plead the injury done me by hesitation.
I feel it, and therefore my pleadings will be natural. It is her
pride to repair the wrongs which others commit. This pride
and this heroism of soul, which I must acknowledge in her are
unaffected, shall be the main engines with which I will work.
Without these perhaps I might despair; but with them hold
myself secure of victory.

Yes, lady of the high sciences, you must descend, and let
my star mount the horizon! The gathering clouds must eclipse
your effulgence, while I shine chief of the constellation!

As for the rest of the family, more or less, they are all fools;
therefore are neither to be feared nor pitied. On her perhaps I

R

may have compassion, when I have taught her contrition, and when she knows me for her superior.

I have written a volume, yet have not half disburthened my labouring mind. Oh that I could present the picture to you complete! That I could paint her as she is; all beauty, all excellence, all kindness, all frost! That I could shew the sweet enthusiast in the heyday insolence of her power; pretending to guide, reform, humble, and subjugate me; while love and vengeance swell my heart, hypocrisy smooths my face, and plots innumerable busy my brain! It is a fruitful, rich, resplendent scene; of which, Fairfax, you have no conception. Me you have known, intimately, and are honest enough to own you have admired: but of her all ideal tracings are contemptible!

Nor should this knight of the magic lanthorn be forgotten; this Nestor[1] junior; this tormenting rival—Oh how I could curse! He who stands, as ready as if Satan had sent him, to feed the spreading flames with oil! He fills his place on the canvas. And who knows but I may teach him, yet, to do his office as he ought? How would it delight me! There is an intemperance of superiority which no human patience can support, nor any acts of kindness compensate. A triumph over her will indeed be a triumph over him, and therefore doubly delicious!

I grant he forbears to prate of the life he gave me. But am I not reminded of the oppressive gift every time he dares to contradict me? Would I endure his interference as I do; would I be shouldered and butted at, by him; would I permit his opinion to be asked, or his dogmas to silence me, were I not burthened with this unasked benefit?

Infatuated lunatic, as I was! But I am in the school of prudence, at present; and suppose I shall learn a little some time; though I do not know when; since, I am told, it is not easy to learn a trade one hates.

Mean while I pay my court assiduously to the two peers, Evelyn and Fitz Allen, who at present are both in town. Nothing must be neglected, nothing left unprepared. Vigilance, foresight, and cunning must do their office, and will soon be in full employment: of what kind I cannot yet determine; or whether it must be open war or covert, or both; but my augury predicts the scene will soon be all life, all agitation, all enjoyment.

Commotion is my element, battle my delight, and conquest my heaven!

This is my hour of appointment: she is expecting me, yet my crowding thoughts will with difficulty allow me to lay down the pen: they rise in armies, and I could write world without end, and never come to an amen. But I must begone. Adieu.

I imagine that by this time you are at Paris; or will be before the arrival of this letter; which, according to your directions, I shall superscribe *Poste restante*.

C. CLIFTON

LETTER LXXII

Anna Wenbourne St. Ives to Louisa Clifton

London, Grosvenor Street

NEED I tell my affectionate friend how great the pleasure is which I receive from her letters, and from that free communication of thought which so effectually tends to awaken the best emotions of mind, and make us emulate each other's virtues? Like her I sit down, now while memory is awake, to relate such material incidents as have happened since last I wrote.

The anger of Clifton is softened into approbation. The most generous minds are liable, from the acuteness of their sensibility, to be unjust. We are once again very good friends.

Not but we have just been engaged in a very impassioned scene. The subject of family consent was revived by him; and, as I intended, I informed him that delay seemed inevitable.

The struggle of his feelings, when he heard it, appeared to be violent. His exclamations were characteristic of his habitual impetuosity; the strength of them excited sensations, and alarms, which prove the power he has over the passions. Oh how I desire to see that power well directed! How precious, how potent will it then become!

One thing, and only one, he vehemently affirmed, could appease the perturbation of his mind, and preserve him from wretchedness which none but those who felt like him could conceive——

And what, I asked, was that?—

He durst not speak it—Yet speak he must, plead he must. Should he fail, phrensy, despair, he knew not what, be something fearful would indubitably follow—

Again, what was it?—

Might he hope? It depended on me; and denial and distraction were the same—

He made me shudder! And, serious when I heard it though I found his demand to be, his manner inspired a confused dread of something repugnant; something eminently wrong.

He ventured at last to speak. I believe he watched his moment. The passions, Louisa, however disturbed, are always cunning. He demanded a promise, solemn and irrevocable, to be his.

Such a promise, I answered, was unnecessary; and, if at all, could only be given conditionally—

There were no conditions to which he was not ready to subscribe—

I replied, too much readiness denoted too little reflection; and not fortitude sufficient to fulfil such conditions.

Fortitude could never fail him, having me not only for an example but a reward. Again he repeated, without my promise, my sacred promise, he really and seriously feared distraction! That this was weakness he was ready to allow: but if it were true, and true it was, should I want love, I yet had too much benevolence not to desire to avert consequences which, beyond all others, are horrible to imagination.

He has surely very considerable knowledge of the human heart; for his tone and manner produced all the effect he intended. I had foreseen the probability of such a request, though not all the urgency with which it was made, and had argued the question of right and wrong. My conclusion had been that such a promise, with certain provisos, was a duty; and accordingly I gave it; stipulating power to retract, should experience teach us that our minds and principles could not assimilate.

At first he was not satisfied. Intreaties the most importunate that language could supply were repeated, that I should make no such exceptions. They were impossibilities; needless, but tormenting. Finding however that I was resolved, he softened into acquiescence, thanked me with all the transports which might be

expected from him, and kissed my hand. He would not have been
so satisfied, had I not very seriously repulsed the encroaching
freedoms which I had lately found him assuming; since which he
is become more guarded.

What latent inconsistency is there, Louisa, in my conduct, which
can incite the alarms to which I feel myself subject? The moment
I had made the promise I shuddered; and, while acting from the
strongest sense of duty, and the most ardent desire of doing good,
I felt as if the act were reprehensible and unjust.—It is the words
of Frank that are the cause: on them my mind dwells, and painfully repeats them, as if in a delirium: like a singing in the ear, the
tolling of death-bells, or the burthen of some tragic ditty, which
memory, in its own despite, harps upon, and mutters to itself!—
'*He is certain that I act from mistaken principles!—To the end of
time he shall persist in thinking me his by right!*'

There must be something amiss, something feeble in my mind,
since the decision of reason cannot defend me from the awe which
this surely too hasty, too positive assertion inspires! It haunts my
very dreams!

Clifton left me; and, being gone, I went into the parlour. Frank
was there. He had a book in his hand, and tears in his eyes. I never
beheld a look more melancholy. Capable as he is of resisting the
cowardice of self-complaint and gloom, still there are moments,
I perceive, in which he can yield; and, sighing over others woes,
can cast a retrospective glance on self. He had been reading the
Julia of Rousseau.[1] The picture given by St. Preux of his feelings
had awakened sympathy too strong to be resisted.

We fell into conversation. I wished to turn his thoughts into a
more cheerful channel; but my own partook too much of the same
medium, not to assimilate themselves in part to his languor.

You seem pensive, Frank. What is the subject of your meditations?

The sorrows of St. Preux, madam.

Then you are among the rocks of Meillerie? Or standing a par-
taker of the danger of Julia on the dreadful precipice?

No, madam. The divine Julia is dead!—[Had you heard the
sigh he gave, Louisa——!] I am at a passage which I suspect to be
still more sublime. I am sure it is equally heart-rending.

Ay!—Which is that?

It is Clara, at the table of Wolmar; where the child, with such simplicity, conjures up the infantine but almost perfect semblance of the dead. If ever laughter inspired the horrors of distraction, it was the laugh of Clara!

It is a wonderful passage. But I find you were rather contemplating the sorrows of the friend than of the lover.

Pardon me, madam. I was considering, since the friend was thus on the very brink of despair, what must be the force of mind which could preserve the lover.

Friendship and love, in such minds, are the same.

Perhaps so, madam.

Can there be any doubt?

When the lover and the friend are united, the heart is reluctant to own its feelings can be equalled.

Ought you not to avoid such a book, Frank; at least for the present?

If it led me into error; otherwise not. I think I know what were the author's mistakes; and he not only teaches but impresses, rivets, volumes of truth in my mind.

The recollection of what had just passed with Clifton forced itself upon me, Louisa; it made me desirous of putting a question to Frank on the subject, and I asked—

What is your opinion of promises?

I think them superfluous, nugatory, and therefore absurd.

Without exception?

Yes——We cannot promise to do wrong: or, if we do, cannot perform—Neither can we, without guilt, refrain from doing right; whether we have or have not promised.

Some glimpse of this truth, for I perceive it to be one, had shot across my mind; but not with the perspicuity of your proposition —I am inclined to be a rude interrogator: I have another question to ask [He bowed]—I own you are seldom wrong, and yet I hope— [I remember, Louisa, that I gave a deep sigh here; and it must not be concealed]—I hope that you have been wrong, once in your life.

Madam!

But perhaps you have changed your opinion—Do you still think as you did?—Are you still *certain that I act from mistaken principles?* [He instantly understood me—Had you seen his look, Louisa—!]

I am, madam.
And *shall persist to the end of time?*
To the end of time.
I could not bear it, Louisa. I burst away.

What rash impulse was it that hurried me forward to tempt this
trial?—Alas! It was the vain hope, for vain it appears to be, he
might have retracted.

My heart is too full to proceed—Heaven bless you!—Heaven
bless you, my dear friend!—You see how weak I am.

A. W. ST. IVES

LETTER LXXIII

Frank Henley to Oliver Trenchard

London, Grosvenor Street

OLIVER, I must fly!—There is neither peace nor safety for me if
I remain—Resolution begins to faint under these repeated and
oppressive struggles—Life is useless, virtue inefficient, time murdered, and I must fly!——Here I can do nothing but doubt, hope,
despair, and linger in uncertainty: my body listless, my mind incoherent, my days wasted in vain reveries on absurd possibilities,
and my nights haunted by the confused phantoms of a disturbed
and sickly brain!—I must fly!

But whither?—I know not!—If I mean to be truly master of my
affections, seas must separate us! Impossibility must be made more
impossible!—'Tis that, Oliver, which kills me, that ignis fatuus[1]
of false hope—Were she even married, if her husband were not
immortal, I feel as if my heart would still dwell and feed on the
meagre May-be! It refuses to renounce her, and makes a thousand
and a thousand efforts to oblige me again to urge its just claims.

I am in the labyrinth of contradictions, and know not how to get
out. My own feelings, my remarks on hers, the looks, actions and
discourse of this dangerous lover are all embroiled, all incongruous,
all illusory. I seem to tempt her to evil by my stay, him I offend,
and myself I torment—I must therefore begone!

Oliver, our hearts are united!—Truth and principle have made them one, and prejudice and pride have not the power to dissever them!—She herself feels this intimately, yet persists in her mistake.

I think, Oliver, it is not what the world or what she understands by love which occasions this anarchy of mind. I think I could command and reprove my passions into silence. Either I mistake myself, or even now, situated as I am, I could rejoice were there a certainty, nay were there but strong probabilities, that her favourite purpose on Clifton should be effected. But the more I meditate, and my hours, days, and weeks pass away and are lost in meditation on this subject, the more does my mind persist in its doubts, and my heart in its claims.

Surely, Oliver, she is under a double mistake! Surely her reasonings both on him and me are erroneous.

I must be honest, Oliver, and tell thee all my feelings, fears, and suspicions. They may be false. I hope they are, but they exist. I imagine I perceive in him repeated and violent struggles to appear what he is not, nay what I doubt he would despise himself for being!

Is not this an unjustifiable, a cruel accusation? Why have I this keen this jealous sensibility? Is it not dishonourable to my understanding?

Yet should there be real danger, and I blind to it! Should I neglect to warn her, or rather to guard and preserve her from harm, where shall I find consolation?

Oliver! There are times when these fears haunt me so powerfully that my heart recoils, my blood freezes, and my whole frame is shaken with the terrific dream!——A dream?——Yes, it must be a dream! If not, the perversion of his mind and the obduracy of his heart are to me wholly incomprehensible!

I must be more guarded—Wrongfully to doubt were irreparably to injure! My first care must be to be just.

Mark, Oliver, how these wanderings of the mind mislead and torment me! One minute I must fly, to recover myself, and not to disturb and way-lay others; the next I must stay, to protect her who perhaps is best able to protect herself!

I have no plan: I labour to form one in vain. That single channel into which my thoughts are incessantly impelled is destructive of all order and connexion. The efforts of the understanding are assassinated by the emotions of the heart; till the reproaches of principle become intolerable, and the delusions of hope distracting!—A state of such painful inutility is both criminal and absurd.

The kindness of the father, brother, and aunt, the sympathising tenderness which bursts from and overcomes the benign Anna, the delay of the marriage——Oliver!—I was recapitulating the seeming inspirations of my good angel, and have conjured up my chief tormentor!—This delay!—Where does it originate?—With whom?—With—! I must fly!—This of all motives is the most irrefragable!—I must fly!——But when, or how, or where, what I must undertake, whither go, or what become, is yet all vague and incoherent conjecture.

F. HENLEY

LETTER LXXIV

Sir Arthur St. Ives to Abimelech Henley

London, Grosvenor Street

MR. HENLEY,

It is now some time since I received your letter. It astonished and I must say offended me so much, that I do not yet know what answer to return. You say I have thrown you into a quandary, Mr. Henley; and I can very sincerely return your compliment, Mr. Henley; for nothing can be more unintelligible than your whole letter is to me, Mr. Henley. And I must say, I think it not very grateful in you, Mr. Henley, nor in my opinion very proper, to write me such a letter, Mr. Henley; that is as far as I understand its meaning, Mr. Henley. I have no desire, Mr. Henley, to quarrel with you, if I can help it; but I must say I think you have forgotten yourself, Mr. Henley. It is very unlike the manner in which you have been used to comport yourself to me, Mr. Henley; for, if I understand you rightly, which I own it is very difficult to do, you threaten me with foreclosures, Mr. Henley; which I must say, Mr. Henley, is very improper demeanour from you to me, Mr. Henley. Not that I seek a rupture with you, Mr.

Henley; though I must say that all this lies very heavy upon my mind, Mr. Henley.

You insinuate that you are grown rich, I think, Mr. Henley. So much the better for you. And you seem to know, Mr. Henley, that I am grown poor: or I think, Mr. Henley, you would not have written to me in a style which I could almost be tempted to call impertinent, but that I wish to avoid a quarrel with you, Mr. Henley, unless you force me to it. There is law as you say, Mr. Henley, for every man; but law is a very fretful and indeed fearful thing, to which you know I am averse, Mr. Henley. Not but there are proceedings, Mr. Henley, which may lead me to consider how far it is necessary.

I must say, Mr. Henley, that my astonishment is very great, after writing me word, as you did, that I might have the money, which I took very kindly of you, that you should now contradict yourself so flagrantly [I am obliged to repeat it, Mr. Henley] and tell me it is not to be had. What you mean by the whats, and the whys, and the wherefores being forthcoming, is really above my capacity, Mr. Henley; and I request you would speak plainly, that I may give a plain answer.

You say you can keep your hat on your head, and look your betters in the face, Mr. Henley. May be so. But I leave it to your better judgment to consider, Mr. Henley, whether you ought to forget that they are your betters.

There are indeed, as you tell me, wheels within wheels, Mr. Henley; for I find that you, and not my son, are in possession of the Edgemoor estate. God bless us all, and give us clean hands and hearts, Mr. Henley! I say no more! Though I must say that, when I heard it, my hair almost stood an end!

You talk a great deal about somebody's son, Mr. Henley. You have puzzled me much; but I think you must mean your own son. Though what you mean beside is more than I can divine. I am very unwilling, Mr. Henley, to think any thing to your disadvantage; and I must say that I could wish you would not speak by ifs, and ands, and innuendos; but let me know at once what you mean, and all you mean, and then I shall know how to act.

Your son, I own, is a very excellent young gentleman; a very extraordinary young gentleman; and no person can be more ready to acknowledge his merits than I, and my whole family. You seem offended with my offer of a commission for him; which I own astonishes me; for I must say, Mr. Henley, that I thought I was doing you an act of kindness. Not that I blame your prudence, sir; or your aversion to the prodigal spendthrifts, who too frequently are fond of red coats and cockades, which are so offensive to your notions of prosperity.

I am not unwilling to own that I, and all my family, are even under obligations to your son. For which reason I am the more inclined to overlook what I must say does not please me, in your last very unexpected letter. Let me tell you, Mr. Henley, that I cannot but hope you will think better of it; and that you will use your kind endeavours to get me the money, according to your promise, which I shall take very friendly of you, sir; and shall be willing to do any thing for your son, in that case, for your sake as well as for his own, which reason can require.

I beg, Mr. Henley, you will consider very seriously of this; and I should hope you would not forget former times, and the very many favours which, in my life, I have done you. I do assure you, sir, I have the utmost desire to continue on a good understanding with you; but I think I have some right to expect your compliance from motives of reason, not to say of gratitude. So, committing this to your consideration, and expecting an agreeable answer, I remain, sir, as usual,

A. ST. IVES

LETTER LXXV

Abimelech Henley to Sir Arthur St. Ives

MOST ONNURABLE SIR,
Wenbourne-Hill

It doth appear as how your onnur be amisst.[1] Whereby I did a partly a queery[2] as much; thof so be as it be no fault of mine. For why? There be reasons and causes. For when as a man has a nothink to fear of nobody, I am of a mind that a may pen his thofts to any man. Why not? Always a savin and exceptin your onnurable onnur.

And ast for a man's a portin[1] himself, there be times and seasons
for all thinks. Whereof as Friar Bacon said to Friar Bungy and of
the Brazen-head, A time was—A time is—And a time is past.[2]
And ast for a threatening about foreclosures, why what have I to
say to a gentleman, if a will not redeem his mortgages when the
time be? The law must look to it, to be sure. Always a savin and
exceptin your onnurable onnur, still say I. So that it be altogether
compus mentus[3] that quarrels and rupturs are none of my seekin.
Whereby your onnurable onnur will look to that. No man can deny
that every man has a rite to his own. For why? A pays scot and
lot,[4] and has a nothink for it but law.

And ast for a man's a growin of rich, why as I do take it a's a not
the worse for that. And ast for a man's a growin of poor, why a
what had I to do, thof so be that some be wise and some be otherwise? Whereof so long as the rhino do ring, the man is the man, and
the master's the master. A's a buzzard in grain[5] that do flicker,[6]
and fleer,[7] and tell a gentleman a be no better nur a bob gudgeon,[8]
a cause a do send the yellow hammers[9] a flying; for thof it might a
be happen to be true enough, a would get small thanks for his pains.
Every man eat his meat, and he that do like cut his fingers. The
foolish hen cackles, and the cunning quean chuckles. For why?
A has her chalk and her nest egg ready.[10] Whereof I tout and
trump[11] about at no man, an a do not tout and trump about at me.
Always a savin and exceptin your onnurable onnur; and not a
seekin of quarrels and rupturs, an they do not seek me. Otherwise,
why so. Plain and positive; that's best, when a man do find the
shoe to pinch.

And ast for law, why he that has a got the longest head will have
a most on't for money: and he that has a got the longest purse will
behappen not to be the first to cry peccavi.[12] Whereof if a man do
don his hat on his head, an a see good cause, why not? For I do a
warrant a will see good cause, an a do doff it under his arm.

Whereby every why has a wherefore. Any fool can a put down
his five nothings; but a's a clever kinchin[13] an a can place a so
much as a 1 afore 'em. Whereof the first frost that brings a white
crow[14] may, in sitch a case, behappen to shew him his betters. For
why? A's a got wherewithall to get more: and a knows the trick
on't too, or a would a never a got so much. Whereby an it comes to
a huff an a gruff,[15] a may not chuse to be arm a kimbo'd,[16] any

more nur another; for a may be happen to have a Rowland for an Oliver.[1] A may behappen to be no Jack-a-farthin weazle-faced whipster.[2] A may have stock and block[3] to go to work upon; and may give a rum for a glum:[4] always a savin and exceptin your onnurable onnur. Showin whereby as I want no quarrels nur rupturs, but peace and good will towards men, if so be as the whys and the wherefores do a bear me out.

Whereof thof a man be but a Mister, a may behappen to buy and sell a knight of the shire: that is under favour, and a savin and exceptin of your onnurable onnur. For why? I be as ready to a quit my hands of quarrels and rupturs as another.

Whereby if the Edgemoor estate be mine, why it is my own. For why? Bein it was my cash that a covered it. Whereof his younk onnur was all a mort,[5] and a down in the mouth, when a did come to me. The world was wide, and a might a gone further and a fared worse. A's a dolt indeed that will part with money, and not have money's worth. Whereby I had a bin starvin, and pinchin, and scrapin, and coilin, and moilin;[6] in heat and in cold; up a early and down a late; a called here and a sent there; a bidden and a chidden, and a forbidden to boot; every body's slave forsooth; whereby I am now my own master. Why not? Who can gain say it? Mayhap a savin and exceptin of your onnurable onnur; witch is as it may be. For why? I wants a nothink to do with quarrels and rupturs, no more nur another; but that's as thinks shall turn out.

Whereby one man's hair mayhap may stand an end as well as another's, exceptin that I wears a wig. An I give the kole, I'll have the dole.[7] And ast for somebody's son, if so be as a man be to be twitted[8] a thisn, after all the gunpowder pistols and bullets, and scowerins,[9] and firins, and bleedins, and swimmins, and sinkins, and risks, and rubs,[10] and sea scapes, and shore scapes, at home and abroad, by land and by water, and savins of precious lives and precious cash, why if so be as all this be to stand for nothink, it is a time for a man to look about'n.

To be sure your onnur is so good as to say my son is a younk gentleman, and so forth. Whereby this gracious and ever mercyfool lovin kindness would go to the cockles of my heart; ay and my chitterlins[11] would crow, and I should sing O be joyfool, if so be as I did find as words wus any think but wind. Whereof when your onnurable onnur is compulsionated, willy nilly, to be so all bountifool as to profess to the ownin of obligations, why that is summut. But fair speeches wonnot heal broken pates; and a mouthfool of moonshine will send a man hungry to bed. Promise may be a fair dog, but Performance will catch the hare.

Whereby had thinks a bin as they might a bin, why then indeed it would a bin summut. But as to the wherewithalls of the twenty thousand pounds, being as it be, why the think is unpossable to be done. For why? The case is altered. Whereof it is best to be downright. Will is free, and money for me.

Whereby this marriage match with the Clifton family, had my oar bin asked, would never a bin of my advizin. For why? I shall not give my lard to butter my neighbour's bacon.

And ast for favours received, why may be so. But what then? Since if so be thof it wus sometimes fair, why it wus sometimes foul. And a good man may behappen to be all as much as a good master. And if a man have a spent his whole lifetime in a pickin, and a cullin, and a coinin, and a furbishin up fine words, to tickle the ears of fine folks, why a ought in all conscience to get the where-withalls for his pains. For if an a gentleman will eat pine apples a must not expect to pay for pippins. Always as aforesaid a savin and exceptin your onnurable onnur. So that if quarrels and rupturs will come, they may not a be said to be of my seekin.

Bein as I am, ever and amen, with all pious jakillations and jubilees of blessins and praise, never failin to pray for due time to repent us of all our manifold sins and wickedness, God of his mercy be good unto us, and save us and deliver us, on our death bed, from the everlastin flamin sulphur of the burnin lake. Amen, an it be his holy will! Umbelly beggin leave to superscribe meself,

                                          ABIMELECH HENLEY

LETTER LXXVI

Anna Wenbourne St. Ives to Louisa Clifton

London, Grosvenor Street

I HAVE had a scene with Frank, which affected me much, and which has occasioned another quarrel, or kind of a quarrel, with Clifton. Sir Arthur had just left the room. He had been asking Frank whether there were any possible way by which he could serve him. We all were his debtors; very deeply; and he should be happy to find any mode of discharging the obligation. Sir Arthur spoke with an earnestness which, in him, is by no means customary. But Frank had nothing to ask, nothing to propose.

I was sitting at my harpsichord, amusing myself; and, Sir Arthur being gone, stopped to tell Frank how sincerely I joined in Sir Arthur's feelings.

I have nothing, madam, said he, to hope from Sir Arthur: but to you I have a request to make, which you would greatly oblige me should you grant—

I trembled, Louisa. I was afraid of some new contest of the passions; a revival of ideas which I myself had so lately, and so inadvertently, called to mind. I am persuaded the blood forsook my cheeks, when I asked him what it was: for Frank, with a tenderness in his voice that was indeed honourable to his heart, prayed, conjured me not to be alarmed—It was a trifle—He would be silent—He would not give me a moment's pain to gratify a million of such silly wishes.

He both moved and revived me. It could not be any thing very dreadful, and I entreated him to speak. There was nothing he could ask I would refuse.

He hesitated, and I then became urgent. At last he named—— His song!—Again, Louisa, he almost struck me to the heart!— He feared he offended me; but there was something so enchanting in the air that he could not forget it, could not resist the wish to possess a copy.

It was impossible to refuse. I went to my papers, and brought it. The evil spirit of thoughtlessness possessed me, and when I delivered it I asked—Is there any thing else?—

' Your kindness, madam, said he, is unalterable. Could I?—
Durst I——?

What?—

He paused—

Speak!—

He laid the song upon the music-desk, and looked——No no—
I will not attempt to tell you how!

Words were needless; they could not petition with such eloquence—A barbarian could not have refused. I rambled over the
keys, hemmed, and endeavoured to collect myself. At last a sense
of propriety, of reason, of principle, came to my aid, and bade me
be master of my mind. I began to sing, but no effort could enable
me to give that expression of which I had before found the words
so susceptible.

Could you think it, Louisa? Do you now foresee, do you forebode what happened?——Your brother came in!—

To have stopped, to have used evasion, to have had recourse to
falsehood would have turned an act of virtue into contemptible
vice. I continued. Clifton came and looked over my shoulder. The
music was on one sheet of paper, the words were on another, in
the writing of Frank. Your brother knew the hand.

When I had ended, Frank took both the papers, thanked me, and
retired. I could perceive the eyes of Clifton sparkle with emotion;
I might almost say rage. He would have spoken, but could not; and
I knew not how safely to begin.

At length, a consciousness of not having done or at least intended
to do wrong gave me courage. I determined not to wait to be questioned: I asked him how he liked the song.

Oh! Exceedingly!——It was very fine!—Very fine!

The words are Mr. Henley's.

I imagined as much, madam.

I thought them expressive, and amused myself with putting a
tune to them.

I am as good as a witch![1]

How did you like the subject?

What subject, madam?

Of the words.

I really don't know—I have forgotten—

Nay, you said you thought them very fine!

Oh! Yes!—True!—Very fine!—All about love——I recollect.

Well, and having so much faith in love, you do not think them the worse for that.

Oh, by no means!—But I thought you had.

Love in a song may be pardonable.

Especially, madam, if the song be written by Mr. Henley.

Clifton!—You almost teach me to despair!—You do not know me!—Perhaps however I am more to blame than you, at present. Timidity has given me some appearance of conscious guilt, which my heart disavows. But, as there is scarcely any error more danger-ous to felicity than suspicion, I own I am sorry to see you so frequently its slave. Never think of that woman for a wife, in whom you cannot confide. And ask yourself whether I ought to marry a man who cannot discover that I merit his confidence?

I find, indeed, implicit faith to be as necessary in love as in religion—But you know your power, madam.

An indifferent spectator would rather say you know yours.

You will not go, madam, and leave me thus?

I must.

In this misery?

I have letters to write, and visits to pay.

You cannot be so cruel?—By heaven, madam, this torment is more than nature can support!

Less impetuosity, Clifton; less raptures, and more reason.

You would have me rock, madam! Unfeeling marble!

I would have you a man; a rational, and, if possible, a wise one.

Stay at least for a moment!—Hear me!—Do not leave me in these doubts!

What doubts?—Do I not tell you the words are Mr. Henley's? The air is mine. If setting them were any guilt, it is a guilt of which I am not conscious. Shew me that it is criminal and I will instantly retract. We must either overcome these narrow, these selfish pro-pensities, or we shall hope in vain to be happy.

I—I—I make no accusation—

Do but examine before you accuse, and I will patiently hear and cheerfully answer to accusation. If you think it wrong in me not to treat virtue and genius with neglect, bring me your proofs, and if I cannot demonstrate their fallacy I will own my error. Let me add, the accusation of reason is a duty; from which, though

S

painful, we ought not to shrink. It is the mistaken accusation of the
passions only at which justice bids the heart revolt.

Here, Louisa, once again I left him, with struggles apparently
more acute than the former. And my own mind is so affected, so
oppressed as it were by crowds of ideas, that I do not yet know
whether this were an accident to be wished, or even whether I
have entirely acted as I ought. My mind will grow calmer, and I
will then begin the scrutiny.

I am minute in relating these particulars, because I am very
desirous of doing right. And who is so capable of being my judge,
or who so anxious I should not err, as my dear Louisa, my friend,
my sister?

All good be with you!

A. W. ST. IVES

LETTER LXXVII

Coke Clifton to Guy Fairfax

London, Dover-Street

OH, Fairfax, if my choler rose when last I wrote, where shall I
now find words hot enough to paint the phrensy of my soul?—
How could I rage and rave!—Is it come to this?—So barefaced!—
So fearless!—So unblushingly braved!—

Fairfax, I came upon them!—By surprise!—My alert and watchful spirit, an adept in such arts, accustomed to them, and rendered
suspicious by practice and experience, foreboded some such
possibility—My knock at the door was counterfeit. I strode up
stairs to the drawing-room, three steps at a time—Swiftly and
suddenly—I opened the door—There they sat!—Alone!——She
singing a miserable ditty, a bead-roll of lamentable rhymes,
strung together by this Quidam![1]—This Henley!—Nay!—Oh!
—Damnation!—Read and tremble!—Read and aid me to curse!—
Set by her!—Ay!——A ballad—A love complaint—A most dole-
ful woe-begone elegy; of sorrows, sufferings, fate, despair, and
death; scribbled by him, and set and sung by her!—By her!—
For his comfort, his solace, his pleasure, his diversion!—I caught

them at it!—Nay they defied me, despised the wrath that drank up the moisture of my eyes, blazed in my blood, and scorched my very soul!——

And after this will I blench? Will I recant the denunciations which legitimate vengeance had pronounced?—

Fairfax—I am not certain that I do not hate her!—No!—Angelic sorceress!—It is not hatred, neither—But it is a tumult, a congregate anarchy of feelings which I cannot unravel; except that the first feature of them is revenge!—Roused and insulted as I am, not all her blandishments can dazzle, divert, or melt me! Were mountains to be moved, dragons to be slain, or lakes of liquid fire to be traversed, I would encounter all to attain my end!—Yes— My romance shall equal hers. No epic hero, not Orpheus, Æneas, or Milton's Lucifer himself, was ever more determined. I could plunge into Erebus,[1] and give battle to the legion phantoms of hell, to accomplish my fixed purpose!—Fixed!—Fixed!——Hoot me, hiss at me, despise me if I turn recreant! No—Then may all who ever heard the name of Coke Clifton make it their byword and their scoff; and every idiot curl the nose and snuff me to scorn!

Recollect but the various affronts I have received, Fairfax, from her and [Oh patience!] Her inamorato! For is he not so?—Wrongs, some of which irritate most because they could not be resented; insults, some petty some gigantic, which ages could not obliterate; call these to mind, and then think whether my resolves be not rock-built! Insolent intrusion has been his part from the first moment to the last. The prince of upstarts, man could not abash him, nor naked steel affright! On my first visit, entrance was denied by him! Permission was asked of a gardener's son, and the gardener's son sturdily refused! I argued! I threatened!—I!—And arguments and threats were so much hot breath, but harmless! Attempts to silence or to send him back to his native barn alike were baffled; and I, who planned his removal, was constrained to petition for his stay. Yes, constrained!—It was do it, or!—Oh!—Be faithful to me, memory!—He was elected president of opinions and disputes, past, present and to come. Appeals must all be made to him, and his sentence was definitive. Law or gospel, physics or metaphysics; himself alone superior to college, court, or convocation. Before him sunk scholiast and schools. In his presence the doctors all must stand uncapped: the seraphic, the subtle, and the singular; the illuminated, the angelic, and the irrefragable[1] to him, were tyros all. Our censor in private, and in public our familiar: like a malignant demon, no respect, no place, no human barriers could exclude him. On no side could the offended eye turn, and not find him there. Disgraced by his company, counteracted by his arrogance, insulted by his sarcasms; obliged to accept the first of favours, life, at his hands; his apparent inferior in the moment of danger; my ministry rejected for his, nay contemned, in a case where the gentleman, the man of the world, and the man of honour merited undoubted preference; and, as the climax of injury, wronged in my love!—Rivalled!—Furies!—

And she!—Has she been less contumelious, less annoyant, less tormenting?—His advocate, his abettor, his adulator, with me only she was scrupulous and severe. I generously and almost instantly forgot all former resolves, and would have thrown myself into her arms—Unconditionally——I, who had been accustomed to give the law, not to receive. I assumed not the dictator. I, whose family, courage, person, and parts have made me a favourite with the brave and fair, though flushed with success, far from claiming superiority, I came to cast myself, my freedom, and my trophies at her feet—Came, and was rejected! Bargained with at least; put off with ifs and possibilities!

I must stop—Must think no more—Or the hurrying blood will burst my veins, or suffocate my swelling heart, and impede just retribution for these and all my other thousand wrongs, which only can be avenged by calm and subtle foresight—Yet think not that the smallest of them is forgotten—Oh no!—

Well then, calm will I be; for I can be, will be any thing rather than not attain this supreme of pleasures, divine vengeance! Yes, anger must be bridled: it has now a second time made me tread backward more than all the steps I had taken in advance. My brain is labouring for some certain and uniform plan, but is at present so disturbed that thought can preserve no settled train.

Previous to this second childish overflow of passion [for if I would succeed childish it is] I had played a master stroke, in which indeed I must own passion was for once my best ally. With most ardent importunity, I with great difficulty wrested a promise from her to be mine. These romancers, Fairfax, hold love promises to be binding and sacred. And this obtained I thought a fair foundation for my fabric.

The current of my thoughts is now wholly turned to this subject. A thousand manœuvres crowding present themselves; nor can I say how many must be employed. I have generally found my brain rich in expedients, and I think it will not fail me now. I recollect having mentioned the maid, Laura: she is secured, and has been for some time past. The fondness of the fool with one less expert would be dangerous; but I have taught her to rail at me occasionally to her mistress, and to praise the favorite, who has never lately been any great favorite with her, having as I guess overlooked her when she had kinder inclinations. She was tickled with the contrivance, which promised to secure her so well from the suspicion of her mistress, and she acts her part tolerably. In fact her mistress seems a being without suspicion, superior to it, and holding it in contempt—So much the better!

This fellow, this king of the cucumber-beds[1] must be removed. I know not yet the means, but they must be found. Present he is dangerous; absent he may perhaps be taught to act his part with safety and effect. My ideas are not yet methodised, but I have a confused foresight of various modes by which this and much more may and must be accomplished.

But no common efforts can be successful—Deep—Deep must be the plot by which she is to be over-reached, the pit into which she must fall: and deep it therefore shall be. There is no art I will not practise, no restraint to which I will not submit, no desperate expedient to which I will not have recourse to gratify my soul's longing—I will be revenged!——The irrevocable decree is gone forth—I will be revenged!—Fairfax, you soon shall hear of me and my proceedings. Farewell.

C. CLIFTON

LETTER LXXVIII

Anna Wenbourne St. Ives to Louisa Clifton

London, Grosvenor Street

THIS letter, dear friend of my heart, is begun in a very melancholy mood. How easy it is to undertake; how difficult to overcome! With what facility did I say to myself—Thus will I do, and thus—How firmly did I promise! Truth appeared so beautiful, so captivating, so omnipotent, that armed by her an infant could not but conquer. Perseverance alone was requisite, and I could persevere. The solid basis of the earth should almost shake ere I would waver!—Poor, vain creature!—Surely, Louisa, we are not all so— Heaven forbid!—

Why am I thus? Why does my heart faint within me? Indeed, Louisa, I begin to fear I have vaunted of powers I do not possess; and prescribed to myself duties too dignified, too mighty for me— And must I abandon an enterprise I deemed so noble?—I have meditated on it, Louisa, till I could weep—

I will not yet despair. At least one effort more, and a strong one, I will make—Alas! I am weary of this promising. My braggart strength is impotency, or little better. But I will do my best; and truth, sincerity, and good intent must be my trust.

My present determination is to relate to your brother all that has passed between me and Frank. I will once more state my feelings, my principles, and my plan. The purity of my heart must be my shield. To contend thus is painful; yet most willingly would I contend, were it productive of the good at which I aim. But instead of gaining ground I seem to lose. Oh that I were more wise, that I better knew the human heart, and that I well could wield the too gigantic weapons of truth! But I fear they are above my force, and pity my own imbecility.

The hour of appointment is come. Clifton will soon be here. I have been preparing my mind, taxing my memory, and arranging my thoughts. Oh that this effort may be more successful than the past! Did he but know all the good I wish him, his heart would surely not feel anger——He shall not die, said Frank!—Can I forget it?——How did my soul glow within me, when, hopeless

but the moment before, I beheld nature again struggling for existence, and returning life once more stir in the convulsive lip! How
did my ears tingle with—'He shall not die!'—I saw a noble quality
exerted, and thought it was but to wish and to have, to imitate and
to succeed——The brother of my Louisa!—A mind too that
might out-soar the eagle, and gaze on the sun of truth!

There must be some cause for my failure, if I fail—With true
simplicity of heart I can say, most earnestly do I wish to do right:
most ardently would I endeavour to prove myself a friend worthy
of Louisa Clifton, and of Frank Henley!—Perhaps the latter is
the cause?—If I have done him wrong, Heaven forgive me! For
I think, were I convicted of it, I could not forgive myself!

The servant has told me Clifton is below. I must take a few
minutes to breathe—I must collect myself. Oh for the tongues of
mediating angels!

A. W. ST. IVES

LETTER LXXIX

Anna Wenbourne St. Ives to Louisa Clifton

London, Grosvenor Street

WHEN last my Louisa heard from me, my mind was depressed.
I almost despaired of the great task I had undertaken. I had likewise an immediate duty, a disburthening of my soul, a kind of
confession of facts to make, from which education has falsely
accustomed us to shrink with pain, and my spirits were overclouded. This rigorous duty is performed; hope again begins to
brighten, and my eased heart now feels more light and cheerful.

Not but it still is tremulous with the sensations by which it has
just been thrilled. I seem to have risen from one of the most interesting and I believe I may add awful scenes, in which I have ever
been engaged. The recesses of the soul have been searched; that
no retrospective accusation of want of absolute and perfect candour
might, as of late it too often has done, rise to assault me.

I found Clifton in the parlour. His look was more composed,
more complacent, and remarkably more thoughtful than it had

lately been. I began with stating that the feelings of my heart required every act, every thought of mine, that had any relation
whatever to him, should be fully and explicitly known. I conjured
him to have the goodness to determine not to interrupt me; that
I might perform this office, clear my conscience, and shew my
heart unveiled, undisguised, exactly as it was; and that he might
at once reject it, if it were either unworthy his acceptance or
incompatible with his principles.

He promised compliance and kept his word. I never knew him
a listener so long, or with such mute patience. I had as I may say
studied the discourse which I made to him, and which I thus began.

It will not be my intention, Mr. Clifton, in what I am going to
say, to appear better or worse than I am. Should I be partial to
myself, I wish you to detect me. There is nothing I so much
desire as a knowledge of my own failings. This knowledge, were
it truly attained, would make the worst of us angels. Our prejudices, our passions, and our ignorance alone deceive us, and
persuade us that wrong is right.

I have before acquainted you of the project of Mrs. Clifton and
Sir Arthur, for our union. I have told you of the unfeigned friendship, the high admiration, and the unbounded love I have for your
sister: or in other words for her virtues. A short acquaintance
shewed me that your mind had all the capacity to which the most
ardent of my hopes aspired. It had indeed propensities, passions,
and habits, which I thought errors; but not incurable. The meanest
of us have our duties to fulfil, which are in proportion to our opportunities, and our power. I imagined that a duty of a high but possible
nature presented itself, and called upon me for performance.

You no doubt will smile at my vanity, but I must be sincere. By
instruction, by conversation, and by other accidents, it appeared
to me that I had been taught some high and beneficial truths and
principles; which you, by contrary instruction, conversation, and
accidents, had not attained. Convinced that truth is irresistible,
I trusted in the power of these truths rather than of myself, and
said here is a mind to which I am under every moral obligation to
impart them, because I perceive it equal to their reception. The
project therefore of our friends was combined with these circumstances, which induced me willingly to join their plan; and to call
my friend sister was an additional and delightful motive. It

appeared like strengthening those bonds between us which I believe no human force can break.

An obstacle or rather the appearance of an obstacle somewhat unexpectedly arose. From my childhood I had been in part a witness of the rising virtues of young Mr. Henley. Difference of sex, of situation, and of pursuits, prevented us till lately from being intimate. I had been accustomed to hear him praised, but knew not all the eminence with which it was deserved. He was my supposed inferior, and it is not very long since I myself entertained some part of that prejudice. I know myself now not to be his equal.

A recollection of combining circumstances convinced me that he had for some time, and before I suspected it, thought on me with partiality. He believes there is great affinity in our minds; he avows it, and with a manly courage becoming his character, which abhors dissimulation, has since confessed an affection for me; nay has affirmed that unless I have conceived some repugnance to him, which I have not nor ever can conceive, I ought as a strict act of justice to myself and him to prefer him before any other.

I should acknowledge the cogency of the reasons he assigns, and certainly entertain such a preference, did it not appear to me that there are opposing and irreconcileable claims and duties. It is my principle, and perhaps still more strongly his, that neither of us must live for ourselves, but for society. In the abstract our principle is the same; but in the application we appear to differ. He thinks that the marriage of two such people can benefit society at large. I am persuaded that the little influence which it would have in the world would be injurious, and in some sort fatal to the small circle for which I seem to exist, and over which my feeble influence can extend.

For these reasons only, and in compliance with what I believe to be the rigorous but inflexible injunctions of justice, have I rejected a man whom I certainly do not merit: a man whose benevolent heart, capacious mind, and extraordinary virtues are above my praise, and I almost fear beyond my attainment.

My memory will not furnish me with every word and incident that have passed between us; and if it would such repetition would be tedious. But I wish you clearly to understand that Mr. Henley has made these declarations to me: that my mode of acting and my reasons have been such as I have mentioned; that I am not myself so perfectly satisfied with these reasons but that I sometimes am subject to recurring doubts; and that I do at present and while I have thought or sense shall continue to admire his genius and his virtue.

If what he has said or what I have done be offensive to you, if you cannot think highly of him and innocently of me, if my thoughts concerning him can possibly be stained with a criminal tinge in your eyes, it becomes you, and I now most solemnly call upon you, as a man disdaining deceit, at once to say so, and here to break off all further intercourse. Esteem, nay revere him I do and ever must; and instead of being guilty for this, my principles tell me the crime would be to esteem and revere him less.

I trust in the frankness of my heart for the proof of its sincerity. My determination is to have a clear and unspotted conscience. Purity of mind is a blessing beyond all price; and it is that purity only which is genuine or of any value. The circumstance I am going to relate may to you appear strange, and highly reprehensible —Be it so—It must be told.

We never had but one conversation in which the subject of marriage, as it related to him and me, was directly and fairly debated. He then behaved as he has done always with that sincerity, consistency, and fortitude, by which he is so peculiarly character-ised. A conversation so interesting, in which a man of such un-common merit was to be rejected by a woman who cannot deny him to be her superior, could not but awaken all the affections of the heart. I own that mine ached in the discharge of its duties, and nothing but the most rooted determination to abide by those duties could have steeled it to refusal—It was a cruel fortitude!

But while it ached it overflowed; and to you more especially than to any other person upon earth, I think it necessary to say that, at a moment when the feeling of compassion and the dread of being unjust were excited most powerfully in my bosom, para-doxical as it may seem, my zeal to demonstrate the integrity and innocence of my mind induced me to—kiss him!

I scarcely can proceed——There are sensations almost too strong to be subdued—The mind with difficulty can endure that mistake, that contortion, which can wrest guilt out of the most sublime of its emanations—However, if it were a crime, of that crime I am guilty—I pretend not to appear other than I am;

and what I am it is necessary at this moment that you should know.

This conversation and this incident happened on the day on which you met him in the corridor, coming from my chamber. A day, Mr. Clifton, worthy of your remembrance and of your emulation; for it afforded some of the strongest proofs of inflexible courage of which man is at present capable. He had been robbed of the hope dearest to his heart, had been rejected by the woman he had chosen to be the friend and companion of his life, had been enjoined the task of doing all possible good to his rival, which he had unconditionally promised, and he left her to——receive a blow from this rival's hand!

Far be it from me, Mr. Clifton, to wish to give you pain, or insult your feelings!——Oh no!——I retrace the picture only because I think it one of the most instructive lessons, for private life, the stores of memory can supply.

I must further inform you that but a few days ago I questioned him, whether he had not changed his opinion concerning me; hoping that after mature reflection he might have thought, as I do, that to refuse him was a duty. But he persists in believing it to be an error. He does not however obtrude his thoughts upon me: on the subject of love an anchorite could not be more silent, or a brother more delicate. That one conversation excepted, he has made no further attempts. A few words were indirectly said, when, as I have just told you, I questioned him; but they were excited by me.

With respect to the song, at which you have last taken offence, its brief history is that it was written, or at least first seen by me, soon after our arrival in France. I found it on my music-desk; and I dare affirm it had been left there by mistake, not design. I supposed it to be his from the hand-writing; and I set it because it affected me.

The day on which you found me singing it to him was the first on which it was ever mentioned by him to me; and then, after he had been pressed by Sir Arthur to know how he could serve him, a copy of it was begged from me as the only favour the family could bestow!——He has done us many favours! Favours which we shall never have an opportunity to repay! Though my hands are impotent, ere my thoughts can be restrained from being just to his worth I must be convinced there is guilt in those thoughts.

How to address myself now personally to you, Mr. Clifton, I scarcely know. The world perhaps would call my views extravagant, my pretensions impertinent, and my plan absurd.——The world must do its will——In the progress toward truth, I have presumed to think you several steps behind me. I have proposed to myself in some sort to be your instructress. I have repeated my plan to the person whom you perhaps may consider as your rival; I have required his aid, and have avowed that I think him very considerably your superior. Each and all of these may be and I suppose are offensive; but the proceedings of rectitude never can be dark, hidden, and insidious. When I have said all that I think of you I should hope you will be more inclined to believe me equitable.

There are many leading principles in which we differ; and concerning which till we agree to proceed to marriage would be culpable. These you were at first eager to examine; but finding the side you took not so clear and well-established as you had imagined, displeased by contradiction, and, in the spirit of that gallantry which you profess to admire, being willing to appear complaisant to the female to whom you pay your addresses, you have lately declined discussion. You think no doubt that the lover ought to yield, and the husband to command; both of which I deny. Husband, wife, or lover, should all be under the command of reason; other commands are tyranny. Reason and not relationship alone can give authority.

You think that the claims of birth to superiority are legitimate: I hold them to be usurpations. I deem society, and you self, to be the first of claimants. Duels with you are duties, with me crimes. Suicide you allow to be generally an act of insanity, but sometimes of virtue. I affirm that no one, who is not utterly useless in society, or who cannot by dying be of greater use than by living, can have a right over his own life: and of the existence of such a being I doubt. You maintain that what you possess is your own: I affirm it is the property of him who wants it most.

These are essential differences. Nor are these all, but perhaps they are more than sufficient to end the alliance we were seeking.

Not that I desire to end it—Far, far the reverse!—You, Mr.

Clifton, are so highly gifted, so distinguished in the rank of intellect, and have a mind of such potency, that to behold its powers employed in the cause of truth, to be myself instrumental in a work so worthy, and afterward to become the fast and dearest friend of such a mind is a progression so delightful, so seducing, that for a time I laboured to persuade myself of its possibility.

These hopes begin to fade; and, did you know how much this circumstance afflicts me, you would at least absolve me from all charge of indifference.

Habits and prejudices which are sanctioned by the general practice, and even by numbers who are in many respects eminently wise and virtuous, are too stubborn to be overcome by the impotent arguments of a young female; with whom men are much more prone to trifle, toy, and divert themselves, than to enquire into practical and abstract truth. In the storm of the passions, a voice so weak would not be heard.

That all these impediments should be removed I begin to believe but little probable; and, till they are removed, as we are we must remain.

The obstacles to marriage are indeed so numerous that I perceive calculation to be very much in favour of celibacy: I mean respecting myself. I ask not riches; but of wealth of mind my expectations by some would be called extravagant. Yet lower these expectations I cannot; for that would be to relax in principle.

I ended; and your brother still sat patient and willing to listen, had I desired to continue. After a short pause, he replied—The profound attention I have paid, madam, will I hope convince you I have not been an idle listener. Your words, or at least the substance of them, have sunk deep in my heart. Your desire that I should remember them scarcely can equal mine. To me, madam, they are so important that the moment I return home, confident as I usually am of my memory, I will not trust it now, but commit them to writing.

What your motives are for this unusual care, or whether you do or do not feel yourself offended, Mr. Clifton, it is not possible for me to divine: but, as I think it alike unjust to conceal what I have done or what I have said, however mistaken my words or actions may have been, I will spare you the trouble of writing, if you think proper, and send you a tolerably correct transcript of my thoughts tomorrow morning. I can easily repeat them, assisted by some memorandums that I have already made, and by the strength of my recollection and my feelings, which I think are in no danger of a sudden decay.

You will infinitely oblige me, madam, and I will endeavour to profit by the favour. My mind is at present as much awake to the subject as yours—I hope you are not unwilling to converse with me on the topics on which we may happen to differ?

Unwilling?—Oh no!—It was your unwillingness that led me almost to despair—But are you in earnest?—Truly and sincerely in earnest?

In earnest, madam: truly and sincerely in earnest.

And will you really reflect, seriously, deeply, on the subject in question?

As deeply, madam, as you yourself could wish.

Mr. Clifton, your present tone and manner rejoice me!—You half revive my hopes!—But let me conjure you to be sincere with your own heart. Examine every thing I have said; every thing; especially what relates to Frank Henley. All that I have observed of your temper, from first to last, obliges me thus seriously to warn you.

Fear not, madam; I will obey your injunctions. I will examine with all the severity you could wish—The cup may have its bitters, but its contents must be swallowed—You will not judge ill of me, madam, for my frankness?

Oh no! Be frank, be true, be worthy of yourself!

Such as you would have me, madam, I must become—All I request is that you would aid me in the task.

And are you indeed as determined as you seem to be?

I am, madam. [I never before, Louisa, saw your brother look or speak with such firmness.] You have been kindly pleased to say you once prescribed it as a duty to yourself to teach, or attempt to teach me your principles.

Not mine, but the principles of truth. Cool and fair enquiry is all I wish. Should any of your principles be better founded than mine, I shall be most happy to become your scholar. I am aware how impossible it is that any two people should think exactly alike on any one subject, much less on all; but on certain great leading points, were you and I to continue as opposite as we are, and were we to marry, felicity could not be the consequence.

Let us hope, madam, it is possible we should make a marriage of opinions, which you think as necessary as of persons.

Quite!—Quite!—Let me conjure you however not to deceive yourself! Pretend to no conviction you do not feel; nor degrade the honest sincerity of your heart by any unworthy indulgence of desire!

Here, Louisa, our conversation ended. Company came in, and the customary occupations of the day took place. But it is with heartfelt pleasure I add that your brother behaved as if he had forgotten his former character, and was at last firmly resolved to assume a new one. I have often endeavoured to encourage hope, but never before felt it in any thing like the same degree. He cannot but be in earnest; his determination for the first time to commit all I had said to writing is an indubitable proof!—May the same propensities continue and increase!—'He shall not die' will again be the burthen of my song!—What a noble mind might his become! —Might?—Let us once more be bold and say will!—Oh that to do were as easy as to say!

A. W. ST. IVES

END OF VOLUME IV

VOLUME V

Coke Clifton to Guy Fairfax

London, Dover-Street

BEFORE you proceed with my letter, Fairfax, read the inclosed paper*!——Read!—The hand-writing is hers!—It is addressed to me! Was repeated to me! Is transcribed for me!—Transcribed by herself!—Read! And if it be possible believe in your own existence! Believe if you can that all you see, all you hear, the images that swim before your eyes and the world itself are real, and no delusion!—For my part I begin to doubt!——Read!—Oh that I were invisible and standing by your side!

Well!—Have you ended?—And do you still continue to breathe?—Are you not a statue?—Would not the whole universe denounce me liar if, knowing me, I were to tell it that words like these were not only spoken to me but are written, lest I should forget the maddening injuries they contain?—What! Make me her confessor?—Me?—No secret sin, of thought, word, or deed, concealed!—All remembered, all recited, all avowed!—Sins committed with the hated Henley!—Sins against love, against Clifton!—Does she imagine I can look on a paper like this and, while my eye shoots along the daring the insulting line, not feel all the fires that now devour me?——Surely she is frantic!

These things, Fairfax, are above my comprehension! My amazement must be eternal, for I never shall be able to understand them.—What! Tell me, Clifton, of her amorous debates

* A copy given by Anna to Clifton, as she had promised him, of all that she had said in her last conversation.

T

with such a fellow? Appoint him her head-usher over me?
Announce him my rival? Meet my eye unabashed and affirm him
to be my superior? Inform me of the deep hold he has taken of her
heart? Own she kissed him?

Once again it is incredible! Nay most and still more incredible;
for, strange to say and yet more strange for her to do, even this
received such a varnish from her lips, her eyes, her beauties, her
irradiating zeal, that reason everlastingly renounce me if I scarcely
knew, while she spoke, whether it were not the history of some
sylph, some heavenly spirit she was reciting?

Yes, Fairfax! There was a moment, a short but dangerous
moment, at which so charmed was I by her eloquence, so amazed
by her daring sincerity, so moved by the white candour of a soul
so seeming pure, that, possessed by I know not what booby devil
of generosity, I was on the point of throwing myself at her feet,
confessing the whole guilt of my intents, and proclaiming myself
her true and irrevocable convert!

And this before the breath that uttered these injuries was cold!

The siren!——All the beauteous witcheries that ever yet were
said or sung do not equal her!—Circe, Calypso, Morgana,[1] fairy
or goddess, mortal or immortal, knew not to mix the magic cup
with so much art!

Not that it was her arguments. What are they? It was her bright
her beaming eyes, her pouting beauteous lips, her palpitating
ecstatic bosom, her—I know not what, except that even this was
not all!—No!—There was something still more heavenly!—An
emanating deity!—The celestial effulgence of a divine soul, that
flowed with fervour almost convulsive!

Had you witnessed her elevated aspirations!—Such swelling
passions so mastered, so controlled, till then I never beheld! Like
the slow pause of the solemn death-bell, the big tear at stated
periods dropped; but dropped unheeded. Though she could not
exclude them, her stoic soul disdained to notice such intrusive
guests!——Her whole frame shook with the warfare between the
feelings and the will—And well might it shake!

I went prepared, and lucky it was that I did. My fixed deter-
mination was to be silent, that I might profit by what I should hear.
That one dangerous moment excepted, I was firm!—Firm!—
Not to be moved; though rocks would, had they listened!

Yes, Fairfax, I did my part. Not that I am certain that to fall at her feet like a canting methodist, own myself the most reprobate of wretches, whine out repentance, and implore forgiveness at the all sufficient fountain of her mercy would not be the very way to impose upon her best.

I begin indeed to be angry at myself for not having yet resolved on one consistent plan. Schemes so numerous present themselves, and none without its difficulties and objections, that to determine is no easy task. Circumstances in part must guide me. I must have patience. At present I can only prepare and keep in readiness such cumbrous engines as this phlegmatic foggy land of beef and pudding can afford. I must supply the fire, if I find it necessary to put the machines in motion.

But, having decreed her fall, my spirits are now alert, and there is not a being that surrounds me to whom imagination does not assign a possible part: and that the part should be well-suited to the person must be my care.

My first exercise must be on myself. Apathy or the affectation of apathy must be acquired—Inevitably must be—My passions must be masked: I must pretend to have conquered them. In their naked and genuine form they are indecent, immoral, impure, I know not what! But catch a metaphysical quirk, and let vanity and dogmatic assertion stand sponsors and baptize it *a truth*, and then raptures, extravagance, and bigotry itself are deities! Be then as loud, as violent, as intolerant as the most rancorous of zealots, and it is all the sublime ardour of virtue.

Yes! I must learn to ape their contempt of all and every terrene object, motive, and respect!

Inclose the strange paper I sent you and return it in your next. I sent it in her own hand-writing, that your eyes might have full conviction. I took a copy of it, but I have since recollected I may want the original. The time may come when she may assail me with accusation and complaint: I will then present that paper, and flash guilt upon her!

I am much deceived if I do not observe in this gardening and improving knight a want of former cordiality, a decrease of ardour, and perhaps a wish to retract—Why let him!—To the daughter's deadly sins let him add new: it will but make

invention more active, and revenge more keen! I will have an
eye upon him: I half hope my suspicions are true!

The aunt Wenbourne too still continues to give laud unto Mr.
Henley!—Damn Mr. Henley!—But she may be necessary; and,
as she is entirely governed by the gull Edward, I must submit to
bring myself into his favour. The thing may easily be done.

The lordly uncle Fitz-Allen is secure. I frequently dine with
him on what he calls his open day; he being overwhelmed with
business, as blockheads usually are; and I do not fail to insinuate
the relationship in which, if care be not taken, he may hereafter
chance to stand to a gardener's son. His face flames at the supposition, and his red nose burns more bright! What will it do,
should I make him my tool, when he finds to what good purpose he
has been an abettor? Be that his concern; it neither is nor ever shall
be mine.

But none of these are the exact agent I want; nor have I found
him yet. They at best can only act as auxiliaries. Laura indeed
may be eminently useful; but the plotting, daring, mischievous,
malignant yet subaltern imp incarnate, that should run, fly, dive,
be visible and invisible, and plunge through frost or fire to execute
my behests, is yet to be discovered.

Were I in Italy, disburse but a few sequins and battling legions
would move at my bidding: but here we have neither cicisbeos,[1]
carnivals, confessors, bravoes nor sanctuaries. No—We have too
few priests and too much morality for our noble corps to flourish
in full perfection.

I know not that all this may be necessary, but I suspect it will,
and I must prepare for the worst; for I will accomplish my purpose in despite of hell or honesty!—Ay, Fairfax, will!—Gentle
means, insinuation, and hypocrisy shall be my first resource; and
if these fail me, then I will order my engines to play!

I have been once more reading my copy of this unaccountable
paper, and though every word is engraven in my memory, it
dropped from my hand with new astonishment! Her history of her
Mr. Henley, the yearnings of her heart toward him, and her unabashed justification of all she has said, all she has thought and all
she has done are not to be paralleled in the records of female
extravagance.

She comes however to the point at last—Calculation is in favour of celibacy—For once, lady, you are in the right!—We may appear to agree on cases more dubious, but on that it will be miraculous if we ever hereafter differ.

I cannot but again applaud myself, for keeping my preconcerted resolution of silence and reserve so firmly. I rejoice in my fortitude and my foresight; for her efforts were so strenuous, and her emotions so catching, that had I been less prepared all had been lost.

C. CLIFTON

LETTER LXXXI

Coke Clifton to Guy Fairfax

London, Dover Street

YES, yes, Fairfax! She takes the sure and resolute road to ruin, and travels it with unwearied ardour!—What think you she has done now?—An earthquake would have been more within my calculation!—She labours hard after the marvellous!—She has been angling again in the muddy pool of paradox, and has hooked up a new dogma!—And what is it?—Why nothing less than an asseveration that the promise she made me is not binding!—Promises are non-entities: they mean nothing, stand for nothing, and nothing can claim.

So be it—It is a maxim, divine apostate, that will at least serve my turn as effectually as yours. To own the truth, I never thought promises made to capricious ladies stood for much; nor were my scruples at present likely to have been increased. If she, a woman, be simple enough to have faith in the word of man, 'tis her fault. Let her look to it!

This is not all: the doctrine is not of her own invention! Mr. Henley, the eternal Mr. Henley again appears upon the scene, from which he is scarcely ever a moment absent!—Were it possible I could relent, she is determined I shall not. But they are both down in my tablets, in large and indelible characters; on the black list; and there for a time at least they shall remain.

My plan, Fairfax, is formed; and I believe completely. When I was first acquainted with her, as you know, my meaning was honest and my heart sincere. I was a fool at least for a fortnight; for that was the shortest period before I began at all to waver. I was indeed deeply smitten! Nor is desire cooled: delay, opposition, and neglect have only changed its purpose. She soon indeed taught me to treat her in some manner like the rest of her sex, and to begin to plot. 'Tis well for me that I have a fertile brain: and it had been well for her could she have been contented with the conquest she had made, and have treated me with generosity equal to my deserts. But a hypocrite she has made me, and a hypocrite she shall find me; ay and a deep one.

She has herself given me my clue: she has laid open her whole heart. She has the fatuity to mimic the perfect heroine! Tell her but it is a duty, and with the Bramin wives she would lie down, calmly and resolutely, on the burning pile![1]

Well then! I will tell her of a duty of which she little dreams! Yes, she shall grant every thing I wish as an act of duty! I will convince her it is one! I! The pretty immaculate lamb must submit in this point to become my pupil; and it shall go hard or I will prove as subtle a logician as herself.

What say you, Fairfax? Is not the project an excellent one? Is it not worthy of the sapient Doctor Clifton? Shall I lose reputation, think you, by carrying it into effect?

I am already become a new man. My whole system is changed. She begins to praise me most unmercifully; and, while my very heart is tickled with my success, the lengthened visage of inspired quaker when the spirit moved was never more demure! I am too pleased, too proud of my own talents, not to persist.

Already I am a convert to one of *her truths*. Do laugh, Fairfax! I have acknowledged that you and your footman are equal! Is it not ridiculous? However I am convinced! Ay and convinced I will remain, till time shall be. She shall teach me a truth a day!— Yet, no—I must not learn too fast; it may be suspicious: though I would be as speedy as I conveniently can in my progress.

The zeal of disputation burns within her; and, as I tell you, I am already one of her very good boys, because the pursuit of my own project makes me now as willing to listen and hunt after deductions, such as I want, as she is to teach and to supply me with those deductions. She starts at no proposition, however extra-vagant, if it do but appear to result from any one of her favourite systems, of which she has a good round number. Rather than relinquish the least of them, she would suppose the glorious sun a coal-pit; and his dazzling rays no better than volumes of black smoke, polished and grown bright on their travels by attrition. She professes it to be the purpose of her life to free herself from all prejudices. But here she has the modesty to add the saving clause— 'If it be practicable.'

Could she, Fairfax, have a more convenient hypothesis? Do you not perceive its fecundity? And, the task being so very difficult, will it not be benevolent in me to lend her my assistance? What think you? Is it not possible to prove that marriage is a mere prejudice?

She shall find me willing to learn many or perhaps all of her doctrines; and in return I desire to teach her no more than one of mine. Can any thing be more reasonable, more generous? Nay, I will go further! I will not teach it her; she shall have all the honour of teaching it to me! Can man do more?

The most knotty and perplexed part of my plan was to find a contrivance to make the gardener's son an actor in the plot. The thing is difficult, but not impossible. I have various stratagems and schemes, in the choice of which I must be guided by circum-stances. That which pleases me most is to invite him to sit in state, the umpire of our disquisitions.

I think I can depend upon myself, otherwise there would be danger in the project. But if I act my part perfectly, if I have but the resolution to listen coolly to their quiddities,[1] sometimes to oppose, sometimes to recede, and always to own myself conquered on the points which suit me best, I believe both the gentleman and the lady will be sufficiently simple to suppose that in all this there will be nothing apocryphal. They will imagine the gilt statue to be pure gold. I shall be numbered among their elect! I shall rise from the alembic a saint of their own subliming! Shall be assayed and stamped current at their mint!

Yet I must be cautious. I would put my hand in the fire ere undertake so apparently mad a scheme, with any other couple in Christendom. Considering how very warm—Curses bite and tingle on my tongue at the recollection!—Considering I say how

very warm I know their inclinations toward each other to be,
nothing but the proofs I have had could prompt me to commence
an enterprize so improbable. But the uncommonness of it is a main
part of its merit; and I think I know the ground I have to travel so
well that I do not much fear I should lose my road.

I am aware that the enemy I have most to guard against is myself.
To pretend a belief in opinions I despise, to sit with saturnine
gravity and nod approbation when my sides are convulsed with
laughter, to ape admiration at what reason contemns and spurns,
and to smooth my features into suavity while my heart is bursting
with gall at the intercourse they continually hold, of becks and
smiles and approving kind epithets, to do all this is almost too much
for mortal man! But I have already made several essays on myself,
and I find that the obstinate resolution which an insatiable thirst
of ample retribution inspires is not to be shaken, and renders me
equal even to this task.

I am well aware however what dangerous quicksands the
passions are; and that a good pilot is never sparing of soundings.
I will therefore not only keep a rigorous watch upon myself, but
take such measures as shall enable me to exclude or retain the
grub-monger,[1] as I shall think fit, during our conversations.

Thus you are likely soon to hear more of our metaphysics; nay,
if you be but industrious, enough to enable you to set up for yourself, and become the apostle of Paris. I know no place where, if you
have but a morsel of the marvellous to detail, you will find hearers
better disposed to gape and swallow.

                                                      C. CLIFTON

LETTER LXXXII

Anna Wenbourne St. Ives to Louisa Clifton

London, Grosvenor-Street

A FORTNIGHT has almost elapsed since I last wrote to my
Louisa, till my heart begins to cry shame at the delay. Could I
plead no other excuse than the trifling occupations of a trifling
world I must sign my own condemnation; but your brother has

afforded me better employment. Our frequent conversations on many of the best and most dignified of moral enquiries, his acute remarks and objections, and the difficult problems he has occasionally given me to solve, have left me in no danger of being idle.

Oh, Louisa, how exquisite is the pleasure I feel, to see him thus determined, thus incessant in his pursuit! A change so fortunate and so sudden astonishes while it delights!—May it continue!—May it increase!—May?—Vain unworthy wish!—It must—The mind having once seized on the clue of truth can neither quit its hold nor become stationary; it is obliged to advance. And when its powers are equal to those of Coke Clifton, ought we to wonder at its bold and rapid flights?

Still the conquests he daily makes over his own feelings cannot but surprise. His struggles are evident, but they are effectual. He even resolutely casts off the strong prejudices he had conceived against Frank Henley, invites him to aid us in our researches, and appeals to him to explain and decide.

'Let us if we wish to weed out error be sincere in our efforts, and have no remorse for our prejudices.'

This is his own language, Louisa! Oh that I could fully communicate the pleasure this change of character gives me to my friend. Yes, the restraint which too frequent contradiction lays him under will soon wear off, and how great will then be the enthusiasm with which he will defend and promulgate truth!

Nor is it less delightful to observe the satisfaction which this reform sometimes gives to Frank Henley. At others indeed he owns he is disturbed by doubt: but he owns it with feelings of regret, and is eager to prove himself unjust.

Yet respecting me his thoughts never vary—Alas! Louisa, I still 'am his by right.' His tongue is silent, but his looks and manner are sufficiently audible. I surely have been guilty of the error I so much dreaded; my cause was strong, but my arguments were feeble; I have prolonged the warfare of the passions which I attempted to eradicate; or rather have left on his mind a deep sense of injustice committed by me——! The thought is intolerable!——Excruciating!

But oh with what equanimity, with what fortitude does he endure his imagined wrongs! Pure most pure must that passion

be which at once possesses the strength of his and his forbearance!
There are indeed but few Frank Henleys!

Surely, Louisa, I may do him justice?—Surely to esteem the
virtuous cannot merit the imputation of guilt?—Who can praise
him as he deserves? And can that which is right in others be wrong
in me?—Yet such are the mistakes to which we are subject, I
scarcely can speak or even think of him without suspecting myself
of committing some culpable impropriety!

Pardon, Louisa, these wanderings of the mind! They are
marauders which uniform vigilance alone can repel. They are ever
in arms, and I obliged to be ever alert. But it is petty warfare, and
cannot shake the dominion of truth.

My feelings have led me from the topic I intended for the chief
subject of this letter.

The course of our enquiries has several times forced us upon that
great question, 'the progress of mind toward perfection, and the
different order of things which must inevitably be the result.'
Yesterday this theme again occurred. Frank was present; and his
imagination, warm with the sublimity of his subject, drew a bold
and splendid picture of the felicity of that state of society when
personal property no longer shall exist, when the whole torrent of
mind shall unite in enquiry after the beautiful and the true, when
it shall no longer be diverted by those insignificant pursuits to
which the absurd follies that originate in our false wants give birth,
when individual selfishness shall be unknown, and when all shall
labour for the good of all!

A state so distant from present manners and opinions, and
apparently so impossible, naturally gave rise to objections; and
your brother put many shrewd and pertinent questions, which
would have silenced a mind less informed and less comprehensive
than that of our instructor.

At last a difficulty arose which to me wore a very serious form;
and as what was said left a strong impression on my memory, I will
relate that part of the conversation. Observe, Louisa, that Clifton
and Frank were the chief speakers. Your brother began.

I confess, sir, you have removed many apparently unconquerable difficulties: but I have a further objection which I think un-
answerable.

What is it?

Neither man nor woman in such a state can have any thing peculiar: the whole must be for the use and benefit of the whole?

As generally as practice will admit: and how very general that may be, imperfect as its constitution was, Sparta remained during five hundred years a proof.

Then how will it be possible, when society shall be the general possessor, for any man to say—*This is my servant?*

He cannot: there will be no servants.

Well but—*This is my child?*

Neither can he do that: they will be the children of the state.

Indeed!—And what say you to—*This is my wife?*—Can appropriation more than for the minute the hour or the day exist? Or, among so disinterested a people, can a man say even of the woman he loves—*She is mine?*

[We paused—I own, Louisa, I found myself at a loss; but Frank soon gave a very satisfactory reply.]

You have started a question of infinite importance, which perhaps I am not fully prepared to answer. I doubt whether in that better state of human society, to which I look forward with such ardent aspiration, the intercourse of the sexes will be altogether promiscuous and unrestrained; or whether they will admit of something that may be denominated marriage. The former may perhaps be the truth: but it is at least certain that in the sense in which we understand marriage and the affirmation—*This is my wife*—neither the institution nor the claim can in such a state, or indeed in justice exist. Of all the regulations which were ever suggested to the mistaken tyranny of selfishness, none perhaps to this day have surpassed the despotism of those which undertake to bind not only body to body but soul to soul, to all futurity, in despite of every possible change which our vices and our virtues might effect, or however numerous the secret corporal or mental imperfections might prove which a more intimate acquaintance should bring to light!

Then you think that some stipulation or bargain between the sexes must take place, in the most virtuous ages?

In the most virtuous ages the word bargain, like the word promise, will be unintelligible—We cannot bargain to do what is wrong, nor can we, though there should be no bargain, forbear to do what is right, without being unjust.

Whence it results that marriage, as a civil institution, must ever be an evil?

Yes. It ought not to be a civil institution. It is the concern of the individuals who consent to this mutual association, and they ought not to be prevented from beginning, suspending, or terminating it as they please.

Clifton addressed himself to me—What say you to this doctrine, madam? Does it not shock, does it not terrify you?

As far as I have considered it, no. It appears to be founded on incontrovertible principles; and I ought not to be shocked that some of my prejudices are opposed, or at being reminded that men have not yet attained the true means of correcting their own vices.

Surely the consequences are alarming! The man who only studied the gratification of his desires would have a new wife each new day; and the unprotected fair would be abandoned to all the licentiousness of libertinism!

Frank again replied—Then you think the security of women would increase with their imagined increase of danger; and that an unprincipled man, who even at present if he be known is avoided and despised, would then find a more ready welcome, because as you suppose he would have more opportunities to injure?

I must own that the men fit to be trusted with so much power are in my opinion very few indeed.

You are imagining a society as perverse and vitiated as the present: I am supposing one wholly the contrary. I know too well that there are men who, because unjust laws and customs worthy of barbarians have condemned helpless women to infamy, for the loss of that which under better regulations and in ages of more wisdom has been and will again be guilt to keep, I know, sir, I say that the present world is infested by men, who make it the business and the glory of their lives to bring this infamy upon the very beings for whom they feign the deepest affection!—If ever patience can forsake me it will be at the recollection of these demons in the human form, who come tricked out in all the smiles of love, the protestations of loyalty, and the arts of hell, unrelentingly and causelessly to prey upon confiding innocence! Nothing but the malverse[1] selfishness of man could give being or countenance to such a monster! Whatever is good, exquisite, or precious, we are individually taught to grasp at, and if possible to secure; but we have each a latent sense that this principle has rendered us a society of detestable misers, and therefore to rob each other seems almost like the sports of justice.

For which reason, sir, were I a father, I think I should shudder to hear you instructing my daughters in your doctrines.

I perceive you wholly misconceive me; and I very seriously request, pray observe, sir, I very seriously request you to remember that I would not teach any man's daughters so mad a doctrine as to indulge in sensual appetites, or foster a licentious imagination. I am not the apostle of depravity. While men shall be mad, foolish, and dishonest enough to be vain of bad principles, women may be allowed to seek such protection as bad laws can afford— It is an eternal truth that the wisdom of man is superior to the strength of lions; but I would not therfore turn an infant into a lion's den.

I am glad to be undeceived. I thought it was scarcely possible you should mean what your words seemed to imply—At present I understand you; and I again confess my surprise to find so much consistency, and so many powerful arguments on a question in favour of which I thought nothing rational could be advanced. You have afforded me food for reflection, and I thank you. I shall not easily forget what has been said.

Tell me, my dear Louisa, are you not delighted with this dialogue; and with the candour, the force of thinking, and what is still better the virtuous fears of your brother? His mind revolted at the mischief which it seemed to forbode: he was happy at being undeceived. And, with respect to argument, I doubt whether he forgot any one of the most apparently formidable objections to what is called the levelling system. But he was pleased to learn that this is only giving a good cause a bad name. Such a system is infinitely more opposite to levelling than the present; since the very essence of it is that merit shall be the only claimant, and shall be certain of pre-eminence.

The satisfaction I feel, my friend, is beyond expression. To have my hopes revived and daily strengthened, after fearing they must all be relinquished, increases the pleasure. It is great and would be unmixed but for——Well, well!—Let Clifton but proceed

and Frank will no longer say—'To the end of time'——! You
know the rest, Louisa——All good be with you!

A. W. ST. IVES

P.S. I thought I had forgotten something. When Frank had
retired, your brother with delightful candour praised the great
perspicuity as well as strength with which he argued. He added
there was one circumstance in particular in his principles concerning marriage, although they had at first appeared very alarming,
which was highly satisfactory: and this was the confidence they
inspired. 'Nothing, he said, gave his nature so much offence as the
suspicions with which, at present, our sex view the men. About
two years ago he had a partiality for a Neapolitan lady, and thought
himself in love with her: but in this he was mistaken; it was rather
inclination than passion. He knew not at that time what it was to
love. Neither this Neapolitan lady, though beautiful and highly
accomplished, nor any other woman his feelings told him could
inspire pure affection, who was incapable of confiding in herself;
and, wanting this self-confidence, of confiding in her lover. Suspicion originates in a consciousness of self defect. Those who
cannot trust themselves cannot be induced to trust others.'

Thus justly, Louisa, did he continue to reason. Nor could I forbear to apply the doctrine to myself: I have been too distrustful of
him; my conscience accused me, and I am resolved to remedy the
fault. I have always held suspicion to be the vice of mean and
feeble minds: but it is less difficult to find rules by theory than to
demonstrate them by practice.

I am sorry, my dear Louisa, to hear that the infirmities of Mrs.
Clifton increase. But these are evils for which we can at present
find no remedy; and to which we must therefore submit with
patience and resignation.

LETTER LXXXIII

Coke Clifton to Guy Fairfax

London, Dover Street

I WILL not suppose, Fairfax, you seek to compliment me, when you say you enjoy the exuberant heat of soul, the fire that pervades my epistles. I am glad you do. I shall not think the worse of your talents. Many a line have I written in all the burst of feeling, and not a few in all the blaze of wit, and have said to myself,—Should he not understand me now?—Why if he should not, dulness everlasting be his portion!—But you take the sure way to keep up my ardour. While I perceive you continue to enjoy I shall continue to be communicative. A sympathetic yawner I may be, but I do not believe I am often the first to begin.

I knew not half my own merits. I act my part to admiration. 'Tis true the combining circumstances are all favourable. I must be a dunce indeed if in such a school I should want chicanery. Our disputations have been continual; nor have I ever failed to turn them on the most convenient topics. But none of them have equalled the last; managed as it was with dexterity by me, and in the very spirit I wished by my opponents. I speak in the plural; for I took care to have them both present. Several remarks which I had heard from him assured me he would second my plan; which was no less than to prove—marriage a farce!—Would you have believed, Fairfax, I should have had the temerity to step upon a rock so slippery; and to have requested this Archimago[1] of Adam's journeymen [Adam you know being the world's head-gardener] to stay and lend me his support?—Yet thus audacious was I; and courage as it ought has been crowned with success!

The thought was suggested by themselves; and, had you or I or any of us vile marriage haters been declaiming against the saffron god,[2] and his eternal shackles, I doubt whether the best of us could have said any thing half so much to the purpose!—Is it not excellent?—

Then had you heard me preach, ay, me myself, against libertines and libertinism!

By the by, Don Cabbage-plant had the insolence to say two or three devilish severe things, dishonourable to the noble fraternity of us knights of the bed-chamber, which if I forget may woman never more have cause to remember me!

However I brought him to own,—I—[Do laugh!] by my very great apprehensions of the effects of such a doctrine, that though marriage be a bad thing it is quite necessary, at present, for the defence of the weaker vessels and modest maidenhood. Ay and I applauded him for his honest candour! I was glad I had misunderstood him! Thanked him for all his profound information! In short made him exactly what I wished, my tool! And a high-tempered tool he is, by the aid of which I will shew myself a most notable workman!——

Not but the fellow's eye was upon me. I could observe him prying, endeavouring to search and probe me. But I came too well prepared. Instead of shrinking from the encounter, my brow contracted increasing indignation; and my voice grew louder, as I stood forth the champion of chaste virginity and sanctimonious wedlock!——The scene, in the very critical sense of the phrase, was high comedy!—

It was well, Fairfax, they went no farther than Paris: had either of them only reached Turin I had been half undone! And had they touched at Naples, Rome, Venice, or half a dozen other fair and flourishing cities, my character for a pretty behaved, demure, and virtuous gentleman had been irremediably ruined!

Upon my soul I cannot put it out of my head!—Had you heard me remonstrate what a horrid thing it would be to have marriage destroyed, and us honest fellows turned loose among the virgins, from whom we should catch and ravish each a new damsel every new day, and had you seen what a fine serious undertaker's face I put upon the business, your heart would have chuckled! To the day of your death it would never have been forgotten!

Perhaps you will wonder how I could draw such a doctrine from these spinners of hypothesis. I will tell you. I had heard them severally maintain—Try to guess what!—Not in seven years, though you were to do nothing else.—You I suppose like me have heard that liberty, security, and property are the three main pillars of political happiness?——Well then, these professors maintain that individual property is a general evil!——What is more, they maintain it by such arguments as would puzzle college, council, or senate to refute. But that I am determined never to torment my brain about such quips and quillets,[1] may I turn Turk if they would not have made a convert of me, and have persuaded me that an estate of ten thousand a year was a very intolerable thing!

My intention was to keep my countenance, but to laugh at them in my heart most incontinently. However, I soon found my side of the question was not so perfectly beyond all doubt, nor theirs quite so ridiculous as I had imagined.

'Tis true, I went predetermined to be convinced, and to take all they should tell me for gospel. I had a conclusion of my own to draw, and if I could but lead to that, I cared not how much I granted.

I know not whether this predisposition in me was of any advantage to their argument, though I think it was not; for, so ready was the solution to every difficulty, I boldly ventured to state objections which I meant to have kept out of sight, lest I should myself overturn a system that suited my purpose. I perceived their eagerness, saw there was no danger that they should stop at trifles even if I should happen to throw them a bone to pick, and the readiness of each reply raised my curiosity. I fearlessly drew out my heavy artillery, which they with ease and safety as fearlessly dismounted. With a breath my strong holds were all puffed down, like so many houses of cards.

By this however my main business was done more effectually. We came to it by fair deduction. It was not abruptly introduced; it was major, minor, and consequent—All individual property is an evil—Marriage makes woman individual property—Therefore marriage is an evil—Could there be better logic?

As for his saving clause, that marriage in these times of prejudice and vice [I have the whole cant by rote, Fairfax.] is a necessary evil, leave me to do that away. What! Is she not a heroine? And can I not convince her that to act according to a bad system, when there is a better, were to descend to the ways of the vulgar? Can I not teach her how superior she is to the pretty misses who conform to such mistaken laws? Shall she want the courage and the generosity to set the first good example? How often have I seen her eyes sparkle, her bosom heave, and her zeal break forth in virtuous resolutions to encounter any peril to obtain a worthy purpose! And can there be a more worthy?

U

Curse upon these qualms of conscience! Never before did I feel
any thing so teazing, so tormenting! And, knowing what I know,
remembering what I never can forget, the slights, injuries, and
insults I have received, how I came to feel them now is to me wholly
inconceivable. She is acting it is true with what she calls the best
and purest of intentions toward me; she believes them to be such;
she sometimes almost obliges me to believe them such myself. She
tortures me, by half constraining me to revere the virtues in favour
of which she harangues so divinely. But shall I like a poor uxorious
lackadaisy driveller sit down satisfied with a divided heart?—
I!—Has she not with her own lips, under her own hand, avowed
and signed her contumelious guilt, her audacious preference of a
rival?—A mean, a base, a vulgar rival!—And after this shall my
projects suffer impediment from cheesecurd compassion?—Shall
the querulous voice of conscience arrest my avenging arm?—No,
Fairfax!—It cannot be! Though my heart in its anger could not
accuse her of a single crime beside, that alone, that damning preference would be all-sufficient!—The furies have no stings that
equal this recollection!

I have been throwing up my sashes,[1] striding across my room,
and construing ten lines of Seneca,[2] and my pulse again begins to
beat more temperately.

Let us argue the point with this pert, unruly, marplot[3] conscience of mine. .

It was not at first without considerable reluctance and even pain
that I began to plot. I almost abhorred reducing her to the level of
the sex, not one of whom was ever yet her equal. But she used me
ill, Fairfax. Yes, she used me ill; and you well know that want of
resentment is want of courage. None but pitiful, contemptible, no-
souled fellows forget insults, till ample vengeance have been taken.
And shall conscience insolently pretend to contradict the decree?

Beside I could not but remember our old maxims, the Cyprian
battles our jovial corps had fought, and the myrtle wreaths each
wight had won.[4] Should I, the leader the captain of the band, be
the first to fly my colours? Was it not our favourite axiom that he
who could declare, upon his honour, he had found a generous
woman, who never had attempted once to deceive, trifle with, or

play him trick, should still be acknowledged a companion of our order, even though he were to marry: but that all coquetry, all tergiversation, all wrongs, however slight, were unpardonable, and only one way to be redressed? What answer can conscience give to that?

Your letters too are another stimulative. You detail the full, true and particular account of your amorous malefactions, and vaunt of petty obstacles, petty arts, and petty triumphs over Signoras and Madames who advance, challenge you to the field, and give battle purposely to be overcome. Their whole resistance is but to make you feel how great an Alexander you are, and that having vanquished them you are invincible! As you will certainly never meet with an Anna St. Ives, 'tis possible you may die in that opinion. But, I tell you, Fairfax, if you compare these practised Amazons to my heroine, you are in a most heterodox and damnable error, of which if you do not timely repent your soul will never find admission into the lover's Elysium.

Bear witness, however, to my honesty; of women I allow her to be the most excellent, but still a woman, and not as I foolishly for a while supposed an absolute goddess. No, no. Madam can curvet and play her pranks, though of totally a different kind; and, being almost mortal at present, mere mortal must become in despite of conscience and its green sickness physiognomy.

At first I knew her not; and, unwilling to encounter logic in a gauze cap, I ceased to oppose her arguments, and thought to conciliate her by resolving to be of her creed. What could be more generous? But no, forsooth! The veil was too thin! To pretend conviction when it was not felt, and to be satisfied with arguments before I had heard them, were all insufficient for her! The prize could be gained only by him who could answer the enigmas of the Sphinx! I must enter the lists of cavil, and run a tilt at wrangling, ere the lady would bestow the meed of conquest! Can conscience pretend to palliate conduct like this?

I then turned my thoughts to a new project, and endeavoured to overpower her by passion, by excess of ardour, by tenderness and importunity. They had a temporary effect, but I found them equally inefficacious. Nor was the art by which I had oftenest been successful forgotten; though I confess that with her, from the beginning, it afforded me but little hope. I tried to familiarize her to freedoms. I began with her hands; but she soon taught me that even her hands were sacred; they were not to be treated with familiarity, nor to be kissed and pressed like other hands! Let conscience if it can tell me why.

In fine, while to this insolent pedagogue she has been all honey-suckle, sweet marjoram and heart's ease, to me she has been rue, wormwood and hellebore: him praising, me reproving: confiding in him, suspecting me: and, as the very summit and crown of injury, proclaiming him the possessor the master of her admiration, or in plain English of her heart.

And now, if after this impartial, this cool, this stoic examination Mr. Conscience should ever again be impertinent enough to open his lips, I am determined without the least ceremony to kick him out of doors.

When this famous conference of which I told you some half an hour ago was ended, and our president, our monarch of morals and mulberries had quitted his chair and withdrawn, I played an aftergame of no small moment. After pronouncing a panegyric on the gentleman, as a legislator fit for truth and me, I read the lady a modest lecture on confidence, informed her of almost the exact quantity which I expected she would repose in me, and declaimed with eloquence and effect against those suspicious beauties who always regard us honest fellows as so many naughty goblins; who, like the Ethiopian monster, voraciously devour every Virgin-Andromeda they meet.[1] But as I tell you, I did it modestly. I kept on my guard, watched the moment to press forward or to retreat; and wielded my weapons with dexterity and success.

Poor girl! Is it not a pity that the very shield in which she confides, her perfect honesty and sincerity, should be destined to fall upon and overwhelm her?—Thus says counsellor Sentiment: and counseller Sentiment is a great orator!—But what say I? Why I say so have the Fates decreed, and therefore let the Fates look to it; 'tis no concern of mine; I am but their willing instrument.

These however are but the preliminaries, the preparations for the combat. Ere long I shall be armed at all points, and what is better by her own fair hands. Nor do I know how soon I may begin the attack. I have been casting about to send this superintendant of the cardinal virtues, this captain of casuists and caterpillars out of the way; and I think I have hit upon a tolerably bold and ingenious stratagem. I say bold because I perceive it is not without danger; but I doubt I cannot devise a better. Without naming or appearing to mean myself, I have suggested to him, by inventing a tale of two friends of mine, what a noble and disinterested thing it would be for him to go down into the country and prevail on his father to remove all obstacles to our marriage——

How! Say you. Is marriage your plan? And if not is not that the way to ruin all?

There is the danger I talked of; but I do not think it great. The scoundrel gardener, I mean the father; who is heartily despised by every body, is desirous that his son should marry Anna. I know not whether I ever before mentioned this sublime effort of impudence. The cunning rascal has so long been the keeper of Sir Arthur's purse, that it is supposed two thirds of the contents have glided into his own pocket. This is the reason of the delay on Sir Arthur's part, which at present I do not wish to shorten. That this son of a grub catcher, a Demosthenes[1] though he be, should prevail on such a father, if he were to go down as I hope he will, is but little probable. However, should the least prognostic of such a miracle appear, I have my remedy prepared. I will generously have a letter written to the senior overseer of the gravel walks, which if the character I have heard of him be not wholly false, shall revive all his hopes, and put an end to compliance.

In Italy, where amorous plotting is the national profession, I was not easily circumvented; and here, where another gunpowder treason would as soon be suspected as such gins and snares, at least by these very honest and sublime simpletons, I laugh at the supposition of being unearthed.

One word more. I think I observe in this knight of Gotham,[2] this Sir Arthur, a more cordial kind of yearning toward our young prince of Babel land than formerly; a sort of desire to be more intimate with him, of which by the by the youth is not very prompt to admit, and an effort to treat him with more respect himself, by way as it were of setting a good example to others. If my conjectures are right, the threats of the old muckworm father have shaken the crazy nerves of the baronet; and I half suspect there is something more of meaning at the bottom of this. Were it so, were he to attempt to discard me, it would indeed add another spur to the fury of revenge! An affront so deep given by this poor being,

this essence of insignificance, would make revenge itself, hot un-
satiable revenge grow more hot, madden more, and thirst even
after blood!—Patience foams at the supposition!

Thank heaven I hear the noisy postman with his warning bell,
which obliges me in good time to conclude and cool these fermenting juices of mine!

C. CLIFTON

LETTER LXXXIV

Frank Henley to Oliver Trenchard

London, Grosvenor Street

MY mind, Oliver, is harassed by a variety of doubts. I believe I
shall soon be down at Wenbourne Hill, and of course shall then not
fail to meet thee and visit thy most worthy father.

The reason of my journey originates in the doubts I mentioned.
I am angry with myself for feeling alarms at one moment which
appear impossibilities the next. If my fears have any foundation,
this Clifton is the deepest, the most hardened fiend-like hypocrite
imagination can paint!—But it cannot be!—Surely it cannot!—
I am guilty, heinously guilty for enduring such a thought!—So
much folly and vice, combined with understanding and I may say
genius so uncommon, is a supposition too extravagant, too
injurious!

And yet it is strange, Oliver!—A conduct so suddenly altered,
so totally opposite to old and inveterate habits, is scarcely recon-
cileable to the human character. But if dissimulation can be productive of this, is truth less powerful? No!—Truth is omnipotent.
Yet who ever saw it hasty in its progress? My only hope in this case
is that the superiority of his mind has rendered him an exception
to general rules.

But what could he propose by his hypocrisy?—I cannot tell—
His passions are violent and ungovernable; and are or very lately
have been in full vigour—Again and again 'tis strange!

But what of this?—Why these fears? Can she be spotted, tinged
by·the stain of unsanctified desire?—Never!—The pure chastity

of her soul is superior to attaint!—Yet—Who can say?—Wilfully her mind can never err: but who can affirm that even she may not be deceived, and may not act erroneously from the most holy motives?

Perhaps, Oliver, it is my own situation, my own desires, but half subdued, in which these doubts take birth. If so they are highly culpable.

Be it as it may, there is a duty visibly chalked out for me by circumstances. Her present situation is surely a state of danger. To see them married would now give me delight. It would indeed be the delight of despair, of gloom almost approaching horror. But of that I must not think. My father is the cause of the present delay. I fear I cannot remove this impediment, but it becomes me to try.

Though I had before conceived the design, this conduct has even been suggested to me by Clifton; and in a mode that proves he can be artful if he please. Yet does it not likewise prove him to be in earnest?

We have lately had several conversations, one in particular which, even while it seemed to place him in an amiable, sincere, and generous light, excited some of the very doubts and terrors of which I speak—If he be a hypocrite, he guards himself with a tenfold mask!—It cannot—No—It cannot be!—

I mean to speak to Sir Arthur concerning my journey, but not to inform him of its purport: it would have the face of insult to tell him I was going to be his advocate with his servant. Not to mention that he has lately treated me with increasing and indeed unusual kindness. If I do make an effort, however, it shall be a strenuous one; though my hopes that it should be effectual are very few. My decision is not yet final, but in my next thou wilt probably learn the result. Farewell.

F. HENLEY

P.S. My brain is so busied by its fears that I forgot to caution thee against a mistake into which it is probable this letter may lead. I mentioned, in one of my last, the project I had conceived of leaving England. Do not imagine I have abandoned a design on which the more I reflect the more I am intent. The great end of life is to benefit community. My mind in its present situation is too deeply affected freely and without incumbrance to exert

itself—This is weakness!—But not the less true, Oliver. We are
at present so imbued in prejudice, have drunken so deeply of the
cup of error, that, after having received taints so numerous and
ingrained, to wish for perfect consistency in virtue I doubt were
vain. Here or at the antipodes alike I should remember her: but
I should not alike be so often tempted and deluded by false hopes:
the current of thought would not so often meet with impediments,
to arrest, divide, and turn it aside.

I have studied to divine in what land or among what people,
whether savage or such as we call polished, the energies of mind
might be most productive of good. But this is a discovery which I
have yet to make. The reasons are so numerous on each side that
I have formed a plan for a kind of double effort. I think of sailing
for America, where I may aid the struggles of liberty, may freely
publish all which the efforts of reason can teach me, and at the same
time may form a society of savages,[1] who seem in consequence of
their very ignorance to have a less quantity of error, and therefore
to be less liable to repel truth than those whose information is more
multifarious. A merchant, with whom by accident I became
acquainted, and who is a man of no mean understanding, approves
and has engaged to promote my plan. But of this if I come to
Wenbourne Hill we will talk further. Once more, Oliver, adieu.

LETTER LXXXV

Coke Clifton to Guy Fairfax

London, Dover-street

COME to my aid, Fairfax; encourage me; feed my vanity; let
hungry ambition banquet and allow me to be a hero, lest I relent:
for, were I not or Lucifer or Coke Clifton, 'tis certain I should not
persevere. By the host of heaven, Fairfax, but she is a divine
creature! She steals upon the soul! A heart of rock could not resist
her! Nor are they wiles, nor woman's lures, nor blandishments of
tricksey dimples, nor captivating smiles, with which she forms her
adamantine fetters. No; 'tis the open soul of honesty; true, sincere,
and unrelentingly just, to me, to herself, to all; 'tis that enchanting

kindness, that heavenly suavity which never forsakes her; that
equanimity of smiling yet obstinate fortitude; that hilarity of heart
that knows not gloom because it knows not evil; that inscrutable
purity which rests secure that all like itself are natively immaculate;
that—Pshaw!—I can find no words, find you imagination therefore, and think not I will labour at impossibility. You have read of
ancient vestals, of the virgins of Paradise, and of demi-deities that
tune their golden harps on high?—Read again—And, having
travelled with prophets and apostles to the heaven of heavens,
descend and view her, and invent me language to describe her, if
you can!

Curse on this Frank Henley! But for him my vengeance never
would have been roused! Never would the fatal sentence have
passed my lips!—'Tis now irrevocable—Sure as the lofty walls of
Troy were doomed by gods and destiny to smoke in ruins, so surely
must the high-souled Anna fall—'Ill starred wench!'¹—I, Fairfax,
like other conquerors, cannot shut pity from my bosom. While
I cry havoc I could almost weep; could look reluctant down on
devastation which myself had made, and heave a sigh, and curse
my proper prowess!—In love and war alike, such, Fairfax, is
towering ambition. It must have victims: its reckless altars ask a
full and large supply; and when perchance a snowy lamb, spotless
and pure, bedecked for sacrifice, in all the artless pomp of un-
suspecting innocence is brought, bright burns the flame, the white
clouds curl and mantle up to heaven, and there ambition proudly
sits, and snuffs with glut of lusty delight the grateful odour.

I know your tricks, Fairfax; you are one of the doubtful doctors;
you love to catch credulity upon your hook. I hear fat laughter
gurgling in your throat, and out bolts your threadbare simile—
'Before the battle's won the Brentford hero sings Te Deum.'²—
But don't be wasteful of the little wit you have. Do I not tell you
it is decreed? When was I posted for a vapouring Hector? What
but the recollections of my reiterated ravings, resolves, threats, and
imprecations could keep me steady; assailed as I am by gentleness,
benevolence, and saint-like charity?

By the agency of subtlety, hypocrisy, and fraud, I seek to rob
her of what the world holds most precious. By candour, philanthropy and a noble expansion of heart, she seeks to render me
all that is superlatively great and good—Why did she not seek

all this in a less offensive way? Why did she oblige me to become
a disputant with a plebeian?—Disputant!—What do I say?—
Worse, worse!—Rival!—Devil!—Myriads of virtues could not
atone the crime!—Yet in this deep guilt she perseveres and glories!
—Can I forget?—Fear me not, nor rank my defeat among things
possible—Be patient and lend an ear.

To one sole object all my efforts point: her mind must be prepared, ay so that when the question shall be put, chaste as that
mind is, it scarcely shall receive a shock. Such is the continual
tendency of my discourse. Her own open and undisguised manners
are my guide. Not a principle she maintains but which, by my
cunning questions and affected doubts pushed to an extreme,
adds links to the chain in which I mean to lead her captive.

Perhaps, Fairfax, you will tell me this is the old artifice; and that
the minds of all women, who can be said to have any mind, must
thus be inveigled to think lightly of the thing they are about to
lose. Granted. And yet the difference is infinite. They are brought
to think thus lightly of chastity: but, should you or any one of the
gallant phalanx attempt to make Anna St. Ives so think, she would
presently cry buzz to the dull blockhead, and give him his eternal
dismission.

Virtue with her is a real existence, and as such must be adored.
Her passions are her slaves; and in this and this alone the lovely
tyrant is the advocate of despotism. She soon taught me that
common arts would be treated by her, not merely with determined
and irrevocable repulse, but with direct contempt. Some very
feeble essays presently satisfied me. No encroachments of the
touch, no gloting of the eye, no well feigned tremblings and lover's
palpitations would for an instant be suffered by her. Take the
following as a specimen of my mode of attack.

Among her variety of hypotheses she has one on mutability.
'Little, she says, as we know of matter and spirit, we still know
enough to perceive they are both instantaneously, eternally, and
infinitely changing. Of what the world has been, through this series
of never beginning never ending mutation, she can form nothing
more than conjecture: yet she cannot but think that the golden age
is a supposition treated at present with ridicule it does not deserve.
By the laws of necessity, mind, unless counteracted by accidents
beyond its control, is continually progressive in improvement.

With some such accidents we are tolerably well acquainted. Such are those which have been destructive of its progress, notwithstanding the high attainments it had made in Greece and Rome. The ruins still existing in Egypt are wonderful proofs of what it once was there; though Egypt is at present almost unequalled in ignorance and depravity. Who then shall affirm changes still more extraordinary have not happened? She has no doubt, some revolution in the planetary system excepted, that men will attain a much higher degree of innocence, length of life, happiness, and wisdom than have ever yet been dreamed of, either by historian, fabulist, or poet: for causes which formerly were equal to the effects then produced are now rendered impotent by the glorious art of printing; which spreads, preserves, and multiplies knowledge, in despite of ignorance, false zeal, and despotism.'

Such was her discourse, and thus vast were her views! Nay, urged on by my questions, by the consequences which resulted from her own doctrines, and by the ardour of emanating benevolence, she astonished me by her sublime visions; for she proceeded to prove, from seemingly fair deduction, 'that men should finally render themselves immortal; should become scarcely liable to moral mistake; should all act from principles previously demonstrated, and therefore never contend; should be one great family without a ruler, because in no need of being ruled; should be incapable of bodily pain or passion; and should expend their whole powers in tracing moral and physical cause and effect; which, being infinite in their series, will afford them infinite employment of the most rational and delightful kind!'

Oh! How did the sweet enthusiast glow, ay and make me glow too, while, with a daring but consistent hand she sketched out this bold picture of illusion!

But, while the lovely zealot thus descanted on splendid and half incomprehensible themes, what did I? Why, when I found her at the proper pitch, when I saw benevolence and love of human kind beaming with most ardour in her eye, and pouring raptures from her lip, I then recalled her to her beloved golden age, her times of primitive simplicity; made her inform me what lovers then were, and what marriage; and what the bonds were which hearts so affectionate and minds so honest and pure demanded of each other.

What think you could her answers to all these questions be?

What but such as I wished? Could lovers like these suspect each other? Could they basely do the wrong to ask for bond or pledge? Or, if they wanted the virtue to charm, could they still more basely ask rewards they did not merit? Could they, with the wretched selfish jealousy of a modern marriage-maker, seek to cadaverate affection and to pervert each other into a utensil, a commodity, a thing appropriate to self and liable with other lumber to be cast aside? No, Fairfax; she played fairly and deeply into my hand. She created exactly such a pair of lovers as I could have desired: for with respect to the truth and constancy with which she endowed them, if I cannot be the thing, I can wear the garb; ay and it shall become me too, shall sit *dégagé*[1] upon me, and be thought my native dress.

Think not that I am a mere listener: far the reverse. I throw in masterly touches, which, while they seem only to heighten her picture, produce the full effect by me intended. Thus, when she described the faith and truth and love of the innocents of her own creation, how did I declaim against the abuse to which such doctrine, though immutably true, was liable!

'Alas! madam,' said I, 'had the unprincipled youths with which these times abound your powers of argument with their own principles, how dreadful would be the effect! How many un-suspecting hearts would they betray!'

I am once more just returned from the palace of Alcina![2] I broke off at the end of my last paragraph to attend my charmer; and here again am I detesting myself for want of resolution; and detesting myself still more for having made a resolution, for having under-taken that which I am so eternally tempted to renounce. Your sneer and your laugh are both ready—I know you, Fairfax—'The gentle-man is sounding a retreat! The enterprise is too difficult!'—No—I tell you no, no, no,—But I am almost afraid it is too damnable!

I pretended to be exceedingly anxious concerning the delay, and afflicted at not hearing any thing more from Sir Arthur. If I did not do this, it might be a clue to lead her to suspect hypo-crisy, considering how very ardent I was at the commencement. And, to say the truth, I am weary enough of waiting; though it is not my wish to be relieved by any expedition of Sir Arthur's, who, as I hinted to you before, does not appear to be in the least hurry, and whose unction for the gardener's son increases.

But had you heard her console me! Had you seen her kindness! The tear glistening in her eye while she entreated me to consider delay as a fortunate event, which tended to permanent and ineffable happiness; had you I say beheld her soul, for it was both visible and audible, Fairfax though you are, the marauder of marriage land and the sworn foe of virginity, even you would have pardoned my tergiversation.

Did you never behold the sun burst forth from behind the riding clouds? The scene that was gloomy, dark and dismal is suddenly illumined; what was obscure becomes conspicuous; the bleak hills smile, the black meadows assume a bright verdure; quaking shadows dare no longer stay, cold damps are dispelled, and in an instant all is visible, clear, and radiant! So vanish doubts when she begins to speak! Thus in her presence do the feelings glow; and thus is gloom banished from the soul, till all is genial warmth and harmony!

These being my feelings now, when I am escaped, when I am beyond the circle of her sorceries, think, Fairfax, be just and think how seductive, how dangerous an enemy I have to encounter— Listen and judge.

'Oh! Clifton'—She speaks! Listen I say to her spells!—'Oh! Clifton, daily and hourly do I bless this happy accident, this delay! I think, with the heroic archbishop,[1] I could have held my right hand firmly till the flames had consumed it, could I but have brought to pass what this blessed event has already almost accomplished! To behold your mind what it is and to recollect what it so lately was is bliss unutterable! I consider myself now as destined to be yours: but whether I am or am not is perhaps a thing of little moment. Let self be forgotten, and all its petty interests! What am I? What can I be, compared to what you may become? The patriot, the legislator, the statesman, the reconciler of nations, the dispenser of truth, and the instructor of the human race; for to all these you are equal. As for me, however ardent however great my good-will, I cannot have the same opportunities. Beside I must be just to myself and you, and it delights me to declare I believe you have a mind capable of conceptions more vast than mine, of plans more daring and systems more deep, and of soaring beyond

me. You have the strong memory, the keen sensibility and the
rapid imagination which form the poet. It is my glory to repeat that
your various powers, when called forth, have as variously astonished
me. To bid you persevere were now to wrong you, for I think I dare
affirm you cannot retreat. You have at present seen too much,
thought too much, known too much ever to forget. In private you
will be the honour of your family and the delight of your wife;
and in public the boast of your country and the admiration of the
virtuous and the wise.'

I fell on my knee to the speaking deity! She seemed delivering
oracles! My passions rose, my heart was full, her eulogium made
it loath and abhor its own deceit; the words—'Madam, I am a
villain!'—bolted to my lips, there they quivering lingered in
excruciating suspense, and at last slunk back like cowards, half
wishing but wholly ashamed to do their office.

By the immortal powers, Fairfax, it was past resisting! Why
should I not be all she has described? The hero, the legislator, the
great leader of this little world? Ay, why not? She seemed to
prophesy. She has raised a flame in me which, if encouraged, might
fertilize or desolate kingdoms. Body of Cæsar, I know not what
to say!

'Tis true she has treated me ill; nay vilely. It cannot be denied.
But ill treatment itself, from her, is superior to all the maukish
kindness which folly and caprice endeavour to lavish. Fairfax,
would you did but behold her! My heart was never so assailed
before!

My resolution is shaken, I own, but it is not obliterated. No; I
will think again. My very soul is repugnant to the supposition of
leaving its envenomed tumours unassuaged, and its angered stabs
unavenged. Yet, if healed they could be, she surely possesses that
healing art——Once more I will think again.

What you tell me in the Postscript to your last concerning Count
Caduke[1] [Consult your dictionary; or to save yourself trouble read
Count Crazy, alias Beaunoir.] is wholly unintelligible to me. But
as you say the name of the gardener's son was several times
mentioned by him, I shall take an immediate opportunity of inter-
rogating the 'squire of shrubs, who I am certain from principle will
when asked tell me all he knows.

Apropos of poetry. The panegyric of this sylph of the sun-beams

gave me an impulse which I could not resist, and the following was
the offspring of my headlong and impetuous muse; for such the
hussey is whenever the fit is upon her. I commit it as it may happen
to your censure or applause; with this stipulation, if you do not
like it either alter it till you do, or write me another which both
you and I shall like better. If that be not fair and rational barter,
I know nothing either of trade, logic, or common sense.

ANACREONTIC

I

WHEN by the gently gliding stream,
On banks where purple violets spring,
I see my Delia's beauties beam,
I hear my lovely Delia sing,
    When hearts combine
    And arms entwine,
When fond caresses, am'rous kisses
Yield the height of human blisses,
Entranc'd I gaze, and sighing say,
Thus let me love my life away.

II

Or when the jocund bowl we pass,
And joke and wit and whim abound,
When song and catch and friend and lass
In sparkling wine we toast around,
    When Bull[1] and Pun
    Rude riot run,
And finding still the mirth increasing,
Pealing laughter roars sans ceasing,
I peal and roar and pant and say,
Thus let me laugh my life away.

III

When dreams of fame my fancy fill,
Sweet soothing dreams of verse and rhyme,
That mark the poet's happy skill,
And bid him live to latest time,
    Each rising thought
    With music fraught,

All full, all flowing, nothing wanting,
All harmonious, all enchanting,
Oh thus, in rapt delights I say,
Thus let me sing my life away!

IV

Oh lovely woman, gen'rous wine,
These potent pleasures let me quaff!
Thy raptures, wit, oh make them mine!
Oh let me drink and love and laugh!
    In flowing verse
    Let me rehearse
How well I've used your bounteous treasure;
Then at last when full my measure,
Tho' pale my lip, I'll smile and say,
I've liv'd the best of lives away.

C. CLIFTON

LETTER LXXXVI

Frank Henley to Oliver Trenchard

London, Grosvenor Street

WITHIN a week, Oliver, we shall once more meet. What years of separation may afterward follow is more than I can divine. I surely need not tell thee that this thought of separation, were it not opposed by principle, would indeed be painful, and that it is at moments almost too mighty for principle itself. But we are the creatures of an omnipotent necessity; and there can be but little need to remind thee that a compliance with the apparently best should ever be an unrepining and cheerful act of duty.

I have had a conversation with Sir Arthur, very singular in its kind, which has again awakened sensations in their full force that had previously cost me many bitter struggles to allay. I began with informing him of my intention to go down to Wenbourne-Hill; after which I proceeded to tell him it was my design to embark for America.

He seemed surprised, and said he hoped not.

I answered I had reflected very fully on the plan, and that I

believed it was scarcely probable any reason should occur which
could induce me to change my purpose.

The thing, he replied, might perhaps not be so entirely improbable as I supposed. His family had great obligations to me. I had
even risked my life on various occasions for them. They thought
my talents very extraordinary. In fine, Oliver, the good old gentleman endeavoured to say all the kind and, as he deemed them,
grateful things his memory could supply; and added that, should
I leave England without affording them some opportunity to repay
their obligations, they should be much grieved. There were
perhaps two or three very great difficulties in the way; but still he
was not sure they might not be overcome. Not that he could say
any thing positively, for matters were he must own in a very doubtful state. He was himself indeed very considerably uneasy, and
undetermined: but he certainly wished me exceedingly well, and
so with equal certainty at present did all his family. His daughter,
his son, himself, were all my debtors.

The good old gentleman's heart overflowed, Oliver, and by its
ebullitions raised a tumult in mine, which required every energy
it possessed to repel. What could I answer, but that I had done no
more for his family than what it was my duty to do for the greatest
stranger; and that, if gratitude be understood to mean a remembrance of favours received, I and my family had for years indubitably been the receivers?

He still persisted however in endeavouring to dissuade me
from the thought of quitting the kingdom. Not finding me
convinced by his arguments, he hesitated, with an evident desire
to say something which he knew not very well how to begin.
All minds on such occasions are under strong impulses. My
own wish that he should be explicit was eager, and I excited
him to proceed. At last he asked if he might put a question to
me; assuring me it was far from his intention to offend, but that
he had some uneasy doubts which he could be very glad to have
removed.

I desired him to interrogate me freely; and to assure himself
that I would be guilty of no dissimulation.

He knew my sincerity, he said; but if when I heard I should
think any thing in what he asked improper, I past dispute had a
right to refuse.

X

I answered that I suspected or rather was convinced I had no such right, and requested him to begin.

He again stammered, and at last said—I think, Mr. Henley, I have remarked some degree of esteem between you and my daughter—

He stopped—His desire not to wound my feelings was so evident that I determined to relieve him, and replied—

I believe, sir, I can now divine the subject of your question. You would be glad to know if any thing have passed between us, and what? Perhaps you ought to have been told without asking; but I am certain that concealment at present would be highly wrong.

I then repeated as accurately as my memory would permit, which is tolerably tenacious on this subject, all which Anna and I had reciprocally said and done. It was impossible, Oliver, to make this recapitulation with apathy. My feelings were awakened, and I assure thee the emotions of Sir Arthur were as lively as in such a mind thou couldst well suppose. The human heart seems to be meliorated and softened by age. He wept, a thing with him certainly not usual, at the recital of his daughter's heroic resolves in favour of duty, and at her respect for parental prejudices. Her dread of rendering him unhappy made him even sob, and burst into frequent interjections of—'She is a dear girl! She is a heavenly girl! I always loved her! She is the delight of my life, my soul's treasure! From her infancy to this hour, she was always an angel!'

After hearing me fully confirm him in his esteem and affection for so superlative a daughter, he added—You tell me, Mr. Henley, that you freely informed my daughter you thought it was even her duty to prefer you to all mankind, even though her father and friends should disapprove the match.

I did, sir. I spoke from conviction, and should have thought myself culpable had I been silent.

Perhaps so. But that is very uncommon doctrine.

It was not merely that more felicity would have been secured to ourselves, but greater good I supposed would result to society.

I have heard you explain things of that kind before. I do not very well understand them, but give me leave to ask—Are you still of the same opinion?

I am, sir.—Not that I am so confident as I was—Mr. Clifton has a very astonishing strength of mind: and, should it be turned to the worthy purposes of which it is capable, I dare by no means decide positively in my own favour: and the decision which I now make against him is the result of the intimate acquaintance which I must necessarily have with my own heart, added to certain dubious appearances as to his which I know not how to reconcile. Of myself I am secure.

And of him you have some doubts?

I have: but I ought in duty to add the appearances of their being unjust are daily strengthened.

Sir Arthur paused, ruminated, and again seemed embarrassed. At last he owned he knew not what to say: turn which way he would the obstacles were very considerable. His mind had really felt more distress, within these two months, than it had ever known before. He could resolve on nothing. Yet he could not but wish I had not been quite so determined on going to America. There was no saying what course things might take. Mrs. Clifton was very ill, and in all probability could not live long. But again he knew not what to say. He certainly wished me very well—Very well—I was an uncommon young man. I was a gentleman by nature, which for aught he knew might be better than a gentleman by birth. The world had its opinions; perhaps they were just, perhaps unjust. He had been used to think with the world, but he had heard so much lately that he was not quite so positive as he had been—— [This, Oliver, reminded me of the power of truth; how it saps the strong holds of error and winds into the heart, and how incessantly its advocates ought to propagate it on every occasion.] He was not quite so well pleased as he had been with my father, but that was no fault of mine; he knew I had a very different manner of thinking. Still he must say it was what he very little expected. He hoped however that things would one way or other go more smoothly; and he concluded with taking my hand, pressing it very warmly, and adding with considerable earnestness—'If you can think of changing your American project, pray do!—Pray do!—'

After which he left me with something like a heavy heart.

And now, Oliver, how ought I to act? The opposing causes of these doubts and difficulties in his mind are evident. The circumstances which have occurred in my favour, being aided by the obstinate selfishness of my father, by his acquired wealth, and as I suppose by the embroiled state of Sir Arthur's affairs, have

produced an unhoped for revolution in the sentiments of Sir
Arthur. But is it not too late? Are not even the most tragical consequences to be feared from an opposition to Clifton? Nay, if his
mind be what his words and behaviour speak, would not opposition
be unjust? Were it not better with severe but virtuous resolution
to repel these flattering and probably deceitful hopes, than by
encouraging them to feed the canker-worm of peace, and add new
force to the enemy within, who rather stunned than conquered is
every moment ready to revive.

Neither is Sir Arthur master of events. Nor is his mind consistent
enough to be in no danger of change.

My heart is sufficiently prone to indulge opposite sentiments, but
it must be silenced; it must listen to the voice of truth.

Did I but better understand this Clifton, I should better know
how to decide. That he looks up to her with admiration I am convinced. She seems to have discovered the true key to his understanding as well as to his affections. Even within this day or two,
I have observed symptoms very much in his favour. How do I
know but thus influenced he may become the first of mankind?
The thought restores me to a sense of right. Never, Oliver, shall
self complacency make me guilty of what cannot but be a crime
most heinous! If such a mind may by these means be gained which
would otherwise be lost, shall it be extinguished by me? Would
not an assassination like this outweigh thousands of common
murders? Well may I shudder at such act! Oliver, I am resolved.
If there be power in words or in reason my father shall comply.

As far as I understand the human mind, there is and even should
he persevere there always must be something to me enigmatical in
this instance of its efforts in Clifton. Persevere however I most
sincerely hope and even believe he will.—But should he not?—
The supposition is dreadful!—Anna St. Ives!—My heart sinks
within me!—Can virtue like hers be vulnerable?—Surely not!—
The more pure a woman is in principle the more secure would she
be from common seducers. But, if the man can be found who
possesses the necessary though apparently incompatible excess of
folly and wisdom, there is a mode by which such a woman is more
open to the arts of deceit than any other. And is not that woman
Anna St. Ives? Nay more, if he be not a prodigy of even a still more
extraordinary kind, is not that man Coke Clifton?

He came in the heyday of youthful pride, self-satisfied, self-convinced, rooted in prejudice but abundant in ideas. Argument made no impression; for where he ought to have listened he laughed. The weapons of wit never failed him; and, while he lanched[1] them at others, they recoiled and continually lacerated himself. Of this he was insensible: he felt them not, or felt them but little. His haughtiness never slumbered; and to oppose him was to irritate, not convince. For four months he continued pertinaciously the same; then, without any cause known to me, suddenly changed. It was indeed too sudden not to be alarming!

And yet my firm and cool answer to all this is that hypocrisy so foolish as well as atrocious is all but impossible—

Indeed, Oliver, I do not seek to wrong him: I do not hunt after unfavourable conjectures, they force themselves upon me: or if I do it is unconsciously. The passions are strangely perverse: and if I am deceived, as I hope I am, it is they that misguide me.

Clifton has just been with me. Some correspondent from Paris has mentioned the visit paid to me instead of him by the Count de Beaunoir, but in a dark and unintelligible manner, and he came to enquire. I confess, Oliver, while I was answering his interrogatories, I seemed to feel that both you and I had drawn a false conclusion relative to secrecy; and that by concealment to render myself the subject of suspicion was an unworthy procedure. However as my motives were not indirect, whatever my silence might be, I answered without reserve and told him all that had passed; frankly owning my fears of his irritability as the reason why I did not mention the affair immediately.

He laughted at the Count's rhodomontade, acknowledged himself obliged to me, and allowed that at that time my fears were not wholly causeless. He behaved with ease and good humour, and left me without appearing to have taken any offence.

I shall be with thee on Tuesday. I know it will be a day of feasting to the family, and I will do my best endeavour not to cast a damp on the hilarity of benevolence and friendship.

F. HENLEY

LETTER LXXXVII

Anna Wenbourne St. Ives to Louisa Clifton

London, Grosvenor Street

ALAS! Louisa, what are we?—What are our affections, what our resolves? Taken at unguarded moments, agitated, hurried away by passion, how seldom have we for a day together reason to be satisfied with our conduct?

Not pleased with myself, I doubt I have given cause of displeasure to your brother. My father was in part the occasion: for a moment he made me forget myself——Louisa!—Frank Henley is going to America! He does not lightly resolve, and his resolution seems fixed!——Good God!—I—Louisa!—I am afraid I am a guilty creature!—Weak!—Very weak!—And is not weakness guilt?—But why should he leave us?—Where will he find hearts more alive to his worth?

Sir Arthur came to inform me of it: he had been conversing with him, and had endeavoured but without effect to dissuade him from his purpose. He came and begged me to try. I perhaps might be more successful.

There was a marked significance in his manner, and I asked him why?

Nay, my dear child, said he, and his heart seemed full, you know why. Mr. Henley has told me why.

What, sir, has he told?

Nothing, child—[Sir Arthur took my hand]—Nothing, but what is honourable to you—I questioned him, and you know he is never guilty of falsehood.

No, sir; he is incapable of it.

Well, Anna, try then to persuade him not to leave us. Though he is a very excellent young man, I am afraid he has not the best of fathers. I begin to feel I have not been so prudent as I might have been; and, if Mr. Henley were to leave England, the father might attribute it to us, and—[Sir Arthur hesitated]——I have received some extraordinary letters from Abimelech, of which I did not at first see the full drift; but it is now clear; every thing corresponds, and my conversation with young Mr. Henley has confirmed all I had supposed. However he is a very good a very extraordinary young gentleman, and I could wish he would not go. I don't know what may happen.

Your brother came in and Sir Arthur left me, desiring me as he went to remember what he had said. Clifton after an apology asked —Does it relate to me? At that moment Frank entered. No, said I; it relates to one who I did not think would have been so ready to forsake his friends!

A thousand thoughts had crowded to my mind; a dread of having used him ungenerously, unjustly; a recollection of all he had done and all he had suffered; his enquiring, penetrating, and unbounded genius; his superlative virtues; a horror of his being banished his native country by me; of his wandering among strangers, exposed to poverty, perils, and death, with the conviction in his heart that I had done him wrong!—My tumultuous feelings rushed upon me, overpowered me, and in a moment of enthusiasm I ran to him, snatched his hand, fell on my knee and exclaimed—'For the love of God, Mr. Henley, do not think of leaving us!'

Clifton like myself could not conquer the first assault of passion: he pronounced the word madam! in a tone mingled with surprise and severe energy, which recalled me to myself——

You see, said I, turning to him, what an unworthy weak creature I am!—But Mr. Henley has taken the strangest resolution—!

What, madam, said your brother, recovering himself, and with some pleasantry, is he for a voyage to the moon? Or does he wait the arrival of the next comet, to make the tour of the universe?

Nay, answered I, you must join me, and not treat my poor petition with ridicule—You must not go, Mr. Henley; indeed you must not! I, Mr. Clifton, my father, my brother, we will none of us hear of it! We are all your debtors, and it would be unjust in you to deprive us of every opportunity of testifying our friendship.

Your brother, Louisa, made an effort worthy of himself, repressed the error of his first feelings, assumed the gentle aspect of entreaty, and kindly joined me.

We are indeed your debtors, said he to Mr. Henley. But I hope it is not true. I hope there is no danger that you should forsake us. Where would you go? Where can you be so happy?

I mean first, replied Frank, to go to Wenbourne Hill; and after that my intentions are for America.

This, Louisa, brought on a long discussion. I and your brother both endeavoured to convince him it was his duty to remain in England; that he could be more serviceable here, and would find better opportunities for effecting that good which he had so warmly at heart than in any other country.

He answered that, though he was not convinced by our arguments, he should think it his duty seriously to consider them. But we could not make him promise any thing further. Previous to his return from Wenbourne Hill he would determine.

Indeed, Louisa, this affair lies very heavily upon my mind. I am incessantly accusing myself as the cause of his exile. And am I not? By the manner of Sir Arthur I am sure he must have said something very highly in my praise. I have gone too far with your brother to recede: that is now impossible. It would be more flagrant injustice than even the wrong to Frank, if a wrong it be, and indeed, Louisa, I dread it is!—Indeed I do!—I dread it even with a kind of horror!

I thought reason would have appeased these doubts ere this; but every occasion I find calls them forth with unabated vigour. Surely this mental blindness must be the result of neglect. Had we but the will, the determination, it might be removed. Oh how reprehensible is my inconsistency!

The rapid decline of Mrs. Clifton grieves me deeply. Your brother too has frequently mentioned it with feelings honourable to his heart. He is now more than ever sensible of her worth. He has been with me since I began to write this letter, and there is not the least appearance of remaining umbrage on his mind. It was indeed but of short duration, though too strong and sudden not to be apparent.

All kindness, peace, and felicity be with you.

A. W. ST. IVES

LETTER LXXXVIII

Coke Clifton to Guy Fairfax

London, Dover Street

I WILL curse no more, Fairfax. Or, if curse I do, it shall be at my own fatuity. I will not be the dilatory, languid, ranting, moralizing Hamlet of the drama; that has the vengeance of hell upon his lips and the charity of heaven in his heart. I will use not speak daggers—[1]

Fairfax, I am mad!—Raging!——The smothered and pent-up mania must have vent—What! Was not the page sufficiently black before?—I am amazed at my own infatuation! My very soul spurns at it!—But 'tis past—Deceitful, damned sex!—Idiot that I was, I began to fancy myself beloved!—I!—Blind, deaf, insensate driveler!—Torpid, blockish, brainless mammet![2]——Most sublime ass!—Oh for a bib and barley sugar, with the label *Meacock*[3] pinned before and behind!—

Fairfax, I never can forgive my own absurd and despicable stupidity!—Marriage?—What, with a woman in whose eye the perfect impression and hated form of a mean rival is depicted?— In colours glowing hot!—Who lives, revels, triumphs in her heart! —I marry such a woman?—I?—

> 'I had rather be a toad,
> And live upon the vapour of a dungeon,
> Than keep a corner in the thing I love
> For other's use.'[4]

I am too full of phrensy, Fairfax, to tell thee what I mean: but she has given me another proof, more damning even than all the former, of the gluttony with which her soul gorges. Her gloating eye devours him; ay, I being present. Nay, were I this moment in her arms, her arms would be clasping him, not me: with him she would carouse, nor would any thing like me exist—Contagion!— Poison and boiling oil!—

Never before was patience so put to the proof—My danger was extreme. With rage flaming in my heart, I was obliged to wear complacency, satisfaction and smiles on my countenance.

The fellow has determined to ship himself for America—Would

it were for the bottomless pit!—And had you beheld her panic?—
St. Luke's collected maniacs[1] at the full of the moon could not have
equalled her!—'Twas well indeed her frantic outrage was so
violent, or I had been detected and all had been lost—As it was I
half betrayed myself—The fellow's eye glanced at me. However
it gave me my cue; and, all things considered, I afterward performed to a miracle. Her own enthusiastic torrent swept all before
it, and gave me time. She was in an ecstasy; reasoning, supplicating,
conjuring, panting. I, her friends, the whole world must join her:
and join her I did. It was the very relief of which hypocrisy stood
in need. I entreated this straight-backed youth, stiff in determination, to condescend to lend a pitying ear to our petitions; to
suffer us to permeate his bowels of compassion, and avert this fatal
and impending cloud, fraught with evils, misery, and mischief—

But marry no!—It could not be!—Sentence was passed—He
had been at the trouble to make a pair of scales, and knew the
weight to a scruple of every link in the whole chain of cause and
effect—Teach him, truly!—Advise him!—Move him!—When?
Who? How?—At last compliance, willing to be royally gracious,
said, Well it would consider—Though there was but little hope—
Nothing it had heard had any cogency of perscrutation—But, in
fine, it would be clement, and consider.

Do you not see this fellow, Fairfax? Is he not now before your
eyes? Is he not the most consummate——? But why do I trouble
myself a moment about him?—It is her!—Her!—

Nor is this all. Did that devil that most delights in mischief
direct every concurring circumstance, they could not all and each
be more uniform, more coercive to the one great end. This poor
dotterel, Sir Arthur, is playing fast and loose with me. He has been
at his soundings [2]—He!—Imbecile animal!—Could wish there
were not so many difficulties—Is afraid they cannot be all removed
—Has his doubts and his fears—Twenty thousand pounds is a
large sum, and Mrs. Clifton is very positive—His own affairs much
less promising than he supposed——Then by a declension of
hems, hums, and has, he descended to young Mr. Henley—A very
extraordinary young gentleman!—A very surprising youth!—
One made on purpose as it were for plum-cake days, high festivals,
and raree show![3]—A prodigy!—Not begotten, born or bred in the
dull blind-man's-buff way of simple procreation; but sent us on a

Sunday morning down Jacob's ladder!—Then for obligations to
him, count them who could!—He must first study more arithmetic!
—And as for affection it was a very wayward thing—Not always in
people's power—There was no knowing what was best—The hand
might be given and the heart be wanting—And with respect to
whether the opinions of the world ought to be regarded, good truth
he knew not. Marry! The world was much more ready to blame
others than to amend itself: and he had been almost lately persuaded not to care a fico¹ for the world. But for his part he was a
godly christian, and wished all for the best. He had faith, hope,
and charity, which were enough for one.

Do not imagine, Fairfax, the poor dotard would have dared to
betray himself thus far, had not I presently perceived his drift and
wormed him of these dismal cogitations of the spirit. He beat
about, and hovered, and fluttered, and chirped mournfully, like
the poor infatuated bird that beholds the serpent's mouth open,
into which it is immediately to drop and be devoured. However,
having begun, I was determined to make him unburden his whole
heart. If hereafter he can possibly find courage to face me, in order
to reproach, I have my lesson ready. 'Out of thy own mouth will I
judge thee, sinner.'

Gangrened as my heart is, I still find a satisfaction in this self
convalescence. The lady of mellifluous speech shall suborn no
more; no more shall lull me into beatific slumbers. I have recovered
from my trance, and what I dreamed was celestial I will demonstrate to be mere woman.

From his own lips I learn that this insolent scoundrel received
a visit from the Count de Beaunoir, which was intended for me:
and, out of tender pity to my body, lest, God 'ild us, it should get
a drilling, he did bestow some trifle of that wit and reason of which
he has so great a superflux upon the Count, thereby to turn aside
his wrathful ire.

I heard the gentleman tell his tale, and tickle his imagination
with the remembrance of his own doctiloquy,² with infinite composure; and, whenever I put a question, took care first to prepare
a smile. Every thing was well, better could not be.

With respect to *Monsieur le Comte*, I'll take some opportunity to
whisper a word in his ear. It is not impossible, Fairfax, but that
I may visit Paris even within this fortnight. Not that I can pretend

to predict. They shall not think I fly them, should any soul among them dare to dream of vengeance. I know the Count to be as vain of his skill in the sword as he is of his pair of watch strings,[1] his Paris-Birmingham snuff-box,[2] or the bauble that glitters on his finger. I think I can give him a lesson: at least I mean to try.

My mother's health declines apace. I know not whether it may not shortly be necessary for me to visit her. The loss of her will afflict me, but in all appearance it is inevitable, and I fear not far distant.

Once more, Fairfax, should you again fall in company with the Count, and he should give himself the most trifling airs, assure him that I will do myself the honour to embrace him within a month at farthest from that date, be it when it will.

Adieu.

C. CLIFTON

LETTER LXXXIX

Anna Wenbourne St. Ives to Louisa Clifton

London, Grosvenor-Street

HE is gone, Louisa; has left us; his purpose unchanged, his heart oppressed, and his mind intent on promoting the happiness of those by whom he is exiled. And what am I, or who, that I should do him this violence? What validity have these arguments of rank, relationship, and the world's opprobrium? Are they just? He refuted them: so he thought, and so *persists* to think. And who was ever less partial, or more severe to himself?

Louisa, my mind is greatly disturbed. His high virtues, the exertion of them for the peculiar protection of me and my family, and the dread of committing an act of unpardonable injustice, if unjust it be, are images that haunt and tantalize me incessantly.

If my conclusions have been false, and if his asserted claims be true, how shall I answer those which I have brought upon myself? The claims of your brother, which he urges without remission, are still stronger. They have been countenanced, admitted, and encouraged. I cannot recede. What can I do but hope, ardently hope, Frank Henley is in an error, and that he himself may make the discovery? Yet how long and fruitless have these hopes been! My dilemma is extreme; for, if I have been mistaken, act how I will, extreme must be the wrong I commit!

Little did I imagine a moment so full of bitter doubt and distrust as this could come. Were I but satisfied of the rectitude of my decision, there are no sensations which I could not stifle, no affections which I could not calm, nor any wandering wishes but what I could reprove to silence. But the dread of a flagrant, an odious injustice distracts me, and I know not where or of whom to seek consolation. Even my Louisa, the warm friend of my heart, cannot determine in my favour.

Your brother has been with me. He found me in tears, enquired the cause, and truth demanded a full and unequivocal confidence. I shewed him what I had been writing. You may well imagine, Louisa, he did not read it with total apathy. But he suppressed his own feelings with endeavours to give relief to mine. He argued to shew me my motives had been highly virtuous. He would not say— [His candour delighted me, Louisa.]—He would not say there was no ground for my fears: he was interested and might be partial. He believed indeed I had acted in strict conformity to the purest principles; but, had I even been mistaken, the origin of my mistake was so dignified as totally to deprive the act of all possible turpitude.

He was soothing and kind, gave high encomiums to Frank, took blame to himself for the error of his former opinions, and, reminding me of the motives which first induced me to think of him, tenderly asked if I had any new or recent cause to be weary of my task.

What could I answer? What, but that I was delighted with the rapid change perceptible in his sentiments, and with the ardour with which his enquiries were continued?

Frank Henley is by this time at Wenbourne Hill. You will see him. Plead our cause, Louisa: urge him to remain among us. Condescend even to enforce my selfish motive, that he would not leave me under the torturing supposition of having banished him from a country which he was born to enlighten, reform, and bless!

There is indeed another argument; but I know not whether it

ought to be mentioned. Sir Arthur owns he is in the power of the
avaricious Abimelech, and I believe is in dread of foreclosures that
might even eject him from Wenbourne Hill. This man must have
been an early and a deep adventurer in the trade of usury, or he
never could have gained wealth so great as he appears to have
amassed.

Past incidents, with all of which you are acquainted, have given
Sir Arthur a high opinion of Frank: and this added to his own
fears, I am persuaded, would lead him to consider a union between
us at present with complacency, were not such an inclination
opposed by other circumstances. The open encouragement that
he himself has given to Clifton is one, and it is strengthened by all
the interest of the other branches of our family. Your brother is
highly in favour with Lord Fitz Allen. My aunt Wenbourne
equally approves the match, and Clifton and my brother Edward
are become intimate. As to me, reason, consistency, and my own
forward conduct, oblige me to be the enemy of Frank.

Louisa, I scarcely know what I write! Think not I have
abandoned myself to the capricious gusts of passion; or that my
love of uncontaminated and rigorous virtue is lessened. No, it is
indecision, it is an abhorrence of injustice which shake and dis-
quiet me.

Write to me; let me know your sentiments; and particularly how
far your application to Frank, when you have made it, is successful.
I am anxious to receive your letter, for I know it will inspire
fortitude, of which I am in great, great need.

                                                    A. W. ST. IVES

LETTER XC
Louisa Clifton to Anna Wenbourne St. Ives

Rose-Bank

OH my dearest and ever dear Anna, what shall I say, how shall
I assuage doubts that take birth in principles so pure and a heart
so void of guile? I know not. I have before acknowledged the mist
is too thick for me to penetrate.

The worthy the noble-minded Frank has been with us, and I

could devise no better way than to shew him your letter. He was greatly moved, and collecting all the firmness of his soul resolutely declared that, since your peace was so deeply concerned, be his own sensations what they might, he would conquer them and remain in England. The heart-felt applause he bestowed upon you was almost insupportably affecting. He has indeed a deep sense of your uncommon worth; and he alone I fear on earth is capable of doing it justice.

But things have taken a different turn; and what can the best of us do, when involved as we continually are in doubt and difficulty, but act as you do, with impartial self denial, and the most rigid regard to truth and virtue?

Alas, dear Anna, I too am in need of support, and in search of fortitude!—My mother!—She will not be long among us!—A heart more benevolent, a mind more exalted—! She calls!—I hear her feeble voice!—Not even my Anna must rob her of my company, for those few remaining moments she has yet to come. I am her last consolation.

L. CLIFTON

I expect you will this post receive a letter from Frank, that will speak more effectually to your heart than I have either the time to do or the power.

LETTER XCI

Frank Henley to Anna Wenbourne St. Ives

MADAM,

Wenbourne-Hill

YOUR generous and zealous friend has thought proper to shew me your letter. I will not attempt to describe the sensations it excited; but, as your peace of mind is precious to me, and more precious still perhaps to the interests of society, and since my departure would occasion alarms and doubts so strong, I am determined to stay. My motives for going I thought too forcible and well founded to be overpowered; nor could they perhaps have been vanquished by any less cause. If one of us must suffer the warfare of contending sentiments and principles, let it be me. It was to fly from and if possible forget or subdue them that I projected such a voyage. Our duties to society must not cede to any effeminate compassion for ourselves. We are both enough acquainted with those duties to render us more than commonly culpable, should we be guilty of neglect.

To describe my weakness, and the contention to which my passions have been lately subject, might tend to awaken emotions in you which ought to be estranged from your mind. Our lot is cast: let us seek support in those principles which first taught us reciprocal esteem, nor palliate our desertion of them by that self pity which would become our reproach. We have dared to make high claims, form high enterprises, and assert high truths; let us shew ourselves worthy of the pretensions we have made, and not by our proper weakness betray the cause of which we are enamoured.

You will not—no, you are too just—I am sure, madam, you will not attribute resolutions like these, which are more (infinitely more) painful to the heart than they ought to be, to any light or unworthy change of sentiment. Superior gifts, superior attainments, and superior virtues inevitably beget admiration, in those who discover them, for their possessors. Admiration is the parent of esteem, and the continuance and increase of this esteem is affection, or, in its purest and best sense, love. To say I would not esteem and would not love virtue, and especially high and unusual virtue, would be both folly and guilt.

But you have taught me how pure and self-denying this love may be. Oh that the man of your choice may but become all you hope, and all of which his uncommon powers are capable! Oh that I may but see you as happy as you deserve to be, and I think I shall then not bestow much pity upon myself.

I have forborne, madam, to intrude the petty disquiets of another kind, from which as you will readily imagine I cannot have been wholly free. Need I say how much I disapprove my father's views, and the mode by which he would have them accomplished? There is no effort I will not make to conquer and remove this obstacle. It wounds me to the heart that you, the daughter of his benefactor, should for a moment be dependant on his avarice. The injury and iniquity are equally revolting, and there are moments when my prejudices falsely accuse me of being a participator in the guilt.

I have had two conversations with my father: they both were animated; but, though he was very determined, his resolution begins to fail; and, as I have justice on my side and am still more determined than he, I have no doubt that in a few days every thing which Sir Arthur has required of him he will be willing to undertake.

However as in a certain sense all is doubtful which is yet to be done, perhaps strict prudence would demand that Sir Arthur should not be led to hope till success is ascertained; of which I will not delay a moment to send you information.

I am, &c.

F. HENLEY

LETTER XCII

Coke Clifton to Guy Fairfax

London, Dover Street

THE moment, Fairfax, the trying, the great, the glorious moment approaches. Every possible contributing cause calls aloud for expedition, and reprobates delay. This gardening fellow is gone. For his absence I thank him, but not for the resolute spirit with which he intends to attack his father and make him yield. He has a tongue that would silence the congregated clamours of the Sorbonne, and dumb-found Belial himself in the hall of Pandemonium. 'Tis certain he has a tough morsel to encounter, and yet I fear he will succeed.

This would destroy all——Marry her?—No!—By heaven, no! If the hopes of Abimelech be not stubborn enough to persevere, they must and shall be strengthened. His refusal is indispensably necessary in every view, unless the view of marriage, which I once more tell you, Fairfax, I now detest. I should have no plea with her, were that of delay removed.

What is still worse, this delay may be removed by another and

Y

more painful cause. My mother it appears declines rapidly: her
death is even feared, and should it happen, I cannot pretend to
insist on the obstacles which her maternal cares and provisionary
fears have raised.

I can think of no certain expedient, for this Abimelech, but that
of an anonymous letter. Neither the writing nor the style must
appear to be mine; nor must the hand that writes it understand its
purport. Tyros and ignorant as my opponents are, in the tricks and
intrigues of amorous stratagem, still they have too much understanding not to be redoubtable.

Those old necromancers Subtlety and Falsehood must forge the
magic armour, and the enchanted shield, under which I fight.
Like wizards of yore, they must render me invisible; and the fair
form of the foolish Clifton they have imagined must only be seen.

Honest Aby, or I mistake him, is too worthy a fellow to desert
so good a cause. And this cloud-capt lady,[1] whose proud turrets
I have sworn to level with the dust, will not descend to plead the
approaching death of my mother, when I shall urge the injustice
of delay—Ay, Fairfax, the injustice! I mean to command, to dare,
to overawe; that is the only oratory which can put her to the rout.
She loves to be astonished, and astonished she shall be. If I do not
shrink from myself her fall is infallible.

My heart exults in the coming joy! Never more will the milky
pulp of compassion rise to mar the luxurious meal! She has been
writing to the fellow, Fairfax; ay and has shewn me her letter! For,
let her but imagine that truth, or virtue, or principle, or any other
abortive being of her own creation, requires her to follow the whims
of her disjointed fancy, and what frantic folly is there of which she
is incapable?

'Tis maddening to recollect, but she doats on the fellow;
absolutely doats! I am the tormenting demon that has appeared
to interrupt her happiness; she the devoted victim, sacrificed
to shield me from harm! The thought of separation from him
is distracting, and every power must be conjured up to avert the
horrid woe!

Never before did my feelings support such various and continual attacks; never did I endure infidelity so open or insult
so unblushing. But, patience; the day of vengeance is at hand,
or rather is here! This moment will I fly and take it! Expect

to hear 'of battles, sieges, disastrous chances, and of moving accidents; but not of hair breadth 'scapes!'[1]—Escape she cannot! I go! She falls!

C. CLIFTON

LETTER XCIII

Frank Henley to Anna Wenbourne St. Ives

Wenbourne-Hill

IT is now a week since I wrote to you, madam, at which time I took some pleasure in acquainting you with my hopes of success. These hopes continued to increase, and my father had almost promised to agree to the just proposals I made, when two days ago he suddenly and pertinaciously changed his opinion.

I am sorry to add that he now appears to be much more determined than ever, and that I am wholly astonished at and wholly unable to account for this alteration of sentiment. I delayed sending you the intelligence by yesterday's post, hoping it was only a temporary return of former projects, which I could again reason away. But I find him so positive, so passionate, and so inaccessible to reason, that I am persuaded some secret cause has arisen of which I am ignorant. Yet do not be dejected, dear madam, nor imagine I will lightly give it up as a lost cause—No—My mind is too much affected and too earnestly bent on its object not to accomplish it, if possible.

I received your letter*, but have no thanks that can equal the favour. I hope the emotions to which it gave birth were worthy such a correspondent. I can truly and I believe innocently say my heart sympathises in all your joys, hopes, and apprehensions; and that my pleasure, at the progress of Mr. Clifton in the discovery of truth and the practice of virtue, is but little less than your own.

I am glad you thought proper to be cautious of giving Sir

---

* It contained the state of her feelings, with which the reader is already acquainted, but no new incidents; for which reason it is omitted.

Arthur any unconfirmed expectations; and I promise you to exert every effort to effect a propitious change in the present temper and resolutions of my father.

I am, dear madam, &c.

F. HENLEY

LETTER XCIV

Coke Clifton to Guy Fairfax

London, Dover Street

WHEN last I wrote my resolution was taken, and I determined on immediate attack. But I went in a seeming unlucky moment; though I much mistake if it were not the very reverse.

The supposed misfortune I had foreseen fell upon me. The 'squire of preachers had fairly overcome his father's obstinacy, and induced him to give ground! Instead of having received the news of his determined persistency, I found her with a letter in her hand, informing her that he had begun to relent, and that his full acquiescence was expected.

To have commenced the battle at so inauspicious a moment would have been little worthy of a great captain. My resolution was instantly formed.

After acting as much ecstasy as I could call up, I hastened home and wrote my projected letter to honest Aby. I threw my hints together in Italian, that they might not be understood by the agent whom I meant to employ. This was my groom, an English lad whom I met with at Paris, who spells well and writes a good hand. I pretended I had crushed my finger and could not hold a pen; and, without letting him understand the intent of my writing, or even that it was a letter, I dictated to him as follows; a transcript of which I send to you, Fairfax, first that you may sigh and see what the blessing of a ready invention is, and next as an example which you may copy, or at least from which you may take a hint, if ever you should have occasion.

'So you have been persuaded at last to give up your point, my

old friend! And can you swallow this tale of a tub? A fine cock and
a bull story has been dinned in your ears? Don't believe a word on't.
I know the whole affair; and, though you don't know me, be
assured I mean you well: and I tell you that if you will but hold
out stoutly every thing will soon be settled to your heart's desire.
She is dying for love of him, and he can't see it! She will never
have the man they mean for her; I can assure you of that; and what
is more he will never have her. What I tell you I know to be true.
No matter who I am. If I knew nothing of the affair how could I
write to you? And if the advice I give be good, what need you care
whom it comes from? Only don't let your son see this; if you do it
will spoil all. You perceive how blind he is to his own good, and
how positive too. Keep your counsel, but be resolute. Look around
you, persist in your own plans, and the hall, the parks, the gardens,
the meadows, the lands you see are all your own! I am sure you
cannot misunderstand me. But mark my words; be close; keep
your thoughts to yourself. You know the world: You have made
your own fortune; don't mar it by your own folly. Tell no tales,
I say; nor, if you are a wise man, give the least hint that you have
a friend in a corner.'

This I dictated to my amanuensis, pretending to translate it
out of the paper I held in my hand, and which I took care to place
before him, so that he should see it was really written in a foreign
language. I likewise once or twice counterfeited a laugh at what I
was reading, and ejaculated to myself—'This is a curious scrap!'

When he had finished I gave him half a crown, praised his hand-
writing, which I told him I wanted to see, for perhaps I might find
him better employment than currying[1] of horses, and sent him
about his business too much pleased and elated, and his ideas led
into too distant a train to harbour the least suspicion.

Nor did my precautions end here. I immediately ordered
my horse, and rode without any attendant full speed to
Hounslow. I there desired the landlord of an inn at which I am
personally known, though not by name, to send one of his own
lads, post, to the market town next to Wenbourne-Hill, and
there to hire a countryman, without explaining who or what he
himself was, to deliver the letter into the hands of honest Aby.
I requested the landlord to choose an intelligent messenger,

and backed my request with a present bribe and a future promise.

My plan was too well laid to miscarry, and accordingly yesterday a mournful account arrived, from the young orator, that judgment is reversed, and he in imminent danger of being cast in costs.[1]

And now, Fairfax, once more I go!— Expedition, resolution, a torrent of words, a storm of passion, and the pealing thunder that dies away in descending rains! The word is Anna St. Ives, revenge, and victory!

C. CLIFTON

LETTER XCV

Coke Clifton to Guy Fairfax

London, Dover Street

ONCE more, Fairfax, here am I.

Well! And how—?

Not so fast, good sir. All things in their turn. The story shall be told just as it happened, and your galloping curiosity must be pleased to wait.

I knew my time, the hour when she would retire to her own apartment, and the minute when I might find admission; for she is very methodical, as all your very wise people more or less are. I had given Laura her lesson; that is, had told her that I had something very serious to say to her mistress that morning, and desired her to take care to be out of the way, that she might be sure not to interrupt us. The sly jade looked with that arch significance which her own experience had taught her, and left me with—'Oh! Mr. Clifton!'

And here I could make a remark, but that would be anticipating my story.

You may think, Fairfax, that, marshalled as my hopes and fears were in battle array, something of inward agitation would be apparent. In reality not only some but much was visible. It caught her attention, and luckily caught. I attempted to speak, and stammered. A false step as it would have been most fatal so was it more probable at the moment of onset than afterward, when the heated imagination should have collected, arranged, and begun to pour forth its stores.

The philosophy of the passions was the theme I first chose, though at the very moment when my spirits were all fluttering with wild disorder. But my faultering voice, which had I wished I could not have commanded, aided me; for the tremulous state of my frame threw hers into most admirable confusion!

'What was it that disturbed me? What had I to communicate? She never saw me thus before! It was quite alarming!'

Madam—[Observe, Fairfax, I am now the speaker: but I shall remind you of such trifles no more. If you cannot distinguish the interlocutors, you deserve not to be present at such a dialogue.] Madam, I own my mind is oppressed by thoughts which, however just in their purpose, however worthy in their intent, inspire all that hesitation, that timidity, that something like terror, which I scarcely know how to overcome. Yet what should I fear? Am I not armed by principle and truth? Why shun a declaration of thoughts that are founded in right; or tremble like a coward that doubted of his cause? I am your scholar, and have learned to subdue sensations of which the judgment disapproves. From you likewise have I learned to avow tenets that are demonstrable; and not to shrink from them because I may be in danger of being misconstrued, or even suspected. Pardon me! I do you wrong. Your mind is superior to suspicion. It is a mean an odious vice, and never could I esteem the heart in which it found place. I forget myself, and talk to you as I would to a being of an infinitely lower order.

Mr. Clifton—

Do not let your eye reprove me! I have not said what is not; and who better knows than you how much it is beneath us to refrain from saying what is?

Do not keep me in this suspense! I am sure there is something very uncommon in your thoughts! Speak!

Thoughts will be sometimes our masters: the best and wisest of us cannot always command them. That I have daily repressed them, have struggled against rooted prejudices and confirmed propensities, and have ardently endeavoured to rise to that proud eminence toward which you have continually pointed, you are my witness.

I am.

Protracted desires, imagined pleasures, and racking pains [and oh how often have they all been felt!] no longer sway me. They have been repulsed, disdained, trodden under foot. You have taught me how shameful it is to be the slave of passion. Truth is now my object, justice my impulse, and virtue, high virtue my guide.

Oh, Clifton! Speak thus, be thus ever!

The moment it appeared, I knew that delay was ominous.

Nay, Clifton—

Hear me, madam!—Yes ominous! I see no end to it, have every thing to fear from it, and nothing to hope—There is a thought— Ay, that verges to madness!—I have a rival—! But I will forget it— at least will try. Who can deny that it is excruciating?—But I am actuated at present by another and a nobler motive. You know, madam, what you found me; and I hope you are not quite unconscious of what you have made me. You have taught me principles to which I mean to adhere, and truths I intend to assert; have opened views to me of immense magnitude! In your society I am secure. But habits are inveterate, and easily revived; and were I torn from you, I myself know not the degree of my own danger. Yes, madam, fain indeed would I forget there is such a person as Frank Henley! Yet how? By what effort, what artifice? Say! Teach me! What though my heart reproaches me with its own foibles, who can prevent possibilities, mere possibilities, in a case like this, from being absolute torments? My soul pants and aches after certainty! The moment I ask myself what doubt there can be of Anna St. Ives, I answer none, none! Yet the moment after, forgetting this question, alarms, probabilities, past scenes and intolerable suppositions swarm to assault me, without relaxation or mercy.

Clifton, you said you had a nobler motive.

I merit the reproach, madam. These effusions burst from me, are unworthy of me, and I disclaim them. You have pardoned many of my strays and mistakes, and I am sure will pardon this. [For the love of fame, Fairfax, do not suffer the numerous masterstrokes of this dialogue to escape you. I cannot stay to point them out.] Yes, madam, I have a nobler motive! Yet, enlarged as your mind is, I know not how to prepare you calmly to listen to me, without alarm and without prevention. Strange as it may seem, I dread to speak truth even to you!

If truth it be, speak, and fear nothing. Propose but any adequate and worthy purpose, and there is no pain, no danger, no disgrace from which if I know myself I would shrink.

No disgrace, madam?

Your words and looks both doubt me—Put me to the proof. Propose I say an adequate and worthy purpose, and let your test be such as nature shudders at; then despise me and my principles if I recoil.

The union of marriage demands reciprocal, unequivocal, and unbounded confidence; for how can we pretend to love those whom we cannot trust? The man who is unworthy this unbounded confidence is most unworthy to be a husband; and it were even better he should shew his bad qualities, by basely and dishonestly deserting her who had committed herself body and soul to his honour, than that such qualities should discover themselves after marriage. There is no disgrace can equal the torment of such an alliance.

I grant it.

You have attained that noble courage which dares to question the most received doctrines, and bring them to the test of truth. Who better than you can appreciate the falsehood and the force of the prejudices of opinion? Yet are you sure, madam, that even you are superior to them all?

Far otherwise. Would I were! I am much too ignorant for such high such enviable perfection.

But is it not possible that some of the most common, and if I dared I should say the most narrow, the most self-evident of these prejudices may sway and terrify you from the plain path of equity? Dare you look the world's unjust contumelies stedfastly in the face? Dare you answer for yourself that you will not shudder at the performance of what you cannot but acknowledge, nay have acknowledged to be an act of duty?

I confess your preparation is alarming, and makes me half suspect myself, half desirous to retract all I have thought, all I have asserted! Yet I think I dare do whatever justice can require.

You think—?

Once more bring me to the proof. I feel a conscious [Again you make me a braggart.] a virtuous certainty.

In opposition to the whole world, its prepossessions, reproofs, revilings, persecutions, and contempt?

The picture is terrifying, but ought not to be, and I answer yes; in opposition to and in defiance of them all.

Then—You are my wife!

How?

Be firm! Start not from the truth! You are my wife! Ask yourself the meaning of the word. Can set forms and ceremonies unite mind to mind? And if not they, what else? What but community of sentiments, similarity of principles, reciprocal sympathies, and an equal ardour for and love of truth? Can it be denied?

It cannot.

You are my wife, and I have a right to the privileges of a husband! A right?

An absolute, an indefeasible right!

You go too fast!

They are your own principles: they are principles founded on avowed and indisputable truths. I claim justice from you!

Clifton!

Justice!

This is wrong!—Surely it is wrong!—This cannot be!

Instead of the chaste husband, such as better times and spirits of higher dignity have known, who comes with lips void of guile the rightful claimant of an innocent heart, in which suspicion never harboured, imagine me to be a traitorous wretch, who poorly seeks to gratify a momentary, a vile, a brutal passion! Imagine me, I say, such a creature if you can! Once I should have feared it; but you have taught my thoughts to soar above such vulgar terrors. My appeal is not to your passions, but your principles. Inspired by that refulgent ardour which animates you, with a noble enthusiasm you have yourself bid me put you to the proof. You cannot, will not, dare not be unjust!

And now, Fairfax, behold her in the very state I wished! Cowed, silenced, overawed! Her ideas deranged, her tongue motionless, wanting a reply, her eyes wandering in perplexity, her cheeks growing pale, her lips quivering, her body trembling, her bosom panting! Behold I say the wild disorder of her look! Then turn to me, and read secure triumph, concealed exultation, and bursting transport on my brow! While impetuous, fierce, and fearless desire is blazing in my heart, and mounting to my face! See me in the very act of fastening on her! And see——!

Curses!——Everlasting curses pursue and catch my perfidious evil genius!—See that old Incubus[1] Mrs. Clarke enter, with a letter in her hand that had arrived express, and was to be delivered instantly!——Our mutual perturbation did not escape the prying witch; my countenance red, hers pale—The word begone! maddened to break loose from my impatient tongue. My eyes however spoke plainly enough, and the hag was unwillingly retiring, when a faint—'Stay, Mrs. Clarke'—called her back!

As I foreboded, it was all over for this time! She opened the letter. What its contents were I know not; and impossible as it is that they should relate to me, I yet wish I did. I am sure by her manner they were extraordinary. I could not ask while that old beldam was present [Had she been my grandmother, on this occasion I should have abused her.] and the eye of the young lady very plainly told me she wished me away. It was prudent to make the best retreat possible, and with the best grace: I therefore bowed and took my leave; very gravely telling her I hoped she would seriously consider what I had said, and again emphatically pronounced the word *justice!*

You have now, Fairfax, been a spectator of the scene; and if its many niceties have escaped you, if you have not been hurried away, as I was, by the tide of passion, and amazed at the successful sophistries which flowed from my tongue, sophistries that are indeed so like truth that I myself at a cooler moment should have hesitated to utter them; if I say the deep art with which the whole was conducted, and the high acting with which I personified the only possible Being that could subjugate Anna St. Ives do not excite your astonishment, why then you really are a dull fellow! But I know you too well, Fairfax, to do you such injustice as this supposes. Victory had declared for me. I read her thoughts. They were labouring for an answer, I own; but she was too much confounded. And would I have given her time to rally? No! I should then have merited defeat.

The grand difficulty however is vanquished: she will hear me the next time with less surprise, and the emotions of passion, genuine honest mundane passion, must take their turn; for not even she, Fairfax, can be wholly exempt from these emotions.

I have not the least fear that my eloquence should fail me, and absolute victory excepted, I could not have wished for greater success.

I cannot forget this letter. It disturbs and pesters my imagination. I supposed it to be from Edward, who has been at Bath; but my valet has just informed me he is returned. Perhaps it is from my sister; and if so, by its coming express, my mother is dead! I really fear it bodes me harm—I am determined to rid myself of this painful suspense. I will therefore step to Grosvenor-street. I may as well face the worst at once. You shall hear more when I return.

Oh, Fairfax! I could curse most copiously, in all heathenish and christian tongues! She has shut herself up, and refuses to see me! This infernal fellow Frank Henley is returned too. He arrived two hours after the express. I suspect it came from him; nay I suspect—Flames and furies!—I must tell you!

I have seen Laura, though scarcely for two minutes. She is afraid she is watched. It is all uproar, confusion, and suspicion at Sir Arthur's. But the great curse is my groom, the lad that I told you copied my letter to Abimelech, has been sent for and privately catechised by her and her paramour! And what confirms this most tormenting of all conjectures is the absence of the fellow: he has not been home since, nor at the stables, though he was always remarkably punctual, but has sent the key; so that he has certainly absconded.

Had I not been a stupid booby, had I given Laura directions to keep out of the way of Anna, but in the way of taking messages for her, she might have received the express, and all might have been well. Such a blockheadly blunder well deserves castigation!

I'll deny the letter, Fairfax. They have no proof, and I'll swear through thick and thin rather than bring myself into this universal, this damnatory disgrace! I know indeed she will not believe me; and I likewise know that now it must be open war between us. For do not think that I will suffer myself to be thus shamefully beaten out of the field. No, by Lucifer and his Tophet![1] I will die a foaming maniac, fettered in straw, ere that shall happen! If not by persuasion, she shall be mine by chicanery, or even by force. I will perish, Fairfax, sooner than desist!

Oh for an agent, a coadjutor worthy of the cause! He must and shall be found.

The uncle and aunt must be courted: the father I expect will side with her. The brother too must be my partisan; for it will be necessary I should maintain an intercourse, and the shew of still wishing for wedlock.

I am half frantic, Fairfax! To be baffled by such an impossible accident, after having acted my part with such supreme excellence, is insupportable! But the hag Vengeance shall not slip me! No! I have fangs to equal hers, ay and will fasten her yet! I have been injured, insulted, frustrated, and fiends seize me if I relent!

C. CLIFTON

LETTER XCVI

Anna Wenbourne St. Ives to Louisa Clifton

London, Grosvenor Street

Louisa!—My dear, my kind, my affectionate Louisa!—My friend!——What shall I say? How shall I begin? I am going to rend your heart.—

Keep this letter from the sight of Mrs. Clifton: if she have not already been told, do not let her know such a letter exists—Oh this brother!—But he is not your brother—Error so rooted, so malignant, so destructive exceeds all credibility!

He came to me yesterday morning, as was his custom. There was something in his look which, could I but have read it, was exceedingly descriptive of the workings of his heart. It was painful to see him. He endeavoured to smile and for a moment to talk triflingly, but could not. He was in a tremor; his mouth parched, his lips white.

His next essay was to philosophise; but in this attempt too he was entirely at fault.

The passions are all sympathetic, and none more so than this of trepidation. I cannot recollect what the ideas were that passed hastily through my mind; but I know he excited much alarm, doubt, and I believe suspicion.

But, though he had found all this difficulty to begin, having begun he recovered himself very surprisingly. His colour returned, his voice became firm, his ideas clear, his reasoning energetic, and his manner commanding. He seemed to mould my hopes and apprehensions as he pleased, to inspire terror this moment, and the excess of confidence the next.

Louisa, my heart bleeds to say it, but his purposes were vile, his hypocrisy odious, and—I must forbear, and speak of foul deeds in fair terms. I know not how many prejudices rise up to warn me; one that I am a woman, or rather a girl; another that I am writing to the man's sister; a third that she is my friend, and so on with endless et ceteras. No matter that truth is to this friend infinitely more precious than a brother. I may be allowed to feel indignation, but not to express my feeling.

But the most distressing, the most revolting part of all is, that he harangued like the apostle of truth, the name of which he vilely prophaned, in favour of the basest, most pitiful, most contemptible of vices; the mere vain glory of seduction. He has not even so much as the gratification of sensual appetite to plead in his excuse. I am wrong; it was not vain glory. Vanity itself, contemptible as such a stimulus would have been, was scarcely a secondary motive. It was something worse; it was revenge. My mind has been wholly occupied in retracing his past behaviour; I can think on no other subject, and every trait which recollection adds is a confirmation of this painful idea. He does not wish to marry me, and I almost doubt whether he ever did, at least fully and unreservedly.

He came to me, Louisa, and began with painting the torments of delay and the pangs of jealousy, which he endeavoured to excuse; and concluded with a bold appeal to my justice; a daring, over-awing, confounding appeal. He called upon me at my peril, and as I respected truth and virtue, to deny his claim.

And what was this claim?——I was his wife!——In every pure and virtuous sense his wife; and he demanded the privilege of a husband!—Demanded, Louisa!—Demanded!—And demanded it in such a tone, with such rapid, overbearing, bold expressions, and such an apparent consciousness of right, that for a moment my mind was utterly confused!

Not that it ceded; no, not an instant. I knew there was answer, a just and irrefragable one, but I could not immediately find it.

He perceived my disorder, and you cannot imagine what a shameless and offensive form his features assumed! I know not what he would not instantly have attempted, had not, while I was endeavouring to awake from my lethargy, Mrs. Clarke come in! She brought me a letter—It was sent express!—The hand writing was Frank's! Agitated as I was, suspicion influenced me, and I retreated a few steps—I opened the letter, and the first words I saw were—'Beware of Mr. Clifton.'—

It contained only half a dozen lines, and I read on. What follows were its contents——

'Beware of Mr. Clifton!—Had I not good cause, madam, I would not be so abrupt an accuser: but I am haunted, tortured by the dread of possibilities, and therefore send this away express—Beware of Mr. Clifton!—I will not be long after the letter, and I will then explain why I have written what to you may appear so strange.

F. HENLEY'

Think, Louisa, what must be the effect of such a letter, coming at such a moment!—I believe I was in no danger; though, if there be a man on the face of the earth more dangerous than any other, it is surely Clifton. But the watchful spirit of Frank seems placed like my guardian angel, to protect me from all possible harm.

My mind debated for a moment whether it were not wrong to distrust the power of truth and virtue, and not to let Mr. Clifton see I could demolish the audacious sophistry by which he had endeavoured to confound and overwhelm me. But my ideas were deranged, and I could not collect sufficient fortitude. Oh how dangerous is this confusion of the judgment, and how desirable that heavenly presence of mind which is equal to these great these trying occasions! I therefore thought it more prudent to suffer him to depart, and suspect vilely of me, than to encounter the rude contest which he would more audaciously recommence, were I to send away Mrs. Clarke, which he might even misconstrue into a signal of approbation. These fears prevailed, and I desired her to stay, and by my manner told him I wished his absence.

Louisa, how shall I describe my anguish of heart at seeing all those hopes of a mind so extraordinary, for extraordinary it is even in guilt, at once overthrown? It was indeed iteration of anguish!

What! Can guile so perfectly assume the garb of sincerity? Can hypocrisy wear so impenetrable a mask? How shall we distinguish? What guide have we? How be certain that the next seeming virtuous man we meet is not a——Well, well, Louisa—I will remember—Brother. My Louisa knows it is not from the person, but from the vice that I turn away with disgust. Would I willingly give her heart a pang? Let her tell me if she can suspect it. She has fortitude, she has affection; but it is an affection for virtue, truth, and justice. She will endeavour to reform error the most obdurate. So will I, so will all that are worthy the high office. But she will not wish me either to marry with or to countenance this error. Marry? —How does my soul shudder at the thought! His reasoning was just; seduction would have been a petty injury, or rather a blessing, compared to this master evil! He was most merciful when he meant me, as he thought, most destruction. I have been guilty of a great error. The reformation of man or woman by projects of marriage is a mistaken a pernicious attempt. Instead of being an act of morality, I am persuaded it is an act of vice. Let us never cease our endeavours to reform the licentious and the depraved, but let us not marry them.

The letter had not been delivered more than two hours before Frank arrived. You may think, Louisa, how hard he had ridden; but he refused to imagine himself fatigued. He brought another letter, which Abimelech had received, but which for some hours he obstinately refused to give up, and for this reason Frank sent off the express. A letter, not of Clifton's writing, but of his invention and sending!

Finding that Frank was likely to prevail on his father to raise the money for Sir Arthur, and obviate all further impediments to our marriage, Clifton, fearful that it should take place, wrote anonymously to Abimelech, to inform him I was in love with Frank, and to encourage him to persist. But read the letter yourself; the following is a true copy of it*.

If such a letter be his, I am sure, Louisa, you will not say I have thought or spoken too unkindly of him; and that it is his we have indubitable proof, though it was anonymous and not in his handwriting.

* The reader has already perused it in Letter XCIV, to which he is referred.

You no doubt remember, Louisa, the short story of the English lad, whom your brother hired at Paris. It was written by him, though innocently and without knowing what was intended. This lad has an aunt, who after having laboured to old age is now lame, infirm, and in need of support. The active Frank has been with her, has aided her with money and consoled her with kindness. The lad himself was desirous of assisting her; and Frank, willing to encourage industry in the young, gave him some writings to copy at his leisure hours. By this accident he knew the lad's hand-writing.

I forgot to mention, in its proper place, the astonishment of Frank at the sudden change in his father, and the firm resolution he took to discover the cause of this change. The obstinacy of Abimelech was extreme; but Frank was still more pertinacious, more determined, and so unwearied and incessant, in his attacks on his father, that the old man at last could resist no longer, and shewed him this letter.

From what has preceded, that is from his manner of acting, you may well imagine what the alarms and sensations of Frank were. He brought the letter up with him, for he would not trust it out of his own custody, and immediately went himself to Clifton's stables in search of the lad, brought him to me, and then first shewed him the letter, which that no possible collusion might be alleged he had left in my keeping, and then asked if it were not his hand-writing. The lad very frankly and unhesitatingly answered it was; except the direction, which this plotting Clifton had procured to be written by some other person.

Without telling the lad more than was necessary, Frank advised him to quit his service, for that there was something relating to that letter which would certainly occasion a quarrel, and perhaps worse, between him and his master: and, as it would be prudent for him to keep out of the way, he sent him down to Wenbourne-Hill, where the lad is at present.

And now what shall I say to my Louisa? How shall I sooth the feelings of my friend? Do they need soothing? Does she consider all mankind as her relations and brothers, or does she indeed imagine that one whose principles are so opposite to her own is the only brother she possesses? Will she grieve more for him than she would for any other, who should be equally unfortunate in error? Or does she doubt with me whether grief can in any possible case be a virtue? And if so, is there any virtue of which she is incapable? What is relation, what is brother, what is self, if relation, brother, or self be at war with truth? And does not truth command us to consider beings exactly as they are, without any respect to this relationship, this self?

But I know my Louisa; she will never be impatient under trial, however severe; nor foolishly repine for the past, though she will strenuously labour for the future.

All good, all peace, all happiness, all wisdom be with her!

A. W. ST. IVES

LETTER XCVII

Louisa Clifton to her Brother Coke Clifton

Rose-Bank

SIR

On Friday morning I received the original letter from Anna St. Ives, of which the inclosed is a copy; and on the following day about a quarter of an hour before midnight my mother expired. I mention these circumstances together because they were noticed, by those who were necessarily acquainted with them, as having a relation to each other; whether real or imaginary, much or little I do not pretend to determine; but I will relate the facts and leave them to your own reflection; and I will forbear all colouring, that I may not be suspected of injustice.

My mother as you know has been daily declining, and was indeed in a very feeble state. She seemed rather more cheerful that morning than she had been lately, and at her particular request I went to visit the wife of farmer Beardmore, who is a worthy but poor woman, and who being at present dejected, in consequence of poverty and ill health, my mother thought she might be more benefited by the kindness of the little relief we could afford her if delivered by me, than if sent by a less soothing and sympathetic hand. I should hope, sir, it would be some consolation to you to learn that my mother's active virtue never forsook her, while memory and mind remained. But of this you are the best judge.

While I was gone the postman brought the letter of my friend; and as her letters were always read to my mother, and as I likewise have made it a rule and a duty not to have any secrets to conceal from her, or indeed from any body, she had no scruple to have the letter opened, because she expected to find consolation and hope: for, till the arrival of this, the letters of Anna St. Ives have lately been all zealous in your praise.

I will leave you, sir, to imagine the effect which a letter beginning as this did must have on a mind and body worn to such a tremulous state of sensibility. Coming as it did first into my mother's hand, the very caution which the benevolent heart of Anna dictated produced the effect she most dreaded. My mother had still however a sufficient portion of her former energy to hear it to the end.

In about an hour after this happened I returned, and found her in extreme agitation of mind. I neglected no arguments, no efforts to calm her sensations; and I succeeded so far that after a time she seemed to be tolerably resigned. She could not indeed forget it, and the subject was revived by her several times during the day.

My chief endeavour was to lead her thoughts into that train which, by looking forward to the progress of virtue, is most consoling to the mind of virtue.

She seemed at last fatigued, and about eleven o'clock at night fell into a doze. About a quarter before twelve I perceived her countenance distorted; I was alarmed; I spoke to her and received no answer; I endeavoured to excite attention or motion, but in vain. A paralytic stroke had deprived her of sensation. In this state she remained four-and-twenty hours, and about midnight departed.

I have thought it strictly incumbent on me to relate these circumstances. But I should consider myself as very highly culpable did I seek to aggravate, or to state that as certainty which can never be any thing more than conjecture. My mother was so enfeebled that we began to be in daily apprehension of her death. I must not however conceal that the thought of your union with Anna St. Ives had been one of her principal pleasures, ever since she had supposed it probable; and that she had spoken of it incessantly, and always with that high degree of maternal affection and cheering hope which you cannot but know was congenial to her nature.

The disappointment itself was great, but the turpitude that attended it much greater. This I did not endeavour to palliate. How could I? I have told you I had no resource for consolation, either for myself or her, but in turning, like Anna St. Ives, from the individual to the whole.

I would endeavour to say something that should shew you the folly of such conduct; for the folly of it is even more excessive than the vice; but, not to mention the state of my own mind at this moment, I despair of producing any effect, since Anna St. Ives herself, aided by so many concurring motives, has failed in the generous and disinterested attempt.

I imagine you will be down at the funeral. Perhaps it is proper. I cannot say, for indeed I do not very well understand many of what are called the proprieties of custom. I own I am weak enough to feel some pain at meeting you, under the present circumstances. But, since it is necessary I should act and aid you in various family departments, if you should come down, I will not yield to these emotions, but considering you as an erring brother, will endeavour to perform what duty requires.

                                                    L. CLIFTON

P.S. Previous to this I wrote three different letters, but they were all as I fear too expressive of those strong sensations which I have found it very difficult to calm. I destroyed them, not because they were wrong, but lest they should produce a wrong effect.

LETTER XCVIII

Coke Clifton to his Sister Louisa Clifton

London, Dover Street

MADAM,

I have received your very lenient, equitable, calumniating, insulting letter; and I would have you put it down in your memorandum-book that I will carefully remember the obligation. It perfectly accords with your sublime ideas of justice to decide before you have heard both parties; and it is equally consistent with your notions of sisterly affection that you should pass sentence on a brother. What is a brother, or all he may have to say, to you; who, more infallible than the holy father himself, have squared a set of rules of your own, by which you judge as you best know how?

Your insinuations concerning the death of my mother are equally charitable, and I have already learnt them by rote. Yes, madam, assure yourself they will not be forgotten. Any suspense of judgment would have ill become a lady so clear sighted. However possible it may be that Anna St. Ives may herself have been imposed upon, and I both ignorant and innocent of this forged letter, yet for you to have entertained any doubts in my favour would have partaken too much of the fogs of earth for so inspired and celestial a lady.

But I must tell you, madam, since you can so readily forego equity in a brother's behalf, I can and will be as ready to forget and cast off the sister. I never yet was or will be injured with impunity: I would have you note down that.

I mean to be at Rose-Bank tomorrow or the day after, to attend the funeral and take such order as my affairs may require; and though I have as little affection for your company as you have for mine, I imagine it will be quite necessary for you to be there: not only that you should be present to execute all orders, but likewise to listen to a few hints which I shall probably think proper to communicate.

In the mean time, madam, be industrious to propagate the report, if you think fit, that I have caused anonymous letters to be written to Sir Arthur's steward, have endeavoured to betray Anna St. Ives, and have been the death of my mother. Spread the agreeable intelligence I say as quickly and as widely as you can, and when you meet me you shall receive a brother's thanks.

C. CLIFTON

END OF VOLUME V

VOLUME VI

Abimelech Henley to Sir Arthur St. Ives, Baronet

Wenbourne-Hill

MOST ONNURABLE SIR, my ever onnurd Master,

I do hear of strange queerums[1] and quicksets,[2] that have a bin trap laid for your ever gracious onnur, and for the mercifool lovin kindness of sweet missee. Whereof I be all in a quandary, for it do seem I wus within an ames ace[3] of a havin bin chouse flickur'd[4] meself. Whereby I paradventerd before to tell your noble onnur my poor thofts on this here Mr. Clifton match marriage, which is all against the grain. And this I do hope your ever onnurable onnur will pry into, and see with your own eyes.

Whereof I have a bin ruminatin of many thinks lately, and of the ups and downs of life, so that I should sing oh be joyfool if as your onnur would but turn them in your thofts, as I have done. Whereby my son has a bin down with me; and I do find that sooth and trooth he be verily a son of my own begettin; and thof I say it a man may be proud of sitch a son; and as your ever gracious onnur wus most mercifooly pleased to sifflicate,[5] a wus born a gentleman, for a has his head fool and fool of fine notions.

Whereby if your onnurable onnur will but a be pleased to lend a mercifool ear to me, why mayhap I should a be willin to come down with the kole to your onnur's heart's content. Why not? For I have a talked matters over with my son, and a has said a many glorious thinks of your onnur and of sweet mercifool missee, all a witch a learned from me. For why? He is my own son, and of the issue of my loins, and I did always giv'n the best of advice. A had his whole feedin and breedin from me, and as a wus always fain to be a man of learnin why I taught him his letters meself; whereof I have now reason to be proud of 'n.

But that is not whereof of a what I wus a goin to think to say.
I wus about to paradventer to proposal to your onnur that, if
thinks might behappen to come to pass in the manner of mercifool
lovin kindness and gracious condysension, the wherewithalls
should a be forth cummin to the tune of fifty thousand pounds:
that is with the betokenin of all proper securities of parchments
and deeds and doosoors[1] to be first signed and stipilated, as hereto-
fore have bin on like future occasions. Take me ritely, your onnur;
I mean for the twenty thousand pounds. For why? I meself will
be so all bountifool as to come down on the nail head with thirty
thousand for my son. And then we shall see who will be a better
gentleman, as your onnurable onnur wus most graciously pleased
to kappaishus[2] him?

Whereby Wenbourne Hill would then be in all its glory; and
mayhap your ever gracious onnur might in sitch a case again go on
with your improofments. And who can say but the wildurness
might a begin to flourish? So that if your noble onnur will but think
of that, why thinks may behappen to begin to take a new turn, and
there may be mirth and merry days again at Wenbourne Hill. For
I do know in your heart your onnur do lamentation the loss of all
your fine taste, and elegunt ideers, and plans, and alterations; all
of a witch have a bin so many years a carryin on and a compassin at
Wenbourne Hill.

Whereof I umbelly condysend to intreat your noble onnur would
a give these thinks a thinkin. For why? The lawyers might a then
be stoptt, and a spoke might a behappen to be put in the wheel
of the foreclosures; witch if not, as your noble onnur already
knows, may not a turn out to be altogether quite so agreeable,
unless your ever gracious and onnurable onnur should be so all
mercifool as to rite to me; whereof I could then give them the
whys and the wherefores, and all thinks would be smooth and
smilin.

I besiege your most noble onnur to ponderate mercifooly of
these thinks, and of a dockin of the entail, and of a settin of the
deeds of the lawyers to work. Whereby every think may in sitch
a case be made safe and secure, not forgettin Wenbourne Hill;
and the willdurness, and mayhap the hermuttidge, and the grotto.
For why, your noble onnur? Where one fifty thousand pound be
a forth cummin from, another may a behappen to be found. But

that's a nether here nor there, a savin and exceptin the death and mortality of man, and the resurrection of the just and of the repentin sinner in all grace and glory.

And so I most umbelly remain, with the thanks givin of goodness, your onnur's most faithfool umbel sarvent everlastin to command,

ABIMELECH HENLEY

LETTER C

Anna Wenbourne St. Ives to Louisa Clifton

London, Grosvenor-Street

No; I will not attempt to console my Louisa, for I will not suppose even at the present moment that she yields to grief, or is in need of consolation. She will not repine at what is not to be remedied, nor debilitate her mind by dwelling on her own causes of discontent, instead of awakening it to the numerous sources of happiness, which by increasing the happiness of others incite it to activity. These are truths too deeply engraven on the heart of Louisa to be forgotten, and it is scarcely necessary to revive them even at this serious moment.

With respect to myself, my friend shall be my judge; my whole conduct shall be submitted to her, with an injunction not to indulge any partialities in my favour, but to censure, advise, and instruct me whenever she finds opportunity. Such, Louisa, has been our intercourse; and we have mutual reason to congratulate each other on its effects.

I have just had a conversation with Sir Arthur. He has received a letter from Abimelech, which he shewed me. Of all the proofs Frank has yet given of energy, this relative to his father is perhaps the strongest. You know the character of Abimelech. Could you think it possible? He is willing not only to raise twenty thousand pounds for Sir Arthur, but to pay down thirty more for his son! He begins to be vain of this son, and has even some slight perception that there may be other good qualities beside that of getting and hoarding money.

But his cunning is still predominant. Having conceived the possibility of this marriage, the accomplishment of it is now become his ruling passion, and has for a moment subjected avarice itself. He neglects no motive which he thinks may influence Sir Arthur, not even threatening; though his language is couched in all the art of apparent kindness and adulation. His letter however has produced its effect on my father, as you will perceive by the following dialogue, which was begun by Sir Arthur.

What think you of this proposal, Anna?

I ought rather to ask what are your thoughts on the subject, sir.

I can scarcely tell. I own it does not seem to me quite so unreasonable as I should once have supposed it; that is as far as relates to me. But if you should have conceived any partiality for Mr. Clifton, I should then——

Excuse me, sir, for interrupting you, but Mr. Clifton is at present wholly out of the question. Were it in my power, which I fear it is not, to do him any service, I should be as desirous of doing it now as ever; but I can never more think of him as a husband.

Are you so very determined?

I am; and I hope, sir, my determination is not offensive to you?

I cannot say at present that it is; for not to mention that I think very well of young Mr. Henley, I own the affair of the anonymous letter was a very improper and strange proceeding. Your aunt Wenbourne and Lord Fitz-Allen indeed seem to doubt it; but, according to the account which you and Mr. Henley give, I think they have no foundation for their doubts.

The behaviour of Mr. Clifton, without the letter, would have been quite sufficient to have fixed my determination.

What behaviour?

The proof he gave of deceit and depravity of principle, by the manner in which he endeavoured to seduce me.

When was that?

The very day on which Frank arrived.

Endeavoured to seduce you?

Yes.

Are you certain of the truth of what you say?

He proceeded too far, and explained himself too openly for me to be mistaken.

Seduce you!—Then you have entirely given up all thoughts of him?

All thoughts of marrying him I have most certainly.

And what is your opinion of Mr. Henley?

What can it be, sir? Are there two opinions concerning him? And if I were blind to his virtues, for whose safety he has been so often and so ardently active, who should do him justice?

I own, Anna, I have often thought you had some love for him, and I am tempted to think so still.

Love in the sense in which you understand it I have carefully suppressed, because till now I supposed it incompatible with duty and virtue; but I acknowledge I begin to doubt; and even to suppose that his view of the subject has been more rational and true than mine; and he thinks it is our duty to form a union, for which he owns he has an ardent wish.

Yes, he has honestly told me all that passed between you; and his sincerity pleased me—But every branch of our family would certainly be against such a match.

I suppose so.

The world too would consider me as having dishonoured myself, were I to consent.

I believe it would.

And would exclaim against the bad example—What ought to be done?

My opinion has been that the world would have cause to make this complaint; but I now think, or rather imagine myself convinced that I was in an error. It appears evident to my mind, at present, that we ought to consider whether an action be in itself good or bad, just or unjust, and totally to disregard both our own prejudices, and the prejudices of the world. Were I to pay false homage to wealth and rank, because the world tells me it is right that I should do so, and to neglect genius and virtue, which my judgment tells me would be an odious wrong, I should find but little satisfaction in the applause of the world, opposed to self-condemnation.

Mr. Henley is a very good young man; a very good young man indeed; and I believe I should even be willing to think of him for a son, if it should not be opposed by the other branches of the family.

But that it surely will.

I am afraid so—Lord Fitz-Allen is half reconciled to us again, and I would avoid breaking with him if possible. Your aunt has a good opinion of Mr. Henley.

But a better of Mr. Clifton.

Yes, so I suppose. I must talk to Edward. Mr. Henley has been his friend.

But Edward does not understand friendship. When he says friend he means acquaintance; and he finds him the most agreeable acquaintance, who tells him least truth; which certainly is not Mr. Henley. I have observed him lately to be rather fond of the company of Mr. Clifton, whom he thinks a better companion.

I own Mr. Henley is very obstinate in his opinions.

If his opinions be true, would you not have him persist in the truth.

But why should he be more certain that what he says is truth than other people?

Because he has examined with more industry and caution, has a stronger mind, and a greater love of enquiry. He does not endeavour to make his principles accord with his practice, but regulates his practice by his principles.

But still I ask what proof he has of being more in the right than other people?

I wonder, sir, that you can put such a question! He has surely given both you and me sufficient proofs of superiority; and though you should doubt the arguments you cannot doubt the facts.

I own he is a very extraordinary young gentleman.

Ah, sir! The word gentleman shews the bent of your thoughts. Can you not perceive it is a word without a meaning? Or, if it have a meaning, that he who is the best man is the most a gentleman?

I know your notions, child, and mine differ a little on these matters. However I do not think you quite so much in the wrong as I used to do; and perhaps there is something in what you say. Many men of low fortunes have made their way to the highest honours; and for what I know he may do the same.

He may and certainly will deserve the highest respect: but if you flatter yourself, sir, that he will seek or accept the titles and distinctions which men have invented to impose on each other's folly, and obtain their own artful purposes, I ought to warn you that you will be mistaken. His whole life will be devoted to the

discovery and spreading of truth; and, individual acts of benevolence excepted, his wealth, should he acquire any, will all be
dedicated to that sole object.

I am afraid these are strange whims, Anna!

I hope yet to shew you, sir, they are noble duties; which it is the
excess of guilt to neglect.

It puzzles me to conceive by what means his father could have
become so rich!

He has all his life been rapacious after money. His faculties are
strong, but perverted. What would have been wisdom is degener-
ated into cunning. He has made himself acquainted with usurers,
and they have made him acquainted with spendthrifts. He has
traded in annuities, and profited by the eagerness of youth to enjoy:
and, since I must be sincere, he has encouraged you, sir, to pursue
plans of expence with a view solely to his own profit.

Well, well; should this marriage take place, it will all return into
the family.

That should be no motive, sir, with either you or me.

I do not know that. You understand your own reasons, and I
mine; and if they should but answer the same end there will be
no harm.

I was going to reply, but Sir Arthur left me; being unwilling to
hear arguments which he took it for granted he should not understand.

Frank came in soon after, and I repeated to him what had been
said. Louisa, I must tell you the truth and the whole truth. Since
I have begun to imagine I might indulge my thoughts in dwelling
on his exalted qualities and uncommon virtues, my affection for
them has greatly increased: and they never appeared to me more
lovely than in the struggles and checks which his joy received, at
the hope of our union, by the recollection of the loss of Mr. Clifton.
He like me is astonished at the powers of your brother's mind,
and at their perversion; and he fears that this attempt, having
failed, will but serve to render that perversion more obdurate, nay
perhaps more active. He seems even to dread lest I am not secure;
which his desire to guard and caution me against would not suffer
him to repress or conceal. His tenderness and ecstasy, and indeed,
Louisa, they were both very strong, were mingled with regret equally
vivid: and Mr. Clifton! Mr. Clifton! repeatedly burst from him.

While I was relating what had passed between me and Sir
Arthur to Frank, and now again since I have been writing it to you,
I accused myself of coldness, and of shrinking from or rather of
half delivering the truth, lest Sir Arthur should think me a forward
girl, or lest I should think myself capable of too sudden a change.
But of the degree of that change do you, my friend, judge. I have
at all times endeavoured to shew you my naked heart, and often
have violently struggled against every disguise. I never concealed
from myself that I thought more highly of Frank Henley than of
Mr. Clifton; but I imagined principle taught me to prefer what
principle now warns me to shun. I am more and more convinced
of the error of marrying a bad man in order to make him good. I
was not entirely ignorant of this before, and therefore flattered myself the good might be effected previous to marriage. I forgot,
when passion has a purpose to obtain, how artful it is in concealment.

I have another quarrel with myself, for having been so desirous
of proving to my own conviction that the world's prejudices and
the prejudices of my family ought to be respected, while that
opinion accorded with my practice; and of being now so equally
alert to prove the reverse. Such are the deceptions which the mind
puts upon itself! For indeed I have been very desirous of acting
with sincerity in both instances. I can only say that I feel more
certain at present; for before I had doubts, and now I have none.
If you suspect me to be influenced by inclination, tell me so without reserve.

All good be with my friend! May she profit by my mistakes!

                                                        A. W. ST. IVES

LETTER CI

Coke Clifton to Guy Fairfax

Rose-Bank

YOU will perceive, Fairfax, I have changed the scene, and am
now in the country. I have a long narrative to detail, and am sitting
in an old hall with gloom and leisure enough to make it as tedious

and as dull as you could wish. My poor mother has taken her last leave of us, and lies now a corpse in the room under me. I could be melancholy, or mad, or I know not what—But 'tis no matter— She brought me here unasked to make the journey of this world, and now I am obliged to jog on. Not that I think I should much care if it were shortened, nor how soon; except that I would live to have my revenge; and that I will have, little troubling myself though the next minute were certain to be my last. It rankles at my heart, and lies there corroding, biting, festering, night and day.

I have quarrelled with my sister, and I am sure shall never forgive her; nor will she forgive me, so that we shall easily balance our accounts. This Anna St. Ives is her supreme favourite. But no wonder——No wonder—It would be strange if she were not! Still to be so ready to give up a brother, and write me such a letter as she did on the death of my mother! If I do not make her repent it Heaven renounce me!

But I consider the whole world as my enemies at this moment; you perhaps, Fairfax, excepted. I say perhaps, for I do not know how soon you may turn upon and yelp at me with the rest.

Forgive me, Fairfax. I am all venom, all viper, and cannot forbear to hiss even at my friend. But let my enemies beware! They shall find I can sting!——These cursed gnawings of heart will not let me begin my story.

I told you I was determined to deny the anonymous letter. I have been very industrious with uncle Fitz-Allen and aunt Wenbourne; and have been equally careful to titilate the vanity of the coxcomb Edward, who is highly flattered with the attention I have paid him, and will I am certain become my warm partisan.

They had all heard the story, but were all ready enough to gape and swallow my tale; which considering it was wholly invention was not ill composed. I begin to hate myself, to hate her, to hate the whole world, for being obliged to submit to such a damned expedient. But I will not recede. I will have my revenge! Were the devil himself waiting to devour me I would on; or were he engaged against me, I would over-reach him!

I concerted my measures, and learning that this lad of mine, who wrote the letter for me, was down at Wenbourne-Hill, I sent my man to inveigle him to come to me, at an inn where I purposely stopped, in my way to Rose-Bank. How durst they suborn my servant?——But—! I will stab and not curse!

My valet executed his commission, and prevailed on the lad to come; though with some difficulty, for he is a stubborn dog; and had not the valet followed my directions, and told him it was to do his old master a service, he would have been foiled. But I took him up at Paris, destitute and in some danger of starving, which he has not forgotten.

This Henley however is a greater favourite with him than I am; as I soon found by his discourse.

I began by sounding him, to try if it were possible to prevail on him to assert he had written the letter at the instigation of Henley, instead of me; but I soon found it was in vain, and durst not proceed to let him see my drift.

I then persuaded him that they had totally mistaken my purpose in writing the letter; that I had done it with a very friendly design; that I had myself a very great esteem for Henley, and that I meant nothing but good to Anna; but that there were some reasons, which I could not explain to him, that had occasioned me to write the letter.

As my next purpose, after that of making him an evidence in my favour, was to send him entirely out of the way, if I failed in the first attempt, I began to remind him of the condition in which I had found him in Paris, which he was ready enough to acknowledge, and seemed indeed afraid of acting ungratefully. I prompted and strengthened his fears, and at last told him that, since I found he was a good lad and meant well, though he was mistaken and had done me an injury, I would give him an opportunity of shewing his gratitude.

I then pretended that I had a packet of the utmost consequence to be delivered to my friend in Paris; meaning you, Fairfax; which I durst not trust to any but a sure hand: and as I knew him to be an honest lad, I expected he would not refuse to set off with it immediately. It was an affair almost of life and death! And, that I might impress his mind with ideas which would associate and beget suitable images, I began to talk of the decease of my mother, of my own affliction at the misunderstanding with Anna, of my very great friendship for Henley, and of the fatal consequences that would attend the miscarriage of the packet.

Still I found him reluctant. He seemed half to suspect me; and yet I made a very clever tale of it. He talked of Henley and his aunt; and he had likewise a dread of Paris. His aunt I find has been maintained by Henley, she being lame and disabled; and as sending him out of the way was a preliminary step absolutely necessary, I gave him a thirty pound bank-note, desired him to go to his aunt and give her ten pounds, and to keep the rest to secure him against any accidents, of which he seemed afraid, in a strange country; with a promise that he should have as much more, if he performed his commission faithfully, on his return.

I further enquired the direction of the aunt, telling him I would undertake to provide for her: and so I must, for she too must be sent out of the way.

At last, by repeating my professions and again reminding him of my taking him up at Paris, I was successful. Though I had more trouble in gaining the compliance of this lout than would have been sufficient, were I prime minister, and did I bribe with any thing like the same comparative liberality, to gain ten worthy members of parliament, though five knights of the shire had been of the number.

He wanted to return to Wenbourne-Hill for his necessaries and trifling property; and this reminded me not only of the danger of doing that but of his passing through London. Accordingly I told him to keep the ten pounds meant for his aunt to buy himself what things he wanted, which I promised to replace to her, and informed him I now recollected that he must take the nearest road to Dover, which I pretended lay through Guildford, Bletchingly, and Tunbridge, leaving London on the left.

The importance, hurry and command I assumed did not give him time to reflect; and the injunctions I gave were such as I do not imagine he would have disobeyed. But for my own security, pretending a fear that he might mistake his way, I sent my valet with him; privately ordering the valet not to part till he saw him safe on board the packet-boat.

And now, Fairfax, it is not impossible but the wise uncle, who has an excellent scent at discovery and no small opinion of his own acuteness, may find out that Henley himself was the forger of this letter; that it was a collusion between him and the lad, that he has himself removed both the lad and the aunt, and that his charity is a farce. I say such an event is possible. You may be sure that the idea shall be wholly his own, and that I will allow him all the just praise which he will graciously bestow upon his penetration.

My directions to the lad were to bring the packet immediately to you; which packet you will find to be blank paper, for I had no time for any thing more, except a short note of which the following is a copy.

'An event which I have not leisure to relate occasions me to send you this by a special messenger. You will most probably receive a letter express from me before he arrives, but if not detain him carefully. Hint not a word of the matter, but make a pretext of urgent business concerning me, for the issue of which he must wait. At all events do not let him escape, till you hear further from

C. CLIFTON'

I was obliged to pretend extreme hurry to the lad, but I gave my valet private instructions to take him round, and use as much delay as he conveniently could. Meanwhile I will send the letter I am now writing away express, that you may be fully prepared; for this is a point of infinite consequence. If you are not in Paris the express is to follow you; and you will be kind enough to take measures that the lad may follow the express. He is ordered to wait your commands, which I told him might possibly detain him a month, or even more; though it might happen that the business would be transacted in a week.

Not that I can hope the real business can now possibly be so soon finished.

You will take care to make your account agree with mine; and circumstances oblige me to require of you, Fairfax, to condescend to get the lad's favour, and not make his stay irksome. You may command me to ten times this amount, as you know.

This is a melancholy scene, and a gloomy house, and a dismal country; and I myself am fretful, and moody, and mad, and miserable. I shall soon get into action, and then it will wear off.

I will have her; ay, by the infernals will I! And on my own terms. I know she is rejoicing now in her Henley. Eternal curses bite him! But I will haunt her! I will appear to her in her dreams, and her waking hours shall not want a glimpse of me. I know she hates me. So be it! If she did not I could not so readily digest my vengeance. But I know she does! And she shall have better cause! I never yet submitted to be thus baffled. She is preparing an imaginary banquet, and I will be there a real guest. I will meet her at Philippi![1]

I wish I were away from this place! I wish I were in my mother's coffin!

I hate to meet this insolent sister of mine. We have had a battle, and I was in such a frantic rage that I could neither find ideas nor words; while she was cool, cutting, insolent, impudent—! I never in my life had so strong an inclination to wring a hussey's neck round.

But I will get away as fast as I can. I am resolved however to turn her out of the house first. She shall feel me too, before I have done. Brother with her is no tie, nor shall sister be to me. Her mother has made but a small provision for her, and has recommended her to my mercy. She had better have taught her a little humility—

Plagues and pestilence! Why do I worry myself about her? I have quite causes enough of distraction without that. I must not turn her out of doors neither, now I remember. If I did she would fly to her friend, and would make her if possible as great a fury as herself.

Why do I say would make? Do I not know that I am her abhorrence? I loved her, Fairfax, better than ever I loved woman; and would have loved her more, have loved her entirely, infinitely, heart and soul, if she had not wronged me. From the first I was overlooked by her, catechised, reprimanded, treated like a poor ignoramus; while her Henley—! If I write any more I shall go mad!—Dash through the window, or do some desperate act!—

C. CLIFTON

LETTER CII

Sir Arthur St. Ives to Abimelech Henley

London, Grosvenor Street

MR. HENLEY,

Sir, I have received your letter, which I must acknowledge is far more satisfactory and in a more proper style than your last, at which I cannot but own I was exceedingly surprised.

With respect to your son, I must say that he is a young gentleman of very great merit; and though a marriage into the family of St. Ives is a thing that he certainly has no right to expect, yet I cannot deny that your proposal deserves some consideration; inasmuch as you now come forward like a man, and have likewise a recollection of propriety.

Neither do I forget, good sir, what you have hinted concerning Wenbourne-Hill, which is far from disagreeable to me. And though there are many impediments, for which I cannot altogether answer just at present, yet I think it very probable that this affair should end in something like the manner you desire. I accordingly expect, Mr. Henley, you will have the kindness to stop proceedings relative to the foreclosures.

In return for which I assure you, on my honour, I will do every thing that becomes a gentleman to bring the affair to a proper conclusion. And as I have a very great respect for your son, and think very highly of his parts, and learning, and all that, I find when things come to be considered that he perhaps may make my daughter more happy, and the match may have other greater conveniences than perhaps one that might seem to the other branches of my family more suitable.

But I know that for the present it will be opposed by Lord Fitz-Allen; and though I do not think proper to be governed by him or any man, yet I could rather wish not to come to an open rupture with so near a relation.

It will perhaps be thought derogatory by some other branches of the family. But my daughter has a very high opinion of the good qualities of your son; and she reminds me continually that he has done us many signal services, which I assure you, Mr. Henley, I am very willing to remember.

When things shall be in a proper train, I imagine it will be our best way of proceeding to pay off all mortgages on Wenbourne-Hill, together with the sum for the docking of the entail to my son Edward, and to settle the estate in reversion on our children and their issue; my rental being made subject to the payment of legal interest to your son for the fifty thousand pounds. But we will consider further on these things when matters are ripe.

In the mean time, be pleased to send me up one thousand pounds for present current expences, which you will place to account. And now I hope, good sir, we shall from this time be upon proper terms: in expectation of which I remain with all friendly intentions,

A. ST. IVES

LETTER CIII

Anna Wenbourne St. Ives to Louisa Clifton

London, Grosvenor-Street

OH that I could write to my Louisa as formerly, with flattering and generous hopes in favour of a brother! Would it were possible! I am already weary of accusation, though I fear this is but its beginning. I cannot help it, but I have strong apprehensions. Not that I will be the slave of fear, or sink before danger should it happen to come.

The lad that copied the anonymous letter has left Wenbourne-Hill! Is run away! No one knows whither! He went the very day on which your brother left London, to be present with you at Mrs. Clifton's funeral; and Clifton now denies, with pretended indignation, having had any knowledge whatever of this letter!—Oh how audacious is he in error! Had the same energy but a worthy object, how excellent would be its effects!

It is a strange circumstance! And what is more strange and indeed alarming, Frank has been to enquire for the lad's aunt, and she is gone! No one can tell what is become of her, except that she went away in a hackney-coach, after having as the people suppose received a present; because she discharged all her little debts contracted during the absence of Frank, and bought herself some necessaries.

What can this sudden and unaccountable removal of these two people mean? They had both apparently the strongest motives to the contrary; and Frank has a very good opinion of the lad, and not a bad one of the aunt.

This is not all. We were yesterday invited to dine with Lord Fitz-Allen; that is I and Sir Arthur, not Frank Henley, as you will suppose. I had a dislike to the visit, though I did not suspect it would have been half so disagreeable. My brother and my aunt Wenbourne were likewise invited; we found them there.

Ever since the scene with Mr. Clifton I have been constantly denied to him, and positively refused all his applications for an interview; conceiving it to be just not to let him imagine there was any doubt on my mind, relative to his proceedings and their motives. We had scarcely sat down to table before he came in, as if by accident. This was a subterfuge. To what will not error and the abandonment of the passions submit?

After apologies for dropping in and disturbing so much good company, and a repetition of—I am very glad to see you, sir; you do my table honour, and other like marked compliments from Lord Fitz-Allen, Clifton seated himself and endeavoured to assume his former gaiety and humour. But it could not be—His heart was too ill at ease. His eye was continually glancing toward me, and there as often met that steady regard which he knew not how to support, and by which he was as continually disconcerted. I did not affect to frown, and to smile would have been guilt. I put no reproof into my look, except the open-eyed sobriety of fortitude, springing from a consciousness of right. But this was insupportable. He talked fast, for he wanted to talk away his sensations, as well as to convince his observers that he was quite at his ease. I know not how far he was successful, for they laughed as much when he failed, or more perhaps, than they would have done had his wit preserved its usual brilliancy. His manner told them he intended to be jocular, and that was their cue to join chorus.

Lord Fitz-Allen was very marked in his attentions to him, which were returned with no less ardour. Clifton indeed evidently laid himself out to please the whole table; but me least, because with me he had least hope; and because he found his efforts produced no alteration in that uniform seriousness on which I had determined.

As soon as the dessert was served up the servants withdrew, and not one of them afterward came in till rung for; which I imagine had been preconcerted. Looks then became more grave, and the conversation soon dwindled into silence. At last Lord Fitz-Allen, after various hems and efforts, for he has some fear of me, or rather of what he supposes the derogatory sufferance of contradiction, addressed himself to me.

I am sorry to hear, niece, there is a misunderstanding between you and Mr. Clifton; and as you happen now to be both together, I think it is a proper opportunity for explanation. You know, Miss St. Ives, that an alliance with the family of Clifton has always met my approbation; and I suppose you will not deny me the favour of listening with patience—Why don't you speak, niece?

You desired me to listen, sir, and I am silent—Let Mr. Clifton proceed.

Clifton after some stammering hesitation began—I know, madam, you have been prejudiced against me, and have been told very strange things; very unaccountable things. I cannot tell what answer to make, till I know perfectly of what I am accused. All I request is to be suffered to face my accusers, and let Lord Fitz-Allen, or Sir Arthur, or this good lady [My aunt Wenbourne] or your brother, nay or yourself, though you think so ill of me, be my judge. I am told something of an anonymous letter; I know not very well what; but if any good evidence can be brought of my having written, or caused to be written, or had any concern whatever in the writing of such a letter, I solemnly pledge myself to renounce the blessing I so ardently seek without a murmur.

Lord Fitz-Allen exclaimed nothing could be more gentlemanlike. My aunt Wenbourne owned it was a very proper proposal. Edward thought there could be no objection to it. Sir Arthur was silent.

His insidious appeal to justice, and being brought face to face with his accusers, revived the full picture of the flight of the lad, the removal of the aunt, and the whole chain of craft and falsehood connected with these circumstances. It was with difficulty I repressed feelings that were struggling into indignation—I addressed myself to Mr. Clifton.

Then, sir, you coolly and deliberately deny all knowledge of the letter in question?

I have told you, madam, that I will suffer Lord Fitz-Allen, your-self, any person to pass sentence, after having examined witnesses.

Answer me in an open direct manner, Mr. Clifton, without ambiguity. Were you not the author of that letter?

I am sorry, madam, to see you so desirous to find me guilty; and I would even criminate myself to give you pleasure, but that I know I must then neither hope for your favour nor the coun-tenance of this good company. I assure you, Lord Fitz-Allen, I assure you, Sir Arthur, and you, madam, and all, upon my honour I am incapable of what is attributed to me.

Do not appeal to my uncle and aunt, Mr. Clifton, but turn this way. Let your eyes be fixed here. Listen while I read the letter; and then, without once shrinking from yourself, or me, repeat as you have done, though in an equivocal manner, upon your honour you are not the author.

I took the letter from my pocket and began to read. When I came to the following passage I again repeated—Look at me, Mr. Clifton—'She will never have the man they mean for her, I can assure you of that; and what is more, he will never have her.' I pro-ceeded to the end, and then added—Once more, Mr. Clifton, look at me and repeat—Upon my honour I was not the inventor and author of those words.

Louisa—! He did look—! I hope I never shall see man look so again!—He stared and forced his eyes to do their office, and repeated—'Upon my honour I was not the inventor and author of those words.'—He stabbed me to the heart, Louisa!—Can he do this?—Then what can he not do? He even felt a complacency at the victory he had obtained, and turning round to Lord Fitz-Allen and the company again repeated—'Upon my honour I am not the inventor and author of those words.'

Lord Fitz-Allen almost crowed with exultation. I am mistaken, niece, said he, if you do not find there are other people who can write anonymous letters: people of no honour; upstarts, mongrels, mushrooms, low contemptible fellows, that would sully the mouth of a Fitz-Allen to mention.

The tone of this lordly uncle was so high, Louisa, and his passions so arrogant, loud, and obstinate, that it was with difficulty I could recover the fortitude requisite to assert truth and put false-hood to the blush. I again turned to my opponent.

Mr. Clifton, I feel at present you are a dangerous man. But I do not fear you. Observe, sir, I do not fear you—[I turned to my uncle] Sir, Mr. Clifton caused this letter to be written. But, if there were no such letter in existence, I have another proof, stronger, more undeniable of which I imagine you will not doubt when I inform you that no third person was concerned. It was addressed to myself. It was a strenuous, bold, unprincipled effort to seduce me. Let the gentleman again look me in the face and tell me I am guilty of falsehood.

I spoke with firmness, and Lord Fitz-Allen's features relaxed, and his eye began to enquire with pain and apprehension. His great fear was of being convicted to want of penetration. Clifton perceived the feelings of the company turn upon him with suspicion; but his art, must I add? his hypocrisy did not fail him. He transformed the confusion he felt into a look of contrition, and with as much ardour as if it had been real replied—

It is that fatal error which has ruined me, madam, in your good opinion, and has occasioned you to credit every accusation against me, however improbable. I confess my guilt. Not guilt of heart, madam; for honour be my witness, my views were as pure as the words in which they were uttered. I was at that time dependant on the will of a mother, whom I loved, and whose memory I revere. My passions were impatient, and I wished to remove impediments to my happiness which now no longer exist. I do not pretend to palliate what is unpardonable, and what I myself condemn as severely as you do; except that I abjure all dishonourable intentions, and meant as I said to be your husband. The strongest proof I can give that this was my meaning I now offer, in the presence of this noble and good company. I require no conditions, I ask for no fortune except yourself, which is the only blessing I covet in this life. I will joyfully attend you to the altar whenever you and your worthy relations shall consent; next week, to-morrow, to-day, this moment; and should think myself the most favoured, the most happy man on earth!

The offer is the offer of a gentleman, Sir Arthur, said Lord Fitz-Allen. If Mr. Clifton had been guilty of any indecorum, niece, [Turning to me] you could not require more honourable amends. This is acting with that dignity which characterizes a man of family, Mrs. Wenbourne; and as it is impossible for Miss

St. Ives to see it in any other point of view, here the affair will
naturally end, and there is no more to be said.

I immediately answered—If, sir, by the affair ending here, you
understand any further intercourse between me and Mr. Clifton,
I must not suffer you to continue in such an error. We are and ever
must remain separate. Habit and education have made us two such
different beings, that it would be the excess of folly to suppose
marriage could make us one.

Miss St. Ives—[My uncle collected all his ideas of rank and
grandeur] Miss St. Ives, you must do me the honour to consider
me as the head of our family, and suffer me to remind you of the
respect and obedience which are due to that head. The proposal
now made you I approve. It is made by a man of family, and I must
take the liberty to lay my injunctions upon you to listen to it in a
decorous and proper manner.

I answered—I am sorry, sir, that our ideas of propriety are
so very opposite. But whether my judgment be right or wrong,
as I am the person to be married to Mr. Clifton, and not your
Lordship, my judgment as well as yours must and ought to be
consulted.

Lord Fitz-Allen could scarcely restrain his anger within the
bounds of his own decorum. He burst into exclamations—Exceedingly well, miss!—Very proper behaviour to a person of my rank,
and your uncle!—You hear, Sir Arthur!—You hear, Mrs. Wenbourne! You all hear!——But your motives and inclinations are
known, miss: I am sorry that it would dishonour the tongue of
Fitz-Allen to repeat them: and I cannot help telling you, Sir
Arthur, that you have been exceedingly to blame to admit such a
fellow to any familiarity with a woman of rank and my niece; a
fellow better entitled to be her footman than her—I will not permit
the word to pass my lips.

I felt the cowardice of suffering worth and virtue to be insulted
without a defender, from the fear that I myself should be involved
in the insult, and replied—

The gentleman, sir, to whom you have twice alluded in terms
of so much contempt, were he present would smile at your mistake.
But there are more people at this table than myself who have been
witnesses how little he deserves to be spoken of in the language of
opprobrium.

Mr. Clifton appeared eager to be the first to acknowledge Mr. Henley was a very worthy person. Edward muttered something to the same tune; and Sir Arthur seemed very willing to have spoken out, but wanted the courage. He began at Turnham Green, but could get no further. Lord Fitz-Allen answered—

What tell you me of Turnham-Green, Sir Arthur? I was stopped once myself, by a highwayman, and my footman fired at him, and sent him packing; but I did not for that reason come home and marry my footman to my daughter.

The full image of Frank and his virtues pervaded my mind, my heart swelled, my thoughts burst from my lips, and I exclaimed— Oh, sir, that you had a thousand daughters, and that each of them were worthy of such a footman for a husband!

Had you beheld this uncle of mine, Louisa!—The daughters of the peer Fitz-Allen married to footmen! The insult was almost agony. The only antidote to the pain which his countenance excited was the absurdity and ridicule of the prejudice. But I perceived how vain it was to expect that in this company the voice of justice should be heard, and I rose. My aunt rose at the same time, to retire with me; but, recollecting myself, I turned and thus addressed Lord Fitz-Allen and Mr. Clifton, alternately:

That I may not be liable to any just blame from your lordship, or you, sir, for want of being explicit, you must permit me to repeat—I never will again admit of the addresses of Mr. Clifton. I have an abhorrence of the errors in which he is now indulging. He himself has told me what a mad and vicious act it would be to marry a husband in whom I could not confide, and I never can confide in him. My persuasion at this moment of his hypocrisy is such that, could I prevail on myself to the debasement of putting him to the trial, by pretending to accept his hand, I am convinced he would refuse. I read his heart. He seeks an opportunity to revenge imaginary injuries; for I never did, do not, nor ever can wish him any thing but good. I think I would lay down my life, without hesitation, to render him all of which his uncommon powers are capable: but I perceive the impossibility of its being effected by me, and I here ultimately and determinedly renounce all thought of him, or of so dangerous an attempt.

Mr. Clifton eagerly started up, and with a momentary softening of countenance, a pleading voice, and something like the tone of returning virtue exclaimed—Hear me, madam!—I conjure you, hear me! My appeal is to the benevolence, the dignity of your heart! Remember the virtuous plan you had formed—!

The combat in his mind was violent but short. Truth made a struggle to gain the mastery, and hope raised up a transient prospect of success, which was as quickly overclouded by anger and despair, and he stopped abruptly. At least his voice and features were so impassioned that, if these were not his sensations, I have no clue to the human heart. Perceiving him pause and doubt, I replied—

It cannot be, Mr. Clifton! You this moment feel it cannot! You have begun a course of fraud, and which the whole arrangement of to-day is only meant as so much pitiful machinery to effect. You are conscious, Mr. Clifton, you are conscious, Lord Fitz-Allen, that our meeting was not, as you have both pretended, accidental. And I here call upon you—you, Mr. Clifton, to tell for what purpose or where you have sent the lad who wrote the letter, and to what place you have removed his aunt? Such an artifice is vile, sir! And to challenge your accusers to stand forward, and with a look such as you assumed to affirm, 'Upon your honour you were not the inventor and author of the letter,' is so much more vile that I shudder for you! Your own proceedings have conjured up a train of recollections that speak a concerted plan of perfidy. You mean mischief! But I once more tell you, sir, I do not fear you! I will not fear you! My fears indeed are strong, but they are for yourself. Beware! The more guilt you have committed, the more you will be driven to commit. Turn back! You are in a dreadful path! It is unworthy of you, Mr. Clifton! It is unworthy of you!

I instantly withdrew, and was followed by Mrs. Wenbourne, who began to express something like blame of the positive manner in which I had spoken, and the high language I had used to Lord Fitz-Allen; but it was too feeble to incite an answer in my then state of mind. I requested she would order her carriage, and set me down. She asked if I would not first pay my respects to my uncle. I answered yes, when my uncle should be more deserving of respect. She said I was a strange young lady. I replied I sincerely hoped there were many young ladies stranger even than I.

She took offence at these retorts upon her words, and I perceived that, though the spirit of my answer was right, the manner was wrong; and explained and apologised as became me. She was appeased, and when the carriage came again asked if I would not go with her to take leave. I answered I imagined my uncle would be glad to wave the ceremony; and, as I thought he had acted very improperly, curtsying and taking leave would but be practising the customary hypocrisy of our manners, which I hoped I should on all occasions have the firmness to oppose.

Accordingly my aunt went herself; and his lordship, still preserving his dignity, pretended to forbid me his presence, till I better understood what was due to the relationship and rank in which he stood. This my aunt reported, and I returned no answer, but left her to make her own reflections.

Thus ended this painful interview—Tell me, what ought I to think? What can be the purport of a conduct so very wrong? Such a string of falsehoods! How different would the behaviour of Mr. Clifton have been, had not conscious criminality oppressed and chained up his faculties! Such persistence in duplicity must have some end in view. Could I consent to marriage, which is now utterly impossible, he has certainly no such meaning. If he had he could not have written, he could not have acted as he has done; and even less in this last instance since his writing than before, for he could not but know that, though he could appear this generous man of honour to Lord Fitz-Allen, he must stand detected by me. It was not possible he should suppose otherwise.

Well! Let him mean me all the harm he pleases; only let me find some opportunity of convincing him what a depraved, unmanly, trivial turn his mind has taken, and let me but give it a different bent, and I will willingly suffer all he shall have the power to inflict. I do not find myself, Louisa, disposed to stand in that dread of baseness and violence which they generally inspire. Virtue is not a passive but an active quality; and its fortitude is much more potent than the rash vehemence of vice.

Adieu, dear Louisa. Peace and felicity guard you!

A. W. ST. IVES

LETTER CIV

Coke Clifton to Guy Fairfax

London, Dover Street

THANK you, Fairfax, for your speed and precautions, which I must request you not to slacken. Do not let the lad escape you: his appearance here would be ruin. Let but my grand scheme be completed, and then I care not though the legions of hell were to rise, and mow[1] and run a tilt at me. I would face their whole fury. The scene would delight me. Let them come all! I burn to turn upon and rend them! The more desperate the more grateful.

I told you, Fairfax, she hated me! I have it now from her own mouth! She feels I am become her foe! My hand is already upon her! My deepest darkest thoughts of vengeance do not exceed her imagination.

And yet she fears me not! Her words, her looks, her gestures are all cool, firm defiance! She is a miracle, Fairfax! A miracle! But I will overmatch her. A heroine! She would have unhorsed Orlando himself,[2] had she lived in the times of the knights Paladin.[3]

I am an insufferable booby, an eternal lunatic, for having first thought of quarrelling with her. But it is too late! I might have foreseen the advantages I give a woman like her. She openly, magnanimously tells me what my intents are, and then spurns at them. She keeps her anger under indeed, but does not repress its energy; a proof of the subjection in which she holds her passions. She once endeavoured to teach me this art, would I but have listened. But that is past!

I could not have thought it was in woman! The poor, wailing, watery-eyed beings I had before encountered would not suffer me to suppose a female could possess the high courage of the daring, noble mind. Never but one short moment did I overtop her: nor are there any means but those I then used. Inspire her with the dread of offending what she thinks principle, and she becomes a coward!

But I will rouse! I will soar above her, will subdue her, will have her prostrate in humble submission, or perish! In the presence of witnesses I feel I cannot succeed; but singly, face to face, passion

to passion, and being to being, distinct and eminent as she stands
above all woman-kind, I will yet prove to her she is not the equal
of the man Clifton.

She herself has even thrown the gauntlet. I have had such a
scene with her! A public exhibition! I cannot relate the manner
of it. I dare not trust my brain with the full reminiscence.

Why did I quarrel with her? She meant me well—Tortures!—
I am a lunatic to tease myself with such recollections. This is a
damned, wrong headed, ignorant, blundering, vile world; and I
cannot see my way in it. I should have had no suspicion that it is all
this but for her.

That Henley shall never have her! I'll murder him first!
Though the bottomless pit were to gape and swallow me, he shall
not have her! The contemptible buzzard, Sir Arthur, is now
completely veered about. But in vain! It shall not be! By hell it
shall not!

This fellow, this Henley must some how or other be disposed of.
The contempt of the arrogant peer, her uncle, will harm him but
little; for the lord, with all his dignity, is no match for the plebeian.

Neither will his lordship hastily seek another combat with his
niece. The only advantage I have, in so insignificant an ally, is that
of hereafter making suspicion alight on Henley, and not on me;
for I mean to carry them both off, Henley and Anna. I know not
where or how I shall yet dispose of them, but there is no other mode
of accomplishing vengeance. They must be confined too. I care
not how desperate the means! I will not retract! They shall be
taught the danger of raising up an enemy like me! I will have them
at my feet! Will separate them! Will glut my revenge, and do the
deed that shall prevent their ever meeting more, except perhaps to
reproach each other with the madness of having injured, aggravated,
and defied a Clifton!

My whole days are dedicated to this single object. I have been
riding round the skirts of this shapeless monster of a city, on all
sides, in search of lonely tenantless houses; some two of which I
mean to provide with inhabitants. I have met with more than one
that are not ill situated.

But I want agents! Desperados! Hungry and old traders in
violence! I care not where I go for them; have them I will, though
I seek them in the purlieus of infamy and detestation. To succeed

by any other means is impossible. She will not admit me in the same apartment with herself, nor I believe in the same world, had she the power to exclude me.

I met her indeed at Lord Fitz-Allen's, where the scene above-mentioned passed; but it was a plan concerted with his lordship, which she easily detected, and publicly reproached him with his duplicity. I gloried to hear her; for she had not injured him. A poor compound of pride and selfishness! Incapable of understanding the worth of such a niece! But she made him feel his own insignificance.

Henley and she are now never asunder. I have mentioned the maid Laura to you. She tells me they have long conversations in the morning, long walks in the afternoon, and at night they have neither of them the power to rise and separate. But I will come upon them! My spirit at present is haunting them, never leaves them, girds at and terrifies them at every instant, during their amorous dalliance! I know it does! They cannot get quit of me! I am with them, weighing them down, convulsing them! They feel they are in my gripe!—Hah! The thought is heart's ease.

When there is no company, and when Sir Arthur is not sitting with them, this maid, Laura, has that honour. Whence it appears that even these immaculate souls have some dread of scandal.

And who is it inspires that dread? It is I! They seem to have discovered that all circumstances, all incidents wear a double face; and that I am the malignant genius who can make which he pleases the true one——Yes! I am with them! I send the Incubus that hag-rides them in their dreams! They gasp and would awake, but cannot!

Why could she not have bestowed all this affection upon me? Why could she not? I once thought a woman might have loved me!——But it seems I was mistaken——The things that go by the general name of woman might; but when I came to woman herself, she could not, though she tried.

Would I were any where but in this infernal gloom! It is a detestable country! This town is one everlasting fog, and its inhabitants are as cloudy as its skies! Every man broods over some solitary scheme of his own, avoids human intercourse, and hates to communicate the murk of his mind. I am in a wilderness. I fly the herd, and the herd flies me. We pass and scowl enmity at each other, for I begin to look with abhorrence on the face of man. There is not a single gleam of cheerfulness around me. The sun has not once shone since the day of my disappointment, which was itself thick darkness.

Would I could get rid of myself!—I am going to take a ride, and make a second examination of a large lonely house beyond Knights-bridge. It lies to the left, and is at a sufficient distance from the road. I think it will suit my purpose. I must not have far to convey them; and Laura informs me their walks are most frequently directed through Hyde-Park, and among the fields at the back of Brompton.

I must be as quiet and appear as little myself as possible; for which reason I ride without a servant. And though I have been industrious in reading advertisements, and getting intelligence of empty houses, I have not ventured to enquire personally. Laura attends them in their walks; but she is secure.

They must both be seized at the same time, and in a manner that shall frustrate all research. It will then be concluded they have gone off together. He is a powerful fellow, a dangerous fellow, and I must be well provided. He shall never have her, Fairfax! I would die upon the wheel, hang like a negro, and parch alive in the sun ere he should have her!

C. CLIFTON

P.S. All society is become odious to me, but chiefly that society which I am obliged to frequent. This uncle Fitz-Allen, aunt Wen-bourne, and brother Edward are three such poor beings, and the censures they pass on a woman who is of an order so much above them are so vapid, so selfish, or so absurd, that it is nauseating to sit and listen to them. Yet these are the animals I am obliged to court! Hypocrisy is a damned trade, Fairfax; and I will have full vengeance for having been forced upon such a practice. The only present relief I have is to make the arrogant peer foam with the idea of his relationship to a gardener's son. This would be an exquisite pleasure, but that it is millions of times more maddening to me than to him!

Anna Wenbourne St. Ives to Louisa Clifton

London, Grosvenor Street

ABIMELECH is come up to town. I am obliged very respectfully
to call him Mr. Henley when Sir Arthur hears me, in compliance
to his feelings: and he has hinted that hereafter, when his name is
written, it must be tagged with an esquire.

The old miser [Well, Louisa, let it be the old gentleman] is so
eager in pursuit of his project that he can take no rest, and is unwilling Sir Arthur should take any. He has a prodigious quantity
of cunning! Whatever he may know of the theory of the passions
as a general subject, no person certainly knows better how to work
upon the passions of Sir Arthur: at least no person who will
condescend to take such an advantage. His discourse is such a continued mixture of Wenbourne-Hill, his money, mortgages, grottos,
groves, the wherewithals, and the young gentleman his son, that
laughter scarcely can hold to hear him. Were the thing practicable,
he would render Frank Henley himself ridiculous.

It is pleasant to remark what a check the presence of this favourite
son is upon his loquacity. He never suspects the possibility of there
being a mortal superior to himself at other times; whereas he has
then a latent consciousness of his own ridicule. The effect which
the absence of Frank has produced, with the favour he is in with
me, and the resolute manner in which he conquered his father when
he last went down to Wenbourne-Hill, have made a total change
in the old man's behaviour to this formerly neglected but now half
adored son. Were habits so inveterate capable of being eradicated,
Frank would yet teach him virtue; but the task is too difficult.

He is certainly in a most delicious trance. His son to be married
to the daughter of his master! That master a baronet! And the
estates of that baronet to be his own, as he supposes, to all eternity.
For the avaricious dreams of selfishness are satisfied with nothing
less. These are joys that swell and enlarge even his narrow heart,
into something that endeavours to mimic urbanity.

Whenever Sir Arthur mentions Lord Fitz-Allen, or the family
consent, honest Aby in a moment conjures up Wenbourne-Hill,

a hermitage, and a wilderness; and for the first day, if he found that dose not strong enough to produce its effect, foreclosures were added to the mixture. Your own heart, Louisa, will tell you what Frank's feelings were at such a mean menace; and, though to stop his garrulity entirely was not in the power of man, he determined to silence him on that subject. But the cunning Abimelech turned even this incident to advantage, by taking care to inform Sir Arthur of Frank's generosity.

Thus, Louisa, things are at present in a train which some months ago I should indeed very little have expected. But such are the energies of virtue! How changed at present do all surrounding objects seem! To me they were never dark; but they were not always pleasant. They are now all cheerfulness and perspicacity. We have the most charming walks and the most delightful conversations, Louisa; and on subjects so expansive, so sublime—! Often do I say—'Why is my friend not with us? Why does she not come and bear her part in discussion? She whose mind is so penetrating and whose thoughts are so grand?' But we shall meet! Days and years of happiness are before us! The prospect is rapture! Yes, Louisa, we shall meet, and I hope quickly!

A. W. ST. IVES

LETTER CVI

Coke Clifton to Guy Fairfax

London, Dover Street

JOIN chorus and rejoice with me, Fairfax, for I feel something like a transient hilarity of heart. I think I am half in a temper to tell my tale as it ought to be told. Time was when it would have been pregnant with humour.

The very master-devil that I wanted has appeared to me, and we have signed and consigned ourselves over to the great work of mutual vengeance! Be patient and you shall hear the manner of it.

Two nights ago I was at the theatre. The king was there; Garrick played; the crowd was great, and no places were to be procured. During the first act I and two more stood elbowing each other at the door of one of the front boxes, the seats of which were all full. The person who was next me was hard-favoured, had a look of audacious impudence, with that mixture of dress which forms the vulgar genteel, and spoke the brogue.

The act being over the audience rose, and my gentleman, with the nonchalance assurance of his character, a total disregard of the feelings and convenience of others, and an entire complaisance for his own, stepped forward into the second seat from the door, on which there were previously four people, its full compliment. But he had noticed they were not all so athletic as himself, and was determined to make them sit close.

The persons next him, observing his redoubtable look, hesitated for a moment, but at length began to remonstrate. They addressed him two or three times without his deigning to appear to hear them; till, either encouraged by his silence or warmed by vexation, they spoke loud enough to call the attention of the people around them.

The Hibernian then sat himself down, threw his arm over the railing of the box, and his body in a careless posture, and very coolly answered—'Pray now be asy, and don't disturb the good company.'

A squabble ensued, and the Irishman continued to answer them with the utmost contempt. In a short time two of them gained courage enough to threaten to turn him out; to which he replied— 'Oh! By the sweet Jasus but I should be glad to see the pretty boy that would dare to lay a little finger upon me!'

After another wrangle, and treating their reasonings and half menaces with the most contemptuous disregard, a gentleman from the next box interfered, and observed it certainly was very improper behaviour. The Irishman turned round, surveyed him from head to foot, and answered—'I find you have all got your quarrelling tackle on board to night; and so as I must fight somebody, and as you, mister, appear to be the most of a gintleman, why I will talk to you when the play is over. For which raison sit down, and make all yourselves asy.'

The beginning of the second act and the impatience of the house to hear their favourite soon imposed silence, and the Irishman kept his seat.

I was so much diverted by the complete impudence of the fellow, that though one of the box-keepers had found me a place, I determined to return, and see how this petty brawl was to end. Accordingly I took care to be round in time, before the curtain dropped; till which the hero of it had kept quiet possession of his usurped seat.

The moment the audience rose he turned about, and with a look which I imagine no man but himself could assume, first on this side of him and next on that, addressed his opponents with— 'Now if any of you are still disordered in the body, and want to lose a little blood, why follow me.'

The two persons that sat next to him were both Jews, and one of them who appeared to have the most spirit had a knotted crab-stick[1] in his hand, and insisted that the Irishman should not leave the company, till he had first given satisfaction for the insult he had committed on them all. The Hibernian replied—'All? Is it all together you mane, or one after another? Perhaps you don't understand the tools of a gintleman, and want to box me! Faith and I should have no great objection to that either, with any half dozen of you, one down and t'other come on. But you must use no unlawful weapons, my sweet fillow.'

So saying, he wrested the Jew's crab-stick from him, laid hold of it at each end, and snapped it in two across the railing of the box; adding with infinite composure of countenance—'This is an improper plaything for you, master Jackey, and you might do yourself a damage with it. Here is half a crown for you. Take it, man, and buy yoursilf a genteel bit of rattan,[2] to beat the little pug dogs away, when they bark after you in the street.'

Insolent as the fellow was, there was no resisting his humour, and the laugh was general. The vexed Israelite endeavoured to persist, and the Irishman drew a dirty letter out of his pocket, from the back of which he tore the direction, and giving it to the angry Jew, said—'If you have any stomach for a good breakfast tomorrow morning, I shall be at home; and the hot rolls and butter will be ready at ten.'

He then strode over the seats and went into the lobby, where he was followed by the crowd.

My curiosity was highly excited, and I requested the Jew to let me read his address.

Imagine, Fairfax, my surprise at seeing the name of Mac Fane! That is, of the gambler and bully who some time ago had been

attempting to plunder brother Edward; and who had been so
successfully opposed by the family knight-errant, Henley! Among
the busy conjectures of my fermenting brain concerning the instruments I might happen to want, should things as they have done
come to an extremity, the supposed qualifications of this hero had
more than once passed in review. The behaviour to which I had
this evening been a witness perfectly confirmed all my former conjectures, which I instantly recollected; I therefore determined not
to lose sight of him.

Before I knew who he was I had been glad to see the squabble
continued, because it drew out the strong traits of this very
eccentric genius; but I grew impatient to put an end to it the
moment I had made the discovery.

The thing was not difficult. His character was too desperate and
determined not to inspire fear; and the humour of his phraseology
and brogue made the laugh always on his side. The passions of his
opponents counteracting each other died away. The farce was
going to begin, and he advised them to 'go, and not lose full eighteen
pennyworth out of their five shillings.'

Finding the morsel was too hard for their digestion, they took
his advice and returned quietly to their seats: while he several
times traversed the lobby, and looked first into one box and then
into another, to let them see that there he was.

My resolution was formed, and I soon found an opportunity of
falling into conversation with him; and as I took care that my tone
should answer the intended purpose, he presently invited me to
adjourn, and take what he called a bottle and a bird at the Shakespeare.

The proposal exactly suited me, and away we went.

He called for a private room, which I should have done if he
had not, though with a very different view. My appearance made
him hope he had caught a gudgeon.[1] He presently began to turn
the discourse upon various kinds of gaming. Billiards, tennis,
hazard,[2] and pass-dice,[3] were each of them mentioned; and, to
encourage him, I gave him to understand I knew them all. He then
talked of cards, and asked if I had any objection to take a hand at
picquet; 'just to pass away an hour before supper.' I answered none.

Accordingly the waiter was rung for, and the cards were presently
upon the table.

He proposed playing for a trifle; from one guinea to five; not more; 'becase as why, he was tied up from deep play. He had lost five thousand pounds within six weeks, and they had had a pretty pigeon¹ of him!—[Had you but seen the form and features of this pigeon, Fairfax!] For which raison he must take care and not be plucked² any more. It was the misfortune of his timper not to know when to stop; and there was not so unlucky a fillow in the three kingdoms. He was always the bubble,³ play at what he would, and every snap-jack⁴ knew him to be his mark.'

Such was the lesson which this fellow had got by rote, and had been retailing to all comers for years. But I have observed of gamblers that they cannot forbear rehearsing their own cant even in the company of each other, and when they are convinced every soul that hears them knows they are lying.

I however had my purpose to serve, and we sat down to our game. The stakes were five guineas a side. According to custom, I won the three or four first games; and he pretended to curse, and fret, and again ran over his bead-roll of being pigeoned, plucked bare, bubbled, done up, and the whole catalogue of like genteel phrases.

The first game he won he proposed, as luck was perhaps taking a turn in his favour, to double the stakes, and I indulged him. He suffered me to win the following game. I say suffered, cheating being taken into the account; for I am certain that at the fair game I am his master. But that is no matter.

The three following games were all his own, and he then began to repeat the remainder of his part. 'By the blissed Jasus he would not believe his own eyes! Three games together!' The fellow swore, with one of the deepest oaths his memory could furnish, such a thing had never happened to him before in his whole life! 'But now that he was in luck, he would as soon play for a hundred guineas as for a thirteener.'

He endeavoured to provoke me to increase the stake; and, by the supper not coming up, I am convinced the waiter and he understood each other, and that the signal had been given. I refused to play for a greater sum, and we continued till he had won fifty guineas, he incessantly swearing—'By the blissed crook! By the hind leg of the holy lamb! By Saint Peter's pretty beard!' and by all manner of oaths, some of them of the most whimsical and others of the most horrible kind, that he had never been a winner so much before in all his life. From the first ten guineas that he won to the last it was still the same tune.

I then rang the bell and ordered supper, thinking the sum sacrificed quite sufficient; though not more than enough to serve my purpose.

While we were eating, he endeavoured by all the arts he knew to excite the passion of gaming in me; and he is a tolerable adept. But my mind was too intent upon another subject. I watched the moment when he was at the height of his hopes, which I had purposely encouraged to produce my intended effect, and then asked him if he did not know Captain St. Ives?

Impudent as the fellow is, his countenance for a moment was fixed, his mouth open, and his eye struggling to get rid of alarm, that it might begin its enquiries. I followed up my blow by adding—

You won three thousand guineas of him I think, Mr. Mac Fane, which I am told were never paid—

The fellow put his hand into a side-pocket, which he had in the body of his coat. I instantly suspected he had a small pair of pistols there, and my suspicions were afterward confirmed. He drew it back, having satisfied himself that they were actually forth-coming, and then recovered himself so far as to ask—

Pray, sir, are you acquainted with Captain St. Ives?—

I am, sir, answered I—I likewise know Mr. Henley.

You do, sir? said the astonished Mac Fane.

I do, sir. I am intimate with Sir Arthur St. Ives, and he is the son of his gardener: a low fellow that acts as the baronet's man of all work; his steward, his overseer, and his cash-keeper.

This contempt thrown on the character of Henley gave the Irishman some relief. By the holy poker, said Mac Fane, but I always thought he was a spalpeen,[1] and no gintleman!

I think you have no great cause to like him much, sir, continued I, from the account that I have heard.

His choler began to rise, and his eyes assumed an uncommon ferocity. Like him! Sweet Jasus snatch me out of the world if I don't pay off an old score with him yet, before I die.

I thought as much, sir, answered I.

Sir! Replied he, again staring with reviving alarm and sus-picion—

I continued.—To tell you the truth, Mr. Mac Fane, that is the very subject which brought you and I into company this evening. I suspected your hate of Henley, and to be sincere I hate him too.

Had you seen the fellow's face brighten, Fairfax, and after brightening begin to flame, you would not have readily forgotten the picture.

But I am rather surprised to meet you in public, sir, added I.

What do you mane by that, sir?

I thought you deemed it prudent to keep out of the way, on account of that affair?

I felt some gratification in playing thus upon his fears—He now once more put his hand into his side-pocket, and pulling out his pistols laid them before him. By Jasus, sir, I don't very well know what you would be at! But when I understand the full tote[1] of your questions, I shall know how to give an answer.

I could not very well digest this oblique menace; but to have quarrelled with such a rascal would in every sense have been madness. You have a well-mounted pair of pistols there, said I, Mr. Mac Fane. I'll bet you the fifty guineas, double or quit, I break this china plate at the first shot, ten paces distant.

By the great grumbler, answered he, but I'll bet you don't! immediately delivering me one pistol, and taking up and unlocking the other himself. Accordingly I placed the plate against the wall, fired, and was not far from the centre. Upon my honour and soul, sir, said Mac Fane, but I find you are a good shot, and I shall be glad to be better acquainted with you.

Having convinced him that I could hit a mark as well as himself, I returned to the subject of Henley; and though I could not bring him to be explicit, I learned from him that he was acquainted with Henley's aversion to prosecute, but does not know on what that aversion is founded. Beside which he confides in a want of witnesses, as I could perceive: except that he has some fear of his accomplice, Webb; a man in whose company this very Mac Fane once attempted to rob Sir Arthur, and whom I suspect he would impeach, but that it would ruin all his gambling views. For he has found means of associating with that whole class of young fools of fortune, whose perverted education leads them to take pleasure in the impudence and humour of such a fellow, as well as in seeing each other stripped and ruined by turns; but who would never admit him as a companion, did they know he had been guilty of an act so desperate as that of going on the highway. Scarcely any thing short of this can expel such a fellow from such society.

But though he thinks himself secure in consequence of the lenity of Henley, he hates him as sincerely as if he were pursuing him to the gallows. The loss of the three thousand guineas is one great motive; and another is that he felt he was out-braved by Henley, whom he could not terrify, but who on the contrary terrified him.

I found he had even formed a scheme of petty vengeance, which was to waylay Henley with some bruising fellows of his acquaintance, for he is acquainted with daring villains of all descriptions, one of whom was to insult, provoke him to fight, and beat him, while Mac Fane himself should keep at some distance, disguised.

It was with some difficulty I could persuade him to desist from this plan, and join in projects of my own. But at last however he was convinced that to rob him of his mistress, and awaken him from all his dreams of imaginary bliss to the torture I am preparing, would be more effectual revenge than a paltry beating. Not to mention that I firmly believe, instead of being beaten, he would conquer the best prize-fighter they could bring; for he is really a powerful and extraordinary fellow.

But you will perceive, Fairfax, I was obliged to inform him of a part of my own views; and that I might fix him I determined to bid high. I told him I had Henley and another person to secure; and that if he would aid me himself and provide other assistants to act under his directions, without seeing or being informed of me, I would give him a thousand guineas as soon as all this should be perfectly accomplished. And, as an earnest of my generosity, I put down the fifty guineas; saying that the wager I had made with him was not a fair one, for that it was fifty guineas to a straw in my favour: he had no chance of winning.

He was quite satisfied with my offer, strengthened as it was by the gratification of his own passions. I told him what a puissant[1] hero Henley is, and of the necessity of coming upon him by surprise. I told him I had seen a house, as before described, beyond Knightsbridge, which pleased me; but that I could not find another near enough, in which to secure Henley.

The geography of the place I mentioned seemed to start an idea in his mind, and he told me, if I would meet him in two days at the same tavern, he would in the mean time not only make preparations and procure assistants, but perhaps bring me further intelligence. As the fellow's brain seemed busy, I did not wish to rob him of the self-satisfaction of invention, and we accordingly parted, making the appointment he proposed.

Of all existing beings, he perhaps was the only one who could in a country like this become the proper instrument of my revenge. And yet, Fairfax, he is a hateful fellow! His language, his looks, his manners, his passions, are all hateful! Courage excepted, there is not a single trait in him but what is abominable! He delights in talking of hocking[1] men, chalking[2] them, and cutting them down! Every time his anger rises against any one, these are its attendant ideas. Such a fellow must come to some tragical end. He can never die of old age, and scarcely of disease. Nothing but the lead and steel in which he delights can end him.

So it is, and I have no remedy. But he shall be to me no more than an implement, with which I will carve the coming banquet.

How minute are the chances and events on which we depend! A few slight alterations of incident, and how different would have been the train of my thoughts! She might have been happy with me, for I loved her, Fairfax. I loved her. I feel it more and more; and were but circumstances a little more favourable, I believe I should turn about and take a contrary path.

But it cannot be! The barrier is insurmountable! An adamantine wall, reaching to the skies! I remember what she said, at her proud uncle's table—'I have an abhorrence, Mr. Clifton, of the errors in which you are now indulging.'——Abhorrence was the word, Fairfax!—It has been at my tongue's end ever since—And when she talked of my errors she meant me.—'I ultimately and determinedly renounce all thought of him!'—This was her language! I knew before which way her heart went; and can I suppose, now she has got a fair excuse, that she will not profit by it? Oh no! I am not so ill read as that in the passions. But I have said the word—They shall never come together!—They never never shall!

C. CLIFTON

LETTER CVII

Coke Clifton to Guy Fairfax

London, Dover Street

I HAVE received your dissuasive epistle, Fairfax. It found me moody and did not contribute to make me merry. To own the truth, no ghost need rise to tell me the methods I use are inclined to the violent. Can you find me better? Nay can you find any other? I care not for consequences; I brave them all.

Time was that I could have been happy with her! Ay and should, but for this fiend Henley. He sleeps securely! Let him sleep on! I will soon awaken him!

I thought I should have been tortured but by one chief passion, and that the love of vengeance would have enveloped me wholly: but they are all devouring me by turns. I certainly hate her, and him I abhor. Yet pictures of imaginary happiness, that might have been, are continually rising, and vanishing in gloomy regret. He too, at the very moment that I could murder him, I am obliged to admire!

Still he shall not have her! Though death overtake him, her and me, he shall not have her! But what is death? A thing to covet, not to dread. 'Tis existence only that is hateful!——Would that my bones were now mouldering!—Why have I brains and nerves and sensibilities?—Oh that I were in the poisonous desert, where I might gulp mephitic[1] winds and drop dead; or in a moment be buried in tornados of burning sand! Would that my scull were grinning there, and blanching; rather than as it is consciously parching, scorched by fires itself has kindled!

I spent all yesterday with that Irish scoundrel. Malignity is his element, and mischief his delight! I suspect by his assiduity that he is poor just at present; for a more industrious demon black Cocytus[2] does not yield. He is already provided with associates, and has found another principal agent for the great work. It is a strange expedient! But these are strange fellows! And yet it is a lucky one; superior to any that I had projected.

When I mentioned the Knightsbridge road at our first interview,

Mac Fane recollected that an intimate of his had just set up what was to him a new trade, in the neighbourhood; that of being the keeper of a madhouse. He determined to go and propose the business to him; and as the fellow was preparing to advertise for lunatics, but had not yet got a single patient, there was a complete opening for such a plan.

He proposed taking me to see this intended guardian of maniacs, and his house; and I ordered a post-chaise for that purpose, that I might hide myself in one corner of it, and not let a living soul detect me with such a companion.

As we were going, I enquired if this keeper were an Irishman? He took offence, and retorted—'What did I mane by an Irishman? Becase he is a rogue you think he is an Irishman! By the holy carpenter you need not come to Ireland for that kind of ware! You have a viry pritty breed of rogues of your own! But he is not Irish. He is one of your own sulky English bugs.'

The description was not inapplicable, for I think I never beheld a more lowering, black-browed, evil-eyed fellow, since the hour I first saw light. He had all the gloom of the most irrascible bull-dog, but without his generous courage. He seemed more proper to make men mad than cure them of madness. But he had two excellent qualities for my purpose; poverty and a disposition to all ill.

I am got into excellent company! But I care not! I will on! All this seems as if it were but the prologue to the tragedy. But be it that, or be it what it will—I care nothing for myself; and I have little cause to care more for them. She never had any mercy on me; and least this last interview, when I was pleading before her pompous uncle.

I have been obliged to hold consultations with these Satanic rascals, to concert ways and means. The most secure we have been able to devise, relative to Henley, is to have a straight waistcoat, to come upon him suddenly, and to encrust[1] him in it before he shall know what we are about. This with a gag will make him safe. But there must not be less than four fellows, and those stout ones. Nothing must be left to chance.

Three more must be provided for the lady, of whom Mac Fane himself proposes to be one. But he means to keep out of sight of Henley, till he is in custody.

I have various preparations yet to make. Mac Fane is to go and hire me the empty house tomorrow. It is furnished; but it must be aired, for I would not have her die a paltry catch-cold death. I would treat her like a gentlewoman in every respect but one; and in that I will have as little compassion on her as she has had on me.

It might have been otherwise! I came to her a generous lover! I saw her and was amazed at her beauties, captivated by her enchanting manners, soothed by her unvaried sweetness! But this sweetness she has turned to gall! I adored her, and was prepared eternally to adore! But injury followed injury in such quick succession that apathy itself called aloud for vengeance!

I own it is true what she said at her uncle's, that I had made a resolution not to marry her. But what were my resolutions? She herself could not but feel she had the power to break them all. But she had not the will, Fairfax! It rankles there! She hates me, and what is more damnable she loves another!

I must turn my thoughts again to this detested mad-house man, and the scenery around it. All the avenues must be examined, and all the bye-paths and open roads that lead toward both houses inspected, that Mac Fane and his emissaries may make no blunder. I will if possible keep out of the action, but I will be near at hand.

I have a secret wish, the moment all is over, to fly the odious scene; for horribly odious it will be: but it would have the appearance of cowardice. It must end tragically! Not even the poor creatures who stand in the place of her natural guardians, tame as they are, can suffer such an insult. Yet which of them dare look me in the face, and call himself my enemy? And, after injuring her, shall I hesitate at trampling upon them?

I must steel my heart, Fairfax, when I go to the encounter; must recapitulate all my wrongs. I have them noted down severally as they occurred! I need but read to rage! What do I talk?—Read?— Can I forget them? No; night nor day! They are my familiars. They wake with me, sleep with me, walk with me, ride with me, glower with me, curse with me—but never smile with me. They are become my dearest intimates. I cherish and hug them to my heart! Their biting is my only pleasure!

I cannot forget this keeper. He is a foul-faced fellow! Has a wry look; a dogged, dungeon hue; of the deepest dusk and progeny of Beelzebub! I wonder by whom, where, and why such fellows are begotten!

There are horrid villains in the world! Villains by trade; that never felt the strong impulse of high-minded passion; that could breakfast in an hospital, dine in a slaughter-house, and sup in the sanguinary field of battle, listening to the groans of the mangled; or toss them on the point of forks, to smelt in a heap! I have heard her talk something of these depraved natures, and of the times when they are all to be humanised. Can you conjecture when, Fairfax? Yet she said they should be, and I was half inclined to believe her.

C. CLIFTON

P.S. I meant to notice that passage in your letter in which you mention Beaunoir; but I forgot it till this moment. So you are at last inclined to think Anna St. Ives must be something more than you every day meet, from the rapturous description of that rodo-montade[1] Count? After all I have written, your faith wanted the seal of such a lunatic? Had you forgotten that the time was when I would have married her? And did that say nothing?

The Count is preparing for England? Let him come! I remember one of his crazy phrases and claims was that he would be her champion, should ever base knight attempt to do her harm. Nor have I forgotten his intended visit, received by Henley. May the winds set fair and blow him quickly over! Should he have any such frolics in his brain, we shall not be long in coming to terms.

This Mac Fane is incessantly importuning me to play, and what is strange has several times excited the desire in me. I took up the dice box, after we had been to the mad-house, and threw half a dozen casts at hazard; but I soon found it was in vain, and checked myself. I know I have the command of my own temper in that respect.

I have been reading over this tedious homily, and find it most ineffably dull. But what is to be done? My gaiety is gone. My high spirits are converted into black bile. My thoughts are hellebore and deadly night-shade, and hilarity is for ever poisoned.

LETTER CVIII

Anna Wenbourne St. Ives to Louisa Clifton

London, Grosvenor-Street

HAVE I been unjust to the brother of my friend? Or had my words
the power over him to turn him from a guilty purpose?—Well;
rather, ay infinitely rather let me be a false accuser than he culpable!
He seeks me no more, offers not to molest me, and I hope has forgotten me; at least has seen the error of endeavouring to accomplish
a purpose so criminal by means so base. I expected storms, but a
sweet calm has succeeded that seems to portend tranquillity and
happiness.

With respect to me and Frank, our union appears to be hastening
to a conclusion. Sir Arthur, impelled forward by his hopes and
fears, proceeds though reluctantly to act contrary to the wishes of
my arrogant uncle. Mrs. Wenbourne is dissatisfied; but her
opposition is feeble, for Edward is reconciled to the match; having
no other motive but the acquisition of a sum of money for his
consent to dock the entail; and of the manner in which this sum
will be squandered we have already had sufficient proof.

I understand Lord Fitz-Allen affects to credit a report of a very
ridiculous, though as some would think it of a very injurious
nature; which is that there was a collusion between Frank Henley
and Mac Fane respecting my brother's gambling affair. The
circumstances necessary to render this probable are so violent as
immediately to expose its absurdity, and to make it matter of
amazement how such an assertion could be invented, or circulated.

What could be Frank's motive?—My wise uncle has his answer
ready—'That of imposing upon the family in order to marry me.'

And what Mac Fane's? 'A bribe' is a short phrase, and soon said.

I imagine it to be some dream of my uncle's, who has an aptitude
for this kind of invention; and who having once put a few incidents
together that seem to agree, persuades himself with great facility
that the fable he has created is fact. Petty calumny like this is
wholly incapable of moving Frank Henley.

The restless crafty Abimelech has prevailed on Sir Arthur to go
down with him to Wenbourne-Hill. He well knows how much his

own power will be increased by the old habits of Sir Arthur, and the ease with which they can be revived by this his interested abettor. Not but I am well convinced, when once every thing shall be settled, and he have no longer any thing to fear from the opposition of Sir Arthur, he will be as little a friend to improving as any of us. Various hints which have dropped from him would have proved this to Sir Arthur, had he not been blind enough to suppose that, he being a baronet, honest Aby is bound ever to remain his most obedient slave and steward; forgetting the proofs he has received that Abimelech at present is more inclined to command than to obey; and that when he parts with money he must have what he calls the whys and the wherefores.

His confidence in Frank however is now so entire that he has entrusted the transaction of certain money business to him, necessary on the present occasion, which he came up purposely to negotiate himself, but which he is now convinced can be done full as prudently and safely by his son. But a few months ago, Frank tells me, he petitioned this father in vain for thirty pounds, who now commits thousands to his keeping.

Not but it is from a conviction that there is no propensity in Frank to waste one of those guineas of which he is so enamoured. Without the least love of money, Frank is a rigid economist. The father indulges no false wants because it would be expensive; the son has none to indulge. Habits which in the one are the fruits of avarice, in the other are the offspring of wisdom.

Abimelech has some confused suspicion that Frank acts from higher motives than himself, and such as he does not understand; but still he hopes they are all founded on his own favourite basis, the love of hoarding. Nor can he very well persuade himself that this love is not the grand mover with all men of sense, among whom he now ranks his son high.

But ah, Louisa, how different are the views of this worthy, this heavenly-gifted son! He is anxiously studious to discover how he may apply the wealth that may revert to him most to benefit that society from which it first sprang. The best application of riches is one of our frequent themes; because it will be one of our first duties. The diffusion of knowledge, or more properly of truth, is the one great good to which wealth, genius, and existence ought all to be applied. This noble purpose gives

C c

birth to felicity which is in itself grand, inexhaustible, and eternal.

How ineffable is the bliss of having discovered a friend like Frank Henley, who will not only pursue this best of purposes himself, but will through life conduct me in the same path, will aid my efforts to promote the great work, and, by a combination of those powers we happen to possess, will add energy to effort, and perhaps render it fifty fold more pervading and effective!

Husband and wife, parent and child are ties which at present claim, or rather extort a part of our attention. But oh how poor how insignificant are they, when compared to the claims of eternal justice; which bind man to man in equal and impartial benevolence over the face of the whole earth, and render the wandering Arab, who is in need of aid or instruction from me, as truly my brother as the one my mother gave me.

I seem now but beginning the journey of life; and to have found a companion, guide, and consoler like Frank Henley is surely no common felicity! May the fates grant my Louisa just such another!

A. W. ST. IVES

P.S. You do not think, Louisa, no I am sure you cannot think that all the ardour I felt for the recovery of a mind like Mr. Clifton's is lost. Far, far otherwise! I still hope to see him even more than my fondest reveries have imagined! But I am not the agent; or at least this is not the moment; or which is still more probable no agent now is wanted. His mind has been obliged to enquire, and though passion may for a time suppress truth, its struggles will be incessant; must be so in a mind of such activity, and must at last be victorious. The grand enemy of truth is the torpid state of error; for the beginning of doubt is always the beginning of discovery. Let us then continue to love this man of wonderful genius; not for what he is, but what he shall be.

LETTER CIX

Frank Henley to Oliver Trenchard

London, Grosvenor-Street

OH, Oliver, how fair is the prospect before me! How fruitful of felicity, how abundant in bliss! Yes, my friend, jointly will we labour, your most worthy father, you, I, Anna, her friend, and all the converts we can make to truth, to promote the great end we seek! We will form a little band which will daily increase, will swell to a multitude, ay till it embrace the whole human species!

Surely, Oliver, to be furnished with so many of the means of promulgating universal happiness is no small blessing. My feelings are all rapture! And yet if I know my heart, it is not because I have gained a selfish solitary good; but because I live in an age when light begins to appear even in regions that have hitherto been thick darkness; and that I myself am so highly fortunate as to be able to contribute to the great the universal cause; the progress of truth, the extirpation of error, and the general perfection of mind! I and those dear friends I have named; who are indeed dear because of their ardent and uniform love of virtue!

Neither, Oliver, are all our hopes of Clifton lost. Anna thinks, and so do I, that he has heard too much ever to forget it all: or rather that he has a mind so penetrating, and so eternally busy, that, having been once led to enquire, it is scarcely in the power of accident wholly to impede the progress of enquiry. And should accident be favourable, that progress would indeed be rapid! By his intercourse with Anna his mind is become impregnated with the seeds of truth; and surely the soil is too rich for these seeds not to spring, bud, and bear a plenteous harvest. Ay, Oliver, fear not. It is not the beauty of the picture that seduces, but the laws of necessity, which declare the result for which we hope to be inevitable.

My present state of happiness meets some slight check from incidental circumstances, not in my power to guide. My father and Sir Arthur are doing what I believe to be a right thing, but from wrong motives. The prodigal Edward, from a very different avarice of enjoyment, is eager to dock the entail. The sum he is to receive will soon be squandered, and he will then be as eager to imagine himself treated with injustice; and will conceive himself left half to perish with want, if his accustomed dissipation be not supplied. But that it must not be. If we can teach him better we will; if not he must be left to repine and accuse, and we must patiently suffer the error which we cannot cure.

Lord Fitz-Allen indulges himself in thinking as much ill of me as he can, and in speaking all he thinks. But this is indeed a trifle. I know that the mistakes of his mind, situated as he is, are incurable; and to grieve or feel pain for what cannot be avoided is neither the act of wisdom nor of virtue.

F. HENLEY

LETTER CX

Frank Henley to Oliver Trenchard

London, Grosvenor Street

I DID not intend to have written again so soon, but an incident has occurred which perplexes all reasoning upon it, and again engenders doubt. It relates to Clifton.

I last night attended Anna to Covent-Garden playhouse, where about eight o'clock I was obliged to leave her, having an appointment with some gentlemen in the city relative to my father's money affairs at that hour; which having settled it was agreed I should return in the carriage for Anna, before the play was ended, to conduct her home. Accordingly having met my men of business, whom on Friday next I am to meet again to receive eight thousand pounds, I drove back to Covent Garden.

It was then about ten o'clock. The coachman stopped at the Piazza. I alighted; but, as I was stepping out of the carriage, whom should I see but the gambler and highwayman, Mac Fane, linked arm in arm with Mr. Clifton! I was struck with amazement, as well I might be. A thousand confused doubts succeeded to each other, which I had neither time nor indeed power to unravel.

However it seemed to me almost impossible that Mr. Clifton should know the man, and suffer himself to be seen in public with

such a character. For certainly a want of self-respect is not one of
the habitual mistakes of Mr. Clifton. I stopped some little time in
this state of perplexity, but at last concluded it would be highly
culpable in me to leave Mr. Clifton ignorant of the character of his
acquaintance. They had gone toward King-Street, and I hastened
after them.

I soon came up with them, and addressing myself to Mr.
Clifton, said—'Sir, it is incumbent on me to inform you of a
particular of which I imagine you are ignorant. The name of the
man you are in company with is Mac Fane. You have heard his
history. He is the gambler who endeavoured to defraud Captain
St. Ives of three thousand pounds.'

I have before acquainted thee, Oliver, of the ferocious character
of this Mac Fane; of which I have now had further proofs. I had
scarcely finished my phrase before he replied, with one of his
accustomary oaths—'You're a scoundrel and a liar'—and immediately made a blow at me.

Being previously on my guard and watchful of his motions, I
stepped quickly back, and he missed me and reeled. This was in
King-Street, where I overtook them.

I turned back, intending not to notice his insult; but he was too
much enraged to suffer me to escape, unless I had thought proper
to run. He is a very muscular fellow, and confident of his own
strength. No man could be more determined than I was to avoid
so absurd a contest, had it been possible; but it was not. He made
several blows at me, two or three of which took effect, before I
returned one of them. But finding that I must be obliged to beat
him in order to get rid of him, and that there was absolutely no
other mode, I began my task with all necessary determination.

The mob collected apace, and we were presently surrounded
by passengers, waiters, chairmen,[1] footmen, hackney-coachmen
and link-boys.[2] It was a strange disgusting situation; but it did
not admit of a remedy. This fellow, Mac Fane, has studied the
whole school of assault, and is a practised pugilist. When I was a
boy thou knowest, Oliver, and before thy worthy father had
taught me better, I was myself vain of my skill and prowess. I was
not therefore the novice which he expected to have found. Not to
mention, Oliver, that energy of mind, if it be real and true energy,

is itself, without any such contemptible knowledge, sufficient to overcome the strongest efforts of tyranny.

Of this I presently made Mr. Mac Fane sensible. After the very first onset, he felt himself cowed; which increased his rage so much that he endeavoured to have recourse to the most malignant and cruel expedients, to obtain victory. This obliged me to give him several hard and very dangerous blows, which I should otherwise have been cautious of doing, and the effects of which he will for some time continue to feel.

He fought however with great obstinacy, and in a manner which proved how much his ambition was wounded by being conquered. The mob, as in all such cases, chose different sides; but much the greatest part was for me. They several times saw the malicious and evil intentions of Mac Fane; and he once received a blow for them, from one of the assistants, which made him more guarded.

It is delightful to the philosopher to perceive how, even in error, justice struggles to shew itself. Those rules which are the laws of honour to the mob originate in this noble principle: and never is the infraction of justice more dangerous than at such moments, when the mind is awakened to full exertion.

Still it was a painful and degrading situation! Wert thou ever at the mercy of a mob? Didst thou ever feel the littleness of thy own faculties, when exerted to make a confused multitude act rationally, at the very time that thou thyself wert apparently acting like a fool, or a madman? If so, Oliver, thou canst conceive something of the contempt which I felt for myself, during this scene. Can a general, thinkest thou, if he be really a fit person to be a general, feel otherwise in the heat of battle? For I am mistaken if armies of the best disciplined men, brought into action, do not more or less become a mob. And added to this sense of imbecility, what must the general's feelings be the next morning, when he goes to view the wretched scene of his own making? Does he go to view it, thinkest thou, or does he shun the fight? If he go he is a fiend; and if he stay away he is worse!

The battle being ended and the rage of Mr. Mac Fane, though perhaps increased, obliged to restrain itself, there stood I, surrounded by my applauding admirers, suffering a thousand ridiculous interrogatories, and confined to the spot for the want of clothes! My hat and coat I had committed to one person, and my

watch and purse to another; taking it for granted the latter would
have been stolen from me if I had not, as was actually the fact, for
my breeches pockets were turned inside out. I had rightly concluded that the chances were more favourable in trusting to a
person I should select, than to the honesty of a mob in the confines
of Covent-Garden.

I was fortunate: the whole of my moveables again made their
appearance; and it gave me great pleasure, because I had trusted
my purse and watch to a poor fellow. The consciousness of his own
honesty was a greater pleasure to him than the recompense he
received from me; though I thought it my duty to reward him
liberally. Beside he had seen me ill treated, and had conceived an
affection for me, or more properly for the justice of my cause, and
he rejoiced exultingly in my victory.

I escaped from the shouts and congratulations of my greasy
well-meaning companions as fast as I could; and after a further
delay of stepping into a coffee-house, to wash and adjust my
appearance as well as circumstances would permit, I joined Anna,
who began to be alarmed, the play being over and the house almost
empty.

I saw no more of Clifton. But that affords me no clue. If he were
before unacquainted with Mac Fane, he would hasten from such a
companion with vexation and contempt: and if the contrary, his
chagrin at being seen by me would equally induce him to shun us.
Mind, as I have always remarked, Oliver, and as I have before
reasoned with thee relative to him, is slow in ridding itself of the
habits of prejudice, even when prejudice itself seems to have ceased.

'Tis true that conjectures disadvantageous to Clifton have, when
Anna and I were considering this incident, intruded themselves
forcibly upon us: but they were only conjectures, and I hope ill
founded. Indeed they are improbable; for Clifton could not know-
ingly league himself with a man like Mac Fane, except for purposes too black or too desperate for even passions so violent as his
to entertain.

I know mind to be capable of astonishing mistakes; nor can I
pretend, when I recollect the proofs on record, to say what are the
boundaries of error; nor indeed what are the boundaries of probability. But I think Clifton could not make himself the associate of
Mac Fane!

I should pronounce more boldly still, but that I cannot conceive how it was possible for a character so legible and gross, as that of this gambler, to impose for a moment on Coke Clifton; acquainted as he is with the world, and accustomed to detect and satirize what he understands to be absurdity! I can only say, if he be proceeding in error so flagrant and deep as this, he is a man much to be feared, but more to be pitied.

F. HENLEY

LETTER CXI

Coke Clifton to Guy Fairfax

London, Dover Street

AGAIN and again, Fairfax, this is an infernal world! A vile, disgusting, despicable, besotted ass of a world! Existence in it is not worth accepting; and the sooner we spurn it from us the better we shall assert our claim to the dignity and wisdom of which it is destitute.

How do I despise the blundering insolent scoundrel with whom I am linked! How despicable am I to myself!

I last night met the fellow again at the Shakespeare. Of all his dirty qualities, not one of them is so tormenting as his familiar impudence! There is no repressing it except by cutting his throat; a business at which he is always alert. Nothing delights him so much as to talk of extinguishing men, treading out their souls, feeding upon their life-time, and other strange revolting phrases, all of the same sanguinary sort.

Having consulted with him concerning the seizure of Anna and Frank, and concluded that the affair should be ended as speedily as possible, I wished to have shaken him off and retired: but the thing was impracticable. I do not choose that my own carriage should attend me on these expeditions; and as it was a rainy night, I knew the difficulty of getting a coach. I therefore staid an hour till the entertainment should be begun, and the Piazza probably more clear.

As there is no sitting in his company without some species of gaming, for his whole conversation, that subject excepted, consists of oaths, duels, and the impudent scoundrels he has put out of the world, I took a few throws at hazard with him; and, as I was very careful to call for fresh dice and to watch his motions, I was a winner; hazard perhaps being the fairest of all games, if the dice be not foul. He ran over his usual litany of being pigeoned, and about ten o'clock I left play, and determined to sally forth; being apprehensive of engaging too deeply at the game, if I staid longer.

The moment we had descended the stairs he impudently laid hold of my arm. My blood boiled, Fairfax! Yet I was obliged to submit.

This was not all! The precautions I had taken were but a kind of presentiment of the vexation that was preparing for me. Just as we quitted the door of the tavern, who should bolt upon us but the hated Henley! I shook with the broad shame! My teeth gnashed curses! How willingly could I have pistoled him, Mac Fane, every being that eyed me, and still more willingly myself!

But there was nothing for it but to walk on, and seem not to see him. He however would not suffer me to depart without a double dose of damnation! The same infernal officiousness, with which from the first moment he saw me to the last he has been seized, came upon him; and though I hurried through the Piazza to escape, like a perjurer from the pillory, he pursued us purposely to inform me I was in company with a rascal, and to warn me of my danger.

I never can recollect my own situation, without an impulse to snatch up the first implement that would deprive me of a consciousness so detestable!

The irascible fury of the bully rid me of my tormentor; he immediately assaulted Henley, and I hastened away from two beings so almost equally abhorrent, but from causes so opposite.

On the following evening, having another appointment with the gambling rascal, I took care to have a coach waiting, and to go muffled up and disguised as much as possible. But for once my caution was superfluous. No Mac Fane appeared.

Not knowing what had happened, and it being night, and I thus properly equipped, I resolved to drive to his lodgings. Being there I sent up my name, and was admitted to the bed-chamber of this doughty exterminator of men. If the temper of my mind were not obnoxious to all cheerfulness, I could almost have laughed, the

bully was so excellently beaten, mortified, and enraged! His head
was bound up, his eyes were plaistered, his thumb sprained, his
body of all colours, and his mind as hotly fevered as Alexander's
itself could have been, had Alexander been vanquished at the
battle of Issus![1]

His impatience to have Henley in his power is now almost
phrensy; and it will be phrensy itself when he comes to find, as
find he will, that though he can tie the hands of Henley his conquest must end there, and that the prisoner will still defy and
contemn his jailor. So would I have him. Henley, though I hate,
I cannot but respect and admire. The other is a creature I detest
myself for ever having known!

Yet who but he could have gratified the unabating burning
passion of my heart? I feel, Fairfax, as if I had taken my leave of
hope, joy, and human intercourse! I have a quarrel with the whole
race, for having been forced into existence and into misery! I have
suffered an accumulation of disgrace, for which I can never pardon
myself! And shall I permit the authors of it to live undisturbed in
their insult and triumph over me? No, by hell, come of me what
will! Lower I cannot be in my own esteem than I already am:
tremble those who made me so!

Beating has but rendered this rascal more impatient and active.
Every thing is prepared. The house is hired, aired, and provided
with a proper guardian. The madman keeper has all his implements ready. We have now only to watch and catch them at a proper distance from all succour, to which in their amorous walks they
have frequently strayed.

Though even you, Fairfax, seem to disapprove my conduct, I
care not. Not to give yourself further trouble with what you call such
positive prudes might be a very good maxim for you, who love your
ease too much ever to be sensible of the boiling emotions of a soul
like mine! You are Guy Fairfax; I am Coke Clifton. Not but I should
have imagined the swelling volumes of injuries I have communicated
would have lighted up a sympathetic flame of retributive vengeance
even in you, which not all your phlegm could have quenched. But
no matter—Though heaven, earth, and hell were to face me frown-
ing, I would on! My purpose is fixed: let it but be accomplished, and
consequences to myself will be the least of all my cares.

C. CLIFTON

LETTER CXII

Coke Clifton to Guy Fairfax

London, Dover Street

SINCE the world began, never yet had scoundrel wight so many damning accessary incidents to contend with, as I have had during the whole progress of this affair! All hell seems busy to blacken me!—I have done the deed—They are secure—But the hour of exultation itself is embittered, and the legitimate triumph of vengeance made to wear the face of baseness—I have them; but as I tell you there is an event, that happened the very moment preceding the seizure, which seems to have been contrived by the most malignant of the fiends of darkness, purposely to steep me in guilt indelible!

After our myrmidons[1] had been three days in vain upon the watch, on Friday last Anna and Henley sallied forth, about two in the afternoon, to take one of their amorous rambles. As usual they were followed by Laura, who had sent me word of their intention, which she had learnt at breakfast time. Henley it seems had previously been into the city.

A scout was on the watch, and when they appeared soon brought the intelligence. All was in readiness. The keeper with three stout fellows in one party, and Mac Fane with four more in another. The earliness of their setting out denoted they intended to lengthen their walk. The great danger was that it should have been directed to Kensington Gardens, as it has been several times lately; but in this instance fortune was on our side.

They went into the park, passed the gardens, walked beside the wall, crossed the Kensington road, and strayed exactly as we could have wished into the fields inclining toward Brompton.

I was on horseback, and by the help of a pocket telescope kept them in view, without the danger of being seen, while they were in the park; but as soon as they had left it I thought it necessary to spur on, and be ready to prevent any blunders. I crossed the road down the lane at the turnpike, passed them, and saw them arm in arm. The sight was insupportable!

From what afterward happened they must have seen me too, though I imagined myself under cover of the hedge.

You know my determination not to be robbed; and indeed robbery at such a time, and in such a place, was a thing I had little reason to expect. But a fellow, who was lying in ambush at the turn of the lane, calculated differently. He imagined nobody to be near, and suddenly presented himself and his pistol, with a demand of my money.

I made a blow at him with the butt end of my whip, which missed his head, but fell on his shoulder. My horse started, he fired and missed, but sprung suddenly forward, and seized hold of the bridle. He had another pistol which he was preparing, imagining I should be more intimidated when I found him so desperate. All this happened immediately after I had passed Anna and Henley; and the latter perhaps having seen the fellow, and certainly having heard the pistol, flew in an instant, leaped the hedge, and just as the robber was again presenting his pistol made a blow, and knocked it out of his hand.

The pistol went off, and the fellow took to his heels. Henley, instead of pursuing him, stayed to enquire with much earnestness whether I had received any hurt.

At this very damning speck of time, Fairfax, the keeper and his scoundrels who had been dogging them came up. There were four of them: two before and two behind. The undaunted Henley severally knocked down the two fellows in front, and in an instant would undoubtedly have been far enough out of all reach; but, in the very act of striking the second rascal, he received a blow from a bludgeon, dealt by the blood-hound keeper, which levelled him with the earth.

Never did my heart feel a twinge like that moment! I thought he was dead! He lay motionless; notwithstanding which the infernal keeper continued his occupation with unconcern, turned the un-resisting body over, slipped on the straight waistcoat, and bound down his arms.

At length he gave a groan! The instant I heard it I galloped off, full speed. It was too much for heart to endure!

I soon afterward heard him shout for aid more than once, but to this they presently put a stop, by forcing a gag into his mouth. They were not very far distant from the house where he was to be confined, and to which he was immediately hurried away.

There he at present remains. His morning dialogues, his noon-day walks, and his nightly raptures are ended. They are things past, never more to return! Of that torment at least I have rid myself; and others compared to that are bliss ineffable! I had sworn it should not be! They might have read the oath largely written on my brow, and ought instinctively to have known it to be the decree of fate!

No, Fairfax! I never asked a favour from him; never by my own consent received one! Not all the tortures of all the tyrants the earth ever beheld should have extorted a consent so degrading! His repeated interference was but a repetition of insult, and as such deserves only to be remembered. I asked not life at his hands; and giving life, instead of a blessing, he did but give torture! The gift was detestable and the giver! Had I perished, he might have been safe and I at rest. I asked not charity of him. No! On any terms I abhor existence; but on those, darkness and hell are not so hateful! It has ulcerated my heart, which not even vengeance itself I find has now the power to heal. For life I am made miserable; but it shall not be a single misery!

While the keeper was acting his part of this gloomy drama, Mac Fane, as you may well imagine, was not idle. He and his un-hallowed scoundrels presently made seizure of the lovely Anna. She stood confused and half terrified at the sudden flight of her enamorato![1] She was more confused, more terrified at the sudden appearance of her ravishers! I charged the scoundrels on their lives to use her tenderly! But what know such hell-hounds of tenderness?

She made I find a brave and by them unexpected resistance: but there were too many of them, and it was in vain! Mac Fane himself is amazed at her beauty; and harangues in his coarse and uncouth jargon on the energy and dignity of her deportment, in a manner which shews that even he was awed.

They were obliged however forcibly to stop her cries. This I imagined would be the case, and I had provided them with a white cambric handkerchief. But what will not the touch of such unconsecrated rascals defile?

Yes, Fairfax, they laid their prophane hands on her, clasped

her in their loathsome arms, polluted her with their foul fingers!
The embrace of a Clifton she might perhaps pardon; but this
violation she never can!

Well then, let her add this injury to the rest! I know her to be
my enemy; sworn, rooted, and irrevocable! And why should I
tag[1] regret to my sum of wretchedness? No! I will at least enjoy a
moment of triumph, however transitory! Let her despise me, but
she shall remember me too!

Give me but this brief bliss, and there I would wish existence
to end! That excepted, pleasure there is none for me; and of pain
I am weary. Yes! I will glut my soul with this solitary, short
rapture; and contemn the storms that may succeed! I fear them
not, shall glory in them, and be glad to find foes, if such should
arise, with whom contention will not be disgrace! I wish and seek
them. Their appearance would give me employment, and employment would give me ease, and ease would be heaven!

                                                    C. CLIFTON

LETTER CXIII

Coke Clifton to Guy Fairfax

London, Dover-Street

ALARM has sounded her horn. The family is all confusion, all
doubt, hurry, fruitless enquiry, and indecision. The absence of
Anna and Henley at dinner threw Mrs. Clarke into consternation;
for Sir Arthur is down at Wenbourne-Hill, with old Henley and
his son Edward. Each is indulging his dreams of improvement,
marriage, docking of entails, and other projects, to which I have
put an eternal stop.

Finding the evening advance, and that the two prisoners did
not appear, the housekeeper sent to the aunt, Wenbourne. She
heard the story and was amazed. She knew nothing of them.

Ten o'clock came, and terror increased. A messenger was dispatched to Lord Fitz-Allen; and he could not at first tell whether
to be sorry or glad, for he did not an instant forget to hope that it
was some rascally act on the part of Henley.

He sent for the housekeeper. She came, and he interrogated her. The answers she gave did not please him, for the tendency of all his questions was to the disadvantage and crimination of Henley, whom she pertinaciously defended. She affirmed so positively, and so violently, that it could not be any plan or evil intention of his, that the proud lord was half angry but half obliged to doubt.

I took care to be in the way, expecting as it happened that a message would be sent to me. I immediately attended his lordship, and learned all that I have been relating. I condoled with him, and pretended to pity the family; not neglecting to lead his thoughts into the channel that would best serve my purpose, and to recapitulate every circumstance I could remember, or invent, that should induce him to believe Henley and Anna had eloped; but affecting candour, and pretending to argue against the possibility of such a supposition.

The effect I intended was produced. He was fully convinced of Henley's being a low, selfish, contemptible scoundrel; and Anna a forward, disobedient, insolent miss.

I offered my services to pursue them, and pressed his acceptance of them violently; but was careful to counteract the offer, by shewing the impossibility of their being overtaken, and by exciting him rather to wish for their escape, that Anna might be flagrantly disgraced, and his penetration and authority vindicated to the whole world.

I did not neglect, before the departure of Mrs. Clarke, to display all my eagerness, by sending round to numerous inns and stable-keepers, to enquire whether any post-chaise had been hired, that should any way accord with the circumstances. Other messengers were dispatched, by my advice, to the different turnpikes; and a third set sent off to various watch-houses, to enquire whether any intelligence could be obtained of accidental deaths, or other mischances.

In short, I was very diligent to hurry the legs of the servants and the brains of their governors into every direction, but the right; and thus for a little while in some sort diverted myself, with the vagaries of the fools upon whom I was playing. One chop-fallen[1] runner trod upon the heels of another, each with a repetition of his diversified nothings; till his lordship thought proper to recollect it was time for his dignity to retire, and not further disturb itself on personages and circumstances so derogatory.

In the morning I was careful to be with him again. I breakfasted with him, and reiterated the same string of doubts, conjectures, alarms, and insinuations.

Mrs. Clarke returned. She had been up all night, and her looks testified the distress of her mind. She proposed sending an express after Sir Arthur; of the propriety of which I endeavoured to make the uncle doubt; but she was too zealous, and her oratory had too much passion, to be counteracted without danger. I therefore, when I saw resistance vain, became the most eager adviser of the measure.

There is no merit in imposing upon stupidity so gross as that of this supercilious blockhead. Mrs. Clarke would be much more to be feared, but that what she may say will be much less regarded. Her affection for Anna is extreme, and a high proof of the excellent qualities of her mistress.

Nor was she one whit less enthusiastic in her praise of Henley. Notwithstanding the forbidding frowns and reproofs of his lordship, she ran over his whole history; and dwelt particularly on an act of benevolence done by him to her niece; that being a circumstance that had come immediately within her knowledge. She spoke with such a fervour and overflow of heart that she once or twice moved me.

She perceived something of the ridiculous compunction I felt, and fell on her knees, wrung my hand, and adjured me, in a tone of very extraordinary emphasis, to save her dear her precious young lady. I scarcely could recover myself sufficiently to ask her which way it was in my power to save her; and to turn the conversation, by exclaiming to the peer—'Ah! Had she but allowed me the happiness and honour of being her protector, I think no man would have dared to do her harm.'

The old housekeeper however continued, and began to denounce impending and inevitable evil on the persecutors of Henley and Anna. I have no doubt she glanced at me, and that her mistress had informed her of the triumph gained over me. Why ay! I should indeed have been the scoff of the very rabble, had I not taken vengeance for my wrongs!

Yet her denunciations seemed prophetic: or rather were feeble descriptions of the excruciating pangs by which I am hourly gnawn!

I grew weary of the dull farce, and put an end to it as speedily as I conveniently could; leaving his sage lordship with the full conviction that the sudden disappearance of Henley, and his niece, could no otherwise be accounted for but by wilful elopement.

I am now preparing for a very different visit. A visit of vengeance! I expect no pleasure, no gratification but that alone! To prove the danger of injury done to me, to punish the perpetrators, to exult at their lamentations, and to look down with contempt at all menace, or retribution, is now my last remaining hope! Let me but enjoy this and all other expectation I willingly relinquish!— I am going—I have them in my grasp!—They shall feel me now!

C. CLIFTON

LETTER CXIV

Anna Wenbourne St. Ives to Louisa Clifton

WHERE I am, what is to become of me, or whether I am ever to see my Louisa more, are things of which I am utterly ignorant. I write not with an expectation that my friend should read, but to memorandum events of which perhaps the world will never hear; and which, should this paper by any accident be preserved, it will scarcely believe.

This vile Clifton—[Surely I ought never again to call him my Louisa's brother]—This perverse man has grown desperate in error! The worst of my forebodings have not equalled his intents! His plan has long been mischief! Hypocrisy, violence, rape, no means are too foul!—Such things are incomprehensible!

I am confined in a lone house, somewhere behind Knightsbridge. I was seized I know not how by a band of ruffians, and conveyed hither. Every kind of despicable deceit appears to have been practised. Frank was decoyed from me. He flew once again to save the life, as he thought, of this base minded man. I know not what is become of him, but have no doubt that he like me is somewhere suffering imprisonment, if he be permitted yet to live.

D d

No thoughts are so tragical, no suspicions so horrid as not to be justified, by deductions and appearances which are but too probable. Yet I will not sink under difficulties, nor be appalled at the sight of danger; be it death, or what else it may. That I am in a state of jeopardy my seizure and imprisonment prove. That Frank is still in greater peril, if still in existence, I have just cause to conclude. There were pistols fired, and one after he leaped the hedge; I know not at whom directed, nor what its fate!——I would if possible ward off apprehension. I know it to be folly, and I will endeavour to steel my heart against this as well as other mistakes. If he be dead, or if he be to die, grief will not revive or make him invulnerable. His own virtue must preserve him, or nothing can; and in that I will confide.

That evil is meant to me it would be absurd to doubt; but of what nature, where it is to begin, or where end, that time must disclose. For I will not permit myself to imagine the trifling indignities, or violence I have hitherto encountered, an evil worthy of complaint.

'Tis true my arms are bruised, and I was rudely dealt with by the vile men who seized me: and that there should be such men is an evil. But to me it is none; or not worth a thought. If I would firmly meet what is to come, I must not weakly bewail what is past.

I am not immortal, neither is my strength infinite; but the powers I have I will use. We are oftener vanquished because we are fearful than because we are feeble. Our debility takes birth in our cowardice, and true fortitude is not to be abashed by trifling dangers.

I meant to write a narrative, but these reflections are forced upon me by my situation. I will proceed.

I was brought here, on Friday*****, by several men of vulgar but ferocious countenances; and my maid Laura with me. I made all the resistance in my power; and the men, without any regard to what I suffered in body or mind, twisted my arms behind me, so that I imagined one of them had been dislocated, and forced a handkerchief into my mouth; handling, tossing, and gripping me, without any respect whatever to decency or pain, till they had conveyed me from the fields, in which I was walking with Frank Henley, to the place where I am.

I scarcely can guess at the distance; but they hurried me away with great violence, crossing several gates, and forcing apertures through hedges, for the space I believe of not more than half an hour: it might be much less.

They brought me to a house walled round; into which having been admitted by an old woman, they hurried me forward up stairs, and shut me into a room decently furnished, with a fire in it and a bed-chamber adjoining; but with the windows barred up, and in which every precaution had evidently been taken to render escape impracticable.

Laura was shut up with me; and there was a slip of paper on the table, on which was written—'Laura is allowed to fetch whatever you may want. Let her ring the bell, and the door will be opened.' —The hand-writing was Mr. Clifton's.

Among other necessaries, there was a book-case, furnished with the works of some of the best authors; and a writing-desk, with pens, ink, and paper.

The same old woman that opened the gate for the men, who brought me, constantly comes to open the door for Laura, when I ring. But this she does with great caution. A chain, similar to what is common for street-doors, is hung on the outside; which she puts up, and looks to see that I am not near, every time she opens the door. The first time she came I stood just behind Laura, and in a morose tone she bade me go back, or she would lock the door again.

After Laura had been several times down stairs, I enquired what discoveries she had made; and, as she informs me, the house appears to have no inhabitants but this old woman and ourselves. The old woman resides in the kitchen. The doors and windows are all secured; and the same care is taken to prevent escape below stairs as above.

The food that has been brought us was good, and well dressed, but almost cold. Laura says she is sure it cannot be dressed in the house, which is most probable.

I communicate but few of my thoughts to Laura, because I fear I have good reason to be suspicious of her. I have long remarked her partiality in favour of Mr. Clifton, intermixed with some contradictory appearances, which I could not solve at the time, but which I now believe to have been aukward attempts to conceal that partiality, and to mislead me; which she in part effected.

The base designs of Mr. Clifton, from the nature of them, cannot have been very recent; and nothing perhaps was more necessary, to carry them into execution, than the seducing of the woman who by her situation could give him the best intelligence.

Since I have begun to doubt her, I have purposely cross-questioned her occasionally, and she has answered with hesitation and incoherency. If however I can perceive the least hope that this letter should be conveyed to the post-office, by any person who may visit the house, and whom she may see but I cannot, I will trust it to her. The trust indeed is nothing, for it cannot increase my peril. The persecution of Mr. Clifton must prove most pernicious to himself. Unless he can deprive me of conscious innocence, it can injure me but little.

Among other ambiguous circumstances respecting Laura, she scarcely seems to repine at her confinement: though she has several times affected uneasiness, which while she acted it she evidently did not feel. Beside she is permitted to stay below, and run about the house; which, whatever caution of bars and bolts may have been used, she would not be suffered to do, as I should suppose, were she really in my interest.

About an hour ago we heard the yard bell ring and the gate open, and she was eager to go down. I encouraged her, and she rung for our turnkey. She had seen me writing, and, without being spoken to, took upon her to suppose it was a letter to my Louisa, and told me she *did believe* she could get it conveyed to the post. I am persuaded this is preconcerted officiousness. But as I said, I have nothing to lose, and there is a bare possibility of hope.

When she came up stairs again, she told me that the person who had rung at the bell was some man of the neighbourhood, who had brought the old woman various trifling articles, and whom she had ordered to return at five o'clock, with tea and sugar.

If contrary to all expectation this should come to hand, Louisa, write to my father; inform him of all you know: and especially write to Mr. Clifton. It will be ineffectual, but write. If there be truth in woman, I would rejoice to suffer much more mischief than he has the power to inflict, could I but by that means restore him to a sense of his own worth; or rather of the worth of virtue!

Why do I talk of mischief, and his power to inflict? I hope to shew him he has no power over me; and that the strength of men, and the force of walls, locks, and bars are feeble, when but resolutely opposed by the force of truth, actuating the will of weak and despised woman!——Injury?——Poor depraved, mistaken man! It is himself he injures! Every effort he makes is but a new assault upon his own peace! It is heaping coals of fire upon his own head; which it has long been the wish of my heart to extinguish!

Had I but any reason to believe Frank Henley in safety, I would not suffer a single sigh to escape me. But I know too well Mr. Clifton dare not permit him to be at liberty, while he keeps me confined. Surely nothing can be attempted against his life? And yet I sometimes shake with horror! There is a reason which I know not whether I dare mention; yet if Mr. Clifton should think proper to lay snares to intercept and read my letters, he ought to be informed of this dangerous circumstance. I know not, Louisa, whether I am addressing myself to you or him; but Frank Henley at the time that I was seized, and he likewise as I suppose, had bank-bills in his possession to the amount of eight thousand pounds!

He had been that very morning into the city, to receive the money on his father's account; and intended as we returned to leave them with Sir Arthur's banker.

If men such as those who seized on me were employed for the same violent purpose against him, and if they should discover a sum which would to them be so tempting, who can say that his life would be safe? Frank Henley, the preserver of Clifton, the preceptor of truth, and the friend of man; the benevolent, magnanimous, noble-minded Frank, whose actions were uniform in goodness, whose heart was all affection, and whose soul all light—and murdered!

Why do I indulge a thought so unhuman, so impossible? It could not be!—No, no; it could not be! A supposition so extravagant is guilt—Yet though I who cannot aid him ought not to encourage such doubts, let those who can be warned, and be active!

I am addressing myself to vacancy! No one hears me! No one will read what I write!

I will be calm. It is my situation, it is confinement, the bars I see and the bolts I hear that inspire these gloomy thoughts. They are unfounded, and certainly unavailing—He may have escaped! He may at this instant be in search of me! Hurrying, enquiring, despairing, and distracted; in much deeper distress than I am: for were I but sure of his safety, I could almost defy misfortune! Let not the world lose him! Oh! If any human creature should in time read this, let him hear, let him shudder, let him beware!

Pardon, Louisa! I do not address myself to you! Too well I know my friend to doubt her! No cold delay, no unfeeling negligence, no rash phrensy is to be feared from her!—Alas! What I am writing she will never read! It cannot be! The man I have to encounter is too practised in deceit, or I should not have been where I am!

Well then, may he himself read! And while he reads, thus let his conscience speak—'There is a man whose worth and virtues are such, that the loss of him would be a loss to the whole human race. From this man I received a thousand acts of kindness: for which I returned ten thousand insults. I repulsed him, scorned him, struck him; and he, disregarding the innumerable injuries I had done him, but a few hours after plunged headlong down the dreadful abyss, to snatch me from the grave. I was dead and he gave me life. In return I have robbed him of what men prize even more than life, of liberty. But if I have put him in jeopardy, if I suffer him to remain in the power of hardened and wicked men, and if he perish, mercy cannot pardon me, justice cannot punish, and charity itself must hold me in abhorrence.'

A. W. ST. IVES

LETTER CXV

Coke Clifton to Guy Fairfax

London, Dover-Street

MY actions are now become one continued chain of artifice. But were that all, and were not the objects of this artifice of a nature so new and so painful, it would afford me amusement, and not be any cause of vexation.

As it is I feel apprehensions which are wholly different from any I ever felt before. To deceive in countries where deception is a pastime, authorised, practised, and applauded, is I find something very opposite to what would seem the same thing, in this gloomy land of apathy and phlegm. There it is a sport and a pleasure. Here it is a business of serious danger and general detestation. But no matter!

I am obliged to watch times and seasons, for I have little doubt that I myself am watched. That old housekeeper I am sure suspects me; and her affection for her mistress is so full, so restless, that it cannot but sharpen her intellects, and make her employ every engine she can imagine for discovery. I walked up to Fozard's as I often do for my horse, and I saw one of Sir Arthur's servants pass the yard, soon after I entered it. I have little doubt but he was dogging me.

I got on horseback and rode slowly down toward Pimlico, and over Westminster bridge, but I saw no more of him.

As soon as I was out of town I mended my pace, and gradually increased it to a full gallop. Passing through Vauxhall, I crossed the Thames again at Battersea-bridge, rode through Chelsea, and presently gained the Brompton road.

My first visit was to the keeper. The fellow has a strange look! A villainous physiognomy! I enquired after his prisoner and found he was safe. The house is well secured; not modern, but in the style of the last century; strong and heavy, and before this affair was thought of had been fitted up for the purposes of confinement, but is now still better fortified. It has a garden, which is surrounded by a high wall, in which the prisoner is suffered to exercise himself; but not without the very necessary precaution of confining his arms in the strait waistcoat, securing the doors, and attentively watching his motions.

I ordered the fellow to see that Henley wanted for nothing, to let a boy he has wait upon him, and to keep out of his way himself, for two reasons of my own. I do not wish Henley to suffer the insults of such a vulgar and narrow-souled rascal: my revenge is of a nobler kind. Neither am I quite certain that this keeper, hardened, obdurate, and pitiless as he is, could withstand Henley's oratory. At least I would not willingly have him subjected to the temptation: though the fellow is so averse to any sense of human pity that I think the danger is very small.

He was offended however at my thinking proper to direct him, and surlily told me he understood his trade.

Here I met Mac Fane, by appointment. He cannot forget the disgrace of Covent-garden, and spoke of Henley with a degree of malignity that would want but little encouraging to become dangerous. I am to pay him the thousand pounds in a few days, and our place of rendezvous is then to be once more at the Shakespeare.

I was glad to escape from the company of these new inmates[1] of mine, these first-born of Beelzebub, and to fly to my other prisoner. I say fly, for I set out with eagerness enough; but every step I took I felt my ardour abate. The houses are more than half a mile apart, and I thought proper to go thither on foot, and not to take any common path, but to cross the fields, as the securest mode.

Laura knew I was to be there, and had her tale ready. She presently came down. I enquired after her mistress, and if her account be true, this heroic woman has not shed a tear, but has behaved with all her apparent customary calm. She is a divine creature!

As I rode along, I made a thousand determinations that all should be that day ended. I cursed myself, pledged my honour, used every method which might have shewn me how much I doubted my own resolution, to prove to myself how irrevocably determined I was! The little remaining firmness I had left wholly died away at the relation of Laura.

I must stay till the calm dignity of her mind shall begin to decline. The nature of her confinement, the fears she cannot but have for her Henley, the recollection of her friends and father, and her apprehensions of me must all quickly contribute to produce this effect.

I do not pretend to deny that I feel a reluctance to a first inter-view: but I am determined the first shall be the only one. I know myself, and know when once I am heated it will not then be Anna St. Ives, a miracle though she be, that can over-awe or conquer me. I have the stubbornness of woman, and the strength of man. I am reckless of what is to follow, but the thing shall be! There is not a particle in my frame that does not stand pledged to the deed, by honour and oath! It is the only event for which I care, or for which I live.

Nor shall I live long when once it is over. I foresee I shall not. But that is not a painful, no, it is a satisfactory thought! I would even present her the pistol, would she but dispatch me the moment my revenge is gratified. I would then sleep, and forget all that is, and all that might have been.

She has been writing. I knew it would be one source of amuse-ment to her, and I provided her with implements. Laura asked and she owned it was a letter to my sister, which she could wish were sent. But that must not be. She means to give it to Laura; I of course shall be the next receiver.

This girl, Laura, acts her part ill. She is not half sorrowful enough. I wonder Anna does not remark it; and Laura says she does not, though that is no very good proof. The complexion of her letter I think will tell me how far she does or does not confide in her maid. I know she holds suspicion in contempt; and yet I think my high opinion of her discrimination would find some abatement, were I certain that she did not suspect this shallow girl.

My soul burns to have it over! And yet like a coward I refrain. But I will not long submit to such contemptible qualms. I will not continue to be diffident of myself; for it is that only by which I am withheld. Not a single wrong is forgotten! I repeat them in my sleep! Ay, Fairfax, such sleep as I have is nothing but a repetition of them; and a rehearsal of the revenge by which they are to be appeased! I will return tomorrow, or perhaps next day; and then—! You shall then hear more from

C. CLIFTON

END OF VOLUME VI

VOLUME VII

Coke Clifton to Guy Fairfax

London, Dover Street

S IR Arthur arrived in town this morning. He brought the usurer Henley up with him in the same carriage.

Young St. Ives set out before them, and was in London last night. He drove directly to my lodgings, and I was fortunately at home. This did not look as if I were in the secret; and if he had any suspicions he had not the courage to intimate them.

I condoled with him, said it was a strange affair, a riddle I could not read, a mystery which time must elucidate, for it baffled all conjecture. He did little more than echo me, and I pretended I would have ridden half over the world to recover his sister, had there been but the least clue; but there was not, and I found myself obliged to sit still in despair and astonishment.

He said it was all very true, and he was very tired. He should therefore drive home, get some refreshment, and go to bed. This fellow, Fairfax, walks on two legs, looks the world in the face, and counts for one on the muster-roll. 'But nature, crescent in him, grew only in thews and bulk.'[1] Yet on the parade, fools and gapers will mistake him for a man.

Contention with Anna St. Ives is honourable, but to seem to shrink from beings like these, or to practise concealment with such mere images of entity, is repugnant to the generous scorn they merit and inspire. Imperious necessity however prescribes law, and I took care to prevent Sir Arthur's visit to me, by having notice sent me of his arrival, and immediately going to the encounter.

To anticipate is to overturn the card-castles of this puny race. Come upon them unexpectedly, stare at them undauntedly, and interrogate them abruptly, and they are put to the rout. Their looks even intreat pardon for the ill they thought, but durst not utter.

Sir Arthur I own beheld me with a suspicious eye; and though he endeavoured to seem to credit me, he did it with an aukward air.

Mrs. Clarke hearing I was there came in, and exceeding even all her former fervour, importuned me, in the most direct and vehement manner, to tell what I had done with Mr. Henley and her dear young lady. She more than ever disconcerted me. Her exuberant passion addressed itself alternately to me and her master. Her tears as well as her words were abundant, her urgency and ardour extreme, and she ended her apostrophe with again conjuring me to tell what was become of her dear, dear young lady!

'Ay, pray, pray do'—whimpered the baronet in a maudlin tone, moved by the unfeigned passion of his housekeeper. I gave him a look, and the driveller added—'if you know.'

I was glad of a pretence to get away, and after telling him the distress of his mind was the only apology for his conduct, I instantly quitted him, without any effort on his part to detain me.

Among other things, Mrs. Clarke repeatedly reproached herself for not having written or sent to my sister; and the knight acknowledged—'Ay, it was very neglectful! But his mind had been so disturbed that he had forgotten it too!'

Why do I misapply my time on beings so imbecile? Maugre[1] all my resolves I have not seen her yet, Fairfax! Nor have I opened her letter! I dare not. Her Henley I am sure is in it, and additional rage would be indubitable madness! Neither is this the thing most to be feared. She has an expanded heart, a capacious a benevolent heart, and she may have said something which were I to see, and yet do the deed which shall be done, it might shew me more fiend-like than even the foul reflection of my present thoughts. Perturbation has done its work; it needs no increase. This quality of benevolence, in which they both glory, is torture to recollect. I say, Fairfax, I never asked their charity. Did I not spurn it from me, the moment I was insulted by the offer? Be pity bestowed on beggars: the partiality that springs from affection, or the punishment due to neglect for me!

I will be with her speedily, Fairfax! Though I linger, I do not relent. Such mercy as the being out of doubt can bestow she shall receive; the pleading world should not wring a greater from me!

C. CLIFTON

P.S. I must be speedy: my sister will hear of the affair by to-morrow's post, and I shall have her whole artillery playing upon me; and in the form of letters I suppose; for I do not think she will hope any thing from personal interview; I made her too sensibly feel her own insignificance when last we met. I expected indeed an attack from her much sooner, for the young lady does not want confidence in her own skill and courage: she is of the Henley school. However I do not intend to peruse any of her epistles. I would send them back unopened, but that it would be an avowal of a knowledge of their contents; and I have no need to increase suspicion, whose broad eyes are already glaring at me. But I will immediately put an end to the witch, and engender black certainty in her stead! The imp[1] shall appear, and shake horrors from her snaky hair!

LETTER CXVII

Anna Wenbourne St. Ives to Louisa Clifton

The Lone House

ONCE more, though but in imagination, let me converse with my friend. I know it is delusion, but it was the sweet custom of our souls, and well may be indulged. Ignorant perhaps of the cause, my Louisa is at this moment accusing me of a neglect which my heart disavows. Let me as usual give her the history of that heart: it is a theme from which she has taught me to derive profit.

This is the fifth day of my confinement. I have the same walls, the same windows and bars to contemplate; and the same bolting, and locking, and clanking to hear. It is with difficulty that I can at some few intervals divert my thoughts from the gloom which my own situation, the distress of my family, and the danger of a youth so dear to virtue contribute to inspire.

Nor do I know what at this moment may be the affliction of my

friend. Should she have heard, she cannot but discover the principal agent of this dark plot; and exquisite indeed would be the
anguish of her mind, could she forget that fortitude and resignation are duties. May they never be forgotten by me, during this
my hour of trial!

My shoulder I fear has received some strain or hurt: the pain
of it continues to be great, and the inflammation is not abated.
The bruises on my arms have increased in blackness, and their
tension is not in the least diminished. The hands of those bad men
must have been as rough and callous as their hearts: they had no
mercy in their gripe.

There is a lonesome stillness in this house, that favours the dismal reveries which my situation suggests. If my handkerchief do
but drop I start; and the stirring of a mouse places Clifton full
before me. Yet I repel this weakness with all my force. I despise it.
Nor shall these crude visions, the hideous phantoms of the imagination, subdue that fortitude in which I must wholly confide.

For these last two days, Laura has pretended to grieve at confinement: but it is mimic sorrow; words of which the heart has no
knowledge. She perceives I suspect her, and her acting is but the
more easily detected.

I know not whether it be not my duty to determine to exclude
her; though that seems like cowardice. I think it is not in her power
to harm me; and for telling, if she have been false, she has done her
worst. I never made a practice of concealment, neither will I now
have recourse to such a fallacious expedient. Yet she sleeps in the
same chamber with me; and ought I not to beware of inspiring
perfidy with projects? 'Tis true my slumbers are broken, my nights
restless, and the cracking of the wainscot is as effectual in waking
me as a thunder-clap could be. I am resolved, however, to take the
key out of the door, and either hide it or hold it all night in my
hand. Mischief is meant me, or why am I here?

I am continually looking into the closets, behind the doors, and
under the beds and drawers. I am haunted by the supposition that
I shall every moment see this bad man start up before me! What
know I of the base engines he may employ, or the wicked arts to
which he may have·recourse?

But he shall not subdue me! He may disturb me by day, and
terrify me by night; but he shall not subdue me! Shall the pure

mind shake in the presence of evil? Shall the fortitude which safety feels vanish at the approach of danger?

Louisa, I will steel my soul to meet him! I know not how or when he will come! I cannot tell what are the vile black instruments with which he may work! Sleep I scarcely have any. I eat with hesitation, and drink with trembling. I have heard of potions and base practices, that make the heart shudder! Yet I sometimes think I could resist even these. He shall not subdue me! Or if he do, it shall be by treachery such as fiends would demur to perpetrate.

Why do I think thus of him? Surely, surely, he cannot be so lost as this! Yet here I am! I own I tremble and recoil; but it is with the dread that he should plunge himself so deep in guilt as never more to rise!

Poor Frank! Where art thou? How are thy wretched thoughts employed? Or art thou still allowed to think? Art thou among the living? If thou art, what is thy state! Thine is now the misery of impotence, thou who hast proved thyself so mighty in act! Thou wouldst not strike, thou wouldst not injure; and yet thy foe would sink before thee, had he not allied himself to perfidy, and had he but left thee free. His most secret machinations could not have withstood thy searching spirit. Thou wouldst have been here! These bolts would have flown, these doors would have opened, and I should have seen my saviour!

He hears me not! Nor thou, Louisa! I am destitute of human aid!

Farewell, farewell! Ah! Farewell indeed; for I am talking to emptiness and air!

Do I seem to speak with bitterness of heart? Is there enmity in my words?—Surely I do not feel it! The spirit of benevolence and truth allows, nay commands me to hate the vice; but not its poor misgoverned agents. They are wandering in the maze of mistake. Ignorance and passion are their guides, and doubt and desperation their tormentors. Alas! Rancour and revenge are their inmates; be kindness and charity mine.

A. W. ST. IVES

LETTER CXVIII

Coke Clifton to Guy Fairfax

Brompton-House

I AM here—At the scene of action—she is in the room above me, and I am ridding myself of reluctance; stringing my nerves for assault. I know not why this should be necessary, but I feel that it is!

I am waiting to question Laura; but I ordered her to be in no haste to come down, when she heard me ring. I would not have my victim suspect me to be here. I would come upon her by surprise, and not when she was armed and prepared for repulse. I will order the old woman to go presently and open and shut the gate; as if she were letting the person out, who came in when I rung.

I expect, nay am certain, her resistance will be obstinate—But unavailing!—I say unavailing!—Neither house nor road are near, and yet I could wish the scene were removed to the dark gloom of a forest; embosomed where none but tigers or hyenas should listen to her shrieks—I know they will be piercing;—Heart-rending! —But—!

I tell you, Fairfax, I have banished all sense of human pity from my bosom: it is an enemy to my purpose, and that must be!— Though the heavens should shake and the earth open, it must!

Yet do not think, Fairfax, bent as I am on the full fruition of love and vengeance, I would use cruelty—Understand me: I mean wanton or unnecessary brutality. I will be as forbearing as she will permit. I fear she will not suffer me to caress her tenderly —But she shall never sleep in the arms of Henley!—She never shall!—I will make sure of that! My mind is reconciled to all chances, that excepted.

As I passed, I called at the mad-house; where I found Mac Fane and the scowling keeper in high divan.[1] They have been horribly alarmed. Henley has attempted an escape, which he was in danger of effecting; but he is brought back, after having led them a short chase.

The apprehensions of these scoundrels concerning future consequences are very great, and swell almost to terror. They talked strangely, asked which way we were to get rid of him at last, and conceive him to be a dangerous enemy. Their thoughts seem tinged with dark lurkings, which they dare not own; and certainly dare not act, without my leave. These fellows are all villainy! A league with demons would be less abominable!—I must close the account, and shake off such pestilential scoundrels!—

Laura comes! I will question her a little, and then——!

Dover-Street

I am returned, and am still tormented by delay!—I cannot help it—I said I would not use wilful cruelty: that were to heap unnecessary damnation!

Laura began by softening my heart with her narrative. Her angel mistress is all resignation, all kindness, all benevolence! She almost forgets herself, and laments only for me! This I could have withstood; but she has been brutally treated, by that intolerable ban dog,[1] Mac Fane, and his blood hounds. Fairfax, how often have I gazed in rapture at the beauteous carnation of her complexion, the whiteness of her hands and arms, and the extreme delicacy of their texture! And now those tempting arms, Laura tells me, nay, her legs too, are in twenty places disfigured and black, with the gripes and bruises she received. Gibbets and racks overtake the wolf-hearted villains! Her shoulder is considerably hurt! It is inflamed, and, as she acknowledges, very painful; yet she does not utter a complaint!

Why did this heroic woman ever injure me? By what fatal influence am I become her foe? Her gentle kindness, her calm, unruffled, yet dignified patience I have experienced—Madman!— Idiot!—Have I not experienced her hatred too, her abhorrence? Did not her own lips pronounce the sentence? And do I not know her? Will she recede? And shall I?—Never!—Never!—No no— It must be.

But I did rightly. This was not the moment. There would have been something barbarously mean, in making her exert the little strength she has with such pain and peril.

I rode to Kensington and procured her a lenitive,[2] with which I returned. The purpose of vengeance excepted, I would feel as generously as herself; and even vengeance, did I know how, I

E e

would dignify—But do not surmise that I would retract!—No, by heaven! A thought so weak has never once entered my heart!

I am restless, and must return—Till it be over, earth has no pleasure for me; and after I am sure it will have none. No—No—I have but this single gleam of satisfaction! The light is going out; give me but one full blaze, and I shall then welcome total darkness!

C. CLIFTON

LETTER CXIX

Coke Clifton to Guy Fairfax

London, Dover-Street

FOR a few days after having secured my tormentors, I enjoyed something like comparative ease: but the ugly imps that haunted me, in fiercer crowds again are swarming round me. I am too miserable to exist in this state; it must be ended. It is a turmoil that surpasses mortal sufferance! If she will wrestle against fate, it is not my fault. I have no wish to practise more upon her than is necessary. But the thing must be.

Sleep I have none, rest I have none, peace I have none. I get up and sit down, walk out and come back, mutter imprecations unconsciously to myself, and turn the eyes of insolent curiosity and ridiculous apprehension upon me in the street. A fellow has just now watched me home; deeming me a lunatic I suppose; for he had seen my agitation, and heard the curses which I knew not were uttered aloud, till his impertinent observation of me brought it to my recollection.

But this shall not be! It shall end! Though I rend her heart-strings for it, I will have ease! The evening approaches; my horse is ordered and I will be gone. I will not, cannot endure this longer!

Brompton-House

I am here, and have talked with Laura. She owns she is suspected, and that her mistress takes the key out of the bed-chamber door, when they go to rest, and hides it: Laura by accident has discovered where. She puts it on the ledge behind the head of her bed, but within the reach of her arm.

This has suggested a thought: I will wait here till midnight and sleep have lulled her apprehensions. It will be better than facing her in the glare of day. Her eye, Fairfax, is terrible in her anger. It is too steady, too strong in conscious innocence to encounter. Darkness will give me courage, and her terror and despair. For it must come to that! It cannot otherwise be; and be it must! In the blaze of noon, when fortitude is awake and the heart beating high perhaps with resentment, nothing but the goadings of despair could make me face her. The words she would use would be terrible, but her looks would petrify!—By this stratagem I shall avoid them.

Nor do I blush to own my cowardice, in the presence of Anna St. Ives: she being armed with innocence and self-approbation; and I abashed by conscious guilt, violence, and intentional destruction.

Why aye!—Let the thick swarth of night cover us! I feel, with a kind of horrid satisfaction, the deep damnation[1] of the deed! It is the very colour and kind of sin that becomes me; sinning as I do against Anna St. Ives! With any other it would be boy's sport; a thing to make a jest of after dinner; but with her it is rape, in all its wildest contortions, shrieks, and expiring groans!

I lie stretched on burning embers, and I have hours yet to wait. Oh that I were an idiot!—The night is one dead, dun gloom! It looks as if murrain,[2] mildew, and contagion were abroad, hovering over earth and brooding plagues. I will walk out awhile, among them—Will try to meet them—Would that my disturbed imagination could but conjure up goblins, sheeted ghosts, heads wanting bodies, and hands dropping blood, and realize the legends of ignorance and infancy, so that I could freeze memory and forget the horrors by which I am haunted!

It draws near midnight—I am now in her apartment, the room next to her bed-chamber.

My orders have been obeyed: the old woman, pretending to lock up her prisoner, shot back the bolts, put down the chain, and left the door ready for me to enter unheard.

Laura has her instructions. She is to pretend only, but not really, to undress herself; and I bade her not lie down, lest she should drop asleep. When she thinks it time, she is to glide round, steal the key, and open the door.

I am fully prepared; am undressed, and ready for the combat. I have made a mighty sacrifice! Youth, fortune, fame, all blasted; life renounced, and infamy ascertained! It is but just then that I should have full enjoyment of the fleeting bliss.

Surely this hussy sleeps? No!—I hear her stir!—She is at the door! And now—!

Heaven and hell are leagued against me, to frustrate my success! Yet succeed I will in their despite—'Tis now broad day, and here I am, in the same chamber, encountered, reproved, scorned, frantic, and defeated!

As soon as I heard Laura with the key in the door, I put out the candles. She turned the lock, the door opened, and I sprang forward. Blundering idiot as I was! I had forgotten to remove a chair, and tumbled over it. The terrified Anna was up and out of bed in an instant. The door opens inward to the bed-chamber. Her fear gave her strength; she threw Laura away, and clapped to the door.

By this time I had risen, and was at it. I set my shoulder to it with a sudden effort, and again it half opened. I pushed forward, but was repelled with more than equal opposition. My left arm in the struggle got wedged in the door: the pain was excessive, and the strength with which she resisted me incredible. By a sudden shock I released my hand, but not without bruising it very much, and tearing away the skin.

My last effort was returned by one more than equal on her part. But I imagine she had set her foot against something which gave way, for she suddenly came down, with a blow and a sound that made my heart shrink!

Still I endeavoured to profit by it, though not soon enough; for the first moment I was too much alarmed. She could not feel pain or blows, and rose instantaneously. I forced the door some little way, and she then gave a single shriek!—It was a dreadful one—and was followed by a repulse which I could not overcome. The door was closed, and like lightning locked. I then heard her begin

to pant and heave for breath—After a few seconds she exclaimed—
Clifton! You are a bad man! . . . A treacherous, wicked man, and
are seeking your own destruction! . . . I am your prisoner, but I
fear you not! . . . Mark me, Clifton: I fear you not!

I hesitated some time: at last I ventured to ask . . . Are you hurt,
madam?

I do not know! I do not care! I value no hurt you can do me! I am
above harm from you!—Though you have recourse to perfidy and
violence, yet I defy you! In darkness or in light, I defy you!

Let me intreat you, madam, to retire to rest.

No! I will stand here all night! I will not move!

Upon my honour, madam, upon my soul, I will molest you no
more to night!

I tell you, man, I fear you not! Night or day, I fear you not!

I request, I humbly intreat you would not expose yourself to the
injuries of the night air, and the want of sleep!

I will sleep no more! I want no sleep; I fear no injuries; not even
those you intend me!

Indeed, madam, you do not know the danger—

Mimic benevolence and virtue no more, Clifton! It is base in
you! It is beneath a mind like yours!—You are a mistaken man!
Dreadfully mistaken! You think me devoted,[1] but I am safe.
Unless you kill, you never can conquer me! Beware! Turn back!
Destruction is gaping for you, if you proceed!

Need she have told me this, Fairfax? Could she think I knew it
not?——But she too is mistaken. Her courage is high, I grant, is
admirable; and, were any other but I her opponent, as she says,
not to be conquered! I adore the noble qualities of her mind; but
great though they are, when she defies me she over-rates them.

I own her warning was awful! My heart shrunk from it, and I
retired; taking care that she should hear me as I went, that she
might be encouraged to go to rest. My well-meant kindness was
vain. She never did confide in me, and never can. I heard her call
Laura, and order her to strike a light, set an arm chair, and bring
her clothes: after which I understood, from what I heard, that she
dressed herself and sat down in it, with her back to the door, there
waiting patiently till the morning.

How she will behave, or what she will say to Laura I cannot

divine. Most probably she will insist on banishing her the apartment; for she never gave servants much employment, and always doubted whether the keeping of them were not an immoral act, therefore is little in want of their assistance.

But let her discard this treacherous and now ineffective tool. I want her no more. I will not quit the house, Fairfax; I will neither eat nor sleep, till I have put her to the trial which she so rashly defies! At her uncle's table she defied me, and imagined she had gazed me into cowardice. She knew me not: it was but making vengeance doubly sure. This experience ere now should have taught her. Has she escaped me? Is she not here? Does she not feel herself in the ravisher's arms? If not, a few hours only and she shall!

Let her not be vain of this second repulse she has given me; it ought to increase her terror, for it does but add to my despair. My distempered soul will take no medicine but one, and that must be administered; though more venomous than the sting of scorpion or tooth of serpent, and more speedy in dissolution.

I left her room that she might breakfast undisturbed. There is something admirably, astonishingly firm, in the texture of her mind. Laura has been down, babbling to me all she knew. At eight o'clock, when it had been light a full hour, Anna, after once or twice crossing her chamber to consider, turned the key and resolutely opened the door; expecting by her manner, Laura says, to see me rush in; for she threw it suddenly open, as if fearful it should knock her down.

She walked out, looked steadfastly around, examined every part of the chamber, and after having convinced herself I was not there, sat down to write at the table where not an hour before I had been seated. When the breakfast was brought, she bade Laura take it away again; saying she had no appetite: but immediately recollecting herself, ejaculated—'Fie!—It is weak! It is wrong!'—and added—'Stay Laura! Put it down again!'

She then, with a calm and determined sedateness, began to serve herself and Laura; treating this perfidious woman [For no matter that I made her so, such she is.] with the same equanimity of temper and amenity as formerly. The mistress ate, for she was innocent and resolved; but the maid could not, for she was guilty and in a continual tremor. 'Be pacified'—said Anna to her—'Compose your thoughts, and take your breakfast. I am much more sorry for than angry at the part you have acted. You have done yourself great injury, but me none: at least, so I trust!——Be appeased and eat your breakfast. Or, if you cannot eat with me, go down and eat it in peace below.'

The benevolent suavity of this angel has made the light-minded hussey half break her heart. Her penitential tears now flow in abundance; and she has been officiously endeavouring to petition me not to harm so good, so forgiving, so heavenly a young lady! I begin to fear she would willingly be a traitor next to me, and endeavour to open the doors for her mistress. But that I will prevent. I will not quit the house till all is over! I have said it, Fairfax!

I will then immediately set Henley free, tell him where she is, where I am to be found, and leave him to seek his own mode of vengeance! Should he resort to the paltry refuge of law, I own that then I would elude pursuit. But should the spirit of man stir within him, and should he dare me to contention, I would fly to meet him in the mortal strife! He is worthy of my arm, and I would shew how worthy I am to be his opposite!

It is now noon, and Laura has again been with me, repeating the same story, with additions and improvements. Anna has been talking to her, and has made a deep impression upon her. She is all penitence and petition, and is exceedingly troublesome, with her whining, her tears, and her importunity, which I have found it difficult to silence.

I learn from her own account she has owned all, and betrayed all she knew; and Anna has been telling her that she, and I, and all such sinners however deep and deadly, ought to be pitied, counselled, and reformed; and that our errors only ought to be treated with contempt, disdain, and hatred. She has talked to her in the most gentle, soothing, and sympathetic manner; till the fool's heart is ready to burst.

Anna has drawn a picture of my state of mind which has terrified her—And so it ought!——She has been sobbing, kneeling, and praying, for my sake, for Anna's sake, for God's sake to be merciful, and do no more mischief! 'Her mistress is an angel and not a woman!'—Why true!—'Never had a young lady so forgiving, so kind, and so courageous a heart!'—True again!—'But it is impossible, if I should be so wicked as to lay violent hands upon her, for her not to sink, and lie for mercy at my feet.'—Once more true, true!—

Mercy!—I have it not, know it not, nor can know! She herself has banished it, from my breast and from her own: at least the mercy I would ask——For could it be—? Were there not a Henley—? No, no!—There is one wide destruction for us all! I am on the brink, and they must down with me!—Have they not placed me there? Are they not now pulling me, weighing me, sinking me?

This is the moment in which I would conjure up all the wrongs, insults, contempts, and defiances she has heaped upon me—— What need I?——They come unbidden!——And now for the last act of the tragedy!

I have kept my word, Fairfax: I have been, have faced her, have——! You shall hear! I will faithfully paint all that passed. I will do her justice, and in this shew some sparks of magnanimity of which perhaps she does not think me capable—No matter—

It was necessary the temper of my mind should be wound up to its highest pitch, before I could approach her. I rushed up stairs, made the bolts fly, and the lock start back. Yet the moment the door opened, I hesitated—

However, I shook myself with indignation, entered, and saw her standing firmly in the middle of the apartment, ready to assert the bold defiance she had given me. The fixed resolution of her form, the evident fortitude of her soul, and the steadfast encounter of her eye, were discomfiting. Like a coward I stood I cannot tell how long, not knowing what to say, she looking full upon me, examining my heart, and putting thought to the rack. Benignant as she is, at such onsets of the soul she feels no mercy.

Self-resentment at the tame crestfallen countenance I wore at last produced an effort, and I stammered out—Madam—

Her only answer was a look——I endeavoured to meet her eye, but in vain.

I continued.—From my present manner you will perceive, madam, I am conscious of the advantage you have over me; and that my own heart does not entirely approve all I have done.

I see something of your confusion—I wish I saw more.

But neither can it forget its injuries!

What are they?

The time was when I met you with joy, addressed you with delight, and gazed on you with rapture!—Nay I gaze so still!

Poor, weak man!

Yes, madam, I know how much you despise me! A thousand repeated wrongs inform me of it: they have risen, one over another, in mountainous oppression to my heart, till it could endure no more.

Feeble, mistaken man!

In those happy days when I approached you first, my thoughts were loyal, my means were honest, and my intentions pure.

Pure?

Yes, madam, pure.

You never yet knew what purity meant!

I came void of guile, with an open and honourable offer of my heart. I made no difficulties, felt no scruples, harboured no suspicions. In return for which I was doubted, catechised, chidden, trifled with, and insulted. When I hoped for sympathy I met rebuke; and while my affections glowed admiration yours retorted contempt. Your heart was prepossessed: it had no room for me: it excluded me, scorned me, and at the first opportunity avowed its hatred.

Go on!——Neither your mistakes, your accusations, nor your anger shall move me—I pity your errors. Continue to ascribe that to my injustice, or to a worse motive, if a worse you can find, which was the proper fruit of your irascible and vindictive temper. Reconcile your own actions to your own heart, if you can; and prove to yourself I merit the perfidy, assault, and imprisonment you have practised upon me: as well as the mischief which I have every reason to suppose you intend.

Then, madam, avoid it! Spare both yourself and me the violence you forebode?

What! Sink before unruly passion? Stand in awe of vice? Willingly administer to shameless appetites, and a malignant spirit of revenge?——Never, while I have life!

Stop!—Beware!—I am not master of my own affections! I am in a state little short of phrensy! Be the means fair or foul, mine you

shall be—The decrees of Fate are not more fixed—I have sworn it,
and though fire from Heaven waited to devour me, I will keep my
oath!—Could you even yet but think of me as perhaps I deserve—!
I say, could you, madam—

I cannot will not marry you! Nothing you can say, nothing you
can threaten, nothing you can act shall make me!

Be less hasty in your contempt!—Fear me not!——Scorn for
scorn, injury for injury, and hate for hate!

I hate only your errors! I scorn nothing but vice—On the virtues
of which a mind like yours is capable my soul would dilate with
ecstasy, and my heart would doat! But you have sold yourself to
crookedness! Base threats, unmanly terrors, and brute violence are
your despicable engines!—Wretched man! They are impotent!—
They turn upon yourself; me they cannot harm!—I am above you!

I care not for myself—I have already secured infamy—I have
paid the price and will enjoy the forfeiture—Had you treated me
with the generous ardent love I so early felt for you, all had been
well—I the happiest of men, and you the first of women! But your
own injustice has dug the pit into which we must all down—It is
wide and welcome ruin!——Even now, contemned as I have been,
scorned as I am, I would fain use lenity and feel kindness. I will
take retribution—no power shall prevent me—but I would take it
tenderly.

Oh shame upon you, man!—Tenderly?—Can the mischief and
the misery in which you have involved yourself and so many others,
can treachery, brutal force, bruises, imprisonment, and rape be
coupled with tenderness? If you have any spark of noble feeling
yet remaining in your heart, cherish it: but if not, speak truth to
yourself! Do not attempt to varnish such foul and detestable guilt
with fair words.

I would advise, not varnish! What I have done I have done—I
know my doom—I am already branded! Opprobrium has set her
indelible mark upon me! I am indexed[1] to all eternity!

You mistake, Clifton!—Beware!—You mistake! You mistake!
[It is impossible to imagine, Fairfax, the energy with which these
exclamations burst from her—It was a fleeting but false cordial
to my heart.] Of all your errors that is the most fatal! Whatever
rooted prejudices or unjust laws may assert to the contrary, we are
accountable only for what we do, not for what we have done.

Clifton beware! Mark me—I owe you no enmity for the past: I combat only with the present.

Do not delude me with shadows. Bring your doctrine to the test: if you bear me no enmity, if what I have done can be forgotten, and what I would do—! Madam—! Anna—!—Once more, and for the last time—take me!

It cannot be!—It cannot be!

Then, since you will shew no mercy, expect none.

Your menaces are vain, man! I tell you again I do not fear you! I will beg no pity from you—I dare endure more than you dare inflict!

I am not to be braved from my purpose! The basis of nature is not more unshaken! High as your courage is, you will find a spirit in me that can mount still higher!

Courage? Oh shame! Name it not! Where was your courage when you decoyed my defender from me? The man you durst not face?—Where is he?—What have you done with him?—Laura has given you my letter—Should your practices have reached his life!—But no! It cannot be! An act so very vile as that not even the errors of your mind could reach!—Courage?—Even me you durst not face in freedom! Your courage employed a band of ruffians against me, singly; a woman too, over whom your manly valour would tower! But there is no such mighty difference as prejudice supposes. Courage has neither sex nor form: it is an energy of mind, of which your base proceedings shew I have infinitely the most. This bids me stand firm, and meet your worst daring undauntedly! This be assured will make me the victor! I tell you, man, it places me above you!

Urge me no more!—Beware of me! You have driven me mad! Do not tempt a desperate man! Resistance will be destruction to you, no matter that to me it be perdition! My account is closed, and I am reconciled to ruin!—You shall be mine!—Though hell gape for me you shall be mine!—Once more beware! I warn you not to contend!

Why, man, what would you do? Is murder your intent?— While I have life I fear you not!—And think you that brutality can taint the dead? Nay, think you that, were you endowed with the superior force which the vain name of man supposes, and could accomplish the basest purpose of your heart, I would falsely take guilt to myself; or imagine I had received the smallest blemish, from impurity which never reached my mind? That I would lament, or shun the world, or walk in open day oppressed by shame I did not merit? No!—For you perhaps I might weep, but for myself I would not shed a tear! Not a tear!—You cannot injure me—I am above you!—If you mean to deal me blows or death, here I stand ready to suffer: but till I am dead, or senseless, I defy you to do me harm!—Bethink you, Clifton! I see the struggles of your soul: there is virtue among them. Your eye speaks the reluctance of your hand. Your heart spurns at the mischief your passions would perpetrate!—Remember—Unless you have recourse to some malignant, some cruel, some abominable means, you never shall accomplish so base a purpose!—But you cannot be so guilty, Clifton!—You cannot!—I know not by what perverse fatality you have been misled, for you have a mind fitted for the sublimest emanations of virtue!—No, you cannot!—There is something within you that lays too strong a hand upon you! Malice so black is beyond you! Your very soul abhors its own guilt, and is therefore driven frantic!—Oh, Clifton! You that were born to be the champion of truth, the instructor of error, and the glory of the earth!—My heart yearns over you—Awake!—Rise!—Be a man!

Divine, angelic creature!—Fool, madman, villain!

With these exclamations I instantly burst from the chamber—Conviction, astonishment, remorse, tenderness, all the passions that could subdue the human soul rushed upon me, till I could support no more.

Of all the creatures God ever formed she is the most wonderful! —I have repeated something like her words; but had you seen her gestures, her countenance, her eye, her glowing indignant fortitude at one moment, and her kindling comprehensive benevolence the next, like me you would have felt an irresistible impulse to catch some spark of a flame so heavenly!

And now what is to be done? I am torn by contending passions! —If I release her there is an end to all; except to my disgrace, which will be everlasting—Give her to the arms of Henley?—I cannot bear it, Fairfax!—I cannot bear it!—Death, racks, infamy itself to such a thought were infinitude of bliss!

What can I do? She says truly: conquest over her, by any but brutal means, is impossible——Shall I be brutal?—And more brutal even than my own ruffian agents?

She has magnanimity—But what have those cyphers of beings who call themselves her relations? Shall they mount the dunghill of their vanity, clap their wings, and exult, as if they too had conquered a Clifton? Even the villain Mac Fane would not fail to scout at[1] me! Nay the very go-between, the convenient chambermaid herself, forgetting the lightness of her own heels, would bless herself and claim her share in the miraculous virtue of the sex! What! Become the scoff of the tea-table, the bugbear of the bedchamber, and the standing jest of the tavern?—I will return this instant, Fairfax, and put her boasted strength and courage to the proof—Madness!—I forget that nothing less than depriving her of sense can be effectual. She knows her strong hold: victory never yet was gained by man, singly, over woman, who was not willing to be vanquished.

I will not yield her up, Fairfax!—She never shall be Henley's!— Again and again she never shall!—I dared not meet him!—So she told me!—Ha!—Dare not?—I will still devise a means—I will have my revenge!—This vaunted Henley then shall know how much I dare!——I will conquer!—Should I be obliged to come like Jove to Semele, in flames,[2] and should we both be reduced to ashes in the conflict, I will enjoy her!—Let one urn hold our dust; and when the fire has purified it of its angry and opposing particles, perhaps it may mingle in peace.

C. CLIFTON

LETTER CXX

Coke Clifton to Guy Fairfax

London, Dover Street

IT shall not be!—She shall not escape me thus!—I will not endure this insufferable, this contemptible recantation of my wrongs! Fear is beneath me, and what have I to hope? I have made misery certain! I have paid the price of destruction, and will hug it to my heart! I know how often I have prevaricated, and have loitered with revenge; but I have not lost the flame: it burns still, and never shall expire!

The night at Brompton, though a night of storms and evil augury, was heaven to the one I have just passed. Sleep and rest have forsaken me. 'Tis long since I closed my eyes; I know not indeed when; but last night I did not attempt it. I traversed my room, opened my windows, shut them again, listened to the discontented monotony of the watchman without hearing him, thought over my never-forgotten injuries, my vengeance, and all the desolation that is to follow, and having ended began again!

There were shrieks and cries of murder in the street, about midnight; and this was the only music by which I remember to have been roused. But it was momentary. My reveries returned, and scenes of horror rose, more swarming, dun, and ghastly!

My waking dreams are eternal—Well, so I would have them!—They prolong revenge!—I would have him by the throat for ages!—Him!—Henley!—Would grapple with him; would stab and be stabbed; not in the fictions of a torturing fancy, but arm to arm, steel to steel, poison to poison! Ay, did I not know he would refuse my fair challenge, hero though he be and cased in innocence, I would instantly fly to let him loose upon me, that I might turn and tear him!—

Why that were delectable!—And can it not be? . . . Can no sufferings move, no wrongs provoke, no taunts stir him to resentment? Is he God, or is he man? To me he is demon, legion, and has possessed me wholly!

Liar that I am! How came I to forget the beauteous sorceress with whom I found him leagued? I have heard them called angels of light; but I have known them only fiends! They goad me with their virtues, mock at my phrensy, defy my rage; and though surrounded by rape, destruction, and despair, sleep and smile, while I wake and howl!

Injury and insult are busy with me! This sister of mine is in town at Sir Arthur's. As she has made the journey I may expect a visit from her soon: but she shall find no admission here. I want no more tormentors!

As I foreboded, she has just been, and has behaved in character. She would take no denial from the valet; he was but an infant to the

Amazon; she would herself see if I were at home, and in she came. The fellow does not want cunning, and he ran up stairs before her, and called out aloud, purposely for me to hear—'You may see, madam, if you please; the door is locked, and my master has taken the key with him.'

He knew I was determined not to see her, and while he designedly made all the clatter he could, and placed himself before the entrance, I took the means he had devised. She came, turned him aside, examined the door, pushed violently against it, and I believe would willingly have broken it open; but finding her good intentions, I set my shoulder to the panel, taking care not to impede the light through the keyhole, which my valet tells me was inspected by her. She ruminated a few seconds and then went away; incredulous and high in indignation.

Well!—I sought for warfare, and it has found me. My former encounters it seems were but the skirmishes of a partisan: this is a deadly and decisive battle!

It is now five o'clock, and I have had a stirring morning. So much the better; action is relief. A message came to me from Lord Fitz-Allen, desiring to speak with me. I had an inclination not to have gone; but reflecting further I determined to obey his summons.

However, when I sent up my name, I desired to know if my sister were there; and was answered in the negative. I then made my bow to his lordship, taking care to inform him that my sister behaved with great impropriety, and that I was resolved not to see her, lest I too should forget that respect due to my family and myself which she had violated. The peer began with circumlocutory hints concerning the elopement—'An unaccountable affair!—No tidings had yet arrived!—Surmises and rumours of a very strange and dishonourable nature were whispered!—Mischief, rape, nay even murder were dreaded!'

I refused to interpret any of these insinuations as applicable to myself. At last his lordship, after many efforts, said he had a favour to beg of me, which he hoped I should not think unreasonable. I desired him to inform me what this favour was; and put some firmness in my manner, that his lordship might see I was not in a temper to suffer an insult.

He answered, for his own part, he had no doubts: he knew my

family, and had always affirmed I could not act unworthy of the gentleman. But, for the peace of mind of Sir Arthur and the other relations of the young lady, he would esteem it an obligation done to him, if I would declare, upon my honour, that I knew nothing of her elopement; of the place she has been conveyed to, or where she is at present.

I then retorted upon his lordship, that the preface to this request entirely precluded compliance; that those who whispered and spread surmises, and rumours, must be answerable for the consequences of their own officiousness; and that with respect to myself, I should certainly, under such circumstances, refuse to answer to interrogatories.

My tone was not very conciliatory, and his lordship knew not whether to be angry or pleased. But while he was pondering I thought proper to make my exit; and leave him to settle the contest between his pride and his puerility as well as he was able.

At my return I found a letter from my sister, which I will neither answer nor open. I have my fill of fury, and want no more!

Damnation on their insolence! They have been making application to the office at Bow-Street![1] A request has just been sent me, a very soft and civil one it is true, from the sitting magistrate, that I would do him the honour to come and speak a word with him, on an affair that concerned a very great and respectable family. I returned for answer that I was engaged, and that I should notice no such messages: but that if any man, great or small, had to complain of me, the law understood its duty, and that I should be readily found at all times.

Whether this be the motion of my superb and zealous sister, or of the arrogant peer, is more than I can divine. But I shall know some day, and shall then perhaps strike a balance.

I have no doubt that emissaries and scouts are abroad, and that I am watched. I was this evening to have met Mac Fane at the Shakespeare; but I will not go. Yet as it is pay night, the hungry scoundrel must not be disappointed. I will therefore write a note to him, and invite him to come and sup with me. He will be an agreeable companion! But even his company is better, at this moment, than solitude.

I will not let my servant carry the note directly to him; for if they have their spies in the field, that might be dangerous. He shall take it to the Mount coffee-house, and there get a chairman[1] to convey it in safety. I will tell Mac Fane likewise to come through the shop door; for I am only in lodgings; and to step immediately out of a hackney-coach. I laugh at their counterplots, and wish I had nothing more to disturb me than the fear of being detected by any exertion of their cunning, even though my kind sister be appointed their commander in chief.

C. CLIFTON

P.S. They might have served the cause in which they have engaged more effectually, had their proceedings been less violent and offensive. They do but nerve me in resolution. The less public they had made the affair the more they would have shewn their generalship. If they be thus determined to brand me, can they suppose that my vengeance shall not outstrip theirs? I own I am perplexed about the means—Invention fails me! I have debated whether I should call in the aid of Mac Fane; but the idea is too detestable!—No! I would rather take a pair of pistols, and dis-patch her first and myself next, than expose her beauties to such ruffian despicable rascals!—Beside I would have her will concerned —And how to conquer that?—I shall be driven, I foresee I shall, to some unheard-of act of desperation!—Drugs are a mean a pitiful expedient: not to mention that she is aware of them, and uses a kind of caution which it would be difficult to overcome. She reserves the meal of one day for the next, after having suffered Laura to eat her part; so that inanity, sleep or other effects, if produced, would first appear in the maid. This perhaps is one of the reasons by which she is induced still to keep her: and were she removed, and could suspect it were for this purpose, I am con-vinced she would eat no more—No!—She must be fairly told the deep despair of my mind! and if that will not move her, why then— Death!

LETTER CXXI

Louisa Clifton to her brother Coke Clifton

Grosvenor-Street

WHERE is Anna St. Ives?—Where is my friend? Where is the youth to whom you owe existence?—Man of revenge, answer me! Oh God! O God!—Is it possible?—Can it be that you, Coke Clifton, the son of my mother, the hoped for friend of my heart, the expected champion of virtue, can turn aside to such base and pitiful vice; such intolerable, such absurd, such deep hypocrisy? And why? What cause? Is this the reward of their uncommon virtues?

And you, Oh man! Did they not labour hourly, incessantly, with the purity of saints and the ardour of angels, to do you good? Was it not their sole employment; their first duty, and their dearest hope? Did they ever deviate? Did they not return urbanity for arrogance, kindness for contempt, and life for blows?—Can you, Clifton, dare you be thus wicked? And will you persist?—

If you have brought them to harm, if your practices have reached their lives, earth does not contain so foul, so wicked a monster!—

Surely this cannot be! Surely you have some drop of mother's blood in you, and cannot be actuated by a spirit so wholly demon!

What shall I do? What shall I say? How shall I awaken a soul so steeped in iniquity, so dead to excellence, so obstinate in ill?—Clifton!—You were not formed for this! You have a mind that might have been the fit companion of divine natures! —It may be still!—Awake! View the light, and turn from crimes, pollution, and abhorrence, to virtue, love, and truth!

Know you not the beaming charity of her whom you perse- cute, if—Oh God!—Surely this is vain terror! Surely Anna St. Ives is still among the living!—

Clifton, once again I say, remember the untainted benevolence of her soul! Is it, can it be forgotten by you? Which of your good qualities was ever forgotten by her? Hear her describe them in her own language!*

These are a few of the commendations with which her descriptions abound. Commendations of you, oh man of mischief and mistake! They are quotations from her letters. Read them; remember them; think on all she has done for you, all she has said to you, and all you have made her suffer!

What shall I say? My fears are infinite, my hopes few, my anguish intolerable!—For the love of God, brother, do not rob the world of two people who were born to be its light and pride! Do not be this diabolic instrument of passion and error! If they still have being, restore them to the human race.—You know not the wrong you do!—'Tis heinous, 'tis hateful wickedness! Can a mind like yours feel no momentary remorse, no glow of returning virtue, no sudden resolution to perform a great and glorious act of justice on yourself?

If you value your soul's peace, hear me! Awake from this guilty dream, and be once more the brother of the agonizing

L. CLIFTON

LETTER CXXII

Louisa Clifton to Mrs. Wenbourne

Grosvenor-Street

DEAR MADAM

You have been kindly pleased to request I would give you some account of the means we are pursuing, in hopes to obtain traces that should lead to a discovery of the very strange affair by which we are all perplexed and afflicted. I am sorry to say that I can do

---

* Here follow numerous extracts from the letters of Anna St. Ives; all expressive of the high qualities and powers of Mr. Clifton, of the delight they gave her, and the hopes they inspired. They are omitted here, because it is probable they are fresh in the reader's memory: if not, it will be easy to turn to Anna's letters; particularly to letters XXIV. XXXI. XXXVIII. XLV. LVI. LXIII. LXVIII. LXXVIII. LXXIX. LXXXII. CVIII.

little more than narrate the distress of the various parties, who think themselves interested in the loss of the dear friend of my heart, and of the youth so well worthy of her affections.

Of the grief of Sir Arthur, madam, you have yourself been a witness: nor does it seem to abate. I should wonder indeed if it could; for though I wish to cherish hope, I own that the secrecy and silence with which this black stratagem has been carried into effect are truly terrifying.

Highly as I esteem and reverence the virtues of young Mr. Henley, I have been free enough to own to you, madam, I never was any admirer of the qualities and proceedings of his father. Justice however obliges me to say that he at present expresses a regret so deep, for the loss of his son, as to prove that he has a considerable sense of his worth. Money has been the sole object of his efforts: yet, though his son had so great a sum in his possession at the time he disappeared, he seems to think but little of the money, compared to the loss which is indeed so infinitely more deplorable.

While I live I shall love and esteem Mrs. Clarke, and her niece Peggy; whose kind hearts overflow with affection, both for my Anna St. Ives and young Mr. Henley. Well indeed may Peggy remember poor Frank. He was her saviour in the hour of her distress. She takes no rest herself, nor will she suffer her husband or her brother to take any. They are all continually on the watch; and to do the men justice, they do not need a spur.

Mr. Webb, her brother, with whose unfortunate history I suppose you are acquainted, gives proofs of zeal which are very affecting. The tears have frequently gushed from me, at seeing the virtuous anxiety of his mind, and at recollecting what that mind was, how and by whom it was preserved, and that its whole activity is now exerted, with the strong and cheering hope of returning some portion of the good it has received!

I know, madam, how great your sorrow must be, as well as that of all the once happy relations of a young lady of endowments and virtues so rare. Yet deep as this sorrow is, I think it scarcely can exceed the anguish I feel; convinced as I am that my mistaken, my unhappy brother is the cause of this much dreaded misery.

I told you, madam, I would go to him. I have been, and could gain no admission. I have written; and have received no answer. These circumstances, added to the perturbation of mind which was so discoverable in him when he was last at Rose-Bank, do but confirm my fears of his guilt.

But as it becomes us to act, and not to lament, while there is any possibility that action should give us relief, I joined Mr. Abimelech Henley in his opinion, that we ought to apply to the civil power for redress. We first indeed prevailed on Lord Fitz-Allen to speak to Mr. Clifton; but it was to no purpose: my brother behaved, as I prophesied he would, with disdainful silence. I own I had some hopes that my letter would have touched his heart: I am sorry to find they were so ill-founded.

Mr. Clifton having refused even to deny his knowledge of the affair to his Lordship, he consented that application should be made to a civil magistrate. But Lord Fitz-Allen is strangely pre-judiced, and is persuaded, or affects to be, that Mr. Clifton, being a gentleman, is incapable of a dishonourable act; and that young Mr. Henley and Anna St. Ives have eloped. The sum of money Mr. Henley had in his possession confirms him in this opinion: and he has several times half persuaded Sir Arthur, and some others, to be of his sentiments.

Hearing this, and finding no positive accusation, and that nothing but surmise could be preferred against Mr. Clifton, whose character was understood to be highly vindictive, the magistrate refused to do any thing more than send a polite request, that he would come and speak in his presence to the parties concerned.

My brother refused in terms of menace and defiance; and we returned home hopeless; yet again having recourse to watching the door of my brother's lodgings, as has been done for these several days. But we have learnt nothing. And what indeed can we learn? Mr. Webb and his brother-in-law have twice followed him on foot, to the livery stables; and have seen him mount his horse, and ride out of town: but the speed with which he went quickly took him out of sight.

The roads he chose were in opposite directions: but that they might easily be, and yet lead to the same place. They are out at present; for their industry is unwearied.

It is in vain to think of pursuing my brother on horseback; for he must infallibly see his pursuer. He went one time over West-minster-bridge, and the other through Tyburn-turnpike up to Paddington. Their present project is, the first time he goes out, to

waylay[1] both these roads, and to get assistants. Mr. Webb is a
swift runner: but the chance of success I am afraid is very small
indeed! However it becomes them, and us, and indeed every body,
not to desist, till the whole of this dark transaction be brought to
light.

I am, madam, &c.

L. CLIFTON

LETTER CXXIII

Coke Clifton to Guy Fairfax

London, Dover-Street

WHY ay! He who opens the flood-gates of mischief is necessarily
in most danger of being swept away by the torrent!——I have
drunken deeply of ruin, and soon shall have my fill!

You warned me to beware of this raven: you told me he scented
carrion!—I laughed at your prophecy!—It is fulfilled!—I am a
gull!—The fleeced, cheated, despicable gull of the infernal villain
Mac Fane!

It was right that I should be loaded with every species of contempt for myself. I have been the fool, the gudgeon, the ineffable
ass to lose a sum of money to him, which to pay would be destruction!—I begin to hate myself with most strange inveteracy! Could
I meet such another fellow, I would spit in his face—Fairfax, it is
true—By hell I hold myself in most rooted and ample antipathy!

I find I have strangely mistaken my own character and talents
——I once thought to have driven the world before me, and to
have whipped opposition into immediate compliance: but it seems
I am myself one of the very sorry wretches at whom I was so all
alive and ready to give, and spurn! These are odd and unaccountable things! And it appears that I am a very poor creature! A
most indubitable driveller! The twin-brother of imbecility! Ay,
the counterpart and compeer of Edward St. Ives, and the tool of
the most barefaced of cheats, as well as his familiar!——Well!
I have lived long enough to make the discovery; and it is now high
time to depart!

I wrote to you but yesterday: but events hastily tread on each other's heels, and if I do not relate them now I never shall. I told you I expected the gambler to supper, by my own invitation—Ay, ay!—I am a very Solomon!—

I dined at home. I knew not indeed to what extremes the St. Ives hunters might proceed: or whether they would make accusation upon oath, sufficient to authorise a magistrate in granting a warrant, to bring me before him; but the attempt must have been impotent and abortive, I therefore determined to brave them: however I heard no more of them or their suspicions.

As I sat ruminating on past events, on my sister and her epistle, and particularly on the zeal with which Anna St. Ives appealed to the letter written by her, which I had received from Laura, my curiosity was so far excited that at last I determined to read them both. I own, Fairfax, they both moved me!—This sister of mine, enraged as I am against her, has somehow found the art of making herself respected. Her zeal has character and efficacy in it: I mean persuasion. I could not resist some of the sensations she intended to inspire. She cited passages from the letters of her friend that were daggers to me! At the very time I was seeking to quarrel with Anna, she angel-like was incessant in my praise!—And such praises, Fairfax—! There was no resisting it!—She thought generously, nobly, ay sublimely of me: while my irascible jealousy, false pride, and vindictive spirit were eager only to find cause of offence!

And yet I know not!—I cannot keep my mind to a point! Surely *I had cause of offence*: real cause?—Surely the retribution I sought had justice in it?—She could not be wholly blameless?—No!—That would indeed be distraction!

I then ventured to read the letter of Anna—On paper or in speech she is the same: energetic, awful, and affecting!

While I was reading this last Mac Fane entered, and soon put an end to my meditations. Did I tell you I had been fool enough to invite him to supper?——He had not been with me half an hour before I was most intolerably weary of his company!

After having vapoured of the feats of himself and the scowling rascal his colleague, to remind me of my high obligations to them, and talking as usual with most bitter malevolence against Henley, he soon began to descant on the old subject; gaming——To ask a madman why he is mad were vain! I was importuned by his jargon—'He had been pigeoned[1] only last night of no less than seven hundred pounds!' Repetitions, imprecations, and lies, all of the same kind, succeeded as fast as he could utter them!

I know all this ought to have put me upon my guard; and I know too that it did not. I believe I had some lurking vanity in my mind; a persuasion that I could beat him at picquet. I was weary both of myself and him; was primed for mischief, and cared not of what kind. If you ask me for any better reason, why, knowing him as I did, I suffered myself to be the tool of this fellow, I can only say I have none to give!

I ordered my own servant to fetch half a dozen packs of cards, and imagined this precaution was some security. What will not men imagine, when their passions are afloat and reason is flown?

To give you the history of how I was led on, from one act of idiotism to another, or how after having lost one thousand I could be lunatic enough to lose a second, and after a second a third, and so on to a tenth, is more than my present temper of mind will permit. It is quite sufficient to tell you that I have ruined myself; and that there is not, upon the face of the earth, a fellow I so thoroughly despise as Coke Clifton; no not even Mac Fane himself! Below the lowest am I fallen; for I am his dupe, nay his companion, and what is worse his debtor! It is time I were out of the world—So miserable a being does not crawl upon its surface.

It is the very heyday of mischief, and I must abroad among it. The exact manner of the catastrophe I cannot foresee, but it must be tragical. I have something brooding in my mind, the outlines of a conclusion, which rather pleases me. I have sworn to avenge myself of Anna, disinherit my sister, and never to pay Mac Fane. These oaths must be kept. Anna must fall! If she will but deign to live afterward, she shall be my heir. And for myself, I know how to find a ready quietus!

My mind since this last affair is better reconciled to its destiny, and even less disturbed than before: for previous to this, there seemed to be some bare possibility of a generous release, on my part, and a more generous forgetfulness of injuries on theirs. But now, all is over! I have but to punish my opponents a little, and myself much, and having punished expire.

C. CLIFTON

P.S. I have not paid the scoundrel his thousand pounds. He proposed a bond for the whole, on which he said he could raise money. This I was determined not to give, and told him he must wait a few days, till I had consulted my lawyer and looked into my affairs, and I would then give him a determinate answer. He was beginning to assume the contemptible airs of a bully; but I was in no temper to bear the least insult. The real rage of my look silenced the mechanical ferocity of his. I bade him remember I could hit a china plate, and that I should think proper to take my own mode of payment. He then changed his tone, and began to commend his soul to Satan, in a thousand different forms, if he had ever won a hundred pounds at a sitting in his whole life before. I sneered in his face, shewed him the door, and bade him good night; and he walked quietly away.

LETTER CXXIV

Louisa Clifton to Mrs. Wenbourne

Grosvenor Street

DEAR MADAM,

As I have taken upon myself the painful duty of informing you of all that passes, relative to this unhappy affair, it becomes me to be punctual. It is afflicting to own that our agitation and distress, instead of abating, are increased.

Finding it impossible to gain a sight of my brother, I determined to attempt to question his valet. Mr. Webb received my instructions accordingly, watched him to some distance from the house, and delivered a message from me, that if he would come to me I would present him with ten guineas.

He made no hesitation, but followed Mr. Webb immediately.

Either he is very artful or very ignorant of this affair. One circumstance excepted, he appears to know nothing.

I promised him any reward, any sum he should himself name, if he could but give us such information as might lead to the recovery of our lost friends: but he protested very solemnly he had none to give; except that he owns having been employed, by his master, to inveigle the lad away, who wrote the anonymous letter, and whom Mr. Clifton, by practising on the lad's credulity and gratitude, sent to France.

The valet indeed acknowledges his master is exceedingly disturbed in mind; that he does not sleep, nor even go to bed, except sometimes tossing himself on it with his clothes on, and almost instantly rising again; and that he has sent for his attorney, to make his will.

I will not endeavour to paint my sensations at hearing this account. I will only add that another incident has happened, which gives them additional acuteness.

I believe, madam, you have heard both my brother and my Anna speak of and describe a young French nobleman, who paid his addresses to her, and who was the occasion of the rash leap into the lake, by which Mr. Clifton endangered his life? This gentleman, Count de Beaunoir, is arrived in London; and has this morning paid a visit to Sir Arthur St. Ives.

He enquired first and eagerly after my friend; with whom, like all who know her, he is in raptures. Sir Arthur, forgetting his character, and the apparently rodomontade[1] but to him very serious manner in which he had declared himself her champion, told him the whole story, as far as it is known to us; not omitting to mention Mr. Clifton as the person on whom all our suspicions fell, and relating to him the full grounds of those suspicions.

The astonishment of the Count occasioned him to listen with uncommon attention to what he heard; and he closed the narrative of Sir Arthur by affirming it was all true. He was convinced beyond contradiction of its truth, for he had himself brought over the lad, whom Mr. Clifton had sent, with pretended dispatches, to a friend of his in Paris.

The lad it appears, suspecting all was not right, and finding no probability of returning, but on the contrary that he was watched, and even refused a passport, had applied to the Count through the medium of his servants, with whom he had formerly been acquainted, to protect and afford him the means of returning to England.

The lad was sent for, his story heard, and he was then questioned concerning Anna St. Ives; and he had heard enough of the affair from Mr. Abimelech Henley, and from the servants, to know that the proposed match, between Mr. Clifton and Anna, was broken off; and that she refused to admit his visits. When Count de Beau-noir last saw Sir Arthur, at Paris, he had assured him very seriously that, should ever Anna St. Ives find herself disengaged and he knew it, he would instantly make her a tender of his hand and fortune: and he had no sooner heard the lad's story than he deter-mined immediately to make his intended journey to England.

My heart shudders while I relate it, but I dread lest it should be a fatal journey, for him or my brother, or both! For he declared to Sir Arthur, without hesitation, he would wait on Mr. Clifton directly, and oblige him either to produce Anna St. Ives, or meet him in the field.

Wretched folly! Destructive error! When will men cease to think that vice and virtue ought to meet on equal terms; and that injury can be atoned by blood?

The Count had left his address with Sir Arthur, and the moment I heard what had passed I flew to his lodgings. He was not at home, and I waited above an hour. At last he came, and I attempted to shew him both the folly and wickedness of the conduct he was pursuing.

He listened to me with the utmost politeness, paid me a thou-sand compliments, acknowledged the truth of every thing I said, but very evidently determined to act in a manner directly opposite. I very assiduously laboured to make him promise, upon his honour, he would not seek redress by duelling; but in vain. He answered by evasion; with all possible desire to have obliged me, but with a fore-gone conclusion that it could not be.

Pardon me, madam, for writing a narrative so melancholy: but sincerity is necessary; intelligence might have come to you in a distorted form, and might have produced much worse effects. For my own part, I have no other mode of conduct but that of writing and of speaking the simple truth; being convinced there is no shade of disguise, artifice, or falsehood, that is not immoral in principle, and pernicious in practice.

I have been very busy. I have sent for the lad whom the count brought over with him, and have made enquiries. The answers he gave me all tend to confirm our former suspicions. He has related the story, at length, of the manner in which he was inveigled away, and prevailed on to go to France.

I next questioned him concerning his aunt; and he knows

nothing of her, has never heard from her, and is astonished at what can have become of her. He means, however, to go this evening to a relation's house, where he thinks he is certain he shall hear of her; and has then promised to come and let me know——But to what purpose? We shall find she has been sent out of the way by Mr. Clifton: and what further information will that afford? None, except to confirm what needs no confirming; except to shew the blindness, craft, and turpitude of his mind!

I am, dear madam, &c.

L. CLIFTON

LETTER CXXV

Coke Clifton to Guy Fairfax

London, Dover-Street

So, Fairfax, you have suffered the lad to escape you; cautioned and entreated as you were! You know, I suppose, by what means; and with whom he is at present?—Well, well!—It is no matter—I have quarrels enough on hand, and enemies enough!—I would fain die in peace with somebody!—I forgive you—I suppose you did your best.

It is exceedingly possible that this may be the last letter you will ever receive from me. Remember me now and then. Should Henley and Anna St. Ives survive me, let them know I was not so entirely blind to their worth as they might perhaps suppose. Shew them my letters if you will: I care not who sees them now! Let the truth be told! I shall be deaf enough to censure.

I have just had a visit from the crazy count; a threatening one. A challenge has passed, and we are to meet to-morrow.

So it is agreed; but I doubt whether I shall keep the appointment. If there be one spark of resentment in the soul of Henley, it is possible I may fail. I mean to give him the first chance. It is his by right; and why should not I do right even to him, once in my life? This farrago of folly, this pride of birth, and riches, and I know not what else lumber, is very contemptible!

Fairfax, the present state of my thoughts force more than one truth upon me. But what have I to do with truth, in a world from which I learned so much error that it was impossible for me to exist in it? These wise people should leave us fools to wrangle, be wretched, and cut each other's throats as we list, without inter-meddling: 'tis dangerous. But Truth is a zealot; Wisdom will be crying in the streets; and Folly meeting her seldom fails to deal her blow.

My mind is made up: my affairs are settled, my lawyer has written out my will, and it is signed. You will find yourself men-tioned in it, Fairfax. I have nominated my sister my executor, and Anna St. Ives my heir. I have been reading Louisa's letter again: it is full of pathos. She has more understanding than I have been willing to allow, and I have relented. She is not forgotten in my will: I would not have her think of me with everlasting hatred.

I know not how it is, Fairfax, but I feel more compunction, at present, than I ever remember to have felt before. I am grown into self-contempt; and the haughty notions, which were the support of my high and sometimes arrogant conduct, are faded. I could think only of Coke Clifton, and I now know Coke Clifton to be a very wicked dolt!

Be not deceived by my present tone: make no false predictions in favour either of myself or Anna St. Ives. Despair and fate are not more fixed than is my plan. My horse will presently be at the door. I shall mount him the moment I have ended this letter, and shall proceed directly to Anna. There, after all is ended, the en-chantment too shall end, and the misventurous[1] lady and her imprisoned knight shall both be set free.

Should Henley, urged by despair to seek revenge, accept my defiance and meet me in the field, the conflict must be fierce, and such as might inspire terror.

To say the truth, were it not to prove myself his equal, perhaps his master and vanquisher, I would not lift my hand against his life. It would be some relief to my soul to fall by his arm. He is a noble fellow, and I have done him wrong. Would he or Anna but charitably strike, I would die blessing them, eased by the expiatory blow. Perhaps they are the only two beings for whom I ever could have had the same admiration; and, if what they tell me be true, admiration continued always ripens into love. They shewed affec-tion toward me, and would, I believe, have loved me. But we did not understand each other, and the mistake has been mutually fatal—Would I had never injured them!—But it is vain!—The die is cast!—We are all fated!—Having accomplished my revenge, and accomplish it I will, they cannot live and not be miserable! They must curse my hated memory, and blaspheme against my honour! —It cannot be otherwise—Let our grave therefore be glorious! They are brave spirits, and will mock my power even to the last. I love their high courage. Perhaps they shall find I have a kindred soul!—Oh would they die forgiving me—!

I know not well whither my thoughts are wandering—They perhaps may refuse to die—They may say it is their duty to live, even though doomed to be wretched—I know them—What they think they will act—Well, well!—Let destiny dispose of events— To me all chances are welcome, all are alike.

As to this count, should Henley refuse vengeance, I owe him no mercy. 'Twas he who prompted me to the frantic act that first made me the debtor of the man I have most injured. I almost contemn a foe so insignificant—Not that he is deficient in bravery, or skill—But what is he?—What are his wrongs?—'Tis lunacy, not anger rankling at his heart!—Or if it were?—The hungry wolf-dog is no fit combatant for the famished lion!

C. CLIFTON

P.S. Fairfax, a new terror has come over me. I told you of the letters of my sister and Anna, and described something of the effect they produced upon me. You may remember I read them previous to my last damned interview with the villain Mac Fane. I recollect having laid the letter of Anna upon the table, and that it continued lying there for some time after his entrance. I had my eye upon it, and meant not to put it in my pocket lest it should be left there, but lock it up as soon as I moved—I forgot it—The letter is lost—I have searched every where, have enquired, have cursed; have threatened unheard-of punishment to my scoundrel, if he have purloined it; but to no effect. He protests he knows nothing of it; and he looks as if he spoke truth—It contained a secret relative to Henley—! Should Mac Fane have taken it up furtively, as I suppose such thieves are always on the watch—? Why, if he should—? Hell hounds!—Blood-thirsty vultures!—If so—! I will be gone this instant!—It is the very era of horror!

FRAGMENT*

WHETHER what I am about to write may ever be found, or whether I the writer may ever be heard of more, are both very doubtful events. It may be of some use to mankind, should this brief narrative hereafter be read; as it may tend to exemplify the progress of the passions, and to shew after having begun in error the excesses of which they are capable. I speak under the supposition that this paper may fall into the hands of persons who know more of Mr. Clifton, and of the affair to which I allude, than even I myself at present know; or, if I did, than I have time and opportunity to relate.

With that hope, and addressing myself to such persons, I will endeavour, as long as I have the means and am able, accurately to recount the particulars of what has befallen me, from the time I was first beset to the latest minute of my remaining where I am; whether my removal happen by death or release; of which, though apparently beyond hope, it would certainly be wrong to despair.

Oh, Anna St. Ives! Should thine eye ever glance over this paper, ignorant as I am of thy destiny, though too well assured it is a fearful one, think not, while I seem to narrate those incidents only which have happened to myself, that I am attentive to self alone; that I have forgotten the nobler duties of which we have so often sweetly discoursed; or that the memory of thee and thy sufferings has ever been absent from my heart!—But why bid thee be just? To whom didst thou ever do a wilful wrong? Oh pardon me!—— Live on, shouldst thou still be permitted to live, and labour with redoubled ardour in the great cause of truth! Despair not! Heave not a sigh, drop not a tear; but sacrifice thy private ills to public good!

Before I begin, it is necessary to notice that I had the sum of eight thousand pounds about me, in bank-bills: for it is this circumstance which seems to have insured my death. Our walk was to have ended by four o'clock, and the money to have been left at the banker's as we returned. I cannot however acquit myself of neglect.

* Written by Mr. Henley in his confinement, and taken from the wainscot in which it was concealed after the catastrophe.

I ought not to have forgotten that money, under our present wretched system, is the grand stimulus to vice; that accidents very little dreamed of daily happen; and that procrastination is always an error.

As I was walking with the lady whose name I have just mentioned, in some fields between Kensington and Brompton, we saw Mr. Clifton pass on horseback, and I believe in less than a minute a man assault him, and fire a pistol, with an intent to rob him as I then supposed.

I ran to his aid; and, immediately after the flight of this real or imaginary robber, I was myself attacked, and laid senseless, by a blow I received on the side of my head; which, as there was no person in front able to strike at me, must have come from behind.

I saw no more for that time of Mr. Clifton. The blow was very violent, and is still severely felt.

When I recovered my senses, I found my arms confined by a straight waistcoat; such as are used to secure maniacs. I endeavoured to call for assistance, but the man who had charge of me, for there were several, thrust his thumb in the larynx, forced open my mouth, and gagged me. He has twice had occasion, as he supposed, to use me thus; and both times with such violence as seemingly to require the utmost effort mind could make, to recover respiration; the thrust of his thumb was so merciless, and the sensation of strangling so severe.

They brought me to a house thoroughly prepared for confinement. It is an old but heavy building, walled round, and provided with bars, bolts, chains, massy locks, and every precaution to impede escape.

I was led by one pair of stairs, to apartments consisting of two chambers; the one roomy, the other much smaller; in which last is a bed.

As soon as I was safe in the room, the master man among them, who as I have since learned is a professed keeper of the insane, ungagged me, took off the straight waistcoat, and then they all left me.

I stood I know not how long in that stupor of amazement which the scene, and the crowding conjectures of imagination, necessarily produced.

At length, I roused my mind to more activity. I then set myself to inspect the apartments. In the largest there was a fire place, and a fire; but neither shovel, tongs nor poker; except a small stick as a substitute for a poker, with which I certainly could not knock a man down. The furniture consisted of a chair, a table, a broken looking-glass, and an old picture, in panel, of the sacrifice of Isaac, with Abraham's knife at his throat. It stares me now in the face, and is a strong emblem of my own situation; except that my saving angel seems wanting.

In the other room, exclusive of the bed and its appurtenances, there was a second chair, which with an old walnut-tree clothes-press was its whole inventory.

In this room was a closet, with several shelves almost to the ceiling; the topmost of them so high as but just to be reached by me, when standing on a chair. I swept my hand along the shelves, and found them as I thought empty.

I then examined the windows. There were only two, one to each room; the remainder having been walled up; and these each of them provided with thick iron bars, so near to each other as to admit but of a small part of the face passing between them. There was a casement to the front room only; and I found a piece of paper tied to the handle of it, on which was written—'You are closely watched: if you attempt to make any signals, or shout, or take any other means to inform persons you are here, your lodging will be changed to one much more disagreeable.'

Having nothing with which I could employ myself except my thoughts, and these flowing in abundance, I sat meditating and undisturbed till it was almost dark. A little before five o'clock as I suppose, perhaps later, for I forgot to say my watch and purse had been taken from me, with a promise that they should be returned, I heard the sound of distant bolts and locks, that belong to the outer gates and doors, and soon afterward of men in loud conversation.

The keeper and two of his assistants came up to me, and once more brought the straight waistcoat, into which they bade me thrust my arms. I hesitated, and told them I did not choose to have my arms confined. To which the keeper replied—'B*** my b**** eyes! None of your jabber, or I'll fetch you another rum one! I'll knock you off the roost again!'

From this speech I conclude it was he who gave me the blow with the bludgeon, when I was first secured.

G g

As he said this, he raised his bludgeon; with which kind of weapon they were all three armed, and had locked the door after them. There was no remedy, and I obeyed.

As soon as they had confined my arms they left me, and remembering the bank-notes which I had in my fob,[1] I began to fear they had come to the knowledge of this circumstance; though I could not imagine by what means. Some short time afterward, perhaps a quarter of an hour, the bolts and chains of my door again began to rattle, and one person singly came in. It was dark, and I could not distinguish his features, but I recollected his form: it was the gambler Mac Fane; the sound of his voice presently put it beyond a doubt.

Without speaking a word, he came up to me and made a violent blow at me. I perceived it coming, sprang upward, and received it on the tip of my shoulder, his hand driving up to my neck. From his manner, I guess it hurt him at least as much as me; for his passion immediately became outrageous, and he began cursing, kicking, spitting at me, and treating me with various other indignities, which are wholly unworthy of remembrance.

His passion was so loud and vehement that the keeper, hearing him, came up. Just as he entered Mac Fane struck me again, and with more effect, for he knocked me down; and was proceeding to kick me in a manner that might perhaps have been fatal, had not the keeper interfered.

I said not one word the whole time, nor as I recollect uttered any sound whatever; and it was with difficulty that the keeper, who is even a more powerful man than himself, could get him away.

I was once more left in solitude and darkness; and thus sat, with fresh subjects for reflection, ruminating on this worthless Mac Fane, my rencontre with him and Mr. Clifton, the extreme malignancy of his temper, and all the connecting circumstances that are allied to events which I cannot now relate.

About eight o'clock my door once more opened, and a little boy of fourteen years of age, as he tells me, brought me a light and some food. The boy imagined me to be mad, and entered the room with great reluctance, his master the keeper standing at the door, cursing him, threatening him with the horse-whip, and obliging him to do as he was bidden! which was to release me from the strait-waistcoat, spread a threadbare half-dirty napkin over the table, set the plates, and wait till I had eaten. The trepidation of the poor boy at setting my arms at liberty was extreme.

The door was not open but ajar, and secured by three chains, between which the boy crept; the keeper standing and looking on, with one arm leaning on the middle chain, and his head only in the chamber.

I observed that the boy had an intelligent countenance, though considerably under the influence of fear; with strong marks of kindness in it, but stronger of dejection.

The furniture, the napkin, knives and forks, and every circumstance denoted the poverty of the man who is my jailer: and his proceedings proved there scarcely could be any guilt from which he would start, to remove this supposed evil. The thought could not escape me, nor the jeopardy in which I should stand, should the money I had in my possession be discovered.

I ate what was brought me, and endeavoured by the mildness and cheerfulness of my look to inspire the boy with confidence. I have no doubt but he was surprised to see so docile a madman, not having yet ever seen any, and being from description exceedingly terrified at the idea of the trade to which he has been forcibly apprenticed. I spoke to him two or three times, apparently to ask him for the trifles he could reach me, but in reality with another view. I likewise addressed him two or three other times in dumb-show, with as much mildness and meaning in my look as circumstances so insignificant would permit.

The effect my behaviour had upon him was very evident; and after beginning in fear and confusion, he left me in something like hope and tranquillity. My prison door was locked, the candle taken away, and I left in darkness. I was no more molested during that night.

My thoughts were too busy to suffer me to sleep. I sat without moving I know not how long. The extreme stillness of all around me added to the unity of the gloom, and produced a state of mind which gives wholesome exercise to fortitude. Deep as I was in thought, I remember having been two or three times roused by the sternness of the keeper's voice, which I heard very plainly, and which was generally some command, closing with a curse, and as I supposed directed to the poor boy.

My bed-chamber door was open, and after some time I removed

into it, and sat down on the feet of the bed, again falling into reveries which fixed me motionless to the place. I cannot tell what was the hour, nor how long I had been thus seated; but I was roused by the sound of a door opening, and once more by the voice of the keeper, which I heard so distinctly as to doubt for a moment whether it were not in my own chamber.

At the same time a broad ray of light suddenly struck against the wall of my bed-room. I followed it with my eye: I was still at the foot of the bed, and its direction was from the left to the right. I had much inclination to pull off my shoes, and endeavour to trace by what aperture it entered; but on further reflection, I concluded it would be best not to excite any alarm, in a mind which cannot but be continually tormented by suspicion and fear.

I paid strict attention however to every circumstance that might aid my memory, in tracing it on the morrow.

The voice of the keeper, for he spoke several times, was now much more distinct than before: he was going to bed, and the question—'Are you sure all is safe?'—was repeated several times with great anxiety, and was answered in the affirmative by a man's voice—'Do you hear him stir?' said the keeper.—The reply was—'No—But I am sure I heard him a little before ten.'

The keeper however could not be satisfied, and in less than five minutes I heard my door unbolting. The keeper and both his men came in with their bludgeons. He asked morosely why I did not go to bed. I answered because I had no inclination to sleep. He went again to the windows, and examined the very walls with the utmost circumspection; and afterward turning away said—'Sleep or wake, I'll be d**** if you have any chance.'

He then left me, and I presently afterward saw the ray of light again, and heard his various motions at going to bed.

I passed the night without closing my eyes, and in the morning began to examine where it was possible the light should obtain admission. I placed myself in the same situation, and looking to the left saw the closet was in that direction, and that the door was open.

Looking into it I found that a part of the flooring, in the left hand corner, was decayed; and that the ceiling beneath had a fissure of some width.

I thought it a fortunate circumstance that sounds were conveyed so distinctly into my apartments: though I speak chiefly of the bed-chamber; for it was the loudness of the keeper's voice, and the stillness of surrounding objects, which most contributed to my hearing him in the front apartment. Not but the decayed state of the building favoured the conveyance of sound, in all directions.

I began to consider how far I could improve the means that offered themselves, and, watching my opportunity in the course of the day, with my fingers and by the aid of the stick left to stir my fire, I removed some of the decayed mortar to the right and left, and increased the aperture on the inside; but was exceedingly careful not to push any flakes, or part of the ceiling, down into the floor below. The attention I paid to this was very exact, for it was of the utmost consequence. Nor was I less accurate in pressing together the rubbish I scraped away into vacant corners between the joints, and leaving no traces that should lead to discovery.

All these precautions were highly necessary, as the behaviour of the keeper had proved; for when he came into my chamber in the morning, as he did early with his customary attendants, he searched and pried about with all the assiduity of suspicion.

At breakfast I was again waited on by the boy, and watched by the keeper. It was necessary I should not excite alarms, in a mind so full of apprehension: I therefore behaved with reserve to the boy, though with great complacency, said little, and dismissed him soon.

In the forenoon the door opened again: the boy was sent in with the straight waistcoat, and the keeper said to me—'Come, sir; put on your jacket!—Here, boy, be handy!'—I once more hesitated, and asked if Mr. Mac Fane were coming to pay me another visit? He did not return me a direct answer, but replied—'If you will put on the jacket, you may go and stretch your pins for half an hour in the garden: if not stay where you are, and be d****!'

After a short deliberation, I concluded that to comply was prudent; and I very peaceably aided the boy in performing his office. As my back was turned to the keeper, I smiled kindly and significantly to the boy; to which he replied by a look expressive of surprise and curiosity.

It cannot be supposed but that my mind had been most anxiously enquiring into the possibility and means of escape, while in my prison; and that the moment this unexpected privilege was granted me, its whole efforts were directed to the same subject.

I walked in the garden overlooked, and in a certain manner followed, by the keeper and his attendants: I therefore traversed it in various directions, without seeming to pay the least attention to the object on which my mind was most busy. But the chance of escape, my hands being thus confined, appeared to be as small in the garden as in the house. It is completely surrounded by a high wall, which joins the house at each end. It had one small gate, or rather door, which was locked and bolted; and had no other entrance, except from the house. After having walked about an hour as I suppose, the keeper asked me, in a tone rather of command than question, if I were not tired. I answered—No. To which he replied, But I am. Accordingly, without saying another word, I returned to my prison.

I will attempt no description of the sufferings of my mind, and the continual fears by which it was distracted: not for myself, for there was no appearance, at this time, that any greater harm than confinement was intended me, but for another. The subject is torturing: but resignation and fortitude are duties. My reason for mentioning it is that it strongly excited me to some prompt effort at escape.

I could think of none, except of endeavouring to convince the keeper it was more his interest to give me my freedom, than to keep me in confinement. Consequently, when my dinner was brought, and he had taken his station, I asked him if he would do me the favour to converse with me for half an hour; either privately or in the presence of his own men.

He did not suffer me to finish my sentence, but exclaimed— 'None of your gab, I tell you! If you speak another word, I'll have you jacketed: and then b*** me, my kiddy, if you get it off again in a hurry!'

I said no more, but ate my dinner; casting an eye occasionally to the door, and conjecturing what were the probabilities, by a very sudden spring, of breaking the chain, for he had only put one up, or of drawing the staple by which it was held, and which, from the thickness of the wood-work, I knew could not be clenched. It was not possible, I believe, for mind to be actuated by stronger motives than mine was, in my wish to escape: the circumstance of the single chain might not occur a second time, and I determined on the trial.

I prolonged my dinner till I perceived him begin to yawn, and at last turn his head the other way. I was about twelve feet distant from the door. I rose quietly, made two steps, and then gave a sudden spring. I came with great violence against the door, but it resisted me, and of course, I fell backward.

After the first moment of surprise, the keeper instantly locked the door, and, in a rage of cursing, called his assistants. They however soon pacified him, by turning his attention to the strength of his own fastenings, and scoffing at my fruitless attempt.

But this incident induced him to change his mode: he stood no more with the door ajar to watch me, but, after sending in the boy, locked and bolted it upon us.

I was in full expectation of the straight waistcoat; and his forbearance, I imagine, was occasioned by the strict orders he must have received to the contrary. His threat indeed, when I attempted to speak, is a proof rather against this supposition; and I can solve it no other way than by supposing that his orders were, if I attempted persuasion with him, he would then be at liberty to do a thing to which he seemed exceedingly prone. His fears for himself, should I escape, must inevitably be strong; and a man, who has waded far enough in error to commit an act so violent, will willingly plunge deeper, in proportion as such fears increase.

The sudden spring I had made at the door, combining with the supposition of madness, had such an effect upon the poor boy that, hearing the door lock and seeing me as he imagined let loose upon him, his fright returned in full force. His looks were so pale, and he trembled so violently, that I feared he would fall into a fit. I went up to him with the utmost gentleness, and said—Don't be afraid, my good boy! Indeed I will not hurt you.

The keeper scarcely stayed a minute before, recollecting I had been long enough at dinner, he opened the door again, but with the caution of the three chains, and bade the boy take away.

I then began to accuse myself of precipitancy; but I soon remembered that every thing ought to be hazarded, where every thing is at stake. My fears were not for myself; and, while my arms were free, could I have come upon them thus suddenly, success was far from improbable. Vice is always cowardly; and,

452 ANNA ST. IVES

difference of weapons out of the question, three to one are not invincible odds.

It now first occurred to me how prudent it would be to conceal my bank-bills, and I began to consider which were the best means. I took them out, examined their numbers, and endeavoured to fix them in my memory.

This was no difficult task; but prudence required that nothing should be left to chance, and I took the burnt end of my stick, and going into the back room, wrote the numbers against the wall, in a place which, from its darkness, was least liable to notice. Indeed I considered there was little to fear, even should the figures I made be seen, for I wrote them in one continued line, which rendered them unintelligible without a key.

I then once more took my chair, and placed it at the closet door; thinking that to hide them at one corner of the topmost shelf might perhaps be the securest place. I previously began to feel, and, at the far end of the shelf, I put my hand upon something; which, when brought to light, proved to be the remainder of a bundle of quills.

I felt again, but found nothing more there.

I then removed my chair toward the other end, and after two or three times sweeping my hand ineffectually along the shelf, I struck the edge of it against the wall, and more than half a quire of paper fell flat upon it.

This led me to conjecture that the shelf had been a hiding place, perhaps, to some love-sick girl, and that it was possible there should be ink. After another more accurate search, and turning my other hand, with which I could feel better to the opposite side, I found an ink-bottle.

I took down my treasure, and examined it: there was cotton in the bottle,[1] but the ink was partly mouldy and partly dried away. However, by the aid of a little water, I presently procured more than sufficient to write down my numbers. But I wanted a pen, and for this there was no succedaneum.[2]

As the safest way of preserving what might become useful, I returned my treasure to the shelf on which it had been found; and for that reason began to consider of another place for my bank-notes. After looking carefully round both chambers, I at last lifted up the old picture, and here I found a break in the wainscot;

in which was inserted, laterally, full as much more writing paper as the quantity I had discovered in the closet. I took away the paper entirely, lest, if seen, it should lead to further search; and, twisting up the bills, laid them so as to be certain of recovering them, when I pleased. The paper I put upon the shelf.

When the boy brought my supper, I asked him his name, how old he was, and other trifling questions, to familiarize and embolden him; and learned from his answers that he had a poor mother, who was unable to provide for him, and that he had been bound apprentice to this keeper by the parish.

At last I enquired if he could write and read?

He answered, yes; he had been called the best scholar of the charity school in which he was bred.

I then asked if he continued to practise his learning?

He replied he loved reading very much indeed: but he had no books.

Did he write?

He had no paper.

Was there a pen and ink in the house?

Yes; but the pen was seldom used, and good for nothing.

Could he get me a pen?

If he had but a quill, he could make me one.

Had he a pen-knife?

No; he had forgotten that: but one of the men had a knife with several blades, and he could ask him to lend it.

And what should he write, supposing he had paper?

A letter.

To whom?

To his mother.

I thought it not right to expose my stores to him, and therefore suffered him to go for that time, without saying any thing more on the subject. But my discourse with him had pretty well driven all apprehension from his mind. I was cautious to speak in a very low tone of voice; and, without being bidden, he had acuteness enough to follow my example.

The next day, at breakfast, I gave him a sheet of paper, and two quills; and told him to make pens of them if he could; one for himself, and the other for me; and to take the paper for his letter. He looked with intelligent surprise—Where did they come from?

was the question in his thoughts; but he said nothing. Madmen were beings whom he did not comprehend.

My kindness to him, however, made him desirous to oblige me. I gave him a part of my breakfast; and he ate what I gave him in a manner that shewed he was not over-fed.

At dinner he brought me both the pens. I asked him why he did not keep one to write to his mother? He said he had written, but had cleaned and cut the pen over again. They were not ill made, considering that, as he told me, the knife was a bad one.

But what will you do for ink, sir? said he. I told him I had a little; but that I should be glad if I had more. Perhaps, he replied, he could get one of the men to bring him a half-pennyworth. I said I had no money, and he answered a gentleman (Mr. Clifton, I suppose) had just given him sixpence, for holding his horse; that he intended to save it for his mother, but that he would spare a halfpenny to buy me ink.

I took the boy's hand, and said to him—'If ever I live to get free from this place, I will remember you.'—The emotions I felt communicated themselves, and he looked sorrowfully up in my face, and asked—'Why, are not you mad, sir?'

The very earnest but mild manner with which I answered— 'No, my good fellow'—both convinced him and set his imagination to work.

I said little more, but finished my meal, wrote down my numbers, and gave him the bottle: but warned him, if he were questioned, by no means to tell an untruth. The boy looked at me again, in a manner that spoke highly in his favour, put the bottle in his pocket, and, as soon as his master returned to the door, removed the things and departed.

He brought the ink with my supper. One of the men had taken his sixpence, but refused to return him any change; and the ink he had emptied out of the keeper's bottle. Such are the habits of vice. The boy related it with indignation, but said he dared not complain. I had nothing else to give, I therefore rewarded the generous boy with a couple of quills, and four sheets of paper for his own use; cautioning him to keep them to write to his mother.

While I wanted the means, I imagined it would have been a great relief to have had the power of writing down my thoughts; but I found they were much too busy, and disturbed, by the recollection of Anna St. Ives and her danger, and by the incessant desire of finding some means of escape, notwithstanding a thousand repeated convictions of its impossibility, to suffer me to write either with effect or connection. I did nothing but make memorandums; some of thoughts that occurred, and others of circumstances that were present. I concealed my papers in the wainscot behind the picture, where I mean to leave this narrative.

The indulgence of my morning walk was continued; and on the sixth day of my confinement an incident happened, by which I almost effected my release.

Confiding in the strait waistcoat and in the strength of his locks and bars, and become less apprehensive from this persuasion, the keeper had left me under the care of only one of his men; himself and the other were employed on something which he wanted done in the house.

While they were absent, the garden-bell rang. The voice of Mac Fane was heard, demanding entrance, by the man who was set to watch me, and fetching the key he opened the gate without hesitation.

My hopes were instantly excited. I made a short turn and crossed him, as if continuing my walk, a few yards distant from the gate. He eyed me however, and I went on; but, the moment he was busied in unlocking and unbolting it, I turned round, sprang forward, and as it opened rushed past.

The violence of my motion overset Mac Fane. The master, whose suspicions had taken the alarm, was entering the garden and saw me. He and his man and Mac Fane instantly joined in the pursuit.

Though I was in the strait waistcoat, yet I happened to be swifter than any of them. The keeper was soon the first in the chase: it was up a narrow lane, with a high-banked hedge on each side. A man was coming down it; and the keeper called to him to stop me. The man seeing my arms confined, and hearing the shouts of my pursuers, endeavoured to do as he was desired. He placed himself directly in my way, and I ran full against him.

We both fell; but the man by the aid of his hands was up rather the soonest. He laid hold of me, and a sudden thought struck me. They were bawling behind—'A madman! A madman!'—and I assumed that grinning contortion of countenance which might easiest terrify, uttered an uncouth noise, and began to bite at the man. Terror seized him, and I again got away, the very moment the keeper was coming up.

I had not run a hundred yards further before I saw another man at a distance, and the hue and cry behind was as hot as ever. The hedge in this place was lower, and I jumped over it into the field on my right. There was a ditch on the other side, of which I had no intimation; and my feet alighting on the edge of it, I once more fell.

My pursuers profited by a gate, which I had passed. It was the field of a gardener, and a man was at work close by. He came and helped me up; but not soon enough: the keeper arrived, and presently after his man and Mac Fane.

I addressed myself to the gardener, endeavoured to tell him who I was, and said I would give him a hundred pounds, if he would aid me to escape: but my efforts were soon put an end to by the keeper, who threw me down, a second time violently thrust his thumb into my throat, and by gagging me prevented further speech.

Mac Fane however thought proper to give the man half a crown, and they all assured him I was a madman; which story was confirmed by the man who supposed himself bitten, and who had joined in the pursuit.

The extreme malevolence of Mac Fane again displayed itself: but his treatment is unworthy notice, except as it relates to what is to come.

I was hurried back to my prison, left with the strait waistcoat on that whole day and night, and was fed by the boy; who shewed many silent tokens of commiseration, though once more watched by the keeper and his two attendants, with the three chains up at the door. All conversations between me and the boy were for several days ended, by the continued overlooking of the keeper and his men.

After the keeper and Mac Fane had retired, I went into the back room, and was standing with my face toward the window, which is beside the closet. The behaviour of Mac Fane had been so extraordinary as already to lead me to suspect he had a wish to take away my life.

As I was standing here, I heard the keeper's bed-room door

open and shut again, and soon after the voices of him and Mac Fane in conversation. I listened very attentively to a dialogue, the substance of which was to me much more alarming than unexpected. It was a consultation, on the part of Mac Fane, on the policy and means of murdering me.

The keeper opposed him, several times mentioned Mr. Clifton as an unconquerable objection, and urged the danger of being detected; for he did not seem to revolt at the fact.

Mac Fane answered he would silence Clifton; of whom his favourite phrase was that 'He should soon do him!'—which he repeated very often, with a variety of uncommon oaths. He even said that, were I fairly out of the way, he could make Edward St. Ives pay him the three thousand guineas.

The curses which Mac Fane continually coupled with my name, and the rancour, the thirst of blood which preyed upon him, were incredible. He a hundred times imprecated eternal damnation to his soul if there were the least danger. The fellows the keeper had with him were of his own providing: they knew he could hang them both: they durst not impeach. [*Squeak*, I recollect, was the word he used.] To take me off was the safest way. Clifton would in reality be an accessary before the fact, and therefore obliged to silence. Beside—'He would do him! He would do him!'—This he confirmed by a new string of oaths.

The keeper however continued averse to the project, said the fellows would hang their own father if he could not bribe them, that there was nothing to be got by putting me out of the way, and that he would not venture his neck unless he saw good cause.

While they were arguing the point, a loud and authoritative rap was heard at the keeper's door, accompanied by the voice of Mr. Clifton, demanding admission. He entered, and the whole story of my escape was related, with that colouring which their own fears inspired.

MacFane darkly hinted the thoughts he had been communicating to the keeper; but, meeting repulse from Mr. Clifton whenever ideas of cruelty were started, he thought proper to use more reserve.

The keeper concluded his account by affirming it would be necessary to continue me in the strait waistcoat, and not to let me walk in the garden any more. Mr. Clifton assented to the latter, but positively ordered my arms to be released. There was no need he said to punish me in this manner, and it should not be. At the same time he gave the keeper a twenty pound note, and repeated his orders to treat me properly, but to take care not to suffer me to escape.

Misguided man! How does your heart pant after virtue! How grieve at the slavery in which it is held! What will its agony be, when the full measure of error is come!

Yet this to me was the lucid moment of hope, for it suggested a train of conclusions which seem like heavenly certainties—Mr. Clifton had made his attempts on Anna St. Ives, and they have been repelled! Even still, and it is several days since, his efforts continue to be ineffectual!—It must be so!—The purposes of vice are frustrated by the pure energies of virtue: for, had they succeeded, I should be released. Heart-cheering thought! Pleasure inexpressible! Yes, Anna St. Ives is safe! Truth is omnipotent; and out of my ashes another, and probably a more strenuous and determined assertor of it may arise! Clifton at last may see how very foul is folly, and turn to wisdom! Would he might be spared the guilt of purchasing conviction at the price of blood!

Three days passed away, after my escape, without any remarkable occurrence. The sanguinary malignity of Mac Fane was more than counterbalanced, by the reasonings of probability and hope in favour of Anna St. Ives.

During my confinement, I had slept but little. Wearied however at length, by the repetition of ideas that were unavailing, I was slumbering more soundly than usual on the night after the ninth day; and was dreaming that my doors were unbolted, the chains rattling, and men entering to murder me; from which I was waked by starting in my dream to run and resist them. It was the real clanking of the bolts and locks of the house doors that inspired this dream; they opened to give some one admission. I know not what was the hour, but it must be very late, and it was completely dark. I soon distinguished Mac Fane's voice. I jumped up, hastily dressed myself in part, and presently heard the keeper's door open—The ray of light appeared on the wall—I crept toward the closet.

The first word Mac Fane uttered was—'I told you I should do him!—I told you I should do him!'

He kept repeating this and other exclamations, which I could not at first comprehend, closing each of them with oaths expressive of uncommon exultation. But he descanted almost instantly from Mr. Clifton, to whom his phrase alluded, to me; adding—it was high time now to do me too.

His joy was so great, his oaths so multiplied, and his asseverations so continual, that he would tread me out, would send my soul to hell that very night, and other similar phrases, that it was some time before the keeper could obtain an answer to his question of—'What does all this mean?' At last Mr. Mac Fane began to relate, as soberly as the intoxication of his mind would permit, that he had done him [Mr. Clifton] out of ten thousand pounds.

Had he got the money?

No——But God shiver his soul to flames if he did not make him pay! He would blow him to powder, drink his blood, eat his bones if he did not!

This was not all—He had another prize! Eight thousand pounds! The money was now in the house!

He stopped short—The cupidity of the keeper was excited, and he grew impatient. Mac Fane I imagine hesitated to reconsider if it were possible to get all the money himself, make away with me secretly, and leave the keeper in ignorance. But he could not but conclude this to be impracticable.

I could not sufficiently connect the meaning of all the phrases that followed; they might depend as much on seeing as hearing; but I understood Mac Fane was acquainted with the circumstance of the money I have in my possession; though whether his knowledge were gained from Mr. Clifton or Anna St. Ives, for they were both mentioned, I could not distinguish. He talked much of a letter, of his own cunning, and of the contempt in which he held Mr. Clifton.

The keeper however was convinced of the fact, for he proposed immediately to murder me, and secure the money.

This point was for some time debated, and I every moment expected they would leave the room, to perpetrate the crime. Mac Fane had his pistols and cutlass, yet seemed to suppose a possibility even of my conquering them. The keeper was much more confident—'He knew how to bring me down; he had no fear of that.' —Mac Fane remembered his defeat, and the keeper his cheaply bought victory.

460 ANNA ST. IVES

They agreed it could not be done silently, unless they could catch me asleep, and the unbolting of the doors would awaken me. They wished the keeper's fellows to know nothing of the matter; they would claim their share.

At last Mac Fane proposed that I should be put in the strait waistcoat the next morning, on pretence of walking me out in the garden; that perhaps it would be best to suffer me to walk there, but not to take off the strait waistcoat any more; that then the doors might be left unbolted, and even unlocked, my arms being confined; and the next night they might come and dispatch me!

The conversation continued long after this, and schemes of flight, either to Ireland or the continent, were concerted, and the riches and happiness they should enjoy insisted on, with great self-applause and pleasure. Poor, mistaken men!

They at last parted, with a determination to execute the scheme of the strait waistcoat. Mac Fane took possession of the keeper's bed; and he as I imagine went to that of his men.

And here I must remark that Mac Fane either forgot or did not imagine that my immediate murder would be an impediment to the payment of the ten thousand pound gaming debt, from Mr. Clifton; which fear afterward actuated him strongly. It could not do otherwise, the moment it was conceived.

According to agreement, in the morning the keeper came, with as much pretended kindness as he knew how to assume, to tell me I might have my walk in the garden again, if I pleased. I answered I did not wish to walk. He endeavoured to persuade me, but he soon found it was to no purpose. He then ordered the boy away, who had brought the strait waistcoat, and quitted his station at the door in great dudgeon.

I soon afterward heard, as I expected, Mac Fane and him in his own room. Mac Fane cursed the keeper bitterly, and supposed that, for want of cunning, he had in part betrayed himself, and rendered me suspicious. The keeper resented his behaviour and cursed again, till I imagined they had fairly quarrelled.

Mac Fane however began to cool, and to talk of another expedient of which he had been thinking. This was to poison me. In this the keeper immediately joined, and began to enquire about the means of procuring the poison. The boy was first mentioned, but that was thought too dangerous. At last Mac Fane determined himself to go to London and buy arsenic, on pretence of poisoning rats, and to set off immediately. On this they concluded, and presently left the room.

My whole attention was now employed in watching the opening of the keeper's door; but there was reason to apprehend they would converse somewhere else on their projects. I imagine however they thought this the safest and most inaccessible place, for a little before dark I again heard the voice of Mac Fane, and they presently came back to their former station.

Mac Fane related the difficulty he had found in getting the arsenic; that several shops had refused him; and that at last he had succeeded by ordering a quantity of drugs, for which he paid, leaving them to be sent to a fictitious address, and returning back pretending he wanted some poison for the rats, asking them which was the best. They recommended arsenic, which they directed him to make up in balls, and he ordered a quarter of a pound. They weighed it, he put it in his pocket, and they noticed the circumstance, telling him they would send it home with the other drugs; but he walked away pretending not to hear what they said.

Mac Fane, glorying in his own cunning, was impatient to administer his drug, and proposed it should be sent up in my tea. The keeper assented, and the boy very soon afterward brought me some tea in a pot ready made, contrary to custom, I having been used to make my own tea.

The keeper was at the door. I asked him the reason of this deviation; and he bade me drink my tea and be thankful. I poured some out, first looked at it, then tasted it, and afterwards threw it into the ashes, saying it was bad tea. I next examined the tea-pot, smelled into it, and then dashed it to pieces on the hearth. I looked toward the keeper and told him there was something in the tea that ought not to have been.

Seeing me take up the candle and begin to move, he instantly shut the door. His conscience was alarmed, and for a moment he forgot the security of his chains. He even called up his men before he opened it again; after which the boy was released, but not before I had time to tell him never to eat any thing that was brought for me. The poor boy noticed the significance with which I said it, and fixed his eyes mournfully upon me. I shook him by the hand, bade him be a good boy, and not learn wickedness from his master.

H h

The remains of the tea-set were soon removed, and a fresh consultation presently began in the keeper's room. Mac Fane was again enraged, and blamed the keeper; who began to suppose there was something supernatural in my behaviour. He said I looked at him as if I knew it was poison, and it was very strange! Mac Fane swore he would dose me at supper, and would go and make me eat it himself, or blow my brains out; but he presently recollected I had not the strait waistcoat on, and altered his tone. It was however agreed that another attempt should be made.

I now began to consider all circumstances; whether it were probable, if I ate a little, that the keeper should suppose it only a temporary want of appetite; what quantity might be eaten without harm, and if it were not practicable to watch the moment when they should come, by night, to execute their wicked purpose, and to pass them and escape? A little reasoning shewed me that I should be in the dark, in a house the avenues to which were all secured, and with which I was unacquainted; that the number I had to contend with now would be four, three of them provided with bludgeons, and the fourth with a hanger and pistols; that release by the order of Mr. Clifton was not impossible; and that, if I began a fray, I should excite cowardice to action; and, having begun, Mac Fane would scarcely miss such an opportunity.

These reasons made me rather resolve to persevere in fasting; which remedy, though it could not be of long duration, appeared to be the wisest. Yet caution was necessary, for, should I make them absolutely despair of poisoning me, they would have recourse to other means.

My resolution was taken, and when the supper came I tasted a bit of bread and drank a small quantity of water, after carefully inspecting it, and without saying any thing more sent the rest away.

The keeper's door soon opened, the ray of light appeared on the wall, and a new consultation succeeded. The keeper again was troubled with superstitious fears; and Mac Fane was persuaded that, having been alarmed at tea-time, I had from suspicion refused to eat any supper.

After a debate, they concluded it would be in vain to attempt

to poison me in my tea, for I should detect it: they would therefore send me a short allowance at breakfast, keep me hungry,
and prepare my dinner for the next day. The keeper proposed
to give me no breakfast, but Mac Fane said that was the way
to make me suspect.

They were both highly chagrined; but Mac Fane was much
the most talkative at all times, and the loudest in oaths and menaces: though I scarcely think even him a more dangerous man
than the keeper.

In the morning, observing they had sent agreeable to their
plan a small quantity, after a little examination I ate what was
brought me, and the keeper retired apparently satisfied.

It was far otherwise at dinner, when I absolutely refused to
eat; and their vexation was greatly increased by my persisting
to refuse the whole day.

Late at night a new council was held, and it was long in debate
whether I should be suffered to live the night out. At last the
cupidity of Mac Fane prevailed, and his fear of not getting Mr.
Clifton's bond for eleven thousand pounds, as he said, though
I understood he had won but ten, seems now to have first struck
him; and this induced him to desist. I understood however that
Mac Fane had still some hopes from his poison, and consequently
that to fast would still be necessary.

Their final resolve was that, the moment Mr. Clifton should
have given Mac Fane the bond, they would then delay no longer:
and, from the threats which he vaunted of having used, he expected the bond to be given the next day, when Mr. Clifton was
to come to the keeper's, if I understood them rightly, after his
visit to Anna St. Ives.

This idea again conjured up torturing images, and fears which
no efforts I have been able to make can entirely appease.

I began this narrative the first day on which I found my life
was in danger, and have continued it to this time, which is now
the twelfth day of my confinement. The desire which the keeper
expresses to possess himself of the money convinces me of my
great jeopardy. He was eager to have committed the murder last
night, during the last conversation I heard. That I should escape
with life from the hands of these wicked men is but little probable;
but I will not desert myself; I will not forward an act of blood by

timidity. Were I to destroy the bank-bills, and to tell them they
were destroyed, I should not be believed. I mean to try another
expedient—I hear them in the keeper's room!

These are the last words I shall ever write. They are determined
on immediate murder—But I will sell my life dearly.   *   *   *
*   *   *   *   *   *   *   *   *   *   *   *   *   *
*   *   *   *   *   *   *   *   *   *   *   *   *   *

LETTER CXXVI

Anna Wenbourne St. Ives to Louisa Clifton

Oh my friend! I am escaped! Have broken my prison and am
sitting now—I cannot tell you where, but in a place of safety.
I have been thus successful by the aid of Laura.

It is now four days since I saw your brother. Lulled to security
by the peaceable manner in which I had submitted to confinement,
and imagining Laura to be still in the interest of Mr. Clifton,
though this silly girl is now a very sincere penitent, the old woman
began to indulge her in still greater liberties. I warned Laura very
seriously against any precipitate attempts, for I saw it was probable this incautiousness would increase, provided it were
encouraged.

No good opportunity offered till this morning, when Laura
was suffered to take the key of my prison chamber, and let herself
in and out.

The moment she told me of it I enquired what other obstacles
there were. Laura said we might get into the yard, but no further,
for there was a high wall which no woman could climb. I asked
her if she thought a man could climb it? She answered, yes, she
had seen men do such things, but she could not think how.

The absence of Mr. Clifton for so long a time, without releasing
me from my imprisonment, made me in hourly expectation of his
return. I therefore did not stay to hesitate, but desired Laura to
steal down stairs before me, and open the door, for that I was
determined to attempt the wall.

Laura was terrified at the fear of being left behind, for she said she never could climb it. 'Alas! What was to become of her?'—I told her she should have thought of consequences long ago; but that she might be certain I would not desert her: on the contrary, I would go to the first house I could find and send her relief, if I should happen to climb a wall which she could not. Though, I likewise added, it was weakness and folly to suppose that men were better able to climb walls than women, or that she could not follow, if I could lead.

The assurance of relief in part quieted her fears: she opened the first door, stole down to the second, I followed, she unlocked it, and we both got into the yard.

The wall as she said was high and not easily climbed; but I had little time for reflection: the old woman saw us through the window, and was coming.

To this wall there was a gate, equally high, but with a handle to shut, ledges running across, and two or three cracked places that afforded hold for the hand. You and I, Louisa, have often discoursed on the excellence of active courage, and the much greater efforts of which both sexes are capable than either of them imagine. I climbed the gate with great speed and little difficulty.

The old woman was already in the yard, and Laura stood wondering to see me on the top of the wall, fearing I should now break my neck in getting down again, and still in greater terror at the approach of the old woman. I made some attempt to persuade the latter to give Laura her liberty; but our turn-key is very deaf, and instead of listening to me she ran for some offensive weapon to beat me off the wall: so, once more assuring Laura I would send her immediate aid, and keeping hold of the gate post with my hand, I let myself down and with very little hurt.

I proceeded along a narrow lane; I knew not in what direction, but hurried forward in great haste; not only from the possibility of being pursued, but because it began to blow and rain very heavily. In less than ten minutes I came to a house: I rang, a man came to the gate, and I readily gained admission.

I was shewn into the room where I am now writing, and another person was sent to me, who perhaps is the master of the house, though from his appearance I should rather suppose the contrary. I asked first if it were possible to get a coach; and he enquired where I came from? I told him, from a house at a considerable distance, in the same lane, where I had been forcibly shut up, and where my maid still was, whom I wished to have released; adding I would well reward any two men, by whom it might easily be effected, if they would go and help her over the wall.

He listened very attentively, stood some time to consider, and then replied there was no coach to be procured within a mile of the place, but that a man should go for one; and that I might make myself easy concerning the young woman (Laura) for she should soon join me. The look and manner of the man did not please me, but the case was urgent, the storm increasing, and I in want of shelter and protection.

I then recollected it would perhaps be safest to write immediately to Grosvenor-Street, to prevent surprise as well as to guard against accidents, and I asked if he could furnish me with a sheet of paper and pen and ink. He answered he feared not, but called a boy, and said to him—'Did not I see you with some writing paper the other day?' The boy answered yes; and he bade him go and fetch it, and bring me the pen and ink.

He then left me, and the boy presently returned, with a sheet of paper, an old ink-bottle, and a very indifferent pen. The boy looked at me earnestly, and then examined the pen, saying it was a very bad one, but he would fetch me a better.

The man who was just gone had told me that nobody could be spared, to go as far as I required, in less than an hour at the soonest; I therefore have time to write at length.

I think there can be little doubt but that my Louisa is long before this in Grosvenor-Street. I would not wish Sir Arthur to be informed too suddenly, I will therefore direct to her at a venture; but for fear of accidents will add to the direction—'If Miss Clifton be not there, to be opened and read by Mrs. Clarke.'—In the present alarmed state of the family this will ensure its being opened, even if both my good friends should be absent.

Good heaven! What does this mean?—I have just risen to

see if the little boy were within call, and find the door is locked upon me!

I have been listening!—I hear stern and loud voices!—I fear I have been very inconsiderate!—I know not what to think!

Where am I?—Oh, Louisa, I am seized with terror! Looking into the table-drawer at which I am sitting, in search of wafers,[1] I have found my own letter; opened, dirtied, and worn! Alas! You know of no such letter!—Again I am addressing myself to the winds!—The very fatal letter in which I mentioned the eight thousand pounds!—Where am I, where am I?—In what is all this to end?

All is lost!—Flight is hopeless!—The very man who headed the ruffians that seized me has just walked into the room, placed himself with his back against the door, surveyed me, satisfied himself who it was, then warily left me, locked the door, and called a man to guard it!—Oh my incautious folly!

I am in the dwelling of demons!—I never heard such horrible oaths!—Surely there is some peculiar mischief working!—The noise increases, with unheard-of blasphemy!

Merciful Heaven! I hear the voice of Frank!—What is doing? —Must I remain here?—Oh misery!——What cries!   *   *
*   *   *   *   *   *   *   *   *   *   *   *   *   *
*   *   *   *   *   *   *   *   *   *   *   *   *   *

LETTER CXXVII

Coke Clifton to Guy Fairfax

London, Dover Street

ALL is over, Fairfax!—I am just brought from the scene of blood!—You see this is not my hand-writing—My hand must never write more—But I would employ the little strength I have, in relating 'the last scene of this eventful history'.[1] My sister is my amanuensis. These surgical meddlers issued their edict that I should not speak; but they found I could be as obstinate as themselves: I would not suffer a probe to be drawn at me till I had written, for when they begin I expect it will soon be over.

I remember I ended my last at the very minute I was about to mount my horse. It was a wintery day. The rain fell in sheets, and the wind roared in my face. My pistols were charged and locked in my pocket.

I rode full speed, but I set off too late! When I approached the madhouse, I heard the most piercing shrieks and cries of murder! —They mingled with the storm, in wild and appalling horror!— I rang violently at the bell! . . . A ready and an eager hand soon flew to open the gate—It was Anna St. Ives!—A boy shewed her the way—It was her cries and his, mingled with the blasphemies of the wretches above, which I had heard!

Her first word again was murder!—'Fly! Save him, save him!'—

I rushed forward—The noise above stairs was dreadful— I blundered and missed the stairs, but the terrified boy had run after me to shew me. I heard two pistols fire as I ascended—The horror that struck my heart was inconceivable!—A fellow armed with a bludgeon was standing to guard the door. My pistols were unlocked and ready: I presented and bade him give way—He instantly obeyed—I made the lock fly and entered!—The first object that struck my sight was Frank, besmeared with blood, a discharged pistol in his hand, defending himself against a fellow aiming blows at him with a bludgeon, Mac Fane hewing at him with a cutlass, and the keeper, who had just been shot, expiring at his feet!

I fired at Mac Fane—My shot took place, though not so effectually but that he turned round, made a stab at me, and pierced the abdomen almost to the spine. But he had met his fate; and the return he made was most welcome!—He fell, and the remaining antagonists of Frank immediately fled.

Frank is living, but dreadfully hacked by the villain Mac Fane. They tell me his life is safe, and that his wounds are deep, but not dangerous. Perhaps they mean to deceive me. If so their folly is extreme, and their pity to me ill placed. I well know I deserve no pity.

With respect to myself, my little knowledge of surgery teaches me that a wound so violent, made with a cutlass in such a part, must be mortal. But mortality to me is a blessing. To live would indeed be misery. Torments never yet were imagined equal to those I have for some time endured: but, though I have lived raving, I do not mean to die canting. Take this last adieu therefore, dear Fairfax, and do not because you once esteemed me endeavour to palliate my errors. Let my letters to you do justice to those I have injured. To have saved his life who once saved mine, is a ray of consolation to that proud swelling heart, which has sometimes delighted to confer, but has always turned averse from the receiving of obligations. I would have been more circumstantial in my narrative, were it not for the teasing kindness of my sister.

Once more, and everlastingly, adieu!

                                        C. CLIFTON

P.S. ADDED BY LOUISA CLIFTON

As to a friend of my brother, sir, I have taken the liberty to delay sending the letter, till his wound has been examined. The surgeons are divided in their judgment. Two of them affirm the wound is mortal; the third is positive that a cure is possible; especially considering the youth and high courage of the patient, on which he particularly insists. I dare not indulge myself too much in hope: I merely state opinion. Neither dare I speak of my own sensations. Of the worth of a mind like that of Mr. Clifton, you, sir, his friend and correspondent, cannot be ignorant. The past is irrevocable; but hope always smiles on the future. Should he recover—! Resignation becomes us, and time will quickly relieve us from doubt.

                                        L. CLIFTON

LETTER CXXVIII

Anna Wenbourne St. Ives to Mrs. Wenbourne

Grosvenor-Street

I RETURN you my sincere thanks, dear madam, for your kind congratulations; and think myself honoured by the great joy you express, at my safety and the deliverance of Mr. Henley. I will not attempt to describe my own feelings; they are inexpressible; but will endeavour to obey your commands, and give you the best account I am able of all that has befallen us.

For this purpose, I inclose the narrative written by Mr. Henley during his confinement; and three letters addressed to my friend, Louisa, but never sent; with a copy of a letter dictated by Mr. Clifton to his friend, Mr. Fairfax. To these be pleased to add the following particulars of what passed after Mr. Henley's narrative breaks off, and the sudden interruption of my third letter by terror.

Mr. Henley heard but had no time to write their last consultation. It was the eagerness of the keeper which overcame the reluctance of Mac Fane to the murder, till he should have procured the bond of Mr. Clifton. The keeper was violent: he had bargained with his two men to assist in the murder, for fifty pounds each; and he told Mac Fane, if he would not consent, they would proceed without him, and he should have no share of the eight thousand pounds.

This argument had its effect: Mac Fane had some doubts relative to the money won of Mr. Clifton; and four thousand pounds was a temptation not to be resisted.

Mr. Henley omitted mentioning a circumstance that occurred of some moment, because he did not know the meaning of it. Probably they had planned it out of his hearing. The day before the attack, the keeper returned him his watch and purse, with the same sum, but not, as Mr. Henley thinks, the same pieces, it contained when delivered. The purpose of this, it appears, was to make him believe the keeper a man of his word.

On the morning of the intended murder, previous to the assault, the keeper came up to Mr. Henley; but not into the room. He talked to him with the usual security of his chains, and proposed that Mr. Henley should deliver up the bank-bills, which the keeper now told him he knew to be in his possession; with a promise that they should be returned, as the watch and purse had been.

An artifice so shallow was not likely to impose on Mr. Henley. He had determined how to act, relative to the bank bills, and answered it was true they were in his possession; but that he would not deliver them to the keeping of any other. Immediately after this repulse, the keeper, Mac Fane, and the two attendants ascended.

The keeper (I speak after Mr. Henley) was much the most confident, and seemed chiefly fearful that Mr. Henley should slip by them. He therefore stationed one of his men at the outside of the door, which he ordered him to lock and guard. Himself, Mac Fane, and the other entered the room; the keeper and the man each with a bludgeon, and Mac Fane with a pair of pistols and his cutlass hanging by his side.

Mr. Henley had purposely kept up a good fire, and had the bank bills in his hand. He bade them keep off a moment, as if he wished to parley; and they, desirous of having the bills quietly, remained where they were. Mr. Henley then took the bills one by one, repeating the amount of each to convince them that the whole sum was there, and then suddenly thrust them into the fire. They all rushed forward to save them, and this was the lucky moment on which Mr. Henley seized the two arms of Mac Fane, who, on account of his weapons, was the principal object, and who, intending to fire at him, in the struggle shot the keeper. The other pistol Mr. Henley wrested from him, during which contest it went off, but without doing mischief.

Mac Fane then drew his hanger, and made several cuts at Mr. Henley, who was attacked on the other side by the keeper's man.

In the heat of this conflict Mr. Clifton arrived; and what then followed, his letter will inform you.

It is necessary I should now say a word of myself, and of the small part which I had in this very dreadful affair. And here I must remind you of the boy, so often mentioned in Mr. Henley's narrative; for to him, perhaps, we all owe our safety. At least, had it not been for him, Mr. Clifton could not certainly have gained admission.

The poor fellow heard and saw enough to let him understand

some strange crime was in agitation. He has great acuteness and sensibility: he looked at me when I first came, in a very significant manner; and would have spoken had he dared.

The door of the room in which I was shut was both locked and bolted; but the man that was set to guard it was wanted, for a more blood-thirsty purpose.

I need not inform you how much my fears were alarmed, the moment I found myself in the custody of the man by whom I had at first been seized. But how infinitely was my terror increased when I heard the voice of Frank, which I did very distinctly, and presently afterward of the horror about to be committed! My shrieks were incessant! The poor boy heard them, and though shrieking with terror almost as violent as my own, yet had the presence of mind to come and set me free.

Mr. Clifton's ringing was heard at the same moment. The top bolt of the gate was high, and I opened it with difficulty; but despair lent me force. It certainly could not have been opened time enough by the boy.

Of this and the following scene, and of the agonizing sensations that accompanied them, I will attempt no further description. I will now only relate by what means, and whose aid, we left this house of horror.

You know, madam, with what activity my dear Louisa exerted herself, and employed every expedient in her power. You are likewise acquainted with the zeal of Mrs. Clarke, her niece Peggy, and the two men, her husband and brother. Their ardour increased rather than abated.

Mr. Webb, whose watchings and efforts were incessant, saw Mac Fane step out of a hackney-coach into the shop where Mr. Clifton lodges. This I understand to have happened on the ninth evening of my confinement. It was natural that this circumstance should immediately excite suspicion and alarm. The coach was dismissed, Mac Fane remained, and Mr. Webb continued hovering about the door, waiting in expectation of seeing him come out, till two o'clock in the morning, but waiting in vain: after which, concluding that he had missed him, he quitted his post.

On the morrow, by very diligent enquiry, he found out Mac Fane's lodgings; but he had not been at home all night. The same ineffectual search was continued during that and the next day; but, on the morning of deliverance, Mr. Webb met a person with whom he had formerly been acquainted, who told him of the house hired by the keeper, and mentioned the names of his two assistants, with rumours and surmises sufficiently dark and unintelligible, but enough to make Mr. Webb suppose it was possible the persons he was in search of were there confined.

The intelligence was immediately brought to Louisa and Sir Arthur, and application as immediately made to the magistracy. Webb had obtained very accurate information of the site of the house; and, what was more effectual, had prevailed on his informer to lend his aid.

The relief he brought, though too late to prevent mischief, was not wholly useless; Mr. Clifton was the first object of our care; for Mr. Henley, though bruised, cut, and mangled has received no serious injury. Laura was likewise sent for and relieved from her prison. Proper conveyances were soon provided, and we all removed as fast as possible from this scene of horror.

You may be sure, madam, we did not forget to bring the boy with us. Mr. Henley has an affection for him, which the poor fellow very sincerely returns; and finds himself relieved from the most miserable of situations, and placed in the most happy.

That I may wholly acquit myself of the task I have undertaken, I must just mention the Count de Beaunoir. He is a gentleman of the most pleasant temper. Urbanity is his distinctive mark, for in this quality most of his flights originate. He has thought himself my admirer, but in reality he is the general admirer of whatever he supposes excellent. When he was told of my being affianced to Mr. Henley, instead of expressing chagrin, he broke into raptures at our mutual happiness, and how much it was merited. He does not seem to understand the selfishness of jealousy.

Perhaps, madam, you have not heard the last accounts of the physical gentlemen, relative to Mr. Clifton. The surgeon who first gave hope is now positive of a cure; and his opponents begin to own it is not impossible, but they will not yet allow that Mr. Clifton is out of danger.

The Count de Beaunoir has paid Mr. Clifton the utmost attention; he visits him twice a day, and, according to the accounts my friend gives me, infuses a spirit of benevolence and affection into his visits which are highly honourable to his heart. Indeed I and

Mr. Henley have several times met him there: for you may well imagine, madam, we are not the least attentive of Mr. Clifton's visitors. It is at present the sole study of Mr. Henley, which way best to address himself to a heart and understanding so capable of generous sensations, and noble energies. There is an attachment to consistency in the human mind, which will not admit of any sudden and absolute change; it must be gradual: but thus much may with certainty be said, Mr. Clifton does not at present, and I hope will never again, treat with complacency those vindictive but erroneous notions which had so nearly proved destructive to all. He makes no professions; but so much the better; he thinks them the more strongly. His mind preserves its usual tone; is sometimes disturbed even to excess, and bitterly angry, almost to phrensy, at its own mistakes; but has lost none of those quick and powerful qualities, by which it is so highly distinguished.

Sir Arthur, madam, has desired me to communicate a circumstance, which I shall readily do, without the false delicacy of supposing that I am not the proper person. It is agreed, between him and Mr. Abimelech Henley, that the marriage between me and Mr. Frank Henley shall take place in a month; to which I thought it my duty to assent. I am sorry, madam, that Lord Fitz-Allen should continue to imagine his honour will be sullied by this marriage: but I am in like manner sorry for a thousand follies, which I daily see in the world, without having the immediate power of correcting one of them.

A. W. ST. IVES

LETTER CXXIX
Coke Clifton to Guy Fairfax

London, Dover-Street

IT is not to be endured! They drive me mad! I will not have life thus palmed upon me! There is neither kindness nor justice in it. I will hear no more of duty, and philanthropy, and general good! I am all fiend!—Hell-born!—The boon companion of the foulest miscreants the womb of sin ever vomited on earth!—The arm in arm familiar of them!——In the face of the world!—This it is to be honourable!—I—I am a man of honour, a despiser of peasants, an assertor of rank!—

Day after day, hour after hour, here I lie, rolling, ruminating on ideas which none but demons could suggest; haunted by visions which devils only could conjure up! And wish me to live? Where is the charity of that? Angels though they be, they have made me miserable! I know I have injured them; I don't deny it. Say what they will, they cannot forgive me—Shall I ask it?—No!—Hell should not make me! I will have no more favours; I am loaded too much already.

For it cannot be true!——Their hearts can feel no kindness for me!—Oh!—

I have lost her!—For ever lost her!—Yet even this deep damnation I could bear, I think I could, had I not made myself so very foul and detestable a villain!——It is intolerable!—The rage of cannibals to mine is patience! I could feed on human hearts; my own the first and sweetest morsel!

Well, well!—Her I have lost; him I have injured!——Injured? ——Arrogance, outrage, contempt, blows, imprisonment, and murder!——These are the damning injuries I have done him!— I took greatness upon me; I mimicked tyranny, and pretended to inflict large vengeance for petty affronts!——I trusted in wiles, and imagined mind might be caught in a net!

Lo how the adder egg of vanity can brood in its own dunghill, and hatch itself[1] to persecution, rape, and murder!—Lo how Guilt and Folly couple, and engender darkness to hide their own deformity!——The picture is mine!——Black, midnight rape, and blood red murder! A horrid but indubitable likeness.

There are but two ways, either to live and pursue revenge, or to die and forget it—Of the pursuit I am weary. I have had a full meal of villany, and am glutted: its foulness is insufferable, and I turn from it loathing. Then welcome death! Again it would have sought me, but for their eternal officiousness. It is in vain. There are swords, pistols, and poison still. Life has a thousand outlets: and to live, knowing what I know and never can forget, would be rank and hateful cowardice! I am determined. I will listen to their glosses no more. Persuasion is vain, and soothing mockery.

Yet one act of justice I will perform before I die. Send me my letters, Fairfax. They shall see me in my native colours!——Send them directly!——There is consolation in the thought——They have dared to shew letters that exposed them to persecution and malice—I will shew what shall expose me to contempt and hatred!——Let them equal me if they can—I am Clifton!—Inimitable in absurdity, in vice damnable!—

Take copies if you will. Proclaim me to the world! Read them in coffee-houses, nail them up at the market cross! Let boys hoot at me, and trulls and drabs pluck me by the beard!——What can they?——It is I, myself, who hold the scorpion whip!—'Tis memory!—What! Envy, rage, revenge, hatred, rape and murder, all possessing one man?——Poor creature! Poor creature!—Pity him, Fairfax!—Pity?—Ask pity?—Despise him! Trample on him! Spit in his face!

C. CLIFTON

LETTER CXXX

Frank Henley to Oliver Trenchard

London, Grosvenor Street

How violent and reiterated are the conflicts, between truth and error, in every mind of ardour!—And, of all errors, the love of self is the most rooted, the least easy to detect, and supremely difficult to eradicate. We can pardon ourselves any thing, except a want of self-respect; but that is intolerable.

I described, in my last,* the dissatisfied state of mind of Mr. Clifton. But, while he imagined he should die and soon lose all memory of a scene become so irksome to him, his dissatisfaction was trifling, compared to what it is at present. Repugnant as the idea was to his habitual feelings, still I have more than half convinced him that suicide is an act as cowardly as it is criminal. Yet to live and face the world, loaded as he imagines with unpardonable

* Omitted.

crimes and everlasting ignominy, is a thing to which he knows not how to consent. To combat this new mistake, into which he has fallen, has for some time past been my chief employment. No common efforts could assuage the turbulence of his tempestuous soul. Energy superior even to his own was necessary, to subject and calm this perturbation. But, in the simplicity of truth, this energy was easy to be found: it is from self-distrust, confusion or coward-ice, if it ever fail.

I have just left him, and our conversation will give you the best history of his mind, which is well worthy our study. I found him verging even toward delirium, and a fever coming on, which if not impeded might soon be fatal. He keeps his bed; but instead of lying at his ease, he remained raised on his elbow, having just finished a letter to his friend. Louisa had described the state of his mind, and I resolved to catch its tone, that I might the more certainly command his attention. Without preface, and as if con-tinuing a chain of reasoning, he addressed me; with his eye fixed, in all the ardour of enquiry.

What is man?—What are his functions, qualities, and uses?—Does he not sleep trembling, live envying, and die cursing?—And is this worth aught?—Is it to be endured?—Why do I suffer life thus to be imposed upon me?

It is not suffering: or, if it be, such sufferings are of our own creation—To the virtuous and the wise, life is joy and bliss.

Perhaps so—Wisdom there may be, and truth and virtue. And, for the virtuous and the wise, the full stream of pleasure may richly flow: but not for me! Pretend not that I may walk with the gods! I who have been the inmate of fiends! I, who proposed glory to myself from the most contemptible of pursuits! I, who could dangle after coquettes and prudes; feed on and inflate myself with the baubles of a beauty's toilette; and, in the book of vanity, inscribe myself a great hero, a mighty conqueror, for having heaped ridicule on the ridiculous; or brought innocence to shame, misery, and destruction! And this I did with a light and vain heart! Did it laughing, boasting, exulting! Satanic dog! Pest of hell! What! Stretch souls on the rack, and then girn[1] and mock at them for lying there! 'Tis the sport of devils, and by devils invented!

Your present indignation is honourable both to your heart and understanding.

I i

Oh, flatter me not!—Vain, supercilious coxcomb!—I spread my wings, crowed in conceit, threatened, resolved, laughed at opposition, and kicked the world before me!—Oh, it was who but I!—And what was it I proposed?—Fair conquest?—Honourable opposition?—No!—It was treachery, covert malice, and cowardly conspiracy! A league with hell-dogs!—Horrible, blood-thirsty villains!—And baffled too; defeated, after all this infernal enginery! Nay, had I been so wholly devil as to have joined in murder, what would have followed? Why they would next have murdered me; and for the justice of the second murder would have hoped pardon, even for the hell-born guilt of the first!

Do not, while you detest and shun one crime, plunge into a greater. This agony is for having been unjust to others; you are now still more unjust to yourself. You will not suppose yourself capable of a single virtue: yet, in your most mistaken moments, you never could be so illiberal to your enemies.

Would you persuade me I am not a most guilty, foul, and hateful monster?—Oh be more worthy of yourself, avoid me, detest me, curse me!

I will answer when you are more calm.

Calm?—Never, while this degraded being shall continue, shall such a moment come!—I calm? Sleeping or waking, I at peace? I pardon hypocrisy, treachery, blows, bruises, prisons, chains, poison, rape and murder? Ministers of wrath descend, point here your flaming swords, annihilate all memory of what manhood and honour were, and fit me for the society of the damned!

Forbear!——(Never before did I address him in such a voice—The last dreadful word of his sentence was drowned, by my stern and awful violence; which reason dictated as the only means of recalling his maddening thoughts, from the despair and horror into which they were hurrying—I continued)—Frantic man, forbear! Recall your wild spirits and command them to order. How long will you suffer this petty slavery? How long shall the giant rage, and expend his strength, in tearing up stubble and rending straws?—Stretch forth your hand, and grasp the oak—Labours worthy of your Herculean mind await and invite you. Away to the temple of Error; shake its pillars, and make its foundations totter! —Be yourself—Shall the soaring eagle swoop at reptiles, the prey of bats and owls?

Do not mock me with impossible hopes—What! Have you not held the mirror up to me, and shewn me my own hatefulness?

Are you a man? Will you never shake off this bondage? Oh it is base! it is beneath you! Of what have you been guilty? Why of ignorance, mistakes of the understanding, false views, which you wanted knowledge enough, truth enough, to correct. Have not many of the godlike men whom we admire most been guilty, in their youth, of equal or of greater errors?—Thus, alas, it happens that minds of the highest hope, and most divine stamp and coinage, are cut off daily; swept away by that other grand mistake of man-kind—'Exemplary punishment is necessary'—So they say—But no—'Tis exemplary reformation! Can the world be better warned by a body in gibbets, than by the active virtues of a once misguided but now enlightened understanding? The gibbet will remain an object of terror to the traveller, who dreads being robbed and murdered; but an incitement to despair, in the mind of the mur-derer!—Banish then these black pictures from your mind, by which it continues darkened and misled; and in their stead behold a soul-inspiring prospect, of all that is great and glorious, rising to your view! Feel yourself a man! Nay you shall feel it, in your own despite! A man capable of high and noble actions!

Here, Oliver, I at this time left him. His eye remained fixed, and he was silent; but its wildness was diminished: the frown of his brow disappeared, and his countenance became more clear. Such associations as these tokens denoted ought not to meet interruption. However I took care to return in less than an hour; fearful lest he should decline into his former gloom, which was little short of phrensy. I had been fortunate enough to reduce his discordant feelings to something like harmony; and the moment I entered his room the second time he exclaimed—

You are a generous fellow! A magnanimous fellow! You can work miracles!—I know you of old—Can bring the dead to life!—Can almost persuade me that even I, by living, may now and then effect some trifling, pitiful good; may snatch some of the remnants, the offals of honour—But aught eminent, aught worthy of—

Be calm.

No! It cannot be forgotten, or forgiven!—Cruel, malignant, remorseless wretch!

Can you speak thus of the present?—You know you cannot!—
And wherefore unjustly insist on the past? Be firm! Conquer this
pride of heart!

Why, ay—Pride of heart! It is the very damning sin of my soul!

Exorcise the foul fiend then, and in its stead give welcome to
firm but unassuming self-respect. Arise! Shake torpor from you,
and feel your strength! It is Atlean; made to bear a world! Cherish
life, and become worthy of yourself! What! Would you kill a mind
so mighty? Do you not feel it, now; possessing you, emanating,
flaming, bursting to spread itself?

Why, that were something!—Could I but once again get into
my own good liking—! You are a strange fellow!—You will not
hate me! Nay, will not suffer me to hate myself!—Damnation!
To be cast at such an immense distance! Oh it is intolerable! It is
contemptible!—But I will have my revenge!—Some how or
another I will yet have my revenge! And, since hate must not be
the word, why——! But no matter—I will have no more vaunting—Yet, if I do not——! I have had a glimpse, and begin to know
you—The soul of benevolence, of tenderness, of attention, of
love, of all the divine faculties that make men deities, infuses itself
and pervades you—Had I but been wholly fool, I had been but
partly villain—But I!—Oh monstrous!—The fiends with whom
I was leagued to me were angels!

Why, ay; contemplate the picture, but do not forget it is that of
a man you once knew, who is now no more. He has disappeared,
and in his stead an angel of light is come!

Stop!—Go not too fast!—I promise nothing—Mark that!—
I promise nothing—Do not imagine I am now in the feverish
repentance of white wine whey[1]—You would have me stay in a
world which I myself have rendered hateful—I will think of it—
I know your arts—You would realize the fable of Pygmalion, and
would infuse soul into marble!

There is no need; you have a soul already; inventive, capacious,
munificent, sublime!

Ay, ay—I know—You have a choice collection of words.

A soul of ten thousand! Nay, an army of souls in one!

And must I submit? Are you determined to make a rascal like
me admire, and love, and give place to all the fine affections of
the heart?

Ay, determined!

Oh, sister!—(Louisa at this moment entered.) To you too I have behaved like a scoundrel! A tyrant! A petulant, ostentatious, imperious braggart!

You mistake! replied Louisa, eagerly. You mistake! You are talking of a very different man! A being I could not understand. You are my brother!—My brother!—I have found the way to your heart! Will make it all my own! Will twine myself round it! Shake me off if you can!

The energy with which she spoke, and looked, and kissed him, was irresistible! He was overpowered: the tears gushed to his eyes, but he repressed them; he thought them unmanly; and, seeing his medical friend enter, exclaimed——I have surgeons for the body, and surgeons for the mind, who cut with so deep yet so steady a hand that they take away the noxious, and leave the wound to suppurate and heal!

Can we do less? said I. Ours is no common task! We are acting in behalf of society: we have found a treasure, by which it is to be enriched. Few indeed are those puissant and heavenly endowed spirits, that are capable of guiding, enlightening, and leading the human race onward to felicity! What is there precious but mind? And when mind, like a diamond of uncommon growth, exceeds a certain magnitude, calculation cannot find its value!

I once more left him; and never did I quit the company of human being, no not of Anna St. Ives herself, with a more glowing and hoping heart. But why describe sensations to thee, Oliver, with which thou art so intimately acquainted? To bid thee rejoice, to invite thee to participate in felicity, which may and must so widely diffuse itself, were equally to wrong thy understanding and thy heart.

F. HENLEY

THE END

EXPLANATORY NOTES

Abbreviations

Grose   Captain Frederick Grose, *A Classical Dictionary of the Vulgar Tongue* (1785), edited by Eric Partridge from the 3rd edition of 1796 (1931; 1963).

Hotten   J. C. Hotten, *The Slang Dictionary* (1859; 1925).

E.D.D.   Joseph Wright (ed.), *English Dialect Dictionary* (1904).

O.E.D.   *The Oxford English Dictionary* (1888–1933).

VOLUME I

Page 1. *the divine Sterne*: Sterne's *A Sentimental Journey through France and Italy* (1768). Cf. Vol. ii, p. 66.

Page 9. *Petrarch*: Francesco Petrarch (1304–74), the most celebrated of early love-poets.

Page 12. (1) *hartshorn*: smelling salts.
   (2) *burnt feathers*: used for reviving those who had fainted.

Page 17. *Bow Street 'bloodhunters' and £40*: the 'runners' from the magistrates' offices in Bow Street were the only effective police in London; the system of payment by results made them eager for convictions. Godwin also speaks of 'bloodhunters' in *Caleb Williams* (1794).

Page 19. (1) *ponderaiting*: pondering.

   (2) *bitt* (bit): 'a piece of money of any kind' (Hotten).

   (3) *kole*: money.

   (4) *kintlin*: child.

   (5) *a ten $\overline{m}$ of*: ten thousand.

Page 20. (1) *shiners*: 'sovereigns; or money' (Hotten).
   (2) *bamboozild*: been cheated of; wasted.

Page 21. (1) *squitterd*: spent copiously, wasted.
   (2) *mag*: talk.

Page 28. (1) *espalier*: lattice-work for training trees.

(2) *quincunx*: group of five (trees).

Page 29. (1) *their remains are laid in their kindred clay, as the poet says*: I have been unable to identify the poet; the sentiment is characteristic of eighteenth-century meditative verse.

(2) *Spanish sheep, buffaloes and Chinese pheasants*: eighteenth-century land-owners were fond of the striking effects to be achieved by the importation of exotic flora, and, less often, fauna.

Page 34. *affection, 'masterless passion, had swayed her to its mood'*: cf. *Merchant of Venice*, IV. i; 'masterless' is Rowe's reading of the Folio and Quarto 'master of passion'.

Page 46. *sailing*: moving 'in a stately or dignified manner' (O.E.D.).

Page 54. (1) *peery*: sly, clever.

(2) *lurcher*: clever fellow (variant of lurker, a swindler).

(3) *quaumee* (qualmish): sickly, weak-stomached.

(4) *pickthank*: mischievous.

(5) *pumpkin* (pumpkin-head): fool.

(6) *kole*: money.

(7) *hulver-headed hulk*: wooden-headed oaf: 'hulver, in the Norfolk dialect, signifying holly, a hard and solid wood' (Grose).

(8) *philistins*: 'bailiffs, or officers of justice' (Grose).

(9) *joulthead*: blockhead.

(10) *thrums*: threepence.

(11) *shiner*: 'sovereign, or money' (Hotten).

(12) *bub and grub*: drink and food.

(13) *duddz*: clothes.

(14) *addle*: gain, make.

(15) *ribb rostit* (ribroasted): beaten.

(16) *Tongue pad*: 'a scold or nimble-tongued person' (Grose); here, criticize.

(17) *ferrit*: worry.

(18) *flickur*: coax.

Page 55. (1) *sir jimmee jingle brains*: fool.

(2) *super nakullums* (supernaculum): the last drops of a drink; here, final reward, money.

(3) *transmogrify*: transfer.

(4) *sifflicate*: play up to. 'Sifflication: a petition, supplication' (E.D.D.). But Aby uses the word in various senses.

(5) *rhino*: money.

(6) *omnum gathrum*: total of stocks; here, acquisitive skill.

(7) *Shave a cow's tail and a goat's chin, an you want hair*: i.e. you have no wits of your own to rely on.

(8) *jerry cum poopz*: acrobats.

(9) *jack in a bandbox* (jack-in-the-box): mechanical toy, plaything.

(10) *master my jerry whissle an please you*: obsequious follower.

(11) *rhino*: money.

(12) *Nicodemus*: timid person.

(13) *bawbee*: halfpenny, trifle.

Page 56. (1) *nobb noddl*: foolish head.

(2) *dust*: money.

(3) *kappaishus*: capable, generous.

(4) *hummdudgin*: deceive.

(5) *foistee fubb*: cleverly deceive.

VOLUME II

Page 63. *Ciceroni*: guides.

Page 64. *Lazaroni*: loungers, beggars.

(2) *Cicisbeo*: gallant, lover of a married woman.

(3) *the purse of Fortunatus*: supposed mythically to be bottomless.

(4) *Mt. Cenis*: Moncenisio, marking the border between France and Italy.

(5) *the 'Cassini', the 'Carnivale', and the 'Donne'*: the pleasure-houses, carnivals, and ladies.

Page 65. (1) *'Cavaliere servente'*: gallant, lover of a married woman.

(2) *in petto*: in my breast, undisclosed.

Page 66. (1) *buckskin*: leather breeches.

(2) *Sterne was in my pocket*: cf. note to vol. i, p. 1.

Page 81. *Jason, the dragon and the fruit*: Jason had to defeat the dragon in order to obtain the Golden Fleece; Clifton conflates the story with others in which fruit is guarded by a dragon.

Page 82. *Cerberus*: three-headed monster guarding the entrance to Hades.

Page 84. *the morals of Epictetus*: the lectures and *Enchiridion* of the Stoic philosopher Epictetus (A.D. 60-100) were edited by his pupil Arrian; they stress the virtues of endurance and abstention. Cf. vol. iv, p. 235.

Page 85. (1) *orange chips*: pieces of preserved orange.

(2) *balsams*: soothing medical preparations.

(3) *surfeit, colic and wormwood water*; medicinal drinks.

(4) *hiera picra*: a folk medicine.

(5) *oil of charity*: a folk medicine.

Page 86. (1) *'put powder in her drink'*: i.e. a love-potion.

(2) *king Minos*: celebrated tyrant of Crete.

(3) *ridden upon the white elephant*: the ceremonial mount of the kings of Siam.

(4) *the Dalai Lama*: ruler of Tibet, famed for his wisdom.

(5) *Great Mogul*: ruler of the Mongol Empire in Hindustan; all-powerful leader.

Page 91. Dun Scotus: Duns Scotus (1265?-1308?), medieval theologian noted for the subtlety of his thought.

Page 92. (1) *rencounter*: meeting, often associated with a duel.

(2) *in my altitudes*: in an extravagant mood.

Page 93. Pindarics: extravagant speeches (from the vigorous Odes of the poet Pindar of Thebes, *c.* 523-442 B.C.).

Page 94. (1) *the pike of Teneriffe*: famous spectacular peak in the Canary Islands; 'pike' is an earlier form of 'peak' (O.E.D.).

(2) *the ass that brayed to Balaam*: the ass saved Balaam's life, and later reproved his master for punishing him; the story is told in *Numbers* 22-4.

(3) *Mufti*: (Turkish) ruler.

(4) *the orang outang his first cousin*: the view put forward by James Burnett, Lord Monboddo (1714-99), that the orang outang was not an ape but a variety of human being, was frequently ridiculed, most amusingly by Peacock in *Headlong Hall* (1816).

(5) *merry andrew, jack pudding, tom fool*: all names for the jester or a mountebank.

(6) *Goliah*: Goliath; fairly common, though incorrect, form (O.E.D.).

(7) *a peck*: a great deal; literally, a quarter of a bushel.

Page 96. Cato, Possidonius (Poseidonius): eminent Stoics.

Page 117. Frank's reading of Shakespeare praised by the French: the discovery of Shakespeare was a notable feature of the development of continental Romanticism. Paul van Tieghem devoted a whole volume of *Le Préromantisme* (Paris, 1947) to 'La Découverte de Shakespeare sur le continent'.

Page 120. eclaircissement: explanation, clarification.

Page 123. '*fitful fevers*': *Macbeth*, III. ii.

VOLUME III

Page 144. (1) *the feast of reason and the flow of soul*: Pope, *Imitations of Horace*, Satire I of Book II (1733), l. 128.

(2) *Mahometan houris*: nymphs of the Mahometan paradise; voluptuously beautiful women.

(3) *Heliogabulus*: Roman emperor (218-222), noted for his excesses.

Page 149. John Hunter (1728-93), the great anatomist and surgeon, had published *Proposals for the Recovery of People apparently Drowned* in 1776 and his ideas, although at first resisted by orthodox opinion, came to be accepted as sound.

Page 162. *flamgudgin*: deceive.

Page 163. (1) *kick down the milk*: destroy your own good fortune.
  (2) *sifflicated*: won over.
  (3) *adasht*: modest.
  (4) *Nicodemus*: simpleton.
  (5) *flamdazzle*: impress.
  (6) *ferretted*: manœuvred.
  (7) *feagued*: encouraged, coaxed.

Page 164. (1) *Gabriel Gallimaufry*: jack-of-all-trades, confused person.
  (2) *all a mort*: lifeless, dejected.
  (3) *rhino*: money.
  (4) *snacks*: shares.
  (5), (6), (7) *marygolds, gilly flowers, yellow boys*: money.
  (8) *bite-bubbles*: gulls, fools.
  (9) *squitter squanders*: careless and copious spenders.
  (10) *chouse chits*: dupes.
  (11) *doosoors* (*douceurs*): 'fee, gratuity, tip' (E.D.D.).
  (12) *the bill for protecting minors against usury*: no relevant Act was passed at this period, but judges gave increasing protection to minors in Equity.

Page 165. (1) *cramp*: constrained.
  (2) *queerums*: strange situations.
  (3) *mag*: chatter.
  (4) *sifflicate*: criticize.

Page 166. *doosoors*: fees.

Page 167. (1) *knatterin*: grumbling at, criticizing.
  (2) *flickers and fleers*: gibes and sneers.
  (3) *humdudgin*: outwit.

Page 168. (1) *kintlin*: young man.
  (2) *quips*: problems.
  (3) *afterclaps*: unexpected blows.
  (4) *chouse clickt*: cleverly settled.
  (5) *a doosoor consideration*: a 'tip'.

Page 173. The Greek philosopher associated with a wooden dish, a lantern, and a tub was Diogenes, the fourth-century Cynic.

Page 176. (1) *whindling*: whining.
  (2) *lackadaisy*: vapid.
  (3) *greensickness*: suffering from a childish illness.
  (4) *affronting*: correcting.

Page 177. *quantum sufficit*: a sufficient amount (term used in medical prescriptions).

Page 178. (1) *the Old Red Lion of Brentford*: a well-known public-house sign.

(2) *budget*: pouch, wallet.

Page 191. *the stone of Sisyphus*: Sisyphus was punished in Hades by having to roll a rock up to the top of a hill, from which it always rolled down: his task was eternal.

Page 194. (1) *a Sydney or a Verulam*: the famous Elizabethans, Sir Philip Sidney (1554-86) and Francis Bacon, Baron Verulam (1561-1626).

(2) *the subject of identity*: the difficulties of this subject had been emphasized by Hume's sceptical discussion in his *Treatise of Human Nature* (1739-40) I. vi; many 'progressive' thinkers of the time held the associationist view of identity propounded by Hartley in his *Observations on Man* (1749). These ideas are clearly discussed by Basil Willey in *The Eighteenth-Century Background* (1940).

VOLUME IV

Page 197. *jack in a band-box*: jack-in-the-box, a mechanical toy.

Page 198. *trammel*: net, trap.

Page 199. (1) *rib-hooked*: attached.

(2) *fico*: fig.

Page 202. *barebones*: skeleton.

Page 205. (1) *destroy with a Gothic hand, as the poet says*: William Cowper, 'Tirocinium' (1785), ll. 913-14:

> Oh, barbarous! Would'st thou with a Gothic hand
> Pull down the schools—what!—all the schools i'the land . . .

(2) Ovid's *Metamorphoses* were frequently translated in the eighteenth century; versions of some of the poems were made by Dryden, Sir Samuel Garth (1661-1719), Nicholas Rowe (1678-1718), and Pope.

(3) The grounds at Stowe, laid out by Richard Temple, Viscount Cobham (1675-1749), were among the most elaborate and celebrated pieces of eighteenth-century landscape gardening. The first epistle of Pope's *Moral Essays* (1734) is addressed to him, and the fourth epistle praises his achievement (*Moral Essays*, Epistle IV, To Richard Boyle, Earl of Burlington, ll. 69-70):

> Nature shall join you, Time shall make it grow
> A Work to wonder at, perhaps a Stow.

Page 206. *Tooke's Pantheon: The Pantheon, representing the Fabulous Histories of the Heathen Gods and Most Illustrious Heroes*, translated from Pomey's *Panteum Mithicum* by Andrew Tooke (1673-1732). This was originally published in 1698 and was widely read. It was revised in 1717 and reached a 35th edition by 1824.

Page 207. (1) *Britons strike home*: a song by Purcell for an adaptation of Beaumont and Fletcher by George Powell entitled *Bonduca; or the British Worthy* (1695).

(2) *Rule Britannia*: the popular song, originally composed by T. A. Arne for the masque *Alfred* by Thomson and Mallet (1740).

The two patriotic songs are both brought in at the comic climax of Sheridan's *The Critic* (1779).

(3) *more than one crow to pluck with him*: more than one score to settle.

Page 214. (1) *a gull queerum*: a foolish mistake.

(2) *transmogrified*: changed.

(3) *komparissuble*: compatible.

(4) *super nakullums* (*supernaculum*): here, simply, money.

(5) *omnum gathurum*: money.

Page 215. (1) *treeved*: fixed.

(2) *chouse flickurd*: cheated.

(3) *flamdudgind*: deceived.

Page 216. (1) *frippery jerry my gingle red coats and cockades*: soldiers.

(2) *squitter squanderin*: careless and copious spending.

(3) *addle brained*: befooled.

(4) *foistee fubbd*: deceived.

(5) *ponderaitin*: pondering.

(6) *Nicodemus Nincompoop*: timid fool.

(7) *the fulhams*: the loaded dice; so called 'either because they were made at Fulham, or from the place being the resort of sharpers' (Grose).

(8) *flib gibberd*: cheated.

(9) *queerumd*: deceived.

(10) *catch me come kiss me*: a country game.

Page 217. (1) *sifflicated*: advised.

(2) *quaumee* (*qualmy*): sickly, weak-stomached.

(3) *kintlin*: child.

(4) *Gaby goose*: simpleton.

(5) *komparissuble*: comparable.

(6) *yellowhammer*: money.

(7) *chink*: money.

(8) *rig roister*: roistering, fooling about.

(9) *Timothy Tipkin*: fool.

(10) *sifflicate*: suggest.

(11) *Peter Grievous*: fool.

(12) *cry peccavi*: admit failure

(13) *flammbite*: trick, deception.

(14) *tale of a tub*: impossible story.

(15) *run rusty*: go wild (of horses).

(16) *the costard monger*: costermonger; fool.

Page 218. Sir Arthur Crabvarjus o' the high ropes: high-handed person.

Page 224. Garrick in Richard III: one of the great actor's most famous roles.

Page 226. cogging of dice: cheating with dice.

Page 229. upon the Captain Copperthorne: argumentative; 'Captain Copperthorne's crew. All officers; a saying of a company where everyone strives to rule' (Grose).

Page 231. (1) *doubt the doctors*: suspect that the dice were loaded.

(2) *spalpeen*: scoundrel.

(3) *smoaked a bail of Fulhams*: discovered a number of loaded dice.

Page 234. (1) *ferae naturae*: wild, untameable natures.

(2) *fillips*: blows.

Page 235. (1) *cogger*: cheat.

Page 236. (1) *the apothegms of Epictetus*: Stoic sayings; cf. note to vol. ii, p. 84.

(2) *men of Gotham*: fools.

(3) *King Cadmus*: founder of Thebes.

Page 238. Nestor: Greek leader noted for his age and wisdom.

Page 240. the Julia of Rousseau: Rousseau's popular romance *La Nouvelle Héloïse* (1761) was translated into English in 1761, 1764, and 1789; its heroine is Julia Wolmar.

Page 243. ignis fatuus: will-of-the-wisp, delusive hope.

Page 247. (1) *amisst*: misled.

(2) *queery*: guess.

Page 248. (1) *a portin*: behaving.

(2) *Friar Bacon, Friar Bungy and the brazen head*: in the traditional story, on which Greene's play of 1594 is based, the head speaks three times, saying, 'Time is'; 'Time was'; and 'Time is past'.

(3) *compus mentus*: understood.

(4) *scot and lot*: all legal dues.

(5) *a buzzard in grain*: a fool.

(6) *flicker*: smile, sneer.

(7) *fleer*: gibe.

(8) *bob gudgeon*: a fool.

(9) *yellow hammers*: money.

(10) *the foolish hen cackles . . . nest egg ready*: it is wisest to keep quiet and make prudent plans; referring to the use of an artificial egg to encourage hens to go on laying.

(11) *tout and trump*: spy and fuss.

(12) *cry peccavi*: admit guilt, give in.

(13) *kinchin*: man.

(14) *the first frost that brings a white crow*: i.e. never.

(15) *a huff and a gruff*: fit of petulance.

(16) *arm a kimbo'd*: with hands on hips; here (unusually) peaceable.

Page 249. (1) *a Rowland for an Oliver*: equal measure.

(2) *Jack-a-farthin weazel-faced whipster*: worthless, thin-faced coward.

(3) *stock and block*: something substantial.

(4) *a rum for a glum*: equal measure.

(5) *all a mort*: lifeless, dejected.

(6) *coilin and moilin*: toiling and drudging.

(7) *the dole*: what is due.

(8) *twitted*: disparaged.

(9) *scowerings*: scoutings, adventures.

(10) *rubs*: obstacles.

(11) *chitterlins*: small intestines; here, innermost being.

Page 252. I am as good as a witch: i.e. I guessed as much.

Page 254. Quidam: certain (here, special) person.

Page 255. Erebus: place of nether darkness on the way to Hades.

Page 256. the seraphic, the subtle, the singular; the illuminated, the angelic and the irrefragable: Bonaventura, Duns Scotus, Occam; Ruysbroek, Aquinas, and Alexander of Hales; traditional appellations of these doctors of the church.

Page 257. king of the cucumber-beds: one of several opprobrious references to Frank's being the son of a gardener.

VOLUME V

Page 270. Circe, Calypso, Morgana: famous enchantresses, the first two encountered in the *Odyssey*, the last in Ariosto's *Orlando Furioso* (1582).

Page 272. cicisbeos: gallants.

Page 274. Bramin wives . . . burning pile: suttee, the concremation of a widow on the pyre of her deceased husband, was officially abolished by the British in India only in 1829.

Page 275. quiddities: quibbles.

Page 276. grub-monger: another approbrious description of Henley, the gardener's son.

Page 280. malverse: corrupt.

Page 283. (1) *Archimago*: chief magician.

(2) *saffron god*: the god of marriage, Hymen the saffron-robed.

Page 285. quips and quillets: quibbles and verbal tricks.

Page 286. (1) *sashes*: windows.

(2) *Seneca*: (*c.* 4 B.C.–A.D. 65) Roman Stoic philosopher.

(3) *marplot*: interfering with a plot or design.

(4) *Cyprian battles . . . myrtle wreaths*: Cyprus was the isle of Venus, to whom the myrtle was sacred.

Page 288. Andromeda and the Ethiopian monster: Andromeda was chained to a rock to be sacrificed to the sea monster, in order to placate Poseidon; she was rescued by Perseus.

Page 289. (1) *Demosthenes*: (*c.* 385–322 B.C.) famous Athenian orator.

(2) *knight of Gotham*: foolish knight.

Page 292. form a society of savages: such ambitions were not uncommon among English Radicals of the time, who derived some of their inspiration from primitivism. For instance, the hero of Bage's *Hermsprong* (1796) is brought up among the Red Indians and contrasts their way of life favourably with that of fashionable Europeans.

Page 293. (1) *'Ill starred wench'*: *Othello*, v. ii.

(2) *'Before the battle's won the Brentford hero sings Te Deum'*: i.e. don't count your chickens before they're hatched.

Page 296. (1) *'dégagé'*: easily, unconstrainedly.

(2) *the palace of Alcina*: Alcina is an enchantress in Ariosto's *Orlando Furioso.*

Page 297. the heroic archbishop: Thomas Cranmer (1489–1556), burnt at the stake for heresy, held in the flames the hand with which he had written the recantation.

Page 298. Count Caduke: cf. French '*caduque*' and Italian '*caduco*'; infirm, crazy.

Page 299. Bull: jest.

Page 305. lanched: launched.

Page 309. (1) *I will use not speak daggers*: cf. *Hamlet*, III. ii.

(2) *mammet*: (maumet), doll, puppet.

(3) *Meacock*: weakling.

(4) *'I had rather be a toad'*, etc.: *Othello*, III. iii.

Page 310. (1) *St. Luke's collected maniacs*: St. Luke's Hospital for lunatics was founded in 1751.

(2) *soundings*: calculations.

(3) *raree show*: special exhibition.

Page 311. (1) *fico*: fig.

(2) *doctiloquy*: learned speech (coinage).

Page 312. (1) *watch strings*: cords for securing a watch to its owner.

(2) *Paris-Birmingham snuff-box*: travellers often reported that expensive trinkets on sale in Paris turned out to have been made in Birmingham.

Page 318. *this cloud-capt lady*: cf. *The Tempest*, IV. i, 'the cloud-capp'd towers'.

Page 319. *'of battles, sieges, disastrous chances'*, etc.: cf. *Othello*, I. iii.

Page 321. *currying*: rubbing-down, dressing.

Page 322. *cast in costs*: defeated (in a legal action) and have to pay costs.

Page 327. *Incubus*: demon which pursues a particular victim.

Page 328. *Tophet*: Hell.

VOLUME VI

Page 339. (1) *queerums*: puzzles.

    (2) *quicksets*: traps.

    (3) *within an ames ace* (ambs-ace): very near.

    (4) *chouse flickur'd*: outwitted.

    (5) *sifflicate*: suggest.

Page 340. (1) *doosoors*: fees.

    (2) *kappaishus*: call.

Page 351. *I will meet her at Philippi*: cf. *Julius Caesar*, IV. iii.

Page 362. (1) *mow*: grimace, mock.

    (2) *Orlando*: a perfect knight, hero of Aristoto's *Orlando Furioso*.

    (3) *the knights Paladin*: the peers of Charlemagne, of whom Orlando was commander.

Page 369. (1) *knotted crab-stick*: strong stick made of crab-apple-tree wood.

    (2) *rattan*: palm cane.

Page 370. (1) *gudgeon*: 'one easily imposed upon' (Grose).

    (2) *hazard*: a game at dice.

    (3) *pass-dice*: (passage) 'a camp game with three dice' (Grose).

Page 371. (1) *pigeon*: 'a weak silly fellow, easily imposed upon' (Grose).

    (2) *plucked*: cheated.

    (3) *the bubble*: cheated.

    (4) *snap-jack*: sharper.

Page 372. (1) *spalpeen*: scoundrel.

Page 373. *tote*: significance.

Page 374. *puissant*: powerful.

Page 375. (1) *hocking*: hamstringing; 'a piece of cruelty practised by the butchers of Dublin, on soldiers, by cutting the tendon of Achilles' (Grose).

    (2) *chalking*: 'cutting inoffensive passengers across the face with a knife' (Grose).

Page 376. (1) *mephitic*: pestilential.
(2) *Cocytus*: river of Hades.

Page 377. *encrust*: envelope.

Page 379. *rodomontacle*: bragging.

Page 385. (1) *chairmen*: men who carry Sedan chairs or wheel Bath chairs.
(2) *link-boys*: boys who carry torches for travellers.

Page 390. *the battle of Issus*: at which Alexander defeated Darius of Persia.

Page 391. *myrmidons*: hired ruffians.

Page 393. *enamorato*: (inamorato); lover.

Page 394. *tag*: add.

Page 395. *chop-fallen* (chap-fallen); exhausted.

Page 404. *inmates*: close companions.

VOLUME VII

Page 407. '*But nature, crescent in him, grew only in thews and bulk*': cf. *Hamlet*, I. iii.

Page 408. *maugre*: despite.

Page 409. *imp*: evil spirit.

Page 412. *in high divan*: in agitated conference; the Divan originally referred to the Turkish Court.

Page 413. (1) *ban dog*: large, fierce dog, held in a band.
(2) *lenitive*: soothing medical preparation.

Page 415. (1) *deep damnation*: cf. *Macbeth*, I. vii.
(2) *murrain*: plague.

Page 417. *devoted*: caught.

Page 422. *indexed*: condemned, by analogy with books on the Papal Index.

Page 425. (1) *scout at*: scorn.
(2) *Jove to Semele, in flames*: Semele insisted on looking at her divine lover and was consumed in flames as a result.

Page 428. *the office at Bow Street*: where the principal Metropolitan police court was situated.

Page 429. *chairman*: man who carries a Sedan chair or wheels a Bath chair.

Page 434. *waylay*: keep under observation.

Page 436. *pigeoned*: cheated.

Page 438. *rodomontade*: bragging.